# Praise for Shadows of the Apt

'The insectile-humans premise is inventive, shaping the world in all sorts of ways'  *SFX*

'Epic fantasy at its best. Gripping, original and multi-layered storytelling from a writer bursting with lots of fascinating ideas'  *WalkerofWorlds.com*

'Superb world-building, great characters and extreme inventiveness'  *FantasyBookCritic* blog

'Adrian is continuing to go from strength to strength. Magic'  *FalcataTimes* blog

'Reminiscent of much that's gone before from the likes of Gemmel, Erikson, Sanderson and Cook but with its own unique and clever touch, this is another terrific outing from Mr Tchaikovsky'  *Sci-Fi-London.com*

'I cannot even begin to explain how much I enjoy the Shadows of the Apt books. Their level of originality and their sheer epic-ness makes for some of the best fantasy entertainment out there'  *LECBookReviews* blog

'Tchaikovsky's series is a pretty great one – he has taken some classic fantasy elements and added a unique (as far as I'm aware) twist . . . Tchaikovsky has created a world that blends epic fantasy and technology'  *CivilianReader* blog

D1384895

# The Sea Watch

Adrian Tchaikovsky was born in Woodhall Spa, Lincoln-shire, before heading off to Reading to study psychology and zoology. For reasons unclear even to himself he subsequently ended up in law and has worked as a legal executive in both Reading and Leeds, where he now lives. Married, he is a keen live role-player and occasional amateur actor, has trained in stage-fighting, and keeps no exotic or dangerous pets of any kind, possibly excepting his son.

Catch up with Adrian at www.shadowsoftheapt.com for further information about both himself and the insect-kinden, together with bonus material including short stories and artwork.

This is the sixth novel in the Shadows of the Apt series, following *Empire in Black and Gold*, *Dragonfly Falling*, *Blood of the Mantis*, *Salute the Dark* and *The Scarab Path*.

## BY ADRIAN TCHAIKOVSKY

### *Shadows of the Apt*

SHADOWS OF THE APT
BOOK SIX

# The
# Sea Watch

## ADRIAN
## TCHAIKOVSKY

TOR

First published 2011 by Tor

This edition published 2012 by Tor
an imprint of Pan Macmillan, a division of Macmillan Publishers Limited
Pan Macmillan, 20 New Wharf Road, London N1 9RR
Basingstoke and Oxford
Associated companies throughout the world
www.panmacmillan.com

ISBN 978-1-4472-2492-1

3 5 7 9 8 6 4

A CIP catalogue record for this book is available from
the British Library.

Map artwork by Hemesh Alles
Typeset by SetSystems Ltd, Saffron Walden, Essex
Printed and bound by CPI Group (UK) Ltd, Croydon, CR0 4YY

Visit **www.panmacmillan.com** to read more about all our books
and to buy them. You will also find features, author interviews and
news of any author events, and you can sign up for e-newsletters
so that you're always first to hear about our new releases.

*To my childhood heroes:*

*Gerald Durrell*

*and*

*Sir David Attenborough*

# Acknowledgements

Picking who to acknowledge is a strange game this far into a series, as it's the same people as before, for the most part: Simon Kavanagh, Peter Lavery, Julie Crisp, Chloe Healy, all the usual suspects at Tor, Annie and my family, all the friends who've supported me and continue to do so. Particular thanks go to Jon Cole, who has turned up un-expectedly at conventions and signings covering a broad swathe of the country; my father, for assistance with the oceanography; to Helen, Joff, Gareth, Frances and Dan for being such tireless hosts every time I hit Oxford; and to Wayne and Krissy for similar honours in London.

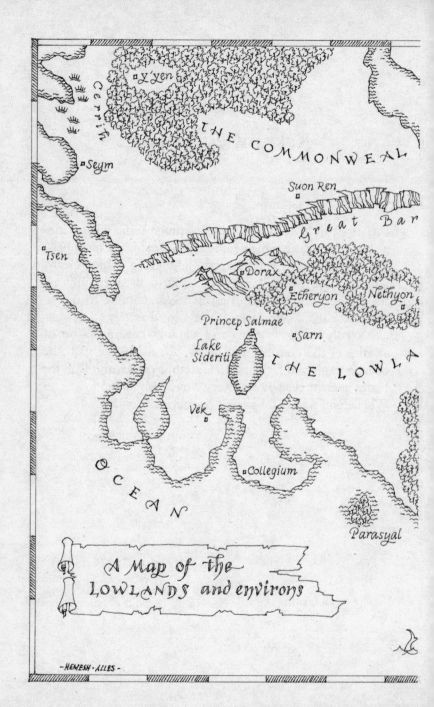

A Map of the
LOWLANDS and environs

-HEMESH·AILES-

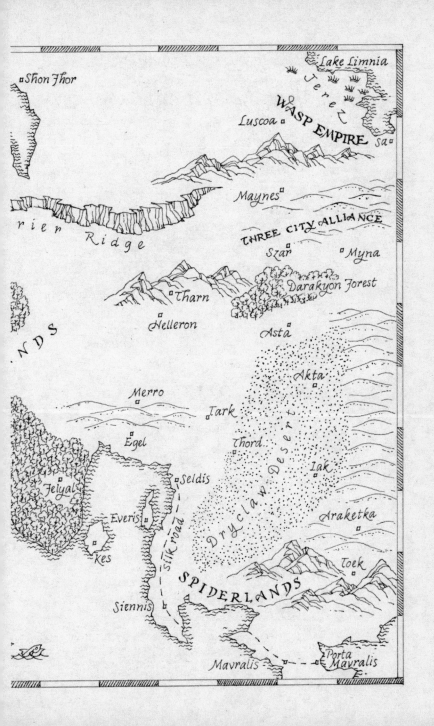

# A map of the SPIDERLANDS

Neoteris

Port Planten

Kanateris

Vancris

Aes

Princep Castella

GOLDEN SKAETHA

BITTER SEA

Sea-Limnis

G R E A T E R   S E A

Escorvis

Hermeth

Midis

Anger

Eryon

Naopte

Bethelme

Forest Erys

—HEMESH·ALLES—

# Summary

Collegium and its allies in the Lowlands have reached an uneasy truce with the Wasp Empire. While the Wasps deal with their internal divisions, the statesman Stenwold Maker finds himself mired in personal battles, hunting his missing ward, Tynisa and awaiting the return of his niece, Cheerwell, from her diplomatic mission to the distant city of Khanaphes.

On the political home front, his efforts to reach peace with the neighbouring Ant city-state of Vek hang in the balance – a peace that is essential if Collegium is to defend itself against the Empire's next encroachment – and the new leadership of Collegium's governing body is shortly to be voted upon, deciding whether the future will be guided by Stenwold's ally, Jodry Drillen, or his bitter enemy Helmess Broiler.

A complete list of characters, places and other things can be found at the back of the book.

## Part One

# Those Who Move on the Face of the Waters

# One

*Four years ago*

Above all, what the boy remembered was the rushing of the waters as his head finally broke through. Paladrya was pushing from behind, forcing him up towards the surface. He could feel the urgency merely through her touch: she who was normally so mild.

Marcantor was ashore already, a tall, narrow form just visible amongst a labyrinth of dark and darker. The boy fell back. It was not because of the air's bitter chill on his skin, at that moment. He did not even recognize the awful emptiness of the sky above. It was that clustering darkness, the darkness of the forest, the knotted overreaching of the clawing trees. Even with the sea still lapping about his calves he realized he was in an alien world.

Marcantor stepped forward, reaching out a hand, but the boy twitched back. The narrow-framed man regarded him bleakly: in the moon's light his face was more than readable, and the boy saw what tight control he exercised. All the boy's fears were written in miniature on the man's face, and the boy knew he should offer him some comforting words, some echo of his heritage, but he had none to give.

Paladrya was beside him, the tide swirling about her

3

legs. She put an arm about the boy's shoulders and hugged him to her. With the seawater still streaming off her he could not tell for sure if she was weeping or not. They shivered together in the unexpected cold, a breeze from within the trees chilling them drier.

'Get the cloaks out,' she hissed at Marcantor. 'He's freezing to death. We all are. Where's Santiren? Must I do everything?'

Marcantor was a foot and a half taller than she was, lean and angular, his armour sculpted – helm and breastplate and bracers all – into flowing lines of pale bone. He had his spear loose in one hand, its barbed-needle head dipping in the water. For a second the boy thought he would use it against her. Paladrya faced him off, though, in her expression only an angry reminder of his place and hers, and the boy's. She was shorter, her body rounded and a little plump where the warrior's was hard, but she had authority. Even in this illicit venture, she was the leader, he the follower. Marcantor scowled and began to cut open a package sealed with a rind of vegetable-leather, using the horny teeth that jutted from the palms of his hands. They trembled now, those hands, from cold or from fear of the unknown. The boy wanted to reach out to him, but his own fear was too great. He had looked up: there was nothing above them but the moon. The world was suddenly without limits and it filled him full of awe and terror. *But that is fitting*, he decided. *What we have done today is also beyond all limits.*

Marcantor thrust something at him: dry cloth, a cloak. Paladrya took it before the boy could, draping it over his shoulders. It was short, thin, barely blunting the wind. He clutched it to himself gratefully. A similar garment went to Paladrya herself, shrugged over the close shift that she wore. Marcantor had acquired something longer for himself, his slender frame half swallowed by it.

Abruptly another tall, thin shape was with them, a

4

woman as lean and towering as Marcantor, each of them reaching seven feet in their peaked helms. She was already cloaked, picking her way, with deliberate care, over the arching, leg-like roots of the shoreline trees. Santiren had been Paladrya's co-conspirator for longer, since before the boy had even been aware of a conspiracy. She had visited this freezing, boundless place before, several times. Her face held no fear of it, only the shadow of their common desperation.

'Any sign of followers?' she asked.

'None.' Paladrya was still shivering. Her face, which the boy had always seen as beautiful, was taut with tension now. 'None yet. And I will return and turn aside any such as do come.'

'No!' the boy said, too loud. 'You can't leave me!'

Paladrya held him out at arm's length. She had been his tutor since his eighth year, and he had loved her a long time, in that silent, awkward way that boys often love their mentors. 'They'll kill you,' he protested.

'Not if I'm back swiftly enough that they cannot suspect me,' she said, but he knew enough not to believe her.

'They'll torture you,' he said.

'And find out what? Santiren has made the arrangements. I know your fate from here on no more than they.'

'But they will *torture* you. Do you think the Edmir will not?'

Her expression was infinitely sad. 'I have hopes that Claeon . . that the Edmir will not do so. I am no stranger to him, no unknown flesh to be torn.'

'He's right, you should come,' Santiren said, and the boy's heart leapt with hope.

Paladrya just shook her head, though. 'I will accomplish more back in the colony. Do not fear for me. There is yet work to be done.'

He did his best, then, to memorize her face in the cold moonlight: the elegant curve of her cheek, her large eyes that the moon bleached grey but that he knew were violet, the dripping ringlets of her hair.

'Be safe,' she told him. 'Your time will come.' She hugged him to her again, and he found that he was crying like a child. 'Santiren,' he heard her say, his face still pressed to her shoulder. 'Your accomplice?'

'Is here, watching,' the tall woman told her. 'Fear not, all is ready.'

'Then the moon and the tides be your friends here,' Paladrya said, her lips twisting wryly as she added, 'Here where there are no tides, and where the moon is too large.'

'And may the luck of the abyss protect you,' Marcantor said from the shadows. 'For you will surely need all of it.'

Paladrya stepped back from the boy, glancing around one last time before retreating away from the straggling treeline, into the water. The boy wanted to go with her, simply because it was her, and because she was returning to the only world he had known all his life. *Surely better to die there than live here?*

It was not his choice, though. He would have to live here, if he could, and she . . .

She would die there. He felt it inside him, the certainty. He was no oracle, as some of his people were, as Paladrya herself sometimes professed to be, but he felt just then that he had worked some small, bleak prophecy nonetheless.

'So where is this land-kinden of yours?' Marcantor snapped. His face said so very clearly, *I do not wish to be in this place*, and the boy wanted to let him go. *But I need him. I need both of them. I need all the help I can get.*

'I am here,' said a new voice, a woman's. A figure stepped from between the trees.

The boy stared at her, for she was different.

She was tall, though not as tall as the two Dart-kinden warriors. Her features were sharp: pointed chin, pointed ears, narrow eyes. She had hair like pale gold, cut short as if with a butcher's uneven hand. She was clad, neck to feet, in brown and green cloth, hard-wearing stuff like nothing he knew. Jagged barbs jutted from her forearms. The boy had never seen anything like her, and it was clear Marcantor hadn't either. The warrior moved to level his spear at the apparition. In a single step she was inside the weapon's reach.

The movement had been too fast for the boy to follow. It left her almost standing next to the man. A small knife was clasped in one hand, close to Marcantor's neck. The woman's expression was still neutral.

'Don't,' she said – or that was what the boy thought she said. Her accent was clipped, equally as sharp as her eyes.

He saw Marcantor tense ready to make some move: a leap backwards, perhaps, to get her at the end of his spear. Muddled in that unfamiliar cloak, over unfamiliar ground, it would not end happily for him.

'Stand down!' Santiren snapped, and Marcantor scowled at her. She was nobody he should need to take orders from. Paladrya was gone.

'Marcantor,' the boy heard his own voice shake, 'please, stand down.'

The tall Dart-kinden regarded him archly for a moment, seeing in the boy only the cause of his banishment to this alien place, then something broke inside him. He grounded his spear, its tip rattling branches, and for a moment his long face held nothing but an exhausted sadness.

'Cynthaen,' Santiren interrupted. 'You know me.'

The knife was gone from the strange woman's hand. Dismissing Marcantor entirely, she focused again on the Dart-kinden woman. 'You I know – these others, not so much.' The boy had to pass her words back and forth in his head before he could interpret them.

'We have our compact,' Santiren said, 'and you understand what I mean. We call upon you.'

The boy watched curiously. This was something he knew nothing of, this touching of fingers across the shoreline. Santiren's kin, though, had come from strange places before her mother made a home within the colony. Paladryra had known. Paladrya always knew.

The land-kinden woman's harsh stare turned suddenly towards the boy. 'You, I know,' she repeated. 'This other, he's like your brother, so I know him, but not this child. Not the woman who was with you. You cannot think I'd help Spider-kinden. No compact binds me to that.'

The boy just stared at her, and he was thinking, *To be all the time in this cold and tangled place? All the time, and never once to step into the waters? How can she live? How can anything live here, exposed to this awful openness?*

'What is Spider-kinden?' Santiren asked. 'We know of no Spider-kinden.'

The land-kinden's eyes flicked in her direction without ever ceasing to look at the boy. He saw the likeness, then, in the way she stood, in that hard-edged face. *She is like the Swiftclaw, I think, save that she has hair and they have none. Is it just the likeness, then? Or is she a killer, inside, like them?*

'Boy,' the land-kinden woman addressed him directly. He saw Marcantor shift, angry at this lack of respect, but that knife was still somewhere, and now the woman was very close to his charge.

'I listen,' the boy said to her. She crouched a little, staring very closely at his face.

'Spider-kinden,' she spat, 'you and that woman. I should kill you here. Were she still here, I would kill her without a thought.' Her eyes, slanting and brown, bored into his. 'You fear me.'

'Why should I fear you?' he got out. He hoped she took any shivering for the cold. *For I can show no fear, not to the Swiftclaw-kinden, nor to her.*

'I can kill you,' she hissed. 'I've been killing Spider-kinden since before you were born. I need no reason.'

He stared into her face, exotic and uncompromising. 'I

have been driven from my home into this dark place by my enemies, yet I do not fear them. How could I fear you, who can do so much less.' His voice was definitely trembling by the end, beyond his control.

He noticed the smallest tug at the corner of her mouth. 'No Spider-kinden ever knew such eyes as you, boy. So large, such a colour.' She straightened up. Without any concrete change, the threat had evaporated from her. 'I am Cynthaen,' she told them. 'Santiren knows me, and we have our compact.' The boy saw Santiren sag with relief at that statement, although she had masked her worry well.

'You cannot stay here,' Cynthaen added, 'not amongst my people. They will not be as restrained as me. They will kill the boy, or give him to the beasts of the forest. He looks too like our enemies.'

'But our compact—' Santiren started to say, and Cynthaen cut her off with a short gesture.

'Our compact holds. I will find your boy somewhere to hide.' A smile made it to her face at last. 'I know just the place, but you must be swift. Follow me and never leave my presence, or you will surely die, compact or no.'

'What's in it for her?' Marcantor demanded, following Cynthaen as closely as he could, through the tangle of roots and branches.

'Quiet, Marcantor,' Santiren warned him from the back.

'Tell me. What's this compact?' he pressed. He was in a foul mood, cold and scratched, limping like all of them. This new place was not kind to bare feet.

'*I'll* tell you,' came Cynthaen's voice.

Marcantor hissed at her angrily, but the boy said, 'I would hear it, if you would tell us. You are helping us, and therefore we have no right to an answer, but I would hear it.'

The land-kinden woman stopped at that, turning back to gaze at him with a slight smile on her face. The boy

9

decided that she was pretty when she smiled like that. Not beautiful like Paladrya, but there was something in her exotic features that could be appealing, when she tried.

'I'll tell you,' Cynthaen said, turning and heading off again. 'Only a little. What little there's left. Go back long enough, you know, we were the masters of everything, or our masters were. Better times then. Age of Lore. Everyone knows it.'

The boy had to strain to hear her, to sieve the words from the quick, accented speech.

'Then it all went to the pyre. We used to roam everywhere. Now, just a few places left where we can keep them out. So many traditions lost. What was a whole Hold once, now just a few families to it. The old ways, gone now, most of them, or going. We're all on each other's toes. Can't keep hold of what used to be the important things. The differences. The traditions.'

She led them on for quite a while without speaking further, and the boy tried to work out if she had answered him somehow, lost in those rapid, disjointed phrases, or not. Then she said: 'They still call us Fisher-kinden sometimes. My family and a couple of others who keep the Sea Watch. We're all that's left of the original Felyal, before all these other types ended up here. They think we're strange. They don't care about us. Still, there's none that can bring in a netful like us. That's right, isn't it, Santiren?'

'That's right,' came the Dart-kinden woman's patient voice. The boy was still trying to come to some understanding of what was being said, the 'Felyal' and the 'netful' and the rest.

'When we go to the beach on the last moon,' Cynthaen went on more slowly, sounding wistful, 'when we dance and cast our gifts, when our seers close their eyes they hear your folk down below. The compact is made again. The others don't understand.'

*I don't understand*, the boy thought, but he thought again

of Santiren's kin, the nomad places where her family hunted. *Magic*, he knew. Magic was in it, this talk of dancing, the magic of the turn of the year: longest night and shortest day, last full moon and winter tides. He was no magician but he realized there was magic in all these things.

Marcantor stumbled and cursed, clutching at his ankle. Cynthaen turned and regarded them pityingly. 'You people never heard of sandals, I'm gathering.'

The boy, whose own feet were sore and raw, said, 'What is sandals?' That took her by surprise, for it was clear she had not been serious. She studied them again, the thin cloaks covering light armour for two warriors, – armour that left thighs and upper arms bare, to move more swiftly. The cloak covering a kilt and then bare skin, for the boy. Something of the strangeness of them – such as they had already seen in her – touched her, and she shivered.

*We are strange reflections of each other*, the boy thought. *And the mirror is the sea's edge*. By force of habit, he tried to fashion a couplet from the thought, but the cold and the pain and the yawning sky robbed him of the power.

'You stay here, now,' she told them. 'Can you hide? Hide, if you can. Don't come out for anyone but me.' She made a spitting noise. 'Fact is, if my people find you, like as not you'll be dead anyway.'

She was gone abruptly, slipping off through the forest of stiff, interweaving trees and into the dark. *So still, here*, the boy thought. *Everything is so still and rigid and heavy, frozen and cold*.

'Hide,' Santiren urged him. 'Marcantor and I will stand and watch.' She hefted her spear, even though, in the close clutter of branches, it would be an awkward weapon.

The boy called upon his Art. That took a few moments, in this unfamiliar place, but he found it calmed him, as the colours rose within his skin, flowing over his arms and legs, matching themselves to the plantlife around him – at first awkwardly, then more and more naturally. He let out a long, calm sigh.

The night forest around them was full of noises. It was another jarring, alien aspect of this place. Things rustled and buzzed and creaked all around him, a constant patter of small life, and some not so small. The boy's eyes, and his companions' eyes, were well used to darkness – there was darkness far greater than this where they came from, places where the limn-lights had never shone – but their darkness was near-silent, not this constant chatter.

Something large moved there, between the trees. They all spotted it at once and he saw the two warriors grow tense, spears levelled. It was tall and slender, and the boy tried hard to make it out, seeing the glint of eyes, the thin spindles of legs, one hooked forearm held close, the other extended forward to aid the thing's careful progress. It regarded them.

*Some kind of claw-kinden thing, but moved to the land.* He knew, without thinking, that this must be the heraldic beast of Cynthaen's kinden. It was close enough to the shrimp they called the swiftclaw, and she herself was close enough to that thing's kinden. The creature was larger than a man, and he guessed it shared a swiftclaw's temper and hunger. Marcantor and Santiren held their spears now in both hands, the thin barbed heads barely moving. The land monster regarded them impassively, huge eyes aglitter in the moonlight.

Cynthaen was there beside it, without warning, putting a hand up to touch its armoured flank. The triangular head cocked to look at her, mouthparts circling, and then it began to creep off, one deliberate move after the next, sometimes solely on the ground and sometimes reaching from tree to tree.

'Now,' she said, and then enquired: 'Where's the little one?'

The boy let his Art flow from him, the dark colours

running like paint until he had recovered his pale skin. Cynthaen watched cautiously. This was obviously Art she had never witnessed before.

The land-kinden woman now dropped something at their feet, pieces of a strange material, crawling with straps. When she realized they did not know what to do with them she uttered a tired sound and took the boy's feet in her hands, heedless of Marcantor's twitch at such presumption. The heavier piece went under his sole, and the straps held it to his foot. It felt exceedingly strange. He saw that Cynthaen herself wore something different, an enclosing sheath of skin that went almost to her knee.

The two Dart-kinden copied the arrangement, with varying success, so that Cynthaen had to correct their crossed and twisted strapping. Marcantor sat very still as she attended to him, but the boy saw his hands constantly clenching, the palms rough with the teeth of his Art. She saw it, too, and grinned up at him wickedly.

'Don't spoil too much for a fight, tall one,' she advised him. 'For my kind, that's wooing.'

Once she was done, she took out something else, a hood of stiff skin. She passed it to the boy. 'Wear it – in case of my people. Now we'd best move. Dawn's getting close.'

'The sun?' the boy asked.

She gave him a look. 'That's what we mean when we say dawn, boy.'

She led them faster this time, although they kept slipping and skidding in their new footwear. They saw no sign of her mysterious, hostile people, but the boy had the sense that she was forever on the lookout for them, deliberately choosing a path to avoid them. All was not peace and harmony amongst the land-kinden.

When the sun came, it was a slow brightening through the trees, first on one side only, and then on all sides. The harsh chill slunk resentfully away, and gradually the night noises gave place to more and different sounds made by the beasts of the day. The boy spotted almost none as large as the swiftclaw-thing of the night, only heard them go quiet as he and the Dart-kinden passed, and then pick up their lives behind them. Once or twice there was the shape of an armoured thing clattering between the plants, or hanging off them. Of smaller things there were legion, and mostly creatures of the air, darting and diving and swarming, glittering in the first light, or clinging to twigs to soak up the sun's warmth.

Cynthaen picked up the pace yet again, until there was a noticeable thinning of the plants around them, a brightening of the light. The heat, where it fell on cloth and skin, was beginning to swelter. The boy saw ahead of them shapes that were obviously not made by nature but by man.

They broke from the trees and were immediately within a gathering of structures that had clearly been put up by some craft or labour, but the boy could not understand how. They appeared so crude as to be the work of halfwits: everything was flat, angular, glaringly ugly, made of blocks and beams that seemed barely finished. He looked on them with horror and could not stop himself from asking, 'Is this where your kinden live?'

'Mine?' Cynthaen glanced back at him. 'Oh, this is none of mine. Don't like it, eh? Then maybe there's some hope for you. They call this place Arvandine. They have built it as close as they dare without risking our wrath.' She led them down paths running between the blocky buildings, ignoring those few residents they met on the way. The denizens of Arvandine were of a quite different kind to Cynthaen: most seemed burly and dark, heavy-bodied men and women bearing burdens of various kinds. One other was almost as dark, but as tiny as a Smallclaw, his head barely reaching to the height of the boy's chest, barely to the Dart-kinden's waists. In a moment this little man, seeing Cynthaen striding straight towards him, had flashed a blur of dancing Art from his back and thrown himself into the air. The boy gasped at this prodigy, staring upwards, watching the man vanish over the rooftops.

*The land-kinden are also air-kinden.* That great unbounded void above them, that had gone from freezing cold to throbbing heat with the coming of the sun, was a slave to these strange and terrible people.

'Here.'

The shabby-looking place they had fetched up beside was a little bigger than most, but no lovelier to look on. Cynthaen banged at a door, while the boy could only think, *How can they live in such ugliness? Even the forest would be better. Cynthaen's kinden have the right idea.*

On the eighth rattling bang, the door was jerked open. A squat, slope-shouldered, dark-skinned man stood there, wearing a sleeved robe that he clasped tight about his broad waist.

'What?' he roared. 'What is it that can't wait for a civilized hour?' His speech was different to the land-kinden woman, a little slower, with the vowels dragged out, but no easier to follow.

'Master Panhandle.' Cynthaen addressed him with obvious scorn.

'Penhold,' he corrected her. He had not even spared a look at her companions. 'What is it, fishwife?'

'I have a gift for you,' Cynthaen told him. 'Your luck has come in with the tide this morning.'

The dark man scowled at her. 'Make sense,' he said.

'I bring three new members for your household,' she told him. 'Rejoice, therefore.'

He stared at her, and the boy wanted to feel sorry for him, but the fact that he himself was being palmed off onto this huge stranger, who obviously bore Cynthaen no love, eclipsed all other considerations.

'Who . . . ?' Penhold glanced past the woman, to see the two Dart-kinden, and then the boy. His face froze, hiding

15

anything that might move behind it. 'Since when did the Mantis-kinden traffic in people?' he enquired slowly, but it was clear that his mind was more concerned with the problem of what this boy and his escort might be.

'You will take them in,' Cynthaen told him. 'Give them a home. Feed them. Work them, if you will. The two tall ones look like they could carry a load.'

The Dart-kinden bristled at that comment, but even Marcantor could tell how everything now hung in the balance.

'And why should I do so?' the big man asked.

'Because I shall bring to you four swords, Panhandle, Mantis-forged rapiers, no less. I know what riches that can bring you.'

Panhandle, or Penhold, stared at her. 'You have no four swords.'

'I will have.'

'You are a catcher of fish.'

'I am a warrior.'

His eyes narrowed. 'Six.'

'Four.'

'Five.'

'Four. Of the very best.'

His eyes flicked again to the boy and the two warriors, as though weighing their worth, and then back to Cynthaen. Something passed between them, some familiarity that made the boy realize that their sparring words hid a longer association than he had guessed.

'I'll bring you a fish, too, if you want,' Cynthaen told him flippantly.

'There's no market for fish.' Panhandle shook his head. 'What am I letting myself in for? Who's after them?'

'No one on the earth is hunting them,' Cynthaen replied, and to the boy the deception seemed glaring. Perhaps it was to Panhandle as well, but if so his face hid it well. He squinted at the two warriors first. 'You'll stand guard, I'd guess,' he decided. 'Guard a shipment, a warehouse? Warriors, in short.'

Santiren nodded shortly. 'We can, once our charge here is safe. We shall not need charity.'

Penhold's eyebrows had risen as he heard her speak, her accent as strange to him as his own was to her. 'And no questions asked, I'm sure,' he muttered to himself. 'Well, then. I am Ordly Penhold, merchant of Collegium. What shall I know you as?'

'Santiren,' the Dart-kinden woman replied. 'And this is Marcantor.'

'And a boy,' Ordly Penhold observed. 'Your servant, is he?'

'I am no servant,' the boy snapped. It had been a long march over a foreign land, passed hand to hand, losing his beloved Paladrya. 'I am Aradocles. I am the . . .' He stopped at Santiren's warning hiss. A whirl of faint colour danced on his skin: shame. *I am hunted, that is what I am.*

There was nothing on Penhold's face to suggest he had understood their exchange but, when he spoke, he said, 'Well now . . . Arad Oakleaves, is it? Perhaps we'll call you Master Oakleaves. Almost a Collegium name that, and a lad like you's better without something too grand.'

Aradocles looked him in the eyes, and saw a man old enough, and wise enough, and outright foreign enough, as not to be easily read.

'Ordly Penhold . . .' He corrected himself, copying the man's own term of address. '*Master* Penhold. Thank you for taking me into your household. I shall do what I can to requite you.'

Only a few scant years later, General Tynan and the Imperial Second Army defeated the Mantids of the Felyal, burned out their holds, drove them from the forest ahead of his swiftly advancing army, and put to the torch every village and trading post they came across. Nor was Arvandine spared.

# Two

To an outsider it would have seemed that the politics of Collegium were of least interest to the politicians themselves. There had been some few moments of silence known to fall during the Collegiate Assembly – they had mostly occurred during the war when to speak into that sudden chasm would have been to volunteer. Business as usual was the constant mutter and murmur of deal-making, deal-breaking, jokes and snickering, and a hundred separate commentaries about current affairs. All too often the only person paying attention to the matter being spoken on was the speaker himself. Sometimes not even that was the case.

'Your big moment soon enough,' Jodry Drillen observed. An experienced Assembler knew how to utter a few low words, amid that babble, which would carry clearly to someone close by, or even to someone halfway around the great bank of stone seats. Drillen, with a voice honed in the lecture theatres of the College, was such a man. Stenwold, sitting two tiers further down and three to the left, heard him precisely and glanced up to see the paunchy, richly dressed man smiling down at him.

*And I am in his party, am I not?* Stenwold knew it. Just sitting here was enough to tell people that he had at last cast his lot. He had never actually taken such a step, it seemed, and yet the men above and below and to either side of him were all supporters of Drillen's faction. The

Assemblers were men and women with enough time on their hands to find significance in anything. In the Assembly, just sitting down was a political act.

It went deeper than that, of course, for Stenwold and Drillen had made deals together behind closed doors. Despite the secrecy it was, paradoxically, well known. There had been an expedition dispatched in Stenwold's name that people had recently started calling 'the Drillen expedition'. It had, rumour suggested, been a great success. Rumour also preceded the expedition's return to Collegium by several days.

Stenwold sat there, surrounded by Drillen's creatures, with an aching void inside him because he had not yet had a chance to confirm some of those rumours. There were a few matters manifestly known about the returning expedition: one College scholar had died, and the Empire had somehow been involved. But Stenwold's interest, for once, shrugged off the political on behalf of the personal.

*What has happened to my niece?*

He had been given no chance yet to speak to the returning scholars. Drillen had grabbed them yesterday at dusk, the moment they arrived. Stenwold had been forced to put his official position ahead of all his personal demands and speak instead to the Vekken ambassadors. What he had heard so far had confirmed his worst fears: Che had not returned with them.

Drillen had promised him access to the two surviving scholars tonight. That was all Stenwold could think about, yet here he was in the Assembly with his name listed to speak.

The Assembly had not seemed itself since Lineo Thadspar died, everyone agreed. Still, while Collegium had been under siege or busy negotiating the Treaty of Gold, that had not seemed to matter. All hands were on the tiller, and pulling the same way. Only with the return of peace had the chaos come crawling in. Without an appointed Speaker the Assembly was deteriorating into name-calling, special interests and personal feuds.

Most of the personal feuds revolved around the identity of the new Speaker. The casting of Lots, the formal process whereby the citizens of Collegium voted in the leaders they deserved, was open all this tenday and Stenwold had already made his choice. Nine Assemblers had put themselves forward as candidates, and Jodry Drillen was one of the front-runners. He was a man with plenty of manifest flaws, to Stenwold's eyes. He was not reliable, trustworthy or honourable. His scholarship had been surrendered to his political ambitions. His patriotism was as fluid as his waist, dependent on his own station within the state. He was nevertheless, Stenwold was forced to admit, the best of a bad field.

*We should select someone at random, plucked out of all the citizens of Collegium,* he thought, and not for the first time. In the absence of a Speaker the role had devolved to the Administrar of the College, as tradition dictated. This meant the task fell on a beaky middle-aged man by the name of Master Partreyn, whose main ambition had hitherto extended to ensuring that the College had sufficient supplies of paper and ink. Used to conducting his life in a quiet monotone, he was usually hoarse through shouting by mid-afternoon, and today it seemed as though the Assembly had a never-ending stream of business. Assemblers would soon start skulking off into the early evening, their patience with democracy exhausted.

Partreyn looked over his scroll where, Stenwold knew, the various Assemblers who wished to take up their fellows' time would be listed, in Partreyn's own neat script. Stenwold's name was amongst them today, to report on the current position with Vek.

*To report success, or some grain of it – and won't that be far less well received than failure.* Not so long since the Ant-kinden of Vek had brought an army up to Collegium's gates. Wounds from the Vekken siege were still open.

People had lost relatives and businesses and property, and gained nothing but scars. News of a glimmer of hope for peace with that violent city would sit badly with many.

*But it is essential, because of the Empire:* the Wasp Empire, which had not been standing still since the inconclusive end to the war. Latest news from Stenwold's agents said that all of the renegade Imperial governors had been pacified and that, of the lands in Imperial hands before the war, only the Three-City Alliance and the Border Principalities remained unbowed. *And when they come for us, we* must *not risk having an enemy to our west.*

'I have Stenwold Maker,' Partreyn got out, forcing his voice over the hubub. There were some cheers, some groans, for Stenwold had never been shy of forcing his company on these men and women. Stenwold pushed himself to his feet, ready to descend and take the floor. Someone else was shouting, though, voice rising high over the general din.

'No! No! This is quite intolerable!' It was a bony Beetle-kinden man who looked slightly Stenwold's senior, sitting near the front row of seats. Several of the men and women beside him began adding their voices to his. He clearly seemed to be the spokesman for some small faction of his own, but Stenwold could not place him.

Partreyn's reply was entirely unheard by anyone further back, but the bony man caught it.

'Three days!' he shouted. 'On the list, three days running, and no time to hear me speak! Do you think my business is not already so injured that I can spare time from it? Hammer and tongs, but you'll hear me speak!'

'Master Failwright!' Partreyn's ragged voice rose in pitch. 'I cannot guarantee—'

'Where's Maker's name on yesterday's list, eh?' Failwright, whoever he was, had a fine screeching voice for such debate. 'Nowhere! Mine's there, not his. Let him wait for the morrow then! Let me speak and be done! Is it so that just because a man goes to the wars, he must always have his way? Are we an Ant-kinden state now? I have business that the Assembly must hear!'

Partreyn looked up and down his list as though he were a seer consulting omens. Stenwold glanced back, and saw Drillen making motions that he should start his speech. *And I could. I could just start shouting with the rest of them, until people started to listen – if they ever did.* There were some others, mostly those who saw Stenwold or Drillen as rivals, who were now calling on Failwright to be given the floor. More though, whom Stenwold guessed as merchants and magnates who, presumably, opposed Failwright, were demanding that Stenwold speak. A few opportunists were now trying to demand that they speak instead. Had there been an elected Speaker, this would never have happened, but Partreyn had neither the formal nor the personal authority to control it.

At last the wretched Administrar looked towards Stenwold with a despairing expression, and Stenwold sat down, sparing his voice the battle. Drillen shot him an interrogating glance and Stenwold leant back to say, 'There's nothing that can't wait for tomorrow, and I'd rather not lose what I have to say in the backbiting that'll follow this. It'll keep.'

Failwright, having abruptly been ceded the floor, seemed uncertain of what to do with it. He glowered defensively at the Assembly from beneath bushy eyebrows. The hum of conversation waxed.

'So who is he?' Stenwold asked.

'Shipping, must be,' Drillen decided. 'That's Ellan Broadrey and old Moulter on either side of him, and they're both dock-merchants.'

Stenwold settled back, preparing himself for a piece of mercantile tedium. The commercial activities of Collegium's magnates had always left a sour taste in his mouth, since there were enough of them who had made a fine profit from the Empire before the war.

Failwright glared around him with a belligerent scowl, as though expecting to be evicted at any moment. Stenwold could not recall ever seeing him before, and guessed he was that kind of Assembler who, once elected, never came to the Amphiophos unless his own interests were threatened. As they were under threat now, apparently.

'Look at you all!' Failwright snapped at the Assembly. His voice carried well, but it set Stenwold's teeth on edge just to listen to it. 'Playing at tacticians and diplomats, as if anyone honestly cared what Maker has to say about the abominable Ant-kinden.'

That caused a scatter of laughter, mostly forced from Stenwold's opponents. *For I have opponents*, he admitted. It was another foot in the mire of politics, and currently it was Helmess Broiler and his adherents who led the chase. Broiler had been one of Jodry Drillen's main opponents for the speakership until recently, when a series of debates and a scandal over cartography had set the man seriously back in his peers' estimation.

'What this city lives on is trade!' Failwright went on. 'We're not Ant-kinden to march, or Spider-kinden to plot. *Trade*, curse you all! And we must act to protect our trade. Are you blind to what has been happening?'

'What has been happening?' Stenwold hissed back at Drillen.

The fat man shrugged. 'No idea,' he said frankly. 'Probably someone's elbowing in on one of his monopolies.'

'The wealth of Collegium is under threat!' Failwright declared dramatically.

'I'm doing fine, thank you!' someone heckled from near where Helmess Broiler sat, to general amusement. Failwright spat out a few half-formed words, furiously, before regaining control of his tongue.

'Oh, yes!' he choked. 'The rail-trade is very well indeed. The airships to Helleron, yes, yes, also well.' His hands clutched and clawed. 'Nobody even asks us how things go for us at the quays!'

'Serves you right for hanging around the docks!' another anonymous wit interjected.

Failwright was flushed with anger. 'Two ships I've lost!' he shouted. 'And in the last three months, eleven merchantment out of Collegium, attacked or disappeared! If you want war, what of the war that pirates have declared on us?'

'Pirates or the weather?' someone from near Broiler called. Had old Thadspar still been Speaker, none of them would have dared, but the absence of his firm hand had given all the malcontents licence to jeer.

'It is an attack aimed at our very heart!' Failwright protested. 'I have papers! I have documented it all precisely. Ships that are robbed. Ships that have been loosed upon by pirate vessels. Ships that simply vanish, no man knows where, with not a single living sailor left to speak of the lost cargo, the ruined investments.' His eyes raked the uninterested Assembly. 'It's Master Maker you call for? Well let him apply himself to some matter of real import for a change!' he shrilled. 'I call on Master Maker to answer this! He who has been so loud in advertising his own imagined threats! What does he say to this?'

The Assembly virtually exploded in a mix of laughter and shouting, some telling Failwright to go away, others calling on Stenwold to stand. The idea of a clash between two firebrands obviously appealed to them.

Partreyn kept waving his hands, mouth open as he shouted inaudibly for quiet. At last the roar died down and left him rasping wretchedly. 'You cannot demand answer from an individual,' he croaked. 'Only if he consents to answer, on behalf of the Assembly . . . Is that not so?' The list of causes was wrung between his hands. 'Master Maker?'

Stenwold took pity on him, standing up to declare, 'I am no expert, save that I defended Master Failwright's docklands from the Vekken, and—'

'And saw most of it burned!' Failwright yelled at him.

Stenwold found himself smiling despite himself at the man's sheer persistence. 'I would more readily answer questions on the Vekken, whether war or peace, than on this, but I'll make a reply if Master Failwright wishes it,' he said, and most of the chamber quietened enough to hear him. 'We are a city of merchants, as Master Failwright observes. We are also a city of scholars. The two complement each other, in fact. We in this hall are gownsmen and townsmen magnates both. The distinction has always been there. We of the College hold our seats here through long tradition that holds that men wise enough to teach are also wise enough to govern. You of the town are elected by our citizens, and thus represent those men and women whose business and practice is successful and notable enough that you can gather the followers and spare the time to play your parts here. And, believe me, the burden of time never seemed to weigh as heavily as this afternoon.'

The expected laughter came and Stenwold paused for it, thinking, *I am getting too good at this. When did I ever want to please the crowd?*

'However, the Assembly has always been deplored by the merchants of this town for interfering in their business,' he went on. 'Not seven years ago, there was a motion concerning the workhouses in Helleron, and whether a clean-handed magnate of Collegium could deal with such institutions, could even own shares in them. It was then firmly stated: the business of a merchant is his own. A year before the war came a motion to ban shares in slaving concerns, for as we outlaw slavery within our city, should our merchants be free to invest in the flesh trade beyond? It was again firmly stated, although hotly contested, that the business of a merchant is his own. Therefore I say to you, Master Failwright, that the business of a merchant is his own. If this Assembly may not dampen his profits, neither may it blow upon the embers of his losses.'

There was a rumble of approval from the lackeys of Drillen, but also from the College Assemblers as a whole. Even as Stenwold sat down, Helmess Broiler was rising to his feet on the far side of the chamber from him.

Partreyn just mutely gestured for him to speak, and Drillen murmured, 'Here we go.'

'Well, historic times, my friends.' Helmess Broiler was a well-dressed magnate, affluently plump, his thinning hair oiled like that of a Spider Aristos. He had proved a thorn since Stenwold's very first speech to the Assembly, resistant to change, greedy for profit, a true spokesman for the Helleron lobby. Stenwold harboured darker suspicions, too, from the man's stance before the war, but none of that was provable. In the end, Stenwold had focused his energy on the Vekken initiative, rather than pursue those he suspected had taken Imperial gold.

Broiler smiled down at Failwright. 'Historic either because Master Maker has come to his senses, or I have,' he said pleasantly. 'I find I agree with him, which I believe is unprecedented. Master Partreyn, you must record it in the books.' More laughter, and Stenwold suddenly felt complicit in it. *And I myself stood where Failwright stands, not so long ago. True, I was arguing for the liberty of cities and not the profit of the sea-trade, but he should merit better treatment than this.*

'Master Failwright, all I shall say is that if you place your investments in a wooden eggshell, so very vulnerable to every turn of tide and wind and roguery,' Helmess continued, 'and if you fail to make provision for an escort or a guard, then on your head be it. On the heads, likewise, of all who cast their money onto the waves. That is why I buy Spiderlands goods imported by way of Helleron, Merro and Tark. They may take longer to reach the markets than your ship-borne

26

cargoes, but at least they seldom suffer from piracy, and no rail automotive has ever sunk without trace.'

The laughter and approval sounded whole-hearted from most, though a little uncertain from Drillen's people. As the furious Failwright stalked from the chamber, Stenwold thought, *I, too, have walked out like that, but I think I chose a worthier issue.* Then the thought of the news from Khanaphes reclaimed him, even as Partreyn announced that any more causes must wait until the morrow, whereupon all thought of Failwright and the shipping magnates left him.

Nevertheless, Jodry Drillen snagged him by the door. 'A word, old friend,' he murmured.

'Now is not the best time,' Stenwold warned him. 'You know—'

'The Khanaphes expedition? Of course I know,' the fat Assembler confirmed. He spread his hands in a helpless gesture. 'If you cannot give me a few moments of your time to impart a warning, Stenwold, then by all means go, but . . .'

'Jodry?'

'There is a matter on the horizon, and you are more than likely to be accused in it.'

Stenwold looked at him levelly. *And how are you trying to twist me now, Jodry?* 'Be quick, then.'

'As a beggar's supper. Come, let's find a room.' Jodry commandeered one of the Amphiophos staff to fetch them some wine, and ensconced himself in a little reading room near the debating chamber. 'While you've been playing nice with the Vekken we've had our own military dictatorship to worry about. I've been keeping the pot from boiling over on this one, but now your name's come into it. I'm talking about the Merchant Companies, Stenwold.'

'What about them?'

'The Companies' was the unofficial name given to the various groups of Collegium citizens put under arms during the recent war against the Empire. They had been trades-men and merchants and itinerant mercenaries organized by profession or by place of residence, and had become the nearest the city had ever known to a standing army. At the end of the war, most had quietly gone back to their civilian lives, perhaps with a pike stowed in the attic or a sword displayed over the mantelpiece.

'For most of them? Nothing.' Jodry paused to receive the wine from the servant, and poured them out two bowls. 'Three Companies have yet to disband, however, and there have been calls to have them formally abolished.'

Stenwold's mind was still on his anticipated guests, news of Che. 'Get to the point, Jodry. Which three?'

'Outwright's Pike and Shot, for one,' Jodry revealed.

'Well, Janos Outwright was always an exhibitionist.' Stenwold dismissed the whole idea airily with a wave of his hand.

'The Coldstone Company, for another,' the other man went on patiently.

Stenwold groaned at that. Coldstone Street had been the furthest intrusion of the Vekken army into Collegium. The men and women who lived there had brought half their own houses tumbling down onto the invaders, then fought as fiercely as Mantids, as doggedly as the Ant-kinden them-selves. When the call had gone out to confront the Empire, the Coldstone Company had been there, not line soldiers but ragged skirmishers, ambushers and desperados. They had made a name for themselves as Collegium's most stub-born and least principled defenders. Stenwold supposed he should not now be surprised.

'And the third?' he prompted.

'Aha, well.' Jodry coughed away a smile. 'They call themselves "Maker's Own".'

A pause. 'Do they indeed?'

'Indeed they do.' The fat man fixed Stenwold with a

measuring eye. 'You might recall them. You took them out with you that time you somehow convinced the Imperial Second to pack its bags and go home.'

'You know what . . .' Stenwold started, and then reread Jodry's expression. 'You don't think . . . ? Jodry, I have not encouraged any such company. Nobody even thought to tell me they were making free with my name.'

'I believe you,' Jodry said drily, 'but who else will is another matter. I had their Chief Officer Padstock here three days ago declaring that, whenever you called for them, they would be ready: that they were just waiting for your word to march on . . . well, pretty much anywhere, I think. The Amphiophos included. If you ever wanted to become Tyrant of Collegium, this is certainly your chance.'

Stenwold looked down at his hands. *So much misplaced loyalty, and yet . . .* 'And there are now calls to have them all disbanded.'

'Of course. Many in the Assembly are somewhat concerned at the prospect of bands of armed militia roaming our city unchecked. Of course, they haven't really thought it through. At the moment the Companies are at least paying lip-service to the idea of civic duty. Disband them and you instantly create three small private armies with a good reason to dislike the Assembly. Then we'd have to pass some law forbidding citizens to own weapons, or some such, and then . . .'

'Then we'd probably be just about ready for the next move from the Empire,' Stenwold confirmed. 'Not to mention that most visitors from, well, from almost anywhere would come with a sword at their belts, and it would be a fine state of affairs to have everyone in Collegium go armed except its own people.' He took a deep breath.

'But we can hardly tolerate private armies in Collegium, either,' Jodry pointed out. 'If they're not disbanded then, soon enough, every Assembler and every magnate will want

29

his own band of cut-throats. Can you imagine what Helmess Broiler would do with a hundred brigands operating under his banner?'

'So what's your plan?'

'I dearly wish I had a plan, right now,' Jodry said. 'I've met with Outwright and the other chief officers, and they're making demands, and I've met with the Assemblers who want them disbanded, and they're making demands, and now both sides are starting to mention you.'

'Well, I can see how it's my problem,' Stenwold allowed, 'but how is it *yours*?'

'Because I plan to be Speaker soon enough, and then all the city's problems become my problems. I want you to back me, Stenwold, because you're the war hero. The Companies will listen to you.'

Stenwold stared at him a long time. 'Will you disband them?'

'I don't know,' Jodry admitted. 'I'm caught between pincers right now, and trying to squirm my way out.'

'Then, when you find your way out, talk to me, and I'll decide if I'll back you.'

For a moment Jodry regarded him sternly, obviously about to deliver a pre-prepared bout of disappointment or chiding, but then he nodded. 'Fair,' he granted, 'but you should apply your mind to it, too. After all, with all your constant talk of the Empire, the future of Collegium's militia should be of prime concern to you. Anyway, off home with you. I hear you've got guests.'

'Guests, yes.' And the urgency flooded back: *Khanaphes. News of Che.* Stenwold nodded hastily to Jodry and hurried off.

# Three

Stenwold's desk had moved house with him twice. It had been part of his life for twelve years, now, through all those hard years of struggle: his attempts to open the eyes of the Assembly to the threat of the Empire; his attempts to second-guess the Rekef; the deployment of his agents and his intelligence-gathering – all played out on this same scratched desktop.

He had returned to his trade, or never left it. It was not the Empire that obsessed him, nor even the Vekken. He was using his profession for ends as selfish and personal as those of any profiteering merchant. He was trying to find his own, but the world was large, and those in it so very small, and he knew now that she did not want to be found.

Tynisa, his ward – Tisamon's child. He had no hold on her, no right to her, and yet he kept trying to find her. The longer he was left without news, the more he feared that she had succumbed to her bloodline; that she had followed her father towards the glorious, bloody end of a Mantis weaponsmaster.

He had letters in from this morning, two at once, and neither containing any comfort. The first was brief, made out in the blocky handwriting of an Ant-kinden who seldom committed his thoughts to paper.

*Master Maker,*

*Got your missive. Will keep searching. Not so many here that a face like hers won't be noticed. Also, all like family here – good will and cheer, you know. She comes here, we'll find her. Maybe you should come here too. Do you good. You'd like what they've done with the place.*

*Am Commander again now. Am told I'm war hero. Load of rubbish, but can live with it. Herself has me in charge of walls now, or will be when walls built.*

*Sperra sends regards.*

*Balkus*

*Commander, Princep Salmae.*

Stenwold read through it once more. *Another pair of eyes now on watch.* He had hoped Tynisa might make for the new city, if only from some memory of Salma. She had been more than fond of Salma, he recalled, before the war and Salma's affections elsewhere had broken them apart. He recalled their last meeting, in Salma's brigand camp. Brief, awkward. It seemed Tynisa had, for once, not known how to act or what to say.

*Balkus will find her if her feet should take her to Princep.* And perhaps Stenwold *should* go himself. The city they were building west of Sarn was founded on all the principles that Collegium and Stenwold both upheld. He should go and see whether they were making good on their intentions, or whether the rot had crept in already.

*My mind is dark this evening.* But then that was hardly surprising, sitting here leafing through the notes of failed searches, while waiting for more bad news from his anticipated guests.

The second letter was written out in a neatly elegant hand, the slightly over-florid style of an educated Beetle mimicking the glorious calligraphy of the Spiderlands.

*My good old friend,*

*I have taken your message to heart. The war scattered many grains and we are all still picking them up. I can guarantee nothing, of course, since this place has grown no smaller since you last saw it. There is no place on the earth where one can more easily find obscurity or dissolution than this city of ours. You know this as well as I, so forgive me the frank words.*

*Still: a Spider-kinden with a Mantis brooch and sword? There are not so very many of that kind. If she does follow in the footsteps of the father, then she'll leave quite a trail behind her. I have sent men to the fiefdom you mentioned, the Halfway House. They are much lessened in numbers following the occupation, but I am informed that they retain their leader from before the war, and so there may be some help found there. If she practises the fighting trade here in Helleron, whether on the streets or in the arena, then I have some hopes of tracking her for you.*

*As an aside, yes, the arena remains, though its builders are flown. The fights there are not strictly to the death, but there have been deaths. I fear my city has been left, after the Wasps, with the taste of blood in its mouth.*

*To return to your concerns: if she has merely passed through our streets on an eastward journey, I will not be able to be of much service. There is some slight hope, though: the Empire remains a wealthy consumer of goods, and now an employer of skilled labour. There are those who speak to me, who are at Sonn or Capitas, and I have asked them to keep an open eye. However, I am reliably told that the Empire is not fond of questions, however innocent. It is a place unfriendly and unwelcoming enough that only their gold makes even a temporary residence there worthwhile. The Emperor may have passed on, but his trappings remain.*

*I hope you find her, Sten.*

*GA*

That last line, that personal voice behind the formal style, tugged at Stenwold: Greenwise Artector, one of Helleron's guiding council, a wealthy magnate and unlikely ally. Nobody but Stenwold knew quite how much he had orchestrated things, behind the facade of public life, to assist the Lowlands in its war against the Empire, even from the heart of an occupied city. Everything Greenwise had seen of the Empire's numbers and movements and capabilities had found its way to Stenwold, and to Salma too, who had used it to slow the Wasp advance until the Sarnesh army was ready for them. It was an achievement worthy of recognition, yet Greenwise had been explicit that it go unrecognized. Stenwold knew exactly why: the Empire still had its people in Helleron, and its ambitions beyond. There would come a time when the Imperial banner would once again come to that city. At which point, Greenwise's fellow magnates would have him handed over without a second thought.

There was a delicate scratch at the door and Stenwold folded the two letters together and put them away, an old instinct he didn't need just now, but might need to take up again soon – just like the sword that hung on the back of the study door.

'You can come in,' he announced.

'You've closed the latch again,' came Arianna's voice, amused. Another old habit, for a spymaster, past or present, valued privacy. He got up and opened the door to her.

He always felt better for seeing her, no matter what the odds. She had sustained him through the Vekken Siege, and it was widely claimed that she and he together had sent the Imperial Second Army packing. Nonsense, of course, but Stenwold was all unwillingly attracting stories that would have done justice to a sorcerer-hero of the Bad Old Days. Having a pretty young Spider girl at his side seemed to coin only envy and admiration, however, rather than the looked-for scandal.

'They're here,' Arianna told him, putting a hand on his arm. 'Cardless is attending to them.' Cardless was Stenwold's third servant since the war, and not given to the gossip and sloth that had seen his master dismiss the other two. He had been Arianna's choice, of course. Stenwold was used to choosing spies and agents, which meant his eye was attuned for different qualities.

He took a deep breath, looking down at his hands. It was time now to resolve the rumours.

Cardless had transformed Stenwold's homely kitchen table into something fit for an important Assembler hosting a Master of the College. There were candles in ornate Spider-kinden holders, and the wine was a good Merro vintage. His three guests held a bowl each already. Two were well known to Stenwold, members of the expedition that had gone under his name. The lean old man was the historian Berjek Gripshod. The younger woman, tall and straight, was Praeda Rakespear, teacher of artifice. There were lines on their faces that had not been evident at their departure. Although they both wore the crisp white robes of their office, the travel of many miles seemed to hang about them, so that Stenwold could almost taste the dust.

The third visitor was a stranger who appeared to fill most of the room, stooping under the ceiling, the tiny bowl a toy in the palm of his hand: a Beetle-kinden, though taller than any man of Collegium Stenwold had seen, and he wore a tunic of a foreign cut, ornamented with gold at the neck and wrist. His bare arms were huge with muscle and traced with scars. He stood beside Praeda with a possessive enough air to be either her lover or a bodyguard. Arianna had met them at the door and then ushered them in to see Stenwold, the perfect Collegiate hostess.

'Master Maker,' said old Gripshod, by way of greeting.

'Master Gripshod, Mistress Rakespear, and . . .' Stenwold looked up at the giant cautiously. He felt that if the man straightened up and flexed his shoulders he would send the walls of Stenwold's house tumbling outwards into the street.

'Master Maker,' Praeda said, 'may I introduce Amnon, formerly the First Soldier of Khanaphes.'

Stenwold blinked at that, reflecting that Praeda had perhaps exceeded a scholar's normal penchant for bringing back research material. 'Well, I'm honoured,' he managed.

The huge man regarded him with a slight, polite smile, the thoughts behind it well hidden.

'Please, sit.' Stenwold gestured to the table. Of course there were only four places set but, even as he noticed it, Cardless was seamlessly inserting a fourth before drifting back with a tray of fruit-bread.

They settled about the table. It was clear to them all that this was not just another case of a townsman greeting the returned explorers. They eyed each other like veterans who might or might not have fought in the same battles, or even on the same side.

'What did you actually know, of what you were sending us into, Master Maker?' Praeda asked him first. 'Or what did Jodry Drillen know?'

'What I knew, you knew,' Stenwold replied. 'And as for what Drillen knew, who can say? I'll say that I don't believe he was trying to stir up trouble anywhere but here in Collegium, but I have no window on his mind.'

'They say he will be Speaker,' Berjek murmured. 'Did we bring that about?'

'Yes and yes,' Stenwold confirmed. 'But there were worse men for the job.' *And am I Drillen's apologist now?* 'If I had thought he was sending you into danger, if I had thought that he was the kind of man to do so, then I'd have had no part of it.'

'I believe you,' Berjek acknowledged, although Praeda looked less certain. 'I opposed you, you know, when you first started your ravings about the Empire. You were right then, so I'll advance credit on your opinions now.'

'Manny was killed,' Praeda stated. 'The Wasps killed him.'

'I'm very sorry.'

She looked to Amnon then, and Stenwold placed his role as lover and not merely a guard. 'If it hadn't been . . .' she began.

Berjek nodded. 'And for the Vekken. It was your idea to have them with us, and I won't say we weren't ultimately grateful. You've spoken with them?'

'As soon as they arrived. I'd left them time to report to their fellows but . . . Ant-kinden, of course – the Vekken here knew, as soon as your ship approached the harbour.' They had told him little else, save that the Empire was there, and involved in an assault on the city, and on the embassy in particular. The interview with the returned Vekken ambassadors had been strange even by their standards. They had left so much out, and he had sensed that it was not just to spite him, but because they lacked adequate words to describe it. Whatever had motivated them to hold to their truce with Collegium, it was not accounted for in the little they had revealed.

'Master Maker,' said Gripshod, 'we know why you've asked us here. It's not merely to welcome the returning explorers and it's not concerning city politics.' He extracted a sealed and folded paper from within his robes, and Stenwold caught sight of the handwriting: his own name inscribed in that too familiar, desperately-trying-to-be-neat hand. He reached for it automatically, but Berjek held it back.

'We need to explain first,' Praeda said. Stenwold's gaze flicked between the two of them, sliding past the chest of the huge Khanaphir soldier. 'Whatever she's written will be her own account but . . . it may not be as reliable as you're used to.'

'What do you mean?' Stenwold was already on the defensive for absent Che without thinking.

The two academics exchanged glances. 'Only that, on reaching Khanaphes, your niece's behaviour was . . . erratic. Increasingly so,' Berjek informed him, a man steeling himself for an unpleasant task. 'She began acting oddly, absenting herself, avoiding engagements. She disappeared two or three times without warning or excuse. She kept odd company: foreign merchants, the Imperial ambassador.' He saw Stenwold react to that last information, and nodded grimly. 'Whatever was preoccupying her mind, it wasn't official duties, Master Maker.'

'She was engaged on some expedition of her own,' Praeda confirmed. 'We all witnessed it. When the attack on the city began she vanished entirely. Everyone thought the Wasps had ordered her killed . . . You do know about the Imperial involvement there?'

Stenwold nodded. 'Word came to me that they were boiling the pot. I'm listed to challenge the Imperial ambassador over it soon, but no doubt he'll say it was all down to rogue elements, therefore nothing to do with them.'

'Who can say?' Berjek said. 'Frankly, I can't see what possible advantage the Empire could have gained, even if they'd ground Khanaphes into sand and dust. Rogue elements would make as much sense as anything.' He drained his bowl and Cardless was immediately at his elbow to refill it. 'Well, you're forewarned, Maker. Read it.' He slid the letter across the tabletop.

Stenwold took a deep breath and broke the seal. That same script greeted him, that had always been a cause of concern for her tutors. The thought came to him of Che diligently practising her letters over and over, a dozen years gone, and he shut his eyes for a moment.

'We should leave.' It was the deep voice of Amnon. Stenwold looked up to meet the gaze of a private man who knew a need for privacy in others, unlike the Collegiates who thrived on the doings of their neighbours. He shook his head, aware that he was being remiss as a host.

'No, no, please, help yourself to my table. I – I won't be a moment.' He should leave Che's letter until they were gone, he knew, but he did not have that kind of strength, not in this.

> *Dearest Uncle Sten,*
>
> *I hope this reaches you soon. I am afraid you will not be very happy with me, but there is not much that can be done about that. I am not coming back to Collegium right away.*
>
> *I cannot explain to you what has happened to me, but it follows from the wounds I took in the war: the losses that I endured. I have healed some of them.*
>
> *Achaeos is dead.*
>
> *I can write that now. It is true for me now, though I am still coming to terms with it. He is dead, but he has left me with his gift – the gift of his kind, and of his Days of Lore. We call them the Bad Old Days sometimes, but I am not sure that is just. They were merely different times, when the Inapt races ruled. I know this now.*
>
> *I must ask you to trust me and I know it will be hard. I have always been the one to follow, to stumble, to make mistakes. I have always leant on you, and trusted you, and been rescued by you. Now you must trust me.*
>
> *I am travelling to find Tynisa. I know where she has gone and I know she is in great danger. It is time for me to mount a rescue.*
>
> *I am not travelling alone, but that is another thing you must trust me on. No doubt the messengers have already told you who I journey with, and no doubt you have already mobilized the army and called for the orthopters to start up their wings.*
>
> *Trust me. I do not say 'Trust him', because I cannot ask that of you, but just trust me, in this.*

*I will come home and, if it is possible, I will come home with Tynisa.*

*Your disobedient niece,*

*Cheerwell*

He looked up from the letter to meet their eyes and there must have been a thunder in his expression that they had not expected. The two academics flinched, and Amnon squared his shoulders as though ready for an assault.

'Who?' was all he asked.

'Master Maker?' Praeda frowned at him.

'Who was she travelling with? She says here, "No doubt the messengers have already told me". So tell me, Masters, who is with my niece.'

'I did not think . . .' Berjek started, but Praeda's eyes widened and she interrupted, 'She must mean the Imperial ambassador.'

Stenwold went quite cold, the letter tearing slightly in his hands. 'To the Empire? The little fool's gone to the *Empire*?'

'I very much doubt it,' Praeda said. 'Has her letter not told you where she was going? She didn't tell us.' At Stenwold's stare she went on: 'The Empire was trying to kill her, last we heard. I can't think that she'd just walk into their hands.'

'Then why is she with—?'

'He'd gone rogue himself,' Berjek said quickly. 'Your niece said his own people were trying to kill him. Another reason the Empire isn't likely to be their destination . . . We . . . ?' For Stenwold had held up a hand. 'Master Maker?'

'Tell me his name.' The foreknowledge, indeed the bloody-minded inevitability of it, made him feel ill and Praeda did not have to say it. He knew already. He *knew*.

His opposite number. His nemesis. His curse. Thalric.

'I should have killed him when he turned himself in to

me,' Stenwold said, and the horrified looks of his Collegiate guests passed him by. 'I should have let Felise gut him. I should have cut his lying throat *myself*.' For a moment he was purely Stenwold the spymaster, whose history and conduct were not at all those of Master Stenwold the scholar and Assembler. In that same moment someone began pounding on his door, a voice distantly shouting his name, and he was reaching for the sword he no longer wore, even as Arianna went to answer it.

Stenwold heard the insistent voice as the door was opened, demanding loudly to see the 'War Master'.

*I am not in the mood.* It was a voice he had heard enough of today already. He heard Arianna trying to put the man off, but for once her charm failed and the intruder had stormed into the room before she could divert him. Master Failwright, Assembler and shipping magnate, clutching a leather satchel stuffed full of documents to his chest.

'Maker!' he spat out, then saw Stenwold's guests and a moment of confusion ensued, before Failwright blurted, 'What's going on here?' as though he had uncovered some conspiracy against the sea trade. Arianna hovered in the doorway behind him with an apologetic expression, but Stenwold told her, by one small shake of his head, that he would deal with this.

'Rones Failwright, isn't it?' Berjek Gripshod observed, in a voice lacking fondness.

'I must speak with you, Maker.' Failwright spoke as though Berjek and the others were just about to leave, as though Stenwold was at the Amphiophos and not in his own home. 'You'll see. You'll see when I—'

'I'll see nothing,' Stenwold said. His voice was leaden, the words like stones.

The man stared at him. 'Maker, they told me you were a man of honour.'

'And?'

'And they sing your bloody praises on every street

throughout this town. You have to help me. They call you War Master, don't they? Well, we're at war, Maker! Not with your precious Empire, but war nonetheless. Our ships are under attack. More and more of them boarded or fired, robbed or sunk, or simply lost without trace where no storm ever was.' He slammed the bulging satchel down on the dining table. A wineglass jumped from the far side with the impact but Amnon caught it almost without looking. He was merely waiting, Stenwold realized, for his host's request to evict Failwright by force.

'It's all here!' Failwright was leafing through a bundle of dog-eared scrolls. 'It's not piracy, but outright war! I tried to tell Broiler's lot, but they're up to their armpits in the Helleron trade. If we go under, they'd do nothing but get richer. Everyone knows he hates you, so you're the only person I can turn to.'

'No,' said Stenwold. The single heavy word halted Failwright's train of thought.

'But everyone—'

'I don't care what people say of me, I was never the champion of one merchant or a hundred. All that I did, I did for my city and the Lowlands. I never asked to be War Master, and if I had, do you imagine a real warlord would care a jot about your disputes?'

'No, no, now look . . .' Failwright took a scroll from his satchel, seemingly at random. 'The ships, I've itemized them all: their cargoes, the men who invested in them, and their fates!'

'Get out of my house.' Stenwold's tone was still calm, but laden with threat.

'Maker, you have a duty—!'

'Yes, I have a duty!' Something broke in him, some barrier that had separated the wartime man from peaceful matters. In that same moment Stenwold wished that he possessed that trick of Tisamon's: the inexplicable sleight that put a blade in his grasp at the merest thought. At the same time he realized that, had he possessed it, Failwright would have died there and then. There was no sword, of course, but Failwright saw it in his eyes. He was still gabbling away, telling Stenwold how it was his responsibility, but in a voice of thunder Stenwold overrode him.

'I have duties to my family, I have duties to my College and my city, but I have no duty to be every man's hired hand. I am not for sale or rent or lease, nor shall I take up your grimy little banner out of public love. I have a ward and a niece lost to me, and friends dead in the war, and an Assembly of men who think that the war was won instead of merely postponed, and *yes*, I have duties, and you now stand between them and me.' He was forcing Failwright back towards the door without touching him, sheer restrained fury boiling off him like steam. 'And if you are still in my sight one minute from now then I swear I will no longer be answerable for my actions.'

Failwright actually tried to thrust the scroll at him, but fell gibbering back when Stenwold raised a hand. Not striking the wretched merchant took more control than not having Thalric killed during the war, when the defecting Wasp was at Stenwold's mercy.

Arianna had reopened the door, and Failwright stumbled backwards through it, still stuttering sounds that were no longer words. The door slammed after him, leaving a moment of blessed silence.

Stenwold turned to his guests, then, and remembered where he was and what he had been doing. 'I . . .' he said uncertainly, still seething with anger that had nowhere else to go.

'I think we should make our exit,' Praeda decided. 'Master Maker, please call upon us if you wish to know more, but it seems there is much your niece told none of us.'

*I should tell them to stay. I am a poor host.* They were right, though. Che's news had broken the back of the evening and it would not recover.

'I'm sorry,' he said, 'this has not gone as I'd hoped.' Even as he said it he was thinking, *Has it not, though? Aside from Failwright's intrusion, did I not honestly expect this after Che failed to come back?*

'We understand,' Berjek reassured him, and they left, quickly making their farewells. Amnon was the last to go, his gaze suggesting he had weighed up Stenwold Maker, and found something there of worth. Stenwold had understood that Khanaphes had little in common with Collegium, which suggested that the man must have been doing a great deal of catching up.

Arianna went over to Stenwold, her slender arms wrapping about one of his. 'For the morning, all of it,' she told him. 'Enough of them, enough of all of them. Put down your duties, warrior, and come to bed.'

That reminded him of the actual war, when his duties could not be put down, when he had burned the oil night and day to save his city. *And, even then, did I save it? The Imperial Second left us because Tisamon finally honed his gift for killing into regicide. What part did I play?*

But the war was currently in abeyance, and long might it remain so. The duties could wait.

On his way to the stairs, he saw that Failwright had been evicted so fast that one of his scrolls lay part-unravelled on the floor near the door. Of all the competing claims on his attention, that was surely the least.

# Four

When he came, he came dressed in plain colours, not in livery nor hooded like a conspirator: a middle-aged Beetle in a leather cap, such as artificers wore to keep their hair safe from sparks, or a soldier underneath his metal helm. His clothes were those of any well-to-do tradesman whose job occasionally required him to get dirty, and his frame was portly, prosperous-looking. The bodyguard was Wasp-kinden but not in uniform, all the trappings of a renegade for hire. There was barely a hint of black or yellow about either of them.

The door these two appeared at was not Helmess Broiler's townhouse, rather a mid-town property he also owned. The line thus trodden was just sharp enough to make him sweat. *Damn the fellow.*

Helmess Broiler was a big man in the Assembly still, for all that Jodry Drillen had clawed himself a clear-cut lead in recent days. Popularity was like cupping water in your hands, forever seeping away. *It will change.* But, for now, Helmess had to accept that he had been wrongfooted. It was not a good time for this meeting, but no time would have been ideal, not after the war.

The servant who opened the door was a man who had been with the Broiler family two generations, with sharp eyes and a tight mouth. Inside, a modest table was already set. This was merely two Beetle-kinden talking business in civilized surroundings, had anyone asked.

'Master Broiler,' said the visitor, pushing the cap off his balding head and smiling with every appearance of cordiality, *And he is enjoying himself*, Broiler thought bitterly. *We both took a fall, after the war, so how come he's smiling and I'm not?*

'Master Bellowern,' Broiler acknowledged. The bodyguard took up his place at a comfortable distance. He was not so evidently a soldier out of uniform as Broiler had feared, but that made it even worse. Paranoia duly raised the spectre of the Wasps' hidden blade: the Rekef. Was this man a Rekef agent? Was Honory Bellowern himself a Rekef agent?

*Of all the people in this city, I am one of only two who truly know to fear the Rekef*, Helmess Broiler thought dourly, *and the other is Stenwold Maker, who would not appreciate the joke.*

And, on the heels of that: *Maker, who put me in this intolerable position by having the bloody gall to be right.*

Honory Bellowern had been a resident of Collegium for a few years now, neatly pre-dating the war itself. He was a model Beetle-kinden, well-mannered, genial, sophisticated and wealthy. One could forget so easily that he was no native, that he was in fact a servant of the Empire. He was not the Imperial ambassador, which role had gone, after the war, to a Wasp called Aagen. Aagen spent most of his non-ambassadorial time touring the factories and the College artificing workshops, and when he stood up to speak to the Assembly, Bellowern was always at his shoulder. Bellowern drew the charts that Ambassador Aagen steered by, and at the same time he was the acceptable face of Imperial policy, a friendly, corpulent statement that *We are like you*. People like Broiler already knew that the Empire was full of such people. Through their factors in Helleron there had been a fine old profit to be made, and that profit was magnified for those prepared to put themselves out a little for their trading partners.

And so it had been natural for Bellowern to have made some business contacts with certain Collegiate magnates. Bellowern had his hand in the coffers of the Consortium, which managed and massaged Imperial trade. Before the war, a lot of that trade had been flowing through Helleron and thence to Collegium, and Broiler had been one of the beneficiaries. Bellowern had not asked so very much, to secure preferential treatment. It was, after all, standard procedure within the Collegium Assembly, denied and decried and assiduously practised. If a citizen of Collegium wanted something done, then he courted those Assemblers most sympathetic. There were gifts and favours, it was how life had always worked. The Empire had become a very comfortable neighbour, and it had been no great sacrifice for Helmess to mouth their words at the Amphiophos. After all, Broiler had been speaking against Stenwold Maker's lunacies, and Broiler had been trading affluently with the Empire, and so a closer working relationship seemed harmless enough.

And then it had all gone wrong, horribly wrong. Stenwold Maker had talked the Assembly into declaring against the Empire, and the Imperial Second Army had come ravening along the coast until it stood at the gates of Collegium itself, since Maker had talked the Assembly into committing Collegium to war.

Even then it had still looked hopeful, and more hopeful for Broiler and his peers than for any others. The Empire was a formidable military force, the Sarnesh had already been beaten once, and Collegium was still battered after the Vekken siege. An Imperial Collegium, with positions of responsibility handed to those the Empire could trust, would have worked out very nicely. *And Stenwold Maker's head on a pike.*

But the Sarnesh and their Collegiate ancillaries had

beaten the Empire at Malkan's Stand, and then the Emperor had displayed the ferociously ill-timed gall to die, dragging Imperial stability with him. General Tynan's Second Army had rushed from the gates of Collegium to secure the man's political future, and Collegium somehow declared it a victory for the Lowlands. The Treaty of Gold was signed, and subsequently there was a peace in which the Empire was remembered as the aggressor and its friends as potential collaborators. Men like Broiler were soon busy erasing whole chapters of their own recent past.

All this could be read quite clearly in the avuncular eyes of Honory Bellowern, now sitting down to eat.

He left it until Broiler's servants had brought out a dessert of honeyed custard, before approaching business. Honory Bellowern possessed a true Beetle appetite, ploughing with gusto through everything that was set before him. But finally he raised a hand, and Broiler's heart sank.

'There's a little matter,' Bellowern began. 'Something that's going to come up.'

He used very similar words each time, and Broiler watched him from across the table, devoid of appetite.

'Within a few days our mutual friends will be the talk of the town again,' Bellowern stated. 'I imagine our colleague the War Master will then become quite agitated. You'd do us the favour of heading up the opposition, surely?'

'What?' Broiler asked flatly. 'What's going to happen?'

'News from the far east, inconsequential really, but you know that Master Maker will try to talk war over it. Collegium needs a cool head in the Assembly, to lay to rest people's fears, Helmess. You can do that, can't you?'

Broiler looked sour. 'And *should* we be fearing, just now?'

'No, no, it's all very, very far away. It's just that Maker gets so very twitchy whenever the black and gold flag is raised. He'll have our ambassador there, anyway, and we've got a few salvos to send over his parapets, but it would be useful to have a little local support, no?'

'Or?' Helmess hadn't meant to say it, but his temper was frayed, and recent developments in his own life – the ones Bellowern was ignorant of – spurred him on.

Honory Bellowern favoured him with a kindly smile. 'You'd rather remain a friend of the Empire, wouldn't you?' he asked. 'You've always impressed me as a man of foresight, Helmess. Tynan's Second nearly broke this city the last time, and it was not the staunch defenders of Collegium that turned them away. You know, we both know, that we'll be back here in time. When the black and gold waves over the Amphiophos, we'll know who our true friends are.' He smiled, white teeth gleaming. 'And, of course, in the short term you need us. You're not the most popular man in the Assembly any more. You're not going to be Speaker, and therefore you need us. If nothing else, you need us to keep quiet about certain aspects of the war.'

'I could deny anything you threw at me,' Broiler stated.

'But who would be believed? You're not the big noise you once were, Helmess. You still have a lot of support, but it's the kind that would melt away like spring frost once you started to smell. You rely on our silence, if nothing else.'

Broiler kept his expression blank, but nodded resignedly. He was a politician, good at dissociating his face from his mind. Bellowern seemed satisfied, anyway. *Ruin me, would you?* Helmess thought. *Well, perhaps I have a little support you aren't aware of. And perhaps there are things the vaunted Imperial spies don't know.*

They concluded their meal, Broiler playing his part as bitter but defeated, and Bellowern seemed to go away satisfied. Broiler stayed by the door a long time after he had departed, considering how much longer he would have to dance to that man's tune. Upstairs, he heard *her* tread.

She'd kept absolute silence all through the meal, not allowing a hint to Bellowern that they had company. Now he heard her at the top of the staircase. A spark struck up in his heart – for her, and for the sheer joy of conspiracy and secret knowledge.

The fog had come as a stroke of luck, for without it the pirate would have overhauled them already. Although the *Pelter* – out of Collegium with a cargo of machined gems, wine and artifice – had been running its engines at top speed for an hour, the other ship's great spread of sail had been gradually closing the distance, and there was no sign of a change in the wind that might give the Beetle engineers an advantage. The *Pelter* was a small ship, and its meagre crew in no position to fight off sea-brigands, so its captain had set a course away from the coast, while cursing the tight-fistedness of the *Pelter*'s owners in a continuous monotone. The weather was becoming rougher further from land, which should affect the pirate more than themselves, and once the coast was out of sight, navigation grew difficult. Perhaps the pirate would turn back rather than risk getting lost.

*Which will leave us lost instead, but that's better than robbed or dead,* considered Tolly Aimark. His career as a ship's captain had seen pirates seize his last vessel, and the *Pelter* was likely to be his final chance to avoid an ignominious dismissal. The merchants back in Collegium would care nothing for the dangers of a seagoing life. They would see only their losses, and punish him accordingly.

Now they had hit a fog bank, which was normally a curse, but which Aimark decided was his first stroke of luck today. He toyed with signalling the helm to turn for shore again, but the pirates would surely be expecting that. If he were on their deck, he would be cutting a course that ran between the coast and the *Pelter*'s last bearing, in anticipation of just such a move. On the other hand . . .

'Two points starboard,' he gave the order, and the *Pelter*

turned further from land, out towards the open ocean. Oh, there were all manner of tales about ships that braved the deep sea, but mostly that such vessels were never seen again. It was a plain fact that the weather was savage there, enough to shred sails and overturn even a little engined steamer like the *Pelter*, but it was now time to see how bold these pirates might be.

'Any sight?' he called out. The *Pelter* still had a mast, though Aimark had no idea when her sails had last been raised. In theory they could continue to make headway if the engine failed, but he had no idea how many of his crew knew even the basics of sailing. He would rely on his artificers to fix the problem, rather than trust to wind and weather to get them anywhere.

The word came back from a Fly-kinden shuttling between him and the lookout. Yes, even through the fog, the great pale swathe of sail could be seen.

'Hold our course,' Aimark ordered. He knew that the pursuers would be listening for the sound of his engines, but at the same time the fog played tricks with sound, deadened and distorted it, and there was a fair chance that, by the time the pirate realized that the *Pelter* had taken an unexpected course, it would be too late.

For a moment the deck shifted strangely beneath Aimark's feet, instantly bringing him out in a cold sweat. *Reefs?* But there could be none here, surely, nor unexpected rocks. The sea beneath them was deeper than any sounding had detected. They were past the Shelf, and there was nothing beneath them but the sea.

The Fly-kinden alighted down beside him. 'Master, they're turning landwards. Hiram saw them tack, before he lost them to the fog.'

A great wave of relief swept over Tolly Aimark. 'Continue on a mile, then we'll plot a course that'll bring us to the coast far from where they're likely to be. Bring my charts up, too, and we'll see where we might end up.'

Even as he spoke the words, something scraped along the hull, but without the solid shock of an underwater rock. Aimark and his crewmen stared at one another, and glanced down the length of the ship, so much of which had become mere shapes in the fog.

A man screamed out there somewhere, and there followed a confused babble of voices. Aimark bellowed for a report, and one of his artificers rushed out of the mist, wide-eyed. 'Dorwell's gone, master! Just . . . vanished. He was there right behind me . . .'

Something grated along against the underside of the hull, and the planks beneath Aimark's feet abruptly flexed and jumped, in time with a splintering sound from below. Incredibly, the ship was still moving, dragging somewhat but not stuck on anything, nor run aground, and yet . . .

There were men rushing up from belowdecks, and he heard calls to man the pumps. Aimark stood frozen, mouth open ready to issue he knew not what order.

Then he spotted the great lumpen shapes appear at the rails, hauling themselves on to deck in a clatter of claws and carapace, and the real terror began.

'Master Sands, Filipo says your man's coming.'

Sands glanced up from his book, noting his underling's careful manner, the respectful style of address stolen from Collegium's upper echelons. *And yet have I not earned it?* Sands believed he had, certainly. The niche for men of his stripe in law-abiding Collegium was a narrow one. The docks and the river district penned in a moderate infestation of unambitious, unprincipled men, but it took someone like Sands to make a healthy living out of doing wrong. He was a Collegiate criminal, and the College and the city had formed him just as surely as it formed the magnates and mechanics and scholars that the place was famed for.

The alley was dark, but his Spider father had contributed enough to Sands's heritage that he could read quite comfortably by moonlight. The moon was waxing, three-quarters full and still bellying out from one night to the next. A murderer's moon, they'd call it in Merro. The Fly-kinden had always been able to turn life's little practicalities into poetry.

Despite his heritage he looked almost entirely Beetle, did Forman Sands. Only closer observation detected the telltale discontinuity of warring kinden in his face. It had been enough, though, between a disinherited birth and a persecuted youth, to set him on a darker path, yet he still considered himself a good citizen of Collegium. He always cast his stone in the Lots, and followed all the major speeches in the Assembly, buying a record of each as soon as the printers could turn it out. If he sired a child, then he would buy a place in the College, with money to spare. Sands had scraped his education together by his own hand, and he valued book learning above all else, not just because of the opportunities it gave but because it made sense of the world in a way that nothing else did. It assisted him as he constructed his own philosophy.

'I still think it'd be easier if you just catch his eye, leave the rest to us. No need for it to be your hand on the knife,' his underling said. He was a plain Beetle man, scarred about the face and missing an ear: competent enough, but with no desire to be anything more than a thug. He was exactly what Sands aspired to distance himself from, symbolically if not actually.

'It must be me,' Sands told him. 'Do you think I'm not capable?'

'No, chief, but—'

'So no argument.' A gesture from Sands sent the man off. He then carefully tucked the book away in the folds of his robe, after marking his page. It was difficult to exist as an intelligent man on Collegium's underside. Collegium preached virtue, humanism, the duty of people to work for each other's benefit, or so the College philosophers claimed.

53

Only thus would the lot of people everywhere, of all kinden and social classes, be improved. Charity and consideration were the watchwords. Even the most grasping of Beetle magnates made a public show of open-handedness. How, in the face of that, could Sands justify himself: the robber and the killer, the agent of corruption?

He had studied long and hard, with the assistance of Spiderland philosophers who had written on the same issues a century ago. They had all manner of glib answers for the conscientious Beetle: good deeds could only exist against a background of evil, the actions of predators promoted excellence in their prey, complacency was ever the enemy of progress. Sands was all the while constructing his own philosophy of the virtue of criminality. Day by day, book by book, he was justifying his own existence.

*And when I am an old man, I shall publish,* he thought, *but, for now, business intervenes.*

His Fly-kinden scout, Filipo, dropped down nearby. 'Coming right now,' he reported curtly. Somehow the Fly-kinden never seemed bothered about right and wrong; Sands envied them such freedom.

'Keep watch,' he directed, and then stepped out into the street.

It was late. His sources had been keeping good track of his target, who was obliging enough to make appointments that continued past dusk. He was hurrying home now, and heading through a good enough area of town. Sands's cronies were twitchy, out of place, while Sands himself was not. No watchman, seeing him there, would have cast a suspicious eye over him: a tall almost-Beetle in neatly folded robes, the very picture of a well-to-do middle merchant or scribe, or else the servant of some wealthy man.

Sands saw his assignation hurrying towards him, a thin Beetle with an agitated step, wrapped up in his own worries, clutching a satchel to his chest. Sands stepped half into his path without attracting his attention, and had to resort to calling out the man's name.

'Master Failwright?'

The shipping merchant stopped, snapped out of his own thoughts, peering at Sands. He saw a respectable, mild-featured Beetle, at least so far as the dusk revealed to him.

'Do I know you?' he asked, suspicious but not alarmed.

'Master Failwright, I am sent from Master Mendawl.'

'I know Master Mendawl,' Failwright allowed.

'Your words at the Assembly have disturbed him, Master Failwright. He was hoping to discuss them with you,' Sands said, and saw how a spark of hope lit up in the man's eyes.

'Of course, of course,' Failwright was saying. 'I knew *someone* would take notice. Let Maker and Broiler and the others stew. He'll see me tonight?'

'He stays up for you in a hostelry near here,' Sands confirmed. 'I'm only glad I found you.'

Failwright nodded, a man with a mission. 'Take me to him,' he directed, and Sands's hand offered the side-street to him. Sands's accomplices had made themselves shadows, and Failwright marched along happily under his direction.

It was simple enough, for Sands had a speed that belied his size. As soon as Failwright was in the shadows, he had a hand over the man's mouth. His other hand, the Spider-Art spines jutting from his knuckles, jabbed twice, once above each kidney, small spots of red spreading in the man's robes. With practised smoothness, Sands spun the man about, slammed his back against a wall and rammed his claws up into Failwright's throat.

The man's eyes were wide, his struggles disjointed. The injuries in themselves, even the last one, were not fatal, but Sands's claws ran with poison. He held his victim firmly while the toxin did its work, locking the man's muscles, a joint at a time, then freezing his breath. He stuck in a few more doses, just to be sure. Beetles were a tough breed, even scrawny merchants like this one.

When Failwright had finally stopped twitching, Sands removed his hand. The man was still alive, just, but not for long. There were a few red specks on Sands's robes, but otherwise it was a remarkably clean way to end a life. Sands's Beetle underling approached cautiously.

'Into the river with him,' Sands instructed, and held out a pouch that the man gratefully accepted. Filipo landed nearby, ready for his cut. Sands left the pair to it. He had a client to see.

*It is all justified,* he thought. *We are the surgeons hacking off the dead flesh.* It was not done for a political cause, for he was no revolutionary. It was done for the sheer sake of it, the philosophical necessity of honing the blade of civilization. He tested that phrase in his mind, found it good, and continued on his way a happy man.


Helmess Broiler had a polished repertoire of smiles for all occasions, but he saved the genuine ones for moments like this.

She stepped down the stairs of his townhouse as though the simple descent was an indecent act, pausing halfway to lean on the banister and grin down at him. She loved him to be duplicitous, he knew. The fact that he had been fencing with the Imperial Bellowern, whilst all the while playing a larger game was meat and drink to her. It was one of the many ways she resembled a Spider-kinden.

It had always been thus, it was true, but formerly it had been a shady habit practised behind closed doors. Beetle men of status and of power, for all that they mostly had wives and families and the like, found in themselves a yearning to exercise their potency through other channels. Mistresses were well known, scandalous when exposed, yet ubiquitous amongst a certain class of Assembler and merchant. A clever young Spider girl or handsome youth who came to Collegium would not lack for opportunity. Oh, it was not always a Spider-kinden, but that was the archetype: beautiful and dangerous and irresistibly charming.

Then Master Stenwold Maker had come along, taking up with a girl young enough to be his daughter and parading her around as though she were one of his war honours. Where there might easily have been a tide of disapproval and horror, instead there had been a strange kind of relief. Master Maker was a war hero, the people's darling who could, just there and then, do no wrong. Keeping a young lover must be *all right*, therefore. This was, Helmess reflected, the one service the wretched old warmonger had ever done for his fellows.

'Elytrya,' he uttered her name, as she looked fondly down on him.

'You keep them dancing,' she observed, and took her time coming down the rest of the steps towards him. He could watch her for ever, he decided.

It was not that she was a Spider-kinden. It was that she was *not* a Spider-kinden, although she resembled them enough to pass as such. That she avoided other Spiders was not unusual, for Spider-kinden were their own worst enemies, so that many ending up in the Lowlands were fugitives from one political struggle or another. If her eyes were of a strange shade and larger than usual, her hair more elaborately curled, then they just assumed that Spiders, with their cosmetics, could do a great deal with their appearance. She was the best thing in Helmess's life, and he loved her, because he loved power, and saw in her his chance to recapture it.

Honory Bellowern had been right: Helmess was much fallen from his former heights, and in no position to withstand a rumour campaign or slanderous accusation about his association with the Empire, especially if that accusation happened to be true. Being in possession of all the facts, the Empire might believe that it owned him.

However, their facts were now out of date, for Helmess Broiler had been cultivating other friendships.

He had no idea how long she had been in Collegium before approaching him, how long she had spent adjusting to the differences, understanding what must have been a bewilderingly alien way of life. She had once let slip that her people, her *faction*, had kept agents in this city for generations, in readiness for what was due to happen so very soon.

When she had come to him first, with her flattery and her promises, she had played at being the Spider-kinden adventuress, whilst sounding him out. Physical attraction had lured him from the start, but she had gauged him well enough, and soon enough, to know it would not hold him. Instead she had appreciated that his working with her, with her unfathomable allies, represented a return to power for him, a power untainted by the Wasp Empire. She had made him an offer too attractive to turn down, and told him a secret truth that he was still trying to digest.

She leant in towards him, wrapping herself about his arm, resting her head on his shoulder. The invisible events of her plot, their plot, were beginning to unfold, in the far, dark places. She had only told him so much, but he could guess much more. The thought that he was the sole Collegiate man to be party to such an abominable act was as sexually exciting as the feeling of her warm body now pressed against him.

There was a knock at the door, but he had already briefed his servants and they let the man straight in. Helmess Broiler's needs for this breed of agent were scant, but a successful merchant was occasionally forced to take decisive action. Forman Sands was always his first choice: not only was the man discreet and reliable, but there was no other paid killer in Collegium who managed to look like a respectable cartel clerk and could make educated after-dinner talk like a College scholar.

'Master Broiler,' Sands said, with a careful nod, first to his employer, and then to his employer's mistress.

'Your news?'

'It's done.' Sands held out Failwright's satchel, which Broiler accepted. It was bulging with scrawled scrolls, the last symptoms of Failwright's fatal curiosity.

'You're a good man, Sands,' Helmess remarked.

'I like to think so, Master Broiler.' Sands took the purse from Helmess's servant almost as an afterthought, as though this wasn't about the money at all.

When the killer had gone, Elytrya hugged Helmess close. Failwright and his annoying questions were done with.

'Do you mean,' he asked her softly, 'to silence an inconvenient question, or to raise yet more? Members of the Assembly cause ripples, when they fall.'

'Either will serve,' she assured him. 'We know that either will serve.'

# Five

*Is this any more honest than my time with the Rekef?*

The copper magnate Brons Helfer and his wife were doing their best to be good hosts. Their spacious drawing room was painted blue, with frescos on two facing walls which Arianna had carefully complimented. They were in the 'Seldis style', which worked out as a bastard approximation of last generation's Spiderlands artists, but hamfistedly rendered by Beetle copyists. Her compliments, not only insincere but downright false, had been gratefully received, for was she not the great Spider lady?

She was not, of course, and never had been. Her family had been hoi polloi of the coarsest character, but in the Spiderlands even the peasantry schemed and feuded. Her departure at a tender age had been prompted by the ruin of her parents, culminating in the death of her mother in a duel. At fifteen Arianna had nothing but her kinden to recommend her, as she scrounged and pilfered her way north up the Silk Road.

There the Rekef had found her, buying her from a fellow Spider, a slaver whose men had snapped her up one night. The Rekef had been explicit and detailed on what other interested parties might have acquired her, that night, what other fates could have befallen her – and might still, if she did not show how very grateful she was to them.

Thereafter she had been trained, and they had infiltrated

her into Collegium with some fake recommendations, but always with a Wasp lieutenant holding her reins. She might be street scum, but she was Spider street scum, which endowed her with a kind of tarnished nobility in Collegium.

Darla Helfer was chattering to her energetically about something, the magnate's wife in full flow as she tried to show their distinguished guest how sophisticated her hostess could be. The woman was plain, stout, wearing fine clothes without flair. Arianna could make homespun look like silk, whereas Darla accomplished the opposite and never knew it. Arianna had just enough self-knowledge, enough bitterness about her past, for her not to enjoy the contrast.

*And yet these Beetles run the world and, as with their clothes, they never see themselves for what they are.* On another wall there hung a small sketch, a copy of a Spider arabesque. It had been produced by some complex device that had rendered a perfect duplicate, line for line, in exacting strokes, the creation of some artificer nephew of the Helfers. The family connection was the only reason it was on display: no other attention was drawn to it. The Helfers plainly regarded it as a piece of mundane trickery, but to Arianna it was infinitely fascinating that these people's machines could accomplish such a thing. It impressed her more than all the derivative clowning on display elsewhere in the room. *If only they would learn to be themselves, what could they not accomplish?* She wondered how much blame her own people should accept for that. The Spider-kinden's very essence was to shine at the expense of others. It was easier to stand tall if you convinced everyone else to kneel.

She had made quite a comfortable home for herself amongst these people. She had backed the right man, becoming a war hero in her own right. People still remembered the moment she had turned up at the breach with her bow and arrows to fight for the city. Nobody seemed to remember that she had betrayed them all first, before turning on her fellow betrayers.

She herself could not quite recall standing there with Stenwold when the Vekken came through the breach. It seemed something that a character in a play might have done, or perhaps in some garish Beetle romance. Had her life seemed so cheap to her, just then? Perhaps it had, for she would have been left with precious few options had Collegium fallen.

It was near evening when she finally got away from the Helfers, with promises to pass on their regards to Stenwold. To the 'War Master' as they still said, but she would do them the service of editing their words. It was a title Stenwold had always loathed.

Cardless was off on some errand, when she reached home. Technically her real 'home' was across town, a fictional separation she had devised for the peace of mind of Stenwold's ailing niece. A selfless decision? No – for the niece's peace of mind was Stenwold's, and Stenwold's was her own. Her position, comfort and opportunities in Collegium were irrevocably tied to him. Recently, the niece had been considerate enough to absent herself, so Arianna drifted between her own residence and Stenwold's as the mood took her.

She wondered what mood she would find him in, being a man of more emotional layers than Beetles were generally accorded, by Spider reckoning. The College demagogue gave way to the clever spymaster, with the inspirational war leader waiting ever in the wings. She had met him, she reflected, at the best of times: he had been all these things.

Now the war had stalled, waiting on like a trained dragonfly up high, and the sharper facets of his life had been carefully packed away, oiled and padded against rust. The sober spymaster lurked behind the throne, while the frustrated statesman took his seat, ground down daily by all the minutiae of a world that was no longer under the immediate shadow of the black and gold. Stenwold the warmonger, they had once called him, and now she could almost feel him daring the Empire to bring back its armies, if only to rekindle that old fire.

She pushed open the door of his study, and stopped short.

He was hunched over the desk, and did not even look up at her. With a lens to one eye, he was poring over a single scroll with immense concentration. She felt a quickening in her heartbeat, out of nowhere, that took her back two years.

This was not the bored Stenwold reading Assembly minutes, nor the frustrated Stenwold sifting through correspondence from the ingratiating and the insincere. War Master Stenwold Maker, the intelligencer and hero of Collegium, had again taken up his old lodgings in the forefront of Stenwold's mind. When he finally looked up, as she stepped into the room, she recognized it in his eyes, that unsheathed edge of a brain working to its fullest.

'What do you make of this?' He thrust the scroll towards her without preamble. The gesture made her smile. His squabblings with the Assembly, his reluctant arrangements with men like Jodry Drillen, he did not involve her in. It was not that she could not have helped somehow, but that he was ashamed of such dealings, ashamed of having to bend his own rules to get what he wanted. Now he was the spymaster again, and she was a spy, and he was including her.

She took the scroll, cast her eyes down the lines of crabbed handwriting, led by his annotations. 'I was never a paper spy,' she warned him. 'They saved me for field duties, you know.'

The *They* was the Rekef, but neither of them needed to mention that name, and they had buried it between them before the war's end.

'Even so,' he prompted, and she nodded.

63

'This is Failwright's grievance, is it?'

'His notes, his summary. Ships out of Collegium heading east. Their captains, their cargoes, their fates, and . . .'

'Their investors,' she noted. 'Who stood to lose money on the deal.' It would not have been instantly visible, amidst Failwright's baffling columns, save that Stenwold had marked it all out, name by name.

'Are you sure you're not just seeing a pattern where none exists? Or that Failwright wasn't?'

'No, I'm not sure at all,' Stenwold admitted. 'After all, the sea trade is an uncertain business. There *are* pirates, there are storms. Ships are lost, sometimes. Such information gets blurred by pure happenstance.' He rubbed at the stubble on his chin. 'But Failwright and his faction were taking it very seriously. Look, a few months ago they sent some ships out with mercenaries on board. Here, look . . . and here. Not touched, not touched, and . . . and then one lost utterly.' Stenwold shook his head. 'And, at the same time, three ships travelling without guard are boarded by pirates.'

'What's this column here?' Arianna's finger marked out one line of scribbled notes.

'I think it's weather reports. Here, where the armed ship was lost, I think he's marked "no storm" but I'm not honestly sure. I need to speak to him . . .' There was the sound of someone at the door, the neatness of its closing bringing the name 'Cardless?' to Stenwold's lips. A moment later the servant found them.

'What says Master Failwright?' Stenwold asked him. 'Delighted to receive the attention, no doubt?'

'Unfortunately Master Failwright was not at home,' Cardless reported.

'You left my message?'

'I did. However, it appears that Master Failwright is considerably overdue. He did not return to his house or his offices last night, and none of his associates knows of his whereabouts.'

Stenwold opened his mouth to speak, then closed it again. His eyes sought out Arianna. Between them was that unspoken history: espionage, agents, sudden disappearances.

'Make further inquiries,' Stenwold directed, as if Cardless was one of his people left over from the war. 'Arianna—'

There was a quick rap at the door and Cardless bowed his way out to go and answer it. Stenwold left the sentence unfinished as he waited. When a Fly-kinden messenger stepped into the room, looking flushed and out of breath, he was not surprised.

Stenwold took the proffered scroll and unrolled it. His face remained blank as he read.

'Tell him I will be present,' was his only response, and the Fly was off on the instant.

Arianna gave him a questioning look.

'The Empire has taken Khanaphes,' Stenwold revealed. 'Jodry's called the Assembly together. I have to go.'

Major Aagen had, to Stenwold's understanding, two expressions only. He was late of the Imperial Engineering Corps, and possessed a zealous fervour for all things technical. He had learned more of Collegiate artifice by way of kindred enthusiasm than had all of the Rekef spying during the war. His other expression was one of stolid acceptance, and Stenwold guessed it would remain the same whether he was faced by a pitched battle or a room full of surly Assemblers.

He was standing even now, holding a scroll in his hands. He had never so far made a response to the Assembly that was not prepared by his shadow, Honory Bellowern, and it seemed mad to Stenwold that Imperial diplomacy should result in a guileless Wasp artificer mouthing statements prepared by a plotting Beetle-kinden handler.

Aagen nodded to Jodry Drillen, whose voice was still echoing a little within the Amphiophos chamber. 'I can confirm,' he read out, 'that an Imperial force is currently receiving the hospitality of the Khanaphir administration.' There was a surprising amount of angry muttering, but then the people of Khanaphes were Beetles themselves, recently popularized as Collegium's backward cousins. Jodry had been capitalizing on his exploratory success, so the average Beetle-kinden in the Collegium street had become newly aware of his distant relatives, in a patronizingly protective way.

'I should stress . . .' Aagen continued. He had been a war-artificer, used to repairing automotives in the heat of battle, so a little shouting would not put him off his stride. 'I should stress that the Empire is present there at the invitation of the Ministers of Khanaphes. You will be aware how the city has suffered recently from incursions by the desert Scorpion tribes, and is therefore in a considerably weakened state—'

'Incursions brought on by the Empire!' someone called out. To Stenwold's surprise, it was not Stenwold himself.

Aagen paused a moment, and Stenwold saw Bellowern's lips move as he prompted. The Wasp went on smoothly, 'The Empire is still dealing with the last of its pretender governors. If one of them has fled into the Nem to rouse the natives into an army to threaten Khanaphes, then the Empire's duty in protecting our neighbours from the results of our own internal conflict is plain. The people of Khanaphes understand this, and I would hope the people of Collegium do so also.' He unrolled the scroll by another hand's breadth, still calm in the face of simmering discontent. 'Furthermore, the Assembly will be aware that the Dominion of Khanaphes is not a signatory to the Treaty of

Gold, nor mentioned therein. In this matter the city of Collegium therefore has no standing.'

That made them even angrier, but mostly because he was right. *And should we have written the whole world into that treaty? And if we had, it would just be broken sooner.* Stenwold ground his teeth and stood up, hearing the chamber fall quiet for him.

'I would ask the Imperial ambassador whether he is aware of the Collegiate observers who were present in the city during its recent troubles with the Scorpion-kinden. They state definitively that members of the Imperial embassy to Khanaphes were later seen assisting the Scorpion invaders, and that the walls of Khanaphes were breached not by native ingenuity but by Imperial leadshotters.'

Again that moment of swift tutelage by the unflappable Bellowern, and Aagen replied, 'I am assured that there was no formal embassy to Khanaphes from the Empress. Master Maker will be aware how most of the pretender governors claimed for themselves the mantle of Emperor. The confusion of his observers is therefore understandable.' As with most of his puppet pronouncements, Aagen delivered the words with a slightly shrug, a bland expression. 'I stress again that this matter does not infringe the Treaty of Gold between the cities of the Lowlands and the Empire. However . . .'

The last word came out unexpectedly and was left hanging. Stenwold narrowed his eyes as Aagen unrolled more of his crib sheet.

'As we are here,' the Wasp said, 'I would like to bring to the Assembly's attention the work that some here are doing to undermine that treaty, and thus bring a return to the conflict that we had all hoped was behind us.'

Stenwold sought out the face of Jodry Drillen, two rows behind him, but the politician shook his head slightly, uncertain where this was leading.

'Imperial agents have recently discovered that elements within Collegium are providing considerable quantities of arms to the Three-City Alliance, most particularly to Myna – to those states that stand immediately on the border of the Empire. This must stop.'

'The Empire does not decide on Collegiate trade,' Drillen snapped, not even standing. 'You yourselves were happy enough to buy Beetle weapons before the war.'

'In arming our closest enemies, Collegium is attempting to destabilize the Empire, to have the Mynans and their allies grow bold enough to attack us, and thereby to start a new war. No doubt when the Imperial army is driven to defend our borders, this will be interpreted as an act of aggression allowing the Lowlands cities to march against us.'

'Myna has a right to defend itself,' Stenwold called out, to some approval.

'As does the Empire,' Aagen replied, with feeling now. 'Master Maker, I was there when we signed the Treaty of Gold. The men and women of this Assembly were responsible for the wording. Why did we stand there, out in the wind before the gates of this city, if we have so little faith in it all? The arming of Myna and its Alliance constitutes an act of war, and a breach of the treaty. I would ask the members of the Assembly to think very carefully before endorsing such a step.'

Honory Bellowern was nodding sagely, the very picture of reasonable respectability. There was a great buzz of talk now, from all sides but most of it centred on Drillen. Across the chamber a familiar figure was standing, waving for silence. Reluctantly, Jodry ceded him the floor, knowing that to refuse would stir up enough protest to forestall any other business. Stenwold turned a loveless gaze on Helmess Broiler.

'Well, here we are,' said Stenwold's perpetual adversary. He said it again, as the chamber quietened. 'Some of us have been waiting for this moment for a year or more, so I'm surprised it's taken so long.' He took a deep, sorrowful breath. 'Masters, what do we want? Do we really want another war, just so we can hand out another round of titles?' *War Master* hung in the air, unsaid, but Stenwold saw enough heads turn his way.

'There are parts of this city still being rebuilt,' Broiler continued, sounding every bit the weary old veteran. 'The city of Tark, for those that are interested, is at least half ruin even now, and they lack the sheer manpower to restore it. Imagine that! A city of Ant-kinden and not enough hands to lay stone on stone?' He let the thought sit in their minds for a moment. 'With apologies to those of us who are, we are not Spider-kinden.' He even raised a small laugh from this. 'If there are those of us who have entered into this treaty with the Empire merely to move the battlefield from our own gates to the gates of Myna, then they are not worthy to speak for their city. We all remember when the Second Army was at our walls. I recall a certain War Master who was even their guest. Did they enact a final vengeance against us, before marching away? Did they put Master Maker's head on a pike? They did not, and from that same forbearance the Treaty of Gold was sieved. How do we repay them now, indeed how do we repay our Mynan allies, if we seek to foment conflict at the borders of the Empire?'

It was a fine speech, Stenwold considered, and he hoped that the Empire had paid good money for it. The Assembly was looking to him now. He glanced at Jodry but there was no help there.

'Anyone who has turned an eye to the lands beyond Helleron,' Stenwold responded heavily, 'will know that there are Imperial troops stationed upon the Mynan border.' He held up a hand to forestall the expected protest. 'No doubt they will claim that they fear Mynan aggression, reprisals from a city that they once enslaved. You will forgive me if recent history makes it difficult for me to see the Empire as victim. What *we* see, here in Collegium, is a fragile balance, like a fencer's pose, and the slightest lowering of our guard becomes an invitation to those forces to begin the work of retaking the Empire's recent losses. Occupation of Khanaphes is hardly the way to assure us that the Empire wishes only peace, and the Empire should remember that the Three-City Alliance *did* sign the Treaty of Gold. War with Myna is war with Collegium, is war with all the Lowlands. I humbly submit to the Empress that she should think very carefully before she resumes the work of her brother, and think also what might happen if the Dominion of Khanaphes calls on its cousins here for aid.'

Rousing cheers, the approval of comfortable merchants who were trading with the Empire even now; of scholars who cared more for who wrote what a century ago than whatever atrocities might happen next year. Stenwold let it wash over him, identifying in that burbling mass only three points of reference: Broiler, Bellowern, Aagen the Wasp. His hand curled around the pommel of the sword he was not wearing.

'I'm sending Mistress Rakespear and that big lad of hers back off to Khanaphes by the swiftest route,' Jodry Drillen declared. After the debate he had repaired with Stenwold to one of the private rooms within the Amphiophos.

Noting his tone, Stenwold asked, 'Sending?'

'Well, in the sense of "I can't stop them going," in that case. So I drew them up some funds double quick and got her transport, and maybe she can bring some sense to the situation. If her friend starts throwing Wasps about the place, though, it won't be worth much.'

'The Empire know our debating styles too well,' Stenwold remarked. 'They know we're stronger in attack than defence. I wasn't expecting them to have found out about Myna.'

Jodry grimaced. 'I never thought that would last. Those what's-their-names, those Rekef Outlander boys, they were just about the only thing in the Empire that came through it keener than ever. They have eyes and ears all over.'

Stenwold nodded, committing the recent debate to memory, to be pulled apart and dissected at his leisure. 'Jodry,' he said, and his voice made it clear this was a new topic. 'I've been thinking about Rones Failwright.'

'Now there was someone we could have done with today,' Drillen said. 'Just to have him piping up about his cursed shipping to put Broiler or the Wasp off his stride.'

Stenwold kept a sidelong glance fixed on the other man's face, watching for reactions. 'I've been doing a bit of thinking about the shipping trade.'

'You're having me on?' Nothing but honest bewilderment. 'Don't tell me Failwright's recruited you?'

'No, no, but . . . when you do the arithmetic, a lot of Collegiate property, a lot of sailors, have been lost over this recent period. Pirate attacks, sunk ships. It's only because of the rail and air trades owning such a loud voice that we aren't all echoing Failwright.'

'You're serious.'

'Reasonably serious. We should at least look into his complaints. What do you suggest?'

'Me?' Jodry rolled his eyes. 'Get a few escorts together. Collegium's crawling with Felyal Mantis-kinden at the moment, maybe hire a score of them and stick them on shipboard. The alternative's to use distinctive cargoes and see where they eventually turn up. Both ways sound expensive to me. You really think there's something in it?'

There was nothing else, nothing whatsoever – no guilt or complicity, just a man who didn't want to be bothered by this particular problem. *Or he's better at hiding it than I am in reading it.* But Stenwold had built a career on making this kind of judgement call.

'I think it would be wise,' he replied thoughtfully. *But I think we'll find, like Failwright, that each time you offer the pirates a poisoned chalice, you'll find they won't drink.*

'I'll organize something,' Jodry said dismissively, but Stenwold was already considering his next move.

'You've been keeping yourself busy, I trust?'

The suite of rooms was located in the best part of the College residences, high up and with a view of the white walls of the Amphiophos. It had been set aside for the use of special guests of the Speaker, but since the war it had become the private, rent-free property of Teornis of the Aldanrael. When the Spider-kinden lord was absent from the city, which was often, the rooms were kept superstitiously immaculate and empty.

Teornis's expression told Stenwold that the man was keeping himself well informed of all that went on at the Assembly. Teornis was not amongst that handful of Spider-kinden Aristoi to be given posts at the Great College, and therefore a voice in Collegium's government. He considered that the actual *work* this would entail was beneath him. For years now he had simply been Collegium's darling, its most sought-after party guest, the leader of fashion, hero of the war and breaker of hearts.

'Oh don't look so downcast, Stenwold,' he said. 'I thought you Beetles liked all that shouting and gesturing.' A couple of magnificently liveried Fly-kinden servants were setting out a cornucopia of finger-food on a low table, along with a carafe of wine. Stenwold wondered moodily if they were slaves or free.

'You know . . .' he started, but it was clear from Teornis's face that the man *did* know, and was merely teasing him. They had stood together, these two very different men, after the Vekken siege had been broken. And that had been this man's doing: for all of Teornis's shameless capitalizing on it, it had been the Spider-kinden ships, the beachhead of their Satrapy soldiers, that had raised the siege.

'Pick a city, any city,' he said.

'I'll choose Khanaphes then.' Teornis was smiling, probably just at the fact that Stenwold had not even had to ask him if he had heard the news. 'Nothing unexpected there, of course.'

'Oh, really?' Stenwold enquired, but Teornis was gesturing for him to sit down, so they took cushions on the floor, Fly-kinden style.

'Sten, your problem is that you've been fighting the Empire too long,' the Spider declared, as one of his people poured some wine.

'Now you're starting to sound like an Assembler,' Stenwold growled, prompting a delighted laugh.

'What I mean is this: you see the Empire do a pointless, violent, cruel thing, and you mark it down as the Wasps simply doing what Wasps do. But I, being who I am, ask why.'

Stenwold frowned. *And a very good question that I should have asked myself.* 'Why Khanaphes?'

Teornis nodded. 'I don't know if you ever saw the place, but it's a sandpit full of grit and peasants. Oh, certainly it has farmland, eked out along the river, but the Wasps have their grain baskets already in the East-Empire. And it has history, too, more than anybody could possibly have any use for, but I doubt that the Imperial army has gone there to write a dissertation on potsherds. So ask yourself, what in the world are they doing in Khanaphes?'

It did not take much thought. 'You think they're coming after *you.*'

'We were at war with them, too, remember? We signed that treaty, just as you did. Neither of us had any illusions that the Empire would stay muzzled for long. No, I'd take this as your own excuse to relax, Sten. When the Empire decides to tear up the paperwork, I'm afraid it looks like Solarno and Seldis destined for the axe, and not Helleron and Collegium – not at first anyway.'

'You must know that we'll defend you.'

Teornis's look was ancient with worldly cynicism. 'Oh, I hope it, Sten, but I can't *know* it and, let's be frank, neither can you.'

Stenwold nodded, sipping his wine. It had a sharp, bitter taste that he was not expecting, enough to set his heart racing for a suspicious moment, before he placed it.

'Mantis-kinden?' he asked.

'It has the twin virtues of being devilishly expensive and really quite unpleasant,' Teornis agreed. 'That puts it into the realm of the exclusive connoisseur. Appreciate it, Sten. That's Felyal graft-wine, and it's not as though there's much more where that came from.'

*After the Empire burned their vines and destroyed their holds.* Stenwold tried to savour the taste, but the wine was like the Mantis-kinden themselves, harsh and unforgiving. 'Tell me, Teornis . . .'

'If I can.'

'You Spider-kinden are good sailors, yes?'

Teornis nodded, his eyes amused.

'What do you know of piracy?'

The Spider broke out into a grin. 'We call it a legitimate tool of statecraft, back home. Mind you, there's little that isn't. I heard that you were cornered over some shipping business. Has it got to you that much?' Before Stenwold could reply, he went on: 'Or maybe you think it's the Empire. You realize that Khanaphes sits on another sea entirely.'

'I know, and I don't know about the Empire, but . . .' *But why not, after all?* 'But Collegium shipping has never suffered like this before, it's true. If the air trade or the rail trade was taking this kind of losses, then there would be rioting in the streets.'

Teornis nodded sympathetically. 'It's our fault, of course – yours and mine.'

Stenwold stared at him, and the Spider waved a deprecating hand.

'Oh not like that, but the bonds we've forged between Collegium and our own lands have put your city on the map, so to speak. South of Seldis, across the far side of the sea, rampant piracy is a normal way of life. There are few great houses amongst us that can't call on a shipful of ocean raiders when needs must. There are whole ports full of scum with a ship and no conscience. They just followed us along the coast, is all, until they found those clunky little buckets your people call ships. My people are used to outrunning or outmanoeuvring pirates, while your lot . . . Sten, I don't mean to pain you, but your people are truly awful at shiphandling. Sail or engine, if the wind's right any pirate down from the Spiderlands would feel she was robbing children. No wonder it's become such a popular pastime.'

Stenwold sighed. 'When I was a child we used to know all the pirates simply by the names of their ships. There would be about a dozen at any time. They were hated and feared and we used to want to grow up like them. They were few, and more skilled at not being caught than catching other ships.'

'Believe me, it's different within the Satrapies,' Teornis told him. 'It's just part of progress, of entering a larger world. Nothing is ever all good. My advice? Have your captains hire an escort frigate at Everis. Now we're your friends, you may as well take advantage of us.'

# Six

It was true, the sea-trade of Collegium had never been much since the revolution. The wealth of the Spiderlands – the art, the silk, the jewellery – travelled north up the silk road to Helleron, then by rail or air to Sarn and Collegium. There were few who would brave the short side of the triangle by sending a boat to hug the coast eastwards to Seldis and Siennis. In the Collegium harbour today there were twelve ships of any reasonable size, six of them boasting Spiderlands sails. The sea was an uncertain partner when it came to trading ventures, so the Beetle-kinden had turned their backs on it.

Normally vice would follow the money, but there was a certain kind of shadowy endeavour that thrived in places overlooked and left behind. There might be only two dozen large vessels here at the best of times, but there was a steady trickle of other boats in and out: fishers, small traders, venturers: smugglers, spies and malcontents. There were inevitably a few drinking dens near the docks where the flotsam of the coast could gather without official eyes upon them.

Despite the solid Beetle architecture of the exterior, this was a Spider-kinden dive that Stenwold had chosen. He had the impression it belonged far more to the average Spider-kinden than did all Teornis's silks and fine wines. The room was dim, the windows shutting out the daylight, and the ceiling and walls were draped with folds of cloth that distorted the shapes of the three or four rooms inside. Men and women sat about on a cushion-strewn floor, conversing in low voices. Two serious Fly-kinden moved pieces about on a dark wooden board, playing some game that Stenwold could not identify in the poor light. Somewhere in the gloomy depths of the place, perhaps even in some cellar below, a musician was playing intricate strings.

He had not come here as Stenwold the Assembler, of course, so he was dressed in hard-wearing canvas and leather, a tramp artificer's battered garments. A reinforced cap balanced on his head, complete with a scarf he could draw across his nose and mouth to ward off fumes, or to hide his face. He carried a sword at his belt, a burden he had not realized how much he missed. People did not normally go armed in Collegium and, now the war was done, the city guard paid close attention to those that did. Yet still, even Stenwold's eyes could see that almost everyone here had a weapon close at hand.

*Evil men and women,* he thought, *undermining the rule of law and civilization for mere profit. The scum of the Lowlands and beyond.* He could not stave off a childish sense of excitement. He was not behind his desk or before the Assembly. He was doing his *own* work. He was investigating again. It was like old times.

He could have sent someone else to ask his questions for him. *Ah, but who could I trust?* In truth he meant, *I am not so old yet that I cannot shift for myself once in a while.*

The Spider-kinden proprietress was an old woman still clutching tenuously to the natural grace of her people. For a single bit, she passed Stenwold a bowl of something acrid and mostly clear.

'New in, master? What's your ship?' she asked him.

'I'm in the market,' Stenwold replied carefully.

'Buying or selling?'

77

'Speculating, just now. If you've a patron interested in talking, I have an hour or so to spare without pressing obligations.'

She nodded. 'Take yourself a seat, Master Speculator, and perhaps you'll hear something to your advantage.'

Over the next hour Stenwold learned more than he could use of the petty doings of the docks. Had he been looking to invest in some unlicensed trade, he would have been doing very well indeed, but nothing shed light on Failwright's notes, still less his disappearance. Once or twice he had the impression that, if he cast aside his feigned disinterest and asked a direct question, he might startle something useful from an informant, but he was keenly aware that he was feeling out an unfamiliar place blind. It was imperative that he did not send advance warning to those he was trying to uncover.

After that he tried a narrow room that lay practically on the waterfront, open to the sea, the interior a forest of columns. Here the Mantis-kinden refugees and expatriates came to talk and drink. They would sit with their backs to the wooden pillars, and plot the downfall of their enemies or tell each other stories of their great days, whilst a young man sang something low and mournful in the shadows towards the back. Stenwold spent an awkward time here, constantly feeling that blades were being unsheathed around the bulk of the column he had set his back to, and he learned very little.

He next tried a Fly-kinden taverna, where the front room was the only space he could physically fit into. The Flies were suspicious of him. Many of them came forward with information, but much of it was patently made up on the spot. They were a clannish lot and, as he left there, he had the sense of being followed. By this time it was getting dark, and he knew he should return home, but he was feeling out of sorts and frustrated by now, awash in a sea of useless information.

He proceeded on to a gambling den set up in what had once been part of the port offices. The Vekken fleet had burned the place out, the Port Authority had relocated, and nothing official had since been found to fill the gap. Now the rotten tooth of the building's shell had been fitted out with tables and chairs, where men and women of many kinden were talking and dicing with one another. Stenwold made himself known to the proprietor, a slab-faced Beetle woman, then elbowed his way to a small table to see what his nets might bring in.

There were two petty smugglers whose boat had been sunk by a rival band, and who were obviously hoping Stenwold would invest in their meagre skills. There was a drunken old man whose rambling lies swooped between versions of events like the moths that skittered between the den's three hanging lamps. Stenwold eventually disposed of the ancient opportunist by giving him some coins for another drink, then sank back into his chair, feeling disgusted with himself.

*If this was Helleron*, he thought, *I'd know what I wanted by now*. Of course, Helleron had no port, no piracy, no tradition of the romantic freebooter that had been fashionable in Stenwold's youth. He remembered stories, songs, even plays. The pirate as anti-hero had enjoyed a brief vogue then amongst Collegium's wealthy middle classes even as some five or six notorious corsairs, and perhaps a dozen anonymous ones, had savaged the previous generation's coastal trade, turning from criminals to posthumous heroes in fifteen years. There had been a Mantis captain known as Arthemae with her scarred face; the ruthless Bloodfly who would slay every crewman left on his prize if one but lifted a knife against him; the Beetle Gavriel Knowless with his ship the *Ironcoat* . . .

A shadow fell over Stenwold, eclipsing the guttering light and cutting loose his reverie. He looked up to see a stout Beetle man leaning over his table.

'Yes?'

'Laem said you're asking questions,' the big Beetle said.

Stenwold shrugged. 'And?' He had already caught the tone: whatever his questions, this man was not here to answer them.

'And you got money,' the man said, reminding Stenwold briefly and inappropriately of a student trying to solve a logic problem. He readied himself.

'Rich men shouldn't come down here. About time you headed home, rich man. But leave your purse.' The big Beetle put his hands on the table and loomed over Stenwold, who sighed.

A moment later he had grabbed his end of the table and whipped it upwards, as hard as he could. The other man lurched forward as his support was yanked away, and his face met the tabletop as it came up, with the crunching sound of a broken nose and dislodged teeth. Stenwold was up in a moment, giving himself space as everyone else in the den started and stared, some reaching for weapons, others just making sure they were well out of the way.

The big Beetle did not stir, so Stenwold guessed he had been knocked cold. Despite his station in life and his pretence at dignity, he could not help but feel a spark of pride.

A moment later two other men were moving towards him, another Beetle and a Kessen Ant-kinden, and they both had drawn swords. His pride evaporated swiftly. *Even thugs have friends*. He had his own blade out, waiting for them, his other hand reaching into his tunic. *I feel I'm about to attract a little too much attention*. His hand inside his coat touched the butt of his other weapon.

He almost missed the little clack of the crossbow, but one of the men was abruptly down on one knee, swearing and tugging at the bolt through his thigh. The Ant whirled, looking for the archer, and a brief shape flitted past his head with a sound like a slap, leaving him reeling drunkenly.

His attacker was a young Fly-kinden man, who touched down on a table almost within arm's reach of him. He had a cudgel in one hand and a knife in the other.

'It's chucking-out time,' the Fly announced. The Kessen stared at him, one hand to his head, sword weighing in his hand. Another Fly, a woman, stepped out from around the table with a little under-and-over crossbow. It would not have done much against a suit of armour, but the Ant-kinden wore nothing but a leather jerkin and breeches.

'Take him,' the Fly woman ordered, 'and clear off.'

The Ant came to the right decision, hauling up his protesting friend and dragging him, limping, out the door. The Fly man hopped to the ground, inspecting the man that Stenwold had knocked out.

'Backswimmer's lads,' he said.

'He always did hire idiots,' added the woman. She sounded a little better educated than her companion, or than most of the people Stenwold had been speaking to all day.

The Fly man stepped close to Stenwold, who regarding him cautiously, sword still in hand. 'Perhaps you should come with us,' the little man said.

'And why would I want to do that?' Stenwold asked. The woman was meanwhile keeping an eye on the den's other patrons, who were making a grand show of ignoring everything. Her crossbow was not pointed at Stenwold, which was a good sign at least.

'You have questions, don't you? Or is this just a way for you to spend an idle afternoon?' the Fly man inquired, adding, with just a touch too much drama, 'Master Maker?'

It was said quietly enough not to carry, but Stenwold twitched on hearing it. *So, I don't play the old game as well as I used to, then. And am I surprised, here in my own town? Even in this dive I'm a public figure.*

'I'll keep my sword,' he said heavily.

The Fly shrugged. 'However you like. But Backswimmer'll send a few lads out here as soon as he hears, just to hammer out the dent in his pride. So perhaps we should taste our legs, now, Master.'

He gave a grin and then sauntered away, with Stenwold following uncertainly in tow. The woman rested the crossbow on her shoulder, the great huntress in miniature, and then followed them outside.

In the old days, the sea had meant rather more to Collegium, not merely for trade but for the mysterious rituals and mummery that the city founders had placed such reliance on. The Moth-kinden had built this city and named it Pathis, or rather they had ordered their slaves the Beetle-kinden to lay stone on stone, according to their plan, but all their precognition had not foreseen the revolution of the Apt, which had cast them down from their power and pre-eminence, and sent them to live like hermits in their distant mountain retreats.

They had chosen well when siting their city, though. Where Collegium stood, the land fell shallowly down towards the sea, where the waters then possessed draft enough for merchantmen to dock. Down the coast from Collegium, the borders between land and sea became starker. There was no good shoreline anchorage for any ship of size, but the coast offered up a warren of little coves, inaccessible beaches, caves, a patchwork of cliffs and shallow bays most of the way to Kes.

This was one such meagre anchorage, a mere half-mile east of Collegium: a crescent of gravel and sand sheltered by the tall, uneven walls of rock that the sea ate away in slow bites at its leisure. The rock was layered in slightly slanted bands: pale, dark red, pink, pale, black, each stripe taller than a man. Helmess Broiler had read a theory once, about a great disaster which had happened an unthinkably long time ago, in which the Lowlands had slumped away from what was now the Commonweal, and where a great wedge of land had simply disappeared into the sea, shearing across the layers of bedrock to leave strata like this exposed forever more. He did not have an opinion on this notion. Events that had happened so very long ago seemed unlikely to encroach on his life, one way or another.

Elytrya clung to his arm, for it was cold tonight: the wind off the sea having nowhere to go save to prowl backwards and forwards about the cove. She did not like the chill, he knew, and even in Collegium's mild winters she complained about it, dressing up in as many layers as she could wear. Now she had two woollen cloaks on, and still she shivered. Nonetheless, she had insisted on coming here. She had ordered the boatman to return for them in three hours, and stay out of sight until that time, on pain of forfeiting payment. The man had given Helmess a knowing leer as he resumed his rowing. *A liaison, the old Assembler and his young Spider mistress?* In truth it was a forbidding place for a tryst, but then Elytrya had business, not pleasure, in mind.

'What are we waiting for?' he asked. There was half a moon in the sky, and he saw no ships, lit or otherwise, casting shadows on the water. The air was clear of fliers, and he heard no engines.

'Wait, dear one,' she said, snuggling closer. Despite her shivering he could see her smiling. She had been planning this for a long time, he knew. He was to meet her allies at last. A moment later he felt her tense in his arms. Of course, her eyes were better in the dark than his. *Or they would be if she were a Spider, which she's not . . .*

'Pass me the lamp,' she said. He had to light it for her, for even the single steel igniter was beyond her, but when she had it in her hand she paced to within a few feet of the water's edge, holding it before her.

*And still no ships.* Helmess listened for the slap of oars, the snap of a billowing sail. There was nothing to be heard.

Elytrya was retreating from the water. Where the lamp-light caught her face, it showed her triumphant. *But no one is coming, my dear, no one . . .*

He thought he saw, in that same moment, a light within the ocean that was no reflection of the moon's. As Elytrya backed towards him, he felt something jump inside him.

Ten feet out from where the waves lapped the shingle, shapes were breaking through the water. Helmess felt a lurch in his stomach, for all that he had halfway been expecting something like this. The seas broke, lapped back, broke again and fell away. A great carapace gleamed under moonlight, huge as a man, legs working nimbly beneath it to skitter up onto the strand. Helmess saw its raised eyes glitter above a flurry of mouthparts, and it raised to the sky a pair of pincers that could have torn steel.

*Cinders and ashes*, Helmess thought numbly, *we're about to be invaded sideways.*

More shapes were following to left and right, as the great crab settled down on its underbelly, claws drawn in like a pugilist's fists. He took them for yet more crustaceans, at first, but they were men. As massive as the crab, more so, but these walked ponderously on two legs, hulking shapes in all-encompassing plates of armour. Helmess sought for any sign of familiarity in them, and found none: in their slab-like mail they were as broad as they were tall, plodding out of the waves with a dreadful inexorability. Whatever they wore was not metal, he realized. The moonlight glinted on something more like the crab's armour, but moulded to them in a way that mere reworked shell could not even approximate. One of them wore something paler, rougher and, as he approached, the others fell into a slow formation behind him, Helmess could hear the plates of his mail scratching together as he walked.

*It can't be*, was all he thought. *It's impossible. How strong would a man have to be to . . . ?*

Elytrya stepped forward as the giant approached, and

Helmess sensed a slight tremor within her. *So this is her employer, is it?* But Helmess could tell there was something more to it than that. A lifetime of unravelling other people's connections told him that there was no leader here, just two lieutenants whose precise positioning was still in flux.

'Rosander,' she said, giving the middle syllable all the weight.

The helmed head nodded, seeming tiny between the great, mounded pauldrons. The man's gauntlets were carved into forward-curving hooks reaching over his hands, and when he raised them, Helmess flinched back, though Elytrya stood her ground. She seemed like just a child, a toy, against the vast canvas of Rosander's armoured breadth.

With surprising delicacy, the hands hidden under those claws pulled free the helmet. Revealed was a narrow, bald head, the skull ridged and braced beneath the skin as though to support the weight of the helm. The man was of no kinden Helmess had ever seen, his face utterly alien in its combination of high cheekbones, small eyes, wispy eyebrows and narrow mouth. The half-dozen men behind him remained faceless, only a narrow slit giving onto the dark beach. Water streamed off them, or seeped out from between the sections of their armour. There were few weapons to be seen aside from the monstrous claws of their gauntlets, that echoed those of what was surely their kinden animal squatting behind them. One held a sword fashioned of some dull metal, its thick blade curving forward to a square-sectioned point. Helmess doubted that he himself could have lifted the weapon even in both hands.

'Report.' Rosander's voice was small and bleak.

'Here's my report.' Elytrya held up a small package sealed with oilcloth against the wet. 'For the Edmir's eyes only.'

Rosander regarded her without love. 'Indeed.' He reached towards her, the tip of his claw narrowly missing her shoulder. Within the cup of the hooked gauntlet his hand was still huge. Elytria carefully placed her package in his palm.

'I see you've brought the heavy stuff,' she said, fingers lightly skimming the coarse surface of his armour. 'A glutton for punishment, then?'

'When we come here in earnest,' Rosander pronounced, 'we shall bring all our might. So we must accustom ourselves.' His accent was slow and strange, the vowels twitched all out of shape. He took another step forward, the sections of his mail grating softly.

*It is.* Helmess abandoned any self-deception. *It's stone. He has a suit of stone armour, yet he's standing right there, holding it up. Oh, it must be lighter in the water, but he won't let that deter him, that much is obvious. Who are these crab-kinden? What do they want of Collegium?* A moment later he caught his breath, for those dark little eyes had flicked towards him. In two stomping strides the huge sea-kinden had eclipsed Helmess's view of sky and sea.

'Nauarch Rosander,' Elytrya kept pace, 'meet Master Helmess Broiler, our man in the city.'

'Land-kinden,' Rosander addressed him, and Helmess managed a small obeisance. The bony, narrow face looked contemptuous. 'Doesn't look like much. You fight, land-kinden?'

So close, feeling the presence of the man pressing on all sides, Helmess managed a brief shake of his head. Rosander made an amused sound, although no humour showed in his expression. Aside from the narrow lips and tiny eyes, his entire head could have been carved from dun wood.

'Chenni!' the huge figure snapped out, and a smaller one stepped out from behind one of his cohorts. Helmess saw a hunchbacked little woman with spindly arms and legs, no bigger than a Fly-kinden. She was as bald as Rosander and, despite her utter disparity in stature, there was a commonality about their closed, taut-skinned faces. She positioned herself a few feet away, further from the giant than Helmess was. With a sudden stab of amusement Helmess realized that by approaching any closer she would have been blocked from the big man's view by the bulk of his own armour.

'How's it coming?' Rosander growled at the diminutive newcomer. His gaze, by Helmess's judgement, was not fierce but fond, however.

'See for yourself, chief,' she told him. 'Going to be a bit of a test. Not sure if it'll hold under the weight.'

'Bring it up,' Rosander instructed her, then swivelled his head back to eye Elytrya. To Helmess's alarm, she clearly did not know what was going on.

'I called you here to take charge of my report for the Edmir, nothing more,' she said, her voice low and dangerous.

'*You* called?' Rosander's lips retracted, showing small, dark teeth. 'You've been away from the colony too long. Things are changing now. I'm not here for you. I'm here for . . . what's your word?'

'An experiment, Nauarch,' said Chenni, her eyes focused on the sea. She spoke faster than him, but with the same accent. 'The machinists back home will be in knots, waiting to hear from us.'

'Rosander . . .' Elytrya started, but he held a clawed gauntlet up to her face, the movement effortlessly swift. At the shoreline, Helmess saw the great crab scuttle sideways in an intricate dance of legs. Behind it something else, something much larger, was dragging itself from the sea.

It had a great rounded front that curved up into little horns on either side. In a wash of water and weed, its snub-nosed leading edge surged forward onto the beach, allowing only the slightest glimpse of the powering legs hidden beneath its over-arching shell. Helmess would have taken it for some other kind of sea-monster were it not for the sounds from within it, the ratcheting and grind and click that told him that gears and springs drove those pistoning legs in place of blood and muscle.

As the sea drained off from it he heard it creak as it supported its own weight. Chenni went tense: the sight was so familiar – an artificer willing her creation to work – that he had to fight down an inappropriate smile.

It held firm, nothing cracked. The hulking sea-automotive lurked on the beach like a house-sized boulder. The little woman made a satisfied noise.

The sounds of its workings intensified, until Helmess feared that some keen ear in Collegium might hear. The automotive lurched forward, clawing its way further across the shingle. Abruptly it began making less healthy sounds, grinding and crunching, and then the unmistakable noise of a stripped gear spinning. Chenni dashed over to the struggling machine.

'Most impressive,' Elytrya declared, but Helmess detected a slight quiver in her voice.

'For a prototype,' Rosander agreed, implacable. 'When we come to seize back the land, we will use every weapon available. You have such things, land-kinden?'

'We do,' Helmess admitted hoarsely. He was thinking of an army of massively armoured men and beasts and machines, sitting invisibly beneath the water, swarming into Collegium from the river and the docks by moonlight, unheralded and unguessed at. 'It is impressive . . . Nauarch,' he said, understanding the unfamiliar word as a title. *Walls staved in, claws rending flesh, seaweed and blood tracked into the halls of the Amphiophos. An enemy that we never even knew we had. And after that night, after the blood-tide has receded, who shall pick up the pieces? Not the Empire . . . and not Maker, either.*

He was unsure exactly when he had lost his last vestige of loyalty to Collegium. Through his dealings as a statesman and magnate, there was no hard line between working for the city and working the city for his own ends. It had been a long time now since he had crossed over into the realms of the parasite.

*Let Jodry Drillen enjoy his term as Speaker,* Helmess thought, *for it may turn out to be the shortest one in history. If the people of Collegium will not give me power, and if the Empire will try to leash me like a beast, then I will seek my allies where I can find them.*

'Gear train slipped,' Chenni reported, arriving back from inspecting the machine. 'Should have seen that coming. Out in the open air there's no water to keep them at their proper pace, so they ran riot. We'll sort it out.'

'Get it back in the water,' Rosander ordered, and his bodyguards turned ponderously and went over to the machine, easing it back into the sea with no obvious effort.

'Remember me, land-kinden,' came Rosander's voice, and Helmess's eyes snapped back to him. That narrow, ridged head was thrust forward between the massive shoulders. 'If you betray us, these hands shall crush you,' the giant threatened.

'And if I do not?' Helmess whispered.

'I'm sure Elytrya has promised you much,' replied Rosander with a sneer. 'Still, the Edmir rewards those that serve him well, as do I.'

'You will need someone governing in your name, who understands the . . . land-kinden.'

'No doubt,' Rosander agreed but, under his bleak stare, Helmess had the uncomfortable feeling of being judged.

The two Fly-kinden had led Stenwold all the way to the curving sea wall before he decided enough was enough. Perhaps it was the sight of the tower and the sea defences, still bearing their scars from the Vekken siege, that prompted him. The Flies were already setting foot on the wall's landward stonework, and he could not see anywhere they might be heading except away from any chance of his calling for help.

'So where are we going?' he asked sharply, and something in his tone brought them up short. The two of them eyed him thoughtfully.

'Now what would that be, Master?' asked the Fly man, looking at the stubby device now gripped in Stenwold's hand.

'A gift from an old student of mine,' Stenwold told them. The little, cut-down, double-barrelled snapbow was surprisingly heavy, and he knew it was barely accurate beyond ten yards, but it was a beautiful piece of engineering, nonetheless. Stenwold remembered the card that had come with it, printed immaculately to resemble elegant handwriting: *Because I owe a great deal to my education.* 'I'll go no further without some answers. Where are you leading me?'

The two Flies exchanged glances. 'Why, Master, you've been all day at asking questions,' the man said. 'So won't you want to go where you'll get answers?'

'And where's that?' Stenwold's gesture encompassed the barren sea wall.

'Look down,' said the woman, jerking her head to indicate the wall's edge. Keeping the snapbow trained, Stenwold cast a careful look over it at the choppy sea. To his surprise there were a few boats moored there, on the wrong side of the wall. He had no idea if this was usual or not – it was not something he had ever thought about asking. One of the vessels was large enough to dwarf the others.

'*Isseleema's Floating Game,*' the Fly man volunteered. 'Scourge of every gambler from Tsen to Seldis, just put in this last tenday to mine the pockets of Collegium. You want answers, Master Maker? We'll take you to where you can find them.'

There was a fair number of people on the deck of the larger ship, and many of them were armed, in a fairly casual fashion.

*This is a very bad idea.*

'Some of us can't fly,' he pointed out. 'Or am I supposed to jump in the water and get hauled out like a barrel?'

'For that purpose we have invented the rope ladder,' the woman told him shortly, obviously someone of less patience than her companion. 'You're a Beetle, therefore you'll work out the basic principles eventually.'

*I could just walk away.*

*But then I'd never know. And even if I came back here with a detachment of the guard, and searched every boat outside the wall, what would I be looking for? What might I have passed up on?*

'I keep this – and my sword,' he said, jerking the snap-bow.

'You can keep anything except standing there,' the woman said. Her wings flashed into life, and she stepped off the wall and floated downwards with enviable ease. Her companion gave Stenwold a slightly embarrassed look.

'That's Despard for you,' he said. 'A short fuse with regard to everything except explosives. Master Maker, my name is Laszlo. I'm first factor of the *Tidenfree*, which you see there on the other side of Isseleema's barge. My people and I want to help you, because we want your help in return. It's simple as that, really.'

'You know what's happening to Collegium's shipping?' Stenwold said, which was more than he intended to.

Laszlo just grinned. 'Oh, Master Maker, we know all about shipping. After all, we're *pirates*.'

After that he could hardly turn them down, so he went hand over hand down the rope ladder on to the barge's deck, where the two Flies had already cleared his credentials with the guards. They led him below, towards a wash of boisterous shouting and cheer and the delights of *Isseleema's Floating Game.*

This deck of the barge had been turned into one large, low-ceilinged room, well lit by lanterns, the curving walls draped with silks in the Spider fashion. Across a dozen tables, a mismatch of patrons were throwing their money away on cards, dice, sticks, even a tiny gladiatorial duel between a pair of hand-sized scorpions. About half the gamblers looked like Beetle-kinden locals, and not always shabbily dressed. Several even looked as though the money they were losing came from a respectable merchant's trade. The balance was comprised of Flies, Spiders and a scattering of other kinden, their differences forgotten in the shifting tides of win and lose. Midway down the long room there was a dais backing against one wall. The only word Stenwold could muster for the Spider-kinden woman there was *enthroned*. She was old – old enough that no trick of Spider-kinden manner or cosmetics could disguise it. Given the difference in their life expectancies, Stenwold guessed she had probably been past her prime before he was even born. She had the look of a woman clinging with clawed hands to the fading remnants of her empire.

Towards the bows, where the room narrowed dramatically, were a series of curtained booths, and Laszlo and Despard were taking him there, pausing impatiently when he could not slip through the crowd as easily as they could, or when some peculiar assemblage of guests caught his eye. Laszlo had to tug at his sleeve as he watched a lean Mantis-kinden woman betting fiercely with three Spiders, without a trace of the murderous loathing her kinden normally felt towards them.

Then it was Despard's turn, as Stenwold stopped to stare at a trio of Ant-kinden women with bluish-white skin. They were not seated at the tables, seeming as much out-of-place observers as he was. They wore dark cloaks and corselets of steel scales, and they stood close enough to

Isseleema's throne that his instincts suggested *bodyguards* first, and then, reconsidering, *ambassadors*? That skin tone indicated Tsen, the odd little Ant city-state on the far western coast, beyond even Vek. *So why are they here? Renegades perhaps? Some private contract?* But there was nothing of the mercenary about the three of them. Ant-kinden that had turned their back on their own cities had a certain look to them – of guilt and regret – and these three did not possess it.

Then Despard retrieved him and guided him over to a booth where the curtain was now drawn back. There were half a dozen Fly-kinden sitting there, and Laszlo had given up pride of place, deferring to a balding man with a huge black beard, quite the most imposing Fly that Stenwold had ever laid eyes on.

'They tell me you're Stenwold Maker, and that it means something,' the bearded Fly addressed him.

'As for the first, I am. As for the second, that depends who you are and what you're looking for,' Stenwold told him. The Fly's head barely came up to his chest, but the smaller man had the solid, calm presence of a general or a Mantis warrior, and there was the same kind of danger about him.

'Laszlo tells me you're looking to find out something maritime, Master Maker,' the man continued. 'Tell me, you're on the Collegiate Assembly, are you not?'

'I am.' To hear this rogue pronounce those words was jarring. The response brought smiles all round, though, and if some of those smiles revealed the odd tooth missing or replaced with gold, Stenwold was prepared to overlook it.

'Call me Tomasso,' the bearded Fly said. 'Master Maker, won't you do me the favour of coming down to our cabin and hearing a proposition to your advantage?'

'Your cabin, is it?' *Is this to be something as mundane as a kidnapping, after all this?* Stenwold had replaced his snap-bow in his belt, but put a hand upon it. Such precautions seemed the norm at the Floating Game. Laszlo's throw-away comment about piracy had seemed disarming in its candour, but there were levels and levels of bluff, after all.

'A little privacy never harmed anyone,' observed the bearded Fly. 'And, besides, there's someone there who needs to be present before any deals are made.'

'Well, you have an advantage over me, Master Tomasso,' Stenwold replied. He felt a precarious balance here, and he looked from face to face, for the menials might well show what their master could hide. There was no sense of impending foul play amongst the other Flies, but a certain excitement. *They want something from me, certainly.* 'I suppose that means you must take me there.'

Tomasso nodded, and his gang of Flies were instantly in motion, passing through the crowd to the point of the bow where stairs led down to a lower deck. Stenwold, though not an overly tall man, had to stoop there, shuffling along the dim, door-lined corridor that presented itself. The Fly-kinden had no difficulties, fluttering down the stairs with a flick of wings, walking down the passageway as though it were the spacious hallway of a palace. When Stenwold encountered another Beetle-kinden coming the other way, he had to force himself into the lee of a door to let the man past.

Laszlo was now holding a door open and steady against the faint pitch of the water outside, and Stenwold followed the Flies into a cabin that was larger than he had expected. There were bunk beds against the far wall, and a low table on the floor surrounded by shabby-looking cushions. A Fly-woman in a grey robe was sitting there by the lower bunk and, after a moment, Stenwold realized that it was because someone was occupying it. He had a glimpse of a lined and weathered face, topped by thinning grey hair.

'Have a seat.' Tomasso reclaimed his attention, taking his own place at the far end of the table. His fellows arrayed themselves on either side of him, like an attentive family.

*Which of course they are.* It was a belated realization but, now Stenwold thought about it, if Laszlo were to grow the beard and age two decades then he would be a fair likeness for Tomasso, and a couple of the others, a man and a woman, bore a good resemblance as well. They all had the same sharp nose, deep eyes, dark hair and skin tanned brown. Despard was quite different, darker and with sandy brown hair, and the girl beside the bed was greyish-skinned, seeming almost a Moth in miniature.

Stenwold sat across from them, feeling keenly the snap-bow digging into his paunch as he lowered himself on to the floor. Tomasso had a wide-bladed knife thrust un-scabbarded through his belt, and Despard was only now untensioning the arms of her crossbow. Another woman present had a bandolier of throwing blades strapped across her chest. For all their size they looked a tough enough crew.

'Now, what would an Assembler of Collegium be doing trawling the dockside dens and making inquiries after the shipping?' Tomasso asked, putting his hands together. 'Be up front with us, Master Maker, is this some private profiteering you're after, or perhaps you've lost a boat at sea, or what is it?'

*A fair question, after all. And maybe if I had been straighter to begin with I'd probably have my answers already without having to come here.* 'Your factor said you were pirates,' Stenwold answered with a nod at Laszlo.

'Did he indeed?' Tomasso said, with a sharp look. 'Well then, perhaps my factor forgets the bounds of polite conversation sometimes.'

'I could have a use for pirates, or those that are familiar with the breed,' Stenwold said flatly, watching his words break across them. To his credit, Tomasso kept any surprise well hidden.

'It's true that, in times past, we might have turned a little piracy in these waters, but that was a very long time ago,' said the bearded Fly, watching him intently. 'Back then we weren't sailing aboard the *Tidenfree*, of course, but a man of your age might just have known us by another name.'

Stenwold felt a smile quirking the corner of his mouth. 'Don't spin that line to me, Master Tomasso, for I do remember a certain Fly-kinden pirate from my father's day, but you're no older than me. You'll have to do better than that if you want me to think you crewed the *Bloodfly*.'

'Will I, now?' Tomasso brought out a long-stemmed blackwood pipe, and Despard lit it for him in a flash of sparks from a little steel-lighter. 'Is Himself sleeping?'

'He is,' said the girl in the Moth-kinden robes. 'Peaceful enough.'

Tomasso jerked his head back to indicate the old man in the bunk. 'He is the third man to bear the name of Bloodfly, and when he closes his eyes for the last time, as he must soon, I shall become the fourth. You have to understand that, amongst our people, business is a family concern.'

*I don't believe it.* But there was not a hint of guile or mockery on Tomasso's face, and the rest of them were as solemn as statues. Stenwold looked from Laszlo to Despard, across the others, and back to Tomasso. In his mind were all the stories and ballads of his youth, celebrating the scourge of last generation's pirates, now that they were safely dead or gone.

*Or perhaps only biding their time* . . . 'If he's the Bloodfly, where has he been?'

'Where business was better. Collegium became poor pickings for pirates since they built the rails to Sarn and Helleron. We've travelled, Master Maker.' Tomasso pulled on the pipe reflectively. 'Up and down the Spiderlands coast, we've travelled. Taking our chances where the winds took us, following the money. Until, at long last, we find ourselves back here, and with Himself in such a way that it seems to me that I should start making plans.'

'And what do you want with me?' Stenwold asked him, 'that you should be willing to help me? I'm no wealthy magnate. What have I got that you could want?'

Tomasso smiled, the smile of man whose carefully baited trap has finally snapped shut. 'Respectability, Master Maker,' he said. 'And you have that by the barrelfull.'

# Seven

'I'm going on a journey,' Stenwold explained. Arianna regarded him for a while before trusting herself to comment.

'This is the Failwright business still, is it?'

'And if it is?'

'Don't you think you're treating it all a little too seriously?' she asked him.

'Arianna, it's been a tenday now since anyone saw Rones Failwright,' Stenwold pointed out. 'Since *we* saw him, as we appear to be the last people to have done so. If Helmess Broiler hadn't lost in the Lots then I'd probably be up for his murder by now.'

'Fine.' She folded her arms. 'When do we leave?'

'Not you,' he told her firmly. He guessed that Tomasso would not accept a second passenger. His arrangement with the Fly-kinden family was tenuous enough already. 'It'll be dangerous,' he added.

'So I'd be watching your back. It'll be just like the war.'

'I need someone to keep an eye on things here while I'm away.'

'So get Jodry Drillen to do that,' she said stubbornly. He saw in her mind then the time he had left her behind for his futile journey to the Commonweal, before the Wasp siege of Collegium.

'I don't *trust* Drillen, not enough to act as my eyes,' Stenwold told her. 'Would you?'

'So,' she said. She was angry with him, still looking for a way to crack his resolve. 'Where now, Stenwold?'

He was intending to stay silent, but he saw her tensing up. 'If I told you that a pack of Fly-kinden was going to show me where the pirates are, would you believe me?'

'What have you got yourself into?' Her face was closed tight now. For a moment he was going to relent. *I'll talk the* Tidenfree *crew into it somehow, why not? Why not bring her along?* He was on the brink.

'I'll be fine.' His words came out automatically. That old reassuring tone that had ceased to work on Cheerwell by the time she was fifteen, let alone on a Spider-kinden. *I don't want you to get hurt,* he thought, but he knew from experience this was an argument that carried no weight with her.

His conversation of last night recurred to him, seeming dreamlike now, with a grinning Tomasso hearing him voice his doubts: *And I'm supposed to believe that the moment I go hunting pirates, I should find pirates already hunting me?*

'Oh no, Master Maker,' Tomasso had said to him. 'We've had our eyes on three or four of your Assemblers for days now. My Laszlo's been watching your home. You were just the first that came to the negotiating table, as it were.'

Stenwold then wondered: *Did they kill Failwright?* But if so, they were playing more double games than he could interpret. His instincts had told him that these friendly, open, heavily armed folk were being straight with him, solely because they were admitting to so much.

'And what do you mean by *respectability*?' he had asked them. 'Quantify it, Master Tomasso. Has the bottom fallen out of the pirate way of life? My sources say not.'

The bearded Fly had glanced about at his family. 'A life of iniquity is all very well, Master Maker. We've taken ships off the Atoll coast and the Silk Road and the Bay of the Mark and not three leagues from where we sit, but there's no future in it and there never will be. We live well day to day, but no better generation to generation, and one day our luck will run out and we'll either sink or swing. When Himself here breathes his last, it's down to me to lead the family, and I want to lead them somewhere else than out to sea. You're a big man in Collegium, Maker. Don't tell me that you can't buy us some respectability.'

'In exchange for what?' Stenwold had asked. 'What do you have for me?'

'Come with us to where the pirates drop their anchors, Master Maker,' Tomasso had said. 'I mean the real pirates, the free thieves of the sea that you won't find drinking in a Collegium taverna. If the answers to all your questions are to be found anywhere, we can find the people who know them for you.' He had smiled again, broad and villainous and honest as a knife. 'Pay us for value received, Master Maker.' With the unspoken words, *and if you don't pay up, we have ways of making you.*

'Stay here,' Stenwold told Arianna. 'Stay and keep watch for me. If you want to watch my back, watch it here where I know I have enemies.'

'I'm going on a journey,' Stenwold explained. The alarm in Jodry Drillen's eyes was gratifying.

'Going where? For how long?'

Stenwold shrugged. 'Two tendays perhaps, three. A sea voyage.'

'A what? Why?' Stenwold had caught Jodry in the Speaker's office, where the man was no doubt deciding on the colour of the new furnishings. Now the fat Assembler looked abruptly like the boy caught trying out his father's outsized sword. 'Stenwold . . . a sea voyage?'

'For my health,' replied Stenwold implacably. It was unfair of him, he knew. He was taking out on Jodry his own guilt over leaving Arianna. *Jodry Drillen, new Speaker for the Assembly. He's earned a little unfairness.*

'This isn't Failwright's lunacy is it?'

'Why? Is it catching?'

'Stenwold, stop *doing* that!' Jodry snapped. 'You can't go. I need you here.'

'You don't need me now. You're Speaker.'

'Not all the Lots are in.'

'You've beaten Helmess Broiler by a comfortable margin already. You don't need me so badly you can't spare me for two tendays.'

Jodry looked wildly about him, putting Stenwold in mind of a big bumbling fly trying to find its way out of a sealed room. 'The Vekken!' he got out. 'Who's going to deal with them when you're away?'

'They're behaving themselves nicely.'

'They're not! They want to see me!' Jodry exclaimed. 'Me and you,' he added awkwardly after a pause.

A worm of disquiet twisted inside Stenwold. 'About what?'

'I've no cursed idea. They're *your* Vekken.'

That Vekken accord, the piece of botch-job diplomacy that Stenwold had been working on for so long, was still important. Stenwold's lifetime had seen two Vekken wars, though he could barely recall the first save as an inexplicable period of fear and commotion during his youth. 'What have you done to sour them, Jodry?'

'Oh no.' The fat man shook his head hard enough to make his jowls wobble. 'Not me. I leave them to you, but this morning I find two of them bothering my secretary for an appointment. You tell me why.'

Stenwold grimaced. Part of him wanted to leave Jodry to fight his own battles for once, but this situation needed him. 'We'll see them immediately,' he decided. 'Send a man for them now.'

'But—'

'I board ship before dusk, Jodry. If you want my help with the Vekken, then you're more likely to get it while I'm still on land.'

After Jodry had sent his Fly-kinden secretary buzzing off to locate one of the Vekken, the Assembly's most likely new Speaker turned back to Stenwold, and eyed him narrowly.

'What's got into you?' he asked. 'What's going on?'

Stenwold stared at him for a long while. *I mostly trust you*, he thought, *but not quite that last bit, Jodry. I'm not so convinced of my own judgement where it comes to assessing my own kinden.* He realized, with a start, that Tomasso the pirate had inspired more instinctive trust in him than this Beetle-kinden of notable family who had done Stenwold nothing but good. *But Tomasso made no attempt to hide what he is, whereas Jodry's whole career is based on impressions and pretences.* The sour afterthought was unavoidable. *And so is my own.*

Jodry was frowning. 'First you're about to laugh at me, and now you look like you want to kill me. Stenwold . . . Is this about your niece?'

'What do you know about my niece?'

'I know she didn't come back from Khanaphes, but Master Gripshod didn't pass her name to me along with Manny Gorget's, so I'm assuming she's still somewhere amongst the living.' The concern in the man's jowly face was genuine, in so far as Stenwold could tell.

'Trust me in what I'm doing.' Stenwold dodged the question nimbly. 'Trust me that I believe it to be in Collegium's best interests.'

Jodry sighed. 'Well, your record is good in that respect. I just hope that what you believe matches what you actually find there.'

The Fly-kinden returned just then, and behind him, walking with a smart military step, was one of the Vekken. The city of Vek had sent four ambassadors, men similar enough in appearance to be brothers, short, stocky, strong-framed, pitch-skinned. Stenwold was able to tell them apart now, from long afternoons of unrewarding negotiations.

'Termes,' he greeted the man.

'Master Maker.' Something had happened on the Khanaphes expedition to change the Vekken's view of Stenwold. When their two delegates had returned, and shared their thoughts with their comrades, a breach seemed to have been made in their blank hostility. All of a sudden they could look at him without reaching for their swords and, when he spoke, they listened. Jodry was right in that.

'Now perhaps we can get somewhere,' the fat Assembler began. 'You people don't like me, but you like Maker here, yes?'

Termes stared at Jodry with antipathy, and Stenwold remarked, 'They don't like me, Jodry, they just dislike me less than most people.'

'This is true,' the Vekken confirmed, his voice clipped and tight as he squared off against the two Beetles. Weight for weight they could have made five of him between them, but Ant-kinden were strong and born to war. They displayed precious little body-language, either, what with living in each other's minds all the time, but Stenwold recognized an Ant preparing for a fight.

'What is it?' he asked. 'What's gone wrong this time?'

'We know that Collegium conspires with our enemies,' Termes said, righteously.

Stenwold would have preferred to deal with one of the two who had made the journey to Khanaphes. The sharp edges had been knocked off their hatred, whereas Termes was still spiky with it.

'What enemies does Vek have these days?' Stenwold prompted.

'We know of the Tseni embassy,' Termes continued implacably.

The response threw Stenwold. For a moment he could not even place the word 'Tseni'. Then his memory supplied it for him: Tsen, that distant Ant city on the far west coast. A city that had no dealings with Collegium or any of the Lowlands, save that it had sent a meagre detachment of soldiers to aid in the war against the Empire, more a diplomatic gesture than any substantial military force.

'Tseni embassy?' he asked blankly. Of course, although a lot of ground lay between Tsen and Vek, every inch of it would have been fought over at some time or other. Ant city-states were never easy neighbours. 'Have you heard of such a thing?' he asked Jodry.

The man looked awkward. 'Well, only today, in fact. Three Tseni turned up from nowhere, just walked into the Amphiophos and started asking who was in charge. Whereupon the news reached our Vekken friends, no doubt.'

Stenwold looked at the dark-skinned Ant. 'It's the first I've heard of it. If they are genuinely ambassadors, then we'll hear them out, but they're not here by our invitation. Do you believe that?'

Termes's dark face neither confirmed nor denied it.

'They must be hoping to trade on their contribution to the war,' said Jodry, matching Stenwold's thoughts.

Stenwold signed. 'Termes,' he said. 'Jodry and I will speak to them now. And then, whatever they say, even if they promise us the moon on a plate, we'll come and talk to you. And then I'm leaving the city for a while – on a matter unrelated to Tsen, Vek or any other Ant-kinden city-state.' Because, otherwise, if he had simply left without stating that, the Vekken would take it as concrete evidence of betrayal. 'And Jodry will pledge to make no agreements or decisions on this matter until I've returned.' *Or until he gets tired of waiting for the Fly-kinden to bring back my body.* He brushed the thought away irritably. 'You see the wisdom of that, Jodry? After all, you're our newest Speaker, so you can explain to the Tseni how very busy you are. Your new role must demand a great deal of organization.'

Jodry gave him a measured nod. 'Oh, yes. After all,

everyone knows how oppressive the bureaucracy here is getting.'

Termes looked from one to the other, expressionless. 'Congratulations on your new appointment,' he said to Jodry flatly, and it was impossible to tell whether he intended humour by it.

The Tseni were not where they had been left. The elegant rooms found for them in the Amphiophos were not only untenanted but devoid of any sign that the Ants had even been there. Arvi, Jodry's Fly-kinden secretary, eventually ran them down in the College's workshops, where they had already started causing trouble.

Jodry and Stenwold arrived to find them dominating a machine room. A crowd of students had been summarily evicted, along with an elderly matriarch who had been teaching them. The three visiting Ant women now held sway over a half-dozen workbenches and a single young Beetle whom they had backed into a corner. He looked slightly familiar to Stenwold.

They had not drawn a sword, for in this place they hardly needed to. They were strung taut with violence in a way that Stenwold's kinden were not. Once he laid eyes on them he found that he knew them, and that he had been expecting to. They were not much changed from when he had recently seen them aboard the *Floating Game*.

*Sneaking into Collegium like brigands*, he thought. *No formal embassies, no welcoming parties, but three soldiers arriving under cover of a Spider pleasure barge.* Even as he entered the room, careless that Jodry was hanging back, he could see the sense of it. *I doubt Tseni ships would have much luck sailing past the harbourmouth at Vek, and the landward route's hardly more appealing.*

They turned even as he entered, noticing how he walked like a warrior, despite the robes. He had not brought his sword, but his stance implied it. He saw three women, alike

as close sisters, mirrors of each other as the Vekken delegates were, and no doubt for the same reason. Their skin
was like fresh ice, their faces strong-jawed and solid. They
had put on a little ornament: simple bands of gold at the
forehead, and something in steel and silver hanging about
the neck that might be a medal. He assumed it must be a
form of show for his benefit, since Ants had no need of
insignia amongst their own.

'What's going on here?' he demanded, and he made it
an open challenge. He would get nowhere with these
strange Ant-kinden unless he carried the full weight of
Collegium invisibly with him into the room.

'War Master, help me,' the Beetle scholar got out.
Although no blade had been drawn he was tucked into a
corner as though he already had a point at his throat.
Stenwold winced privately at the old title, but on the other
hand it would do no harm.

'What are you?' one of the Tseni asked casually.

*No avoiding it.* 'I am Stenwold Maker – lately called War
Master – of the Assembly of Collegium,' Stenwold told
them. He met their eyes without wavering, giving not an
inch. 'You, I am told, are ambassadors from Tsen. You are
not behaving like it.'

He felt Jodry shuffle in the doorway, as if to caution,
*Steady on . . .* There was a brief, blank moment in which
the three must have been mentally comparing notes.

'War Master, they've . . .' the scholar choked out. Thin
and gangling for a Beetle, he looked to be about eighteen,
surely in his last year of studies. Any of the Tseni could
have snapped him in half.

'First things first,' Stenwold decided. 'You, come here
and stand by me.'

The scholar hesitated, but the three Tseni obviously
decided that maintaining a heavy hand was unlikely to work
here. They allowed the boy room, and he fled to Stenwold's
side.

'Now, who are you and why are they bothering you?'

'Maxel Gainer, Master Maker,' the scholar replied. 'And they've come to steal—'

'If you will talk of theft,' said one of the Tseni, 'then let us talk of theft.' Her hand was on her sword-hilt. *Always we get to this point, with Ant-kinden,* Stenwold thought. *It was like dealing with the Vekken all over again.*

'So talk then,' Stenwold invited. 'Explain yourselves. Why has Tsen sent the world's smallest invasion force to take over Collegium one room at a time?'

To his surprise one of the Tseni's lips twitched in a swiftly-suppressed smile. Ants did not smile amongst themselves, since they grew up sharing such nuances of thought and sensation invisibly amongst themselves. Therefore only contact with other kinden could start to teach them what varying expressions and intonation were for.

'I knew a man of Tsen once,' he said. 'His name was Plius, and he turned out to be an agent of your city, although I didn't know that for a long time. He sent for troops to fight the Wasp Empire, and he died bravely fighting alongside Ant-kinden of two other cities. History in the making. Perhaps we shall start again, and make a better job of it this time. I am Stenwold Maker, this lad is apparently Maxel Gainer' – *whose name is maddeningly familiar, but from where?* – 'and you . . . ?'

'Kratia,' replied the Tseni who had done all the talking. She shared a moment with her fellows. 'It appears we have not been correct in the manner of approaching our grievance,' she said. 'You will understand we are not much used to dealing with other kinden.'

The bald lie drew grudging respect from Stenwold. *Used enough to sail all the way here in a Spider ship. Used enough to throw my kinden's thoughts about Ants back in my face.* 'What do you want with young Gainer, Officer Kratia . . .' Again there was that unexpected ghost of an expression that led him to correct himself. 'Commander Kratia, then?'

She nodded curtly. Stenwold was reclassifying her and her companions already, not soldiers but spies, agents: the sort of people he had been dealing with most of his life.

'This one is in possession of mechanical secrets belonging to our city,' she said, 'and that cannot be tolerated. As its former allies against the Empire, we are sure Collegium will make proper restitution.'

*And I reckon the Vekken are lucky you're not here to stir up a war against them*, Stenwold thought. 'Gainer, does this make any sense to you?' he asked, mainly to give himself more time to think.

'Master Maker, they want to take the *Tseitan*,' Gainer replied. 'All the plans and everything! Ten years of work!'

'*Our* work—' Kratia started, but Stenwold held a hand up.

'Enough. Jodry?'

The Assembly's new Speaker bustled forward. 'Here.'

'It is clearly an issue of considerable weight that has brought these three women so far. Therefore think of it as your first proper diplomatic spat.'

To his surprise Jodry made no complaint, or perhaps he was just trying to display solidarity before the Ants. 'I'll take it from here, Sten. It's obviously nothing to do with the . . . with your friends. Thank you for your help. Good sailing, or whatever one says in such situations.'

Stenwold went home, and managed to finish off his packing whilst arguing once again with Arianna. She wanted to know why he couldn't take her, and towards the end of the dispute he realized that it was not that he *couldn't*, exactly, but that he *wouldn't*. He could have talked her past Tomasso and his crew, and he was not expecting so much trouble during his absence that he needed her in Collegium. When he dug deep enough in his heart to find the real reason, it left him sad, and ashamed of himself.

*And is having a young Spider mistress not enough to make me feel young, but I have to go mimicking the misadventures of my youth, charging about with nothing but a sword and my wits to rely on? Am I getting so old, in truth, that I have to prove my vigour even to myself?* He had no answer to that, but he stuck to his position, leaving Arianna angry and unhappy behind him.

The *Tidenfree* had nudged its way in between merchant-men, sitting openly in Collegium's harbour. It bore no overt sign of being a pirate ship and, in truth, it was not the *Bloodfly* of recent legend, instead a graceful single-masted slender thing that would have done a Spider proud as a yacht.

It was only as he set foot on board that the name '*Tseitan*' abruptly made sense to him. Not a word he had heard before, but one derived from a name he should have remembered. The artificer Tseitus, who had died in the Vekken siege of Collegium; the Ant-kinden Tseitus, with his blue-white skin like Plius, like Kratia. Tseitus, whose submersible craft had sunk the Vekken flagship, and for whom the new model – Gainer's improved prototype – was named.

# Eight

'Boats are like the kinden that make them,' Tomasso expounded. Around them, the crew of the *Tidenfree* was casting off. From below decks the surprising sound of a solid little engine was thudding, dragging the ship backwards out of dock, whilst a half-dozen Fly-kinden had fluttered aloft, ready to bring out sail. A remarkably stocky woman was ordering them about in a voice that would have done credit to a leadshotter.

Stenwold nodded politely, sensing that Tomasso's metaphor was about to give his people a rough time.

'Beetle boats,' Tomasso continued, sure enough, 'are. fat and solid and slow, begging your pardon.' He grinned a glint of gold Stenwold's way. 'Spider ships are pretty and they move well, but they're far too clever and they can never go anywhere the straight way. Mantis boats are quick and vicious, and it's impossible to steer them anywhere.'

That brought a bark of unmeant laughter from Stenwold, although he felt guilty about it afterwards. Tomasso's smile widened.

'And what about Fly-kinden ships, Master Tomasso?' Stenwold asked him. 'Tell me about those, will you not?'

'Oh, they're fast, Master Maker, and they're good for any seas, and they'll make use of any trick to get where they're going.'

Stenwold looked astern, seeing the Collegium harbour

receding. This was the first time he had ever gone to sea. His travelling had been towards the Empire, always.

'If you plan on killing or kidnapping me, now's the time,' he said evenly.

Tomasso roared with laughter that was twice as big as he was. 'Oh, surely, Master Maker, surely, but we're as good as our word. You can give us something that only a high-up of Collegium can, and it's something that we can't steal. In return we can get you to places that only a third-generation villain knows about. Now, come.' He strutted across the deck, beckoning Stenwold to follow. The swell was building, now that they were beyond the sea wall, and the Beetle had to reach out for his balance a little before he was able to proceed. He heard a little smirking from the crew.

'People you should know,' Tomasso called back to him. 'At the tiller is our sailing master, Gude.' He indicated the broad Fly woman, who gave Stenwold a stony nod. 'If she ever tells you to do anything aboard this ship, then you do it. I may be the head of the family, but once we're under sail, her voice overrules mine.' Gude's stern demeanour made Stenwold believe it.

'You've met Despard, of course. She's below at the moment with the engine, and that's her doman. Your other chaperone is . . .' Tomasso glanced about, and then bellowed, 'Laszlo! Get your backside on deck!'

'Right behind you, chief.' The young Fly dropped from the rigging without warning, making Tomasso's hand twitch for his knife-hilt.

'You, you troublemaker, can look after our guest, and make sure he doesn't end up over the rail. Laszlo's our factor, Master Maker. He buys and sells ashore. While we're on board, though, he might as well look after you, so ask him for anything you need.'

'Thank you.'

'And I meant it about the rail. This ship wasn't designed

with your kinden in mind.' Tomasso's gaze took in a railing that would come up to Stenwold's knee.

*A ship designed for people half my size who can fly.* He made the requisite mental adjustments.

'Oh, and you should meet Fernaea as well, to make sense of some answers I'll give to some questions you'll certainly ask a little later,' the bearded Fly continued, dragging Stenwold, and Laszlo, back towards the bows again, where stood the grey-robed Fly girl who had been tending to the sleeping old man on the *Floating Game*. 'Fern, this is Master Stenwold Maker, magnate of Collegium.'

She nodded at him, as reserved and close-faced as her Moth-kinden name suggested.

'She's . . . a seer,' Stenwold guessed.

'Oh, well done. You're a man of uncommon experience, then, for a Beetle?'

'You might say so,' agreed Stenwold. Fernaea was staring at him, defensive and tense, and he wondered what mischance had brought a Moth-trained magician into the ragged crew of a pirate ship. Nothing happy, that was certain.

'What about your . . . ?'

'My uncle, you mean. Himself,' Tomasso finished. 'Isseleema's an old friend, which means that, when she's accepted a hefty purse to look after Himself, I can be reasonably sure that's just what she'll do.' His cheer vanished abruptly. 'Time, Master Maker, it's just a myth to a lout like Laszlo here, but you and I are old enough to hear its wings on the air. Himself . . . Himself has time sitting, counting by his bedside, and there's no magic nor artifice on all the wide seas that can do anything about that.'

'I'm sorry,' Stenwold said automatically.

'We're all sorry,' Tomasso acknowledged. 'But it's my job to find us a future, and if the best means to that is helping you, then here's my hand on it.'

He didn't offer his hand, so Stenwold chalked that one up to *Figures of speech (Fly-kinden pirates)*. While he was doing so, Tomasso looked him up and down critically.

'You'll pass, for where we're going. For such a Big Man you dress down nicely.'

Stenwold was wearing his hard-weather gear: a suit of reinforced canvas and leather with toolstrips and pouches, such as an artificer would wear to go to war in. He had an oilcloth cloak over that, to keep as much of the sea out as would prove practical. The Fly-kinden around him all wore long-coats, or what amounted to long-coats on them: shiny with wax and oil, wool-lined on the inside, appropriate clothing for the rain and the cold wind. Most also had a woollen cap on, save for Laszlo, sporting a leather helm, and Gude, who went bare-headed, the breeze tugging ineffectually at her short light-dyed hair.

'You're armed?' Tomasso asked, and when Stenwold twitched back his cape to show his sword-hilt, the Fly sniffed. 'Anything else?'

'In my luggage,' Stenwold allowed.

'Good. The port we're headed for, it's not good to be too subtle about these things.'

'And where *are* we headed, Master Tomasso?'

'Kanateris.' The name meant nothing to Stenwold, save maybe for its last syllable.

'Is that near Seldis?' He racked his brains for the ports along the Silk Road.

'Oh, we're not pointing ourselves east, Master Maker. That's the long way round.'

'What do you mean?'

'You're an educated man, so you see the same maps I do. It's quicker to cut straight south, if you want to see where the Spiders live.'

*Which is correct, of course, and yet we don't.* Stenwold had learned that, and not questioned it, because sea travel had never been of interest to him. *It goes to show how knowledge is never wasted.* One of the College's mottos, that, and how very true. 'Enlighten me,' he said.

The *Tidenfree* was making good headway now, the coast-line receding smartly. He would have said, *the familiar coastline*, but of course he was no seagoer, so it could have been Solarno or Seldis or some city on the moon for all he would recognize the view.

'Laszlo.' Tomasso singled out the younger Fly. 'Make yourself useful to Master Maker. I need to go and plot our course with Gude.'

The young Fly strutted up to Stenwold, the salt wind tugging at his coat. 'You want the secret, Master?'

'Is it a secret?'

'Oh, isn't it? But if the chief says tell, I'll tell. Where would you sail, in order to do business with the Spider-lands, Ma'rMaker?' Laszlo gestured expansively, as if trying to encompass all of creation with his hands. His rapid speech condensed 'Master Maker' into a babble. 'Why, down the coast, of course, hoping the ships of Felyal and Kes aren't too hungry, past the forts of of Everis and into Seldis or Siennis, a long old way. And there you'd trade with Spiders who'd charge a fortune for the goods up the Silk Road, yet pay a pittance for yours, for the chief occupation of everyone in those cities is taking bribes and levying taxes. Believe me, I know. Or, if you were a foolish man, you'd take your ship down the desert coast and look to sell to the Spiderlands direct. Know what happens to people who do that?'

'They don't come back,' Stenwold suggested.

Laszlo nodded energetically. 'Not cos the Spiders are mean, you understand, but it's a death warrant to go that way and trade, not knowing how they do things. Eventually you bribe too much or too little, bribe the wrong man, say something you never realized was an insult, fail to compli-ment the women, drink in the wrong taverna. The next day, well, you're lucky if you're in chains and gone from being a trader to being stock in trade, if you get me. So your lot, all you get are the dog-ends from Seldis, and at a ruinous poor price, too.'

'But you know how to get on with the Spiders?'

'We could sail along the desert coast with no trousers and we'd get away with it,' Lazslo replied. It was hard to tell just how old he was. He looked like a man of twenty years, but his enthusiasm was six years younger. 'However, we don't need to. There are two reasons why even those who know better still sail the coast road to Seldis, Ma'rMaker. Firstly, once you're out of sight of the coast, it's cursed hard to plot a course just by sun and stars. You reach the far shore and you're a hundred miles from where you should be, and you with your water running low, and who knows what family owns the next port. More than that, there are the weed seas. The sea's got forests, like the land does, with weed so tall it reaches from where the sun don't shine all the way to the open air. Your ship gets caught in that, there's no steering out of it, and then you starve or die of thirst or . . . well, they say there's things that live there that'll soon put you out of your misery. Other problem is the weather. It's rare enough to get across without a storm, and I'd bet you a bit to a Helleron central that we'll see one this trip. Tear a ship apart, bring the mast down on you, rip your sails off, they can. Wind, lightning like the sky's on fire, waves that come between you and the sun—'

'Sea-kinden,' Gude interrupted unexpectedly.

Laszlo snorted. 'Nobody believes in sea-kinden,' he said. 'And, with all that storm going on, who'd need them? Faced with that kind of weather, the coast road looks awfully inviting.'

'But you've got a way through?' Stenwold prompted.

'Oh, surely,' Laszlo confirmed. 'Come up and stand by Gude now, Ma'rMaker.'

'Stenwold. Just call me Stenwold,' the Beetle insisted, clumping up from the deck level to the wheel. Gude gave Laszlo a warning glare, but he ignored her blithely.

'Now, I'm betting you know what these toys are,' he said.

They were battered and weather-worn, not the workshop-mint pieces that he had seen previously, but Stenwold was artificer enough to pick them out. 'I see an absolute clock and a gimballed compass,' he said.

'And with their help, and charts, and a reckoning taken from the sky, and some fairly taxing mathematics, Ma'r Stenwold, we find our way to wherever we want to be.'

'And you also calculate your way through storms, do you?'

Laszlo still smiled, but abruptly it was the smile of an older man. 'Oh, Master Stenwold Maker, this is the other part of the secret.' He leant close, forcing Stenwold to bend nearer to him. 'Do you believe in magic?' he said.

Stenwold paused a long while before answering. His instinct was 'No,' of course, and nearly any other Beetle would not have hesitated to say so, but he had seen too much, encountered too many other kinden. 'Yes,' he said at last, and reluctantly.

Laszlo's smile changed again, without moving, like the sea colours in the sunlight. 'Well,' he said, with a little less flippancy and a little more respect. 'Magic? Now there's something. I personally find it hard to credit, but there comes a point when you have to say, "I see that something's making something happen, whether it's magic or not." Yes?'

'Yes,' Stenwold agreed.

'Well, when we hit a storm, as I reckon you'll be seeing, we ship the mast and Despard sets the engine to run, but it's Fern there who calls the course. She's a dab hand at reading storms, Ma'rMaker. But this is how the Bloodfly and his crew have skipped the seas for a generation now, ever since your lot first built those clocks. We never put out without an artificer and a seer, and a halfway decent back-up for both, and with that we're as free as anyone in this world, and we'll take you to Kanateris in a fifth of the time, and you'll find all the answers that there are to be had.'

Jodry Drillen was celebrating. He had a great deal to celebrate, having beaten Helmess Broiler, and a handful of other hopefuls, to be appointed the new Speaker for the Assembly. Moreover, his agents across the city had already begun to characterize his spell in office in glowing terms, before the ink was even dry on his letters of appointment. Not for him the fate of poor old Lineo Thadspar, who had lived to see his city under siege, his world shattered by war, and who had died without seeing it put right. Jodry was a man bringing peace and prosperity, people were telling one another excitedly – as though he had come with both commodities in a bag, to be given out in handfuls. Just now, everyone loved fat, jovial, avuncular Jodry Drillen, and he was capitalizing on it for all he was worth.

Arianna had to admit there were worse people to throw a party. Jodry was a good host: neither gaudy in his ostentation, nor parsimonious in his hospitality. He trod a fine enough line that a Spider-kinden could come to his grand townhouse and be neither offended nor bored. She had to admire his choice of guests, too: there was a delicate balance of Assemblers, ambassadors, magnates and wits, enough to keep the conversation moving. A few of his selections betrayed Jodry's barbed sense of humour, for there was one of the interchangeable Vekken there, awkwardly unarmed but standing in one corner with clenched fists, no doubt complaining inside his head to his colleagues elsewhere in the city. The loathing in his eyes was not for any of his Collegiate hosts, but for the Tseni woman Jodry had brought in to balance him. It was a bold move of Jodry's but, surrounded by such cheer and licence, the two Ants were cowed into keeping their dislike to a civil silence.

Even better, and greeted lavishly when he walked through the door, Helmess Broiler himself had been invited. As Jodry had made this publicly known, his adversary could not have stayed away without being jeered at. His arrival, to the covered smiles of at least half the room, had displayed a kind of wounded dignity. The sparkling, bejewelled woman on his arm had also served to deflect the mockery. Only Arianna smiled further on seeing her. *Oh you have a Spider-kinden woman on your arm, do you? It's a shame that Beetle eyes aren't so good for the fine details, Master Broiler, for she's no true-blood Spider. There's some halfway blood in that one.* The thought was petty but, following Stenwold's departure, she had a fair store of pettiness to expend, and she was not sparing with it.

There had been a string of entertainers performing in the house's large common room, Fly acrobats and jugglers, an old Spider-kinden man who sang, then a pair of Beetle clowns whose satirizing would have offended half the room, Jodry included, had it not been done so cleverly. Now a tall, sallow woman came up, that Arianna recognized as a Grasshopper-kinden, either an imperial fugitive or a rare traveller from the Commonweal. She carried some elongated stringed instrument, which she tuned with a few practised tweaks of her fingers. Arianna decided that she had heard enough music for one evening, it never being one of her joys, so she slipped out and up the stairs to the roof garden. Here, against a tastefully gaslit trellis maze of twining plants, a few other guests had taken refuge, either for trysts or private words. Arianna found a stretch of balcony between two spiny-leaved shrubs and looked out over the sleeping city: the streets of Collegium picked out in lamps and lit-up windows.

It was strange to think that Stenwold was not in the city. It made her wonder why she herself still was.

She heard someone step behind her and she tensed out of old instinct. *Once a spy* . . . The needles of bone that her Art gifted her with had already sprung from her knuckles.

'Missing Master Maker, my dear?'

She straightened at the tone, because there were different kinds of authority. Some were assumed, like the titles that the Beetles loved to bedeck each other with. Some were innate.

'Lord-Martial Teornis,' she said, turning. She had seen him before, greeting Jodry. Their host had been resplendent in a white robe draped with folded cloth of gold, whereas Teornis, ever the gracious guest, had come dressed one step down, in a robe of black hung with red but in the same Collegium style. If there was a circlet of rubies half hidden amid the dark curls of his brow, well, he wore it well and he would be forgiven it. For a man who could have stolen the evening from under Jodry's feet, it was pure diplomacy.

She felt dowdy in comparison with him. She had been too long away from her own kind, and too lowly and poor, even then.

'I should probably tell you not to "lord" me, but frankly it's a pleasure to find someone who gets our titles right. I've been Master-lord-magnate-chief-Spider too often in recent months. These Beetles can never understand the virtues of simplicity.'

She smiled, still shy of him. He was Aristoi, a scion of the Aldanrael family that held a solid slice of the power and influence in Seldis and Siennis. Her family had been nothing, mere dirt compared to him, hoi polloi of the worst order. When she was still young, they had become nothing more than dust at last, caught in the jostling of two noble houses and milled like flour.

'I'm surprised to catch you alone, my dear, for I hear

you're quite the social celebrant these days. Old Stenwold's been a good step for you to climb.'

'I doubt he'd like to be described that way,' she replied defensively.

'Come now.' Teornis stepped forward, almost close enough to brush her shoulder as he stood beside her at the balcony rail. 'Quite a sight, these Beetle cities. All that heavy stone, all those glorious artificial lamps. Such a contradictory people.'

She felt frozen by his closeness. It was not a matter of attraction although, had he wished, no doubt he could have drawn her to him. It was pure, rank fear, the fear that any low-birth Spider-kinden learned, if they survived. *Do not tangle with the Aristoi. Obey them, respect them, but, most of all, avoid them. You are* nothing *to them.* Her mother's voice, her dead mother who should have listened better to her own advice.

'But we were talking about the social advantages of bedding Stenwold Maker,' he continued, still looking out at the city. His smile was patiently amused, as though watching a clever child perform some prodigal task. 'You can't be so very touchy about that, surely? Sentiment?'

'You'd pretend we have no feelings, Lord Teornis?' she asked, forcing the words. In that moment she wanted him to drop this pretence, to turn on her like a lord of the Aristoi and cast her aside like the ragged renegade she was. Instead he smiled at her, as genuine a smile as anyone ever practised in the mirror.

'We alone are gifted, amongst all the kinden, are we not? We feel as much as they, we love, we hate, we take joy, and yet we never lose our minds or practicalities amid the sea of our emotions. Small wonder that, alone of all the rulers of the old times, we still possess our palaces and our slaves. Feel what you want for Stenwold Maker, my dear, but don't let that cripple you.'

'And I thought you liked Stenwold.'

He laughed at that, with unfeigned delight as far as she could tell. 'Oh, I do, truly. He's a remarkable man. He's more than half Spider, inside his head. A loyal ally, a man of principle, a halfway decent intelligencer, and an inspiration to his underlings. The man's a constant source of amusement. I don't mock you, Arianna. If you were going to ride to prominence on the wings of a Beetle, you chose the right man.'

She folded her arms. It was impossible to believe he was not still making fun of her, despite the sincerity in his expression. 'I'm glad you approve.'

'One might ask where now, of course?' He was gazing over the city again, lost in contemplation. 'You must feel the sides of your cage here begin to chafe – being what you are.'

'And what *am* I, Lord Teornis?' she demanded, expecting him to name her low-born, fugitive, a whore even, waiting for him to put the blade in.

'A Rekef spy.'

That left her speechless, and her expression made him grin boyishly.

'Oh, not now, not any more. My dear girl, you look so horrified that I almost wonder if I've hit on something I'd not known. No, no, we all know you've put away the old black and gold since the war, but still, do you imagine anyone's *forgotten?*'

All she could think was that he was going to discredit her somehow – some way of ruining Stenwold. 'So what?' she got out. 'It's no secret.'

'Nor is it a criticism,' he rebuked her gently. 'A Rekef-trained agent with a working knowledge of the Wasp intelligence networks, Master Maker's lucky to have you. Assuming, of course, that he's putting all that fine training of yours to work.'

Again she was silent, though for different reasons. She had never noticed any of Teornis's agents watching her, she had not felt anyone fingering the pages of her life. Of course, given who he was, she would not have done.

'Owing to certain . . . developments within the Empire we've lost a fair few of our deep-cover people within the Rekef. Either dead or forced to flee. Bothersome, as I'm sure you can imagine, since Master Maker and I agree that the Empire won't be mending its nest for ever.'

This time he waited until the prolonged silence forced some words out of her.

'Are you making me an offer, Lord Teornis?'

He looked directly at her. 'Girl, you're clearly very resourceful. You escaped the Spiderlands. You survived the Empire. You maintained a cover here in Collegium, and you led one of this city's cleverest sons about by the nose. You then dropped the black and gold and lived to tell about it, and you're currently living the high life as a socialite and a war hero. Not a bad run, given the start the world gave you. So why be surprised if my family can see a use for your talents?'

'You want me to leave Stenwold?'

He shook his head, his smile sardonic. 'Oh, dear, no. Think before you speak, dear girl. You'd be so much less use to us if you did that.' He held up a hand. 'Before we witness any upsurge of sentiment, I'll stress my hope that Maker would never find out. Under ideal conditions, he'd enjoy a long life and go to his grave without suspecting. We're allies, after all, and, more than that, I like the man, but that doesn't mean that my family wouldn't relish having someone close to him who can, let's say, make the occasional well-timed suggestion.'

'Well, Lord Teornis, forgive me if I haven't had your upbringing,' Arianna replied. There was not much room at the balcony between Jodry's foliage, but she put what distance she could between them. 'I, however, must talk in more mercantile terms. How much did you imagine you could buy me from him for?'

'Adoption,' he said, and in the quiet that followed he beckoned over one of Jodry's servants to light his pipe. It was a Beetle habit, and not even a sophisticated one, except when Teornis was involved. She imagined, numbly, that the practice would suddenly become fashionable now. The smoke from the brass bowl of his pipe was sweet, not the old burnt smell from Stenwold's study.

'Of course I'm serious,' he continued at last. 'It's a fair price in exchange for what you've built here in Collegium. If I set the best of my agents on to it, they'd never quite reach the heights of influence you can now command, not if they slept with the entire Assembly, men and women of all kinden. And besides, aren't you bored? To be servant of just one master: what Spider was ever happy with a life that uncomplicated? And I'd rather you wrote your reports for me, rather than sending them back to your former Rekef masters. At least Stenwold and I are on the same side.'

'Adoption . . .' she murmured. Nobody belonging to another kinden could quite understand the scale of it: he might as well have offered her the moon. It meant nobility. It meant that she would become Arianna of the Aldanrael. It meant filling all those gnawing absences that had plagued her childhood.

'Think about it,' Teornis urged her. 'You don't need to make a decision now. In fact, you might never have to choose between old Stenwold and me. Report to me, live with him, and let's do our work as though we were partners in the same business. I'd hope the time might never come when you would have to discover where your true loyalties lie.'

He gave her a brief bow – more than a jumped-up commoner should ever have merited – and then he was off to greet some Assembler in warm tones.

Arianna clung to the balcony as though she were drowning.

★

123

Stenwold was not taking well to seaborne life. The motion of the boat kept him constantly off balance, and he had already almost pitched over the side more than once. He now sat miserably before the mast as the Fly-kinden crew flew and skittered across the woodwork all around him. Three days out now and, according to Tomasso, making good time towards this mythical Kanateris, there was nothing to see but sea.

That was what he found most disturbing: horizon to horizon there was only the sky and the waters. It felt like falling. *My kinden must be more earth-bound than I thought. Give me a dozen seers and seven different clocks and compasses, and I'd still be hugging the coast, thank you very much.* He couldn't see that the Flies would fare any better than he would, if some catastrophe should suddenly strike the ship. He doubted that any human being alive would have the stamina to make it ashore from here.

''Ware weather!' came the shrill call from the bows. Stenwold's head jerked up. The little robed figure of Fernaea had its arms outstretched, facing along the ship with her face shadowed by her cowl, a Moth-kinden in miniature.

'What course?' Gude bellowed back.

'Two points starboard and tie everything down!' the Fly seer returned. Stenwold noticed Gude take a deep breath.

'You heard her! Get everything ready for the Lash!'

The crew, who had seemed to be busy enough a moment before, were abruptly in a frenzy. They swarmed across the deck, leaving nothing loose behind them, in such a fervour that Stenwold was mildly surprised not to find himself stowed in a locker.

He stood up, leaning on the mast for purchase. 'What should I do?' he asked.

Laszlo touched down beside him, without warning. 'Depends, Ma'rMaker. You reckon you're any good at climbing rigging?'

'I've been nothing but ballast so far.'

'Ballast? Good nautical term,' Laszlo grinned.

'What's the Lash, Laszlo?'

The grin widened, though not without a little tension underlying it. 'It's the sea out hereabouts, Maker, when the storm takes it. It's why nobody but us does anything so stupid as venture this way. Come forward a moment.' He skipped off, leaving Stenwold to lumber behind him, up to where Fernaea was standing.

'What's the news, Fern? How long?' Laszlo was asking.

She had her hands on the railing, staring ahead, but she glanced back as he hailed her. Stenwold was almost surprised to see that she had blue eyes, rather than the white orbs of a Moth. 'See for yourself,' was all she said.

The sky ahead of the *Tidenfree* was fast losing the light. A darkness was gathering there like a swarm of locusts, a great weight of cloud blotting out the blue. The wind was freshening, too, gusting now as a pale harbinger of the storm.

Stenwold could think of nothing but the occasion when they had destroyed the *Pride*, in the yards outside Helleron. The rail automotive's engine had called up a storm when it exploded, returning its lightning to the sky.

The crew behind him were furling the sail. They no longer coursed freely through the air but swung from rope to rope of the rigging, and he saw the wind contending with them over the disposition of the canvas. Seeing the crew down on deck securing themselves with lines, Stenwold pointed to them.

'Should I be doing that?' He found that he had to raise his voice a little, as the lines all around them started to keen as the wind tugged at them.

'Can you fly?' Laszlo demanded.

'No!'

'No point, then. You'd end up in the sea and we'd never be able to haul you out during the Lash. At least we folk can just drag along in the air like a kite until we're hauled in. Mar'Maker, maybe you'd better get below.'

Stenwold bared his teeth. 'Is there nothing I can do? I'm sick of being luggage.' He ducked as something swung close to his head, and then Tomasso had skidded to a halt beside them.

'*Someone* go kick that idiot Despard,' the bearded Fly shouted. 'Because the sail's down but the engine isn't up, and we've got about ten minutes to put that right.'

Laszlo and Stenwold exchanged glances. Overhead, the day was being blotted into dusk by the clouds' vanguard.

'Now *that* I can help with,' the Beetle declared, and hurried as best he could towards the hatch, watching Laszlo disappear through it ahead of him with enviable speed.

He had got just three steps down towards the cramped confines below, when something solid struck the ship and sent every plank, spar and line thrumming. Stenwold's boots skidded from under him and he took the rest of the stairs all at once, keeping his feet at the bottom by jamming his arms against the narrow walls. Laszlo was hovering in the air before him, utterly still though the walls of below-decks lurched about him,

'What was that?' Stenwold demanded, although he already knew, in truth.

'That was the Lash!' Laszlo told him, already retreating down the little wooden corridor, and Stenwold followed, bending almost double. He could hear others of the crew pitching below: heading, he guessed, for the cargo hold to tie everything down and get themselves out of the weather. He just hoped the weather didn't come indoors after them.

They were abruptly in a room large enough for him to stand in, and his best guess was that it was at the very stern of the ship. From the fittings about the walls, he saw that there had been a big steam engine in here once, but the oil-burner they had hauled in to replace it was half the size, leaving enough room for even a Beetle-kinden to get round it. The engine was a Collegium-made piece, modified over and over by small and nimble fingers. Despard was half obscured by it, artificer's goggles down over her eyes and a wrench in one hand.

'Chief wants to know why so quiet,' Laszlo told her cheerily.

She shot him a vile look that the goggles only helped send on its way. 'Seized up since we left harbour, can you believe?'

'I can believe chief wants it working right now, Despot.' Laszlo's sanguine calm was already getting on Stenwold's nerves and, from her present reaction, he wondered how Despard had managed to share a ship with him so long.

'Can I help?' he asked.

'You know engines?' she snapped back.

He bit down on the part where he reeled off his College accredits and just said, 'Yes. What can I do?'

'Give me tools when I ask for them, hold things down where I tell you, and punch Laszlo in the face if he so much as opens his mouth.' She ducked back behind the engine.

The ship lurched again, and stayed lurched, the room canting twenty degrees off vertical. Stenwold proceeded hand over hand, hanging from the remnants of the old steam engine, finding Despard's tools as her tight voice rapped out a demand. He could hear the whole *Tidenfree* complaining as the wind dragged at it, timbers shifting one against the other. The floor beneath him was never still, jumping and sloping without pattern. Each time it moved, the two Fly-kinden were momentarily airborne, wings blurring by pure instinct, keeping them steady. Stenwold could only cling on and curse the limitations of his kinden.

'Stand back!' Despard shouted. Stenwold did his best, squeezing himself into a corner as she dragged down on a lever with all her weight, wings flurrying for extra purchase.

With a roar the engine came alive, filling the room with

the smell of burning. From above, Stenwold could hear Fernaea's voice somehow, high and clear even over the tearing wind that was making every rope on the ship shriek and sing. Even Gude's bellowing replies were lost, but the seer's directions rode the wind like a nightmare. Stenwold imagined her clinging to the very point of the prow, the stormwinds catching and dragging at her grey robe, eyes facing the skies, and somehow, somehow, working some magic to find their way through the storm. *And backed by good Collegium artifice, no less. These Flies have stolen the best of both worlds. No wonder they've survived on the seas for three generations.*

The *Tidenfree* shuddered again, the vibration of the engine merging with the shaking of the timbers as the ship began abruptly turning into the wind. There was a sound like a great vat boiling over, hissing and steaming, and a moment later Stenwold realized that it was the ferocity of the rain pounding the decks above him. The ship boomed hollowly as another fist of wind struck it, and water was running down the stairs and washing round the soles of his boots.

'Are we sinking?' he cried.

'Just the rain, Ma'rMaker!' Laszlo assured him. 'If it gets too bad, we'll pump.'

Stenwold had gone to the entrance, hunching over with the vague intention of going up on deck. The two Flies shouted at him.

'I can't just stay here,' he said. The sound from above was unimaginable, the wind shrieking through the lines, the waters crashing and thundering. He could not imagine what it might look like from abovedecks. If he discovered three sea monsters tearing the vessel apart between their pincers, he would not have been surprised. Still, it could not be worse than being trapped down here and *not* knowing. The very planks beneath his feet were grinding and shifting, never level, tilted now this way, now that. The *sea*: he could feel the sea trying to get him, with teeth and claws grating on the other side of the hull.

'You'll be over the side in an instant, if you go up there!' Laszlo warned him. 'Most of the crew will be below now. Only Fern and Gude and maybe a couple more to help Gude with the oar. Everyone else will be down in the hold or the cabins.'

'What if we sink?' Stenwold demanded.

'Then we drown!' Despard snapped. Stenwold felt his legs give way as the floor shifted again. Abruptly he was sitting down in the water that washed back and forth in sympathy with the waves outside. *It shows how much we turn our back on the sea.* He had never thought of drowning, not once, but now the idea seemed so terrifying to him that his innards were locking up with it. He had thought to die on a sword's point, perhaps, or burned by the sting-fire of a Wasp, or falling from the sky with the tatters of an airship's gasbag torn open above him, but not this: not dragged into the pitch cold dark of the sea.

'Where will the wind take us?' he demanded. 'To what shore?'

'The wind takes us nowhere while this engine's running!' Despard declared.

'Other than that,' Laszlo added, 'to no shore any man knows. When the Lash is driving, it'll drag you all the way out into the grand ocean. If you're lucky, your corpse might wash up on the Atoll Coast, but other than that . . . nobody ever sees you or your sails again. Some say there's a whole graveyard of broken ships out there, far past the horizon. Maybe some day we'll go look.'

Stenwold clung to the old engine fittings. It was not illness that afflicted him, not the sea-malady he had heard of. Beetles had iron stomachs, as a rule, and even the pitching of the waters was not undoing his constitution. No, his sickness was entirely bred of fear. *We have no business being out here. I have no business being out here.*

Beetles were never meant to go to sea and Master Failwright could go hang himself, if he wasn't already dead. *Why did I think this was a good idea?*

'Tell me . . .' He had to speak, had to wrench his mind away from thoughts of the grasping waters. 'The Atoll Coast, you've been there?' A casual conversation, save that he was shouting at the top of his voice to get the words heard over the storm.

'Not us!' Despard called back. 'Himself did a lot of business there, I think, but the chief's contacts are mainly down the Strand.'

'She means the Spiderlands coast, Ma'rMaker,' Laszlo put in. The floor was abruptly sloping a good thirty degrees the other way, and Stenwold clung on gamely to avoid sliding away into what was now the low corner of the room. The two Flies had merely taken to the air briefly again: every time the ship around them shifted and shook, their wings flickered to lift them from the deck and keep them stable. They did it without even thinking, a Fly-kinden's version of sea-legs. Stenwold was bitterly envious.

'You never went to Tsen, then?' he asked. *Tsen. Collegium politics. The business with the Vekken. Anything else but the sea. Not the drowning hungry sea, at all.*

'Never. Heard of it, though,' Laszlo stated. 'Why?'

'I heard they have some . . . interesting boats there,' Stenwold got out. The water was like a little river flowing into the room now. Despard flitted over to the engine and began making adjustments.

'They're mad there,' she called over her shoulder.

'Submersibles!' Stenwold shouted, like a curse.

'Come over here, Beetle, and make yourself useful!' was her answer to that. He hauled himself towards her, half falling down, half climbing up. He saw that she had rigged up something with a handle.

'You use those big arms of yours to get this going!' she ordered him. 'Pump, Beetle, pump!'

'Where does the water go?'

'Out! There's a set of double-lock valves. Don't worry, it all goes out and nothing gets in.' As he started working the pump, surprisingly heavy work for something manufactured for Fly-kinden, she yelled, conversationally, 'Submersibles, is it?'

'I hear so!'

'Well, I heard the same,' she admitted. 'Never believed it, though. You hear all sorts of odd about the Atoll Coast. Himself told Tomasso something, 'cos now he won't go near it. Different world, they say. Ports that aren't on any maps! Sea reaches that eat up ships! Sea-kinden, that sing you on to rocks and then pick your bones!'

Stenwold let the solid routine of the pump engross him, yet he could see it having no effect on the water swirling about his boots. For all he knew, it was just a joke at his expense – or simply to keep his mind busy. He tried to think about the Tseni ambassadors, the *Tseitan*, the damage it would do if the Vekken now walked away from Collegium. He found that, just then, he didn't care. He could return home to find the black and gold waving over the Amphiophos, and all he would care about would be that he was back on dry land.

# Nine

Helmess Broiler reclined awkwardly. He was not a slender man, and Beetle seating tended towards straight-backed wooden chairs, which made his shoulders and neck ache after too long. He was too ungainly to lounge on couches like a Spider-kinden, and he could hardly squat on the floor like a Fly. Instead he had invested in a big padded chair, called a College chair locally for its associations with an academic's study. It was not overly dignified, for an Assembler, but it was at least comfortable. His consolation was that Elytrya would come and sit at his feet, in what he could think of as an adoring manner. He could put a hand down and stroke the coiled waves of her hair, which was pleasant enough.

In such a way did he greet Forman Sands when the killer was ushered into his sitting room. Sands was dressed noncommittally but well, the picture of a modest but tasteful tradesman. It gave Helmess a certain pleasure to know that, had any unwanted company burst into his house just then and discovered his hired murderer in the ante-chamber, they would have found Sands perusing his books or admiring his art. It was so good to know that the man was *civilized*.

'Have you news to please me, Sands?' he asked.

Sands shook his head, face set: the modest tradesman about to report that the goods were not yet in stock. 'We put out, went halfway to Vek, Master Broiler. No sign of them.'

Broiler played magnanimity well, if only because Elytrya had given him foreknowledge of Stenwold's elusiveness. He waved a gracious hand. 'Well, there will be other chances. You'll get your claws into Maker sooner or later, either on land or on sea.'

'As you wish, Master Broiler,' Sands said, with a brief bow. 'You have anything more for me?'

'Just wait on . . . no, hold. I'd be grateful if you had someone go to the dockside and see if Maker's ship is known, at all. I do have to wonder who he's playing with these days.'

'I'll attend to it myself,' Sands promised, still the pleasant man of business. He did not even cheapen their conversation by asking for money. He knew Helmess was good for it, and honest men of commerce did not need to sully themselves with such details unless it was absolutely necessary. *He really is quite the find*, Helmess thought, as Sands backed out of the room. *Where else would I find a killer that I could introduce to my mother?*

'All as you said,' he noted. 'You're sure your people went both ways along the coast? East and west?'

'Oh, yes,' Elytrya assured him. 'And there were ships, but not one of that description. Otherwise your Master Maker would be having his bones picked by the crabs even now. He has some clever friends, I think.'

'You think they set him down on land somewhere close? Maker was an intelligencer in the war, so he might be trying to follow Failwright's trail covertly, while people think he's gone. No doubt he'll turn up in Collegium wearing a different hat and asking questions. I should have had Sands keep an eye out for him.'

'Or . . .' she leant back against his legs as he trailed a finger down the angle of her jaw.

'Or?'

133

'Or they went to sea, Helmess. Just out to sea.'

He pondered the thought. Before embarking on this campaign with her he had researched his ground as a good Beetle academic should. He knew the routes that ships took between Collegium and any port worth naming. He had first assumed Stenwold was going to his friends in Vek, and had posted Sands to catch him there if Elytrya's allies failed. Still, caution was a virtue, and her friends had been waiting for that little Fly boat on the other route too, in case Maker had been heading for Kes or the Fly warrens, or even the Spiderlands.

Instead that ship had simply vanished, or gone nowhere. *But nobody just goes out to sea.*

'Or they went out to sea,' he allowed, reflecting that he had been living with a lot of impossibilities, recently. 'But what in the world for? What does Maker expect to find out there?'

When Stenwold came to his senses, the world seemed unnaturally calm. The boards beneath him clung together still. He heard the wash of water, the creak of timber and rope and the sounds, surprisingly few, of the *Tidenfree*'s crew going about their business. After the Lash it seemed like another world.

The storm had been no brief squall, either, He had not realized, after they had the engine working again, and the ship was shouldering through the waves by main force, that they would have to keep at it hour after hour through the embattled seas. Night had come, and only the compass had kept their course through the darkness, the clouds that swallowed the moon, the wind and surging seas that dragged them this way and that. From his labouring post within the engine room, Stenwold had seen none of it, but he could see in his mind's eye how tenuous was the path the Fly-kinden were treading. They relied on Fernaea to give them a course, using whatever doubtful tricks and sleights the Moth-kinden had taught her in their far mountain retreats. She called out, high over the storm, to Gude and her crew at the steering oar. Gude was Inapt, too, and Laszlo had claimed that the best seafarers all were, that they retained some instinctive connection with wave and weather that the Apt could not match. Still, for that very reason, Gude could not read the compass nor set a course by it. The ship's second artificer had been clinging up there beside her, taking the readings from clock and compass rose, and relaying them in a manner that Gude and Fern could master. It was a lunatic's dream, and the thought had loomed large in his mind throughout the night that it would only take one of these small mariners to misjudge, and the land would never again feel the tread of Master Stenwold Maker, nor even know his fate.

Still, some other part of him could not help but feel a grudging admiration. *Fly-kinden, they'll cheat and exploit anything, even the basic laws of nature.*

He could not say for sure when the storm had finally abated, or when they had passed through it. He had been at the pump in the engine room, and the work that had seemed trivial at first had become crucial soon enough. Even with the hatches bolted down, enough water came in from above to swamp them. Despard was continually at the engine, hovering above it much of the time with utter concentration. Laszlo apparently knew just enough of the trade to act as the absolute last-ditch, stand-in, backup artificer, or at least enough to pass her the tools Despard cried out for as she made adjustments and small repairs, wings blurring here and there, while the engine laboured on.

There was no rest. Stenwold pumped away the water until his arms burned, and then he pumped some more. He had done the work of two Fly-kinden at a time, and he had carried on doing it all night. *I may not fly. I may be huge and heavy and slow. I can work, though.* Beetle-kinden won no sprints at the Collegium games, but give them a track long enough and they would be lumbering on when even the fleetest of their competitors had fallen.

Still, he was not young and his endurance had its limits. He could not say when he had reached these, for his memories had become fragmented by fatigue. He only knew that he was waking up now, feeling every part of him complain, feeling his arms scream at him for the abuse he had heaped on them. He was rousing from an exhausted sleep, who knew how long after, and the storm had passed.

He lay on the floor of the engine room, half curled protectively about the engine. He winced at that. Had something slipped a gear then he would have known about it the hard way. There was a slight pressure against his kidneys which he identified as Despard, fast asleep while sitting up, and using him as a broad pillow. He was loath to wake her but, now that he had returned to consciousness himself, every part of him that was crushed against the hard boards was letting him know about it. He shifted as carefully as he could, hoping he would be able to let her down gently, still sleeping. At the first movement, she twitched and gave a small cry, instantly on her feet – no, not her feet, but airborne for a moment, then coming down a yard away from him.

'Beetles,' she said, still half asleep, but in unmistakable tones of disdain. She yawned and stretched, grimacing. 'Don't like Beetles, as a rule. Big, clumsy bastards. You're all right. Can find a use for you.'

Stenwold sat up slowly, regretting every inch of it. 'That's from the orphanage, then, that you don't like us?'

He heard the tiny whisper of a knife clearing its sheath. Despard was in the air again, hovering inches above the deck, staring down at him. 'How do you know . . . ? *What did I say?*'

He looked sadly at the tiny knife she held, wondering what untold miseries he had just unwittingly brought back to life. 'A Fly with a Beetle name? There're only so many ways that can come about. A student of mine, a half-breed, he's gone through life with a Fly name for the same reason. Not that he ever disliked Flies, to my knowledge.'

She touched down on the floor again, carefully putting the little blade away and seeming embarrassed by her reaction. 'Only natural,' she said. 'After all, we're much nicer, as everyone knows.' Her bleak smile belied it. 'Believe me, the wedding was the first good thing that happened to me in all my life.'

Stenwold frowned, still intent on the slow and painful business of getting to his feet. 'Wedding?'

It took her a moment to catch his puzzlement. 'Family, Maker. We're all family here. That's how the Bloodfly business works. That's how you get a third-generation pirate like Tomasso. So, if someone can do something useful, like fix an engine, or like Fern's charlatanry, then you get them hitched. Believe me, at the time it was a good deal.'

Stenwold, upright now, tried to stretch, calling on all the Art of his ancestors just to straighten his arms. 'Who's the lucky fellow?' A thought struck him. 'It's not Laszlo, is it?'

Despard burst into a peal of incredulous laughter that utterly erased her earlier brooding, and then there came a voice from outside the room, 'Please, Ma'rMaker, I have standards,' and Laszlo himself slipped in. From his bright smile to his clean clothes there was no suggestion that he had actually been on the same vessel with them the previous night. He was almost painful to look at in his neatness. 'You might want to come up on deck now, Ma'rMaker. We're in sight of Kanateris.'

'Already?' Stenwold levered himself forward step by strained step.

'Well, you don't think we'd go through all that if it wasn't *quicker*, do you?' the Fly asked, hopping ahead of Stenwold, then up the steps and into the half-light.

They were under sail again, the crew buzzing about the rigging keeping everything shipshape, Stenwold assumed, whatever that meant. Off the port bow he saw land as a darker shadow against the lightening sky.

'Dawn over the Bolas Islands,' Laszlo proudly announced.

Stenwold glanced about, seeing Tomasso standing on the aft deck once more. Gude still had the oar, and Stenwold wondered if she ever tired, or whether she had taken the Lash in shifts along with her fellows. Of the more fragile Fernaea, Stenwold saw no sign, and he guessed that she was exhausted by her card-tricks throughout the storm.

'And where might the Bolas Islands be?' he asked them. 'Except on the other side of the Lash, that is?'

'The Strand,' Laszlo said, 'as the long coast of the Spiderlands is called, has an enormous bay bitten out of the middle of it. The biggest Spider cities are located there, and all the major houses have holdings scattered about that bay. It's about as big across as . . . oh, say the distance from Collegium to Vek. And a bit more, maybe. Anyway, the line of this bay must continue on under the water, like it's a big bowl on the seabed, because there are shoals you have to watch for and, around the rim, some little fingers of it stick up above the sea. That's the Bolas Islands, and on the biggest of those is Kanateris.'

'What is it? Some noble's retreat?'

'Oh they'd love that.' Laszlo's intolerable grin grew ever wider. 'No, Kanateris is pirate country. All the seaborne scum of the Spiderlands ends up there eventually, either to buy or sell.'

'Hmm.' Stenwold went to lean on the rail, and found it too low, of course. He settled for resting a foot on it, holding on to one of the shrouds of the jib for balance. The wind was steady and the sea was calm enough as a result. 'And the Spider nobles, they just put up with that, do they?'

He saw from the Fly's face that he was being foolish to ask, even before Laszlo answered.

'There's not a noble house that doesn't keep a few privateers on the books, that call themselves pirates. Everyone says how terrible that Kanateris exists, but nobody does anything about it. This is the Spiderlands, Ma'rMaker, and they're awfully clever about everything they do.'

'I suppose . . .' Stenwold paused, frowning. 'Do I hear . . . music?'

'That you do,' Laszlo confirmed.

It drifted towards them over the waters, as they neared the island and started cutting across the wind. At first he caught only tattered snatches of it, a melody and harmony he could not make out. Then they were past the island's near point and tacking into the land-cupped harbour. The chief of the Bolas Islands was a mountain jutting from the waters, its slopes thick with tenacious greenery. In the centre of the bay was Kanateris, a town smeared up across two hundred yards of rock, and it was singing.

Stenwold heard some strange, shifting pattern of strings at the heart of it, switching and changing tone in a pattern that followed no laws of music he knew. Above it, though, he heard two score instruments adding their voices, and each in perfect pitch with the others, each following the strings and working out fantastic elaborations on the simple, erratic changes. The sound swelled and broadened as they neared, woodwind and strings and horns each succeeding the last, and being succeeded, but the tune evolving and evolving again from moment to moment. It became vast and intricate and sad and wise, that music, like nothing tame Collegiate ears had ever heard: music made for and by men and women who lived in a world older and more vibrant than his own.

*Inapt* music, he reflected. Collegium scholars might debate, but Stenwold knew for sure that, just as he knew how to fix a slipped gear or work a lock, so there were some things his own life would never quite encompass. He did not have to believe in magic to sense swathes of life that he would never truly enter. Even as Gude and the crew could move with the sea, and handle a sail with an instinct that no Apt mariner could quite match, so too was this astonishing lift and crescendo of music, that washed over him and through him, belittled him and humbled him, and spoke in a hundred voices, only a dozen of which he could understand. He felt something catch in his heart, catch and then pass on, as if to say, *I have moved you: I hold you in the palm of my hand, and yet you cannot hear me, not truly.*

As the *Tidenfree* tacked back again, the music reached its utmost, the notes hanging in the air over the island like a vast, invisible cloud. Then it began dying away, even as the sails were being furled, even as a low galley ploughed out to meet them and pilot them the last stretch of the way. Stenwold realized that the last of the underlying strings had gone, and from that cue the other musicians ceased one by one, each one drawing their line of the symphony to its conclusion. He was now close enough to see a few musicians up on the rooftops, packing away their instruments, making ready to start the day.

Even Laszlo had fallen silent in the face of that, and his voice held some last trace of reverence although, Apt as he was, he too was denied the music's full breadth. 'They string a couple of harps up, either side of the bay,' he explained. 'When the wind catches them, they sing and, if you've the ear for it, you can tell what the day's weather will be, just from the pitch and sound. Of course, after a while people began playing along. They love their music, the Spiders, and any musician who's particularly good can find herself a patron that way. So it got more and more, I reckon, until every morning most Spider ports greet the dawn like that. Quite something, isn't it?'

Stenwold didn't trust himself to speak.

'The Spiders have a special name for your kinden,' Laszlo added. 'They call you the "noisy, silent people".'

Still half-lost in the music's last fading echoes, Stenwold nodded. 'They may have a point.' For a moment he and Laszlo stayed silent in the bows, as the oarsmen of the galley hauled away at the sweeps to bring the *Tidenfree* into dock. They were chained to their oars, Stenwold noted grimly, but then he should not be surprised at that.

Looking from the toiling rowers on the galley to the town itself, he found his eye being led up and up. Kanateris was just strewn up the mountainside, as though all the buildings had been originally heaped at the top and left to distribute themselves all the way to the waterline.

Seeing the direction of his gaze, Laszlo put in, 'So, you can't fly then?'

'No.'

'Can you do that trick where you climb up the sheer walls?'

'Not that either. Never an Art I thought I'd have much use for.'

'Splice me, Ma'rMaker, but what *can* you do?' the Fly exclaimed.

'Tread up stairs for as long as it takes.' He gave a brief laugh. He was remembering Myna, which had also been a stepped city, albeit of a kinder gradient. He recalled the mad flight from the invading Wasps so long ago, how Tisamon had hauled and bullied him up step after step. *If only I could have predicted what I'd face, one day, I'd not have complained.*

'Listen up!' came Tomasso's voice from the stern. The *Tidenfree* was now at one of the spindly piers that Kanateris extended into the water like long, rickety legs. Two of the crew were tying up, and their chief had just thrown a few coins down to the tug galley. Now he had his arms clasped behind his back, surveying his followers and looking every bit the pirate captain. When he had their attention, he went on: 'Laszlo, Piera, you two and I will take our passenger to where he might learn what he needs to know. For the rest of you, nobody goes ashore. I want all hands waiting to take us away from here quickly, just in case. I don't recognize most of the sails here.'

He met Stenwold amidships, where a plank had been put out to reach the pier. 'Master Maker, perhaps you should go arm yourself fully?'

'Three or four weapons is this season's Kanaterese fashion,' Laszlo added.

Stenwold nodded and was halfway to the hatch just as Despard appeared, staggering under the burden of his piercer.

'I took the liberty,' she grunted, proffering it with difficulty. The hefty, four-barrelled thing was almost as big as she was.

'You certainly did,' he agreed. He lifted it away from her to reveal a grin almost as big as Laszlo's.

'It's a beauty,' she announced, though it was clear that neither Tomasso nor Laszlo were overly sure of what it was. 'Marlwright-Verwick design, isn't it?'

*I never met an artificer but they loved explosive weapons,* Stenwold considered. 'You know more than me, anyway,' he remarked. She had loaded it well, he saw, for the four javelin-like bolts were neatly placed. He rested the piercer on his shoulder, thinking it would be a strange thing to walk into a town like this, sword, piercer and miniature snapbow. He felt like a brigand. Still, Tomasso had two long knives and a handful of throwing blades stashed in his belt, and Laszlo had armed himself with a bladed hook on the end of a rope – a Fly weapon that Stenwold had no fond memories of.

Piera turned out to be a sullen-looking Fly girl wearing a corselet of leather and chitin scales. She had a strung shortbow straining over one shoulder, and a fistful of stubby arrows thrust into one of her tall boots. A jagged scar across her forehead said that she was no stranger to a brawl.

'Don't we look the fearsome raiders,' Tomasso declared. 'Come on, Master Maker, let's find you your answers.' And he led the way to shore, over the timbers of the pier that creaked alarmingly when Stenwold followed.

'Why no shore leave, chief?' Laszlo asked as they set foot on to the brief strip of grey sand that served Kanateris as a beach.

'Fern said "Old Friends" when I asked her about the future,' Tomasso revealed. Seeing Stenwold's look he grimaced. 'Oh, I wouldn't look to divination if we were off Collegium's coast, Master Maker, but here in the Spiderlands I've learned to trust it. In this part of the world there's scarce a ship's captain that'll put out to sea without a fortune teller's seal on it.'

There had been a brief bustle about the piers themselves, as the early risers from two dozen craft of around the *Tidenfree*'s size began stretching and yawning and calling lazy insults to one another. The streets themselves, steep tiers of uneven steps that Stenwold trod carefully, seemed mostly deserted. What he had at first taken for buildings were mostly little more than booths and shacks: cloth over timbers that were set into the sheer rock. Each was covered up with an identical grey screen that billowed slightly in the dawn breeze. Those few locals that were out so early looked ragged and dirty, obviously those who could not even boast a roof of canvas for the night. Still, they were Spider-kinden mostly, and that drew stares from Stenwold. Back in Collegium the least of the Spiders graciously deigned to pose as equals with College masters and town magnates. Now he saw why there were so many of their kind scattered across the Lowlands, away from their homelands. Here were Spiders of no family or import, the lowest and the meanest. What nearly broke the heart was that they were still beautiful, men and women both. They stood there in their tatters with their grimy, exposed skin, and he saw beggars that would have provided a graceful ornament to any Collegium Assembler's arm. When they caught and held his gaze he guessed that begging was not their only source of income. *But, then, Collegium morality has never applied to the Spiders.*

Something stirred near his foot and he jumped back, as hairy, spindly legs abruptly hooked up under one of the booths' screens. In an instant there was a big grey spider there, as large as any of the *Tidenfree*'s crew, industriously unravelling and consuming the curtain's threads to reveal the booth's interior. He gazed up along the vertiginous street and saw that almost every booth now boasted a worker, carefully undoing what must have been an evening's patient work.

His expression drew a smirk from Laszlo.

'Easy, Ma'rMaker,' the Fly said, 'they're only house-spiders.'

'Every spider of that size or larger within a tenday's walk of Collegium was hunted down generations ago,' Stenwold grunted. 'You can still find old houses where the nursery has a grill over the window, for fear of them.'

'Oh, a shame, that is,' Tomasso spoke from over his shoulder, as they laboured up the slope. 'There's never an animal anywhere that'll train up as well as a spider, and they find all manner of use for them in these parts. In fact, most Spider-kinden sea-captains will take a couple of fellows like these for the topmast. Curse it, but I remember when we were duelling ships in a storm with Ebris of the Ganbrodiel. One time we passed close enough to loose arrows at him, as he tried to board us, and I saw a nest of little beasties up in his rigging, mending his sails and straightening his lines.'

Stenwold knew that he should not find this at all surprising or upsetting, since his own kind, with their Art, had domesticated so many different beetle species, after all.

Still, there was none amongst those beetles that might creep up the wall one night, poisoned fangs aglitter . . .

'Of course, everyone's heard at least one story of someone who got dead drunk around here,' Laszlo said cheerily, 'And then they fell asleep in the gutter and someone found them next morning, drained like last night's wineskin. But that's just stories.'

'You're not helping,' Stenwold told him. Laszlo's answering grin replied that he knew it full well.

Now, a hundred trudging steps up, the flimsy shacks either side of them were giving way to something more permanent. At least there were roofs on many of the little huts, made of thin strips of tightly interwoven wood. Still they had no stouter walls than cloth could supply them, and the only protection they had from any curious neighbour with a knife would be whatever arachnid sentry happened to be crouching alertly within.

Kanateris was waking up now. The network of streets clinging to the island's rocky sides filled up quickly, and Stenwold witnessed a strange dance of precedence, of people moving aside for each other to a pattern he could not discern. Everyone in the port except himself seemed to know exactly who to give way to and who to brazen past, and he could only stumblingly follow Tomasso's lead. Every so often he saw an unresolvable difference, two groups that would not give way. Then hands found there way to sword hilts, insults were called, cloaks thrown back to show knives and armour. He saw no blood spilt, though. Always someone decided the game was not worth it.

Because the streets were narrow he was frequently shouldered into one stall or another, enduring a moment of entreaty from its owner before they could get on their way again. Once he found himself surrounded by wicker cages, each one with its eight-legged denizen, whilst a Spider-kinden man in gleaming silks tried to persuade him that he badly needed such a guardian to watch over him as he slept. A second time he found himself walled in by fantastically complex tapestries, and the woman there offering to weave his future for him. Seeing her work, so full of symbols and allegory that he could not begin to guess at, he could almost believe it was true.

The people of Kanateris proved a varied lot. Most were Spiders, but Stenwold reckoned almost half were of other kinden: Flies and Grasshoppers, Ants of strange cities and a good few he did not recognize. Once they quickly whisked themselves out of the way of a veiled Spider lady whose two guards were Mantis-kinden with pale, pearly skin, and who wore ornate silver slave-bracers as if they were a mark of pride.

Looking back down towards the water he almost fell. The cavernous drop behind them seemed to drag at him. He had not realized they had climbed so high.

'How far up are we going?' he asked.

'How far *in*,' Tomasso corrected. 'Your own people may give place to those with the highest houses, but here it's who's nearest the *centre* that's important. Anyway, we're close now.' He stopped by the entrance to some kind of tavern, whose interior reached further back than Stenwold expected, cut into the rockface. It was sheer gloom inside, with only a few sulking lamps to ward off utter darkness.

'Hoi, Grampos!' Tomasso hailed, and there followed a disturbance inside, someone pushing their way through the half-dark between close-packed bodies. What emerged, like a grub into the sun, was something like a Spider-kinden: a man of their general look, but burlier and longer of limb. He was stripped to the waist, his exposed body almost woolly with coarse dark hair.

'Well, if it's not Skipper Tomasso,' the man Grampos observed neutrally. He had hobbled, on his way out, and Stenwold saw that one of his ankles had been ruined a long time ago. The image of a slave's shackles was unavoidable.

'Grampos, does Tyresia the Prophetess still keep to her old haunts?' Tomasso asked him.

'Moonlight Circle now,' Grampos replied. Stenwold had to fight with his accent to wrest sense from the words.

The answer seemed to please Tomasso, anyway, and he flipped the retreating Grampos a coin, before they continued on their way. 'She's getting on in the world,' the Fly captain commented. 'Always good news that, when someone owes you a favour.'

'Prophetess?' Stenwold said doubtfully. 'I'm not sure . . .'

'Master Maker, these are the Spiderlands. Real magicians, if you accept there being such, would never be so coarse as to announce it. So: anyone calling herself a prophetess is something else entirely.'

Their course changed now, creeping between stalls perched along precipitous ledges, or even heading down a few steps – heading further *in*.

They found Tyresia within a great tent of coloured silks, which was pitched to one side of a broader street. Her enclosed space was nonetheless cool and light, with shimmering clear panels set into the woven ceiling. She was an elegant Spider-kinden woman who looked to Stenwold's eyes to be of at least middle years, and was therefore surely much older. She wore a plain robe of golden brown, with a single brooch shaped like a butterfly her only ornament, and thereby made the simplicity seem sumptuous. Tomasso and his party waited at a polite distance while she finished her conversation with a pair of copper-skinned men Stenwold identified as Fire Ants. Money changed hands, given not to Tyresia herself but into the palm of a Fly-kinden girl who fluttered out from a back room on cue. Then the Spider matriarch reclined back on her couch and waved Tomasso over.

There was another couch, but Tomasso sat on the floor,

leaving a low table between him and his hostess. Stenwold, glad of a respite for his legs, lowered himself down beside Tomasso, while Laszlo lounged in the entrance, close enough to hear what was being said. A scrabble from above indicated that Piera had taken up a watch from somewhere around roof level.

The Fly servant, or at least so Stenwold hoped she was, came out with a tray of small cups. There were rooms and rooms extending behind Tyresia, Stenwold saw, but only odd glimmers or shafts of light gave anything away about them. When he looked down again there were two thimble-sized receptacles before him, one steaming with something dark, the other containing something clear.

Thanking the Spider kindly, Tomasso knocked back first one then the other, in quick succession, as did she. Trusting to his race's noted constitution, Stenwold did the same.

He had hoped for drinking chocolate, a Spider-kinden delicacy currently popular in Collegium, but his nose gave him the lie even before he tasted it. The hot liquid was bitter enough for him to suspect poison, then the clear one was harsh enough to clean spoons with, evaporating from his throat in a freezing mist. Just as he was about to gag, or possibly beg for a doctor, a marvellously warm and sooth-ing aftertaste followed. He suspected that his expression must be causing some well-hidden amusement while, from his companions' faces, they might have been drinking plain water.

'How is my cards partner these days?' Tyresia asked politely.

'Getting old,' Tomasso admitted. 'Lady, each time I visit, another winter has passed for me, so how is it that they never touch you?' The words were neither hurried nor sincere, but Tomasso was obviously following some prescribed code of etiquette. There then followed further careful compliments from each to each, feigned humility, enquiries after old friends. Stenwold knew enough about

Spider-kinden to know that an 'old friend' or a 'dance partner' was an enemy of some sort, whereas a 'card player' was, if not a friend, then at least an acquaintance that the speaker was not currently at war with.

He had not yet heard Tomasso ask a question at all, but abruptly Tyresia laughed, as free and innocent as a young girl, putting one hand to her mouth to stifle it. 'Forgive me, my dear, forgive me. You mean the Barbarous Coast, do you not?'

That drew a sour look from Stenwold which surely did not go without notice, but Tomasso was nodding amiably enough. 'I have set sail there of late, it's true.'

'Oh you poor dear, how can you stand it?' Tyresia shook her head sadly. 'Alas, I do not make enquiries that way, these days. So little of interest ever happens there. Since I came to the Moonlight Circle I have had my eyes on wider horizons.'

Tomasso ran his fingers through his beard. 'Of course, one such as you is highly regarded in your profession, so your lessers must all know you.'

'And I know them,' she finished. 'You would be wise to speak with Albinus, dear heart. He has a feeler or two still in that direction.'

Tomasso nodded. 'Perhaps our paths shall cross some day.' Even as he got to his feet, though, Tyresia held a hand up. The gesture was so direct that it put Stenwold on his guard.

'Because I love you, little one, know that Ebris of the Ganbrodiel is in port.'

'Does he know I am?' Tomasso had gone very still.

'Not from me, dear one, but he will know your hull when he sees it. I'm surprised that you did not recognize his.'

'Ah, well, last time we met, I gave him a gift of firepowder that fair burned his ship out from under him. I'd guess he has a new one now.'

'He sails the *Storm Locust*,' she confirmed. 'Take care, little one. I don't want to hear that you have come to grief.'

The path to Albinus took them in an arc all round Kanateris, slowly closing back towards the docks. Tomasso seemed tense now, and he and his crewmates kept a constant eye on the sky. Stenwold did even not need to ask. It had become clear that there was precious little brotherhood amongst pirates.

They ducked inside a chocolate house situated barely twenty yards above the quay, before plunging into smoke-perfumed darkness. Stenwold just let Laszlo tug him along by the sleeve, unsure whether this was their destination or whether they were merely sidestepping some danger. Abruptly they were up against a door, and it was a moment before Stenwold realized the significance. It was the first actual door that the town had presented him with. No spider had woven this.

'Skipper Tomasso of the *Tidenfree*, buying,' the Fly called out, knocking. A moment later came the click of a latch. The lamplight that fell on them was not bright, but it seemed blinding after the gloom. Beyond was a little room done up in a Lowlander style, even down to the solid chairs and a desk. The guards standing by at the far wall were Bee-kinden, but of no city that Stenwold could name. Seated at the desk, Albinus himself was an Ant. He was aptly named, for his skin was ghostly in the lamplight, his hair colourless to the point of transparency. His eyes were a stark, unhealthy pink, raw as those of a man after a night's hard drinking.

He grinned at them without humour. 'Skipper,' he acknowledged with a nod towards the other seats. 'Kind of you and your purse to come pay me a visit.'

Tomasso remained standing, but Stenwold was not too proud to rest himself. His first thought was that Albinus, robbed of the colouring of his brothers, must be a man without a city, a renegade. It was perhaps what he was intended to think, but he had been around the Vekken for too long to believe it. He knew Ants now: it was the brotherhood inside their heads, not mere skin pigment, that made them what they were. Knowing that fact, and hearing the man's speech, he guessed that Albinus was probably still on the payroll of the city of Kes. That island nation would have an interest in keeping an eye on the Spiderlands trade routes, and what better disguise for a patriotic spy than to pose as a freelance one?

There was no sign of the elegant niceties that Tomasso had employed on Tyresia. 'You're the man to talk to about Lowlander shipping, they say?'

'They're kind to say it,' Albinus replied. When he smiled, his deathly white face was like a skull. 'The *Tidenfree* sails the Strand, does she not? Why would you want to know?'

'Perhaps the Strand is a little prickly these days.'

The Ant nodded, as if satisfied with that. 'So ask, Skipper.'

'I hear someone's throwing their weight around against the Collegium boats.' Tomasso's accompanying gesture seemed to make Stenwold his co-conspirator, just some Beetle profiteer who didn't care about harming his own kin. 'Now, if I'm going to cut myself a slice of the Barbarous Coast, I want to know who might come looking for me. Or else maybe I'll just offer my ship to them, if they're recruiting.'

'They're not, Skipper. They have all the hands they need.' Albinus's voice remained flat, but Stenwold's heart leapt just at the words. *He was right. Failwright had the right of it. There is a conspiracy.* His fingers clutched at the arms of his chair, but he made himself sit still.

'Then tell me who to steer my course clear of. How much for it, Albinus?'

The Ant calculated silently for a moment. 'Two-thousand-yard. And don't try haggling, little man. We Ant-kinden have no patience for it.'

Tomasso gave no reaction, but Laszlo could not keep in a whistle of appreciation. Whatever the currency, it was clearly a great deal of money.

'I have . . .' he started, thinking of the Helleron-minted coins in his purse.

'I pay him. You pay me later,' Tomasso cut him off. 'Just remember our agreement.' He signalled, and Laszlo came forward and started counting out big coins, twice the size of a Helleron central and looking like solid gold. He stopped at twenty, making two neat stacks of them.

'The name?' Tomasso prompted.

Albinus smiled his death's-head grin. 'The Aldanrael,' he said.

# Ten

Stenwold felt numb when they reached daylight again, leaving the dimly lit cavern of Albinus the spy behind them. *Aldanrael.* The thought made him feel ill. For a moment he wished, he really wished, that Rones Failwright had brought his wretched papers to someone else. Anyone else.

*But, of course, I suppose Rones Failwright was killed on his orders.* The Aldanrael were as well loved in Collegium as ever a Spider house had been. Were they not friends and heroes? Had they not fought against the Vekken and the Empire, to keep the city free?

*And now this: piracy and plunder. A secret war against our shipping. But why?* He saw Teornis's face, handsome and laughing, in his mind's eye. *Never trust a Spider, they say, but surely* . . . He tried to tell himself that he was a fool to take the word of some strange washed-out Ant-kinden speaking against a man he had known for years, but something leaden inside him seemed already to know the truth.

*I cannot just accept this. I must be sure.* The implications, the delicate relationship Collegium had built with the Spiderlands, the cities of the silk road, there was so much to lose.

Almost crashing into Tomasso, he looked up.

A dozen men and women had taken possession of the street in front of them. Most of them were Spiders, armed with long knives and rapiers, and a couple of others with bows. One man stood in the centre, prudently keeping further away from the Flies and Stenwold. He was an elegant, slender figure in a heavy greatcoat that seemed too big for him. He wore his hair long, as many Spiders did, but it was combed forward so as to cover half of his face. The burns were still visible beneath his fringe. On either side of him stood two huge Scorpion-kinden men in chain hauberks, shields and axes at the ready.

'Look who we happen to have bumped into,' the Spider-kinden leader called out. Stenwold was aware that the street was fast emptying around them, leaving only Tomasso's small party confronting their antagonists. 'Little Skipper,' the Spider went on, 'you have plotted a poor course, to bring you here.'

'Ebris,' Tomasso named him, 'you're looking well.'

'Seas curse me when I ever want the opinion of a *Fly* on how I look,' Ebris spat.

Tomasso had his hands on both his knife-hilts, standing feet apart, smiling calmly at the Spider captain but appearing tense as a drawn bow to his own companions. 'You should know, Ebris, you'll now have these waters to yourself. I'm setting sail for the south. We need never meet again.' Stenwold saw that Piera had her bowstring half drawn back, and Laszlo's hooked blade was in his hand, the rope already loosened from his waist. Carefully, without any eye-catching movements, Stenwold unshouldered his piercer, running a quick eye over it to be sure it was still charged and loaded.

'We need not meet?' Ebris echoed. 'Oh, Skipper, you underestimate my sentimental attachment to you. I'd not dream of letting you breeze away without a keepsake or two.'

'Be careful what you dream of,' Tomasso replied levelly.

The Spider's face twisted, baring the livid, shiny skin

where the flames had caught him. 'You burned my ship!' he spat.

'I hear you have a new one,' said the Fly, still quite steady.

'*You burned my ship!*'

'You were robbing mine at the time, Ebris,' Tomasso snapped at last. 'And if I happened to pop a couple of pots of firepowder and a fuse in amongst the cargo you stole, well, it was your own choice to rob your brother thieves.'

'You stain my family to three generations, if you call yourself my—' Ebris started and, even as he was speaking, Tomasso's fingers flicked out. His hands had left his dagger hilts, and two throwing blades were in the air even as the Spider spoke. One of the Scorpions twitched his shield up before his master's face at the last second and, on the other side of Ebris, a Spider-kinden woman's head snapped back with the small, hiltless knife in her eye.

Stenwold heard Piera's bowstring twang, and Laszlo was abruptly airborne, slinging his blade in a wide arc. A couple of Ebris's crew rushed Tomasso, but the Fly had his fighting knives out now, catching their rapier blades and turning them aside, fighting half on the ground and half in the air, his lack of height and reach becoming an irrelevancy. Ebris was meanwhile shrieking at his people to kill all of them.

The *Tidenfree* crew had seized the initiative, but the numbers were against them, and Stenwold saw that, had he not been there, they would surely have taken to the skies and fled for their ship.

*Up to me to finish it, then*, he said to himself.

'Ho, Spider!' he bellowed, and levelled the piercer. The two Scorpions obediently clumped before their captain, bracing their shields. It was clear that none of them had any idea what Stenwold was holding, beyond that it was a weapon.

'And who are you to address me, slave?' Ebris of the Ganbrodiel demanded.

'The future,' said Stenwold, and pulled the trigger.

The sound alone stopped the fight, sent the Spiders reeling back, virtually knocked the Flies from the air. What kept the fight stopped was what those four long metal bolts had accomplished. The Scorpions had been faithful body-guards, but the piercer had struck through their shields, splintering the wood like kindling, ripped open their mail and torn their bodies up so that they looked as though some wild beast – a mantis or a hunting beetle – had been at them. Their last service had been in vain. Two of the bolts had retained enough force to take Ebris squarely in the chest. Now they stood proud of his body, as though waiting for someone to run a flag up them.

For a moment, everybody just stared. Stenwold calmly put the piercer down and reached for his belt. He might be a long way from home, but he knew people – people of any kinden – and there was always one.

A scarred Spider-kinden, older than Ebris had been, probably a loyal family retainer, yelled something wordless and went for Stenwold with his sword. Before Tomasso could get in the way, Stenwold had loosed both barrels of the little snapbow Totho had made. True, one bolt flew straight over the man's head, but the other one caught him beneath the collarbone and stopped him in his tracks. He dropped to his knees with a disbelieving look, and keeled over onto his side.

'Anyone else?' Stenwold demanded, brandishing the weapon. The piercer was discharged, the snapbow empty, but his Inapt adversaries had no idea of that. *Keep your superstitions*, he found himself thinking. *Leave to me the foundry and the forge, and we shall see who carries the day.*

They melted away, the remnants of Ebris's crew. By that time Laszlo was calling for aid, and Stenwold turned to see that Piera had taken an arrow in the belly, even during that short moment of skirmish.

They rushed her back to the *Tidenfree*, convulsing and weeping in Stenwold's arms. As the ship cast off, Despard and Fernaea both tried all the tricks of modern and ancient medicine to keep some life in her, but before Kanateris had reached the horizon she was gone.

Jodry Drillen employed three secretaries now, with standing instructions to take away and deal with anything that did not require his specific and valuable attention, yet still each morning there appeared a neat pyramid of scrolls on his desk: petitions, proposals, complaints, agendas, reports from his own people or invitations from the high-placed. *Why did I want this, precisely?* It seemed out of all proportion to the effective worth and influence of his new position. Locals had great difficulty persuading foreign visitors that the Speaker did not actually rule the Assembly or the city. His role was just that of a glorified bureaucrat. Collegium was ruled by the vote of the Assembly as a whole, not by the word of one man, just as the Assembly and Speaker both were selected through the casting of Lots by the citizens at large. Visitors found it an astonishing system. Jodry had seen them walking about the streets of Collegium with a nervous, expectant air, as if waiting for the howling mobs of anarchy to descend at any moment.

*So why would any sane Beetle want to be Speaker, one might ask?* Oh but, of course, there were perks. The Speaker was the city's face when it came to foreign diplomacy. The Speaker met ambassadors and hosted gatherings. The Speaker was not expected to raise motions himself before the Assembly, but he drew up the list of who spoke and when. It was not in Jodry's power to ban any Assembler from making a speech or putting a matter to the vote, but his whim determined whether a petitioner had the midmorning hours, when the Assemblers were sharp, or the early-morning slot when they were half-asleep, or later when their minds were on which chop house would receive them for lunch. Or else the next day, if there were enough wanting to be heard. In its own strange way the influence of the Speaker was as great as any Spider Aristos, and perhaps only the Spiders truly understood its implications.

Still, he had perhaps underestimated the baggage entailed. Here he was, scarcely an hour into the morning – on a day when the Assembly was not even in session, yet! – and already the business was piling up.

'Ambassador Aagen wants to talk with you about the next games,' said Arvi, and the position of his finger along the scroll he read from showed that he was barely halfway through. The Fly-kinden was all immaculate perfection, giving the impression he could waste Jodry's time all day, if he needed to.

'Don't we have a committee ruling on the games?' Jodry complained. 'I'd swear we gave old Nemmie Linker some money for it.'

Arvi's nose wrinkled. 'Aagen's a Wasp, Master. He's used to a single person being in charge, and usually a man.'

'Well, put him off.'

'Very good.' The Fly made a small cross on the scroll. 'Master Outwright came with a delegation about the future of the Companies. They know that there's a motion to disband them, and now they're spitting teeth about it.'

'Did you mention that the war is over? Perhaps he hasn't heard,' Jodry muttered.

'I suspect he would reply that it was not as simple as that, Master,' said Arvi smartly. He was quite the most humourless Fly that Jodry had ever known, but also the most efficient.

'I'll see them this afternoon.' Jodry paused to think for a moment. 'Have my gorget and sword fetched and polished, or whatever they do to them to make them look good. I might as well look the veteran myself.'

'Very good.' Arvi's finger moved on. 'A delegate from the Council of Thirteen in Helleron wants to talk about the railroad. It's Jandry Pinhaver, so—'

'So I can't very well ignore him. Well, invite him for drinks this evening. He should appreciate that. Take up two bottles of the '500 Seldis Glorhavael. I hear Pinhaver knows his wine.'

'Very good. Then we have another thirteen personal petitions for justice.'

'Look through them yourself. If there's anything that looks as though it's genuine, bring it back on tomorrow's list.'

'And the two genuine petitions from yesterday?'

'Bring them back tomorrow, too, and that one from the day before.' Jodry sighed. *And I imagined that I would have time for a few good causes.* He had tried that, over the first few days, and not only because he knew Stenwold would have expected it. The problem was that, on digging deep enough, so few causes retained their virtue for long. 'Come on, man, what else?'

'Stenwold Maker stepped on to the docks this morning from the *Tidenfree*, a Fly-run vessel of no provenance,' Arvi reported, before rolling the scroll up neatly.

Jodry stared at him, open-mouthed, before gathering himself enough to say, 'And you couldn't have told me that first thing? Seventeen days he's been gone!'

'Would you have wanted to deal with the rest, if I had started with Master Maker?' Arvi raised one eyebrow.

Jodry gave him a sour look. 'Don't think that I can't dismiss you, without references.'

'But think of all the petitions for justice I would raise, Master,' the Fly replied, deadpan.

*Not humourless,* Jodry conceded. *If only.* 'Send for him.

I want to see him the moment we're both free. I'll fit it in around anything else. Tell him I need him to help stop a third Vekken war, that should get the truant bastard's attention.'

'Very good,' Arvi responded, and bowed his way out of the door.

He had gone to Arianna first, after he stepped ashore, but only because he had been making plans while aboard ship. The *Tidenfree* crew were fully briefed, and they would meet with him later.

All the way home a single thought: *The Aldanrael* had sat like a lead ball in his stomach. He had been trying to disbelieve Albinus's words, through fog and wind and the Lash. *I will have proof.* Even if the pallid Ant had spoken the truth, it would be a grave step to point a finger at the Lord-Martial Teornis of the Aldanrael. To jump to conclusions and mislay the blame, well . . . Teornis was popular amongst the citizens of Collegium, but peace was even more popular. Stenwold had no doubt that he would slide from war hero to warmonger in an eye-blink.

Arianna had been glad to see him, at least. She had held him long and hard, and he thought she might even have wept, although her eyes were dry when she finally let him go. It reminded him of how they had been during the Vekken siege, in the first flush of their relationship.

He had been going to tell her more, to ask her advice even, but in the end he found the words would not come. He simply did not want to lay this burden on her.

One of Jodry's people had found him, soon enough, and called him to an urgent conference. Stenwold regarded the prospect sourly. *Was it too much to hope that, by becoming Speaker, he would stand on his own feet and not treat me like his personal servant?* He was being harsh, he knew, but Jodry's dire warnings about the Vekken smacked of cheap sensationalism. *I will see our new Speaker in my own good time.*

Instead he had taken to his study and written a note, very carefully phrased, though it was not addressed to any particular name. In truth, Stenwold had three or four possibilities in mind for whom those same words would serve, as he was not sure who was in the city just now, or who would be most willing to oblige. That gap in his knowledge threw him, as though he had found one of the stair treads missing on his way down to breakfast. *I'm losing my touch. I should know these things already.* He wondered then, sitting in this study which had seen so many years of plots and agents, *Am I still an intelligencer, a spymaster, in truth? Or am I just become another fat Assembler with a war record?*

Then Arianna had come in with a mug of chocolate for him. He hastily hid the letter away by instinct, beneath another sheet of parchment, then felt guilty for the action. She would work out soon enough that he was up to something. Meanwhile, she was waiting still to hear what had taken him off to sea for almost two tendays, and he did not want to lie to her. As she draped herself over his shoulder, he almost told her again, but bit back the words, found something pleasant and banal to say. The knowledge had already poisoned him. He did not want it to sicken her as well.

Later, after he had called up some Fly-kinden messengers to carry his letters, he and Arianna found other points of agreement, and his secrets were almost forgotten. Elsewhere, in the new Speaker's townhouse, Jodry Drillen stewed and stamped and went without Stenwold's company and, for him, Stenwold spared not a moment's thought.

Jodry's man was knocking at his door barely after dawn on the day after, though. Cardless diverted him, putting him off and sending him to walk about the streets for another hour or so, but by that time Stenwold knew that the Speaker, like a fly on old food, would not be swatted off without inevitably circling back.

He left the bed and, without waking Arianna, dressed in his best College robes, and headed off to the Speaker's offices. *Let's get this over with. I have other things to do with my time.*

The messenger caught up with him on the very steps of the Amphiophos, swinging through the air to match pace with him faultlessly: a young Fly woman, neat as a button, handing him a folded paper. The circular badge of her guild gleamed, freshly polished, on her chest.

Stenwold unfolded the paper, holding it close. His eyes flicked over the few words, before he enquired, 'Who gave you this?'

'Master Maker,' the Fly told him, reproachfully, 'this was *left* in our offices. Nobody saw by whom.'

Stenwold felt a worm of unease, for the paper had read, in stark, sharp letters, '*Tell Maker I shall be there.*' *Still, there's nothing that can be done about that, until the time . . .* He was about to move on but the Fly skipped in front of him, coughing politely.

'Ah, so you've not been paid for it.' He made a wry face and passed her a couple of coins. She bowed neatly, feet already leaving the ground, and was off and away over the city.

Jodry was to be found at his desk, and not alone. A young Beetle lad that Stenwold recognized as Maxel Gainer was sitting mournfully in a chair nearby, as though he was a student about to be disciplined. He looked up hopefully when Stenwold was ushered in.

'What's the emergency?' Stenwold asked. He had not heard that Collegium was now at war with Tsen or Vek, or any Ant city-state, and he was sure that someone would have mentioned it.

Jodry raised his eyebrows. 'Am I allowed to ask just where you've been these last two tendays?'

'On a cruise for the good of my health,' Stenwold replied curtly. 'Jodry—'

'I need your diplomatic acumen, Stenwold. You know these Ant-kinden better than I do.'

*So I'm now Collegium's special envoy to the entire Ant race am I? What a prime job that would be.* He took a seat, with a sidelong look at Gainer. 'What's he done now?'

'Nigh on started a war,' Jodry said dismissively. When Gainer began to protest, he held up his hands. 'Oh, not deliberately, and more down to old Tseitus than him, but, hammer and tongs, Stenwold! You'd not believe the tight-ropes I've been walking, and I'm not a man constitutionally suited for that, I can tell you.'

'So how have things fallen out with the Tseni and their submersibles, then?' Stenwold asked. The thought that submersibles might become useful in Collegium's near-future had not passed him by. *If the Spiders attack, they will come by sea again.* The other thought, which he could not keep from his mind, was *And how friendly is Jodry here with Teornis – with the Spiderlands?* It had always been the Empire, with Stenwold. He had always been hunting for the Imperial agents and sympathizers, marking down men or women as hands that took Wasp coin. He had never stopped to think that others, too, might have designs on his city and on the Lowlands.

'Their case is that the *Tseitan* is essentially a stolen design,' Jodry explained. 'They're making a big deal of it, as though it's going to be the next snapbow. Personally, I think it's just about political leverage and that they want something else from us.'

'Well, what exactly is the *Tseitan*?' Stenwold pressed. 'Is it ours or theirs or what?'

Jodry signalled to Gainer, who cleared his throat. 'The original submersible, my master's old boat, was manufactured in Collegium, but Master Tseitus brought along a good half-dozen innovations with him – in his head but ready-made, if you see. I always reckoned they were his.' The young artificer looked harassed, a man clearly out of his depth. 'He could have learned them in Tsen, maybe. But we did a lot of our own work on her too, and the *Tseitan* throws out at least a couple of the ideas Master Tseitus came up with, for better ones. He kept improving the design all the time.' He looked downcast. 'Wish he was here with us now, I tell you that.'

'So what do Kratia's Tseni want?'

'War with Vek,' Jodry replied. Seeing Stenwold's reaction, he smiled bleakly. 'They haven't said as much, but that's what it is. As soon as they got wind that we were cosying up to the Vekken at last, they started to sweat about it. Vek's armies have been pointing east a long time, so if they're suddenly happy about relations in our direction, it makes sense that they might turn to Tsen for their next war games. After all, there are a lot more Vekken than there are Tseni.'

'Well, they can whistle for their war,' Stenwold said sourly. 'I've spent too long building the peace.'

'Ah, but these Tseni, I hate to say it, are clever bitches. They're not like your average Ant-kinden ambassador. They've been going about the people, making themselves known. They've been guesting with Assemblers. They've been talking up Tsen's role in the war: how they sent soldiers so many miles to fight off the Empire and die in front of Sarn. And Tseitus . . . Well, you'll laugh.'

'They're saying he's a hero,' Gainer put in, sounding equally baffled and proud.

'I thought they were saying he was a thief?' Stenwold demanded.

'That's what happens when you go off on a cruise for your health,' Jodry observed pointedly. 'The world doesn't just wait. It turns out now that Tseitus was a hero of Tsen come to help his good friends in Collegium. I've already had one request that his work in the war be recognized officially, Sten. His work in sinking the Vekken flagship, of course.'

Stenwold nodded dourly.

'And let's face it, he did.' Jodry threw up his arms. 'And, yes, the Vekken were trying to kill us all, and that's not exactly ancient history. So people are starting to mutter.'

'I can imagine.' For Stenwold, it was like feeling the leaden, icy waters close over his head. He was drowning in Collegium politics yet again. 'Let me think on this. There must be a way.'

'Take all the time you need – but not too much,' Jodry said. 'Master Gainer, at least, has profited from this. Not only is he seen as a hero's apprentice now, but the donations towards the *Tseitan* project have now become almost adequate. Throwing good coin at a boat that sinks looks like madness to me, but you never can tell with people.'

'I just want to continue Master Tseitus's work,' Gainer said stubbornly. 'I don't care about all this other stuff.'

'My advice is to use it while you can,' Jodry recommended. He turned back to Stenwold. 'Now, are you glad I called you in so quickly?' he gave a broad, sardonic smile.

'No,' Stenwold replied shortly. 'But you were right to do so, curse you. The last thing we need right now is trouble with the Ants. With any Ants.'

Jodry nodded. 'You're probably also aware that those Wasp soldiers sitting near Myna's borders haven't gone anywhere. They're saying the whole Eighth Army is marching up and down there like it's the Empress's birthday or something. War here in the Lowlands is probably just what they're waiting for. If we have to look away for ten minutes, we'd probably find that the whole Three-City Alliance has vanished like a conjurer's hat by the time we look back.'

*And how much more true will that be if we end up crossing swords with the Spiderlands*, Stenwold reflected. *They'll celebrate all over the Empire, if they find that their two great enemies have come to blows. And then they'll march.*

As he stepped out of the office, he paused to run over the conversation in his head, prying at the gaps. *Any suggestion of betrayal there? Any hint of a Spider lurking behind the words? Perhaps Jodry's just too accomplished a statesman.* In truth his gut feeling was that Jodry had nothing to do with the piracy business, but he knew he could not take the chance of assuming so. Absolute secrecy, then: the knowledge, burning inside him like hot metal, would not be let out that way. *And, in all honesty, if he is innocent of any complicity, he is better off not knowing, and Arianna the same. I will keep this between me and the* Tiden-free *until I know for certain.*

Stenwold trailed his slow way home, still carrying the burden of knowledge he felt unable to vouchsafe to anyone.

# Eleven

He paused in the doorway of the Merraian Taverna, and a moment of bittersweet nostalgia caught him, seeing its familiar interior. The place had been a landmark of his intelligencing work since long before the war. The owner knew him well – and his money – but it was something more than that . . .

*How long has it been?* Three years and more since he had sent them off. It had been the end of innocence for his niece and his ward and two of his students. *Except Tynisa had already killed a man the night before, and Salma had known more of loss and death than any youth of his age should do.*

Standing there, in the doorway of the little Fly-kinden establishment, he felt such a fierce stab of loss that instead of heading on to the back room he sat down, dropping to the floor beside one of the low tables, overwhelmed by his memories. *I've lost them all. Hammer and tongs, but I've lost them all.* Tynisa had fled who knows where, and Totho was now a deserter from the Imperial army, become some kind of artificer-prince off the Exalsee. Che was running wild with Thalric – *Thalric!* – as her only companion, and Salma . . . well, the war had claimed him, dying with sword in hand at the place that they were now calling Malkan's Folly or Malkan's Stand, depending on whose side you had fought.

*Add them all to the list.* The Moth, Achaeos, had died of his wounds in Tharn, and Scuto during the Vekken siege. Tisamon, Nero, Marius lanced by a crossbow bolt in Myna so long ago, Atryssa in childbirth. *I'm running out of friends.*

The obvious question loomed: *Who will be next? Will my games get Jodry killed perhaps, or Arianna? Maybe I'll cut a swathe through the* Tidenfree *crew.* He felt sick with it, but forced himself to stand, nodding to the owner as he ducked into the back room.

They had been waiting for him: Tomasso and Laszlo were already sharing a jug of light Fly beer under the dim light of a guttering gas lamp.

'Master Maker,' the bearded man said, as Stenwold settled down opposite from them. 'You've spent the meantime wisely, I hope?'

'I have.' In the three days since he had stepped off the *Tidenfree*, Stenwold had been receiving reports from the docks, perusing manifests, asking questions.

'You look troubled,' Tomasso put in.

'Nothing relevant to our business.' *Or I hope so, at any rate.* 'You're docked . . . ?'

'Beyond the wall again,' Tomasso replied. 'There's no harsh weather expected, and we'll attract less notice there.'

'How?' Stenwold pressed. 'How is it that the port authorities don't run you off, or drop rocks on you?'

'Because the Collegium harbour has a long history of corruptibility that probably goes back to before the Revolution, for all I know,' Tomasso explained. 'Besides, there's nothing in your laws that says which side of the wall a ship must moor. Believe me, I've looked. A few coins here and there makes sure it isn't publicized. It's only a secret because so few ever go out onto the wall and look over, and because the goings-on at the docks seldom reach eminent people like yourself, Master Maker.'

Stenwold nodded, wondering whether he should feel moved to do something about this little pocket of lawlessness he had uncovered, but finding no motivation whatso-ever. 'How is . . . ?'

'Himself? No better, but breathing still, thank you for asking.' Tomasso drained his bowl and had Laszlo refill it. 'Business, then?'

'We're not complete yet,' Stenwold noted. 'I was hoping for—'

Laszlo coughed pointedly, and Stenwold went still. The back room was not large, nor yet cluttered, but he saw now how the two Flies were sitting oddly close to each other, for men with all the intervening space to choose from. He closed his eyes for a moment, listening hard, scent-ing the air, because he needed to re-experience the room, re-evaluate it and take it *all* in this time, without being fooled. What he guessed at now was an Art that he had known Tisamon use, sometimes, but not as skilfully as this.

She was there when he reopened his eyes: not invisible, not shading into the background, but keeping so very still that she had slipped by him, his eyes flicking over her towards the Flies, without registering. She was kneeling before the table, close enough to have already stabbed him: a Mantis-kinden woman with dark hair cut close and a pointed face. She would have looked young, even pretty, without the scars, for a jagged blade wound stretched from her chin to the mess it had left of her left ear, now long healed over. One of her hands was shiny with burn marks that he recognized as Wasp-sting, although she moved the fingers easily enough as she took the beer jug off Laszlo. She wore a leather cuirass studded with chips of chitin, and bracers of bronze-inlaid wood cut to let her arm-spines stand free. To one side of her belt were two short blades, narrow as rapiers but no longer than shortswords. They had guards that hooked back down their hilts in a clutch of jagged spurs.

Stenwold produced the brief note he had received from the messengers. 'Yours?' he asked.

Her eyes barely glanced at it. 'I'm here, aren't I?'

'And you are . . . ?'

'Danaen,' she said. He knew her by reputation, by notoriety. It was what he had been looking for. The Mantids of Felyal had not been good neighbours always. The Collegium-spawned logging towns at the edge of the Felyal had been profitable, but they had sent tales back with the lumber: fights, people disappearing. Every so often some pedlar would go into the woods and not come back, or a merchant who assumed too much would be found with his throat cut. Sometimes, once every decade perhaps, things would go bad and the Felyen would close their borders for a month or so. It was part of the trade.

That was the least of it, of course. Longships from Felyal plied the waves between their own treeline and the isle of Parosyal, and they were jealous of their seas. Every so often they would come out in force, and then the ships of Kes or Collegium would have to take care, and keep some goods back ready to appease them. Of course the Mantids' real targets had been Spider-kinden merchantmen. Whenever the raiding days came upon them, brought on by some irregular and inscrutable calendar all their own, no Spider-kinden was safe on the seas.

That was all in the history books now, even if the ink was still not dry. Felyal was no more, and the rebuilding was like to take generations the way the Mantis-kinden went about things. The Imperial Second Army had scythed down the flower of the Felyen warriors, burned out their holds, and driven them like chaff until many of the survivors came to Collegium. They had fought the Wasps with a will, loosing their long arrows from the walls and killing the Imperial soldiers in the air, but now that it was peace they were a mutinous and violent minority kicking their heels in the poorer areas of the city, always on the point of drawing a blade.

Danaen had been a longship captain, back in the day. She had done some little trading down the coast, but her name was spoken of as a raider – another kind of pirate. *I am in good company here today.* Most importantly, a woman like Danaen could be trusted in one thing: she would be no friend to the Spider-kinden or to the Aldanrael. They had not bought her, could not buy her: rich as they were, they had not the currency. She was just what Stenwold needed but, looking on her ravaged features, he found he feared her. Mantis-kinden were unpredictable, quick to take offence and just as quick to kill over it. *She is not Tisamon, I must remember.*

'To business, then,' he said. He met Danaen's cool, slightly contemptuous gaze. 'How many followers do you have who would sail with you?'

She shrugged. 'Who can say? It has been too long since they were called upon, perhaps – too long since the black-and-gold burned our ships. Some have taken the coin of your merchants. Some have gone to the Ant city, to be their scouts for when the Empire comes again. The old ways are dead, Beetle.'

*Perhaps we can breathe life into them yet.* Stenwold did not say it, though. He felt profoundly uncomfortable at using one such as Danaen. It was not that he did not *like* the Mantis-kinden, but they understood their honour far more than they would ever understand such things as diplomacy or necessity. 'You'll not need your own ship for this,' he said. 'I want Collegiate ships protected from piracy. Particular Collegiate ships.'

Her lip curled into a sneer. 'So, you are just one more merchant offering your gold.' Still, she made no move to go.

'No.' He gathered himself. 'I do not want you striding about deck, waving flags and frightening them off. I will have your people below decks and hidden. Only when the ship is boarded, if it is, will you make yourselves known.'

Something had come alive in her expression. 'And fall upon them?'

'Take their ship, if you can. Force a surrender – a *surrender* – if possible. Find proof as to who gave them the orders, whose is the ship. You understand me?'

'We fight,' she said.

'You will be under the command of Tomasso here or whoever he designates,' Stenwold told her sternly. 'This is not blood for blood's sake. I must know the truth.' *And I will not mention the Spiders, not yet. I don't want your people believing they have my licence to gut every Spider-kinden in Collegium.* 'Answer me, Danaen.'

He could almost feel her will bucking against him, but he held her gaze placidly. It was she, in the end, who glanced away. 'I will obey the Fly-kinden, if that is your wish. If our enemies throw down their arms, we will spare them.'

'Whoever they are?'

She looked at him again, lips twisted. 'Do you wish me to sign one of your papers? Which ship are we to sail on?'

'Ah well, there's the question.' Stenwold's time had so far been spent in drawing up a mental picture of the vessels that had been the pirates' prey: a picture based on cargo, on ownership, on the make-up of the merchants and investors behind the voyage. He had isolated a few vessels sailing within the tenday which would make a tempting target. *And, yet, it's plain that whoever is behind this, the Aldanrael or not, will be keeping their eyes on the docks. They are well-informed, as Failwright's figures show. So, then, will they not notice a score of Mantis marines embarking, and will they not then mark that ship down as one to avoid?*

'You will board Tomasso's *Tidenfree*,' Stenwold instructed. 'Tomasso will then rendezvous with the vessel I nominate. The captain of that ship will receive a sealed letter from me, explaining that I have paid for some added security for his trip. Believe me, every shipping magnate and consortium is very aware of the dangers, and I hope that my name will be sufficient to convince them to take you. From then . . . well, it's always possible you'll get a very pleasant voyage to Kes and back, but if not, you'll be ready.'

'We will,' she agreed. In her mind she was sharpening her swords already.

'Three Centrals a man for the voyage. Five Centrals bonus each if the ship's attacked. Another five each if I get the proof I want.'

Mantis-kinden did not haggle, nor were they much for the value of money. She nodded without comment.

'We'll get ready to sail, then,' Tomasso stated, standing. Danaen was abruptly on her feet as well.

'I shall gather my warriors,' she declared. 'It will be good to smell blood and the sea again.'

She left through the fallback hatch in the ceiling, a flutter of wings and then a slam of wood. *What price incorruptibility?* Stenwold asked himself, and not for the first time.

There was a bright summer sun in the gardens of the Amphiophos. A Beetle woman in Assembler's robes was entertaining a youth half her age, waited on by a pair of servants with wine and figs imported from the Silk Road cities. Arianna watched them sourly, sitting on her own in the greenery. The Beetles were not great gardeners, she decided. When they had set out to make this city theirs, those centuries ago after the revolution, they had been concerned with more practical matters. The Amphiophos, like some parts of the College and a few other buildings, was left over from the city's former masters, though, and the Moths had possessed an eye for beauty. Even though the place was more ordered now, and though there was a mechanical sundial that chimed the hour, and some fountains recently put in, to the Inapt mind the gardens were still a restful place. Except that she could not relax.

*I did everything I could to arouse his suspicions*, she thought. *Everything but actually tell him.* When Stenwold had come back from his voyage, from wherever it had taken him, Arianna had been nervous, unsure of herself and of their continuing closeness. When he had lain with her, she had clutched at him like a desperate woman, as she had when they had first come together. Surely he had seen the parallel: the way she had been when she was a Rekef deserter who lived only by his graces, and fought the Vekken alongside him because her life was inextricably reliant on his own. But, no, there had been no hint of suspicion in his eyes.

*I asked almost nothing. Surely he was suspicious that I did not even ask where he had been.* She had been denying herself temptation. If she had heard something of any significance, then it would have dragged her down – down towards the next betrayal in a life that was a string of them, like pearls in a necklace. She had passed over the subject of his absence as though he had simply stepped out to order wine and victuals. *Stenwold the Spymaster, surely that omission spoke to you?*

And it had not. If anything, Stenwold had simply been grateful not to have to explain himself, and that was all. He bumbled on his way, like a Beetle did, engrossed only in his own business while a world of meaning and subtlety passed by above his head. *How can he not see where I am? That I am on the brink? Does he* want *me to betray him? Does he not care?*

Their few years together had been a union born in the fires of one siege, tempered in the next, but now peace had come, and he was a different man – or she was a different woman. *I preferred it when we were fighting.* Now she had everything she could want, or at least everything that this Beetle city could give her, and it would have been enough had Teornis not spoken to her, had he not made her the offer. She had not realized what she was missing until his sly words drew it out of her.

*Stenwold takes me for granted*, she thought, and then

knew it for the truth. Stenwold cast no suspicious eye over her because she was his now, and the thought that his possession of her might only be a temporary matter, like a phase of the moon, had never occurred to him. Beetles were used to building in stone. What they put in place stayed there, generations on. Spiders built in silk that could be taken down and respun each morning.

If she was adopted into the Aldanrael, even as their most junior tyro cousin, she would want for nothing. More than that, though, she would have to be on her guard every moment. She would inherit their feuds and their alliances: she would learn the steps to their dances. Her life would never be as secure as this again, never more lived between stone walls. *Trapped. I am trapped in Beetle society as though it was amber. It is very pretty, very comfortable, but there is no fire to it. The fire between Stenwold and me was the war, the Empire, the thought that we could lose.* It was gone, now, that fire: leaving only the smoke rising from the candles of the Empire's defeats: Myna, Szar, Solarno, Malkan's Stand.

*I would have continued living as Stenwold's mistress for a long time indeed, had Teornis never come to me and opened my eyes.* She did not feel grateful for the revelation, rather she hated the man for it. Still, she could not undo the knowledge he had given her. She could not crawl back into that comforting shell.

*And, after all, it is as Teornis said,* she considered. *He and Stenwold are friends, or almost. There is no reason why I should have to choose between them. I can play a double game as long as I need.*

She leant back. 'Tell your master I agree,' she whispered, and heard the scuffle as the unseen auditor drew away, then crept off to find Teornis of the Aldanrael.

The tiring rooms of the Amphiophos had been the traditional scene of last-minute politicking for centuries. Generations of Collegium Assemblers had suffered crises of conscience, double-crossed their allies and rediscovered their principles here, within a short stone's throw of the debating chamber itself. The walls were hung with white drapes, which would originally have been the robes of the Assemblers, before it became custom for them to possess their own. Now these little rooms did nothing but provide a place of conspiracy.

Jodry beckoned Stenwold in as soon as he put his head round the door. 'You cut it fine sometimes, Maker,' he observed, rubbing his hands. Jodry always experienced a bout of nerves at the last moment before addressing the Assembly, yet when he actually stepped out before them, he would be steady as iron. 'You know Master Outwright, of course,' he added.

'Who doesn't?' Stenwold remarked wryly. Janos Out-wright had been a persistent annoyance to the Assembly at large for over ten years, occasionally even overtaking Stenwold himself as the man whose speeches were most dreaded. He was a bald, stout and extremely short states-man who had cultivated a bushy moustache. He had clung to his seat in the Assembly by stunts and exhibitionism, rallying the mob for some pointless cause for just long enough to win some votes, before abandoning them for some other piece of business. Stenwold hoped that his involvement in the Merchant Companies was not another such brief-lived scheme.

'Master Maker, delighted.' Outwright clasped hands with Stenwold in what he believed was a warrior's grip. Over his Assembler's robes he wore a blue-enamelled gorget and breastplate, the latter etched, in silver, with a wheel of pikes and snapbows and the words *Outright Victory or Death*.

Stenwold nodded to him politely, feeling a little diplo-macy was wise. *What clowns we end up standing beside*, he thought but, as of recent developments, he knew that the longevity of the Companies had become a matter of some import.

'And this is Elder Padstock, Chief Officer of . . . well . . .' Jodry could not suppress a pointed smile.

'Of Maker's Own,' Stenwold finished for him. Padstock was a stocky, heavy-set woman, her greying hair tied back. She had come in one of the knee-length coats of buff hide that many of Collegium's defenders had taken to, little more than an artificer's work coat. Her breastplate was plain, but she wore a red sash over it, with a golden sword-and-book stamp and the words *Through the Gate*.

'I knew you would not abandon us, Master Maker.' She clasped his hand firmly, and held it a moment. Stenwold searched her face for clues. *I cannot recall ever seeing this woman before.* But then the men and women who had insisted on accompanying him from the city had been helmed, anonymous. He had assumed he was going to his death, and would have preferred to do so without their company. It was the merest chance of timing – and an Imperial general's sense of honour – that had made them heroes and not corpses.

She was trembling slightly, he noticed, and there was the faintest glint of tears in her eyes. That moment, that suicidal moment, was still with her, no doubt the greatest day of her life, forever being told and retold. The naked adoration in her gaze made him profoundly uncomfortable but he clasped her hand again and thanked her.

'No sign of the Coldstone boys yet,' Jodry said.

'Perhaps that's just as well,' Stenwold considered. 'Jodry . . . at least tell me their livery doesn't show a mound of dead Vekken or something. Working with Vek isn't exactly easy going at the best of times.'

Jodry gave a snort of amusement. 'You'd think so, wouldn't you?' Then his expression soured. 'They use a white helm in profile as their device. The motto is, *In Our Enemies' Robes*. You understand that?'

Stenwold nodded grimly. By the time the Vekken had been turned back, it was said that there was not a resident of Coldstone Street left living that did not own an Ant-made hauberk, sword and shield. He was willing to bet that a fair number still had Wasp-crafted kit stowed in the cellar or the attic, as well.

'Well,' Jodry declared, 'let's go face the people.' He stretched his arms, waggling his fingers to release the tension. The door opened even as he reached for the handle. Revealed beyond was an Ant-kinden man, some renegade Tarkesh with waxy-white skin and steel-grey hair. He wore a tunic of grey-blue and a cloak a little darker, and he had come armed: a shortsword sat at his hip with what they called a knuckle-shield, a little wood-and-leather buckler with metal studs in its face. The promised white helm and motto were absent, along with any other decoration.

Jodry said, 'Coldstone?' and the Ant nodded.

'Officer Marteus,' he introduced himself, nodding to Padstock.

'Well then, we are all met,' Jodry concluded, although it was clear he would have been happier without this disreputable-looking figure standing beside them. The three Merchant Company officers regarded him distrustfully, as well they might. 'Let us understand entirely what I am offering you, before we go in,' he informed them sternly. 'You know how many of the Assembly are calling for the Companies to be disbanded. Private armies are all very well in Helleron, they say, and I agree. However, I have found one other way out and, with Master Maker's blessing, there should be sufficient voices to carry the motion. I won't disband the Companies. I'll legitimize them. Your three surviving forces will be recognized by the city.'

They nodded soberly, and Jodry went on, 'I've had my secretary prepare some regulations: how many to be permitted in the complement, how often they must train, arrangements to borrow snapbows from the armouries, and the like. There will be a stipend, recognition, but only if you keep to the rules. This way the city will feel safe with you, you keep your pride and . . . well, I don't need to tell you the third advantage.'

'Collegium has an army,' Stenwold concluded.

'An army of shopkeepers,' Jodry agreed, 'and reason help us all. Let's go and establish our military dictatorship, shall we? They were foreclosing on an orphanage this morning, so it's all good works today.'

'The future of the Companies is the future of Collegium,' Elder Padstock declared, with utter conviction. 'The Empire shall come again, won't it, Master Maker?'

'Without doubt,' Stenwold agreed. *But I fear we shall have need of you sooner than that – sooner than any of you know . . .*

# Twelve

Jaclen Courser had first come to the *Migrating Home* as an apprentice engineer fresh from the Great College. She had worked hard since then: from artificer's mate to chief engineer, to navigator, to the *Home*'s master, taking orders only from the cartel that owned the vessel. When they were out of port, hers was the only commanding voice, or so she was used to.

*Stenwold Maker*, she thought. Oh, but she remembered Maker from College, twenty years ago: a plump, idealistic youth a year younger than she, always hanging about with his mad friends: that crazy Mantis and the Spider girl everyone liked so much. The Mantis had died in the war, she had heard. Some said he had ended up killing the Wasp Emperor. What had happened to the Spider, nobody seemed to know, save that Stenwold's ward looked mightily familiar to Jaclen, the one time she had seen the girl.

Still, Maker had done well enough for himself, and Jaclen didn't begrudge him. *He did some fine work in the war, they say.* The war was a sore point. Like most of Collegium's merchant fleet she had been caught outside the city when the Vekken blockade came in, and had therefore not been able to lift a finger to help. *Still, I'd rather Master Maker did well for himself in the world without involving me.*

She had his note in her hand now. As per instruction, as grudgingly per instruction, she had not so much as broken the seal until the *Migrating Home* had pulled out of harbour. She did not like being any man's game piece, but it seemed that her fate had now been commandeered by Collegium's War Master.

*To the Master of the* Migrating Home, the note had begun. *Complaints have been brought to the Assembly of increasing attacks upon the shipping of our city on its journeys east.* That was Rones Failwright's work, Jaclen well knew. The man had been agitating in the Amphiophos for an age about the pirates. Now it seemed that someone of moment had finally noticed him. *Why all the secrecy, though?* she asked herself. Stenwold's note had gone on: *I am arranging for a vessel, the* Tidenfree *under Master Tomasso, to catch up with you once you are under way. You will take on board a detachment of guards who will serve to deal with any raiders or brigands of the sea that you should meet. This is at my expense, and no demands will be made of your employers.* Which was all very well, and terribly generous of the man, but Jaclen could not help wondering why they hadn't just marched the guards on board there at the docks, with fanfare and ceremony, to let all eyes know that the *Migrating Home* was no longer free prey for piracy. The only logical conclusion was not a happy one, namely that Stenwold Maker was playing a game. He did not want to warn the pirates off, but instead was setting a trap for them. *And I'm to be the bait, curse the man.* Jaclen morosely watched the Fly-kinden corvette coming in, reefing its sails and letting its engine match speeds with the chugging *Home*.

Twenty years, woman and girl, she had kept the *Home* afloat, and in that time she had been boarded by pirates eight times. Once, when the attackers had been some wildly overconfident raiders from Felyal, she had ordered them driven off with crossbows. The other times she had called on her crew to stand down and stand by, while the pirates removed the best of the cargo. Of those eight occasions, five had occurred over the last year and a half. If that had not been the case she would not have willingly gone along with this ploy, but matters were now growing desperate. Keeping her ear to the ground, she knew that the consortium that owned the *Home* was tottering, reeling from its losses. Other merchants had been broken, left penniless when their ships came back empty, or sometimes did not come back at all. Many were abandoning the sea trade for other business less fraught with difficulty.

It had occurred to her that this venture might be piracy wearing a different hat. If Maker had gone bad, then he might be using his good name to have ships stand quietly by and be boarded. She did not quite believe that, for she had never before known pirates who worked by appointment.

The Fly vessel, sleeker and smaller than the *Home*, drew close with careful steering. Jaclen ordered the engines stopped, and lines cast over to secure them. Even before the two vessels were linked a pair of Fly-kinden had hopped over, wings glittering briefly in the sunlight. One was a young man and the other old enough to be his father, with a striking bush of a black beard.

'You'd be this Master Tomasso, then?' Jaclen enquired curtly, as the Flies landed before her.

'I'm none other,' the Fly said, grinning. 'Permission to come aboard, Skipper?'

'Granted, I suppose.' She then cast an eye over the *Tidenfree*'s deck. 'Master Tomasso,' she asked, her voice tightly controlled, 'what do you intend?' Her hand crept towards her belt and the knife she kept there. Gathered ready to board her vessel was a pack of Mantis-kinden, armed to the teeth: just the sort of sea-reavers that she had always tried to steer well clear of.

Tomasso glanced back at his ship and gave a laugh at the sight, startlingly loud from such a small man. 'I can see why you'd worry. Never fear, Master Courser, they're not about to descend on you with claw and sword. These are

Maker's bodyguards, here just to make sure you get safe and sound to wherever you're headed.'

Jaclen put a hand to her head, feeling a pain coming on. 'We're bound for Everis, Tomasso: the Spider-kinden. I don't see them being in the market for *that* particular cargo.'

'We'll just keep them below decks and quiet-like, once you get there,' Tomasso replied, still grinning broadly. 'After all, let's hope they don't even have to draw a blade all voyage. On the other hand, if you are overhauled by some ragbag of pirates, then who would you rather have at hand to see the villains off?'

Jaclen shook her head. Even as she watched, the Mantids began jumping or flying aboard, scarcely a one of them deigning to walk the gangplank like civilized people. They were a rough lot: claws and rapiers, longbows and arm-spines and battle-scars. Most wore leather jerkins or great-coats, or cuirasses of chitin scales, and a couple even had pieces of the old-style carapace armour, which sold for a fortune when it was sold at all, and which nobody even knew how to make any more, since the Felyal burned. Her own crew were meanwhile keeping a good distance, and the Mantis-kinden were soon standing on her deck as though they had already taken the ship.

'Well, it's too late to refuse you now,' she remarked drily, and Tomasso laughed again.

'I'll be leaving my man, Laszlo, here to watch over them,' he explained. 'You tell him, then he'll tell them. Maker's orders were for our friends to heed him.'

'Let's hope they remember that,' Jaclen said. Most of her – the solid, businesslike majority born of twenty years' hard work – felt that this situation was a barrel of firepow-der just waiting for the spark. Some small sliver of her youth had reawoken within her, though. Wasn't this one of those dreams that she'd had: to give it all over and turn raider? To raise sail and haul oar with the Mantis-kinden as they made free with the sea and all its plunder? And now she had her own complement of Mantis marines to spring on the next whoreson of a pirate that tried to take advantage of her.

The third time the *Migrating Home* had been taken, her Master at the time had tried to put up a fight. As the cargo was pillaged, the pirates had hanged the man and three of the *Home*'s crew from their rigging, just to make their point. It had been by random lot, and it could have been Jaclen left dangling and kicking, as easily as anyone else. A little core of steel inside her would be waiting with anticipation for the sight of a hostile sail.

The fight with the Assembly had seemed harder even than the Vekken siege, objection after objection hurled from the seats to strike home. Had Jodry not been Speaker, then the Companies would have been dissolved, with all the consequent trouble that would bring. As it was, there had been just enough of the Assembly who were proud of the city's recent history to ensure that Outwright, Padstock and Marteus retained their commands, under the direct authority of the Assembly itself. It was not much of a force compared with the Ant city-states or a single Imperial army, but it would give Collegium a core of trained and well-armed soldiers when they were needed, which volunteer companies could then be formed around at need.

Of course, news of the Beetles' new martial standing had spread fast, especially to the various foreign embassies, leading Stenwold inexorably on to his next piece of diplomacy.

He had chosen the room carefully: one of the College's many odd little teaching rooms. So many of the College's original buildings pre-dated the revolution: built to the Moths' plan for their own inscrutable purposes, though built by Beetle hands. After the city – and the future – had changed hands, the people of the newly renamed Collegium had done their best with the spaces that the

Moths had left them. However, it was not entirely the room's dimensions that had attracted Stenwold, but its ornament. College rooms tended to inherit whatever random decoration had been bequeathed to the institution, so any blank space of wall was fair game for showing some masterwork or certificate or piece of gaudy tat that some kind benefactor had seen fit to give away. Stenwold now positioned himself beneath this room's artistic burden and waited.

The three Vekken ambassadors arrived on the stroke of noon. They entered the room cautiously, as they always did: three pitch-skinned Ant-kinden, almost mirror images of one another, wearing tunics and sandals and sword belts. They had never learned the lesson the Tseni seemed to have picked up, that other kinden took note of ornament and spectacle. If Stenwold had passed them in the street, he would have assumed them too poor even to be itinerant mercenaries. He now named them, in his head: Accius, Malius, Termes.

'Thank you for coming,' he greeted them. They stared with their usual watchfulness, two looking at him, one turning away to keep an eye on the door.

'You wished to discuss the threat of Tsen,' the one he thought was Termes declared. 'It is past time to do so.'

'And that is indeed why I asked you here,' Stenwold assured them. They were still suspicious, wanting to know why they were here at the College and not at the Amphiophos, clearly expecting an ambush either metaphorical or literal.

*Well, I have my ambush all set out*, Stenwold reflected. 'You see the etching behind me?' he prompted.

Two pairs of eyes regarded it in silence before Termes said, in a remarkable display of politeness, 'The likeness of yourself is very good.'

Stenwold hadn't thought so, but he suspected that Collegiate aesthetics made higher demands of representational art than would Vekken tastes, and that for Ant-kinden the face was the least part of identifying fellows. 'Do you know what occasion this was?' he pressed them. They fell silent again, although he could almost hear the hum of their internal dialogue. He turned to look at the piece himself, conceding that it was nothing much: a competent piece of work, acids etching on copper. The technique was slightly old-fashioned now, since machines existed to cut a much crisper image. Still, Stenwold himself was recognizable, and he could have named a few of the other faces even had he not known who they were meant to be. He remembered that day well, even at this remove: standing on the steps in front of the Amphiophos, before the crowd – a show of solidarity and triumph. There was Lineo Thadspar, who had been Speaker at the time. There was Balkus, the Sarnesh renegade, and over there was Parops, the Tarkesh exile. Also there was Teornis, of course, and Stenwold's stomach lurched on seeing the handsome, smiling Spider-kinden, backed by his grab-bag of mercenaries and Satrapy conscripts.

'I do,' said Termes. Enough displeasure permeated his normally level tone to let Stenwold know that he did indeed understand.

'I think you know me well enough to accept that I would not bring you here merely as an insult, or to offend you. I hope so, anyway.' This was the crucial point. They would now leave and his work would be undone, or they would stay and he could continue to build his tottering bridge towards them.

Again they were silent, hidden thoughts darting between them. He allowed them time.

'Speak your piece,' said Termes eventually. It sounded hostile but their continued presence indicated his victory.

'The artist has here created a view of those left in possession of the city, after your siege was lifted,' he said. 'Contained in this etching is Collegium's great secret: why we have not been conquered, by Vek, or by the Empire.'

*And now the Spiderlands will try its hand, apparently. We are the pearl in everyone's oyster, it seems.*

Their eyes were focused on the picture once again, seeking some hidden weapon amidst the background, some coded message. He let them look. The secret he mentioned was in plain view. Any College student could have named it by now, but the Vekken were not used to thinking in such a way. He was trying, against all tenets of Ant-kinden culture and nature, to wrench their collective mind around to it.

'Do you see?' he asked, eventually.

He assumed they were going to say no. Termes was about to, he was sure, but one of the others, Accius he thought, said, 'We see.' There was a moment of silent disagreement between them, suggesting Termes plainly did not, but then the answer was made plain to him and he fell into step with the other two.

'Collegium itself could not stand against the Vekken army,' Accius stated. 'The siege was relieved from without.'

*Almost, but not quite.* 'The lesson goes further than just the one engagement or just the one war,' Stenwold replied. 'Our strength is in our friends, in those who will give of themselves to keep us free.' He could almost catch the thought that flew between them. 'I know you think that walls and swords and automotives provide a surer strength, and that if you rely only on yourselves, nobody can let you down. Well, that's true, and we'd all be fools not to strengthen ourselves as much as possible. We'd be fools to rely entirely on the grace of others. That's Helleron's folly, and that's why Helleron fell so swiftly to the Empire – and will fall again.'

'It did not fall. It climbed down of its own accord,' Termes noted acidly.

'Oh, I agree. I'll not defend them.' Stenwold sighed. 'There was a time when swords and walls and well-trained soldiers were enough, and a city-state could stand on its own against all comers, hold the rest of the world at sword's length.' *The time of the Ant-kinden, although I'd not be so tactless as to say it.* 'That time is gone.'

They showed no reaction, just waited.

'The Empire brought that to an end,' Stenwold went on. 'The Empire, which controls dozens of cities, and draws its power from them all. No single city can stand against it – Tark was not the first Ant-kinden city that fell to the Imperial armies. Any city that pursues a course of isolationism is conniving at its own destruction for, when the next great aggressor comes, whether it be the Empire again, or the Spiderlands, or even the Commonweal, that city will fall for want of friends.'

'We are not blind to what you mean,' Termes stated.

'I mean more than you think,' Stenwold warned him. 'Yes, I am offering you Collegium's hand of friendship, and I will break heads and twist arms in the Amphiophos until I get the city behind me. We do not want a third war with Vek. Nobody has profited from the last two. All that has happened is that both of our cities were left weaker at the end.'

'That is true,' agreed Termes. Ant voices were never expressive, but there was the slightest hint there of a degree of emotion kept otherwise submerged.

'So let us talk about Tsen.'

The sudden juxtaposition did not seem to throw them. 'You are proposing an alliance,' Termes observed.

'Not the alliance you mean,' Stenwold told him firmly. There was a moment of silence, and he could see their minds working on that. No hands dropped to sword hilts – they did not leap to the conclusion that Collegium would league with Tsen against them. He had brought them that far towards Collegiate thought.

'I am proposing an Alliance between Vek and Tsen,' he said quietly.

'Impossible.'

'Entirely possible. Look behind me: Sarnesh and Tarkesh soldiers standing side by side.' Stenwold realized belatedly that the etching did not show the different Ant-kinden skin-tones, but he knew they would remember who had been ranged against them. 'Tseni and Tarkesh soldiers fought alongside Sarn against the Imperial Seventh at Malkan's Folly. What I am trying to tell you is that the world has changed.'

'The Tseni will never accept this,' said Termes disdainfully.

'But you would?' When the Vekken did not respond, Stenwold continued: 'If the Tseni could be brought to it, would you? I am offering to broker a truce, at least, between your cities. Collegium will then stand with a hand out to each of you. You cannot deny that Sarn has profited well from its trade with us. We offer the same to you, and you will have to trust the Tseni just as they trust you, because if either should break faith, then the aggressor will find Collegium set against it, and perhaps Sarn as well – and even the Ancient League states, and who knows what else. I know the Ant-kinden understand the value of strong walls but, these days, walls of stone are not enough. A treaty may be only paper, but a wall of paper can be stronger than stone. If Vek continues to stand alone then one day its walls will not suffice, and it will fall. It will not fall to Collegium, because we have no armies, but inevitably the day and the enemy will come, and it will fall.'

'You threaten us,' Termes challenged him. 'You use your peaceful nature as a club.' For a moment Stenwold thought he had lost it all, but then he thought over the man's words again. *Humour?* Without any clue evident in face or voice, it was impossible to tell, but it would not be the first time he had sensed a sardonic edge to this particular Vekken.

'This city has survived on its ability to make and keep its friends,' Stenwold said. 'We will act as broker between

Tsen and Vek, if not to forge a friendship, then at least an understanding. Your understanding is that the best way to be strong and safe is to vanquish your enemies, but if you make them your friends, you are stronger still.'

'You give us much to think about, Master Maker,' Termes told him. 'We accept the fact that your proposal is important, and must be considered carefully. It runs contary to our way of life, but you are correct when you say that the world has changed. Malius will travel to Vek with your words. The king shall hear them.'

'I can ask no more than that,' Stenwold confirmed. 'And for that I thank you.' *Because Collegium is about to lose a few old friends, I think, and so we are in great need of new ones – or at least of losing old enemies.* He was keenly aware of the image of Teornis beaming down on them all. His choice of room was now beginning to oppress him.

When the three Vekken had filed out, Stenwold waited a good ten minutes – his own thoughts darkening and lightening in turns – before he called, 'You can come out.'

This room had another advantage, besides its ornament, for the Moths had built it with a secret space. A wooden panel behind a hanging was pushed aside, and Kratia of Tsen stepped out. She regarded Stenwold warily.

'Well?' he asked her.

The blue-skinned Ant grimaced. 'You are a very dangerous man and I should kill you here and now.'

He raised his eyebrows. 'We're alone.'

'Are we?' She looked around. 'How am I to know that there aren't more of these little coffins hidden in the walls? You could have the entire Sarnesh army waiting to leap out on me.' Her tone was light, but deliberately so. She was shaken enough that it showed, even through her Ant reserve. 'An alliance between Vek and Tsen?'

'So the rumour goes. You and your people have shown yourselves adept at spreading rumours, but I think our citizens will find that one interesting.'

'How can you think that it will work? The Vekken—'

'The Vekken claim that you're the unreasonable ones.'

'Very clever, Master Maker.' She folded her arms. 'They will take advantage of your trade, but they will be waiting for the chance to bring another army here.'

'Oh surely,' he agreed. 'But all the time they wait, they will grow prosperous and more comfortable, they will profit from new ideas and inventions, they will send their students to the College – as spies at first, but also as scholars. Eventually their time for aggression will arrive, and if we have held them off long enough they will then ask, "Why? Why fight to take what we can be given? Why give away everything we have already gained?"'

'You think so?'

'It worked with the Sarnesh,' Stenwold declared. 'I would be the first to admit that the Vekken are a harder shell to crack than Sarn ever was, but they're not mad and they're not monsters, merely frightened. The first war with Vek came about after the Sarnesh alliance was signed. They assumed we would turn on them, because it's what they would have done. They think – forgive me but it seems that most Ant-kinden think – of survival and security in terms of eliminating threats. And so we come to you.'

'Are *we* a threat?' she asked, playing the innocent.

'If someone had asked me a few tendays ago, I'd have said no. Now you've had the chance to run around Collegium a while, yes. Commander Kratia, you are yourself a very subtle woman, capable of doing a considerable amount of damage in this city just by some well-chosen words. However, I believe that your actions spring from the same motive as the Vekken siege: you want safety for your city. But in your case, safety from Vek. I am now offering this, just as I am offering Vek safety from you.'

'Master Maker, you do not understand. Vek is three times the size of my city.'

'Then I suggest you invest in a few allies. May I suggest

the city of Vek? They're ideally placed to assist you. Or do you think all my words were for the Vekken only?' A barbed piece of deception, that, to place her where she could believe she was gaining an advantage over them, as though she and Stenwold were conspiring together, when in fact . . . 'Besides,' Stenwold added, 'Tsen may be small, but it's clear you make up for it in artifice. You may find that profits you more in trade than ever it did in self-defence. Perhaps you, also, would like to send a message to your city and its court.'

'And if they say no?'

'You disappoint me. The Vekken have already worked that one out,' Stenwold said. He felt absolutely merciless in taking all the deeply held tenets of Ant-kinden society and twisting them in his hands. 'What do you *think* will happen, if you say no but the Vekken say yes?'

The *Migrating Home*'s funnels had belched smoke for two miles of coast, but the sails of the other vessel only came nearer. Jaclen Courser had taken a good look at it through her glass: a swift and slender corsair with a magnificent spread of grey canvas, slowly but inexorably outstripping her own labouring vessel. Laszlo had watched their own ship's progress, shaking his head. The steam engine below was a charcoal-burner, and not a bad piece of artifice for something ten years old. The oil-burner aboard the *Tiden-free* would have shifted the *Home* along a good deal faster, but whilst engines gave a steady push come wave or weather, with a favouring wind a good sailing ship would always outreach them.

Jaclen had conferred with Laszlo. If they were due for this mummer's show, then they would have to give the other vessel no reason to think the *Home* was playing them false. If the pirates suspected a trap, they might put an arrow into everyone on deck before they boarded. *I will get through this game of Maker's without losing anyone from my crew* had been the thought written plainly on Jaclen's face. The pursuing ship would expect them to use all efforts to outrun it, and so she had ordered the *Home*'s own mast to be cranked into place and its sails spread. It was to little actual purpose, since the Beetle vessel scarcely made better headway and its crew were no sailors. They spent as much time steering it away from the rocks of the coast as they did trying to put distance between themselves and their hunter.

The approaching vessel was now off the aft starboard quarter, between them and the open sea, and inching its way forward still. The *Migrating Home* was being left with no option but fight, surrender, or wrack against the coast.

'She's the *Very Blade*,' Jaclen identified her, training her glass on the other ship's bows.

'Means little,' Laszlo commented. 'This end of the coast, any pirate sails under false name when they're raiding.' When she looked at him, he added, 'Or so I'm told, anyway,' a little too hastily.

'We're coming to the endgame,' Jaclen decided. 'We've made our best efforts. It's clear we'll not outrun them, and to push our luck further will invite a kicking.' Even as she said it, they saw a billow of smoke from a point near the *Blade*'s bows. A hollow knocking sound floated to them just as a spout of seawater leapt skyward between the ships.

'I make out a couple of smallshotters at the rail,' Jaclen announced. 'Little man, you go tell my crew that, when we get to where the metal meets, I want anyone tending those weapons brought down. I want no holes in *my* hull.'

Laszlo nodded and kicked off into the air, darting down the length of the *Home* while spreading the word. Jaclen sighed, feeling a knot in her stomach. *I could order the hold barred, confess all to the pirates . . . but then I've still got a hold full of Mantis trouble, and odds are the pirates'd burn my ship to be rid of it. Maker's now committed me to his cursed plan. Well, if this goes wrong, I'll have his hide as a foresail, I swear that much.*

Her own crewmembers were all nervous, but she hoped it would appear as the nerves of sailors faced by pirates. None of them sported more than a knife, but there were a surprising number of places on a ship where swords and crossbows could be hidden, to be near at hand when trouble came calling. Jaclen took a deep breath and then called out for them to drop sails. She felt the change beneath her feet as the *Home* lost the wind by degrees. The *Very Blade* was angling in towards them, trimming its sails with exquisite precision, ready to coast alongside.

The previous incidents of piracy that Jaclen had experienced had not been devoid of bloodshed, but the raiders tended to spare anyone who had surrendered and just pillage the hold. She knew the logic. A pirate crew did not want to have to fight to the death over every cargo, so they made sure that their prey knew the drill: either fight and die, or cast down your weapons and live. No guarantees, of course, for there had been murders, rapes, mutilations. If the pirates had been experiencing a few bad days, or if they had been forced to chase for a little too long, then they might decide to take it out on the crew. *It's not as though there are any guarantees.* It was the thought of those crewmates she had lost, especially in more recent attacks, that steeled her now to the thought of what was about to happen.

She had a good look at the *Very Blade*'s crew as the pirate ship came in closer, seeing that they were a mongrel bunch. Almost a dozen were Ant-kinden, bronze-skinned Kessen, either rogue or mercenaries. They wore light ring-mail vests and steel helms, and many of them held crossbows levelled at the *Home*'s decks; one even had a new-fangled snapbow, stolen from who knew where. The rest of the crew, a good three dozen men and women, were a ragbag of Spiders, Fly-kinden, halfbreeds and a couple of hulking Scorpions. There was little armour but much ornament, men and women carrying their wealth on their person. Each one was armed to his or her own taste: rapiers, knives, shortswords, hooked pikes and boarding axes.

Laszlo had ended up by the helm, where his own bow was tucked. To his experienced eye, their attackers looked like any other pack of masterless sea-thieves. *So was Albinus right or wrong?* If it was the Aldanraels, then whether Stenwold got his proof depended on how long a leash the Spiders kept their pets on. Laszlo knew pirates, though, and that breed did not work well for anyone. Given usual practice back off the Spiderlands coast, it seemed likely that some servant of the Aristoi would be on board the *Blade* to ensure that its crew remembered whose ships were to be counted fair game.

'Now you all stay stood, and nobody get any fool's ideas!' the Ant with the snapbow bellowed in a parade-ground voice that reached them with breath to spare. A moment later the bows of the *Blade* ground teeth-jarringly along the *Home*'s side, making the best part of both crews stagger, and then the ropes came out. Whilst the Kessen crossbows did not waver, a dozen pirate sailors secured the vessels one to the other. *You might come to regret all those knots in a moment*, Laszlo considered. He kept his breathing easy, leaning on the rail and looking relaxed. The Beetle helmsman beside him kept clenching and unclenching his fists. He had a crossbow of his own hidden in a locker at their feet, and Laszlo just hoped he would let matters take their course before he tried to snatch it up.

'I thank you for your cargo, kind Beetles,' the Kessen boomed at them. 'Give my regards to the College folks, now.' His crew bunched at the rail and then began to jump aboard, heading for the aftmost of the *Home*'s two hatches. Stenwold had asked, when they were concocting this plan, why the pirates didn't often take possession of the actual ships along with the freight. It had been for Tomasso to point out to him that the pirates would be sailors all, and not engineers. Odds were that none of them would fancy trying to tow or manhandle a big steam ship like the *Home* into some distant safe port, without either sinking her or running her aground.

A motley bunch of Spiders, Ants and half-breeds had strutted over to the hatch. Laszlo risked a look at the four crossbowmen left behind at the *Blade*'s rail, noting that they had lowered their weapons slightly, seeing nothing evident in the *Home*'s crew to give them concern. The three-foot iron barrels of the smallshotters were still mounted near the pirate's bows, but the Beetle-kinden woman and the half-breed youth, who were apparently the *Blade*'s artillerists, were paying little attention to their charges.

The lead pirate levered the hatch up, and Laszlo was close enough to hear him say, 'Now let's see what—'

He saw what soon enough – saw it coming straight at him. Danaen's vanguard came straight out of the hold into the pirates' faces: a half-dozen Mantis-kinden in a flurry of wings and blades, Danaen herself at their fore. Laszlo saw one Mantis man take a crossbow bolt clean through the shoulder in that first instant, the shock of it knocking him sprawling on to the deck beyond. By that time four pirates were dead and the others at the hatch had turned to make an escape they would never complete. Everyone was shouting and reaching for their weapons.

*Just like old times*, Laszlo thought. He had his bow in hand, an arrow already nocked. In his mind he recalled the *Tidenfree* latched on to some Spider merchantman, where the crew had decided to make a fight of it. The *Tidenfree* Fly-kinden would be shooting down from the rigging, whilst whoever they had paid as marines would be swarming the decks: Scorpions or Ants or some band of Spider brigands. He was grinning like a madman as he loosed his first shaft.

The Beetle-kinden artillerist was dead, picked off by one of the *Home*'s better shots. The halfbreed youth swung his piece towards the swirling chaos of the Beetle ship's decks.

More and more Mantids were flying and climbing out from the hold, whilst Danaen and her firstcomers were already sprinting for the rail. Laszlo had an impression of the pirates trying to recover from the shock. Some were shouting one order, some another. The Kessen with the snapbow bellowed for all hands. Laszlo tried to sight on him but the man was too far away. He settled for putting an arrow into one of the enemy's crossbowmen, lancing the man in the side. As the Beetle helmsman beside him finally got his own weapon loaded, Laszlo took off for the spars above, nocking another arrow as he flew.

The pirates' great chance would have been to pen Danaen's people aboard the *Home*. Mantids were no great fliers, and if the fight could have been held at the railing, then they might have won through by attrition. When the Mantis-kinden struck, though, leaping over the rails in a glitter of wings and howling for blood, the crew of the *Blade* gave way in terror. There were enough jokes about the Mantids to be heard in any sailor's taverna: how they were backward, they were gullible, they were crippled by their oaths and honour. Even then, the laughter had a slightly nervous ring to it, and if a handful of Mantis reavers walked in, their jokes would freeze into silence.

*Curse me, but they're fast*, Laszlo had to admit, but it was not all Danaen's way. By the time she had her feet on the *Blade*'s deck, half a dozen of her followers were already dead or badly injured, but the Mantids just didn't stop. The wounded were left to fend for themselves, and they took no prisoners, heard no cries for mercy. Laszlo just watched them for a moment: he saw Danaen herself duel briefly with a Spider-kinden, twin blades to twin blades, a spinning dance of steel on both sides that would have won prizes at the Collegium games, but here was played for higher stakes and prizes. She broke off from that to kill an Ant-kinden who had tried to stab her from behind, spinning to lance his throat over the rim of his round shield, and then turning back as the Spider lunged at her. She caught both his blades on one of hers and ran him through an eye. Another Mantis, a golden-haired youth, had left his spear rammed through the chest of a Kessen crossbowman: now he fought only with the spines of his forearms, but he was tearing open armour with them and parrying swords. A handful of Danaen's people were now in the rigging with Laszlo, standing with shifting balance and no handholds, bending bows that were as tall as they themselves were to let their long arrows fall on the foe.

Laszlo found the loud Kessen again. The man had his snapbow to his shoulder, sighting carefully. A moment later he was reloading, although Laszlo had no idea what he had shot. He looked satisfied enough with himself. *Still too far for a sure shot, so time for a little heroics.* He took flight again, letting his wings cast him over the *Blade*'s decks.

That was a mistake, he discovered shortly enough. An arrow slashed past him, and he returned the compliment, grazing the shoulder of a Spider-kinden archer up in the pirate's own ropes. He darted about the other side of the mast, snatching another shaft from his quiver, seeking out the Ant with the big voice. That same voice was being put to powerful use as the man roared for his crew to form a fighting line and pen the Mantis-kinden against the railings. *Good plan, at that.* Laszlo swung about, another missile darting wide of him, and spotted his target.

The Kessen saw him as he came in. He had been sighting along his weapon's long barrel, but now he dragged it upwards. Laszlo gave his wings their freedom, doubling pace as he sped past the man at a distance of barely a dozen feet. The other man loosed first, but the sudden burst of speed had thrown his aim, the little bolt hurtling off to oblivion. Abruptly, Laszlo turned, flying backwards, fingers releasing the bowstring as he did so. He was rewarded by the sight of the Kessen's head snapping back, the arrow almost clipping the rim of his helm before it drove in. Then another three shafts dotted the sky about Laszlo and he fled for the relative security of the *Home*'s mast.

It was a fragile refuge. He heard a concussive sound and the rigging around him was trembling like saplings in a storm. The pirates' other smallshotter had loosed a round at the *Home*'s mainmast and, although missing, it had severed one of the stays. Thankfully the Beetles built things to last, and there were enough ropes to take the strain. Laszlo swung around the mast, letting his wings carry him back towards the *Blade* whilst his hands placed another arrow at the ready. By then the pirate artillerist had been shot down by Jaclen Courser herself, and the Mantis-kinden reavers were busy spitting any enemy who still held a blade. They were spitting a good few that weren't, too, and Laszlo didn't like that – if only for reasons of personal precedent. 'Take prisoners!' he shouted, nipping overhead. 'Leave them be if they surrender, curse it!'

Danaen glared up at him, clearly not familiar with the custom.

'We'll want to question them!' Laszlo called down to her.

'What's the point?' she demanded. 'What will they know?'

'If we don't question them, we'll never find out.' He dropped almost to her level, but still far enough, he reckoned, to get himself out of the way of her blades. 'Stenwold would want it that way,' he added, hoping that they held that degree of loyalty to their ostensible employer.

She scowled at him again but, at a gesture from her, the few surviving pirates were soon left, kneeling and unarmed, but alive. At that point the doors to the rear cabins were thrown open. The *Very Blade* had a high rearcastle to it, but nobody had issued from it during the fight, so Laszlo had assumed it was deserted. Now four more pirates, Spiders all, dashed out with drawn rapier, not on the attack but ready to defend themselves. In their wake came . . .

Laszlo let out a sharp breath at the sight of her. She was tall and elegant, immaculately dressed in a neatly tailored hauberk of hide, chitin and silk armour. Her shirt and breeches were of striking red, and there were rings aplenty on her hands. The Spider-kinden master of the vessel, surely, and she stared around at the mob of Mantids, not even deigning to draw her rapier.

'What is this?' Her voice cut clear and crisp through the confusion, and everyone fell silent for it. Danaen snarled and moved in on her, blades extended in a fighter's crouch. The Spider woman eyed her disdainfully. 'What is this rabble that comes to infest my ship?' she demanded. 'How *dare* you?'

Laszlo could sense her Art radiating off her in waves, blazing away at all around her: command, dread and the crushing hammer of her authority. He saw Danaen's advance falter, the Mantis hunching behind her swords as though warding off a physical blow. Laszlo had never before witnessed a bona fide Spider-kinden Arista unleashing all of her Art and will.

'Leave this ship while you still can,' the Spider snapped and, incredibly, Danaen took a backwards step. Laszlo felt any words freeze in his throat. This single woman was facing down the entire Mantis boarding party.

Or not the entire party.

She began, 'If you—' and then pitched backwards so fast that only later did Laszlo register the long-shafted arrow that had struck her. Danaen gave a yell of fury and launched into the dead woman's bodyguards, her own people following right on her heels.

That was the end of it. Laszlo had some of Jaclen's crew secure the few survivors aboard the *Migrating Home*, whilst Danaen's people continued scouring the *Blade* belowdecks for any other latecomers. They obviously considered it a great victory, but Laszlo had long noted that Mantis-kinden seemed to take no great joy from these events once the killing was done. They would sing and drink, he knew, but mostly to commemorate their own fallen. The kinden had made melancholy into a national pastime, and he found them incomprehensible. The Mantids had left the Spider-kinden dead out on the *Blade*'s decks, apparently as a sign of disrespect. The other fallen, whether their own or the balance of the pirate crew, they pitched into the sea for the crabs and fish to eat their fill of, after stripping them of anything worth taking. By the time Laszlo began his own search of the vessel, the Mantids were standing about, looking grim and private, as though resentful that there had not been more of a fight.

He entered into the aft cabins, where the Arista had emerged from, and it was not hard to identify which was hers. She had not stinted on her finery, even on this rough vessel, for the walls were draped in coloured silks, and there was a padded couch and a writing desk. He rooted around for a short space of time, collecting some coins and a fistful of papers. There were several documents strewn about, and the scroll tacked out onto the desk was evidently a work half-finished, but none of it revealed a comprehensible word. Each page bore a complex, coloured pattern of interlocking shapes, as though the Spider captain had been engaged in some peculiarly styled abstract art.

Laszlo nodded glumly. This was Spider code, he knew from experience, and impenetrable unless one knew the secret of it. Because, as a kinden, they were their own worst enemies and fiercest rivals, Spiders usually went to extremes of complexity in disguising their secrets. Why, they said that Spider-kinden pattern encryptions were so fiendish that even they themselves struggled with it . . .

He paused, frowning at the incomplete missive spread out on the desk. He was no spy, but he imagined that one would have to be extremely skilled just to compose something like that in one's head. Of course, Spiders as a whole were a subtle lot, but the woman who had ventured forth from this cabin had seemed more forthright than most . . .

And there it was. His heart leapt with glee when he noticed it. There was a little scrap of parchment pinned alongside the coded message she had been working on, and there, in absently elegant handwriting, was the original: the words that she had been painstakingly encoding, to be destroyed, in some never-to-come future, after she was done.

*My dearest Aderonis*, Laszlo read, *I am conceiving a loathing for this business. I would rather stay with you and let these villains have their way but, without my reminding them of the family's direct authority, who knows what they would do? Not what was demanded of them, certainly. Bide well, then, and know that I do think of you, despite the water that lies between us. It will take more than tides and hard weather to keep me away from you.*

He stopped reading. It had, indeed, taken more than that, but a boatload of Mantis raiders could put a hole through anybody's plans. He wondered who Aderonis was, and what he would think when no word came, and then when word finally did come. *The family's direct authority*, he thought unhappily. No mistaking the meaning of that. *You did it, Master Maker*, he considered. *You put one over on the Spider-kinden. I just hope you feel happy with yourself after they find out you killed one of their Aristoi.* Killing a tattered renegade like Ebris of the Ganbrodiel would raise no great waves, but a female of the family Aldanrael . . . *Could I have stopped the Mantis-kinden?* He had not even known that a bow was being drawn on the woman until after the arrow had hit its mark.

*I think the war has just started.*

He stowed the papers inside his jerkin and flitted back out for the decks. Jaclen could continue to Everis, but Laszlo and Danaen's people would be steering the *Very Blade* back towards Collegium, because Stenwold Maker needed to hear of this as soon as possible.

# Thirteen

The name hung in the air after Stenwold had spoken it: *Aldanrael. A* name grown familiar to the folk of Collegium, a name that spoke of friendship and rescue in dark days. He did not rush the silence but looked from face to face, those few there with him in his study: Jodry Drillen, of course, who was looking as though he had just been stabbed; brooding, bearded Tomasso, keeping his peace before the Speaker; Laszlo and the Mantis, Danaen, as witnesses; the reliably solid figure of Elder Padstock, Chief Officer of the Maker's Own company; and Arianna.

She stood behind his chair, her hands on his shoulders. Those hands had twitched as he named the Spider house, and he had merely thought, *She understands what this means, crossing swords with the Aristoi.*

'Can . . . can you be sure, though?' Jodry managed at last. 'Towards the Spiderlands, things are seldom clear, they say . . . don't they?'

'Things have been well concealed from us for over a year, if Failwright's notes are to be believed,' Stenwold replied. 'We have accomplished that rarest of achievements: we have stolen a march over the Spider-kinden. They did not know we were warned of them until Danaen's people hacked down their hirelings. There was a Spider-kinden master of the ship that Danaen sailed into harbour, and she left papers.' Stenwold gave a half-smile. 'The Aldanrael is named.'

'Stenwold,' Jodry almost whispered. 'Stenwold, we can't
. . . you know what this means. There must be another
way. You are bringing us to war.'

'*No!*' Stenwold snapped. 'That's exactly the rumour that
Teornis will stir up. That is the muttering that people like
Helmess Broiler will raise, who bear neither of us any fond
feelings. They will say, "There goes old Maker, desperate
for another war so he can play soldier again." I did not
bring us to this, Jodry. I have uncovered a plot, a hidden
war against our city.'

'Then what are you proposing?' Jodry demanded.

'We confront them. We expose what we have discovered, and call their bluff. I'd hope they'd back down,
blame everything on someone else, and give up whatever
scheme it is that they're about. Either that or we'll exchange
the Aldanrael for some other house less interested in our
shipping. You know how the Aristoi families feud. Believe
me, Jodry, I did not go looking for a war with the
Spiderlands.'

Jodry glanced over Stenwold's shoulder. 'My dear, what
say you? You can perhaps know the mind of your people
better than we.'

Arianna looked down at Stenwold's bald head, and then
across at fat Jodry. 'I do not think the Aldanrael, or the
Spiderlands, will simply walk away,' she told him sadly.
'You've killed one of their own.'

'Can we deal with this quietly?' Jodry asked. 'Perhaps
we can just get Teornis in a room and talk him round.'
Stenwold could not see Arianna's expression, but from
Jodry's reaction he guessed that it was not encouraging.

'I'm not sure Teornis and the Aldanrael will let this be
settled quietly,' he murmured.

'But they're *Spiders*. I thought they liked all that hole-
and-corner stuff,' Jodry complained.

Stenwold sighed. 'Teornis knows we don't want another
war, not so swiftly on the heels of the last. He will hope

that we sue for peace, submit to whatever terms he demands, rather than fight. And meanwhile the Empire's building up forces near Myna. It wouldn't take much distraction on our part to see the Empress acquire a few more provinces while our back's turned. Teornis knows all this.'

'There will be panic, uproar. We'll throw the whole Assembly into a horror, statesmen and merchants and scholars all,' Jodry said direly.

'But, more than that,' Stenwold stated, 'our people have been robbed, some have been killed. Master Rones Failwright, a member of our Assembly, has vanished, and it seems plain that the Spiders did away with him once his voice grew too loud. I don't think we can hide this, but also I'm not sure that we should. I don't think the Spiders want a war either, and a show of defiance now may forestall all of that. Collegium must be *strong*, and we may just face down Spiderlands and Empire both.'

'If you go begging to them,' Danaen agreed, 'they will give you only knives. They will cut you and cut you, and make you ask them to cut you again. Spiders must be met with sword in hand. There is no other way.'

'Thank you for that.' Jodry grimaced. 'I'd accuse you, Stenwold Maker, of being a man who refuses to take the easy way out of anything. However, in this case, I'm not sure there's an easy way. I wish you weren't right quite so often, is all. You're prepared to handle this at the Assembly?'

'When have I ever shied from bringing unwanted truths before the Assembly?' Stenwold reproached him.

'Then I'll call you, tomorrow, first thing.'

Stenwold nodded and took a deep breath. 'Chief Officer Padstock.'

'Yes, War Master.' The woman looked as though she had been waiting for this moment all her life.

'Tomorrow I would like you to assemble your company

before the Amphiophos. Take no action unless ordered to, or unless violence is offered you, but I want a reminder that Collegium is more than books and words and coin to be taken.'

'It will be my pleasure, War Master,' she said, and only then did he realize that she had used the title a moment before.

*Well, perhaps it is time to don that robe once again,* he thought, without joy.

One by one they filed out until, after they had gone, it was just Arianna left there in Stenwold's study with him. He was fretting with his papers and she knew, from that old habit, that he had more to say.

*Did Teornis know this was coming?* she asked herself. *Did he broach me because of this?* She guessed not, or he would have detailed some more active work for her already, given her some specific instructions. *But he knew that he would lock horns with Stenwold, sooner or later.* A saying of her people, of her family, returned to her. *You cannot stop how fast the world turns.* The world had ground her family into pieces. Now she herself would have to stay one step ahead of it.

Stenwold was regarding her with a slight smile on her face. 'I know,' he said.

Her heart stuttered. *He knows?* 'Sten?' she asked, her voice smooth and easy. There was an art that all Spiders learned, to keep a gap between the mind and face so that no shock to one caused ripples on the other.

'This situation, I know it's not like going up against the Empire, sword against sword. I know Spiders are a different game entirely.'

*Oh, if only you really did, though.* He was proffering her a tiny scroll, a curl of paper barely the size of her little finger. She took it numbly, opened it to find a single line of elaborate script. 'Welcome to the Dance,' she read. She had no doubt that it was in Teornis's own hand. Anything else would have been bad form.

'It came to me via the very messenger I sent to fetch Jodry,' Stenwold explained.

'You know what this means?' she pressed. She felt a clutch of tension inside her, but she did not know whether it was for Stenwold's future or her own.

'I know that "the Dance" is what they call politics, amongst the Spider-kinden, so I suppose Teornis is just telling me that he knows what I've done. His people must have recognized the *Very Blade* as soon as Laszlo brought her into harbour.'

'Oh Sten . . .' she sighed. 'You do not understand what he means, not at all.' *Which could cost you your life.*

He frowned at her. 'What, then?'

'Oh, it's high praise of a sort,' she said sadly. 'He means that, by uncovering this you have proved yourself a peer in his eyes. He considers you a worthy opponent. It means that he will make no allowances for your kinden. You are a Spider to him, and he will not spare you, nor expect you to spare him.'

'Ah.' Stenwold looked at his hands. 'Well, that seems plain. Should I be expecting the assassin's knife, then? Should I start preparing my own food?'

'Oh, that would be poor form,' Arianna explained. 'Inelegant. To commission the death of your chief enemy is an admission of defeat – or next to it. Spider-kinden do not simply have their dance-partners killed: they destroy them, piece by piece, until death would seem a mercy. I do not think Teornis will seek to have you killed unless you leave him no other choice by backing him into a corner. Your friends and allies are under no such protection, though. It is a long-standing tradition to attack someone through their household. Take Jodry, for example.'

'Jodry?' Stenwold shook his head. 'Jodry's the Speaker for the Assembly, after all. I can't see Teornis causing that much trouble just to get to me. In fact, it's more likely he'll kill me to inconvenience Jodry, surely.'

'No, Stenwold, no,' Arianna insisted. 'What does Teornis care about Beetle ranks and titles? What makes the true adversary is skill, not . . . public office. You are his enemy. You are the man he will dance with. For the rest – Jodry, your Fly-kinden, the Mantis and her crew, that militia-woman – fair game, Stenwold, all of them.'

'And you?' Stenwold pressed.

'Oh, who knows what Teornis would do with me,' she said, looking straight into his face and thinking, *I am telling you, Stenwold. Listen when I tell you. Understand me!* But he did not understand her. There was only concern in his expression.

'I should have you leave the city,' he started, and raised a hand to cut off her immediate objection. 'And I know that would solve nothing. Distance is no shield. Instead I must make use of you. Your help here will be the difference between life and death, it seems.'

*Oh, very likely.* 'What do you want from this, Stenwold? What will you count as a victory?'

'Keeping Collegium safe,' he replied immediately. 'I do not know what the Aldanrael think to gain from this piracy – they would not risk so much just for plunder. Whatever it is, though, they must walk away from it. My people will be nobody's prey.'

'And if Teornis offers a compromise?'

'If he does, is it likely to be sincere? Or merely a trap?'

She shrugged. *And I cannot answer that. I cannot see what Teornis seeks either.* 'It may be. But, even so, if he does?'

'Will I treat with him, you mean? I would be a fool not to listen to what he might have to say, but I will not simply bare my city's back for the rod. Men have died. Ships have been lost. If we offer some meek submission, then we simply invite worse.'

*And that is true also*, she thought. 'Think carefully on what you will tell the Assembly,' she warned him.

'I know. Words said openly cannot then be unsaid.' He rubbed at his face.

*And am I advising him now for himself, or for Teornis?* she asked herself. *What can I say that is not a betrayal of one man or the other?* 'If you give him no other alternative, he will fight,' she said. 'I know the Mantis say we are cowards, my kinden, but that is not true. It is just that direct violence is considered the last and ugliest way of solving any problem. We will take up the sword, if no other choice is left to us, but if you leave him an escape, he may take it. Public face is very important to us. When you make your speech, at least allow him some graceful way to step away. You never know, if the Aldanrael's plans are still young, they may prefer to abandon them rather than risk a confrontation. Teornis himself may jump at a chance to wash his hands of the matter.'

'I understand.' Stenwold nodded soberly. 'I will choose my words carefully.'

She left him at his desk, staring at a blank parchment.

Downstairs, she had Cardless prepare her a tisane, while she took stock of her options. *Tell Stenwold* was one of them, but the time for telling him had now come and gone. She should have mentioned it as soon as they were alone together. She should have mentioned it as soon as he returned from his voyage on the *Tidenfree*. Every moment that passed took her further away from the moment when confession would bring her absolution rather than blame.

*Can I just walk away and vanish?* She knew she could not. She could betray Stenwold, but never abandon him. She could not stand apart, and know that he was facing this fight, and not know what would become of him. *If I am by his side, whoever's side I am on, then there may come the moment when some act from me can . . . Can what? Save or destroy him, which?* Teornis would not let her run, either. He would judge her more harshly for taking flight than he would for remaining loyal to Stenwold, although he would not hesitate to be rid of her in either case. Even as Stenwold's ally, she was valuable to Teornis as a means of applying pressure, while as a runaway she would be despised and worthless – fit only to be hunted down like an animal so that her incriminating knowledge could be capped.

*And if I go to Teornis now?* It was worse than that, of course. If she did *not* go to Teornis now, he would want to know why. His note to Stenwold showed he was well aware that swords were being drawn. He would not believe her if she pleaded ignorance, and she was not sure she could lie to him convincingly in any case. *Every minute I stay away invites him to conclude that I've betrayed him.*

*Stenwold. Teornis.* The big, lumbering Beetle with the sharp mind, or the elegant, laughing Spider. *Stenwold, who roused the whole city against the Wasps. Teornis, who held the entire Fourth Army with just two hundred men and some clever words. Stenwold, who kept the Vekken at arm's length for days. Teornis, whose relief force drove them off.*

*Stenwold, who gave himself to the Empire to save me from the crossed pikes.*

*Teornis, who will make me one of his family.*

She felt her selfishness stir, at last. Who was she to sit in judgement on either the War Master of Collegium or an Aristos of the Aldanrael? She was just Arianna, Spider orphan of a failed family, also Rekef deserter, exile from her old home and parasite on her new one. What were honourable causes and noble sentiments to her? She had joined the Rekef readily enough when it suited her, and abandoned it just as swiftly. She had then taken up with Stenwold . . . well, Stenwold was the Big Man in Collegium in those days. Now her association with him had surely taken her as far as it could go. She might be the toast of the city, but this was a Beetle city and, however much they tried to mimic the glories of the Spiderlands, they would never seem more than clowns in borrowed clothing.

Teornis would make her one of the Aristoi. She would be part of the Dance. She would be wealthy, and have slaves and riches and all good things. More, the Dance never stopped and she would never be *bored*. Beetles might strive for a comfortable life. Spider-kinden strove only to *live*.

She slipped out of the house. If Stenwold had any sense, he might begin to suspect. She knew that he would not, though. He was a spymaster, and there were few of his agents that he held in total trust, but she was his agent no longer. She had stepped in too close, and he would no more suspect her of betrayal than he would have suspected Cheerwell his niece.

'I've been expecting you.'

One of Teornis's people had led her to a townhouse overlooking the harbour, which still bore some blackening from the Vekken incendiaries. From without, it was just another two-storey Beetle tenement, squat and flat-roofed. Inside it had been draped with silks in the Spider style, and she found Teornis upstairs, stretched out on a couch. A Fly servant offered her wine as she came in, and she took it but did not drink.

'You knew it would come to this when you first approached me,' she accused him.

'Time spent stating the obvious is time wasted,' he reproached her. One hand indicated the couch opposite from him, and she sat there stiffly. 'If you think I've misled you, then go back to your Beetle lover.' He was smiling, and there was nothing harsh in his voice, but his words cut her nonetheless.

'What is going on?' she demanded. 'Collegium's shipping? Why so much trouble over so little?'

'Oh, it's not gentlemanly to bore a great lady with one's plans.' Teornis sipped his wine, watching her carefully. 'One presents the finished work, or not at all. So . . . ?'

'Stenwold will speak before the Assembly tomorrow.'

Teornis steepled his fingers.

'Raising the stakes on his very first move, very bold,' Teornis noted. 'Who is in his cadre?'

The word was used by Spiders for an Aristoi's closest agents and followers. 'Jodry Drillen,' Arianna recited, knowing that she might be signing death warrants even as she spoke the names. 'Some militia officer called Padstock. A crew of Fly-kinden mariners led by a man called Tomasso. And Danaen, who leads the Mantis reavers that took the *Very Blade.*'

'Mantis-kinden,' said Teornis disgustedly. 'You'd think they'd be grateful that I allowed them the glory of destroying the Fourth. Well, I've dealt with them before, and I can deal with them again. Speaking of dealings, how is our Beetle manipulus? Front or back foot?' Meaning, on the attack or preparing a defence.

'Standing firm,' she told him. 'But he will talk, if you will. I hope I have persuaded him not to make any direct accusations tomorrow, therefore to hold open the chance that some . . . agreement can be reached.' She stopped because he was giving her a sharp-edged smile.

'It is a noble and respected tradition to play two sides off against each other, and thus to pull their strings,' Teornis remarked, very pleasantly. 'However, you are not so skilled as to be able to play both myself and Maker for fools, girl. Content yourself with taking my instructions, and you will prosper. Try to turn this into your own dance, and I cannot vouch for your future.'

She began to say something, but the words would not come out.

He nodded slowly. 'My dear Arianna, do not think that I do not understand sentiment. I am fond of Maker myself.

I do not want to rid the world of him, for we will need him, like as not, when the Empire stirs again. Still, we must make him tractable, and he must learn that drawing a sword on the Aldanrael is not to be advised.' He put down his goblet on a tray that his servant proffered. The metallic clack of it seemed very loud. 'My cousin Elleria had command of the *Blade*, and Maker's people killed her,' Teornis said flatly. 'The family will want blood for that. I cannot simply throw up my hands and abandon the plan. Whatever *agreement* is reached, however it may look to the dull Beetles and their Assembly, it will be a victory for us. If Maker will give way, then all the better, and we can then work out some mummery to make him look strong and us blameless. If Maker will be stubborn . . . Aristoi blood has been shed, so we *cannot* back down.'

Abruptly he sighed, and Arianna had a brief window onto a genuine unhappiness. 'Far be it from me to criticize the women of my family,' he continued, 'but Elleria was a fool. Why else would they have placed her in such a demeaning role? And even that she got wrong, and then she got herself killed. If there was any justice in the world, then she'd be denounced as a rogue element, and we'd all be friends again. However, she *is* family, and Maker's agents killed her. I have sent to Everis to raise a fleet, a proper armada that will make the force that broke the Vekken siege look like a scouting party.' His face was all brittle brightness and good humour again, in contrast to her aghast expression. 'It will be up to us, my dear, to bring Maker to his knees in submission before that becomes necessary, however. Do not fret: outfitting an armada takes time. We have a few months, I would guess, before their sails are seen.'

There was an expectant hush as Stenwold took the podium, called to speak without warning, unscheduled and before any other petitioners. *Has word got out?* he wondered. It was not impossible that Jodry had failed to keep the matter to himself. Looking at the Assemblers, though, he guessed not. It was simply that an old instinct had been reawakened amongst them. They were used to this: Stenwold Maker had been away from the city; Stenwold Maker had returned; Stenwold Maker would now come before the Assembly full of dire warnings. He had conditioned them to it, over the last ten years and more.

*Only now perhaps they'll believe me*, he considered, and the thought gave him a strange feeling of anxiety. *Did I think I was safe, back then: was I secretly glad that, no matter what I said, nobody would pay any heed? Now that my words have consequences, I must be careful what I say.*

His gaze caught that of Teornis. The Spider-kinden was here by right, as an ambassador, but he seldom bothered to exercise that right unless he knew that something of importance would be said. He nodded coolly to Stenwold. *We know*, his look seemed to say. *You and I, only we two know fully what we are about here.*

Stenwold had spent a long time countering the machinations of the Empire. The Wasps were almost like old friends now, for he knew them and their ways. The Aldanrael, however, were unknowable and subtle. For all Arianna's assurances, he had not discounted a direct attempt on his life. He wore his sword, and a tunic of hide and steel plates beneath his robes.

'My fellows of the Assembly, Masters and Magnates of the city of Collegium,' he addressed them, 'as you hear my voice, I would ask you to consider another voice that has been strangely silent of late. The man I refer to was not shy of disturbing our councils here with his worries, and yet where is he now? I speak of Rones Failwright. Who of you here has asked himself where that man has gone? Not one of you?'

He allowed them the pause, then took up again before they could start discussing with their neighbours.

'Perhaps you are simply glad that the old ship-handler is no longer nagging us all about his lost profits?' An undercurrent of mirth, and Stenwold frowned at them thunderously, for all he had engineered it himself. 'Master Failwright has disappeared. He has not been seen for near three tendays now. I believe he is dead. I believe he was murdered.'

That quietened them, and Stenwold took a deep breath. Now that he was under way he did not so much as glance at Teornis of the Aldanrael.

'Should I not take this to the militia, you ask? Is this a matter on which to try the patience of the Collegiate Assembly? Well, Masters and Magnates, I have undertaken my own investigation into the issues that Master Failwright would so often raise before us. Why kill such a man, unless he had uncovered a truth amidst all his complaints? You will recall his grievance, of course: he claimed that the shipping of Collegium was under attack, that there was some force or pattern behind the loss and pillage of ships, something more than mere chance and independent brigandage could account for.'

They were shuffling a little, shifting on their stone seats, wondering where he was going with this. Only a handful of merchants still actively involved with the sea-trade were listening attentively.

'I took the liberty of conducting an experiment, as a good College Master should,' Stenwold told them all. 'I had, stashed aboard a trader bound for Everis, a hidden cargo of swords, just to see what might befall.' He had them again, with that revelation. 'As it happened, there was a pirate vessel out there that took an interest in my cargo. A vessel going by the name of the *Very Blade* overhauled our ship and tried to board her. Our crew and our marines threw them back and took their ship. It lies in the harbour even now.'

There was a cheer at that, which surprised him. Perhaps

they thought that was all: old Maker playing War Master on the waves for his own amusement, striking a few little blows for Collegium against the lawless. He raised a hand to hush them.

'There was evidence aboard the vessel to suggest that Master Failwright was correct in his beliefs,' he told them. 'There was a hidden hand behind the actions of this pirate ship – and who knows how many others?'

He had his silence, at last. It was a rare thing in the Amphiophos, that stillness.

'What documents were recovered suggests an involvement from the Spiderlands, and I am sad to say that the family Aldanrael is named.'

It was like dropping a stone on to clear water: the moment's graceful fall, and then chaos. Fully half the Assemblers there were trying to say something: to each other, to him, to the chamber as a whole. Many were horrified, protesting that he could not possibly be right, for the Aldanrael had proved themselves firm friends of Collegium. *I can only agree. I cannot see why they would do it, but here we are, nonetheless.* Others, especially the shipping men, were calling down shame on the heads of all Spider-kinden, demanding justice and reparation.

Stenwold's eyes sought out the Imperial ambassador: Aagen was expressionless, but behind him there was a curious look on Honory Bellowern's honest face – a man given an unlooked-for gift of incalculable value.

Jodry stepped in just then, selecting someone at random from the crowd simply to shut the others up. Stenwold saw a solid, greying woman he could not put a name to rising to her feet.

'This is preposterous!' she snapped. 'The Spiderlands? What gain is in this for them? Since the siege, we've been getting along famously with them, so why would they start robbing us?' There was a fair amount of support for her, and yet a lot of muttering, too. *Because they're Spiders and you can't trust them,* seemed to be the meat of it.

Jodry singled out another, but his finger drifted too close to Helmess Broiler, and his old adversary stole the moment, standing and holding his arms up for quiet. He had enough supporters still that he got it, or at least a semblance of it. 'My fellows!' he called out, and Stenwold braced himself for more opposition. What Helmess said instead, though, was, 'We should not dismiss this just because we laughed at Failwright.' This was sufficiently surprising that the rest of the Assembly started listening. Helmess looked left and right, his gaze stern. Stenwold had to admit that the man had a fine debating manner, crammed with authority.

'We will see Maker's evidence, of course. Master Maker and I are old friends in this chamber. We have crossed swords often and, although the admission must be wrung from me with pliers, he is a man who always has the city's interest at heart, whether his suspicions are true or false.' He smiled slightly, just for Stenwold's benefit. 'Surely it is time that we turned to the accused, Master Speaker. What do the Spiders say?'

*What is he after?* Finding himself apparently on the same side as Helmess Broiler made Stenwold feel very uncomfortable indeed, and Jodry was obviously thinking the same thing. Nevertheless the Speaker nodded and waved towards Teornis. 'What say the Aldranrael?'

The Spider Aristos stood up smoothly, utterly untroubled. 'These are grave words, Master Speaker. By all means, let us examine Master Maker's papers, for I cannot think he would raise such a storm over nothing. Perhaps one of my family's rivals seeks to drive a wedge between us. Our mutually profitable friendship has drawn envy in many quarters, I am sure. Perhaps it is some enemy of yours that seeks to plant the seed of conflict. Perhaps my own family has kept some plan from me.' He spread his hands, seeming the soul of reason. 'I place myself at the Assembly's disposal, so that we may divine the truth in all of this.' Teornis now looked Stenwold directly in the eye. 'I'm sure that we would all prefer to explore every possibility before we commit ourselves to something unwise.'

# Fourteen

'I have had word from Everis,' Stenwold informed his co-conspirators. They were all in his study again: Arianna, Jodry, Danaen, Laszlo and Tomasso. Cardless had just poured the wine and absented himself.

'Not encouraging word, I take it,' Tomasso put in.

'Well, I know at least that the *Migrating Home* was able to dock, unload and leave unmolested, which I suspect is part of how this Spider "good form" business works. However, my eyes in Everis say that a fleet is being assembled: warships, supply ships, troop carriers. A fleet in its infancy, as yet, but there are a lot of new sails along the Silk Road coast, and Everis is where they're all bound.'

'An armada, they'll be calling it,' Tomasso supplied.

Stenwold nodded. 'That they do. There's precedent, then, for this?'

'Oh, it's a rare honour,' the bearded Fly replied. 'A whole load of Spiders have to be facing in the same direction at the same time to get an armada together, and none of them putting knives in the backs of the others, either. You've fired up the Aldanrael, Stenwold, and sounds like they're putting most of what they've got into this one. Normally it takes a rebellious satrapy to kick up this kind of response. Of course, we know what hasn't helped.'

'The Arista on the *Blade*,' Stenwold agreed.

'Someone's favourite daughter, no doubt,' Tomasso concluded glumly.

'She deserved her death,' Danaen said contemptuously. 'She deserved a worse death. An arrow was too clean. Do not tell me now that we should have spared her.'

'Laszlo has explained to me the circumstances,' Stenwold said, 'and you did what you had to. Still . . . she was a fool to try and face you down. If she had been wiser, she would have lived, I'm sure.'

Danaen's expression was not so sure of that, but Stenwold did his best to overlook it. *Save me from over-zealous allies.* 'Well, if it comes to that,' he said, 'we'll have to see how Collegium artifice matches up to Spiderlands cunning. The Vekken did not find it so easy to take us, either by land or sea.'

'The Vekken, however, did a lot of damage – and so did the Empire after them,' Jodry said miserably. 'We cannot go on fighting wars. We cannot afford the cost in lives or goods. Stenwold, have you thought about finding allies in some other Spider house?'

'Which?' Stenwold asked him.

'Well, I have no idea, but the Aldanrael must have enemies.'

'Spider politics, Jodry. As you say, we have no idea. They change their faces daily in that part of the world. Each morning they get up and learn a new list of who their friends are, and who their enemies. Arianna, am I right?'

'You would not lack for people willing to profit from you,' she conceded, 'but you would never know their hearts. Anyone you dealt with could easily be an agent of the Aldanrael. Do not enter those waters. You have neither compass nor chart.'

'As an example of this, I received a message from the enemy, last night,' Stenwold announced. 'It was left on my pillow.' He showed them the small slip of parchment. 'It says no more than this: "You have heard your spies.

Perhaps you would now wish to listen to us. State your time and place, if you would not have the ships sail." I suspect I shall hear no more from my agent in Everis. He has done what the Spiders wished and told me of the threat to Collegium that they are assembling.'

'But Teornis wants to talk,' Jodry prompted.

'Supposedly.' Stenwold took a deep breath.

'You cannot talk with Spiders,' Danaen spat scathingly. 'Every word is a lie. Every promise is made to be broken. The only peace to be had with Spiders is after you've killed them.'

Jodry coughed. 'Yes, well, for my part I say we have to meet with him. He won't want a fight, so we can surely find some way through this mess that doesn't see a hundred ships blockading our harbour and landing soldiers all the way down the coast. The Spiderlands is *vast*, Stenwold. We have no idea what they might send. They have plenty of artificers amongst their subjects, too. Don't think it will just be sailing ships and swords.'

Danaen was scowling at Jodry, and looking daggers at Arianna as well. The two Flies sat back, waiting to be of some use. Stenwold put a hand to his forehead. 'I will meet with him,' he stated.

The Mantis made a hissing sound. 'If you so much as hear them speak, they will corrupt you, – or kill you. There is *no* dealing with them, save with a blade.'

'That is not our way,' Stenwold snapped, with enough authority to beat her down. 'This situation is slipping out of control. Spider-kinden who have lived in Collegium all their lives are fearing to show their faces in the streets. Honory Bellowern, of all the cursed people, sent me a message of support from *the Empire*, in our time of need, and if this cannot be resolved – if Spider sails reach our harbour – then no doubt the Eighth Army will march into Myna so as to bring that support so much the closer. We have to act, therefore. I will meet with Teornis.'

'Stenwold Maker, listen to me,' the Mantis declared fiercely. 'I will kill Teornis of the Aldanrael.'

Stenwold stared at her. 'I don't . . .'

'I will take a score of my people and I will go to where he is, and kill him and his servants and guards and all who lodge with him,' Danaen stated flatly. 'That is the only way to negotiate with Spiders.'

'And what will that accomplish?' Stenwold demanded. 'We're not at war with just Teornis, we're at war with his whole cursed family. All that would achieve is ensure that we would never again be able to negotiate any kind of peace.'

Danaen folded her arms sullenly. 'Where will you meet him then? How will you deal with him? He will twist your mind with his Art. He will have his agents hiding, ready to poison you or slay you.'

'Some neutral party, perhaps, to mediate . . . ?' Jodry started.

'Who?' the Mantis snapped at him. 'Who, indeed, that they have not bought? Who, that you can fully trust? You can trust only my kind, to be rid of all the influence of his kinden, and we say *kill*.'

'And who could we trust with the knowledge of what would be said at such a meeting. No third parties, Jodry. If we do talk to Teornis then we must talk fully and frankly.'

'Well, then,' the Speaker for the Assembly looked grim, 'the Mantis is right, Sten. How could you be sure it wasn't a trap?'

'Arianna says he won't just have me killed out of hand, since it's not their way,' Stenwold told him.

'With respect, Master Maker,' Tomasso put in, 'their way is to win.' He had sat in silence for a long time while the others talked, with Laszlo fidgeting at his side. Now his voice drew their attention. 'Spiders play Spider games with each other, and the top Aristoi will tell you how they keep to their little rules. But, Master Maker, those rules are only for those at the very top, only for the people that move the pieces around.'

Stenwold thought of Teornis's earlier note, welcoming him to the Dance. *Or was that just to lull me into a false sense of security? Do I really believe that a Spider Aristos would consider me an equal?*

'And besides,' Laszlo put in, 'doesn't mean they don't off each other *sometimes*.'

Stenwold opened his mouth, then closed it again, the words gone. After a pause he said, 'There *must* be a way. I want to believe that Teornis just wants a way to back out gracefully, without making himself look a fool before his family. But I see what you say.' He sighed. 'There must be a way,' he said again.

'Perhaps it will come to us,' Jodry said thoughtfully. 'Some place, some mediator, some guarantee of safety. Let me think about it. I'm sure something will spring to mind.'

'Well, if not, then the armada,' Stenwold agreed. 'While you're racking your brains, spare a thought for our sea defences too.'

After his informant had left the parlour, Helmess Broiler settled down on his couch thoughtfully. 'Who would have thought . . . ?' he kept repeating to himself. Elytrya draped herself across the back of the couch and traced her fingertips across his scalp, waiting patiently for him to unpack his thoughts to her.

'This whole Spiderlands business has taken me quite by surprise,' he told her eventually. 'In this life you learn to be wary of apparent good fortune, especially where a Spider is involved. However, perhaps life has finally decided to give back to me some of what Stenwold Maker has taken away.'

'Perhaps killing that man Failwright was a mistake,' Elytrya suggested.

'Apparently not, for they're blaming the Aldanrael for it, and that makes me a very happy man.' Helmess poured her some wine. It was a good Spiderlands vintage, and he reckoned that it would be in short supply soon. 'You had better keep yourself indoors for the moment,' he added. 'After all, *I* know you're no Spider-kinden, but the general populace of Collegium are unlikely to be as enlightened in that particular respect as I am.'

'So there will be war,' she observed. 'You people always seem to be having wars.'

'Only because Maker insists on dragging us into them,' Helmess retorted. 'Well, let him try to drag himself out of this one. He'll find it won't be so easy.' He paused, thinking. 'Although he has a clever mouth on him, does Maker, and I can't deny it. I don't think we can allow him and Teornis to hammer out an accord. That wouldn't suit us at all, now, would it?'

'You want your Spider fleet to come sailing into the harbour here, do you?' she said, gently mocking.

'Why not? Would a few dozen wooden ships pose any difficulties for your warriors?'

She snorted. 'Rosander's Greatclaw-kinden would sink every last one of them before they had any idea what was going on.'

'Well, then, you may even become the heroes of the hour, until everyone realizes that you're not stopping with just the Spiders.' Helmess laughed. 'We must try to arrange for Maker to be standing front and centre when that happens. Have him hold out his hand in friendship. I want to see Rosander pincer it off at the wrist.' Abruptly his mood darkened. 'Or maybe not. Maker's too clever by half, and he could talk a Fly out of the sky. I think maybe the Spiders should do him in.'

'That would make sense,' she agreed. 'Why should Failwright be the only martyr?'

He laughed at that. 'Oh, yes, a martyr. I'll pay for the statue myself, once he's dead.'

Elytrya studied his expression. 'And you have a plan.'

'I may have.' Helmess nodded. 'I think I need to set up a meeting, as a concerned and patriotic Assembler of Collegium. Our little informer must needs earn his keep. Go and fetch him back in again, would you?'

She straightened up and glided over to the door, while Helmess's eyes followed her every move. *I am doing well out of this deal*, he considered. She was no true Spider-kinden but she was as beautiful as they, and with a liquid, sly grace that he actually preferred. *And as duplicitous as any Spider, no doubt, but that just adds to the thrill.*

She brought in the neatly dressed young Beetle man, and Helmess addressed him from the couch. 'Master Cardless.'

Stenwold's servant gave Helmess a polite little bow. He had proved to be quite the find: a well-educated man who had been dismissed from a good position in Helleron after certain irregularities had turned up in his master's finances. Bitter and ambitious, he had arrived in Collegium prudently after the war, just when old Maker had been looking for a new servant. Helmess had leant on a few acquaintances to provide Cardless with glowing references, whereupon Maker had taken him on without a thought. Moreover, Helmess was sure that Cardless was an exemplary servant, with not a financial irregularity to be seen. After all, he was now drawing *two* salaries without even having to put a hand into another man's pocket.

'I have a job for you, Cardless,' Helmess informed him. 'Something a little more than your usual watch-and-report.'

The servant's stance altered in a way that indicated, though with impeccable politeness, that special duties carried an additional charge.

Helmess smiled sourly. *At least he is predictable in his villainies.* 'Oh, you'll get yours, don't worry, but I want you to bring me that Mantis woman you mentioned to me.'

'Danaen, Master Broiler?' Cardless wrinkled his nose. 'That savage?'

'None other,' Helmess confirmed. 'Tell her I'm a concerned citizen that wants to talk about the evil Spiders, and who better than their traditional enemies to set me straight, eh?'

'Very good, Master Broiler,' Cardless agreed. His answering smile was superior enough that Helmess decided to take him down a peg.

'And now you're asking yourself whether I've ever wondered if you'll sell me back to Stenwold Maker,' he guessed, seeing the truth of the accusation instantly written across the other man's face.

'Master Broiler, I would never—'

'Save it. I know you,' Helmess cut him off. 'Understand this: Stenwold Maker is an honest man, and he'd have no time for a traitor in his own house, confessed or not. The best you'd get out of him then is a kick out the door and a bad reference. You keep doing what I tell you, Cardless, and you'll profit from it, so don't get any clever ideas. Now go find me that Mantis-kinden. I'll see her tomorrow, if you can arrange it.'

After Cardless had gone, Helmess stretched out luxuriously, feeling very pleased with himself.

'Tomorrow,' Elytrya asked him, 'and not tonight?'

'I prefer to do dark deeds in daylight,' Helmess murmured. 'People aren't expecting them then. Besides, I thought you and I could explore a different branch of villainy tonight, no?'

'I must say, our Master Maker is rather getting into the spirit of things,' was Teornis's remark, when Arianna had finished recounting her news. The Spider lord's townhouse had changed since she had last seen it. The calibre of his staff was subtly different now: fewer fancily dressed Fly-kinden menials and more obviously armed men. She had spotted at least a half-dozen Kessen Ant-kinden – mercenaries she presumed – standing alert with repeating crossbows in hand, and there were some newcomers as well: arrogant, strutting Dragonfly-kinden wearing armour of chitin and wooden plates. Those on the roof had extravagantly recurved longbows, and those indoors carried single-edged swords. They were an import from some satrapy of the Spiderlands where the Aldanrael held sway.

'Of course,' Teornis went on, 'he's still a Beetle, plodding and cautious and devoid of style.' He was sitting at a desk, leafing through papers, and in that looked to Arianna like any Beetle merchant or academic. When he glanced up to meet her gaze, however, she noticed the quirk at the corner of his mouth, and realized he was doing so deliberately for his own amusement. *Or for mine.* Very few outsiders understood that a great deal of what comprised a Spider-kinden was a sense of humour, especially when times were hard. The ability to step on to the scaffold and offer one last jest to the crowd was the mark of a true Aristos.

'He will agree to meet if terms can be proposed that will satisfy his people.'

'Meaning the mad Mantis,' Teornis sighed, and the smile slipped. 'Whatever terms we baffle Maker into offering, I'll see her dead. Let them be ignorant savages in their own forests all they want, but when they kill one of my blood, then blood shall follow. They think that they have a sole monopoly on grievance and revenge? Well, I look forward to giving that creature Danaen a *real* reason to hate my kind. I'll strip her skin off, an inch at a time, and make her eat the flesh of her followers.' The words were matter-of-factly spoken, his eyes fixed on her face to gauge her reaction.

'She's nothing to me,' Arianna told him. 'I'm sure she'd kill me in an instant if she thought Stenwold wouldn't know about it. It wouldn't matter how loyal I was, or to whom, because to her I'm just another Spider.'

'It's Maker's error to employ such volatile servants,'

Teornis agreed. 'Well, now, I shall find some convenient place that even the Mantis cannot object to. Let me confront Maker face to face, and we shall see what he will not do to avoid another war. My agents are already abroad in the city, stirring up fear, turning the people's anger away from our kinden onto their reckless leaders. Soon he'll accept any terms I offer him just to avoid a riot.'

'I don't think so,' Arianna said, before she thought about it. There was a moment of silence in which Teornis's expression revealed nothing of his own thoughts. *And so at last I act like something more than a mere servant*, she considered. *You promised me adoption into the family, Teornis. Don't forget that.*

He nodded shortly. 'You're right, of course. I do our Master Maker wrong. He's better than that, and he won't bend so easily. He listens to that fat fool Drillen, though, and Drillen is just a . . . what are those flying machines? He's just a great bloated *airship* buoyed up by the opinion of the hoi polloi. Once they turn on him, he'll soon force Maker's hand.'

Arianna nodded cautiously. 'That seems likely.' *And so Jodry Drillen's life is saved, because his cowardice is more useful to us alive than his death is as a warning.* She found herself surprisingly relieved, having not realized how she had grown so used to the portly Assembler.

'I will need a little acting out of you, at some point, if things come to it,' Teornis informed her. 'Maker has other traits than his plodding to recommend him as an opponent. For a start, he is sentimental. It is a noble quality, perhaps, but a true manipulus should know when to abandon sentiment. If my enemy put a knife to the throat of my sister, or my mother, then I would demonstrate my love of family in the vengeance I took thereafter, not in bending the knee then and there. Maker is not like this, as we have seen.'

Arianna had a sense of what was coming, and shifted uncomfortably.

'Who does Maker hate most in all the world?' Teornis asked abruptly.

'I'd have said it was the Empire, until just a tenday ago. Now maybe it's you,' said Arianna, testing how frank she could be with him.

'Oh, no, no, no. The Empire, always the Empire,' reprimanded Teornis. 'The reason he's so agitated by this current tangle is that it distracts the attention of the city *from* the Empire. He wants *us* as allies, in the end. So he'll scheme for that, tell us all his tedious rote about common enemies, over and over again. He hates the Empire far more than us, and with good reason. They're unpleasant fellows, at the best of times, and their manners are even worse than the Beetle-kinden. *But* . . . But he put himself in their hands, of his own free will, for your sake.'

'That was then.'

'Oh, my dear, no. He did it then, and he will do it again now, if need be. For you, my dear one, only for you. If Stenwold Maker proves himself devoid of reason, and will not nod his head like a good loser, then it's time to threaten what he holds dearest: you yourself, – you and only you. Play along, if it comes to that. I know you can.'

*And how far will such playing have to go? Will I have to keep acting even while you cut my throat?* But he did not seem to think he was asking anything unusual, just one more deception.

'Of course,' she replied.

'Of course,' he echoed. 'But it may not come to that. On the other hand, it may go considerably further.' Teornis shook his head, looking genuinely regretful. 'There is one other little duty you may have to shoulder, if things proceed to their worst. I'd rather not impose it on you, and I swear I'll do what I can to find any other way, but I shall be honest with you in this. You may have to kill him.'

She said nothing, and kept her expression as still as she could.

'Inelegant, I know,' he said, apparently in the belief that he was mirroring her thoughts.

*I told Stenwold it would not come to that,* she reflected. *To simply eliminate an opponent is graceless, for the Aristoi, until they have ripped everything else from him. But, of course, how better to demonstrate that a man has nothing left, than to have his death come by the hand of the one closest to him? Oh, yes, that would be elegance indeed.*

'I would rather not have you break cover in such a gauche manner,' Teornis drawled. 'However, certain circumstances may require it, so I give you fair warning. Stenwold Maker is not the only one who might need to fear violence at our negotiations.'

'Stenwold wouldn't—'

'Oh, surely he himself wouldn't,' Teornis agreed, 'but I want your blade at his throat if anyone in his party *would.*' Seeing her expression he smiled again. 'I understand how you must feel about this, my dear, but you perhaps have been living amongst their kind for too long. You have forgotten your true self. When your shell of Beetle-ness has been cast aside, you shall emerge as the pure Spider, I assure you, and such thoughts will no longer trouble you.'

Helmess returned home later than he had planned, delayed by unwelcome business. Honory Bellowern had summoned him peremptorily to another meeting at Helmess's other townhouse. This time the Imperial Beetle's manner had been shorn of the sly, his usual cunning almost submerged by the great tide of good fortune that had swept him up.

'Well now, are you ready to receive the benefits of a friend of the Empire? They may be yours sooner than you think,' Honory had declared, the moment they were alone together.

'You mean this business with the Spiderlands,' had been Helmess's reply, sounding as disdainful as he could manage. In truth he suspected that the rift between Stenwold and the Aldanrael was far more of a boon to his own plans than to anything the Empire might be seeking, but he kept *that* well and truly to himself.

'We require another favour, Master Broiler,' Bellowern had told him, predictably enough. 'We'd like you to fan the flames, if you would. Rattle some swords towards the Spiderlands. Go shake Stenwold Maker's hand and call him a true patriot.'

Helmess's sour smile had not needed much feigning. 'I've started on the path.'

'Your initiative has been noted,' had come Bellowern's patronizing response. 'I've not had orders back, of course, but I anticipate that, once the sails are in sight of the harbour, there will be an army ready to march to repatriate Myna and the other so-called Alliance cities back into the Empire. The bleeding hearts of Collegium will be too busy fighting for their much-vaunted freedom to object. After that, Helleron, then the Lowlands, frankly. By year's end we'll be investing Sarn with a couple of full armies, and you and I will be dining in the Amphiophos, under the black and gold. How's that sound to you?'

Helmess's smile had been broad and genuine, though the thought behind it had been, *Oh you have no idea just how many players there are in this game, Master Bellowern. The black and gold might receive a little surprise, if it comes down the coast again.* 'Just let me know what you wish me to do,' he had invited, before setting off home to meet his next unwitting tool.

Danaen strode into Helmess's parlour displaying all the confidence in the world, but these Mantis-kinden were not as inscrutable as they thought they were. If she had been a Spider or a Moth, then Helmess would have had no window onto her soul. In her expression, though, he registered naked curiosity. She would not be well educated about Collegiate politics, but no doubt she had heard that Helmess and Stenwold were not best of friends.

He had sent Elytrya away, during this interview, since it would not do to be seen with anything resembling a Spider-kinden at his side.

Danaen folded her arms, looking contemptuous, and Helmess thought, *Five centuries ago, and your kind might have been justified in that expression. Nowadays you're just a joke in bad taste, but perhaps I will get the chance to laugh at you, after all.*

'I asked to see you because I know you have the ear of Master Stenwold Maker, and he so seldom listens to me,' Helmess began mildly. The Mantis woman just stared back at him impudently, but he assumed the demeanour of a concerned, perhaps slightly ineffectual Beetle statesman, as he knew she must view him, and continued. 'We were all extremely surprised when he told us about the Spider situation,' he continued. 'After all, it was his people who brought Teornis and the Aldanrael family into the war with the Vekken, and with the Empire too.' He watched her carefully, from behind his avuncular exterior. There was no suggestion that she had heard the rumours – in fact the extremely accurate rumours – that he had been collabor-ating with Imperial agents. *But, of course, Mantis-kinden wouldn't* deign *to listen to Beetle gossip, and how I shall now exploit that.* 'A lot of us are worried about how Master Maker will handle this.'

Her scowl of derision deepened: no doubt she took him for the peace-making kind. Helmess let her believe so for a moment, then said, 'Many of us in the Assembly fear that after all this, after the blood that has already been shed, Maker will simply roll over and get back into bed with the Spiders as though nothing has ever happened.'

She raised an eyebrow. 'That makes no sense. Why would he even tell you, then? Would any of you fat Beetles even have known, had he not opened your eyes?'

'Well, perhaps not.' Helmess picked his words with care. 'But, then, Master Maker has achieved his current rank amongst us by taking us into wars. That has been the subject of our many disagreements, and I am less certain about his means of taking us out of them. He has become known as a . . . compromising man. You know of the Vekken siege a few years back, yes?'

He received a curt nod.

'Well, you must know that Maker is even cosying up to the Vekken these days.'

And she did know – he saw it in her eyes – and he had planted his seed of doubt. She said nothing, but her posture was now different, less stand-offish, more receptive.

'So, he's got us into another fight. Well, if what he says about the Spiders is true, then perhaps that's fair enough. What I'm worried about, what many of us are worried about, is that now he's made himself the centre of attention all over again, he'll just make some deal with Teornis and then hush the whole thing up.' Helmess steepled his plump fingers. 'And what will that solve? Really, I mean, what? Will it stop them taking advantage of us? I really rather doubt it. I'm not too proud to admit that the Spiders are a clever lot. I'd not want to talk terms with one of them. You never know what you might be agreeing to.'

She nodded, just a little, and he thought, *Prejudice is such a wonderful thing*.

'Your people, of course, you know the Spiders. When I heard that you and yours were involved, well, that offered a spark of hope, I can tell you. I was hoping that Maker would just put your talents to their best use: a strong, solid strike against the Spider-kinden, to show them we're not to be toyed with. Nothing seems to have happened, though, since Maker made his big announcement. Some of us are getting worried that he's going to go soft on us again.'

She cocked her head to one side, watching him narrowly. 'What are you saying?'

'Would you kill the Spider lord, if you had the chance?'

'Of course.' She did not pause for a moment.

'But I'd guess Maker doesn't want that, or he'd have given you the order already. After all, Teornis is right here in the city.' *And how that must gall her. She must almost be able to smell him from twenty streets away. Yes, look, there go her hands to her weapon hilts, just at the thought . . .*

'He's . . . thinking,' was all Danaen's voice said, though her body language betrayed a great deal more.

'Oh, well, thinking is always a wise precaution.' Helmess made a great show of holding his hands up in despair. 'Tell me, please, are my fears justified? Is he going to meet with them?'

'He might. That's what he's thinking about,' said the Mantis. She had come here wearing a full suit of distrust, but he was easing her out of it piece by piece. 'But he has found no meeting place he can be sure of.' Her expression shifted to a sneer. 'If not for that, no doubt he'd be meeting with *them* already.'

'Then perhaps that's what he should do,' Helmess said frankly. Danaen was frowning, caught off guard, but he pressed on. 'If he and the Spider meet somewhere secluded, somewhere private, then who knows what might happen?'

She merely stared at him, and he saw he would have to elaborate.

'Some isolated spot free from interference,' he went on. 'Where the Spider's agents and creatures would not be able to intervene, let us say. If, at that meeting, the city's interests were not being upheld – if they were being sold to the Spiderlands through craven negotiating, perhaps – then a bold sword stroke could accomplish a great deal.'

She did not seem to realize that he was trying to lead her into iniquity, or perhaps he was only giving voice to thoughts that had been running through her head already. He had no doubt that she saw no betrayal in all this, for to her, as to so many of the old-style Felyal Mantids, hatred

234

of the Spider-kinden was a great and noble cause, and anything that furthered it could not be considered bad. He watched her closely, trying to interpret her thoughts from her expression. In the end she said, 'Perhaps, but it will not happen. There is no such place.'

*And my work is almost done.* 'And if I have already thought of such a place?'

He now had her utter, focused attention, and it was a frightening thing. Her victims must feel as he felt then, he realized. Her unsheathed concentration had razor edges.

'Where?' she asked, and he told her – and was treated to a genuine Mantis smile.

Stenwold mulled the proposal over slowly, trying to see it from all angles. He had with him only his most able people, now. He had not summoned Elder Padstock, because he did not want to sully her loyalty by revealing the inner workings of diplomacy. He had not called Jodry Drillen, because he knew the man was already under pressure from the Assembly. Stenwold still respected his opinion, but now, when Jodry spoke, Stenwold could hear the voices of a great many other Assemblers behind him.

Arianna and Tomasso, he had therefore boiled his council down to. Arianna and Tomasso and Stenwold himself, gathered here in Stenwold's study to hear Danaen out.

'A ship?' Stenwold pondered. 'Your advice is a ship?'

'My advice is: let me kill these Spiders. Do not meet with them,' Danaen replied firmly. 'If you must, meet them somewhere away from this clutter of stone. Meet them where they can arrange no ambushes, no surprises. Have a ship, a big flat trader-ship, towed out to the open sea. We come to it by sea and so do they. We send some over, perhaps your little Fly-kinden, to search for hidden knives. When we are sure there are none, then we row you there by boat – you and just so many others. Meet the Spider there, talk if you must. Or let me kill him.'

Stenwold glanced at Arianna. 'Your thoughts?'

She took her time answering, which reassured him. It was always good to have another well-thought-out viewpoint.

'I think it might serve,' she said at last. 'I'd guess that Teornis would accept it. Given what you're fighting over, he would find it appropriate, I think.'

Stenwold's gaze turned to Tomasso.

The Fly-kinden was already nodding. 'It's cursed hard to sneak up on someone on the open sea in broad daylight,' he remarked. 'You'd see a sail miles off, and even an engined vessel without the high profile of a mast would be spotted in time to take action. The *Tidenfree* will be your transport, Master Maker, since you know yourself there's precious little that can outpace or outmanoeuvre her. If the Spider lord does try to bring in more force, we'll spot them and get you out before they arrive.'

'Then we'll do it,' Stenwold declared, and he found himself immensely relieved that he would at last get to wrestle with Teornis directly. *I have known the man long enough, and yet I cannot see why he has jeopardized so much for so little. I must first understand. Then perhaps I can solve this business without another pointless conflict.*

'I shall provide your escort,' Danaen declared.

Stenwold frowned, thinking of short Mantis tempers and mocking Spider words. 'Perhaps just you and a couple of your people. I'll recruit a few of Padstock's company, as well. Myself and eight others, say, that should be manageable, and Teornis to bring along the same, and have the same chance to check over the ship as we have. I can't think of anything fairer than that.'

Danaen looked disgruntled, but made no complaint. In an ideal world, Stenwold would have preferred to go without any Mantis at his back – and that was a strange thought to have, given his history – but if there was a trap, if negotiations broke down beyond recovery, then he knew

236

that he could rely on nobody as much as on Danaen's people. They would be prepared to die, not for him but for their age-old hatred of the Spider-kinden.

'A messenger,' he decided. 'I'll pass our proposal to the Aldanrael, and let us hope they accept it.'

'I cannot think that they will not,' Arianna predicted, but any subtleties in her tone passed him by.

# Fifteen

The sea was choppy and the *Tidenfree*'s hull jolted and bounced as it cut across the waves towards its goal. Stenwold stood at the bow and brooded, with Laszlo perched on the rail beside him to keep him company.

Someone had found a suitable ship for his meeting with Teornis, and if he did not personally find it fitting, there was no point in saying so. The broad, flat barge that they had moored out here, beyond sight of Collegium harbour, was already known to him. It had been one of the Vekken supply vessels during the late siege, the last survivor of the flotilla of great flat-bottomed vessels that the Vekken sailors had navigated along the coast as part of their invasion force. Somehow it had avoided being burned, sunk or sailed away from the city by those that captured it, and now here it was, serving this peculiar duty.

It did not escape Stenwold's recollection that the sailing ships that had taken those barges, smashed the Vekken warships and raised the siege had been under the command of Teornis of the Aldanrael. How glad Stenwold had been to see the man then, how the Spider had been the hero of the hour, most popular man in Collegium. And now . . .

*How did we let it come to this? How did he let it come to this? Why, for the world's sake?*

'Is something wrong, Ma'rMaker?' Laszlo asked him.

*Many, many things are very wrong indeed.* 'No, just

thinking,' he replied, not entirely convincingly. 'Tell me, is there some significance to where you moored her?'

'Edge of the shelf, Ma'rMaker,' Laszlo said, and noticed that this had failed to edify. 'What I mean is, the sea's not the same all the way across. It gets deeper some, as you go on.'

'I think I knew that,' Stenwold told him, shrugging his shoulders to settle his artificer's leathers more comfortably.

'Well, of course – but it's not like a wine bowl or anything. It gets deeper all of a sudden and a lot deeper in one go. Any further out than that girl is and you'd never be able to drop anchor, not with all the length of chain you could carry. That's where the real deep sea starts, and where ships don't go beyond. Unless they're us, of course. If we get some urgent running away to do, I reckon the chief'll just turn us for open water, see if them Spiders will follow us and risk the Lash and the weed seas. I'd lay odds they won't.'

'Let us hope it won't come to that,' Stenwold told him. He glanced back along the deck of the *Tidenfree*, which was busy today. There could be seen Elder Padstock and a dozen of her company, clad in helm and breastplate, and with snapbows newly signed out from the city armouries. Beyond them, scattered about the deck with no apparent order or plan to them, was a score of Mantis-kinden. Danaen might only be bringing a brace of them to the negotiating table, but if things went wrong, the *Tidenfree* would bring a whole world of trouble as fast as her sails could propel her. Stenwold was sure that someone on Teornis's ship would have a telescope, and the Aptitude to use it, and he wanted his Mantis marines in plain view and obviously spoiling for a fight. *Just for a little insurance.*

'There's our man,' Laszlo pointed, and Stenwold followed his finger to see a pale sail coursing in at an angle to their own line of approach. Unfolding his own glass, Stenwold made the best examination he could. Teornis's transport was similar in shape to the ill-fated *Very Blade*, albeit smaller and swifter. It was still almost as long again as the *Tidenfree*, and he saw that Teornis had also cluttered the decks with reinforcements, although it was too far to see what calibre of swords he had brought with him.

'We're faster,' said Laszlo, obviously attempting to read his mind. 'If it comes to it, we'll sail rings around them. We've taken larger ships than that, and carrying less muscle than we are now, too.'

'Good to hear it,' said Stenwold weakly, wondering whether those 'larger ships' had been peaceful merchant-men in desperate flight from the notorious pirate Bloodfly. 'Who's going over to check out the ground?'

'Me and Solli and Fernaea,' Laszlo said. 'And I'll be one of your eight when you go over yourself, if you don't mind. After all, come trouble, I'm your best bet for getting word back to the *Tidenfree* without getting shot into the water.'

'Fast, are you?'

'Could have been a messenger, me,' Laszlo confirmed.

They were making good speed towards the barge, and so was Teornis. Stenwold took another peer through his glass, noticing the burnished armour of Kessen mercenaries at the rails of his adversary's ship, and others less recogniz-able but sporting longbows. Then his view wheeled wildly, and he took the telescope from his eye to see the Spider ship coming to, and lowering sail.

'Time to earn my keep,' Laszlo said, and kicked off from the rail, casting himself across the deck to come down near the mainmast. Two of the *Tidenfree* crew were waiting for him there, and one handed him a shortbow and a quiver of arrows. He waved to Stenwold and grinned broadly, but his accomplices looked more serious.

*And rightly so, since we don't know what they might find.* He did not reckon that Teornis would have hidden men aboard the barge: Fly-kinden had keen eyes, and the *Tiden-free* would easily outdistance the Spider vessel in a race back to Collegium harbour, or into the wilds of the open sea. Still, if Teornis was just a little too overconfident, or uncharacteristically unsubtle in his methods, then Laszlo and his friends might flush out more trouble than they could handle. Stenwold remembered the Art that had allowed Danaen to blend in with her surroundings, to let the eyes of others pass over her. Spiders knew that Art, too, Stenwold was well aware, *But I do not think that Teornis would risk an assassin being discovered. Such Arts are not certain, and Flies are notoriously inquisitive.* Yet he felt a lurch in his stomach as the three intrepid scouts lifted off from the *Tidenfree*'s deck and veered over the dancing waves towards the barge.

They were specks only as they dipped and dropped on to the deck, and through his glass Stenwold saw them pause for a moment, bowstrings drawn back. Then they were quartering the deck, swiftly and professionally. A moment later they had gone below.

It was a long, anxious wait. Stenwold meanwhile fidgeted with his telescope and shuffled his feet, intensely aware of a boatload of Mantis-kinden at his back, who wanted any excuse for a fight. *Pray we do not give them one.*

A movement at his elbow resolved itself into Tomasso. The bearded Fly had spent the journey so far beside Gude at the helm. Now he unlimbered his own telescope, not Stenwold's pocketable one but a proper seagoing piece, extending to half as long as the Fly was tall.

'You should know,' he grunted, making a great show of examining the instrument, 'I'm now the fourth Bloodfly – as of the early hours of this morning.'

It took Stenwold a moment to disentangle that one, but then he understood. 'My condolences,' he said, thinking of that old, old Fly-kinden man he had seen just once, aboard *Isseleema's Floating Game*, who had been a notorious pirate, from a line of notorious pirates, in his prime.

Tomasso nodded shortly. 'It doesn't change our bargain,

Master Maker. It only makes me want to remind you of it, because it's time for my family to try out respectability, for a generation or two.'

'I hope you know me well enough by now to trust my word,' Stenwold remarked.

'I think I do, at that,' allowed Tomasso. 'Mind you, you're a man who seems to be trying to arrange his own death at any given moment.'

'Well, as to that,' Stenwold said, with a strained smile, 'I went over the disposition of my affairs recently, and I've left what assistance I can to you, should this venture go wrong. Believe me, you and your people have been more help than I could have asked for.'

'Looking after our investment, nothing more,' Tomasso said gruffly. 'Ah, and here come our intrepid explorers.' He fixed the glass he carried to his eye, and Stenwold followed suit. Laszlo and his fellows had come up on deck again, tiny figures even through the lenses. Laszlo himself hopped up and stood on the barge's rail, where he waved a white cloth theatrically at the Spider vessel, finishing with a flourishing bow. Stenwold heard Tomasso snort.

'Boy's going to get himself killed one of these days,' observed the *Tidenfree*'s master, 'while baring his arse at a Spider lord, probably.'

Laszlo and the other two remained standing at the barge's rail, waiting. Stenwold turned his magnified gaze towards the other ship and saw a trio of figures lift off from it, with the barge clearly as their destination. The whole process, search above and below decks, was now to be repeated by Teornis's people. The Vekken shipwrights themselves would never have gone over the craft in such fine detail.

'Oh, there's nasty,' Tomasso murmured.

Teornis's auditors were not Fly-kinden, as Stenwold had expected. A closer examination showed that they were

Dragonflies, wearing light armour of chitin and wood, and carrying fantastically carved longbows. They were not the civilized and elegant Commonwealers that Stenwold had guardedly dealt with during the war, but the denizens of some Spider satrapy, gone half savage. Stenwold was vaguely aware that, back in the Days of Lore, at some point long before the Collegiate revolution, the Commonweal had suffered some kind of great exodus: malcontent nobles and their followers being forcibly ejected into the wider world. Dragonfly soldiers had supported Teornis when he raised the Vekken siege, and there was a city of piratical Dragon-flies on the Exalsee to trouble Solarno's shipping, and who could know where else they had found safe havens?

Stenwold could wish that Teornis had not been so wise in choosing his soldiers. Tomasso's present discomfort was well-founded, for Dragonflies were as nimble as his own kinden in the air, whilst being almost as swift and deadly as Mantids when it came to a fight.

'There are so many things that could go wrong with this,' the bearded Fly muttered, 'and if it goes bad, it'll go stinking rotten and all at once.'

'Oh, yes,' Stenwold agreed. He searched for his own feelings on this and found not fear, but a flutter of excite-ment. *It's like shipping out with these Flies in the first place. I used to live like this once, before I got respectable. Being finally seen to be right about the Empire has nearly blunted me.* He felt an odd, lost yearning again for those fast-and-loose days before he had shouldered the burden of being a war hero and a statesman to whom people listened. *Oh, Tisamon, what I wouldn't give to have you here right now.*

He had to hope that Danaen would prove to be the next-best thing.

There was a footstep on the deck behind him, and he turned to see Arianna. She had come attired for battle, wearing a leather cuirass, and with a strung shortbow holstered across her back. It was what she had worn, close enough, when she had come to fight at his side against the Vekken, and he found himself smiling at her wanly.

'The boat's ready,' she told him, 'for when they are.'

'They're coming up already,' Tomasso remarked. Indeed, the Dragonfly-kinden were back on deck, all three of them, their search having obviously been cursory. *Is this Teornis telling me something?* Stenwold wondered. *Has he told them to be brief to show he trusts me? Or are they just better at killing than at diligence?*

The Dragonflies were now airborne, heading back towards Teornis's vessel, and a moment later Laszlo and his comrades were winging back towards the *Tidenfree* as well. Stenwold took a deep breath and headed amidships for the boat. It was a narrow launch hung out over the *Tidenfree*'s side, ready to be winched down by two of the more Apt members of the crew. His boarding party were standing ready: Elder Padstock and two of her people, with snapbows at the ready; Danaen and two of hers, with swords and bows, arm-spikes and Mantis bloody-mindedness.

Stenwold joined them, with Arianna at his back, and a moment later Laszlo dropped down in their midst, making the Mantis-kinden twitch and scowl.

'You know what we're about,' he addressed them. 'Keep your eyes open, shout out if you see something out of place. We're taking no chances. Do *not* act, unless they act first, or unless I order it. If we see violence today, I do not want my party to be the instigator.'

'Very good, War Master,' Padstock assured him.

'Then let us be about it,' he said, and carefully stepped down into the rocking boat. They joined him one by one, with Danaen's warriors taking the oars. Last down was Laszlo, who perched himself at the bow as the boat was winched into the water. He had his bow ready, an arrow to hand, a small but martial figurehead.

As the Mantis-kinden hauled on the oars, Stenwold took his glass out again and tracked down the other ship's launch. It was a grander, broader affair, and four of Teornis's eight were rowing, and making no greater headway. The Spider lord himself could be clearly seen, reclining in the stern. *Assuming it is him and not some lookalike relative,* the unpleasant thought came to Stenwold. At this distance, though, he could not bring that face into sharp focus no matter how he adjusted the lenses.

*At least we can be glad of one thing regarding his Dragonflies,* another idea struck. *If they had been some Apt kinden, Flies even, then perhaps they could have set some incendiaries or explosives within the ship. Be thankful for Inapt enemies.*

They were nearing the barge, a low-sided craft, cumbrous and bulky in the water. The Vekken had been no great shipwrights, and what skill they possessed they had reserved for their warships. The barge seemed so close to the water that any large wave would swamp the rails. *Hammer and tongs, if the weather grows poor she may founder and sink out here, and would that not be an irony? Teornis and myself clinging to the same plank.*

Laszlo's wings hauled him into the air before the prow of the launch nudged the barge's side. He had tugged a rope ladder with him, and after a moment's securing he let it down. Danaen stood in the launch, shifting her balance in perfect time with the waves, and let her own wings bring her up to the barge's deck, and her people followed suit as Stenwold tied off the launch. *A wise precaution, bringing Mantis-kinden who can fly.* He was uncomfortably aware of his own shortcomings in that regard, and how much of a trap this ship could become, and beneath it all, of the appalling depth of water below, which could swallow all the schemes that he and Teornis together might hatch until the end of time.

He put such thoughts out of his mind and began climbing.

Of the two launches, he had arrived first, and he chose the stern as his standpoint. Padstock and the two from the Maker's Own company fanned out behind him, snap-bows cradled in their arms. Stenwold watched as the three Mantis-kinden took their stand to one side, further forward than he would have liked. Danaen's hands were seldom far from her sword hilts.

There was a light touch on his shoulder, and he took Arianna's hand briefly. She looked serious, nervous even, but he supposed that was only natural. *Teornis is one of the Aristoi, after all, and it must take a lot for Arianna to set herself against him.*

Laszlo had fluttered over to look over the far rail, and now he was on his way back. 'Guests are here,' he said shortly as he looked upwards, and Stenwold guessed he was missing a handy spread of rigging to find a seat in. The Vekken barge was moved by steam-engine, though, and not sail.

A moment later, a pair of Teornis's Dragonflies dropped on to the deck, barely twenty feet away. The violence nearly started then and there, with weapons springing into the hands of the Mantids and the Dragonflies responding with half-drawn bowstrings. The moment passed, though, and a few moments later the man himself appeared.

The Spider Aristos looked like a tragic hero from some high-class play. *No*, Stenwold corrected his first impression, *he looks like the man those actors are trying to resemble.* He wore a long jacket of black silk, glittering with complex traceries of silver thread that were thickest at the cuffs of his full sleeves. Over this he had donned a cuirass of chainmail worked fantastically fine, looking lighter and easier to move in than Stenwold's leather and canvas. *I'll bet he can swim in that, if need be,* and then, *Fine mail over silk, maybe enough to slow a snapbow bolt?*

The headband that Teornis wore was plain gold, setting off the darkness of his hair and narrow, pointed beard. At his belt he had a rapier with an elaborately twisted guard, while on his left hand he wore a heavy glove of embroidered leather, a duellist's parrying tool. He even had a knife hilt visible in the top of one of his high boots.

His followers had filed up after him: two more Dragonflies, and a quartet of the Kessen Ant-kinden with their large shields and shortswords. *But not snapbows,* Stenwold noted. *We have that advantage yet.* He was uncomfortably aware that, by bringing Laszlo as messenger and Arianna as adviser, he was putting himself at a disadvantage if it came to brute force.

'Lord Teornis,' he said, letting his voice ring out as though he was in the Amphiophos.

'Master Maker,' the Spider allowed.

Stenwold stepped forward until he was at least level with Danaen. 'I thank you for agreeing to meet with me.'

'Why should I not meet with my old friend, Stenwold Maker?' Teornis answered. 'Albeit he has levelled some hurtful accusations at my own family recently.'

'We will talk frankly, or there is no point to this,' Stenwold told him. 'We are here without witnesses other than these, who are sworn to each of us. If we cannot speak openly of what we know, what's the point of any of it?'

For a moment Teornis's expression admitted nothing, but then he smiled readily. 'Well then, speak.'

'Pirates under orders from your family have been preying on Collegiate shipping,' Stenwold started. He stopped when Teornis raised a hand. 'If you'll deny that, then—'

'When pirates take orders, Master Maker, they are privateers, and that is a different game entirely,' Teornis corrected him. 'Do proceed.'

'Why? Why give such orders?'

'I am not obliged to lay out the plans of the Aldanrael to you, if you cannot fathom them for yourself,' Teornis replied evenly.

'And now? Will you declare war before the Assembly?

Or will I have to make public the papers we took from the captain of the *Very Blade*?'

'After her death,' Teornis put in coldly.

Stenwold stared at him. 'Do you claim that she was none of yours?'

'Oh, she was mine, Maker. She was my cousin, Elleria of the Aldanrael. She always was too bold and incautious in her dealings, poor creature, impatient of the proper precautions when dealing with codes and letters. She was, in short, a fool, and doubly a fool for being willing to play pirate captain rather than practise prudence on land. But she was family, and your minions killed her.' His eye took in the three Mantis-kinden with barely disguised loathing.

'She was leading an assault on Collegium's citizens,' Stenwold pointed out, angry at being put so spuriously on the defensive. 'Do you call her death an injustice?'

Teornis's smile had an edge on it that would put Danaen's blades to shame. 'No, Maker, I do not. It was just, because she was killed in due reprisal for her actions. It was just, because she was killed by her own recklessness. However, she was *family*, a true member of the Aldanrael's female line, and her death has set in motion events that care nothing for Beetle *justice*. Your people speak at endless length about rights, Stenwold. They bleat on about humanity's mutual regard, and who can do what to whom. There are no rights. You are entitled to only what you can cut or charm out of life. If our armada does bring its full force to bear on your city, and breaks your defences, and kills your soldiers, and enslaves your people, then, *yes*, that will be unjust, but the world will not care. Justice is like some unnatural hybrid flower you people have bred. It will not live long unless you keep it sheltered and warm.'

'And is that what you want? Collegium in chains?' Stenwold asked him, privately considering that Sarn and the Ancient League and, yes, perhaps even Vek might have something to say should those ships arrive.

'No, of course not,' Teornis said, seeming genuinely angry, frustrated even, 'but you are binding my hands, Maker. My family will not be easily pacified now. I advise you to find a means of mollifying them, for if the armada sets sail, then nothing in the world will stop it, and it will make the fleet I led against the Vekken seem like nothing. And we both know what will happen while we are at each other's throats. The Black and Gold will be at Sarn's doorstep before we're done, and probably Seldis's as well.'

'So you propose,' Stenwold laid out slowly, 'that in return for your family plundering half of the eastbound cargoes Collegium has sent out over the last six months, killing our mariners and practising this deceit on us – in return for all of this we should offer some grand gift and beg your forgiveness for having offended you?'

'As I say, manifestly unjust, but then consider your alternatives,' Teornis told him.

A new voice spoke up, 'I have an alternative.' It was Danaen.

Stenwold frowned at her uncertainly for a moment, but decided to follow her lead. 'My Mantis-kinden would have me give the order to kill you,' he said. 'Is that what you want?'

'Are you suggesting that would solve anything?' Teornis asked him.

'It would solve my immediate problem. Perhaps it would send the right kind of message to the Aldanrael. But, no, it is not a course of action I am eager to try. I remember when you and I stood on the same side, Teornis. I never looked for anything but your friendship, but neither can I stand by and let my city fall victim to . . . pointless acts of brigandage. So what am I to do?'

'Let me kill him,' Danaen said promptly.

Teornis curled his lip. 'Your Mantis makes great presumptions about her capabilities.'

'This is not helping,' Stenwold stated. 'We came to talk, not to fight.'

Danaen spat. 'I've told you, Maker, there's only one way to deal with Spiders. If you won't take that step, I will.'

'You will not!' Stenwold snapped in return.

Her eyes blazed rebelliously. The Dragonfly-kinden that Teornis had brought were reaching for arrows.

'Felyen! To me!' Danaen yelled out. There was a moment's startled pause and then a half-dozen Mantis-kinden were clambering over the sides of the barge, dripping wet but armed to the teeth. The Dragonflies had their bows bent instantly, and Teornis's Ants formed up around him, with shields raised.

'Why, Maker? Why use Mantis-kinden?' Teornis cried out. 'Any other race might possibly exercise some self-control, some rational restraint, but *Mantis*-kinden? You might as well have cut the throat of any chance for peace between us.'

Stenwold was barely listening to him. 'Danaen, what is this?' he demanded, aware that Padstock's people had brought their snapbows up.

'You do not need to ask, Beetle,' the Mantis leader told him. Her reinforcements had now spread out across the deck in a loose crescent, ready to descend on Teornis's guards.

*And on Teornis's ship someone will be watching the sky to ensure nobody comes flying to our aid,* Stenwold thought wildly, *but they will not be watching the sea. Who would think that they could just* swim *over?*

'What of Mantis honour,' he demanded, 'that commodity you speak so highly of? The Mantis-kinden I have known would not betray me so!'

The look Danaen turned on him was of pure scorn. 'The Mantis you knew was a blood traitor, a breeder of abomination,' she hissed at him. 'Do not think you know us, Beetle. Do not think you know us, at all.'

Stenwold must have missed a signal then: not from the Mantids but from Teornis himself. The next thing he knew was the cold line of a dagger against his throat, and someone holding him tightly from behind. His first thought was that it was one of the Mantids, but then he heard Arianna's voice whisper, 'I'm sorry.'

'Everyone still now,' Teornis commanded. 'Mantis swords back in Mantis sheaths, and you Beetles can aim those bows down at the floor. If you're talking about *justice*, Maker, your people have a poor way of showing it.'

Stenwold stared only at him, because to twist his head to look at Arianna would hurt too much, above and beyond the knife. He expected to see contempt in his opponent's face, that a man who set himself up as a follower of the Dance should fall for such a transparent trick, but instead he surprised a pinprick of sympathy in the man's expression.

'Now, we will talk,' Teornis declared.

'You mistake us, Spider,' Danaen said, with evident relish. 'Have your traitor gut the fat old man if you wish. What is he to me?'

Teornis's reserve held. 'He is the spokesman of your new adopted city, or would you betray that as well?' he demanded archly.

She sneered. 'In even considering dealing with the likes of you, he has betrayed all right-thinking people. Kill him, or I shall kill him. I care not which.'

Teornis's eyes found Stenwold's gaze again, and his expression seemed to carry the accusation: *Your death be on your own head, since you chose to deal with these fanatics.*

*And it's true*, Stenwold thought, but the Mantis meant nothing to him just then. It was another betrayal that had cut him deeper.

The four Kessen Ants grouped tighter about Teornis,

each sharing thoughts with the next, ready to fend off the sudden Mantis strike that must be only seconds away. Stenwold could imagine Padstock and her people on the very edge of doing something unwise to Arianna, whose knife edge was like a razor at his throat. He could hear her ragged breathing and her arm about his neck was trembling slightly. *Her regrets are going to kill me at any second, but at least she has them.* The Dragonflies had bowstrings drawn back.

'Any bloodshed here and my ship will move in and rid the world of all of you,' Teornis declared flatly, 'Mantis bravado or not, you gain nothing here. The armada will still sail, and if you shed a drop of my blood my kin will . . . a—' He stopped speaking, mouth still open, his eyes fixed entirely elsewhere. A ripple of uncertainty ran through the cordon of Mantis-kinden, staying their hands for a precious second or two.

'Arianna . . .' Stenwold got out.

'Just stay still,' she whispered. 'I don't want to hurt you, Sten. I really don't want to hurt you. Please, please call them off.'

'I don't think I can . . .' he started to say, and she screamed and pushed him away from her.

He assumed she had been shot, but there had been no sudden crack of a snapbow. Then he thought she had sliced him, for pain lashed across his neck, but it was nothing but a shallow nick left by the sudden withdrawal of her knife. Then chaos and devastation were let loose, for Arianna's scream had set the Mantids in motion.

They made no subtleties about it, simply charging the Ants with savage speed in an attempt to overrun them. They clashed, with the Kessen trusting to their mail and shields, and their constant watch over each other, to turn the many swords away. One of the four Ants went down, Danaen's narrow blade curving over his shield's rim to pierce the armour at his throat. Another Mantis was felled and writhing, pinned to the deck by a long arrow, and one more had his face gashed by a Kessen shortsword. Stenwold tugged at his own blade, turning to see—

To see what Teornis and Arianna had seen, and it stopped him in his tracks, too. It was an eye.

It jutted out from the waves, set into a pointed crest of rubbery flesh tall enough to overlook the barge's low side: a mottled-yellow eye with a broad slash of black for a pupil, and measuring larger across than a man's torso.

All around him they were fighting, Teornis's people and his own. He heard the explosive snap of Padstock's bow, and her voice calling out, '*Through the Gate!*' which must have bewildered everyone there save for her own followers. The Dragonflies were aloft, sending down shaft after shaft at any Mantis that offered a clear target.

Teornis went down without warning. Stenwold thought he had been shot, then that a Mantis had got him, for his Kessen bodyguards were being overwhelmed, though they put up a stubborn and furious fight. Then Stenwold saw, and the sight made his stomach lurch.

Something had grabbed Teornis by the leg. Something like a leathery cable had snagged his ankle and was hauling him towards the rail. He had his rapier out, but its narrow blade was ill-suited to cutting, and his people were too busy fighting to hear his cries for aid. The sight was so horrible that Stenwold himself made a move towards him, with no other aim in mind but the rescue of his enemy.

In a flurry of wings, Laszlo landed beside him. 'I'll head for the *Tidenfree!*' the Fly called out.

'Laszlo, look!' But, when Stenwold pointed, the terrible eye was gone. The Fly skipped into the air a moment later, eager to be away, and an arrow zipped past close to where he'd been.

Stenwold turned to find himself not five feet away from Arianna, with his sword to hand. Her knife was still out, his blood decorating the edge. Their eyes met.

Something slapped at his leg and, assuming it was an arrow, he dropped into a crouch, one hand raised uselessly to ward off the next. A moment later he was sprawled on his back, the breath exploding from his body. He kicked out desperately, feeling a tightness about his calf, almost losing hold of his sword.

A sudden contraction hauled him two feet along the deck towards the railing and he realized that *it* had him.

Stenwold jackknifed up, crying out as he saw the thick tentacle that had snaked across the deck to encircle his leg. He lashed at it with his blade, just as a new convulsion rippled down the length of it, and he was dragged another half-body length towards the sea.

His nerve broke. The thought of that eye, belonging to some unspeakable sea-thing lurking just beyond the barge's rail, the thought of all that *water*, that all-consuming depth just yards away, was too much. Stenwold screamed in revulsion and fear, and hacked wildly at the grasping tentacle. His first blow glanced off its thick, oozing hide, while his second merely gashed open his own thigh. Another tug hauled him inexorably closer to the edge. He cast about wildly, still shouting for aid. He saw one of Padstock's company go down, spitted by an arrow. The Mantids were finishing off the Ants, and some were sending arrows up at the circling Dragonflies.

Teornis—

With a snarl of pure futile savagery, Teornis vanished over the barge's side, his rapier spinning from his hand. A moment later Stenwold's free foot kicked against the wooden rail.

He tried to brace himself against it, feeling the appalling strength as the monster's muscles seethed and pulsed. He hacked again, barely penetrating the creature's thick skin.

'Ma'rMaker!' Laszlo was beside him in an instant. The Fly's expression showed that, life of piracy or no, he had never encountered anything such as this before. His dagger was out in an instant, though, and he laid hands on the coils wrapped around Stenwold's leg and began cutting. He should have been halfway to the *Tidenfree* by now, but Stenwold had never been so glad to have his orders disobeyed.

Another surge of strength sent agony tearing through his leg and made the railing creak and splinter. Laszlo was using both hands to drive the dagger deeper, now, heedless of whether it skewered Stenwold as well.

'One moment, Ma'rMaker,' the Fly hissed between his teeth. 'Just one moment . . .'

His eyes met Stenwold's, and there was a moment of shared horror between them as another leathery whip crawled over the side and lashed itself about his chest. Laszlo opened his mouth to yell, but in the next second he was airborne, not by his own wings but whipped from the deck in a single convulsive spasm, and a second later the sea had claimed him.

Stenwold struck the limb that held him a solid blow, aiming for where the Fly's knife had scored its skin. It tugged yet again, and this time the railing half gave way. He had no wits left now for tactics or clear thinking; the sword was forgotten. Stenwold was clawing at the deck with both hands, a pointless struggle to stay clear of the dark and hungry ocean. He began howling something, some desperate plea. There was nothing left of War Master Maker but a sheer dread of the deep.

A hand grasped his wrist and hauled on it. He looked up into the fear-twisted face of Arianna.

'I have you!' she shouted.

'Don't let go!' He was weeping, trying to kick out with his snared leg, trying to dig his nails into the wood, all craft and Art lost to him.

'I have you, Sten!' she cried again, dragging at him, stealing back precious inches from the sea. 'I'm sorry, Sten,' she was saying. 'I'm so sorry!'

Stenwold saw the sword's point leap from her chest before he realized what it was. For a moment it was simply an image he could not make sense of, just as that great yellow eye had been. Then Arianna arched back, blood exploding from her lips, her grip gone from his wrist. As she fell, she revealed Danaen behind her, grinning like a madwoman, arms bloody to the elbows. She spared a moment to catch Stenwold's gaze, and her expression was pure triumph.

He screamed in grief and rage and terror at her, and then the tentacle hauled once again, and he slid past the broken rail and into the sea.

*Part Two*

# The Abyss Gazes Also

# Sixteen

The first thing that came to him as he awoke was the warmth of the muggy, humid air. It had a scent to it of sweat and the sea. His leg ached and burned, and he recalled how he had hacked at it in his haste, as it had been tugged and mauled by . . .

*The sea monster,* thought Stenwold. *Hammer and tongs, it's swallowed me.*

Other fragments of his situation began to touch him, one by one. He was lying on a curving, hard surface, not cold like metal but feeling more like bone or shell. His uneasiness increased. There was a pulsing sound in the air, heavy and insistent, and with each pulse the floor jerked, and his innards told him that he was in motion.

He was soaked to the skin. Somehow, perhaps because the air seemed saturated with water, that sensation came to him only just before he opened his eyes.

Opening his eyes was not an improvement.

There was light, but like no light he had ever seen before. It was an oppressive reddish-purple, and he could see very little by it. His face was shoved close against the curving inside of whatever held him, be it beast or box.

He tried to keep still, to avoid awakening the further ire of the sea monster, but the horror of his situation clung to him, refusing to be dislodged. Caught by that obscene tentacle, hauled towards the waters, the desperate struggle to free himself, the yawning maw of the ocean.

*Arianna.*

Her face as Danaen had run her through. Arianna who had tried to betray him, but had not been able to. Arianna who had died in a final act of loyalty, but died nonetheless.

With that he could no longer keep it in. At first his shoulders shook, and then his whole body. He tried to reach out, to grasp at the insides of the monster to stop the upwelling of emotions, but he found he could not move his hands, which were pinioned behind him. A shudder racked him, and Stenwold wept for dead Arianna, and for his exchange of the sun for the bowels of a beast.

There was a sound nearby, over that relentless, slightly erratic pulsing. Only a moment later did he realize that it was speech. It was weirdly drawn out and accented, and he caught not a word, but it was a human voice. He tried to twist round, only to find himself tied or webbed with leathery, slightly pliable ropes. The voice continued, joined by another, still uttering words he could not quite catch. He forced himself to calm down. *Where there are live men, there is hope, and they do not sound as though they expect to be consumed.* The tone of the speakers was jarringly conversational. Stenwold took hold of his grief and loss and fear, and this time he forced it down, steadied himself, and listened.

They were speaking familiar words, he finally realized, but with a strange inflection. He caught the odd piece of meaning, and then put together strings of words at a time, until he heard:

'. . . Not what I looked for in a land-kinden at all. Such ugly things, these two, anyway. Why these?'

'Ask Arkeuthys,' the other voice said, or that is what Stenwold thought he heard. He was unsure, until the first voice answered, whether it was a name, or simply a phrase he had not understood.

'*You* ask him,' said the original speaker. His voice was a little higher than the second one. He sounded younger.

'You've never talked to Arkeuthys, have you?' said the older-sounding voice, a man's voice as were they both, although Stenwold had not been sure of that initially. 'You're scared?'

'I don't need to talk to him to be scared,' said the younger. 'Seeing him's enough.' Stenwold was following their talk more easily now. They sounded close enough to be crouching just behind him, speaking only loud enough to be heard over the . . .

*Over the engine* . . . The revelation surged through him. No heartbeat this, but some manner of engine. He had heard nothing like it before, but he was more and more sure that the sound was mechanical in nature, and part of nothing living, for all it had no definite rhythm. He had already identified that each thundering pulse jerked them forwards, and could only guess at the means of propulsion that he bore baffled witness to.

One of the men gave out a ragged groan, without warning, and for a moment Stenwold thought the other must have stabbed him. Then there was some ragged breathing, and the younger voice continued, 'Arkeuthys says . . . ?'

Stenwold took a deep breath and gave a determined twist at whatever held him, resulting in him flopping onto his back, crushing his bound arms beneath his own weight, He had a brief view of the pale curve of a close ceiling, with some kind of lamp shedding the sanguine light, and then he heaved himself round again so that he was facing away from the wall.

There was far less space here than he had first thought. The erratic surge of the engine had given the cramped chamber a false sense of distance. Instead, he now found himself staring at Teornis.

The Spider lord was awake but lay very still, so Stenwold

guessed he had been playing dead for the benefit of their captors. He had opened his eyes as Stenwold moved, though, and now he winked once, very deliberately. His fine clothes were torn, and his hands were also bound. *So, this was not a Spider plot, then, but who . . . ?*

Beyond Teornis were two men, obviously the two speakers. The ceiling was low enough to have them kneeling, and the bloody light made things uncertain, but Stenwold thought they were pale-skinned and dark-haired. There was a younger and an older one, as he had surmised, and they made surely the strangest pair ever to be crewing any kind of automotive.

They were savages. That was his instant first thought. They were barbarians, primitives from some underdeveloped tribal land. They wore almost no clothing beyond kilts that extended to mid-thigh, but they made up for that in other finery. On his arms, the younger man wore some bracers that were inscribed with elaborate arabesques, and a torc encircled his neck. The older had metal tracery running all the way from wrist to elbow, work as delicate and intricate as Stenwold had ever seen, as light and complex as if it had grown there frond by frond. His collar was comprised of more of the same, an expanse of branching and rejoining tendrils of metal that covered most of his shoulders and upper chest. About his brow, his long hair was confined by a twining band of the same material. It was impossible to be sure in the strange light, but something about the glint of it suggested gold to Stenwold – gold in a quantity to make a Spider Aristos raise an eyebrow, and of a workmanship to match anything he could imagine man or machine achieving.

The younger man was lean and slender, and he had a short beard cut square, of the same dark lustre as his hair. His senior was paunchier, broad across his bare midriff, more jowly about the face, and with a beard that had been carefully styled so that it curved upwards and rolled into itself. Beyond all this, though, came the revelation that, despite Teornis's captivity, these were Spider-kinden.

Or no, they were not *exactly* Spider-kinden, not quite, but there was a similarity between their faces and Teornis's that showed them to be some sort of kin, some offshoot of the same root-stock, linked by a trick of ancestry.

And an errant thought occurred to him, *Have I not seen this before in someone recently, that I took for a Spider?* But he could not pin down the idea and it soon escaped him.

'Arkeuthys says . . .' the older man stammered. He was looking strained, to Stenwold's eye. 'He says he saw their two leaders trading insults, and it was these two he grabbed.'

'And what about the other one? Did you—?'

'Of course I did.' The older man glared at his fellow. 'He says it's just some land-kinden who got in the way. He *cut* Arkeuthys, the little one did.'

'So we don't need him, then?' To Stenwold's alarm, the younger man took a knife from his waistband, a vicious-looking weapon with a wicked inward curve. Stenwold craned his neck to follow the man's gaze, and spotted a third captive: the tiny trussed form of Laszlo, looking bruised and still unconscious.

The older man's eyes abruptly moved to meet Stenwold's own, and there was a shock of alien contact, reinforced by Stenwold's meanwhile working out who 'Arkeuthys' must be. Of course, there was an Art for speaking with beasts, though you seldom heard of it these days. But one could only speak with animals appropriate to one's people . . .

*Founder's Mark!* he whimpered inwardly. *These are sea monster-kinden.*

Noting his distress, the man with the coiled beard smiled. 'Kill the little one now. He can't be worth much,' he said.

'Hoi!' This was a new voice, emerging from somewhere

ahead, towards the vehicle's direction of travel. 'None of that!'

'Keep out of it,' the older man snapped.

'Nobody's killing anyone!' the new voice insisted. It was a higher pitch than theirs, clearly a woman's voice, but high even for that. Her accent was slightly different, too, drawling the vowels less, but also stressing her words in unexpected places. Stenwold found it even harder to follow.

'Arkeuthys says—' one of the first two began to argue.

'Don't care. If we've got three land-kinden, then we bring *all* three land-kinden back to the colony, alive.'

The look on the face of the older man showed resentment and loathing. '*I* am the voice of the Edmir here.'

'And I'm the handler of this barque,' the woman shot back.

'So?'

'So if you even want it to get as far as your Edmir's city, you keep me sweet, or I'll push off for the Stations or Deep Seep, or wherever I choose.'

'You wouldn't dare—'

'And *furthermore*,' the woman's voice continued, ploughing straight over the older man's words, 'if you suggest killing someone just because they're *small*, then I'll get Rosander to pincer your piss-damn arms off at the elbows, got it?'

The look on the man's face was, Stenwold found, exactly the look of a Spider thwarted by someone undesirable. 'The Edmir shall hear of this, Chenni,' he growled.

'I'll pit your chief against mine, any day,' the woman jeered at them. 'And at least tell me you equalized them. Did you do that one thing right?'

'As they're not crushed and dead, of course we did,' the younger man spat back. 'We know our business. You keep to yours!'

The one thing that came through, across this chasm of different cultures, was the thought: *They are divided*. Even here, trapped and grieving and, he had no doubt about it, in some kind of submersible automotive deep beneath the waves, he had a tiny spark of hope. If there were factions, there would be politics and, whatever his talents, he was a statesman.

And they would let Laszlo live, and that gave him an ally. *And maybe Teornis as well, for all that they look like Spiders. These are no more his people than mine.*

Then the older man snarled with frustration and signalled for his colleague to put away the knife and, to enact that frustration, he kicked Teornis in the kidneys and then stamped on Stenwold's gashed and abused leg. The sudden flare of pain was savage enough to rip consciousness away from him.

He awoke again to a firm and nudging pressure against his better leg, slowly jolting him from the morass of oblivion. He opened his eyes to see the grim reddish light, and shut them again. The nudging continued. It felt like a foot.

*Arianna.* The thought came to him from nowhere, a thought orphaned and without issue, passing him like the lights of a distant ship. He clenched his fists, feeling them tug and stretch at the stuff that was binding them.

'Maker.' The voice was soft, barely on the edge of hearing.

'Teornis?' he murmured in reply, as quietly as he could, trusting to the Spider's hearing.

'None other,' came the response. 'Our jovial friends have gone fore. How much of their talk did you hear?'

'Some. I understood less, though. And you?'

'The same. However, they're a bloody-handed lot, it's clear.' Stenwold had to strain his ears to hear the calm, measured tones. 'And Apt, it seems, for I take this to be a machine of some kind.'

'That's my guess, though the walls and floor are made of nothing I've ever seen manufactured.' There was movement from nearby, and they fell silent at once. Stenwold heard two people, he assumed the same two, shuffle up closer and hunker down.

'What's the order?' enquired the younger voice.

'Get them cloaked and hooded. The Edmir wants nobody to set eyes on the land-kinden. He'll send men to take them directly to his cellars.'

There was a little shifting around, and Stenwold heard the younger man whisper, 'What if *she* wants them for Rosander?'

The older man let out a long breath. 'We'd better hope the Edmir gets more men to us quicker than the Nauarch can.'

Absently, Stenwold wondered whether his own future would be more secure in the hands of this Edmir or the one they called Rosander. He recalled that their pilot, who had spared Laszlo's life, had been acting for Rosander, but he had a gloomy suspicion that there were no such thing as safe hands now waiting to receive the captive landsmen.

*Waiting where? Where in all the maps are they taking us?* But there were no answers to that, no more than there were maps.

The lurching motion of their craft was slowing, he noticed, accompanied by a few bucking shifts of direction. His stomach clenched at the realization that, whatever port they were heading to, they were shortly due to arrive.

They suddenly plunged – there was no other word for it. It was as if they were in a flier that had abruptly lost its grip on the air. Stenwold heard one of their captors groan at the motion, that had sat quite easily with the Beetle. *Inapt are they?* Then, just as suddenly, they were rising, the curious vessel bucking a little against some external current, their unseen pilot wrestling, no doubt, with the levers.

A moment later the lurching of the engine ceased, the interior becoming vastly silent without it, and the motion of their conveyance, that had been so strange, became jarringly familiar. They were bobbing on calm water, just as if they were in nothing more than a rowing boat.

'Fat one first,' Stenwold heard quite distinctly, accent or no, and then their hands were on him. In the cramped space they were awkward with him, and it was plain they were trying to hurry as well. Stenwold let his body go intentionally slack, but after they had fumbled him a second time, they did something to their hands – something he instinctively recognized as Art – so that they latched onto his clothes and skin with a painful sureness. As they hauled at him, he felt as though they were going to rip strips of his hide off, and he yelled with pain and started cooperating with them as best he could. They laughed at that, and he wondered if they had known that he was awake all the time.

'Hood him,' snapped the older man, just as the light ahead changed in character from the infernal red of the vessel's innards to something greenish-blue, no more natural but considerably more pleasant. A moment later some kind of bag was dragged over Stenwold's head, the texture of it unpleasantly slick, after which he had to rely on guidance from his captors to get him out of whatever hatch the vessel possessed and onto stone that was worked in some smoothly undulating pattern.

They hurriedly dumped him, and he heard the younger man call out, and others coming over. There was a rapid conversation that he did not catch, save for several mentions of the name 'Rosander' again, and the instruction, 'Watch him.' Then he guessed his two captors were returning inside for Teornis and Laszlo.

The surface beneath him had felt like stone but, as his questing hands examined it, it had a peculiar texture to it, the polished surface still bearing faint indentations and pockmarks. The air about him was neither hot nor cool, laden with a kind of stagnant damp, and he could smell fish, and the sea, and the men around him possessed an oily, fishy odour of their own, which was unlike anything he had come across before.

Something dropped across his legs, making him cry out in pain. The unseen burden writhed and slid off him, and he guessed from its size that it was Laszlo. Then he heard approaching feet, and a current of agitation ran through his unseen guards. Someone barked something that could only have been a challenge, and then the shouting started.

Stenwold tried his best to follow what was being said, but the words escaped him, too fast and too foreign to make any sense. A pattern came to him, though, of thieves bickering over the spoils. *And I'm a spoil.* He could pick out the voice of the older man who had ridden in the submersible with them, and there were a lot of other voices backing his case. The opposing camp seemed to have far fewer participants, but their voices were of a very different character, certainly not the near-squeak of their pilot. In fact, their bass rumble put him in mind of very large men indeed, as big as Scorpions or even Mole Crickets.

He heard, in the midst of this cacophony, the distinctive sound of steel, the touch of blades: not put to use, yet, but sliding across one another, ready for blood. He scraped his head across the ground, trying to dislodge the bag, but it was no use. *This is maddening.*

Then there was a sharp rapping, surely a staff against the stone floor, and quiet followed meekly in its wake. Stenwold heard enough shuffling to imagine the two warring parties separating reluctantly.

'That is quite enough,' someone said, a new voice that was clearly used to being obeyed. 'Now, who leads these . . . ah, and is it Chenni I see there?'

There was a pause, and then the high tones of their pilot. 'Aye, your Eminence.' She sounded flustered, if Stenwold was any judge.

'Kindly tell your Nauarch, my ally the good Rosander,

that he need have no fear. He may approach me for speech with the land-kinden at any time.' The new voice spoke smoothly, but then it gained a new edge: 'And if your bannermen do not disperse this moment, do not think that Rosander can save them from being dismembered, joint by joint.'

'You . . .' Whatever Chenni was about to say, she clamped down on it.

'I don't dare?' The new voice was dangerously soft again. 'Your Rosander is not the sentimental fool you take him for. He'd not wish to upset me for a few worthless lives like these. Be thankful that you yourself are currently somewhat more dear to him than most. Now go. Your services with your machine are appreciated, but it is time for you and yours to quit this place and bother me no more.'

After the scuffling and shuffling that surely meant Chenni and her 'bannermen' dispersing, the order came, 'Get them to their feet.' Stenwold was unceremoniously hauled upright, supported between two men, and a moment later he was being hustled forward, stumbling over the unseen ground. He could only hope that Laszlo and Teornis were still nearby. The route was complex enough that he lost track entirely of how many turns they took, save that their journey was more often upwards than not, struggling and slipping on ramps of grooved stone that his boots could not properly grip. His captors were ruthless in their progress, using their Art to maintain their sticky grip on him whenever he threatened to fall.

At last they stopped, and he had the sense of a large space echoing with a murmur of voices. *A council chamber? A court of law? Am I to be tried for the crime of being land-born?*

'Land-kinden,' said the leader's voice more softly, 'from here you shall go to the cells, beneath my great halls, and I cannot say if you shall ever venture forth from them again.

I think it only fair, therefore, that you see, just this once, some small piece of your people's doom.'

A moment later the bag was dragged from Stenwold's head. He closed his eyes, anticipating a shock of sunlight, but instead there was an overcast, almost twilightish gloom, relieved only by patches of wan light, globes of blue-green or green-white or purplish-red. Those lights went back and back, though, and multiplied with distance. Stenwold found himself standing on the brink of a balcony of moulded stone, looking down into a vaulted space between curved walls swelling in the shadows and then narrowing to a pointed ceiling, which some half-seen walls were seamed into radial symmetry by elegant buttresses, as though they were standing within a vast stone gourd. Even in the dim light, Stenwold saw that, between the ridges, the ceiling and walls were folded and worked until they seemed more like the natural interior of some great shell than the work of hands. Below them a multitude bustled in the many-coloured dusky light, figures large and small, and none seen clearly, but no glimpse of any looking like kinden Stenwold knew. There were figures as small as Flies, or as large as Mole Crickets, or as slender as Mantids, and most of the throng wore little for garments – kilts, cloaks, perhaps a sash. A few clumped through the crowd in armour that made them seem as ponderous and powerful as automotives, broader across the shoulders than Stenwold was tall.

He glanced to either side, finding Teornis and Laszlo staring as aghast as he. Their captors mostly resembled the men from the submersible – the not quite Spider-kinden. The women amongst them were high-cheeked, fair and lustrous of hair, the men with elaborate beards, and all of them decked out in gold and a dozen kinds of precious stones that Stenwold could not identify. Others, standing like servants and subordinates, were taller and thinner, lightly armoured in breastplates and tall helms of what might be chitin or even boiled leather. These were cloaked and held long spears, and their faces, hollow-cheeked and elongated, were unlike any kinden Stenwold knew.

At his shoulder stood a man he immediately knew as the leader. He, too, was of the Spider-kin people and, although they were all attired like Aristoi, this man boasted an additional level of luxury. His dark, curled hair was shot through with a coiling net of gold and glinting gems and he wore gold leaf, like tattoos, from wrist to shoulder of both arms. His cloak was fashioned from the hide of some beast, picked out in curving abstracts of shimmering colours, and his torc was a crescent moon of mother-of-pearl that gave back all the colours of the unhealthy lamps.

'What think you, O land-kinden?' he asked, keeping his voice still low. 'Do you like your new home?'

'There has been a mistake. We're not your enemies . . .' Stenwold started hurriedly but, at a gesture, the bag was jammed over his head again, and he was marched away.

# Seventeen

They uncovered his head again somewhere else, some-where far less spacious that was reached by descending an incline. The glistening lamps shone a sallow greenish-yellow here, and the floor was set with intricate, irregular stone gratings. Even here in this oubliette, the walls and ceiling were ridged and patterned, painstakingly carved into organic whorls and ridges with such all-encompassing detail that at last Stenwold began to think in terms of 'grown' rather than 'made'. Half their guards had gone, leaving a handful of bearded men still holding on to them. Stenwold saw Teornis glancing about brightly, putting on an optimistic expression that Stenwold was sure he could not genuinely be feeling.

'Separate cells,' instructed the leader's voice. Stenwold followed the sound of it to see his shadowy form standing in an archway, just a dark shape in the darkness, there for a moment, and then turning to vanish off into the gloom.

For a moment Stenwold could see no cells, but then one of their guards pried open a floor-grate. Beneath them was a dank space enclosed by bars that were just folds and pillars of stone, some miserable grotto that combined the worst qualities of underwater and under the earth.

Teornis went first. He accepted it gracefully, stepping to the edge like a man going defiant to the gallows. One of their guards raised a hooked knife, and Stenwold felt a moment's panic before the man merely severed Teornis's bonds, before moving on to free the wrists of the other two.

'Thank you,' the Spider said, impeccably courteous.

'He didn't say to cut them loose,' another guard objected angrily.

'He didn't say not,' replied the man with the knife. 'If they're land-kinden, where are they going to go?'

When the angry one still looked stubborn, the knifeman poked Stenwold in the gut with a finger. 'You, fat man, you know where you are?'

Stenwold shook his head dumbly.

'Let them have their hands, poor lost bastards,' the knifeman declared, and Stenwold only belatedly recognized an awkward sympathy on his face. 'Look at them, their whole world's been cracked open.'

There was some laughter over this, even from the angry man, but the man with the knife didn't join in. As Teornis let himself down into his cell, another grate was levered up for Laszlo. The Fly-kinden looked so rebellious, Stenwold wondered if he might suddenly take wing and go . . . where? For their captors were correct, of course: Laszlo might buzz and batter his way through these sculpted halls forever. At last he climbed down into the hole, and only as his grate was lowered again did Stenwold note, *He didn't fly. Does that mean he's hurt? No, clever lad, he doesn't want to show them that he can.* For, of course, not one of the sea-kinden they had seen, amongst that briefly glimpsed bustle, had been airborne. *It's good to have a secret in reserve.*

'Now you, big man,' said the man with the knife. Another pit was yawning for Stenwold.

'Are you permitted to hear me speak?' Stenwold enquired, without hope.

'Say what, now?' The knifeman frowned at him. Stenwold repeated himself slowly, and the other shook his head without rancour.

'You speak all you like to the Edmir, when he comes for you. Now get in.'

Stenwold peered down, aware that little of the unwholesome light would reach him, down there. *At least Teornis and Laszlo can see better in the dark. I shall be blind.* The space was not great: enough room to sit down with his legs bent but certainly not enough to lie flat. The drop to the floor was about eight feet, he guessed.

Hands took hold of him and, rather than be cast into that stony grave, he lurched forward, took hold of the edge, and lowered himself gradually down.

The grating was dropped above him, making surprisingly little sound, then the guards padded off, their bare feet almost silent on the stone.

The gloom was all-pervasive, for the loathsome little lights seemed to illuminate nothing but themselves. In lieu of anything else, Stenwold fixed his gaze on them, seeing that they did not even flicker, just gave out their steady, sickly glow. *More like the phosphorescence of a fungus than a real lamp.*

After a moment he heard a dry chuckle that he identified as Teornis's. He reached towards the sound, his hand encountering the slick and uneven stone columns that stood boundary between his cell and the next. 'What?' he demanded. 'What's so funny?'

'I was just thinking,' Teornis's calmly amused tones issued from the murk, 'that even War Master Stenwold Maker of Collegium can't blame this one on the Empire.'

*How can he stay so calm?* But, of course, such grace in the face of adversity was part of the Spider way. They must maintain face until the very last. With that thought, something subsided within Stenwold, and he felt the Spider's example lending him a tenuous stability. The humour in Teornis's remark abruptly came to him, and he even managed a wretched laugh.

'That's better. I thought we'd lost you,' the Spider Aristos remarked. Stenwold thought that he now could just make out the other man's form moving amid in the forest of lumpen pillars.

'So, about this honest and frank discussion we were having,' Stenwold ventured, and guessed that the other two prisoners managed to raise their spirits a little at that, from Laszlo's snickering and the Spider's polite laugh.

'Yes, we made a hash of that, didn't we?' Teornis admitted. 'Or, well . . .'

'Or I did,' Stenwold declared flatly.

'Ma'rMaker, that isn't so . . .' Laszlo rushed to his defence.

'It was Danaen that broke the truce, and it was my decision to bring her along,' Stenwold observed. *And there, it is out, and I feel better for owning up to it.*

'Danaen's your Mantis, I take it,' Teornis said. 'Well, you're not the first taken in by the stories they tell about themselves, all guts and honour. They even believe it themselves, most of the time, but they're human just as we all are. Just as, I hope, our captors are. It was also your idea to hold our little meeting afloat, I recall.'

'Actually . . .' Stenwold frowned, 'that was Danaen also.'

Teornis left a pause before answering. 'I don't quite know what to make of that.'

'Those Felyal Mantids, Ma'rMaker, they're all sorts of boatmen,' Laszlo said slowly. 'Those longships of theirs turn up all over. Maybe . . .'

'Maybe they sold us to the sea-people,' Stenwold finished. 'I find it hard to credit, but . . .'

'But here we are now,' Teornis finished for him. 'Perhaps it was just too much temptation after I trusted my life to their forbearance. Ah, well, a lesson learned, although it's hard to see what use one might make of such a lesson now.'

Stenwold grasped at the intervening bars, feeling the texture of the ridged stone smooth beneath his hands. 'Honest and frank, Teornis? You're still willing to talk?'

'Talk all you wish, Master Maker.'

'Then tell me *why*.' When Teornis did not immediately reply he pushed further. 'Were the Aldanrael so disillusioned by our trade agreements and treaties that they had to push us into war?'

'Ah, that,' said the Spider, as though it was nothing, merely some child's game from long ago. 'Master Maker, I do regret it. I even spoke up against it, but when the matriarchs of the Aldanrael command, I must obey. I'm surprised you haven't fathomed it yet. Trade, Stenwold – it's as tawdry as that. Collegium relies heavily on trade coming through Helleron, both by rail and air. Even when the Empire had taken the place, there was still a surprising traffic continuing between your kinden's cities. However, during that occupation the sea trade increased in leaps and bounds. Your man Failwright and his people did well then, as did many of my own people. It's clear as glass that Helleron will surrender again, the moment the Empire so much as looks west. All we wanted, once that moment came, was to be in a position to profit from having an absolute control of the sea lanes – nothing more sinister, more dramatic, or more worthy than that. As I say, I myself felt it was beneath us and that there were better ways of exploiting our relationship with Collegium, but my damn-fool cousins decided they wanted to play pirate. Frank and honest enough for you?'

'And Arianna?' The words came out before Stenwold could stop them. 'Why . . . ?' But he let the sentence tail off and die, not wanting to hear his own voice tremble.

'Because I offered her the chance to live as a Spider should, and not as some surrogate Beetle-kinden,' Teornis explained. 'If it is any consolation to you, I was never sure truly whether I had her. I don't think she was sure, either.'

'It's no consolation.'

'Still, there may be grounds there for some reconciliation, in the unlikely event that we ourselves ever see land or daylight again. After all, our current circumstances surely put such matters into perspective.'

'She's dead. Danaen killed her.'

Teornis allowed a respectful interval to pass by before he responded to that. His eventual comment was, 'Well, I suppose I can claim my share of blame in that. I put her there, with a blade in her hand.'

Stenwold had no response to that, and an uncomfortable silence fell. In the end it was Laszlo who took up the slack.

'I'm sorry, Ma'rMaker. I had an arrow ready for her myself, when she put her knife to you, but I held off. I didn't think you'd want . . .'

'Thank you,' said Stenwold emptily. 'But I suppose Teornis is right. In the face of this' – he made a gesture that their eyes would pick out better than his own – 'it all of it seems a little pointless.'

'Sea-kinden . . .' Teornis pronounced. 'Well, my excuse is that it is hard to account in one's plans for the formerly mythological.'

Laszlo laughed bitterly. 'All those old maps,' he said. 'Sailors' stories. The sea-kinden – they say you could hear them singing out of the weed forests or from old rocks, to lure ships to their doom, you know? The maps, sometimes they would have them drawn on the empty spaces: beautiful girls down to the waist but, like, lobsters or something underneath. Bit daft, if you ask me.'

'Abominations, they would call those,' Teornis clarified, 'and merely an artistic convention. But these sea-kinden here are real enough, and human enough. Your people have no records of such, Stenwold?'

'Not that I've ever heard. Possibly our mariners have stories, as Laszlo says, but none that came to me.'

'And so we go on pushing at the borders of the world,

until we wish we'd left them well alone,' the Spider intoned softly, obviously quoting from some source Stenwold was unfamiliar with. 'Did you ever hear of the City of Bones, either of you?'

Laszlo anwered no, and Stenwold shook his head, trusting to the Spider's eyes to catch the gesture. His own vision was slowly adjusting to the pallor of the lamps, not to the gloom, so much, but the strange tricks they played with shape and shadow.

'It is an excavation, past the desert margin beyond Irroven. Scholars from our academies have been digging there nigh on ten years now. Nobody's ever seen anything quite like it.'

Stenwold frowned, not perceiving anywhere relevant this was taking them, but he let the man speak. In truth, Teornis's calm, conversational tones were helping a lot to ease his own disturbed mind, and perhaps the Spider knew it.

'There was a city there once, how long ago I cannot say, save that no Spider histories record it. No modern-day city is nearby, and the region has a poor reputation, for the sensitive. In uncovering the streets of this old ruin, our academics found something appalling, fascinating – a massacre.'

'No need to go digging for that. I could point you to plenty in our lifetimes,' Stenwold remarked sourly.

'It looked as though some invading force had overrun the walls, killed every living thing and then left the place to the desert. But the true surprise was in the nature of the bones unearthed. Bones of people, certainly, but bones of animals as well. Horses and goats and sheep, but also . . . other kinds of animals. Dozens of kinds of animals, freakish and unheard-of creatures. I have seen some of the pictures the scholars drew, to represent what they believed these dead beasts looked like. The world is best off without them: monsters such as you cannot imagine, horned and tusked and fanged. But dead, all dead, their bones lying where they fell, in the centre of a city lost to all maps. Their last stand, perhaps – but against who?'

Stenwold shivered, throwing the unpleasant images off. 'What's your point?' he asked.

'My point is that the world holds stranger things in it than we know. Even these sea-kinden are closer kin to us than whatever race lived in that dead city. Our chiefest captors here were enough like me that I must even accept them as some lost offshoot of my people. So, let us inventory what we know of them, and a plan may then suggest itself.'

'We know precious little,' Stenwold complained. 'Not least, we know no reason why they should wish us any harm – we who have not so much as looked at them before.'

'Start smaller,' Teornis suggested. 'Let us look at our current lodgings. What does this place suggest, to you?'

Stenwold frowned again, putting a hand to the nearest column of his cell. He felt the smooth, rounded, stone, formed as though it had once flowed like water and then set. 'No seams,' he said. 'This is all of a piece.'

'Have you ever seen a Mole Cricket sculpture?' Teornis put in. 'They could build this, I think, with their Art.'

'Caves,' Laszlo said unexpectedly. When they prompted him, he elaborated, 'There are sea caves I've seen, like this. I don't know how it works, but it's like the stone's dripping from the ceilings. You get spines and pillars, and all sorts, just like it was all frozen in mid-thaw. Only, I'd not put money on getting a lot of close-together little cells like this formed out of it.'

'Sea caves . . .' Stenwold felt a sudden irrational twitch of hope. 'Could we be . . . there's a lot of coast lies east and west from Collegium. There must be a lot of caves that nobody's ever gone to.' His mind was recalling to him that arched space that their captors had let them gaze out on, surely too great to be some little cave tucked into a cliff, but he overrode the thought. 'Perhaps we're even in easy march of Collegium, if only we could break out and—'

'You are not near your home.' The unfamiliar voice startled all three of them to silence. It was a woman's voice, accented like their captors', save that it was not coming from above, but from down there amongst the cells.

Stenwold scanned the dim vaults uselessly, seeing the dark shapes of Teornis and Laszlo, but no other. A moment later, Teornis's voice snapped out, 'Show yourself, if you please.'

Stenwold saw nothing immediate, but he caught Laszlo's sudden intake of breath.

'You are land-kinden? Truly?' the woman's voice resumed.

'My lady, we are,' Teornis confirmed, with some noticeable respect. 'I am the Lord-Martial Teornis of the Aldan-rael, and this is War Master Stenwold Maker of Collegium. His comrade is not known to me.'

'Laszlo, off the *Tidenfree*,' the Fly piped up, not to be outdone. 'Pleased to meet you, Ladyship.'

Stenwold caught a glimpse of movement, and located a shadow that must be her: the tenant of another cell of this stone honeycomb. 'Then I am Paladrya,' she told them simply, 'and whatever ranks or titles I once had, I am shorn of them now, and I can offer you only my apologies, my most sincere apologies, for the harm that I have done you.'

'What harm might that be, Bella Paladrya?' Teornis asked her softly.

'It is my doing you are here,' she told them. 'It is my doing that your people are in danger. All that now befalls you is my fault.'

# Eighteen

When he had taken hold of this colony of Hermatyre, after the troubles had been put down, he had asked the builders if they would open out a section of this antechamber of his so that he could see the waters.

With their skill and their Art, they had bidden the substance of Hermatyre retreat, and in its place they left the transparency of membrane, so that he who claimed, at least, to be their lord and master could view this broad slice of his domain. In truth, of course, the builders had no masters, no lords, save perhaps the unknown plan or design that induced them to tolerate all the trespassers – the Obligists – who dwelt here under the roofs that they created. On those few occasions in Hermatyre's history when an Edmir had displeased the builders, his reign had ended then and there, and it did not help that none could say for sure just what their errors had been. The Edmir Claeon, as with all those before him, therefore trod a careful path that he would never know the precise boundaries of.

*But I pushed far to claim this throne,* he considered, *and every day I must push further to hold it.* The name 'Rosander' came to him and he scowled. *If only things were otherwise I'd leave that tiny bald head of his out for the fish to clean.* But Rosander was a necessary evil, one it seemed that, each day, a little more time and effort went into handling. *But now we have the land-kinden, and everything will change. Rosander will have his war and then be out of my way.*

The view through his transparency was of the mottled sea floor, some distance below him, and stretching away until even Claeon's eyes could see no more. It was far from featureless because, beyond the boundaries that the builders had set on Hermatyre, there were outposts, weed farms, lobster runs, all the complex play of labour that furnished the people of Hermatyre with what they needed to survive. Save for the builders, of course, for the builders lived by their own graces, and cared nothing for those that eked out a living within their creations. *So why do they tolerate us, if they do not need us?* It was the question preoccupying every Edmir since the first, and Claeon would not be the one to answer it.

Something monstrous and vast moved across his field of vision, blotting out the rounded shells of farms and the coloured sparks of the limn-lights. Claeon watched as the great coiled length coursed across his view, waiting again until the great leviathan had bunched itself together in a vast knot of limbs and baggy, creased flesh, and then drifted back to press a broad, yellowish eye to his window. This view, this transparent membrane, was one of Claeon's private pleasures. His people were not permitted to swim up to ogle their ruler, and there were guards outside to enforce his whims. Some creatures of Hermatyre did not consider themselves bound by such laws, however. Just now, Arkeuthys was letting Claeon know of his desire for a conversation.

Claeon had heard of how it was, for other kinden, when they used the Speech-Art. Their charges were dumb brutes with simple desires, and they were easily instructed, chided and controlled. Claeon's people had always suffered a more challenging relationship with their own beasts, for the great octopuses of the reef had minds that could reason like a man's, and as for Arkeuthys . . . Arkeuthys was well over a century old, the largest, wisest and most ancient of his kind, and the undisputed ruler of all his people. Arkeuthys was another necessary evil without whom Claeon would not stand where he now stood.

*You play a dangerous game.*

In Claeon's head, the voice of the octopus-king was like stones grinding and rattling in the far, cold depths. Normally it was the human mind that opened the channels of Art-Speech, but Arkeuthys had seen human generations come and go, and understood their minds better than they did themselves.

'Because I must,' Claeon whispered, knowing that Arkeuthys would feel his thoughts, read his lips, draw his meaning out despite membrane and water.

*These prisoners . . .*

'Are safe.'

*Are you not concerned that you have gone too far?*

'I got where I am by taking risks. You know that.'

*Word about the land-kinden is across the city already.*

Claeon frowned. 'How is that possible? I took every precaution—'

*You left your own men and the Nauarch's men alive as witnesses, and you humans do love to talk. Probably there is not one of you who does not now speculate about the Edmir's new prisoners. You had best make quick use of them.*

Claeon nodded. 'You were absolutely sure of your prey, were you?'

*Two of them were leaders, the third merely an annoyance.*

The Edmir stared into the horizontal slash that was Arkeuthys's pupil. 'And how would you know a land-kinden leader?'

*I can tell a leader of men by the way that he stands*, the leaden voice of the octopus ground out the words.

Claeon's expression soured a little, wondering if some criticism was meant there. Did he, Claeon, *stand* like a leader of men? Arkeuthys was silent on that point, and to ask would

283

be to show weakness. 'We shall see what we can squeeze from them that I can then feed to Rosander.' He grinned suddenly, teeth glinting amid his dark beard. 'What of you? Do you, too, not speculate about the fabled land-kinden?'

*What are they to me, or to my kind? Less than nothing,* came Arkeuthys's reply. The huge body bunched itself about the frame of Claeon's window. *There is trouble coming, Edmir. I sense the currents shift. Do not be unready.*

Then the enormous length of the great octopus was spiralling away, surging off into the open water, casting a many-limbed blot over the peaceful and pastoral seascape.

One of his people came to him shortly after, bowing low and waiting to be acknowledged. She was Sepia-kinden, her pale skin currently set with a spray of red-brown freckles that pulsed slightly as she breathed. Claeon regarded her proprietorially: one of his more decorative servants, and possessing a keen mind for her kind – or at least keen enough to want to keep her master happy.

'What do you bring me?' He stood with the great sea-window at his back, and beyond it the midnight reaches of his domain.

'An envoy from the Littoralists awaits your pleasure. It is Pellectes, Your Eminence,' she announced, keeping her eyes modestly lowered. Like all the Sepia-kinden she was slight of build, her body rounded and soft, her nature, he supposed, as passionate and expressive as they were claimed to be. He could not immediately recall her name, but that was surely secondary, as was the fact that she had proved herself a fair majordomo since he appointed her three moons ago. She had lasted longer than all of the last three officials put together. Mind you, Claeon had been going through an impatient phase, just before her appointment, and he was a man intolerant of small failures. *After all, why spend so much in gaining the Edmiracy, to let fools balk me still?*

*And speaking of fools* ... 'The Littoralists can wait until the coral grows over them,' he snapped, seeing her skin flush in points and swirls of blue and green at his sharp tone. Pellectes would want the land-kinden handed directly over to him, of course, but Claeon did not need the Littoralists as much as he once did. *One necessary evil that is now losing its necessity.* And he had only one response to unnecessary evils.

'Send some of my guards to fetch me a spokesman from the prisoners. I will see how these creatures dance,' he directed his majordomo. *Haelyn* was her name, he now recalled. He would have to detain her, after she had passed on his orders. It would not be the first time, and she would be glad of it, or at least wise enough not to show any different. It would set him in the right frame of mind for torturing a land-kinden.

'Your fault?' Stenwold asked, trying to discern more of the woman Paladrya in this poor light.

'I am in no position to make amends,' she said, her voice halting, tentative. 'Grant me one wish, though, land-kinden. Tell me, is he well?'

This was so unexpected that not even Teornis had an answer for her. When the silence stretched out, she begged them, 'Please, tell me, is he hurt? He . . . he cannot be dead, surely?' There was a ragged edge to her tone now.

'Lady, we do not know of whom you speak,' Teornis told her gently.

'But surely he must have sent you . . . ?' She trailed off. 'If you do not follow Aradocles then why are you here?'

'A very fair question, but the answer lies below the waves and not above it,' the Spider replied.

'We were snatched from our ship by your sea monster,' Stenwold explained, unable to keep a shudder from his voice. Even to think of that moment, the creature's arm coiled about his leg, the sudden lurch, the waters closing over his head . . .

'But I see this is not some prison made especially for landsmen, then,' Teornis intervened brightly. 'You are a native yourself, I perceive. Are the sea-kinden so very law-abiding that you are their one criminal? What are your circumstances, that you must endure our company?'

Stenwold could make her out more clearly now. She looked very pale against the surrounding gloom, the sallow lights catching her skin. Like all the sea-people she wore very little, just a kilt and a cloth pulled about her breasts. Her appearance was gaunt, and the way she held herself showed a woman hurt and vulnerable.

'This is the Edmir's own oubliette,' she pronounced. 'These spaces are reserved for those valuable enough to keep, and too dangerous to ever let loose. I am here because I am a traitor to the Edmir, and yet . . . and yet he has not steeled himself to kill me.'

'This Edmir, he's your lord, is he? The ruler of this place?' Teornis pressed, and Stenwold had to strain to see her nod. The Spider continued, 'And what is this place? What is it called? If it is no cave, then what is it?'

'This is the colony of Hermatyre,' she told them, obviously considering the words self-explanatory.

'A town?' Teornis asked and, when she did not respond, 'There are many people in this colony of yours?'

'Oh, thousands,' she told them. 'Hermatyre is the largest of all the colonies, and that's not counting the Benthist trains.'

'Well, who'd count them?' said Teornis drily, still chipping away at his bafflement. 'Excuse us for these questions, but we find ourselves strangers and prisoners in a very hostile place, and you are the first person who has had pleasant words for us.'

'Why are you to blame for us being here?' broke in Stenwold, perhaps impoliticly. 'Or do you take that back now, now that we are none of your . . . Aradoces, or whatever the name is.'

'I am to blame,' she confirmed sadly. 'It was I who turned the Edmir's eyes towards the land. I have endangered not only you but all your kinden . . .' She stopped fearfully, and at that point Stenwold heard movement above. Before his eyes, Paladrya faded, her pale skin greying until, lost in the dimness, she had blended with the stone around her. *What good can it do her*, he wondered, *since she is still in her cell?* He guessed this hiding Art was pure reflex, her last attempt at defence, slipping beneath the notice of her captors so as to escape one more beating, or worse.

A knot of the sea-kinden had entered the room from above and were peering down at them through the gratings: four men and a woman, gold ornamentation glittering in the sick light against fish-white skin and lustrous dark hair. 'Land-kinden,' one of the men called.

'We hear you,' Teornis said.

'You are the leader here?' they asked him.

'No one else is.' Teornis risked a glance at Stenwold, while squaring his shoulders. The unspoken thought was there: *I will meet this, whatever they intend.* Stenwold wondered whether the thought of poor Arianna's fate lay behind the man's bravery, and he was seeking to make amends.

The sea-kinden hauled up the stone grille, and Stenwold realized that nothing but the hatch's own weight kept it in place: no locks or latches. He wondered if he might be able to shoulder it open, if he managed to climb up there. The grille looked like a four-inch thickness of stone, and must be a prodigious weight, but surely not impossible to shift.

Teornis held his arms up towards the gap, and they could just reach down to take hold of his wrists and haul him out, his boots kicking at the sides to stop him being scraped against the stone. He stood in their midst like some lord, with nothing of the captive about him, and for a moment they hung back a little uncertainly. Then their spokesman smacked him across the side of the head, and another shoved him in the back, making him stagger, and they jeered at him as they manhandled him out of sight.

Stenwold hoped the Spider's considerable resourcefulness would help him survive whatever was to come. *But, of course, he is Teornis of the Aldanrael, so he'll come back on a litter carried by a dozen virgins.* The sentiments rang hollow, though, and Teornis, his enemy of only the day before, had now become one of the most familiar points in Stenwold's world.

Laszlo let out a long sigh. 'And then there were two, Ma'rMaker. I'm of a mind to go scout out this Hermitty place, before they drag me off as well.'

Stenwold made a wry face. 'Sounds like a grand plan, Laszlo. Perhaps I'll go with you once I've picked up some Mole Cricket Art and can walk through walls or something.'

'Fly-kinden Art beats all,' Laszlo announced. 'But we were talking to the lady. Hey, lady, you still there?'

Stenwold was watching for it now, and saw how Paladrya now paled and shaded gradually from stone-colours to the pallid white that served these sea-kinden for skin tone. It was nothing like the Art Danaen had used to become so very still that Stenwold had overlooked her: this was simply a camouflaging, a blending of shades.

'I am here,' she told them.

'What will happen to Teornis?' Stenwold demanded of her.

She looked downwards. 'I cannot say, for I do not know what they want, of you. Possibly they will torture him, if the Edmir is so inclined, or if they think that he knows anything of Aradocles.'

'We know nothing of him – assuming it's even a him,' Stenwold told her. 'Why should we?'

'Because, some years ago, I took him to the shore and sent him away on to your land, to escape the Edmir. I had hoped he would come back, perhaps with an army of land-kinden, but I have heard nothing. I hoped that you . . . that he had sent you here.'

Stenwold shook his head wearily. *Other people's problems*, he thought, *as though I don't have enough of my own.*

'Lady, if I walked out from here, what would I see?' Laszlo interrupted.

'We are beneath the Edmir's palace,' she told him. 'There are many tunnels down here, and quarters for his most trusted servants and guards, and rooms for his pleasures.' There was a catch in her voice on that last word. *Torture*, Stenwold at once surmised, remembering her mention of it, and then he looked at Paladrya again and guessed that she had undergone her share of that treatment as well.

'And then?' Laszlo pressed her eagerly.

Looking at him, the ghost of a fond smile appeared on her face. 'And then, small one, you would come to the main halls of the palace, and from there it would be but a step to the Cathedra Edmir. And from there to anywhere in Hermatyre that you might choose, if you but knew anywhere – or anyone.'

Laszlo nodded, obviously seriously considering this further. 'Well since our hosts have seen fit to give me a cloak, how much would I stand out, up there? I saw a few fellows around my size, when we looked out over the market or whatever you had there.'

'You might be taken for a Kerebroi child, perhaps, or one of the Smallclaw-kinden,' Paladrya guessed. 'Although you have hair, and none of the Onychoi do.'

Stenwold could only blink at these unfamiliar terms, but Laszlo shrugged casually.

'I'll try and keep my head covered,' he said. 'Now, let's see about this grating.'

Stenwold folded his arms, and watched as Laszlo's wings flared in the dimness, and took him to the top of his own cell, until he was clinging to the grille.

He heard Paladrya gasp in astonishment 'That is your Art?' she said in awe. 'But that is amazing, impossible . . .'

'Lady, that's just flying,' Laszlo replied offhandedly. 'Still, I reckon your fellows up there wouldn't expect me to end up at this end of the bottle.' He had twisted himself now until he had his feet firmly anchored against the wall, his shoulders pressed to the grille. For a moment he paused, breathing heavily, then his wings flared and flickered, spread out flat against the grating, and he used all their upward force to push at it.

It did not move. He might as well have been trying to pry the stone of the bars apart.

Laszlo collapsed back to the cell's floor with an expression of astonishment. 'Well, I thought I'd at least shift it a bit. How much can it weigh?' he muttered.

'The hatches have water-locks,' Paladrya explained. 'Unless you possess the Art, and know where to pull, they will not open for you. I'm sorry.'

'The Art?' said Laszlo grimly.

'The Kerebroi Art,' she confirmed. 'The gripping Art.'

Stenwold recalled how the guards' hands had latched on to him, raising weals on his skin and biting into his clothes. He heard Laszlo curse in frustration, his earlier confidence utterly misplaced, and Stenwold half expected him to take wing again and start battering about the top of his cell in a desperate bid to find a way out.

The next moment they heard raised voices, and then a group of people approaching above, some of them with very heavy footfalls indeed. The guards reappeared, and not alone. All four men were trying to keep a trio of newcomers out, but they were severely out-sized. The figure in the lead was huge, easily as wide as two of the guardsmen together, and armoured in a suit of curving, overlapping plates. There was no scrape or clatter of metal about him, so Stenwold guessed that it was chitin mail, or whatever local substitute they used here. Nothing of the man was exposed, from his clumping, segmented boots all the way up to his massively broad pauldrons and the surprisingly small full-face helm that allowed only a slit to observe the world through. The guards kept shouting at him, trying to bar his way but obviously unwilling to start anything violent. The enormous man just shouldered forward, one plodding step after another, until he was standing at the foot of the ramp. He raised both hands up to shoulder height, and the guards backed off hurriedly, for his gauntlets each bore a forward-hooking claw that jutted a good six inches from the knuckles.

Behind the huge man, almost in his shadow, came two others. One was Fly-size, bald-headed and hunchbacked, wearing only some kind of short smock. The other was as tall as anyone there, lean and muscled and as bald as his smaller companion, with some kind of Art-growth protruding about his fists.

'You dare defy the Edmir?' one of the guards was berating them. 'Do you think he will sit still for this insurrection within his colony?'

'The Nauarch just wants to talk to a land-kinden. Is that so bad?' said the smallest figure, who appeared to be in charge. With a start Stenwold realized he recognized that voice: the pilot who had transported them to this place, in that cramped and blood-lit submersible. He craned his neck to get a better look. She had something at her belt, some unfamiliar-looking bundle, but when he saw it more clearly he felt that it must be something like an artificer's toolstrip. *Apt*, he decided, *but only her?* The guards, in their kilts and barbaric splendour, seemed unlikely candidates for engineers, and the small woman's two companions looked no better suited. When he had looked out over that crowded chamber earlier, there had been nothing to suggest any mechanical industry going on here and, under the sea, how could it? *And yet that submersible . . .* someone *had made that. Maybe she is some freak, a solitary maverick.*

'The Nauarch can go peel himself,' growled one of the other guards, perhaps unwisely. In an instant the lean, bald man had struck him, punching the offender in the jaw, and whipping his head round with the force of it. The victim collapsed back into his fellows and then slumped to the floor.

The other guards had knives out then, the same broad, hooked blades Stenwold had seen before. Against the armoured giant and the horn-fisted man they seemed paltry.

'If you slay us, we who are servants of the Edmir, you will never set foot in this colony again,' one of the guards warned desperately.

'And wouldn't that be a shame,' said the Fly-sized woman. 'Now, your Edmir said something to me when we brought these land-kinden in. Some of our bannermen wanted to do the Nauarch's will by taking a landsman away with them, there and then, and ol' Claeon, he said that my Rosander wouldn't tear up their alliance just because a few of our people got killed. Well, I reckon that's true, but it cuts both ways. The Edmir finds you torn apart and hung about like bunting, he's not going to go to war with Rosander over it. You Kerebs are hardly important enough, so keep out of our way and hush your mouths.'

She then looked down for the first time, to see the two land-kinden. To Stenwold's chagrin she addressed the Fly. 'You're the boss here?'

'Oh, that would be grand,' said Laszlo acidly, still smarting from his failed escape attempt.

'I am War Master Stenwold Maker of Collegium.' Stenwold spoke up to draw her attention to himself. He did not like where this might be going, and if someone else out there wanted to torture the land-kinden, then it would not be Laszlo's back bared for the lash.

'That sounds very high and mighty,' the woman re-marked, and her name came back to Stenwold: *Chenni*.

'I would be glad to act as ambassador to your leader,' he announced.

She smirked at that. 'Well, that's just dandy.' Her head snapped up again to focus on the guards. 'Get this open,' she commanded.

They stared at her sullenly, the three of them still standing upright. They had given up on evicting the intruders from the oubliette, but that was a different thing to actively helping them.

'None of you?' Chenni prodded, and then sighed. 'Well, I was just trying to make it easy for you.' She stood back, gesturing to the tall, lean man. 'Do the honours.'

The bald pugilist flexed his arms and rolled his shoulders, crouching down before the hatch to Stenwold's cell. His fists were huge, with a chitinous shell formed over their knuckles and a vicious, backwards-pointing spike alongside the edge of his palms. As Stenwold watched, the spikes flexed, snapping forward like daggers, and then slowly folding back again. As Art-grown weapons went, they were as formidable and complex as he had ever seen.

While reflecting on that, he missed the motion. The man above him became a blur, and the grating smashed into fragments that rained down on Stenwold, rebounding painfully from his head. He ended up half-sitting against the cell wall, arms raised for protection, surrounded by hand-sized fragments of shattered stone. Numbly he noted that they were hollow: honeycombed with irregular chambers like magnified pumice. *Probably not heavy at all, just held tight by this 'water-lock' thing until . . .*

He looked up wonderingly. The man was now extending a shell-knuckled hand down towards him. 'Don't make me come down and get you,' he warned, and Stenwold did not need to be told twice. He reached tentatively up, feeling the strength in the other man's grip, and then the mailed giant had taken hold of his comrade and, between them, Stenwold was dragged up through the ruins of the hatch.

The edges of it were razor-jagged, ripping his clothes and grazing his skin, but his new captors obviously cared nothing for his comfort, dumping him at their diminutive leader's feet.

'Someone wants to meet you, landsman,' Chenni told him, and then instructed her companions, 'Pick him up and carry him. We're moving out.'

# Nineteen

As soon as they had him beyond the oubliette, they had bundled Teornis in hood and cloak again. He made no attempt at a struggle, sensing that his captors were all too eager to inflict some punishment on him. He tried to keep track of turns, of slopes up and down, but this place, this Hermatyre, seemed to have been laid out by madmen, and within moments he had lost all track of where he was, what direction they had taken. He sensed few other people nearby, though, so either the passage of the guards was being given a wide berth or they were using some secluded back way.

*They do not want any of us seen. No doubt the land-kinden would cause quite a stir.* And that was another piece to work with: firstly a division between the factions of their captors, then a separation between the captors and the general populace. This was all grist to Teornis's mill, which was good because that mill had been perilously short of material to feed it for too long now.

He had said a lot to Stenwold that his family would have frowned on. He now played out the recriminatory interview in his head: his mother or his eldest sister glowering down at him.

*You revealed the family's plans to your enemies. That is outright betrayal,* either one of them would accuse him.

*We were trapped in a cave beneath the sea, with no hope of ever leaving it,* he heard his own voice replying.

*That is no excuse*, would come the severe response – and it was true. To talk so carelessly, even when all was lost . . . But, then, Stenwold Maker, that plodding, workmanlike intelligencer, would never believe the real driving force behind Teornis's need to speak. He would only have heard the usual light tone of voice, never guessing how brittle it was: the low, low ebb of the worst hour of Teornis of the Aldanrael.

*Despair. I've never before known despair. It is not a feeling Aristoi are supposed to harbour.* He tried to feel blithe about it, but the hand of that alien emotion still lay heavy on his shoulder. It had touched him first there on the barge, when he had realized how grievously he had miscalculated. *I got it wrong, after so long. Did I underestimate the Beetle? No, rather I overestimated him. I did not fear his treachery, and thus overlooked the fact that there are more ways than one to be betrayed.* Lured out to a death-ship, outwitted by that dull blade of a Mantis. Oh, Teornis had a further score Dragonfly-kinden waiting on his ship, who had taken flight for the barge as soon as they saw the trouble, but that was not the point. He had been *outmanoeuvred*. He had slipped during the Dance. It was gauche and clumsy, and had torn a rent in a self-image that had been twenty years in the making.

And then here, this grim place; these dour, cruel people. A captive, for reasons he could not understand, of a people whose existence he had been blissfully unaware of. A man dragged from the Dance he knew into another where the steps were strange, and performed for the highest stakes. He was so *ignorant* here.

And so he had despaired, and made his confession to Stenwold Maker, who had then seemed the only familiar face in the whole world.

Or perhaps his family might have understood if they could be persuaded to see that this fat, balding Beetle was a worthy adversary after all, was in fact a man fit for the

Dance. There was a camaraderie, after all, between those that took a turn together out on the floor. One did not *hate* one's greatest enemies. One thanked them, for making life worth living.

'Let him see,' said a voice, and the hood jerked from his head, as the cloak was ripped away.

The room was not large, around the same size as the chamber he had seen above the cells, and of a similar construction: windowless and low-ceilinged, irregular in outline, but someone had been busy here, devising furnishings. There were frames of some yellowish, bone-like material, hung with loops of greenish rope. There was a rack of gleaming blades, curved and jagged, and another one of whips, single- and many-headed. Seeing it all, Teornis laughed.

He sensed his captors drawing back from him in surprise and he glanced around at them: the near-Spider faces narrowed in suspicion, hands on the hilts of knives as though he had become a dangerous threat all of a sudden. He chuckled again, for good measure.

'Such mirth,' said the same voice. Teornis looked away from the guard to see the speaker, seated in a chair built from curving sections of shell that glistened with mother-of-pearl. It was the same man who had given them that one snatched glimpse of the undersea marketplace, for Teornis recognized the pearl crescent of his torc, the hide cloak, the exquisite goldwork. He was powerfully built, broad at the waist, and his beard and curling hair gleamed with a rainbow of oils in the wan light. Teornis stared him in the eye, registered the face with its hooked nose, the dark eyes, all the lines of casual cruelty, and decided that no true Spider would have such truths written so plainly on his features for all to see.

The man arose from the chair and stalked over to where the guards held Teornis. 'Why does this amuse you, land-kinden? Do you not know what you see?'

Teornis replied slowly and clearly, to overcome the difference in their accents. 'I had thought, when I was first brought to your city, that my life had reached its worst day. But there is always another step down, it seems.'

The man considered him for a moment, without any sign of having understood his words, and then a muscle twitched at the corner of his mouth.

*Good*, Teornis thought. *More to work with.*

A nod of the man's head, and Teornis was bundled over to one of the frames. They had to bend him back to secure him there, the ropes tight at his wrists and ankles, and the contours of the frame stretching his joints. He had been expecting that, though, and he kept the despair at arm's length for another turn.

'Is this for pleasure, or something to do with Aradocles?' he ventured, hoping that he recalled the name correctly. The man with the pearl torc had been poring over the rack of knives, but now he went very still. Without looking back, he growled, 'What do you know of that name?'

'Your woman, in the cells, gave it to me,' Teornis told him. 'Would I be in the presence of the Edmir, then?'

The man did turn at that, although he had a knife in his hand as he did so. 'I am the Edmir Claeon, undisputed ruler of all Hermatyre, land-kinden. Choose your next words carefully.'

The trio of abductors did not care much for bundling Stenwold up to hide him from the masses. The huge, armoured man brought up the rear, so that if Stenwold slowed a step he would be bounced forward by that broad, shell-clad chest. The lean, bald pugilist went ahead, sheer belligerence radiating from his every joint. Chenni pattered along beside him, almost companionably.

*Use your eyes*, Stenwold told himself. *Remember everything you see.* From the ramp they shouldered through a series of tunnels lit only sporadically by the phosphorescent blisters. The workmanship, if it was workmanship, was all of the same organic style, with no defined edges, not a single visible tool-mark. Once or twice they ran into one of the Spider-looking people, dressed poorly, just a loincloth and less jewellery in most cases, and these moved out of their way hurriedly and offered them no resistance. Through it all, the armoured form behind them clumped on so stolidly that Stenwold began to wonder if it was not some impossibly advanced automaton. Then the bald man ahead called out a remark Stenwold didn't catch, and a grunt of hollow laughter came from the armoured one's helm.

Now they were moving upwards, Stenwold stumbling and slipping on the slick stone surface, until they had come out into a larger chamber, a space divided into four lobes by curved ribs that rose to a point in the ceiling. There, a half-dozen of the broad, mailed figures were stood as if spoiling for a fight. Their clawed gauntlets held hooked daggers and forward-curving, heavy-ended swords, and one carried a beaked maul whose head looked like twenty pounds of gold capped with bronze. They had corralled in three others: two of the Spidery sort and a woman of another kinden yet again, whose skin kept coursing with pale colours, white and blue.

'We're moving!' Chenni announced to them. 'Thank these people for their hospitality here and let's be going.'

The warriors made a ponderous turn, with a scrape and slide of their shelly armour, and then the entire party, with Stenwold now in its midst, was making what appeared to be a quick exit. Their armour blocked much of his view of wherever they were going next, those enormous rounded pauldrons forever in danger of smashing him in the face. For all their bulk, the big men managed a solid, tireless progress, and they gave the impression that precious few barricades could have slowed them down.

'I don't suppose I can ask where we're going?' he got out, despairing of even being heard.

'Man in charge,' replied Chenni's voice from somewhere above and behind him. Stenwold had been wondering how she avoided being crushed underfoot, but now he craned his neck back to see her perched on the shoulder of one of her cohorts. 'When you get there, land-kinden, maybe you'll not be so eager to find out,' she added.

*Joy.*

They pushed on through a great hall that seemed very elaborately carved or crafted, and for a moment he thought he glimpsed some kind of statuary around them. Then there was a brief shout and a scuffle. He saw tall, thin men with spears being shunted effortlessly out of the way, and sensed that his abductors' onward progress was aided by the fact that nobody actually wanted to start a fight, that all here were *supposed* to be on the same side, so it would have gone badly for anyone striking a blow in anger.

And then they were out into the open air.

Not the open air. Of course not. For a moment the sense of space and light had deceived him. The light was nothing more than the glowing bulbs, although for a second the bluish shade had seemed too wholesome to be anything other than day. He had a glimpse of a great many people hurrying out of the way of his escort, faces of kinden he did not know, or kinden that looked familiar but were not. He caught glimpses of temporary structures, something like a marketplace perhaps, or the shantytown of refugees that he had seen around Sarn during the war. He got no sense of a mood that would have allowed him to distinguish between those extremes, for his swift-moving escort created a wake of curiosity and alarm that blacked out all else.

There was some shouting from behind, and a quartet of warriors dropped out of step and turned to await their pursuers. One was the man with the mace, and Stenwold took a good look at it as he was hustled past. Despite the alien light, he was now sure it was gold. *Gold-plated, surely?* But he had already seen a great deal of ornament and finery so far, suggesting it could be solid. If the sea-kinden could mine gold in such quantities, what could they possibly want with the land?

He mentally kicked himself for thinking like a Helleron merchant. If they had that much gold, it could hardly form the basis of their currency. *If they even use a currency.*

Then they were back in the tunnels again, but pausing, clustered together as a knot of little pallid men wove around them. The newcomers' white skin was intricately tattooed, their faces devoid of expression. There was something disconcerting about them in their silence and their purpose: they seemed just the fingers of some greater unseen hand. Whoever they were, Chenni and her warriors stayed quite still as they passed, obviously not wanting to jostle them.

Stenwold heard her say, after the small men had moved on, 'And where are *they* going? What's got them riled?'

'Never worth trying to second-guess them,' the lean man replied. 'Let's just hope it's none of our business.'

Shortly after that they began heading down and down, and the quality of the chambers they passed through was definitely deteriorating. There were no more great markets, but Stenwold spotted plenty of people, many of them looking like cousins of Chenni. They stared a lot, and there was tension in the air. The lights grew fewer and further between, and still they were going downwards.

*How large is this colony?* he wondered. *Where is the sea from here? In what direction is Collegium?*

There was another of the armoured men ahead like a living door, already lumbering aside to let them pass, and then the escort was breaking up, the various warriors trudging off on their own errands, until just the original trio delivered Stenwold into a long, low room. There was only one lamp, a broad disc set into the ceiling, which rippled slightly with odd movements of its contents. The washed-out light it cast showed Stenwold a single figure at the room's far end, seated in a great stone throne carved into a basket of interlocking loops. This delicate-looking framework seemed incapable of supporting him, for he was big enough for three, and his armour made him even more so. As they got closer Stenwold saw it was not composed of the shell segments of the warriors but of some other, paler material. This warlord wore no helm, revealing a narrow head as bald as Chenni's, heavily ridged across both brow and jaw, with a low crest drawing the skin tight over the crown of his skull. His nose and mouth were small, his eyes deep-socketed and suspicious, while his skin was the brownish-yellow colour of old bones.

'Chief, this here's the land-kinden's War Maker, or that's what it sounded like,' Chenni announced. 'Land-kinden, I give you Rosander, Nauarch of the Thousand Spines Train.'

Rosander stood up, and the plates of his mail grated across one another with a sound neither like metal nor shell. Stenwold stared at him in silence.

'This all they had?' the Nauarch grunted.

'They had a hairy little shrimp about my size,' Chenni told him. 'Just him and fatty here. Fatty says he's in charge. You know how Arkeuthys reckoned he'd grabbed their leaders.'

'Leaders of what?' Rosander spat contemptuously, fixing Stenwold with a doubtful gaze. 'You look like some Gastroi weed-farmer to me, landsman.'

Stenwold glanced about. He had been left alone standing in the middle of his room, his escort having stepped away from him. He squared his shoulders. 'I'm happy to say I don't even know what that is.'

Unexpectedly, Rosander smiled, showing square, yellowing teeth. 'You're the leader of the land-kinden?'

'We have no single leader,' Stenwold told him.

Rosander made a face at that, the corners of his mouth turning down. 'Well, I know what that's like. Still, you'll tell me about your people's weapons, no doubt, and how many warriors they can muster. In time, you will, anyway.'

Stenwold took a step towards him, waiting for the guards to tense in readiness. They did not, and no wonder, for Rosander looked as though he could have torn the Beetle prisoner in half with his gauntleted hands. The colourless light fell on the incised planes of his armour, and Stenwold's impossible suspicion grew and grew. *Stone? Stone mail. How can you carve stone into a suit of armour?*

'Nauarch Rosander,' he said, trying hard to copy Chenni's intonation that stressed the middle syllable of the name, 'it seems you bear my people some ill will. I am a diplomat, a statesman. We are from different worlds, worlds that have not touched until now. I cannot see what quarrel can have arisen between us.'

He tried to draw back as the Nauarch's arm moved but, in mid-speech, he was too late to avoid the hard pinch as the forward-jutting claw of Rosander's gauntlet snagged his arm. The big man now held one of those hooked knives in his hand, its point upwards, and the edge rested lightly against Stenwold's wrist, his hand pincered neatly between its metal blade and the gritty hardness of the claw.

'In the Benthic trains we have no time to be subtle,' Rosander growled. 'When a man insults me, or fails me, or endangers my people, I take his hand off and abandon him in the wastes. Do not tell me that we have no quarrel, landsman.'

It was very easy to imagine one twitch of Rosander's arm crushing Stenwold's wrist, slicing through flesh and snapping bone. He remained very still. 'Then we do have a quarrel, it would seem,' he said quietly. 'Tell me how I can lay it to rest.'

Rosander's tiny eyes frowned at him from beneath heavy brows. 'Well he sounds like nobody I ever heard before,' he remarked to Chenni. 'He can only be a landsman, though he's not what I expected. Can he be speaking the truth? Can they really have *forgotten*?'

Chenni shrugged her hunched shoulders. 'Chief, if they take it from you, *you* remember. If you take it from them, well, maybe it doesn't stick in your mind so much.'

'What have we taken from you?' Stenwold demanded, as urgently as he dared. 'Why would you send your warriors against us?'

'To take it back,' Rosander replied shortly and, when Stenwold's baffled expression remained, he went on, 'To take it all back, the home of our ancestors, the place you drove us from – or so they tell me.'

He searched the Beetle's face for some sign of understanding, but all Stenwold could say was, 'When?'

'When history began, when the Seven Families arose,' the Nauarch said slowly, speaking words containing the rhythm of ritual. 'We were driven into the sea, and only the beasts of the sea saved us. We found our paths. We built. We journeyed. We lived within our hosts. We dwelt in shadow. We are greater now than ever we were when your people drove us into the waves. We have never forgotten, though. Always we have the Littoralists to remind us, telling the old tales.' The spade-toothed smile returned. 'I wouldn't care so much, landsman, for it's all history to me, but my warriors are restless and the Edmir has promised me my war.'

There was movement behind them, and Stenwold felt a slight tightening of the grip on his wrist, a slight wetness of blood where the dagger's edge dug in. He did not dare turn.

'I bring a message from the Edmir,' said a woman's voice trying to sound calm.

'And you are . . . ?' Rosander addressed the speaker. 'No, you must be Claeon's latest pet.'

'I am Haelyn, his majordomo. For now.'

That smile again. 'Until he tires of you?'

'Indeed, Nauarch, but until then he has asked me to enquire after an errant prisoner who may have escaped from his oubliette.'

'Did he put it in those words, little majordomo?'

'He left the wording to me.'

Rosander laughed at that, and when his armour rattled Stenwold saw that it was indeed stone. He recalled how fast the man had moved to seize his hand.

'It so happens we have caught this strange creature,' the Nauarch declared, releasing Stenwold's wrist abruptly. Stenwold risked a glance behind, and saw what he thought might be the same woman that Rosander's raiders had been menacing earlier.

The sea-kinden continued their careful pantomime. 'This creature here would match the description,' Haelyn confirmed. 'I have men outside, waiting to escort him back.'

The man of Rosander's kinden who had been with Chenni earlier was abruptly standing behind the newcomer, blotting out the light.

'You're sure the Edmir would not prefer that I keep him? It seems foolish for him to trust his prisons, if men like this can so easily walk out of them.'

Stenwold saw Haelyn's skin flush and dance with nervous colours. 'Alas,' she said, keeping her chin high, looking Rosander straight in the eye, 'I fear he would be most displeased with that.' *Displeased with me*, was the meaning obvious in her bearing.

Stenwold glanced back at the Nauarch and thought he saw some sympathy register in that narrow face.

'You are worth more than your master,' the big man rumbled. 'Take your prisoner. Inform Claeon that I will speak to all his charges soon. If not, then my train may become restless yet again, and there are more ways than one to make him "most displeased".'

'Thank you, O Nauarch,' Haelyn replied, and Rosander pushed Stenwold, almost gently, towards her.

'Your Edmir had better place more guards upon his oubliettes,' Rosander commented. 'For if another prisoner were to escape, we might start losing confidence in him.'

Haelyn looked hard at Stenwold, obviously seeing something as strange in him as he saw in all his current surroundings. Then she was heading carefully around the hulking warrior, and Stenwold felt he had no choice but to follow.

# Twenty

When Stenwold was returned to the oubliette, the smashed grate had been replaced and the Edmir's guards lowered him back in, under Haelyn's watchful eye. Stenwold had noticed, while still up above, that their original quartet of warders had now been doubled. He wondered whether that would deter Rosander, should the man want another chat.

'Where's Teornis?' was the first thing he asked.

Laszlo shook his head grimly. 'Didn't bring him back, not yet.'

'They may not, ever,' Paladrya's ghostly voice spoke from the gloom. 'The Edmir has certain . . . tastes. With two land-kinden in hand, he may choose to test his third one to destruction. He believes that enjoying the pain of others is a prerogative of rulers.'

She had appeared from the dark, her skin losing its stone colours. Stenwold pointed a finger at her, angry with her because he had no other target. 'You!' he snapped, and she flinched. 'Start telling me something useful.' When she just stared at him he went on, 'To start with, tell me about this nonsense that we're supposed to have driven you into the sea.'

'It is nonsense,' she agreed, which was the last thing he had expected to hear. 'Just an old, old story, and one that nobody cares about, except the Littoralists. Nobody else believes it now.'

'Your Rosander seemed to believe it,' Stenwold retorted hotly but, even as he said it, he was not sure it was true. Rosander had just been passing on the myth, and Stenwold knew a hollow excuse for warfare when he heard it.

'I could not say what the Nauarch believes,' Paladrya said meekly. 'In truth, I would guess that we did once live on the land, for although we have Art to breathe the water, this air is still more natural to us. Our home is here, though. It was not long ago that anyone claiming that we should go back to the land would have been laughed out of the colony, and the Littoralists were considered a bad joke. But now the Edmir humours them, and gives them power. Now people who laugh at them often meet a bad end. And then there is Rosander,' she added. 'Rosander has been promised his war . . .'

'A war on my people,' Stenwold confirmed.

'Any war, but Claeon finds in your people an enemy fit to match Rosander's power.'

Stenwold sought out Paladrya's pale face, trying to maintain his ire, but his basic decency was already sapping it, telling him that this woman was not, herself, deserving of it. He sighed deeply. 'Look, tell me some of the things that you just take for granted here, will you? What's an Edmir. What's a Nauarch? What's going on between Rosander and this Claeon? How does this place *work*? Can you teach me that without just muddying the waters?'

'I was a tutor, once,' Paladrya said sadly.

'And I was a student. We're well met, therefore, so tell me.'

'This is the colony of Hermatyre. There are other colonies, but none are close by. The sea . . . perhaps it is different on land, but the seabed is mostly barren, deserted. It is hard to live, in those great expanses, and dangerous. So, whenever the builders found a colony, there are many who come—'

'Builders?' Stenwold interrupted. 'Explain builders. Who builds? Your people?'

'The Arketoi,' she told him. 'They build the colonies, layer on layer. They are always building them, over and over. They are the start of it all. In the distant past they began to form Hermatyre, and then my kinden came, and all the others, the great families.' She was scanning his face for signs of understanding. 'Ways of life,' she told him. 'It is not easy to live in the open water, as I have said. Few are the kinden who can manage alone. Those who live in the colony are called Obligists.'

'That's a kinden?' he asked, bewildered.

'No, no. It is just a way of life. The Obligist path is to live within the colonies that the Archetoi build. Obligist because we are obligated to them: everything we have we owe to them.'

'They are your masters? This Claeon . . . ?'

'No, no,' she repeated, clearly finding it hard to accommodate his level of ignorance. 'They barely notice us, do not care at all for us. Certainly they do not rule us. They simply create these spaces into which we creep to live our lives, and where we hope not to offend them. When the colony is attacked, as when the Echinoi raid, then we defend our homes with our lives, and perhaps that is all the builders see in us: expendable soldiers who will die for *their* creations. Who can fathom their minds?'

'I'm finding it increasingly difficult to fathom even your mind,' Stenwold said acidly, and immediately regretted it as she flinched. 'So Claeon's not an Architect? So what is he, then? Where does he come in . . . and Rosander?'

'Claeon is Edmir. The Edmir rules the colony, or at least the Obligist population within it, the Kerebroi and Onychoi and all the other great families.'

Stenwold just stared at her pointedly, and he had the sense that she was trying to work out where best to start.

Even the youngest child she might have taught would take for granted matters that were a complete mystery to these land-kinden.

'I am of the families of the Kerebroi. The kinden of the family of the Kerebroi are the majority here in Hermatyre. Claeon is Kerebroi, but of the royal line, and he is Edmir over the colony. Also in Hermatyre there are others. There are the kinden of the families of the Onychoi. Rosander is of the Onychoi, as were his servants that took you from Claeon's care.'

Stenwold seized on that. 'Rosander is Nauarch of the . . . of the something train.'

'The Thousand Spines. Rosander and his people are Benthists. They travel the wastes, where they scavenge and trade. Normally they would arrive at a colony like this and be gone back into the darkness, but Rosander's people have been here for five years now. Claeon brought them. Claeon keeps them here.'

'And they're getting restless,' Stenwold saw. 'Rosander has a lot of warriors, yes? His people are fighters by nature. And I'd guess yours aren't?'

She nodded. 'You begin to understand it, land-kinden. Claeon lets the Littoralists speak to Rosander of their ancient, stupid grievances, and then Rosander plans his conquests. He has been to the land already, so they say.'

Stenwold shivered at that. *Is this a serious threat?* He imagined Rosander's giants ranged against snapbows. How strong was that armour? *But then they're hardly likely to issue a formal declaration of war.* He wondered how much of the dockside and the riverfront a determined raiding party of Rosander's creatures could strip bare before anyone could work out what was going on. *And then back into the sea before anyone understood . . . and beyond any retribution.*

He felt as though he should say something positive. '*We must do something,*' or, '*We have to get out of here*' or suchlike, but the sheer impossibility of the challenge rose up against him, trapped here in an oubliette beneath a palace in some kind of colony beneath who could know how many leagues of sea.

'I have met Rosander,' he said slowly. 'Now tell me of Claeon.'

'Edmir of Hermatyre, usurper and tyrant,' she said softly. 'My lover, once.'

He let that sink in. 'I suppose that came to an end when he threw you in here.'

He saw her pale hands gripping the stone bars of her cell. 'No, land-kinden, it stopped when he discovered that I had betrayed him – when he had me whipped, when he had me raped.' Her voice was flat and toneless. 'But he must feel something for me, even now, for though I have been kept here two years, I am still alive. He has not ordered my death, nor broken my bones, nor harmed me beyond repair.' Her voice threatened to break at last, but she held it together mercilessly. 'No doubt you have no such people where you come from. Please believe that, of my kinden, of all the sea-kinden, Claeon is a poor ambassador. And even he was not so, once. When his brother lived, before temptation was put before him, he was . . . a different man.'

Stenwold had more questions, but in the face of such misery he had not the heart to ask them.

Claeon re-entered the chamber, looking in a rather worse temper than before. Teornis braced himself. He had been left strapped to the whipping frame since the Edmir had been called from the room. Some development had obviously displeased him in the meantime, which doubtless boded no good for Teornis's future health. The interruption had occurred just after a few lashes of the whip, which Teornis had tried to bear manfully, and which had doubtless been meant as a polite introduction to the Edmir's hospitality. Teornis suspected that Claeon now intended to start a more meaningful conversation, probably with the knives he seemed so keen on fondling.

*Well, I have had a chance to prepare my speeches, O Edmir,* he considered. *Let us now see whether there is anything left of my skills.*

The most wretched aspect of it was that all he felt for Claeon was contempt. Oh, it was not that a Spider-kinden would never stoop to a little torture for a pastime, but it would either be simply a pastime, or it would be the serious interrogation of a knowledgeable but stubborn prisoner. If their positions were reversed, and if Teornis had captive an ambassador from a hitherto unguessed-at culture who might know all the secrets under the sea, then he would not waste time in indulging some petty personal inclination for inflicting pain. Either he would have a skilled professional torturer sifting through every nerve and fibre of Claeon's being for what he knew, or he would be plying his own charm to win over the stranger to the cause of the Aldanrael. Since this second option plainly had not occurred to the Edmir, it would be up to Teornis now to place that thought in his mind.

Claeon stared at the Spider's arched form, but his mind was for the moment elsewhere. 'I would give a great deal,' he muttered, 'to have that oaf Rosander here in this room and at my mercy.'

Teornis took a deep breath. His back still stung, from the ministrations of the lash, and his joints and muscles were sorely strained from having hung here for so long. With an ease born of long practice, he expelled the discomfort from his mind, made of his voice a pleasant thing and said, 'There is one other, I think, you'd rather have here than just me.'

Claeon started at his words, and Teornis thought, *Not used, I think, to having the meat address him. I must work fast before he decides I'm better off without a tongue.* 'I can get Aradocles for you. How would that please you, O Edmir?'

The expression on Claeon's face became instantly guarded. 'You do not even know who Aradocles is,' he accused.

'True, save that I know he has escaped you, therefore he is your enemy.'

Claeon was stalking closer. His hand brushed down the line of knives, twitching at them, but none of them had found his grip yet. 'No doubt you think I would send you back up to the land on receiving your word of honour to return with the boy. You land-kinden must be very simple.'

*Oh. indeed.* 'I expect you would send some of your warriors along with me,' Teornis said mildly. 'But I can give you something more than that, to prove my good faith.' His reasonable tone, not pleading, not desperate, nor distorted by fear, was intriguing the man. *My fish is on the very point of the hook.*

Claeon did not speak, but he nodded by a fraction of an inch as if to say, go on.

'Allow me to make a presumption, O Edmir,' Teornis put forward. 'I may be wrong, but you are in a splendid position to educate me if that is the case.'

An unwilling smile tugged at Claeon's mouth, almost lost amid the wealth of his beard. 'Then presume,' he prompted.

'Your monster took us from our ship near one particular city – colony – picked out of the length of a very extensive coastline.' Teornis watched the man's face to make sure that words like 'coastline' had meaning here. 'Why would you be concerned with that one place, considering you are the lord of the sea?' he added, assessing Claeon as a man not immune to flattery. 'It must be because you have an interest there. But what interest? Can it be linked with the disappearance of your enemy Aradocles on to the land?'

'I see Paladrya betrays me even from my oubliette,' Claeon growled. 'She talks too much to you, too little to me, even when I have her here in this very room. She claims she does not know where the boy went, having left such decisions to the servants that fled with him. Still, this land-colony is the closest place of any size to where she confessed she took him. Why should your colony not feel my wrath, if it shelters my enemies?'

'Why indeed?' Teornis forced a smile. 'Especially as it is not my colony.'

'Explain yourself,' Claeon snapped.

'Willingly. My own colony lies a great distance from that place, but a quarrel has grown between my people and the locals. When your monster captured us, we were meeting to argue over our differences.' He made his smile broader. 'I see you don't believe me, and if our positions were reversed I'd be doubtful too.' *And may our positions be reversed one day, O Edmir, and you shall then see how a truly civilized kinden takes revenge.* 'You must have agents in that colony, though, or how else could you have known where we would be? Since you have your people hidden there, in that place, send to them, I beg you. Send to them and ask them how matters stand between that colony and the Spiderlands. Ask them about me, Teornis of the Aldanrael, and see what they say.'

Claeon studied him for a long time, and now his expression became as hooded and hidden as that of any Spider Aristos. At last he called out, and another man of his kinden came in, clearly one of his guards.

'Take this prisoner to one of the upper chambers,' the Edmir murmured. 'Have him fed, but watched and guarded carefully.' He cocked an eye at Teornis. 'If what you have said is true, you'll have no objection if I replace you with one of your cell-mates, no doubt?'

'They are my enemies, just as they are yours,' Teornis said, and if he felt a stab of shame, it was lost in the physical relief of being released from his bonds.

*

'Day or night, do you reckon?' Laszlo asked.

Stenwold prodded unenthusiastically at the bowl of something unfamiliar that had been passed down to him. His stomach, only a moment ago a riot of hunger, suddenly had other business. Whatever it was smelt of fish – or even more of fish than everything else here – but had the consistency of porridge.

He pondered the Fly's question, and realized with alarm that he had no idea. 'I . . .' He could not bring himself to admit that his internal clock had not survived the loss of the sun. 'Day,' he concluded, sounding as confident as he could.

'It is night.' Paladrya had relapsed back into stone colours, and her voice rose ghostly from the gloom. 'The tides sweep towards the sea's edge. The nautili rise from the deep places.'

'How can you tell?' Stenwold demanded. 'Why would you people even need to know?'

'We feel the moon as it passes above. We feel the sea enliven with a thousand thousand growing things in the sunlight. We feel the cold creep in as the darkness rises from the depths, where it lives always,' she stated.

Stenwold shivered. The thought, *I'm going to die here*, surfaced in his mind, and he watched it bobbing there like a drowned thing before it sank once more. *Die, without ever seeing the sun again, without ever seeing Cheerwell or being there when the Wasps come again. Die without ever seeing Arianna, but then that has become a given.* A shudder racked him, of loss and loathing. He was aware of Laszlo watching him with concern, and wished that Fly-kinden eyes were not so sharp in the dark.

They heard sounds above, then. They had more visitors, it seemed. Stenwold stood up, hoping that it would be Teornis being returned to them at last, but there was a conversation going on above, something more than just dropping off a prisoner.

'Change of shift?' Laszlo suggested quietly. He was standing, too, braced for action, ready to employ his Art. Stenwold wasn't sure, but he suspected the Fly was going to try some impossible piece of theatrics if the cells were opened, jumping the eight or ten guards above, in a bid to gain the pitiful span of freedom it would win him. He knew he should dissuade his companion, but the voice in his head was telling him that it would be better, surely, to be killed in some futile endeavour than to rot away down here in the dark.

'Then you take it up with the chief,' he heard a woman's high-pitched voice say. 'You read what's there, and if you want to go interrupt him when he's getting himself all worked up, then fine.'

'Since when are you on the staff?' one of the guards demanded, and then, 'Hey, I asked you—!' There was someone already halfway down the ramp before the first guard got to them. Stenwold thought it was Chenni at first, but then he saw it was another woman of her kinden, diminutive and hunched.

'In case you hadn't noticed,' the woman said, turning with raw vitriol in her voice, 'the chief's staff changes with every phase of the moon, mostly because they get on his nerves all the time by not doing what they're *told*.' The guard loomed over her, but she seemed utterly unflapped.

'Three of you – for two prisoners?' another guard objected. The ramp was getting cluttered now. There were at least four of the jailers there, and a sharp-faced man a little taller than they were, also as bald as half these sea-people seemed to be. Another knot of guards was gathered about someone else still at the top of the ramp.

'You don't think we can handle them?' the woman asked, stepping down off the foot of the ramp and forcing a pair of the guards to follow her.

'Himself's just doubled the watch here,' her opponent objected. 'Doesn't make sense, him just sending three . . .

three I-don't-know-what-you-are's to take care of this pair. They're important, these are.'

'All the more reason for you to do what you're told. You've seen the orders,' the woman rejoined.

Stenwold was becoming very aware of Laszlo. The Fly had gone very tense, and now he half flew, half climbed to the top of his cell, where he waited silently, obviously ready to act on the instant. *Something's up.* The guard had been listening to the woman's words, but Stenwold realized that Laszlo had been reading something into her tone. Something was not ringing true. Something was up.

'Look, I'm not having this,' the chief guard decided. 'Maybe Himself has a few Onychoi on the staff to do the dull jobs, but I never heard of him hiring a Polyp.' He gestured back up the ramp. 'I mean, why would anyone?'

'Because we can do this!' snapped another woman's voice, and abruptly two of the guards at the top of the ramp were falling, just dropping down into the oubliette itself. They were twitching as they hit the ground, spasming and fitting.

The chief guard was shouting some kind of oath as he pulled his knife from his belt-loop. The small woman was marginally quicker, whipping out her own dagger and ramming it hard into his groin, and then into his throat, to choke off his scream. On the ramp it became utter chaos. The bald man had gone into a frenzy, lashing out at all around him with his bare hands. Stenwold recognized his kinden as like the man with Chenni, who had smashed the cell grating with his bare hands. The newcomer had the same Art-bulked fists, with his spines set forwards like knives, and he carried a pair of stilettos jutting upward in his hands as well. As he fought, Stenwold spotted the kinship he had missed before: just as Paladrya's people resembled Spiders, so this man was a cousin to Mantids.

Now the other woman was coming down the ramp, also lashing out with her bare hands. She drove two of the guards before her and, although they had blades out, they were keeping well out of her reach, so much so that the bald man killed both of them from behind before they realized how far down they had backed away. They got a spine in the back of the neck each, as brutal and surgically precise a blow as anything Stenwold had ever seen.

There were no more guards, after that. The final man had been going after the small woman with his curved dagger when he had trod over Laszlo's cell and the Fly had snagged his foot through the grate, tripping him. The woman's steel had done the rest. Now she was looking down at Laszlo as he hovered at the very top of his cell, desperate to be out of it.

'Well, that settles that,' the little bald woman said shakily, staring at the blur of the Fly's wings. 'They really are land-kinden, not just hoaxes.'

'Time,' grunted the bald, Mantis-looking man, and the small woman nodded enthusiastically.

'Right, Phylles, open up the lids.'

The other woman, who had created such an affray with the guards, came to crouch by Stenwold's cell. He looked up at her curiously. On the one hand she was a kinden he had not seen before, not the Spider-like elegance of Palad-rya or the guards, nor possessing Rosander's squat bulk. Yet from another point of view, she was familiar. She wore more clothing than the other locals, to start with. Whilst practically every other sea-kinden went about in a state of indecent undress, by Collegium standards, this woman was wearing a long leathery coat over some kind of tunic and, although she was barefoot, she wore something approaching breeches too. She was heavily built, her hair spikily short, and her skin looked bruise-purple in the fickle light. In her face and build, though, she was not unlike Stenwold himself, not unlike all those Beetle-kinden he knew back under the sun. Although it meant nothing, although she would be no more a Beetle than Paladrya was a Spider, the sight gave him heart.

'Stop staring,' she growled at him, and put her hands to the grating. She closed her eyes for a moment, feeling it out, and then had it lifted off without effort. She reached a hand down to him, grinning, and seemed surprised when he took it. Only then did he remember the way that the guards had been trying to keep clear of her touch. Something squirmed within her grip, and he nearly let go, but some obscure sense of keeping face made him hold on. She hauled grimly, and he kicked and scrabbled at the stones to help her, and between them they soon had him lying gasping on his belly on the oubliette floor, legs still dangling down into his cell. By the time he had found his feet, Laszlo was free as well, and had taken up one of the dead guards' knives.

'Now, come on,' the small woman urged them, her voice low and urgent.

'And who says so?' Laszlo demanded. He was keeping his distance from the newcomers but had dropped out of the air.

'Some weighty people want you out of here,' she said, squaring up to him, meeting him eye to eye.

'So maybe we'll make our own way.'

'Laszlo,' Stenwold struggled into a sitting position, 'where would we go?'

The Fly looked unhappy. 'What about her?' he asked, pointing downwards.

'*Time*, Wys,' the bald man repeated pointedly. He was already standing near the top of the ramp, half crouching in the shadow of the doorway.

'Her who? Who else is down there?' The small woman – Wys? – squinted at where Laszlo was pointing. Paladrya's skin shimmered reluctantly before she let herself be seen.

'You a land-kinden?' Wys asked doubtfully.

'I am not,' answered Paladrya.

'Then you're not in my brief. Let's go, landsmen—'

'She stays, I stay,' Laszlo said stubbornly. 'She's a prisoner too.'

A pair of men arrived above, not expecting trouble, perhaps merely come to investigate where the guards had gone. Stenwold caught only a brief glimpse of them before the bald man struck. His hands lashed out, blurring with speed. Stenwold didn't notice whether it was dagger-points or the spikes of the man's Art, but he had taken the unsuspecting pair down in an instant. He looked pointedly down at the others.

'Get her up, Phylles,' Wys said, exasperated.

Phylles gave the world a look of resentment and frustration, and hauled the grate off Paladrya's cell, reaching down to pull her up with a lot less effort than she had Stenwold.

'Spit me,' Wys said, staring. 'It's the Traitress.'

In the brief silence that followed Stenwold tried to catch Paladrya's reaction to this accusation, but she would not meet his eyes.

'Oh, we'll bring her too, all right. There'll be a nice bonus when we hand her over,' Wys said enthusiastically. 'Now, let's move. Any funny business and we'll be delivering a land-kinden with one arm or something.' She was pattering up the ramp even as she spoke. Phylles meanwhile gestured for the land-kinden and Paladrya to follow.

When Stenwold got close he whispered, 'Traitress?' but the woman would not answer him.

They passed through the vacant guard room, strewn with oddments of jewellery and clothing that must have belonged to the dead men below. On a flattened-off lump of stone that protruded directly from the floor there was some kind of board, showing a series of concentric rings marked into segments, and black and red stones were arranged partway through an unfamiliar game.

Stenwold tried to recall the route that Chenni's party had taken earlier, and realized quickly enough that they were not following it. Instead they seemed to be heading downwards, and he had the feeling that they were going yet deeper into the Edmir's palace – or whatever edifice they were in. When he tried to ask questions, he got such a vicious look from the bald man that the words died in his throat. Paladrya looked drawn and frightened.

*Brigands*, he thought, *mercenaries*. But they were well-connected ones. They obviously had some kind of seal or document they had used to get into the cells, even if it had not quite convinced the sentries. *And they were cursed quick in dealing with the guards, after that.* He bore the deceased men no love, but the ferocity with which Phylles and the bald man had culled the oubliette's warders was chilling.

Then the passage they had been following came to a strange kind of end in a round wall with a star shape incised into it. Stenwold did not interpret it as a door until Wys pushed at it, and it split into tooth-shaped sections that folded away from them. There was a small room beyond, with an identical kind of hatch, making it seem a pointless little antechamber to Stenwold.

When they were inside, Wys hauled on one of the curled-back fangs, and the door they had entered through flexed shut again, moving like a living thing. A strange premonition came to Stenwold and he pointed, 'What's through there?'

'The sea, idiot,' the small woman told him, and moved towards the second hatch. Stenwold had a moment of lurching horror, then he had almost hurled himself at Wys. The bald man snagged his belt halfway and hauled him back, but he still clipped the small woman's shoulder, staggering her. She had her knife out instantly, and Stenwold saw the bald man's spiked fist poised above his face. Laszlo's blade was in his hand as well, and Phylles had a hand out towards him, eerily reminiscent of a Wasp about to sting.

'We'll drown!' Stenwold choked. 'The sea . . . We'll drown. You'll drown us.'

For a moment Wys stared at him, open-mouthed, then her eyes flicked to her comrades. 'Spit me,' she said. 'Piss-damn land-kinden. This job just gets more stupid.'

'Cauls,' the bald man suggested.

Wys smirked at that, then nodded. 'Stay here, watch them,' she said, and then had the first toothy door open again, and was scuttling away.

# Twenty-One

Their ship was a shell. His wonder at the sight of it, hanging in the pale glow of the colony like a spiral moon, was all that stopped Stenwold from going out of his mind.

Wys had come back quickly, too quickly, which suggested that the missing prisoners, and the slaughter of the guards, had not gone unnoticed. Stenwold guessed that the Edmir's pursuers were expecting them to attempt a flight into the colony proper, not to use this marine exit, but the thought surely would not evade them for long.

'Get these over their heads,' the small woman snapped impatiently. A moment later, the woman called Phylles was trying to drag a bag of clear membrane over Stenwold's face. He tried to fight her off and she jammed an unkind knee into his stomach, then unrolled the filmy material so that his head was entirely within it. It smelled like rotting fish and the waxy membrane made a blur of the world beyond, and he tried to pry it off, convinced he could not breathe. Phylles hit him again, unsympathetically, and he gasped, finding out that the bag did not cling to his face, and that there was a little air sharing its interior with him.

He had meanwhile lost track of what else was going on, so the wash of water caught him by surprise. He tried desperately to kick himself away from it, but Phylles held on to his collar, and he was buffeted fiercely as the room filled up within moments. Her bare feet seemed somehow glued to the floor, and she handled him as though he was a kite in a high wind, until the inflowing current had subsided. Then she began grimly dragging him away, and the walls receded behind them, until he realized that they were outside the colony and under the vast weight of the water.

It was hard to breathe then, not from the caul – which had puffed out against the sea – but from the cold, clenching weight of ocean all around him. He had closed his eyes when the water came at him, and he only opened them again after he had re-established a rhythm to his breathing. To his astonishment the membrane about him, which had made his vision so smudged and grainy in the air, showed his surroundings crystal-clear.

Behind them the colony glowed out a thousand colours. His heart skipped to see it, looking so alien and beautiful. Yes, for all that he had been its captive, he could not deny that it was beautiful. It was huge, too. The irregular, bulging walls rose up and up, in towers and domes and spires and intricate skeletons of white stone, draped with fronds and frills and gills of waving plantlife, and all illuminated by great bulbous lamps of ghostly greens and bloody reds, brooding purples and violently bright blues. For a moment he forgot about the fathoms of water around him, the monsters that swam in it, the horror of drowning, just gazing at that sight that filled his whole horizon. The colony was a city. The colony was immense.

The colony was alive, he saw then. It was alive in that sea life swarmed across it. The lights picked out a million sparks of fish in ever-changing constellations, the clinging slick hands of octopuses, high-stepping crabs picking their way sideways up the colony walls, shrimp the size of a man's arm darting here and there in a flurry of beating legs. The colony was alive beyond all this, though, for its outer walls were built of life: cells and cells of it, each with its rosette of tiny arms. When a fish skimmed the stone, he saw a flurry of motion as the colony-builders dragged their tendrils in, then spread them out again once the intruder had passed.

*Builders*, Stenwold thought. *Their builder-kinden, the . . . the Archetoi, Paladrya said. Surely not . . . ?* But he thought of the smashed grating, and how it had been nothing but a honeycomb of hollows within. *Cells built on cells built on cells, until . . .* The magnificence, the overwhelming sight before him, showed how far that 'until' had gone.

Then Phylles was yanking him along and, in her sure grip, he turned helplessly in the water and saw the ship.

He understood, then, the peculiar internal geometry of the vessel that had kidnapped them here. The sea-kinden did not build what nature itself could build better. Wys was already swimming swiftly ahead of them, where her destination hung in the sea, pale and banded in the suffused glow of the colony Hermatyre. It was a coiled spiral, and Stenwold had seen such adorning pendants in the Collegium marketplace, brought in by beachcombers and of a size to fit neatly within a man's hand. Perhaps something like this washed up occasionally, whole or in pieces. A lucky beachcomber could have lived inside it.

Phylles reached her arms about his chest, linked her hands together, and then kicked off towards the shell, giving him a better view of it. The cavity that the shell's original owner would have occupied served as a hatch now, with some manner of artful contrivances flanking it. Opposite that, at the rear, a circular stencil of sections had been cut out and covered over with something transparent, and a pale light could be seen glimmering from within. He tried to make out a propeller or limbs, or any other propulsion device, but there was nothing there he recognized.

Wys had already disappeared through the shell's entrance, towing Laszlo, and the bald man shepherded Paladrya after them. Stenwold felt Phylles give an extra kick to propel them inside, and he was let go within a narrow, circular-sided chamber. He found that he himself was having to breathe heavily by now, although she had done all the work. Collegium scholars had known for years that the goodness in the air, necessary to keep a flame or a man alive, could be used up, so he guessed that the caul was nearing the end of its effectiveness. He understood the purpose of this small room, though, even before the water drained swiftly from it, and he had the filmy hood off before Phylles could help him with it.

'You,' she said accusingly, 'are pissing difficult to move.'

Still feeling the bruises, he looked back at her stubbornly.

Wys had opened another of those segmented doors, and beyond lay what must be the vessel's main chamber, a long, upward-curving room lit by two of the phosphorescent lamps. There were nets hung on the walls, with a few bundles slung inside them, but otherwise it seemed a bare sort of place.

'Lej?' Wys called. 'Lej? Hey, *Spillage!*'

Something loomed ahead of them, and Stenwold recoiled from it before realizing what it was: the head and shoulders of another man of Rosander's kin, but poking vertiginously down from beyond the upward curve of the ceiling.

'Chief?' the apparition said.

'Get us moving,' Wys told him shortly, and he instantly withdrew into the upper reaches of the vessel.

'What will you do with us?' Paladrya asked. She had her arms wrapped about herself in the very picture of dripping misery.

Wys grinned unpleasantly. 'With these two land-lads, I'll be handing them over, and I've not the faintest clue why someone wants them, save that they'll do better for being out of Claeon's raspy little hands. For you, woman, I'd guess a traitor's death, and why not?'

Paladrya dropped to her knees and then fell over on to her side, and Stenwold thought that she had somehow willed her own death in preference to execution. She was still breathing, though, and her eyes were wide open. When he knelt beside her she only shook her head, saying, 'I'm sorry.'

Phylles put a hand on his shoulder, to haul him off, but Laszlo stepped in between them, wings flickering momentarily, and she backed off, obviously unsure about land-kinden Art.

'Leave her alone. What's she done to you?' the Fly demanded.

'She gave Hermatyre to Claeon,' Phylles spat.

'Oh, and you're all such concerned citizens, are you?' Laszlo, half her size, stood with hands on hips defiantly.

Wys snorted in amusement. 'He's got you there.'

Phylles glared at her, and then at Laszlo. 'Well, she's a murderess,' she declared, although without much conviction. Stenwold guessed he had witnessed only a fraction of the blood on her hands.

'I didn't,' Paladrya said, so quiet only Stenwold heard.

Laszlo, meanwhile, was obviously spoiling for a fight. 'And you're a charitable institution now, are you? And all those guards you and him chucked around, they're all sitting up again with headaches, are they?'

'We *rescued* you!' Phylles yelled at him indignantly.

'No, you didn't.' Laszlo folded his arms, chin jutting pugnaciously. 'You're going to sell us to someone else, right? If this is a proper rescue, take us to Collegium docks, please.'

'She said she didn't kill anyone,' Stenwold said loudly, because what little patience Phylles possessed was obviously being eroded by the moment. The woman glared at him, and he saw something move in her hands, as though she held some twisting creature there. A moment later she had stomped off along the upward curve of the deck.

'The Traitress can say what she likes, but she killed the

real Edmir,' Wys said, not unsympathetically. 'I'm no Obligist. The little sprat was probably an obnoxious turd and deserved it, but a death's a death.'

'Aradocles,' Stenwold pronounced slowly. Under his arm, Paladrya nodded weakly. Stenwold felt slow-witted, continually numbed and baffled by his surroundings, to not have perceived the link. 'This Aradocles was the Edmir?'

'Would have been, surely, after his father died,' Wys replied, frowning.

'His *father*?' It took a moment for Stenwold to catch up. *Hereditary titles.* He understood that the Commonweal managed things in the same way, and of course there was the Imperial family of the Wasp-kinden, but really . . . government by bloodline? Neither the Wasps nor the decaying Dragonfly state encouraged him to place any faith in it.

Abruptly the giant shell containing them shuddered and lurched, and Stenwold knew they were under way. He looked to the window ahead, cut into the shell's rear face, and saw the seabed beneath them recede. *We're going backwards,* he thought, and felt the same intermittent surges of motion that had confused him in Chenni's smaller vessel.

Wys wore a strange expression. 'Spit me, but you really are land-people?' She glanced from him to Laszlo.

'That we are,' Stenwold confirmed.

'This must all be complete babble to you, then?' she observed.

Stenwold laughed at that, although Paladrya flinched as he did so. 'Oh, you could say that. But this Aradocles of yours isn't dead, not the way *she* tells it. That's the story the Edmir's put out, is it?'

Wys's smile grew cynical. 'Sounds like some things are the same, land or sea, but I believe he's dead, anyway. He disappeared: great big hunt on for, oh, two years or so – where was the missing heir? Then word came out there'd been some dirty business in the palace. One of the lad's own staff, his tutor, had done for him. They had her killed, they said, and Claeon went from being regent to Edmir. Big ceremony, not that any of us got invited. But it was *her*.' She jabbed a finger at Paladrya. 'They led her through the streets with a chain about her neck. I was there for that. I remember her face.'

'She swears she took him onto the land,' Stenwold stated.

'Hah, well, good as dying, that, isn't it . . . ?' He saw the new thoughts crowding into Wys's mind even as she said it. 'So Claeon's swiping land-kinden, is he?'

Stenwold mutely gestured at himself and Laszlo. The small woman looked thoughtful. 'We've taken on more than we thought, here,' she muttered. 'For a start, I didn't believe you were really landsmen. I'd thought that was just a Littoralist story. Spit me, what are we involved in here?'

'Oh you think *you've* got problems?' Laszlo remarked, and she chuckled at that, looking him up and down.

'We should shave you, boy,' she told him. 'Could make a Smallclaw of you yet. Spit me, I'm minded to hand your big friend and the Traitress over and hold on to you. A man who can hang in mid-air like that would be worth his keep.' The eye she turned on him was so cheerfully acquisitive that Laszlo could find no ready reply.

'Where are we going?' Stenwold asked. 'Now we've got the threats of execution out of the way, can you tell us?' In his arms, Paladrya struggled to sit up, still shaking slightly. Now he saw her in the stronger light of the ship's interior, she was clearly a woman ill used, and ill used for some time. There were marks on her pale skin that even her Art could not hide, and she was gaunt and hollow-eyed.

'Just a place, some farm my paymaster's commandeered. Owners are sympathizers, probably. This is political. It's more important for you to know who you're going to get handed over to, than where the deal's done. I'd guess they're some of the old Edmir's party – Claeon's brother's lot. After all, it's only because of the Thousand Spine mob that they didn't wind Claeon's guts out on a spear, whether Aradocles was dead or not.'

*Thousand Spine . . . That's . . .* Stenwold fought for the correct words. *That's Rosander's train, his warband or whatever. That means Claeon took over, and he used Rosander as muscle, yes. So now I've got Obligists who live in the city – the colony – and I have Benthists who don't, only some Benthists, like Rosander, do because they're invited, and the Obligists are split into rival camps anyway . . .* He clenched his fists in frustration, because he was trying to understand the result of millennia of divergent history, and he *had* to get it right. His life would depend on it.

'Wys,' he addressed her, and she nodded. 'Wys, your people are . . . where do you fit in?'

'Freeloaders, landsman. And we don't fit in. We don't take to the open seas, and we don't live in the colonies, we just take our opportunities. Me, Phylles, Fel and that useless bastard Lej up in the engines, we're Wys's Hunters.'

'Mercenaries,' Stenwold agreed, and when she looked blank he added, 'For money? You understand money, here?' He suddenly thought of the wealth of precious metal he had seen, but Wys was nodding.

'Of course we have *money* – what do you think we are? *Mercenaries* . . .' It was clear the word was new to her. 'Oh, I like that.'

'There can't be many like you,' Stenwold said. *Particularly if you don't even have a word for what you are.*

'Money's only good at a colony,' Wys agreed, 'and there's not so many things an Obligist needs to hire someone from outside for. We're a select group.'

*And I'll wager you're bandits whenever the money dries up,* Stenwold reflected. 'Are we free to wander on your ship?'

'Our barque?' Wys's gesture took in the limited coil of the living space. 'Don't get in Lej's way, don't annoy Phylles, and Fel will be watching you. Aside from that, you've a little while till we arrive. We're fighting against current to get there. I'd advise sleep, but it's your call.' With that pronouncement, she did something quick and complicated with one of the nets on the wall, and turned it into a hammock. She bundled herself into it fully clothed, or at least without removing her brief tunic, and was apparently asleep in an instant.

Stenwold and Laszlo exchanged glances. 'We're getting somewhere, slowly,' the Beetle murmured.

'In understanding these madwigs, maybe.' Laszlo shrugged. 'No closer to getting back to the light and air, though, Ma'rMaker.'

Stenwold nodded. In truth he was trying not to think about that. It was hard to retain any composure when his mind was playing host to the yawning chasm that lay between him and home. *I think if I saw some black-and-yellow down here, I'd embrace it. But, no, Teornis was right. Even the Empire can't reach us down here.*

*And if the sea-kinden reach upwards?* He had no idea of their capabilities, though they had enough aptitude to make these submersibles, however the ships worked. They produced the light and, somehow, the air . . .

'The air . . . ?' He frowned. 'Paladrya . . .'

She was watching him fearfully, as though bracing herself for a blow. She had not, he guessed, found much to trust or like in people since her incarceration.

*And she had been Claeon's lover, she said. And she'd betrayed him for this Aradocles, and then Claeon found out, and locked her up, and worse . . .*

*And where in the bloody world has this Aradocles been, if she pitched him landwards years ago?* The obvious answer loomed, but he fought it down. *If this heir is dead, that's no use to me. But if he can be found . . .*

It was the bait for his hook, in order to catch some chance of getting back home. Surely they would want their precious heir returned to them? But first he had to understand them, lest he put a foot wrong, and this abyssal world then swallow him for good.

'Paladrya, tell me about the air,' he said gently.

'I don't understand.' It was clear in her expression.

'You people can breathe underwater. Why haven't I just drowned? Why keep those caul things?'

A flicker of something like humour crossed her face, which must have been a rare visitor of late. 'You mustn't take offence,' she said, 'but the cauls are for children. It is the earliest Art any of us learn, but not before the age of six, perhaps, or seven . . . so we have the cauls. The Benthists developed them, they claim. They need them more, when they're travelling.'

Stenwold let the subject of the Benthists go by for the moment. 'But the air,' he pressed her. 'Air goes stale, even my people know that. How are you . . . are you making air? You have machinery of some kind?' *It can't be an Apt solution, unless they've been Apt for, what, thousands of years, long enough to be forgotten by the rest of us, all ties with the land severed.*

'We accreate it, of course,' she said, voice tailing off by the end of the sentence when the word made no impact on him. 'Accreation,' she enunciated, as though to a fool or small child. 'We extract it from the water.'

'There's no air in water,' Laszlo jeered, 'Or else you wouldn't drown.'

She gave the Fly a level stare. 'There is indeed air to breathe in the water, if you possess the Art to free it. It's the simplest form of accreation.'

Stenwold and Laszlo exchanged looks. 'What else can you . . . accreate?' the Beetle enquired slowly.

'There are many things in the water,' she told him, 'if you can but draw them out. The limn-lights, for example, are simple work.' A twitch of her hand took in the pale globes illuminating the inside of the submersible. 'But most of what we need, we make – we accreate. Shell, bronze, gold, membrane, stone, all of it can be formed by someone with the skill and Art for it. Some things the sea makes for us, like the shell that this barque is made from, but almost everything else is made by accreation.'

'So you just, what, conjure all your raw materials out of the water?' Stenwold asked incredulously.

'Raw materials?' she asked, frowning again.

'Ask him this question,' broke in a new voice. Phylles had come back, and Stenwold guessed that the curved nature of the ship meant that no conversation could be private. The purple-skinned woman crouched on her haunches, still trying to look angry but obviously intrigued. 'How do you people ever craft things on land, land-kinden, if you don't accreate from the sea?'

'We . . . make things,' Stenwold said unhelpfully. 'Someone mines the raw materials – the metal ore say – from underground, and then it gets smelted into the metal, and maybe cast in a mould, or else a smith beats it into a shape and finishes it off, or perhaps a machinist cuts the metal into the right shape, if it's precision work . . .' He broke off, for she had drawn a knife out. Only later he would remember that she needed no knives to fight with. She laid the blade before him, and he saw it was four inches of razor-sharp bronze with a hilt fashioned of some pearly shell.

'So you people would, what, get a lump of bronze, and just sort of *force* it into looking like a knifeblade?' she asked him, sounding utterly disbelieving.

'Well, heat it up and beat it flat, over and over . . .' *And I've seen not a single fire, not a naked flame, and what on earth would they burn here, unless they can 'accreate' coal or something. The cells weren't warm, but they weren't cold either, they don't have much need of clothing other than for a minimal modesty . . . they can't make fire. They make things without fire.* 'And you . . . don't do that?'

Her face was doing something strained, and he realized she was not-quite-laughing at him. 'Beat it flat? Like with a rock or something? Over and over . . . ?' She lost the battle and a delighted crow of derision erupted from her. Stripped of her customary ill humour she looked even more like a discoloured Beetle-kinden from some far-off city.

'Very funny,' Laszlo snapped angrily. 'And you do better, do you?'

She gave him a pitying look. 'Man in the Hot Stations made this for me. They're good with metal there. I told him what I wanted, and he set out a tank, and I came back three days later and he'd got the blade formed. I did the hilt myself. I make most of the fittings round here.' She took up the knife, and Stenwold saw that the blade was plain, but the grip was lightly incised with intricate, geometrical patterns that were picked out with verdigris as neatly as though jade had been inlaid. *Which she made by this accreation*, he realized. *Not cut, not carved, but simply laid in as part of her plan, as she sieved the materials from the seawater.* He recalled all that fantastically intricate jewellery he had seen in Hermatyre. *So they can just grasp gold from the sea, and shape it how they will without need of the whitesmith's art. I wonder if they realize they could just* buy themselves *a chunk of the land, no need for invasion?*

*And what are the limits of this Art of theirs?* The question inevitably followed on from his previous thoughts. *What could they not make?*

Phylles was still smirking at him, but there was a degree of uncertainty behind her expression, that had perhaps underlain her earlier hostility as well. *She's scared of us*, Stenwold saw. *We are land-kinden, and we are strange to her.* 'Do you believe that my ancestors drove yours off of the dry land?' he asked her. 'Do you dream of going back?'

'I saw the land once,' she told him flatly, raising her belligerence like a shield. 'Up on the surface, while cack-handed Lej was getting this thing moving again. Dry and barren, it was, and I could feel my skin cracking just being up there, out of the water. You're welcome to it, land-kinden. Just don't you lot try coming down here.'

She stormed off again, heading up the slope where their engineer had appeared from. Stenwold smiled slightly after her. She might be a sea-kinden of some unspecified type, but he had met a lot of other people like her, as easily offended and overly defensive. He decided he knew how to handle Phylles, whatever she was.

'Right,' he said vaguely, glancing up at the bald Mantis-cousin, Fel. Throughout the conversation the man had not offered a single contribution, just standing there with his arms hanging loose by his sides, as though he would be fighting at any moment. *Very like a Mantis*. 'No chance of anything to eat, I suppose?' he asked. 'Anything that's not fish, ideally, although I accept there's small chance of that.'

For a moment Fel just looked at him, with the spikes on his fists flexing slightly, but then he stepped sideways and started rummaging one-handed in one of the cargo nets.

'Do you feel able to answer more questions?' Stenwold asked Paladrya. 'It sounds as though whoever hired these mercenaries isn't going to kill you out of hand at any rate.'

She was still pressed against him, held in the embrace of one arm. She had stopped shaking, but he had the sense of keeping stable some very precious, fragile thing. 'Ask,' she said quietly. 'I cursed you to this, by my interference, so I will make amends any way I can.'

'Well, then . . .' For a second Stenwold floundered in the ocean of his own ignorance. 'This Hermatyre that the Edmir rules . . . there are other colonies, there must be . . . ?'

'There are,' she agreed. 'There is Deep Seep, down in the dark and the cold. There is Grande Atoll, I have heard, beyond even that . . . and the Pelagists tell of colonies further still.'

'And Hermatyre's relations with them? Might there be allies against Claeon? He doesn't sound the diplomatic type,' Stenwold mused. Paladrya was already giving him what had become her usual look, when he said something that puzzled her.

'Relations?' she asked. 'Well, there is some trade. The Benthist trains call at those places, sometimes, and there are the Pelagists . . .'

'But surely they care, if their neighbour is taken over by a tyrant?' Stenwold pressed.

'Why?' she said simply.

'Well . . . what if Claeon decided to take over this Deep Seep, as well, and sent an army over?'

'This happens on land?'

'It happened to my home city – colony – very recently.'

She flinched at the thought. 'It takes the Benthist trains many moons to travel between colonies, even if they follow direct paths, and usually their chief interests are in scavenging the depths. The Pelagists are swifter, but even they . . . they are so thinly scattered that to see five of them in one place is cause for surprise. How should such a thing be accomplished?'

'A desert,' interjected Laszlo soberly. He was obviously quicker to grasp the idea than Stenwold. 'The sea floor is a desert. These Benthists are like nomad tribes – like the Scorpions in the Dryclaw, say. You exchange a few messages, a little trade, some raiding probably, but each colony's got to shift for itself alone, I reckon. Which means that each colony's also its own worst enemy, come to that. Which gives us this mess we've run into. Lady, tell us something we need to know, will you?'

'Speak,' Paladrya invited. Fel was back with them then, no doubt disappointed that they had not tried to take advantage of his being distracted. He handed them strips of something tough and stringy. Stenwold tried it cautiously, and found it infinitely welcome, just like dried beetle jerky and, best of all, only tasting very slightly of fish. *I suppose a lobster is just an aquatic beetle, when it comes down to it.*

'Tell us about your kinden, your sea-kinden,' Laszlo continued, and in the Fly's face was the avid look of a traveller learning something that nobody else of his country has ever known. 'These families of yours . . . ?'

'The Seven Families, yes,' Paladrya echoed, 'although that's just tradition. There are always rumours of other families, other kinden within the families we know . . . in the deep places, in the far places, other colonies . . .'

'Hold.' Stenwold put a hand up, glancing at their guard. 'No chance of something to write with, and write on? I should be making notes, at least.'

Fel looked as though he had been asked for the moon on a stick, but after a moment he brought over a rounded sheet of thin, leathery cloth, and a thin seashell that had been capped with something like horn. There was ink inside it that wrote somewhat messily, as though Stenwold was scribing on blotting paper, but it was not so different from the reservoir pen sitting on his desk back in Collegium. The letters he formed, though, were obviously unfamiliar to his hosts. *Well, I suppose that, whenever they were exiled down here, it must have occurred before literacy was well established.*

'The Seven Families,' Paladrya repeated, and Stenwold remembered that she had been a tutor, once. 'First of the Seven is the Kerebroi, who rule the colony of Hermatyre and all its farms and land,' she recited as if by rote. 'Of the Kerebroi, we Krakind are the mightiest, but those who are Dart-, or Sepia-, or Wayfarer-kinden are our cousins, and ought not to be slighted that they lack our skill at governance.'

There was a snort from Phylles, who had come back down to hear the lesson. She obviously had other ideas about the predilections of the Krakind.

'Hold on,' Laszlo said, holding a hand up just like a schoolboy. 'Krakind, you said, as in "kraken"?'

'What's kraken?' Stenwold asked him.

'Well, Mar'Maker, that beast that hauled our arses down here would be a kraken to most mariners, and no mistake. You hear stories, you know? Like how they're supposed to be really smart, rescue drowning sailors and all that . . . Guess that's a load of rot, then.' He raised his eyebrows at Paladrya. 'So you're one of them, are you? Octopus-kinden?'

She nodded. 'As is Claeon, as is Aradocles, and their royal line which has governed Hermatyre for eleven generations.'

'Go on, though,' Stenwold prompted. 'The Seven Families?'

'Next is the Onychoi, the people of the claw,' she told them. 'Some live within the colonies, but most are Benthists, travelling the ocean floor. Many live in the Hot Stations now, I'm told. You have met Rosander, and Wys, and Fel here. They are all Onychoi of one kind or another.'

*That's a lot of variety to fit in just one kinden*, Stenwold thought, contrasting Wys and Rosander. *Or, no, they're not* kinden, *but several kinden all within the one family: crabs and shrimp and whatever Fel happens to take after, I suppose, but they're all kin. I suppose that means they're the closest kin to us, as well, of all the sea-kinden.*

'Next come the Archetoi, who build the colonies and allow us to live within them,' Paladrya went on, her voice acquiring a sing-song pattern, a rhyme for children. 'They are the Builders, and worthy of honour, and none who relies on the colonies should offend them or stand in their way, for we survive by their grace. After the two great families and the Builders, there are also the lesser kinden,' Here Paladrya threw a very pointed look at Phylles. The dark-skinned woman scowled but said nothing, as Paladrya went on, 'There are four of them, and usually the Polypoi are counted first of these.'

'You leave me out of this,' Phylles said gruffly. 'I don't want any part of your stupid Obligist hierarchies.'

338

'The Polypoi are lonely and self-reliant,' Paladrya went on, and then Phylles broke in with, 'Loners. *Loners*, not lonely. We do just fine on our own.'

'Perhaps you can set the record straight after we're done,' Stenwold suggested, which drew her frown on to him.

'No skin off my nose whether you get a proper education,' she told him, and made a great show of stomping off again.

Paladrya took a deep breath. 'Well, the Polypoi live beside the colonies, mostly, in outlying farms and homesteads, or just on their own like hermits. Or sometimes there are Onychoi hermits, and the Polypoi live near them. We claim that they are lonely, or why else would they stay just outside, rather than simply going on their own ways?'

There was a sound of derision from elsewhere in the vessel, but Stenwold gestured for Paladrya to continue.

'Then there are the Medusoi, who constantly travel the oceans, and have little to do with the colonies at all. They are the greatest of the Pelagists, meaning those who swim freely, although there are Kerebroi and Onychoi who also feel no ties to a colony or train. The Medusoi are strange and dangerous. Sixth of the Seven Families are the Gastroi, the lowly. The Gastroi live mostly outside the colonies, but they keep the farms and herds that feed us. They are quiet and uncomplaining and dutiful, and in turn we must protect them from the dangers of the sea. They are also skilled at accreating, and at working the shells and stones that the sea leaves us with.'

She appeared to have finished there, so Stenwold indicated on his fingers that even land-kinden could count to seven. She had become something brighter for a brief moment, given the chance to teach, but now she retreated into herself again.

'The Seventh family is . . . different. Those I have told you about, they are part of our society, even peripherally.

Even the Medusoi recognize where they fit in and, although they are dangerous if crossed, they will not seek out danger. The Echinoi are different, however. The Echinoi have no laws. We do not even know if they have language. They are . . . something other than human, it is said. Some claim they resided within the sea long before the other families came, and resent us for our intrusion. Certainly they, of us all, have no need of air. How their children manage, we cannot guess. The Echinoi are the spine-kinden, and they roam the vastness of the seabed. When their bands find victims – a farm, a train, even a whole colony – they attack without mercy. They are the enemies of us all. Hope that you never see them, land-kinden. They would not care who or what you were. They would feast on your bones.'

'Lovely,' Laszlo muttered darkly. 'Just when you thought you were surrounded by thoroughly unpleasant people, there's worse.'

Fel had remained blank throughout Paladrya's lecture but, at that, he smiled, showing neat, predatory-looking teeth.

# Twenty-Two

'How does it go?' Stenwold asked. He had left Paladrya asleep, and Laszlo picking over the vessel's cargo nets, while he clambered and slithered until he could get within sight of what he took to be the engine room. It was tucked into the innermost coiling of the vessel's shell, and Wys's engineer seemed barely able to fit there. It was the first time Stenwold had seen one of the big Onychoi unarmoured, and the man still looked very broad at the shoulders. He was probably a full foot taller than Rosander, too, and would have given a Mole Cricket-kinden a fair run in a wrestling match. One careless backhand would have sent Stenwold himself rattling all the way back along to the vessel's entrance hatch, and probably worse, too, because there was a great serrated claw curving from the back of each hand. The spiked gauntlets of Rosander's banner-men had obviously sheathed Art-grown weapons like these. The man's name was Lej, Stenwold recalled, or possibly Spillage.

'Go?' The engineer turned to him questioningly. That face was frightening at first, tucked between those bunched shoulders, with a ridged and hairless skull and a heavy jaw. Lej possessed the mildest blue childlike eyes that Stenwold had ever seen, though, which somewhat took the edge off his grim visage. 'Oh, heap big magic, Lowlander,' he said. 'You wouldn't understand.'

Stenwold raised his eyebrows. 'Well, I see you've got a spring-wound clockwork behind you, that's feeding tension into two separate engines for some reason. What I can't work out is what the engines are doing to make the sub-mersible move like this.' If any vessel he knew were to make progress in this lurching series of thrusts, he would have sent it back to the dockyard for repairs.

Lej was staring at him, jaw actually dropping. 'You're Able?' he said.

'Apt, yes. There's a lot you don't know about the land. Almost everything, for a start. The same's true of what I know of the sea.'

The Onychoi was now grinning, showing teeth like yellowed pegs. 'Oh, landsman, there's precious few who'd know this was even an engine. Oh, I'm impressed. I really am impressed. Do you have these gear-trains, then, where you're from?'

'Clockwork? Certainly. They're . . . new, then?'

'This barque was fitted out just two years back,' Lej told him. 'But they've been making these engines for . . . what, six, eight years? The first ones were rubbish, though, between you and me. Swimming was better. It's only in the last few years they sorted out the strain ratios, and the like. I hear some of the designs coming from the Hot Stations these days are slick, real slick.' Here was an engineer talking about engines, and Stenwold had a moment of utter dislo-cation. *I could be in the College workshops right now. I can almost hear Totho in this sea-kinden's voice.*

'So what happened to start it off?' he asked. *They can't have gone from Inapt to Apt in just eight years. It must have been there long before, waiting for a trigger, something . . .*

'Springs,' Lej informed him. 'The idea's been about since before I was born, the way they tell it, but it's about getting a good enough spring to hold the tension. The Hot Stations, now, they worked out how you accreate spring-steel, like we've got here. Before that you had to do

342

it by tensioning shell or bone, and that gets you nowhere, frankly. Come here and see.'

Stenwold tried to approach, but skidded on the curve of the shell. A broad hand grabbed his shoulder and stopped him sliding away out of sight entirely.

'Why've you got those things on your feet? No wonder you can't stand up properly,' Lej enquired. He meant Stenwold's boots, and with that came the understanding why, however over- or under-clad, everyone in this undersea world went barefoot, for almost all of the floors Stenwold had been sliding about on were smoothly uneven. Cursing himself for a slow student, he unlaced his boots and threw them off, hearing his footwear bang and rattle all the way down to the main hold.

'Look at that,' Lej observed. 'Land-kinden got toes, too.'

With the new traction from his bare feet, Stenwold was able to clamber closer. 'I see your spring,' he said, privately thinking how this would all barely pass for a prentice-piece back in Collegium, 'but what is it powering. Propellers? Legs? How does this shell move?'

'Like it did when it was alive,' Lej replied, obviously puzzled. 'How else?'

'I have not the first idea how shells move,' Stenwold told him. *Natural history was never my strong point, and who'd have thought it would be a matter of life or death one day?*

'Siphons,' Lej explained, and saw that the word carried no meaning. 'We pull in water at the front, and then squirt it out of the siphons, left and right, to make us go forward. If we want up or down it gets harder. We either flood the inner chambers, or get some air into 'em. Smooth, eh?'

*If only I was not a prisoner. If only Collegium was not under threat from land and sea. If only . . .* For he was seeing something here: he was seeing history. The sea-kinden had discovered their aptitude, and Stenwold was witnessing what must be the first stages of a technical explosion like the revolution that had freed his own people from the yoke of the Moths five centuries before. 'It's very impressive,' he said, suddenly feeling hollow. 'Thank you for showing it to me.'

He slid carefully back down to the main chamber, where Laszlo eyed him expectantly, but Stenwold just managed a wry smile and found himself somewhere to sit, resting his back against the sloping wall as best he could.

*I cannot say what might happen, if it came to war between us and the sea-kinden. They have the advantage of surprise, and they have unknown Arts, and for a long while we would be unable to strike back.* He reflected, oddly, about the Moth-kinden of Tharn during the war, and what they must have felt when, after generations of mounting attacks against the Helleron mining concerns, a Wasp airfleet had arrived on their doorstep. *We would manufacture our battle submersibles, no doubt, even if they drove us from Collegium entirely. In time, we would take the war to them. Whatever the upshot, whether we turned them back, or whether they claimed the coast from us for ever, this moment of theirs, this delicate unfurling of their new way of life, would be crushed in the fray. There is so much to learn here that we will never know if Rosander gets his war.*

He saw that Wys had now woken up and was standing before the many-paned viewport cut into what was either the fore or the aft of the shell, depending on how flexible his thinking was. Stenwold took a moment to admire the workmanship, where some tireless craftsman had sawn out a hundred interlocking gaps in the foot-thick hull, each one then covered over with some transparent material that had no doubt been accreted into place. The spars and struts left between the panes were cut into curls and spirals, the entire design a thoughtless work of art. The sea-kinden, with their very industry governed by imagination rather than the hard labour of hands, seemed incapable of achieving anything plainly or simply.

'Wake up your new friend,' Wys instructed him, gesturing at Paladrya.

'We've arrived?'

'Close on. You're about to become someone else's problem.'

The window showed them approaching some kind of wedge-shaped bivalve shell, one of as massive proportions as the vessel they were travelling in and picked out by bulbous, fading swirls of phosphorescence. Beyond it was a dark wall that Stenwold assumed was just empty water at first, but then he noticed a slight motion caught by the luminescence shed from their ship, and he sucked in his breath.

'Weed seas,' Laszlo murmured, beside him. 'How many ships have run foul of those? These ones must go all the way to the surface?' The barrier was a wall of weed, a dense forest of anchored fronds that dangled upwards towards the unseen, distant air.

'Reaching for the sunlight,' Wys confirmed. 'How else?' A frown. 'Or do you not—?'

'Yes, we grow crops. It is one of the primitive skills we land-kinden have mastered. Along with wearing shoes and not living in the arse-baiting *sea*,' Laszlo snapped pointedly. 'You are really getting on my nerves, you know that?'

'Laszlo—' Stenwold started, because Fel and his killing fists were very close, and he had lost track of where Phylles was, and it was not so very long ago that sea-kinden had been debating how expendable Laszlo was. Wys was laughing, though, a hand pressed to her mouth to hold it in.

'You're priceless,' she told Laszlo, fondly patronizing. 'I'd love to keep you. Business intervenes, though.'

They had pulled nearer to the shell, which was now turning out to be considerably larger even than the ship. Stenwold saw motion near the base of it, where an octopus of considerable size was squatting in a rosette of coiled tentacles, one baleful eye regarding them. Something else dashed past the window, and he received only the blurred impression of some dart-like shape with trailing streamers, and a figure impossibly mounted upon it.

'That's our patron's steed, I reckon,' Wys observed. Phylles had come out from some hidden nook, and padded across to her, peering outside.

'Looks it,' she agreed. 'And that's . . . Pelagists of some sort. What are we into here?'

As their viewpoint rounded the shell, she had picked out another sea-monster lurking there. This one looked at least more acceptable to Stenwold: something like a flattened woodlouse with an anchor-shaped head. It was comparable in size to Wys's submersible.

'You people ride these monsters?' Laszlo demanded.

'Well, yes, on them or inside them, for those without the know-how to work one of these beauties,' Wys replied, patting the shell-ship's hull. 'How else to get about? It'd take for ever to swim. Spillage, hold us here!'

There was a vaguely affirmative noise from above, and for the next few minutes the submersible jockeyed about in the water, shifting from side to side, and then dropping a good distance quite suddenly. Bubbles flashed past the window on their long journey back to the mother air.

Phylles was at the land-kinden's elbow, proffering a limp handful of translucent membrane. Stenwold accepted the caul from her reluctantly. Travelling in this machine, for all its strange construction and motive power, had seemed the closest to normal life since the monster Arkeuthys had ripped him from the barge.

Stenwold was readier this time, when the rush of water coursed over him. As Phylles took hold of him, he did his best to kick a little, to help her progress, but he remained little more than inconvenient baggage, bobbing and twisting at the end of her arm. He gained confused views of the coiled submersible, and then of the great stony mound they were heading for. The place had a single hole cut into it – at the hinge where the two halves of the shell met – and they entered through another pair of twin hatches. *Just like a lock*, Stenwold decided, thinking of canals and water levels, *only more so. How do they make the doors work?* The doors here were not those neatly folding segments, but a kind of curved plug of thick, whorled stone, or possibly just more shell. The inner surfaces, he noticed, were slick with mucus that sealed them wetly against the open sea.

The shell-house's innards were lit in dull shades of blue by a dozen small lamps, and a ramp carved out from the building's inner wall curled down from the hatchway to the floor below. The place was cluttered with bales of what Stenwold took to be dried weed, and at first there was no welcoming party to be seen. Wys did not seem discouraged by that, and led them down to stand in the midst of the little empty space available. Stenwold glanced left and right, and saw Fel and Phylles watching warily.

'Let's get this over with,' Wys called out. 'Some of us have other business.'

The figure that stepped out was one of the Kerebroi, Paladrya's people. He was tall and lean, with a hooked nose and a magnificent beard ending in twin forks that coiled like ram's horns. His hair, above a high forehead, was swept back in elegant waves. Beyond a cloak and a kilt, all he wore was a fortune in gold and jewellery, his bare chest almost hidden by an entire vest of linked pearls.

'You have the Edmir's prisoners?' he asked suspiciously. Stenwold now saw movement behind him: four or five very tall, thin men and women wearing peaked helms, breast-plates and greaves of some pale substance. They carried spears with long needle points, but held them loosely, without threatening Wys's party.

'You doubt me?' Wys asked. 'I'm hurt. I have more than that, councillor. I have land-kinden.'

The tall man's hooded eyes narrowed. 'You no doubt imagine I will pay more if I believe so.'

'Oh, boss,' Wys said, 'I'll hold you to the asking price, but these are the real deal. You, boy, do your trick.'

Laszlo glared at her but, after Fel had prodded him, he let his wings flare and ascended halfway to the distant, gloom-shrouded ceiling. The expressions on the faces of the spearmen were caught between fear and wonder, but their master merely nodded, still frowning.

'As good as your word,' he said. 'And your reward is well earned in this case. Would you stay with us for word of another assignment?'

'Pay me for this one first,' Wys growled. 'And, while you're at it, how much for her?'

She hauled on Paladrya's hand, dragging the woman forwards. The tall man's eyes widened for a moment, his mask of disinterest slipping.

'*You?*'

'Heiracles,' she named him dully.

Two of the thin guardsmen had levelled their weapons, on her appearance. Stenwold saw something barbed squirming alongside the narrow spearpoints.

'What is this?' Heiracles demanded.

'From the Edmir's private cells – not dead at all,' Wys elaborated.

'Well, then, that can be rectified. My people will be glad indeed to know that justice was truly brought upon the Traitress. We always suspected that Claeon lied.' He nodded at his men. 'Kill her. We'll preserve her head for proof.'

'Hold on, chief. She says your boy might be alive too.'

A twitch of Heiracles's hand halted his spearmen, his eyes fixed not on Wys but on Paladrya herself.

'They said you killed him,' he murmured. 'Claeon said so . . . we assumed you were in it together, and then he disposed of you. He was not best known for his sentimental nature. You, on the other hand . . .'

'Why would I kill Aradocles?' Paladrya asked quietly.

'You were Claeon's lover.'

'And yet I did not love him. I loved the boy, as a tutor should.'

Wys coughed delicately. 'Ah, boss . . .'

'Pay her.' At a gesture from Heiracles, one of the spearmen came forward with what looked like an oblong, carved stone. He set it before Wys, who opened it up along an invisible crack. Within, Stenwold saw sheaves of the thick, leathery stuff they used as paper, colourfully inked. Wys counted through these, as though they were deeds or promissory notes, and was obviously satisfied.

'A pleasure, Archon,' she said, beaming. 'Now, you had something else for us, before we head on to the Stations?'

'Stay and listen to our counsels, and then I may,' Heiracles told her. 'Come, bring them all. Follow me.'

Laszlo had landed again by now, bored with being stared at. Heiracles allowed himself just one worried glance at the two land-kinden, before leading them among the stacked bales. His people had cleared a private little space there, and another pair of his guards was waiting, along with someone of another kinden, a broad figure with dark brown skin not unlike Stenwold's own, wearing a coat of grey hide over his bare chest. He seemed to have white stubble covering his head and chin, but on closer inspection, Stenwold saw that this was not hair at all, but little nodules of something that resembled stone.

'When are the rest of your people arriving?' Heiracles asked him, and received a weary shake of the head in response.

'They'll be here when they get here,' the man grumbled in a hoarse voice. 'Doesn't work like for your lot, all living next-door. We've been travelling for days, and Nemoctes will be here, oh, half a day maybe. Or two hours perhaps. Or a day. Depends on the currents. The others? All of the others? We could be waiting till your lads with the spears die of old age.' His long-suffering eyes found the newcomers. 'Who's this?'

'Land-kinden, Gribbern,' Heiracles announced, as though they were his personal discovery. 'Now are you interested?'

'No. Nothing to do with me,' the man called Gribbern replied, in the same miserable tone. 'Just here because Nemoctes told me someone should be, and guess who was luckless enough to be closest?'

'You speak for the Pelagists, though?' Heiracles pressed.

'Don't know that anyone speaks for the Pelagists. Not Nemoctes. Not me, certainly. All I know's Nemoctes told me to be here, and most folks tend to listen when he says things. Don't know why – just going with the flow, me. Don't know nothing, does old Gribbern. Besides, technically, I'm a Profundist, and not a Pelagist, but as there's few that might understand the distinction . . .'

Heiracles had obviously lost patience, for he turned back to Paladrya. 'Hermatyre believes that you killed the heir, and then Claeon executed you for it. The second proposition is obviously false, so tell me about the first.'

Paladrya took a deep breath. 'After Rosander's train moved in, to keep the peace as Claeon said, I knew that Aradocles was in danger. Claeon trusted me, and he talks . . .'

'He talks to his bedfellows, we know,' Heiracles finished for her coldly.

'He did not tell me outright that he sought the heir's death, but he could not quite hide it, either. He was too full of his plans for his future as Hermatyre's ruler. I understood that Rosander's people would be coming for Aradocles, to make him vanish, so to legitimize Claeon's Edmiracy. The boy was nearly of age, and Claeon had grown to love his position as regent too much. So I took him away to the only place where Claeon could not follow.' She glanced at Stenwold, then, and Heiracles frowned.

'How?' he demanded. 'How could you take him *there*? The land is death.'

'We have listened to our own counsel for too long,' Paladrya said gently. 'The other kinden, often they keep old secrets and we never think to ask. There are ancient pacts, I was told, between certain families of the Dart-kinden and certain powers of the land, pacts of mutual respect and acknowledgement. I did not ask the details: all I knew was that there was a channel by which to send word. I sent Aradocles on land with two followers, to await . . . to await I know not what. I knew only that if he remained in any place that Claeon could reach, he would die.'

'The Hot Stations,' Heiracles objected. 'Deep Seep perhaps.'

'Claeon has eyes and hands active in each,' she told him. 'You know this. You know Claeon also. He possesses none of his brother's wisdom. He is just a small man who clings to the idea of being a great one.' She gathered her self-possession, fighting to slough off all the fear and help-lessness that being a prisoner had layered her with. 'So, Heiracles, you yourself remain loyal to the true succession, even though you've believed him dead? Is that the case?'

'Do not question me,' he told her sternly, and Stenwold saw Wys waggle her eyebrows, obviously amused. Then again, most things seemed to amuse Wys.

'Or is it just because Claeon has not included you amongst his creatures?' Paladrya jabbed.

Heiracles glared at her. 'Claeon is a murderer and a usurper, and some of us did not share his bed.'

She shrugged that off. 'And what have you done mean-while? Aradocles has been gone for more than four years, and I have been in the oubliette for two. What about you? What grand plan do you have, Heiracles?'

'With Rosander's bannermen all over the city, there is little that can be done,' he told her flatly. 'I have my spies inside the palace. I have gathered information. Recently

I have arranged to extract some curious prisoners I had received word of. Do not make me regret it.'

'And if Aradocles returns?'

Heiracles regarded her without expression. 'Oh, yes, if the boy-Edmir returns then no doubt the colony will rise up, although there is the small fact that they will be rising right into the claws of Rosander's thugs. But you sent him onto the land, and the land is death. Only the Littoralists pretend otherwise.'

'And the land-kinden?' Paladrya said stubbornly. 'Heiracles, send these two land-kinden to find Aradocles, and bring him back. Rosander's not unbeatable.'

Heiracles's smile was not pleasant. His sharp eyes turned on Stenwold. 'You'd do that, would you?'

*Oh, hammer and tongs, yes!* 'Return me to the land and I will do whatever you want, believe me.'

The expression on Heiracles's face grew disdainful. 'Oh I'm sure of it, *if* you could be trusted. Why should these landsmen care for our troubles? No doubt some relative of theirs has skinned and eaten the boy already, if they even go so far as to prepare their food.'

'Claeon believes he's still alive,' Paladrya insisted. 'Why else would he take land-kinden captive?'

Heiracles gave her a pitying look. 'Claeon believes many things. Some say he even believes the Littoralists, and looks to make conquests above the waves. But I believe otherwise. I believe he has tired of feeding Rosander's Thousand Spines and looks elsewhere for a means to keep the colony under his thumb. I believe that these land-kinden are to form his new militia within Hermatyre: a captive slave army that could only do his bidding, or drown. Besides, what creature that must eke out its living beneath the burning sun and dust would not leap at the chance to live as we do? No, I will not trust these savages.'

Coming from a man wearing little but a kilt and some gold baubles, Stenwold found this a little rich. Laszlo was clearly gathering himself to deliver some invective, until Wys cuffed him across the back of the head.

'Don't reckon anyone wants to hear my thoughts,' Gribbern's droning voice broke in, 'but I don't see how this concerns the Pelagists, or even the Profundists, of which technically I am one. I don't see how even Nemoctes, who's a good deal more sociable than me, would want to get involved in this.'

'Then why did he send you?' Heiracles demanded of the man.

'Don't see as he did *send* me,' responded Gribbern's mournful voice. 'He *asked*, mind, because he cares about Hermatyre, on account of even Pelagists having to moor up there sometimes, and Profundists as well. But it doesn't sound like anything there's going to change unless you somehow magic the boy back, and it seemed to me as though you're not even interested in that . . .'

'I said nothing of the sort,' Heiracles protested, and hastily, which piqued Stenwold's interest. 'I simply said I cannot see that we should trust these . . . outlanders. Of course I'd wish Aradocles back, if I believed there was any chance.'

'There is a chance,' Paladrya insisted.

'Enough from you,' he snapped. 'You're still under threat of execution. Push me too far and . . . what now?' For one of his spearmen, still dripping from the sea, had clattered in amongst them, past the bales.

'Archon,' the man gasped, 'you must leave. The Edmir's men are coming.'

# Twenty-Three

'You look like a man who has received some bad news,' was Teornis's understatement. In truth the Edmir's face was like thunder. The messenger luckless enough to bring that same news must have had little time in which to regret it. Teornis had already gauged Claeon's character by the way he treated his underlings. Good Aristoi inspired loyalty, rewarded good service, and were utterly ruthless when necessary. Claeon's temper was like a beast unchained. He lashed out at the undeserving when angry, and that bred only resentment. His power alone prevented reprisal, and Teornis had seen men just like him fall very quickly once their one crutch was kicked away. *And may my foot do the kicking one day, O Edmir.*

'Tell me of your companions,' Claeon snapped, hurling himself down onto the woven mattress of the bed.

Teornis took a moment to compose his words, contrasting the relative comfort up here with the cell down in the oubliette, or with Claeon's torture chamber for that matter. These guest chambers, or whatever they were, were at least spacious and furnished, adorned with the sea-kinden's customary artistic flair for pointless arabesques, and there was even a small extent of rubbery window giving out on to the endless dark waters. 'Of the small one,' he started, 'nothing need be said. He is a servant, no more than that.'

Claeon grunted in acknowledgement. In truth, Teornis

had no particular feelings for Stenwold's Fly companion one way or the other, but he was not going to risk himself to keep the little vermin alive.

'The other, though, he was always my chief opponent in the war between his people and mine. He has considerable power and influence amongst his own colony.'

'A clever man?' the Edmir muttered.

'Oh, clever certainly.' *So what's wrong?* Claeon's displeasure was intense enough to stop any other clues getting through. *Has Stenwold died?* It was a bitter thought. *Perhaps he tried some ridiculous escape attempt and the guards killed him. Perhaps the guards just killed him for sport. They seemed fit servants for their master, from what I saw.* 'A valuable prisoner, for bargaining, I would say. And a man who knows a great deal of useful information.'

Claeon's look grew only darker.

Teornis grimaced. 'O Edmir, if I have displeased you, then only let me know how . . .' he tried.

The Edmir glanced up at him, as though seeing him for the first time. 'You? Oh, I still have you, and I see I was wise to keep you separate like this. You are a man of influence also, so you say?'

'With my people, yes,' Teornis allowed cautiously. 'With many people above the waters, indeed. You wish me to use this influence of mine on your behalf?'

'And you are an enemy to those other two?'

'Our peoples are enemies, it is true.'

Claeon let out a long hiss. 'As you have guessed, I have my agents on land. The Littoralists indeed have their uses. Your people – or your enemy's people – they have agents amongst my own, I now discover.'

Teornis blinked at that, momentarily left without words. 'I . . . had not thought so, O Edmir,' he said at last.

The Edmir glowered at him. 'If you play me false, landsman, I shall give you over to Arkeuthys to devour.'

'O Edmir, we have never known of your people – or

355

your colony. Perhaps there are some land-kinden that once did, though. Perhaps those who formerly ruled the places where now your other prisoner's people stand once knew. They knew a great deal that they neglected to share with others. For his people, though? No, surely not. I cannot imagine that they could have such knowledge, and not trumpet it all over the land. They are not subtle as you and I are. They do not understand the value of secrets.'

'Then it is a rot within the colony, that someone has dared such a thing,' Claeon murmured, more to himself than Teornis. 'Perhaps it was *her* they came for, after all, and they took away the landsmen just because they were there. I am betrayed. There are spies in the palace, there must be. Who can I rely on?' He looked up keenly. 'Your fellow prisoners, they knew nothing of Aradocles? You swear it?'

'That name was unknown to all of us,' Teornis confirmed.

'And yet . . . perhaps they might now find him, if he remains alive to be found,' the Edmir told himself.

'As might I,' Teornis put in carefully.

Claeon stood up abruptly. 'I do not trust you,' he told the Spider. 'I will not trust you unless I must. Your comrades have escaped, but I shall regain them. My hunters seek them out even now. I shall have them back and, when I do, I shall rework them on my benches so that they shall not be capable of flight a second time.'

He stormed out, leaving Teornis rubbing his chin speculatively and feeling pieces of a plan begin to fall into place.

Heiracles's face tightened on hearing the news. 'In what form?' he demanded.

'Dart-cavalry are close. Our scout signed for Onychoi as well,' his man reported.

'Hold them off,' the lean man ordered, and the messenger went running for the hatch, ascending the ramp in great strides. Heiracles looked round at Paladrya and the two land-kinden. 'They cannot breathe water, I take it?' he snapped, indicating the caul that Stenwold still held.

'Boss, there's precious little they *can* do,' Wys told him.

'I cannot carry them with me. My entourage and I rode here, and it were best they left here separately, so as to confound pursuit. Gribbern . . .'

The dark man sighed. 'Don't reckon I much fancy it but, then, Nemoctes would do it if he were here. Shame he's not, really.'

'Gribbern, just give me a straight answer!' Heiracles held his temper with difficulty.

The other man gave a monumental sigh. 'Reckon I might take one, just about. Just one, mind. My Pserry won't fit more, is my thinking.'

'I'll take the little one,' Wys put in quickly.

'This wasn't what I wanted from you—' started Heiracles.

'It's what you *need*, though, right? We can talk payment when we meet again.'

'Gribbern can hide in the weed. Your barque will never outdistance dart-riders.'

'My barque, chief, can look after itself. They'll hit rough waters if they come after me,' she promised. 'You, squib, you're mine.' She dragged at Laszlo's arm, and the little man gave Stenwold a wide-eyed look.

'Go with her. We'll meet again.'

'But where? These clowns haven't even got a *plan*, Ma'rMaker!' Laszlo protested, pulling against Wys. 'Who's going to look after you?'

'Just go.' Stenwold forced a smile. 'Be safe.'

'I'll send word by the Pelagists,' Heiracles told Wys.

'Right, boss.' She hauled Laszlo up the ramp, with her crew following. The last Stenwold saw of the Fly was a caul being dragged over his still-protesting mouth.

'Paladrya, will you ride with me?' Heiracles proffered a hand.

'Do I have a choice?'

'Under the circumstances, no.'

'Then I would be delighted,' she said pointedly. 'Land-kinden . . .' She turned her wide eyes on Stenwold, who was losing familiar faces by the second. For a second she stared at him, despite Heiracles's obvious need to be gone.

'Paladrya,' Stenwold acknowledged and, to his surprise, she embraced him briefly, a moment's clasp, her cheek to his, and then she was pulling away. 'Good fortune.'

'And you,' Stenwold said. He turned to Gribbern, seeing little to inspire confidence in that dour, stone-pocked countenance.

'Reckon you'd better come with me,' the man grumbled, and headed up. Stenwold met Paladrya's eyes once more before he followed.

In the water once more, back in the grip of the cold and the breath-stopping clench of the sea, Stenwold saw Gribbern kick off from the shell's hatch and descend towards the bottom, his grey coat billowing around him like shabby wings. With no option, Stenwold did the same, paddling ineffectually at the water, while feeling a gentle current drift him towards the wall of tangled weed. He never really landed at all, only got close enough to the mud of the sea-floor to kick it into clouds of sediment, as he lurched and bobbed towards Gribbern's waiting figure. The sea-kinden was gazing upwards, his arms dejectedly by his sides. Stenwold glanced up and saw shapes passing in the faint light of the shell-house's lamps. They were swift, stream-lined, and they were duelling as fiercely as any Exalsee aviators, darting against each other in a swirl of speed. Two clashed together, and he had a glimpse of riders crouched over couched lances, closing, then breaking apart in a swirl of dark blood.

*Or ink?* They were riding squid, he saw, and riding them bizarrely backwards, with the beast's head and trailing tentacles to the rear. They carried nothing more than lances, no bows or thrown spears or anything like modern weapons, and he wondered how far a crossbow bolt would travel with any force, down here.

He saw Wys's barque move off ponderously through the water, banking across the face of the weed. One of the darting squid made a pass at it, but turned abruptly as it got close, zigzagging wildly away and almost unseating its rider.

Something caught at his sleeve and he thought instantly of clutching tendrils, and tried to kick away. His eyes found Gribbern's long-suffering face, though, and the sea-kinden was pulling him along, not swimming but walking over the seabed in great, bounding strides. Stenwold caught his breath, such as it was, when he saw their destination: the woodlouse-thing, grazing quietly at a stand of weed, with its long antennae flicking mildly at the water.

*I'm running out of air already*, Stenwold thought. *I can't just sit atop that thing while it waddles off*. Gribbern's tugging was insistent, though, and soon they found themselves in the shadow of the enormous creature. Abruptly, Stenwold was released, feeling himself begin to choke inside the caul. Gribbern had kicked off from the bottom, and vanished briefly behind the curved horn that was the near side of the monster's head. Then he reappeared, gesturing urgently, and Stenwold made a tremendous effort, and jumped.

He made precious little headway, but it was enough for Gribbern to catch his outflung hand and pull him effortlessly the rest of the way. There was a gap there, like a vent or gill where the beast's head joined the first segment of its body, and it was just large enough for a man to squeeze into. Gribbern seemed intent on forcing him through there and, with no other option, Stenwold pulled and grabbed and wriggled until he was suddenly inside a small chamber beyond. A moment later, Gribbern had joined him, not without some effort, and he ended up with his knees jabbing Stenwold's chest, and Stenwold's elbow in his eye. The chamber shook, and the wall at Stenwold's back parted, spilling water into a further space beyond. He fell backwards, fighting to loosen the caul, and got it off with a great whoop of breath.

The air was stale-smelling in here, and there was only a single yellowish lamp. There was precious little for it to illuminate, either: a few seamless-looking lumps of shell that Stenwold guessed were containers, and a scattering of clothing that included another coat like Gribbern's, a pair of thick leathery gauntlets and some long strips of cloth of uncertain function.

'Where are we?' he asked. The water that had come in with him was now draining away somewhere.

'Home,' Gribbern said shortly. The entire room pitched sideways, and then righted itself, and Stenwold realized that they were inside the monster, and that the monster was under way.

'You . . . live in this thing?'

'Pserry and I live together.' One of Gribbern's hands rose to stroke the room's side with surprising tenderness. 'Been forty years now, for Pserry and me. We're too old for all of this chasing about, but we were the closest, more fool us, and Nemoctes and the others couldn't get here in time. Our bad luck, that. Yours, too, otherwise you'd have had better quarters, no doubt. Still, you're here now, so we'll both have to make the best of it.'

'How can you . . . where are we going?'

'Away,' Gribbern told him. 'Pserry knows: he sees, and I see what he sees, or what he feels. Most of the time, there's no light where we roam, we Pelagists. Though technically I'm a Profundist, me. Deeper than anyone, I go. Only mistake is coming up to the shallows, like this, is the way I see it.'

'The *shallows*?' Stenwold could not stop himself.

For the very first time, Gribbern smiled, but not pleasantly. 'Oh, you're a land-kinden, that's right. Well, land-kinden man, there are depths and depths, and then there are the depths that we've seen, Pserry and me. After that it gets *real* deep.'

No sooner had Laszlo been bundled aboard the shell-ship than Wys was shouting for Lej to get them moving. The previously lazy drift of the ship turned into an abrupt surge, sending Fel and Phylles clutching for the netting, and Laszlo into the air with a flick of his wings. Wys was grinning fiercely.

'Heading?' bellowed her engineer.

'Go deep around the weed!' she called back. 'We've some company we need to lose.'

'Are we faster?' Laszlo asked her.

'No.'

'Then how . . . ?'

'We don't get tired, and they don't know the first thing about barques like this one. Let them break all the spears they want against our hull,' she boasted proudly. A moment later something flashed knife-like across their view: a brief glimpse of a lean, spindly man crouching low in a high saddle, the beast beneath him just a pale blur in the shell-ship's lamplight. The only impression Laszlo had of the steed was an enormous round eye.

A moment later there were more of them, coursing back and forth before them, and he realized that they were fighting. They lashed through the water with astonishing swiftness, the riders leaning sideways to jab lance points into the paths of their opponents. These were warriors such as Heiracles had commanded: tall, thin men and women clad in light, sculpted armour. Their free hands mostly held additional spears and they clearly disdained shields. Although their lightning offensives seldom connected, Laszlo saw one of them run straight through by the force of a strike, the lance piercing through breastplate and torso to drive deep into the mantle of his mount. The monster instantly bucked away in a cloud of ink and blood.

*Was that one of Heiracles's men? Or one of the Edmir's?* There was no sure way for him to tell, although the fighters themselves obviously had no difficulty in discerning. It seemed impossible, in the dim water for them to recognize the faces of their enemies, yet they wore no uniforms, carried no emblems. A thought came to Laszlo, and he asked, 'These cavalrymen of yours . . . ?'

'The Dart-kinden,' Wys confirmed, still intently watching her ship's course. She was close by the window now, hands poised near what might qualify as some kind of levers.

'They have the Art-speech with their beasts?'

'Of course,' was her prompt reply. 'Most people do, who can't get better transportation.' At which she patted the vessel's side affectionately. Her words held the familiar contempt of the technologically superior.

Laszlo nodded. He guessed then that the riders must be taking their cue from their mounts, who would recognize their own stablemates by scent or taste or something. Such Art-speech was something he had seen little of, back on land, but he had heard of it. It was seldom practised, there, save in a few notably backward places. The world had moved on. *But obviously not down here.*

A second later Wys jumped back as one of the riders skimmed past the window, jabbing at it with his spear. Laszlo experienced a frozen moment of waiting for the membrane to tear like paper, but it held firm at the cost of an ugly white scar left in the spearpoint's wake.

The rider was coming back for a second pass. It was clear that he did not fancy a head-on charge, but was trying to angle himself to make the most of his mount's speed. Wys hauled down on some device, but with no visible effect.

Laszlo braced himself. He had the dripping caul ready

to hand, still, though if the ship was breached he guessed it would be little enough use. He glanced at Fel and Phylles, and saw them calm.

When it seemed that the rider was just about to run his mount's pointed end right through the shell-ship's hull, the beast twisted aside beneath him, jerking and flailing with its tentacles. It righted itself, facing clear in the opposite direction, and Laszlo had a moment of watching the rider fight furiously to turn it round before it vanished at top speed into the murk.

'A little concoction from the Hot Stations,' Wys explained, sounding very pleased with herself. 'They don't like the taste, you see.'

Another couple of Dart-kinden riders appeared briefly within their view, but their animals began veering off even as they did so. Shortly thereafter, there was nothing but the submarine blackness to be seen.

'And we're clear,' Wys announced, stepping back from the window. 'Heiracles's boys must have given them a fair old run, and there's going to be some heads rolling amongst the Edmir's guard today. He's not a man you ever want to report a failure to, I hear.'

'Let's hope it is a failure they do report,' Laszlo pointed out.

'Oh, if I'd know you were such a sour one, I'd have left you,' she reproached him, grinning. 'Now, listen up, you're crew until Heiracles tells me what to do with you. That means you do what I say.'

'Oh, it does, does it?' Laszlo bristled.

'Or you can swim,' she pointed out. 'You reckon you get to be a passenger when we all have to work? You can pay your passage, can you?'

Laszlo opened and closed his mouth a few times, then folded his arms sulkily. 'So what do I do?'

'Oh, Phylles can start you off on something simple.'

'Wys, they were talking earlier, and he can't even

accreate,' the larger woman complained. 'And unless you want lots of things reaching down from high places, that trick of his isn't exactly useful for much.'

'Find something suitable for him,' Wys directed. 'Hey, Spillage!'

'What now?' came the engineer's voice.

'Chart us a course for the Hot Stations.'

Phylles was frowning. 'Why?'

Wys smiled. 'Because we've worked for Heiracles enough for me to know where he prefers to do business. He'll want these land-kinden far away from Hermatyre, and he had friends at the Stations, last I heard. Mark my words, we'll get some grubby Pelagist turning up sooner or later to tell us just that, so we might as well anticipate him. Besides, Stations are good business.' She grinned at Laszlo. 'You'll like them, land-boy. The Hot Stations are where it's all *happening*.'

# Twenty-Four

There was precious little room in the space behind Pserry's head, which Stenwold considered was no real surprise. The space there smelt strongly of Gribbern, who must presumably spend much of his life living there. For now, Stenwold's reluctant rescuer was mumbling away to himself, hunched over inside his coat, while Stenwold was sitting almost back to back with him, staring at the wall and feeling the gentle rocking motion as Pserry the woodlouse, or whatever it was, clattered over the seabed.

'Where are we going?' he asked. Being deprived of any visual clue was maddening.

'Don't reckon that fellow rightly told me where I should be headed,' Gribbern broke off his mutterings to answer. 'Still, don't see as how I much want to get collared by the Edmir's people, for all we Pelagists are s'posed to be above all that. Or Profundists, as—'

'Technically you're a Profundist, yes,' Stenwold finished for him. 'Please, Master Gribbern, just tell me something of what's going on.'

'*Master* Gribbern,' the sea-kinden echoed, as if tasting the title. 'Sounds impressive. If I ever meet a *Master* Gribbern, I'll give him your regards. This just-plain-Gribbern says that we're into the weed now, where their darts won't easily follow, and won't follow fast even if they do. We can make good time down here on the bottom, and I always say that steady's the best way.'

'And after that?' Stenwold prompted. 'You have a plan?'

'Don't reckon it's up to me to be coming up with plans. Reckon that Heiracles fellow, he'll go speak to Nemoctes or someone else, depending on who's closest, and the word will get passed on.'

'You could always take me to the land's edge,' Stenwold suggested. 'Since I'm obviously an inconvenience to you, what's there to lose?'

Gribbern harrumphed. 'Besides from the fact that I don't reckon it's a good idea, on account of how a lot of people might get annoyed at me, Nemoctes included, Pserry couldn't manage it. There's the land-wall in the way: too steep to climb, and there's no way we're swimming it. Besides, I rightly hear that going close to the land is just inviting death. No sense in taking chances, say I.'

'Landwall?' Stenwold asked, baffled.

'Surely.' Gribbern twisted round against his back, so as to peer at him. 'You know all this, rightly? I'm sure it pleases land-kinden to play all kinds of games with us regular folk.'

'I know nothing,' Stenwold said, with patience. 'Please educate me.'

'Well landwards of here there's a great wall where the seabed just rises on up and up. Now Pserry can't make it, can't swim so well, but I hear some can swim so close to the surface that they get over it, while some of the Onychoi can go climbing it. Takes many days, they tell me. But up there the water's shallow, shallower and shallower and not healthy to be in, and then comes the land. Dreadful place, so I'm told, nothing but the emptiness above, and it's cold and dry and hot and dry all the time, they say.'

*Laszlo told me . . . he said, 'the Shelf,'* Stenwold recalled abruptly. *We were anchored at the edge of the shelf, where the water got deeper.* A picture arose in his mind of the Barrier

Ridge, the great cliffs that served as the border between the Lowlands and the Commonweal. Perhaps this land-wall, this Shelf, was another such, but wholly under the sea, forming an instinctive border to the sea-kinden world.

*Only they can swim over it . . . but then we can fly over the Barrier Ridge, but few enough do it, because the Commonweal's strange and unwelcoming and there's nothing we want there.*

'Then . . . how tall's this weed?' he asked, trying to assess it.

'All the way to the top, or so they say,' came the vague reply, and then Gribbern was mumbling again, holding some curious little conversation with himself. Stenwold began to wonder whether it was Pserry that he was confiding in.

*Let's hope Laszlo got clear as well – and Paladrya.* He wondered what would happen to Paladrya now. He had wanted to reassure himself that her life could only get better now that she was out of from Claeon's clutches, but he did not trust Heiracles one inch. The man was too much like the Spider Aristos he resembled, and Stenwold had no doubt that if it became convenient to denounce Paladrya as regicide and traitress then Heiracles would do so without compunction. The thought upset him, for the Krakind woman had a rare strength in her, to have endured so much in Claeon's dungeons.

'*Master* land-kinden,' Gribbern said abruptly. 'You know anything about Littoralists?'

'Only what you people have told me,' Stenwold said, reflecting, *And that's little enough.* 'They've got a grudge against the land, it seems, want to go back there and wipe my people out, that kind of thing. Don't tell me you believe that business, how we forced your ancestors into the sea?'

'Don't rightly know and don't see that it matters these days, anyway,' Gribbern replied. 'Way I see it, we got ourselves the best of the bargain. Still, I hear them Littoralists got loud voices in Hermatyre these days.'

Stenwold grunted. *Why am I answering* these *questions about their own world?*

There was a little more murmuring and then, 'They got people in your places, the Littoralists?' Gribbern pressed.

'How would . . .' Stenwold frowned. 'Yes, I'd say they must have. It wasn't chance that saw me snatched down here. Someone tricked us into going by boat, and someone was ready for us when we did.'

Gribbern made a mournful sound, whispering to himself again, and Stenwold was unable to stave off the impression that the other man was relaying everything he said. *To his animal? Surely not.* He tilted his head back, trying to pick out individual words.

'It sounds as though Claeon is well established there,' he heard, but the voice was faint and hollow, a deep-voiced man speaking from a great distance. It was not Gribbern.

Stenwold felt his stomach twist, abruptly feeling the cramped space behind him contained more than merely Gribbern's hunched form. 'Who said that?' he demanded. 'Who's there with you?'

'Don't see anyone here with me but you,' Gribbern answered, maddeningly slowly. 'But I was talking to Nemoctes.'

'Who . . . how?'

'Just Art, land-kinden,' Gribbern told him, as though enlightening Stenwold was a personal tragedy. 'Only Art. We spend so much of our lives alone, we Pelagists – or we Profundists, as I say. We spend our time so many leagues from one another, and you can go years in the deep places, in the far reaches of the sea, and never see a beast or barque that another human being lives in. We sit well with solitude, we do, but still we cannot pretend that we do not miss the voices of our fellows. We have an Art, is all, all of us drifting kinden. We speak to one another from time to time.'

'How far?' Stenwold asked him. *Is there anything like this amongst the kinden I know?* But he knew there was not. This was not the Mindlink of the Ants: the distances were too great, and Stenwold had actually *heard* Nemoctes's voice. The sea-kinden had another impossible trick up their sleeves.

'Oh, it varies,' Gribbern said placidly. 'Perhaps you should talk to Nemoctes yourself. It might be of some use. I'll pass on what you say to him. Nemoctes, I'm letting you talk to him now.'

The faraway voice came, from some indefinable point before Gribbern. 'Land-kinden, do you hear me?'

'My name is Stenwold Maker.'

'He says his name's Stenwold Maker,' Gribbern murmured. 'Sounds a strange kind of name to me. Over-fancy, I'd say. Still, what do I know?'

'I am Nemoctes, Stenwold Maker,' spoke the voice. Even tiny and echoing, it gave Stenwold the impression of a confident and powerful man.

'You're the leader of these Pelagists?' Stenwold asked, Gribbern's low voice shadowing his words.

'There is no such thing,' said the absent Nemoctes, sounding amused, 'but enough of them will listen to me. I represent some of us who have come to dislike Hermatyre under its current rulership.'

'Nemoctes,' Stenwold said, with as much patience as he could muster, 'I appreciate there's all kinds of politics going on down here, but it's nothing to do with me, and it's nothing to do with my people. All I want to do is go home.'

There was a pause as Gribbern relayed that message faithfully, and then a longer one, while Stenwold had nothing to do but stare at the confining walls of Gribbern's cramped home. At last Nemoctes replied. 'I understand that,' he said. 'If it were as simple as you say, then I would take you to the shore myself, but what you say is not true. You yourself have confirmed it. Claeon has an interest in your world. The Littoralists are already spying there, and no doubt they have gathered allies. Whether it is war against you, or a plot to bring your people here to serve him, Claeon intends no good, and you are part of his plans. I regret, I deeply regret, but I cannot just let you return.'

'If something is going on up above,' Stenwold insisted, 'then the best way to deal with it is to let me go up there and sort it out. I don't want sea-kinden agents amongst my people, any more than you do, and nothing that Claeon might be planning is going to mean any good for us. Let me help you by acting where you cannot.'

'That seems logical,' Nemoctes said, but his tone gave Stenwold no hope. 'It may well be what is eventually agreed. However, we must have a genuine conclave first, we Pelagists and Heiracles's people, I hear rumours that the heir may yet be alive. We must let the water clear before we can see what is the best course.'

'Right,' Stenwold said. Abruptly the sense of confinement, the feel of Gribbern's back pressing against his, the dim light, the stale air, it was all too much for him. He felt like weeping in frustration.

'I give you my word that you will be allowed your say, and I will not have you used merely for Heiracles's political ends. We will do with you what is best for our people, but also what is best for yours if this is possible.'

Stenwold found that he believed the distant voice, but it gave him no joy. One man's oath was such a little thing in the wide sea.

'Nemoctes,' Gribbern said, then.

'Speak.'

'Reckon I have to break in here. We're not alone.'

There was a moment as Stenwold and the far-off Nemoctes considered these same words.

'We are followed,' Gribbern explained, and there was the faintest tremor in his voice.

'Who's there?' Nemoctes demanded, with Stenwold joining in, 'Followed how? By who?'

'Pserry says it's Onychoi,' Gribbern reported. 'Not so far behind and tracking us through the weed.'

'Speed?' Nemoctes pressed.

'Oh, reckon it's close to ours,' Gribbern said miserably. 'Three, maybe four of them.'

'Head deep and keep moving,' ordered the tiny, Art-born voice. 'I am coming for you now. I am not so far away.'

'Don't think I'm so worried about them,' Gribbern muttered. 'Pserry reckons they've been behind us since we set off, and getting no closer nor further, and we can run for longer than they can, but Pserry says there's something else now, something moving in the weed above us, keeping pace.' His voice jumped in pitch, just for a moment.

'Stay calm, Gribbern,' Nemoctes told him. 'I am closing. I will be with you.' There was a quality to those remote tones, though, that cut through the confidence he was trying to instil. Neither Stenwold nor Gribbern remarked on it, but they were both thinking the same thing: *He is not so close. He is too far.* Stenwold had no idea, in truth, what distance separated them from the invisible Nemoctes, but Nemoctes obviously knew, and his own voice betrayed him.

'Don't reckon anyone else is out there, then?' Gribbern said. There was a faint tremble against Stenwold's back, something being held in. 'Who hears me?'

A new voice picked up immediately, sounding like an old woman's: 'I hear you, old Gribbern. I'm on my way.'

'I'm close by Hermatyre,' said another voice, overlapping, young and harsh this time. 'Can you turn for me?'

'Don't think I can, at that,' said Gribbern gloomily. 'Onychoi'll have me if I do anything but head straight.'

'I am near,' said a new voice, and the sound of it raised the hairs on Stenwold's neck: a woman's voice but strange and ethereal, as though it had been made solely to be heard disembodied and ghostly. 'I am coming.'

'Only . . .' Gribbern choked on the word, and then

continued gamely, 'Only Pserry's telling me there's something real big over us, and I've got a nasty feeling . . .'

'I'm on my way, so just keep moving,' Nemoctes insisted. Other voices added their encouragement, but Stenwold could feel Gribbern shaking.

'Nemoctes,' the sea-kinden whispered. 'Pserry's *scared*.'

'I'm close now,' Nemoctes said, but there was a haggard edge to his words.

'Gribbern, be strong,' said the strange woman's voice.

Stenwold could clearly hear Gribbern's breathing growing quicker and more ragged as though the exertions of his beast were transmitting themselves to him. Pserry was definitely moving faster now, the gentle rocking motion becoming a bouncing jolt as the creature scuttled between the weed stalks.

'Land-kinden,' Gribbern said, sounding immensely calm, 'reckon you'd better take that caul up.'

'What good will that do?' Stenwold asked. Caught up in the other man's fear, he had not been thinking of himself. Now the appalling weight of water returned to mind, the drowning crush of it. How long would the caul give him? Five minutes? Less? 'Gribbern, I cannot survive out there.'

'Take it up, is my advice. Maybe Nemoctes . . . in time, maybe . . .' Abruptly he lurched forwards, as though stabbed. 'Nemoctes!' he hissed. 'They sent *Arkeuthys*!'

Stenwold felt the same blade of horror in his own gut. It was the sea monster, the great sea monster whose horrifying eye had observed him on the deck of the barge, whose many arms had plucked him down into this cursed world. Arkeuthys, the name that inspired terror even in its own allies.

'Gribbern, listen to me,' Nemoctes was saying, though in truth neither of them was listening to him. 'Keep straight, let the weed protect you. Even Arkeuthys . . . Gribbern, hold out! Just hold out!'

A moment later Stenwold was slung sideways as Pserry

turned without warning, the entire bulk of the creature slewing sideways and then taking off again, even faster than before. 'What is it? What happened?' Stenwold shouted, but Gribbern had no words for him. With equal suddenness Pserry turned again, practically bounding over the uneven seabed, jostling and bouncing its two passengers.

Gribbern cried out.

Stenwold slammed backwards into him, their little box-like world abruptly jolted forwards so that for a moment the wall Stenwold was facing had become the ceiling, and Pserry's tail must have been pointing straight up. Then they landed in a great clatter, and began scrabbling desperately away again. For a moment Stenwold thought they had pitched down a crevasse, but then his heart went cold.

*It almost had us then*, he realized. The monster was right above them.

'Not going to let you down,' Gribbern said, though whether it was spoken to Stenwold or Pserry or the absent Nemoctes was unclear. The woman's voice was still saying something, but Stenwold could not catch it. Gribbern turned to him, twisting round awkwardly, his shoulder clipping Stenwold's chin. 'Put the caul on!' he insisted. 'Put it on!'

He had meanwhile taken up something, some kind of weapon, from the clutter lying around them, some kind of beaked mace.

Stenwold dragged the caul over his face as Pserry lurched over some obstacle. Stenwold could almost hear the frantic skitter of legs.

A moment later the chamber was full of water, of the sea rushing in. It hammered Stenwold onto the floor, but Gribbern was manhandling him, shoving him towards the abruptly opened hatch. Stenwold went through in a tangle of limbs, flailing wildly into the open water, almost dragging the caul from his head in an instinctive terror of drowning. He had expected pitch-dark, but there were lights here, gleaming globes the size of a man which were tethered throughout the weed, illuminating its tangled, claustrophobic snarl of waving green.

Stenwold touched the seafloor, kicked off without meaning to, his arms waving helplessly. He saw Gribbern, the mace like an anchor drawing him down to the mud, his coat spilling out around him.

He saw Pserry: the valiant beast was still scurrying, its bluntly curved head shoving onwards through the weeds, but there was a greater shadow around it, a multitude of arms folding the weed out of the way. Vast and formless, it hung impossibly over the fleeing creature, and Stenwold had to remind himself that Pserry was the size of a big hauling automotive, and so Arkeuthys was . . .

The seething coils of the enormous sea monster struck, all together, ripping Pserry from the seabed, turning the wretched beast half upside-down. Stenwold caught a blurred glimpse of that great slit-pupilled yellow eye, and a scything beak like a giant's shears. He felt the crack as those jaws hit home, crushing down on Pserry's side, grinding through the thrashing creature's shell. Again and again Arkeuthys's severing beak descended, with Pserry's limbs flailing futilely, until the water all about the monster was strewn with pieces of cracked armour and broken legs.

Gribbern gave Stenwold a shove, bowling him along through the weed. There was no word for the expression on the sea-kinden's face, but his free hand was making some signal, some piece of sign language whose meaning was clear. *Go!*

*Go where?* The interior of the caul was already feeling dangerously close. Then Gribbern's next shove turned Stenwold around, and he saw the problem. Arkeuthys had not come alone, of course.

The Onychoi were picking their way between the weed stalks: massively armoured men, as broad as they were tall, perched on high-stepping, sidestepping crabs that would have measured a quarter of Pserry's size. Gribbern pushed Stenwold again, and then turned, the beak-headed mace raised in his fists. Stenwold was fumbling for a weapon, a knife, anything, but unlike Laszlo he had not re-armed himself since their capture. He had nothing but his bare hands.

One of the Onychoi jumped down from his high seat and fell slowly to stand before Gribbern. He had a sword of sorts, a heavy, streamlined thing with a forward-curving, pick-like point. Despite his almost graceful descent, he stumbled slightly as his feet touched the bottom, and Gribbern did not let him recover, swinging the mace in a ponderous arc so that the beaked point, with all that weight behind it, chipped into the Onychoi's shoulderguard. The impact barely rocked the inhumanly broad figure, and then his sword was sweeping down in a cleaving stroke, all appearing so gradual that it was as though they had choreographed it beforehand. Gribbern, using some Art to gain solid purchase on the seafloor, managed to twist out of the weapon's path, and then his lazy backswing caught the Onychoi's helm, lashing it sideways.

The pincer caught Gribbern's free arm without warning, moving more swiftly and deftly than either of the men. The Onychoi's mount had taken a delicate step in and plucked its master's opponent neatly out of the duel. A moment later the second claw caught Gribbern about the waist and closed hard enough that the water instantly filled with a ballooning cloud of blood.

Stenwold screamed in grief and horror and tried to flee, struggling and kicking at the water and the mud. He saw the Onychoi begin to move towards him, each stride resembling a leisurely leap. The sickly light of the lamps was becoming much brighter, showing him far more than he wanted to see. The crab was busy feeding, a dozen mouthparts working industriously, shredding the remains of a tattered grey coat. The Onychoi took another step and paused, sword cocked back. Everything was light. Even the weed was glowing.

But it was not the weed. A draping curtain swept over Stenwold, a veil of tendrils that gleamed with their own pale luminescence. Some were so slender he could barely see them, others were coiled into drifting helixes or ornamented with lacy frills. His breath was growing laboured now. The caul had done almost all it could for him.

The Onychoi was retreating now, fumbling backwards towards his mount. Stenwold took no joy in it for, above the crab-riders, the louring cloud that was Arkeuthys boiled forward in a flurry of tentacles.

It touched the first outpost of that shimmering wall and instantly recoiled as though slapped, the great, fluid bulk of the monster flailing and contracting into itself. The one great eye that was turned towards them flared in almost-human rage and pain.

Stenwold, growing faint, fell back, let himself drift, and looked upwards.

*The moon*, he thought, as the world fell away from him. *The moon has come to save me . . .*

# Twenty-Five

'I thought we didn't like Benthists,' Laszlo complained, in tones intended to be heard in the engine chamber. There was a questioning grunt from Lej, up above, and Laszlo repeated himself louder.

He heard a scuffle and a scrape, and then the huge engineer let himself down into the submersible's main compartment. 'Why'd you say that?' Lej asked.

'Well, Rosander's lot,' Laszlo pointed out, 'they're Benthists, right? Onychoi?'

'Surely,' said Lej, obviously puzzled by his attitude. He lumbered over to join Laszlo at the window. Outside, the rugged, rocky mud of the seafloor played host to an entire Benthist encampment, its long line of animals and conveyances coiled into decreasing loops that presumably put the most vulnerable in the centre. There were over two score of gigantic armoured beasts, all pincers and legs and craggy carapaces, each one burdened with bulging nets of cargo or peaked howdahs made of shell and fishskin, some drawing laden travois. As well as the animals, Laszlo observed some kind of automotive there as well, a great bronze walker made into the form of a stylized lobster, which was splendid enough that he guessed the Benthist chief – their 'Nauarch' – must travel on it. Above them a dozen or so squid-riding Kerebroi traced graceful paths, darting off into the darkness beyond the train's lamps and then arcing back, obviously watching for danger. A single submersible sailed with them, a slender thing made out of a razor shell that could only just have fit a single pilot of Wys's size.

'Rosander we don't like. Benthists we're happy with. Onychoi? I'm Onychoi. Wys is. Fel is,' Lej rumbled. 'Nothing wrong with Onychoi. Nothing wrong with Kerebroi. People are people. Just certain individuals we're not so keen on. Besides, we're for hire. Not our job not to like people.'

Wys, Fel and Phylles were outside there amongst the Benthists with Heiracles's chest of money, apparently trading for something. The sight of the Benthist camp had been wholly welcome to them.

'Problem with Rosander,' Lej continued, choosing his thoughts carefully, 'is that he doesn't *act* like a Benthist. The Thousand Spines have been in and around Hermatyre for years now. Benthists should be on the move. Nobody's happy with them just *sitting* there.'

Laszlo nodded, still staring out at the busy caravan. The Benthists were out in force, certainly. Parties of them kept appearing from the gloom, tracking their way across the ocean wastes. Laszlo assumed they had been off fishing or foraging or something. The seabed looked so inhospitable he was amazed that there could be enough there to keep so many mouths fed. He guessed that there must be at least four hundred Benthists in sight, with who could know how many more off scavenging. Most of them were Onychoi: plenty of people resembling Lej, both in and out of their massive suits of armour. Others were of Wys's kindred, diminutive crouched forms scuttling or sculling everywhere, checking the animals and goods. All of them seemed to be wearing a great deal more clothes than the people of Hermatyre, but perhaps the open water was cold whereas the colony was muggily warm. After a while Laszlo was able to pick out a scattering of other kinden: aside from the Kerebroi sea-cavalry above, he spotted a few people like Paladrya in amongst the heavy, broad forms of the Onychoi, and a couple of others he simply couldn't place. There was even a thickset young man who could have been Phylles's brother, lounging atop one of the beasts, with his back against some kind of extraordinary flower-like outgrowth that waved a hundred tendrils on the unseen current.

When he mentioned this to Lej, the big man shrugged.

'Why not?' he asked, with his customary patience. 'Someone wants to ride with the Benthists, why not? The life's not easy. Easier in a colony, for all you have to do things in a certain way. But freer out with the Benthists. Sometimes that's what people want: not all fenced about by walls, not to go drifting about alone like a Pelagist. Some people like it that way.'

'Did you ever do that? Travel with a train?' Laszlo asked him.

'Born in one,' Lej confirmed. 'Got off at the Station, when I was fourteen. Worked there, got trained. Here, now.'

'You like machines?'

'Surely.' Lej grinned, which transformed his face, made him look younger and more human. 'Good to be able to do something lots of other people can't. Like you. You know what I'm saying.' He meant Aptitude, of course. Laszlo was trying to put together a picture of how many people were actually Apt down here. He had the impression that the talent was mostly confined to the Onychoi, and there were obviously a lot of them who, like Wys, were Apt but had never really thought about mechanical things, and therefore tended to assume there was some impenetrable mystery about them. Laszlo's casual acceptance of the submersible's workings had got him a great deal of unearned respect from Lej, even though he was in no real position to help out. It was not that his knowledge of artifice – minimal as it was – would not have been some use; it was just that the gear trains that kept the barque moving were made with

379

someone like Lej in mind, and Laszlo would barely have been able to wrestle a single gear about. Even winding the engine was done by hand and by the sheer power in Lej's broad shoulders.

'Here's Herself,' Lej murmured, pointing to where Wys and the others were just emerging from the inner reaches of the spiralled train.

Laszlo chuckled, drawing a curious glance from the mechanic. 'We say that, sometimes,' he explained. 'We'd say "Himself's in a bad mood" or something. Odd that you do, too.'

Lej gave him a long, considering look. 'Land-kinden, I don't know why you and me, we even understand a word each other says,' he remarked.

Laszlo stared at him, startled by the thought. Words were words, after all. They meant . . . They had meaning. Intrinsic meaning. He was sure he had read that, somewhere.

Fel and Phylles were both laden down with sacks and jars and strangely moulded pearly containers. Wys was in deep conference with an Onychoi woman of Lej's kinden, who seemed to be wearing overalls done up at all the joints, and overlaid by piecemeal armour. She was just as broad and heavily built as the male of the species, and Lej had identified her as Epiphona, the Nauarch of the Three Red Fish train. Sure enough, several of the armoured draft-beasts sported simple square banners with a trio of crimson dots. To Laszlo's eyes there appeared little fish-like about the emblems.

Epiphona watched Wys's hands carefully as the tiny woman's fingers flew in the hand-speech these people used when outside under the open water. Her own hands moved in return, just a few signs but decisively. A moment later Wys and her crew were heading back towards the submersible.

'Must have got some bargains,' Lej mused. 'She looks happy.'

Laszlo had seen the stuff they used as money: leathery pieces of thick, uneven paper printed with fantastical designs. Apparently Hermatyre just churned this stuff out to the Edmir's order, and anyone working for the city got rewarded with some. Laszlo had opined that it must be easy to make your own, and had learned that there was some complicated business with the ink and the patterns, so that even a skilled accreator would have difficulty in duplicating them. It seemed a mad system to him, but he decided he would have to take their word for it. After all, they were clearly not going to be moving to the Helleron gold standard any time soon.

Shortly afterwards, Wys and the others came stomping inside, the dregs of seawater running off them. They had food, she announced, and some fresh-woven clothes, and something called 'leitwater' for Lej, which was apparently strong drink of some kind. Lej then asked a lot of questions about vintage, which boiled down to finding out which individual had distilled the stuff out of seawater. The thought made Laszlo feel quite ill, as there were surely lots of unpleasant things in seawater, and every fool knew it was poison to drink it. Still, these people were insane enough to actually *live* in the sea, and even *breathe* it on occasion, so he shouldn't be surprised at this fresh example of their lunacy.

'Any word?' he demanded of Wys, as soon as he could get a word in.

'Hmm?' Wys raised her feathery eyebrow, the only tufts of hair on her head. 'Oh, of your friend? Nothing. They've met a few Pelagists, but none that recently, and it's not likely the news would be bandied about that freely. Don't worry, they'll find us.' She smiled at him, obviously believing that she was being reassuring. 'Nothing bad will have happened to him. He's probably reached the Stations already.'

★

He remembered the darkness closing on him.

He remembered something lancing into his side, a feeling like burning, then fighting to breathe.

The surging, hanging bulk of Arkeuthys rolling forward in the water, like an angry cloud, tentacles reaching out but then suddenly recoiling.

Himself rushing upwards through the water, dragged by the thing in his side, into . . .

Stenwold remembered . . .

*Light.*

And woke to it, bright enough to claw at the edge of his eyelids. He lay on a yielding surface, and felt a dull ache in his side where something had pierced him. The light was so white, he could see it despite his closed eyes. White and bright and pure, like nothing he had seen since they took him away from the sun.

For a moment he thought . . . but he was not back on land. There was no fresh breeze, no open space. Around him the damp, neutral air reverberated to a soft, rhythmic sound, like a rush of water heard from three rooms away. *A submersible, it must be . . . ?* But not like the jetting dart they had kidnapped him in, nor even Wys's coiled home. There was motion evident in the padded surface beneath him, but it was different to the almost violent stop-start of siphons that Lej had shown him earlier.

He opened his eyes, or tried to. The light was just too bright. He was surrounded by glare. He raised a hand to blot it out, feeling his joints ache. Something in him was ready for a sharp stab of hurt in his side, but there was now only the distant and fading memory of pain.

*Yet another strange place. Every time I ever try to understand* . . . Chenni's barque, then the oubliette, Wys's vessel, the shell-house, the claustrophobic cabin behind the head of Gribbern's poor sea monster . . . and now this. Where was *this*?

*I hope Laszlo did better than this. I hope* Teornis *did, too, wherever he is.* He felt that he would have kissed Teornis, to see him just then, enemy or not.

He finally risked peering through his fingers. Everything around him seemed to glow pale, as though he was sitting under the full moon. There were arching walls around him – no, a dome, a dome above. The walls kept undulating softly. He could make out grey shapes within them, worms and sacs and . . .

Like intestines. Those dim forms within the translucent walls were like the guts of some creature, and beyond them was . . .

The sea. The water. He spotted the darting forms of fish as they approached to butt at the light. He looked down.

Looking down was definitely a mistake. There was less light emanating from down there. The floor was nigh on transparent, and below was only sea – yet not only sea. There was a drifting trail there, too, like the forest of weeds but floating, hanging in the water, going on for ever and for ever until the white light could no longer penetrate. Strings and coils and glittering strands of jewels. Tentacles.

*Not a submersible.* He held himself very still. That there was air here, and not simply some kind of digestive juice, suggested he was now the guest of some other type of sea-kinden, but that failed to inspire him with any great confidence. He saw a fish darting in amongst those lazy strands. A single touch, a mere brush against the slimmest tendril and the creature was twitching, spasming and then still, stuck somehow on the near-invisible thread. Then the creature he was inside began to haul up the line, contracting and contracting again, as it dragged its victim in smoothly towards some hidden orifice.

*Just like me?* He remembered that lance of pain, that tug. *How can they* live *like this? Why don't they go mad with revulsion? Everything here is so hideous!*

'Tell me how you feel.'

His head moved automatically to find the source of the voice.

'Oh,' gaped Stenwold.

She was not hideous. She was anything but hideous, and he knew instantly what land-kinden her people must once have been cousin to. Those blank white eyes, that pale skin that shone softly, constantly brushed with muted sheens like mother-of-pearl. He remembered the girl that Salma had loved, who had once been known as Grief in Chains, and who had danced and been ethereally beautiful – somehow not fit for Stenwold's or Salma's world of blood and war. This woman was the same. She was more so. Her skin was so alabaster-pale that he dared not look too closely lest he discern *her* organs beneath it and, besides, her skin was all that she possessed, that and her long, pale hair that rippled and twitched as though it felt the sea current shifting beyond those filmy walls. She knelt, sitting on her heels, and stared at him with those huge, featureless eyes and no expression at all on her face.

'What . . . ?' he managed. He felt as though he had been off-balance for days now, reeling from one incomprehensible sight to another, as though any moment he would be out in the water again, in a cell, or in the jaws of a monster. He was shaking and, as he noticed it, the shaking became worse and he could not stop it. All he could do was just stare bleakly back at this sea-kinden woman.

'Tell me how you feel,' she repeated.

He opened his mouth to frame an answer, but even posing the question to himself made it impossible to utter. *Lost*, he thought. *I feel lost.* And he was truly lost. No other son of Collegium had ever been so adrift, surely. *I want to go home.* Not because he was War Master Stenwold Maker, hero of Collegium, who would save his city from the Spiders as he had, somehow apparently, saved it from the Vekken and the Wasps. He wanted to go home for the same reason a wayward child cries for its mother. *I want to see something familiar. Walls, doors, roofs, my friends. Not . . .* The image of Gribbern's death appeared abruptly in the front of his mind: the blindly mechanical apparatus of the crab's mouthparts going about their delicate work of ripping a man to shreds and consuming him. As he recoiled from the thought, his mind's straining seams finally sprang. They all came out, all the old faces. *Tisamon, you bastard, where are you when I need you?* Nero sketched slyly, he who had died hundreds of miles astray in Solarno . . . Salma, Totho, Tynisa . . . The dead and the lost.

Arianna. He relived her death, Danaen's cruel blade separating her from her life's last seconds with typical Mantis precision. Arianna who had betrayed him and betrayed for him and tried to kill a general for him, and who might even have loved him, in some brief moment between wars.

He was aware that he was falling sideways, but his arms were too busy trying to hold himself together. The surface that he fell on to rippled with alien life as he landed, and he wished it would swallow him up, absorb him, divide him from this killing ache of loss just as the Mantis blade had severed Arianna from him.

He felt her presence, then: delicate fingers trailing across the tattered clothing over his back, exploring textures tentatively, unsure quite what to do with him. When they touched skin they shrank away. She might almost have been floating in the air above him, as he shuddered with pent-up grief. Some instinct or memory had obviously touched her, for her arms were then around him, an encircling embrace only an inch from contact, head bent low so the fronds of her hair twined slowly, blindly about him. He shook and sobbed under her tentative guardianship, and at last, when it had all been wrung out of him, and sheer exhaustion triumphed over the draining wells of emotion, he slept.

★

He awoke to voices, and for a moment he was kicking frantically in Gribbern's tiny cramped cabin, because it was the distant echo of Nemoctes drifting to him from far away . . . and when she answered, when his mysterious benefactress spoke, he recognized her voice from the ghosts that had haunted Gribbern, in those last headlong moments before he and his mount had died. 'I am near,' she had assured him, but she had not been quite near enough.

'He returns to us,' she said now, without looking round at him, somehow sensing even the opening of Stenwold's eyes. She was sitting, her knees drawn close to her chin, facing away from him.

'Stenwold Maker of the land-kinden, do you hear me?' came the scratching sound that distance and their Art made of Nemoctes's voice.

'And if I do?' Stenwold replied weakly.

'He hears,' the woman confirmed.

'I am glad that you still live, land-kinden.'

'I'm not sure I share that pleasure,' Stenwold told the air. 'What do you want?'

There was a pause after she had relayed his words, and then Nemoctes said, 'I have told Lyess to bring you to the Hot Stations. We will meet there – with Heiracles and other loyalists if possible. Claeon will not dare act too openly for fear of the Man.' That one word was spoken as a title of some weight. 'I will find your friend, the other land-kinden. He will be brought to you there.'

'Good,' Stenwold responded, thinking that was the least they could do if they could not take him home. Then shame struck him, and he muttered, 'I'm sorry about your friend.'

'As am I,' and so he was, for Nemoctes's bitter sadness could be heard quite clearly. 'Sorrier still as I am the cause, the one who has brought some of my fellow Pelagists into this conflict. I do not intend to see any more of my people slain – or any others under my care, yourself included.'

'Then take me to the land,' Stenwold demanded promptly. 'Free me.'

He did not hear Nemoctes's sigh, but his mind inserted it into the pause that followed. At last the unseen sea-kinden said, 'If I was free myself to act, then I would hold no prisoners. Freedom is the life of a Pelagist, so I would never willingly deny it to any. I can only pledge that Heiracles and his people must advance some definite cause against you, or purpose for you, otherwise I shall return you to your people myself, and your friend also. No more waiting. No more holding you behind their backs in case of need.'

Perhaps that was fair, and a fine thing to promise, but Stenwould could not find it so. 'Well,' he said, without direction. 'And what now?'

'You shall be in the Hot Stations as soon as time and the currents allow,' Nemoctes told him. 'Until then, Lyess shall care for you. There are few dangers in the ocean likely to trouble her, I hope.'

Stenwold remembered how Arkeuthys had flinched back, stung by the tendrils of whatever sea-monster he was now travelling in. Under other circumstances, he would have wondered at how much more closely these sea-kinden lived with the creatures whose Art they bore, how much more they relied on them, and had been affected by them in turn. As it was he just felt the whole situation somehow vile. Then the woman – Lyess he assumed – turned about to stare at him again, milky arms wrapped about her knees.

'I . . . suppose we are to be companions for a while, then,' he said awkwardly. An answering expression came to her face, but it was one for which he had no name. It was not joy, certainly, at this prolonging of his company. It was closer to fear, perhaps, but a fear of something the land did not encompass. 'How long is it to these Stations? You have supplies, I take it?' He looked about the bell-shaped chamber, with its rippling walls, seeing there was no place that cargo might be stored. In fact he could see clean through to the sea, in all directions.

'We will provide,' she replied.

He guessed that 'we' included her creature, whose busy flesh surrounded them. The thought made him shudder and he shuffled forward, and at once she drew back from him, hands extended out a little, as though she was a Wasp who might sting. That wordless expression on her face intensified.

'What?' he asked her, having no reserves of patience to spare her feelings. 'What is it?'

'I have not borne one like you. I have not admitted one like you to this place. Ever.'

'That's hardly surprising,' he said dismissively, 'since, for some reason, we land-kinden don't like to come down here very much . . .'

But she was already shaking her head. 'I . . . have had no guests at all. I am not like Nemoctes, to have many dealings with the Obligists. I have only the voices of my peers. We travel far and deep, we Pelagists. There may be years without meeting any other. Some of us that drift in the furthest currents never meet another of their kinden – of any kinden. We are made to be solitary throughout the great width of the sea. I am not used to . . . not being alone. Even with other Pelagists we have met only briefly, before we have passed on our ways. Even my mother and my children . . . There are only the voices – the Far-speech of our Art. I have lived in a world of voices for so long. It is . . . difficult to know another face.'

There was a question in his mind ever since he had deciphered Gribbern's mutterings, and he had never had the chance to ask it of poor Gribbern. 'This Art of yours, it is through your creatures? Do they talk mind to mind at such a distance?'

'No,' she said simply. 'You are thinking of Pserry, perhaps. Pserry had a mind, although only Gribbern and his kin could speak to it. That is a different Art, the speaking-with-beasts. My companion here,' and her arm encompassed all that was around them, 'has no voice, no mind. So we are a different partnership.'

That plural was beginning to make him feel uncomfortable. 'But how can you direct it?'

'We are joined, but there is only one "I". *I* am Lyess, so *we* are Lyess. There is no other mind, only an echo. An echo within a great space of memory.'

'I don't understand.'

'Mind is the enemy of memory, sometimes. There is a great memory, a memory of thousands of years. It speaks very faintly, so faintly that even Nemoctes's voice – that we heard just now – would drown it out. There is no other voice, though, when I am here alone, and so, if I listen carefully, I can hear that memory. It is an ancient memory. Our kind are amongst the oldest, the very oldest of them all.'

Some vague ramblings of the less reputable Collegium philosophers were recalled to Stenwold: mutterings about insect race memories, of a great space of conjoined mind that the animals somehow existed in, or else what was it that people connected to, when they called upon their Art? Last generation's crackpot theories ... He looked into her face, pale and delicate and beautiful, as Grief in Chains had been beautiful, and could believe almost anything.

*I feel that Rosander and Paladrya were like brother and sister to me in the face of this.* 'But how, then?' he pressed on. 'Art is from the beast, from the perfect and ideal concept of the beast – if you believe that. Fly-kinden can fly, because flies can fly.' His words obviously bewildered her but he forged ahead. 'How can you use this Far-speech? What could cause you to learn such powers?'

'Loneliness, land-kinden,' she told him. 'Nothing but loneliness, here in the long dark night of the sea.'

# Twenty-Six

'How long to these Stations?' Stenwold asked her, looking out at the passing sea that was lit only by the illumination from Lyess's steed, the thing she called her companion.

'Time,' she said, and when he looked exasperated she just tilted her head to one side. 'We shall take you there, land-kinden. We shall sleep and wake, and sleep and wake, and more . . . and we shall be there.'

'What am I supposed to do before then?' he asked her.

'Rest,' said Lyess simply. 'Claeon shall not trouble you while you are in my care, nor shall Rosander's bannermen find you. Rest, and watch the waters pass.' Her voice became musical when she spoke at length, like a crystal chime. It seemed to reverberate about the chamber, as though arising from the substance of the creature that carried them.

'Your waters give me no joy,' he told her, brooding on them. A school of fish flurried past, each one with mirror-scaled sides that scattered the light back at him. He had no doubt that they would suffer their share of casualties once they encountered the deadly train beneath. The fact that their substance, peculiarly processed by Lyess's creature, would later feed him made him feel ill.

'That is sad,' she told him, staring intently at him again. Sometimes she patrolled the circumference of the chamber, one outstretched hand leaving a ribbon of colour flowing along the wall wherever she touched it. Sometimes she just knelt as if she were meditating. She seldom blinked, and her eyes were almost always fixed on him. She did not know what to do with him, but sharing her domain plainly unsettled and fascinated her. *She does not even care that I am from the land,* Stenwold thought. *She would stare at any of the sea-kinden just the same.*

'I am not meant to be in this place,' he told her. 'This . . .' – his hand described the great emptiness about them, above and below and to all sides – 'this just seems like a desert to me, a desert of water.' *Give me the spires of Collegium over this. Hammer and Tongs, give me a Wasp slave camp, even!* A pair of legs and a quick mind might free him from the Wasps. Here the only way of escape was to drown.

'There is much to see, if you but wait,' she promised him. 'There is beauty in many forms, and struggle also. But, most of all, there is calm. Calm is something you have experienced little of, I think.'

He could not help looking at her, as she spoke to him. *Beauty, yes, but surely not to touch.* She looked delicate as glass, ready to shatter in a man's hands, but he remembered how she had put her arms about him, before, and he had sensed far more strength hovering there than he would have guessed from her looks. That had been a strange gesture for one who had known so little of society. Perhaps some instincts persisted despite all the degrees of separation the sea and a difference of kinden could impose.

'The thing I most want to see is something the sea cannot provide,' he told her. The thought occurred that he must seem a dour guest, but she had it in her power to return him to land, he was sure – yet she would not. He was a prisoner, still, albeit of a different oubliette.

'Would you like me to show you the sun?' she asked him.

He felt something within him come close to breaking apart. 'Yes.' It was barely a whisper.

He felt a change, then, in the ceaseless pulsing of the creature around them . . . an ascension, perhaps? The dim sea told nothing of it, uniform in its obscurity. *What time of day or night is it, even? How can she even know there will be a sun? I have almost stopped believing in it, almost begun to think the sun is one of those myths of the Days of Lore – like the great Moth magics in the stories.*

Her ceaseless regard was beginning to unnerve him, but his eyes were already tired of the depthless water, the obscure shapes that marred the translucent walls of this latest prison. *What could make anyone seek out this way of life? They must have been desperate. Perhaps we did drive them to it, after all?*

'Rest,' she told him. 'I will wake you.'

It was clear that they were not soaring upwards on swift wings so, with his back to Lyess, he lay down on his side, feeling the surface give and stretch unpleasantly beneath him. He closed his eyes against the persistent light and fought for some kind of sleep. His body rhythms were hopelessly adrift by now, and he had no idea how many days had passed in the world above. These sea-kinden seemed to have some clock to live their lives by, but it escaped him. Without sunrise and sunset, he was lost in time.

He was later never quite sure whether he truly slept, that time, only that he was suddenly aware of her being close, and surely some time must have passed. He opened an eye and saw her, at the corner of his vision, crouching over him. For a moment he wanted to kick out at her, nightmare thoughts of her draining his blood as the Mosquito-kinden did in the stories, but he held still and forced himself to turn his head and look at her.

She was already moving back even as he did so. Her hair, which had hung down over her face, recoiled first and seemingly of its own accord, retreating from him to loop itself about her shoulders. For a second, his world was captured in her eyes, huge and sightless, and deeper than the sea could ever be. Then she had withdrawn, back across the chamber floor almost bonelessly. 'We are here,' she announced.

'Where?'

'Above.'

He looked up, and almost cried out. There was light, but it was not just that cold, sterile light given off by her creature. There was a *blue* above him that he had almost forgotten, and he lunged to his feet, one hand extended as if he could grasp the sun and hold it close to him, take it down to burn away all the horrors of the depths.

'I have to go outside,' he told her. 'Please, I have to *feel* the air.'

She had retreated all the way across the chamber from him now, as though he had suddenly become a dangerous madman. He did not notice any signal from her, and certainly she did not voice her permission, but there was an opening now, where a moment before the floor had been unmarred. Water was instantly washing about his ankles, and he knew he would somehow have to swim – out from under the monster's bulk – but in that moment he did not care about its stinging tendrils, or the drag of the water, or his own inability. He pulled the caul over his head and simply dropped through the gap into the sea.

For a moment he was sinking, but he was still within a forest of tentacles, and they allowed him purchase. He struggled through them, finding that a path opened which-ever way he turned, fighting his way through the dense geography of the creature's underside, knowing only that the air was there somewhere beyond, if he could only reach it.

There came a moment when there was nothing above him but the water, and Stenwold kicked and scrabbled, flopping and grasping his way up along the curve of the creature's side, until his head broke the lapping surface of the water and he could pull the caul from his face.

It was a bright day: the sky was near cloudless and the Lash was not clogging the horizon. Stenwold Maker fought his way up on that rubbery, giving slope and, from there, on to that scant section of Lyess's companion that broke the surface Once there he collapsed onto his back, arms outstretched and looking into the vast, welcome emptiness of the sky, smelling the fresh salt air.

*If I could only fly*, the thought came to him. But he knew the answer to that one: if he could fly, he could maybe escape Lyess, but never the sea. He could not know what direction to go in, and nobody, of any kinden whatsoever, could possess the stamina to make it to land from this remote spot. There was nothing but water from one end of the horizon to the other, and not a sail to sully the endless waves.

Still, it was sweet. It was a pleasure he had taken for granted all his life, but it was so sweet now.

How long he lay there, his tattered clothes drying, stiff with salt, he could not have later said, but at last the thing beneath him began to move, to subside slowly into the water. *Damn her*, he thought, instantly bitter. *Was this so hard? Is Nemoctes's schedule so rushed? Do we not have 'time'?* He tugged on the caul and slipped back into the sea, knowing that he would have no option save to return to that captivity or else to drown. This time the sea-monster's tentacles brushed him forward in rippling eddies, almost dragging him to the point where the open mouth waited to swallow him again. Cursing all sea-kinden he dragged himself through, feeling it close so swiftly that the cold, gelid flesh of it slobbered against his foot.

He gave out a cry of disgust and turned to glare at Lyess. 'What news?' he ordered of her. 'I assume there must have been some news, that we must now hurry to these Hot Stations?'

Kneeling with head bowed, her hair flowing over her face, Lyess made no answer.

'Speak to me,' he insisted. 'What has happened that we have to go under again?'

'We had to descend,' she confessed, very softly, and then looked up at him. Stenwold heard himself make a strange sound. Her skin, the skin of her face, was cracked and wrinkled, as though she had aged decades. 'The sun harms us,' she told him. 'My companion and I, we cannot bear its touch.'

*Would you like me to show you the sun?* she had asked. He felt ill. 'Your face . . . will you . . . ?'

'I will be well soon,' she assured him. 'But the sun will kill us if we let it. That has been known. We are much more of the sea than the other sea-kinden. To us, the land is only an echo in the memories. We were the first – or almost the first.'

'I'm sorry,' he said.

She just stared blankly back at him and asked, 'What for?'

Laszlo woke at the words 'Hey, land-kinden', finding that he understood them, and his current situation, without any clutching confusion. He was lying in one of the cargo nets that draped the interior of Wys's barque, and had found it served as a hammock by any other name. He opened an eye to find Phylles regarding him suspiciously.

'Someone here you should see, Wys says,' the Polypoi woman told him. She kept her distance, mostly, and he guessed it was because she was unsure of what dangerous Art he might possess. *Which would be a wise thought, if I was something other than a Fly.*

He dropped down from his roost with a flicker of wings

that made Phylles back up several steps more, then saw immediately who she had meant. Wys and Fel were both standing near the hatch, along with a tall, broad-shouldered man in armour.

'Who's he?' the Fly asked. 'How'd he get here?'

Phylles flicked a finger past his shoulder, towards the window. There was something hanging in the water, and Laszlo had to stare at it a while before he understood. It was of almost the exact size and shape as the submersible, save that it was still living. Where Wys had placed her hatch sprouted the head and arms of a sea monster, The eye was enormous and white, with a tiny pinprick of a pupil, set beneath a mottled leathery flap that looked to Laszlo like some kind of poorly fitting cap. There was a forest of writhing tendrils in front of the eye, far more than any creature could surely find a use for. Compared to Arkeuthys, Laszlo decided, it looked placidly inscrutable, as though it knew a great deal that it wasn't letting on about.

He marched over to Wys, determined to see what mad-man had come sailing to them aboard such a beast. The newcomer looked as though he was some kind of Kerebroi, and a powerful and elegant one, at that. His skin was darker than Paladrya's, or that of the oubliette guards: the sort of faded brown that bones turned to out in the desert. He had a high forehead, long black hair curling from a widow's peak, and his beard gleamed with oils. His armour impressed Laszlo the most, if only because it was comprehensible to him as something that could be manufactured and worn. The individual pieces had obviously been accreated: moulded out of something like crabshell into the form of breastplate, shoulder-guards, greaves and the like, and fantastically wrought into the shape of waves and sea-wrack, scallops and coiled snails. But at least it was a suit of plate armour such as land-kinden might wear, rather than the monstrous, all-encompassing carapaces of the Onychoi. Hanging from a loop at his waist was a truly nasty-looking weapon, a crowbar crossed with a pickaxe, that must be of some use in levering both men and monsters out of their shells. There was also a shield slung across his back.

He was possibly the most normal person that Laszlo had seen in some while.

'Little land-kinden,' Wys gestured, 'meet Nemoctes.'

Laszlo gave the man a grudging nod. He remembered that name, at least, from their interrupted conference.

Nemoctes regarded him evenly. 'Greetings to you, land-kinden.'

'The name's Laszlo. Where's Master Maker?' Laszlo saw no particular reason to be polite about it.

'Safe,' Nemoctes assured him. 'As safe as we can make him. There were complications or I would have sent word earlier.'

'What complications?' Laszlo wanted to know.

'Gribbern is dead, but another who heeds me rescued your friend,' Nemoctes declared. 'They head for the Hot Stations – as I discover Wys had already guessed. We will hold a fresh conclave there, beyond Claeon's reach.'

'Good for you,' Laszlo replied stubbornly. He half hoped the man might take offence, showing what he was made of, but Nemoctes simply nodded.

'It's war, isn't it?' Wys said unexpectedly. 'Any way you look at it, Hermatyre's going to fight with itself.'

A shadow crossed Nemoctes's face. 'If these land-kinden can secure the heir for us, then perhaps the bloodshed will be little, and within the palace only. Otherwise . . . it may be a uncertain situation indeed, if Heiracles raises the mob in his own name.'

Wys made a rude noise. 'I'd not follow Heiracles out of the sun unless he paid me. I don't know what they think of him in Hermatyre, but I don't reckon it's much.'

'You may be right.' Nemoctes shrugged, the plates of his armour scraping. 'My people have helped him as much as we can, and more than we should in some cases. We have no army to fight on his behalf, though, and nor would we, anyway. I do not care, myself, what blood runs in his veins, but enough others do, and therefore will not accept him even though they bear Claeon no love.'

'Maybe I'll start trading out of Deep Seep soon,' Wys mused. 'Don't recall anybody caring much about wars down there.'

'Too cursed cold down there, is the reason,' Phylles muttered, and Wys nodded glumly.

'Well, you go talk to your folks,' she told Nemoctes. 'We'll see you inside the Stations, and then we'll see what's where.'

The tall man nodded, and opened the hatch, stepping into the small room beyond. Once he was gone, Wys sighed long and deep. When she looked up, her eyes were bright, though.

'Fel, Phylles, Lej,' she addressed them, even the unseen mechanic, 'It's one of those times.'

'You mean where we either get rich or dead?' Phylles asked sourly.

'We've been rich so far, haven't we? And not dead even once?' Wys was grinning. 'With such a record, how can we go wrong?'

Both Phylles and Fel were still looking highly unenthusiastic, so she dismissed them with a wave of her hand. 'Land-kinden,' she beckoned, 'Laszlo, come to the window with me. Let's see Nemoctes off.'

Laszlo followed her over to the far end of the chamber. Nemoctes must already have reached his mount, for now the creature was lazily departing, retreating ponderously backwards off into the darkness.

'Tell me about your people, landsman,' Wys prompted him.

'You mean my kinden?'

'I mean your people. There are some folks up there

who'd want you back, yes? Someone must have shed a tear when your barque docked again at your colony, and you weren't on it.'

'My family,' Laszlo replied. *Or at least they'd better have, rotten bastards.*

'Pay to get you back, I'd wager,' Wys considered.

Laszlo shot her a sidelong look but she was watching the passing waters idly. 'They would, at that,' he informed her, though with the same mental caveat as before.

She nodded. 'I'm a woman used to making my own way in the world, Laszlo,' she said, 'and you may have noticed that I've taken a shine to you. You're not so different to us, for all you're clueless. I keep wanting to shave your head in order to make a civilized man of you, but otherwise you're just a human being, like we all are.'

*A fair sight more than you or your crew*, Laszlo thought, but he just nodded diplomatically.

'Heiracles, Nemoctes, and Claeon even, none of them have the brains of a stone,' Wys observed thoughtfully. 'What do they see in you? That you're either a threat, or something to conquer, or some kind of, what, captive militia to rule the colony with? No, no, no, stupid, all of them. I've seen you. You go and talk to Spillage like you're an engineer. Your clothes are in a poor state, and you wear more of them than anyone could want, but I can see they were tailored well enough. Your people have potential.'

'Well, thank you,' said Laszlo acidly, and she put up a warning hand before his face instantly.

'You just rein in that tongue and listen to someone when they're telling you something to your advantage,' she snapped. 'Wouldn't it be a tragedy if we never got to the Stations at all, but left you somewhere where you could just kick off for home, up above the waves?'

His breath caught and he wanted to shake her, to clutch her tight. 'Home?' he whispered.

'Your people make things differently to us. That means

they must make different things from ours,' she said. 'Things we've never seen. Things that are common as dirt to you will be like crab's ink down here,' she said, which he assumed was a rare or non-existent commodity. 'Things we take for granted, well, your lot'd tear each other apart for them. You see where I'm going with this?'

'Trade,' he replied.

'Surely, trade,' she agreed. 'Stuff Heiracles and stuff their war, I say. If your people, your family, were of a mind for barter, then why not? All anyone's ever said about the land was that it was death, that the landsmen – if there even were any – were murdering savages, and that everything up there was like poison. Now here you are, and if we haven't managed to poison you, I reckon you're not likely to poison us. So how about we forget the Stations and start making some money?'

'What about Master Maker?' Laszlo asked her.

'Nothing to do with me,' she said. 'Heiracles will sell him somewhere, or Nemoctes, or who knows what. This is between you and me, Laszlo.'

*Home. My family.* This was the best offer he was likely to get and surely, once there, he could do something to rescue Stenwold . . .

That seemed unlikely, he had to admit. By the time any reliable contact was established between the *Tidenfree* crew and Wys's people, Stenwold would have gone on to whatever fate the sea held in wait for him.

Inwardly, Laszlo swore.

'Don't take this the wrong way,' he said slowly, 'but I do have to get Master Maker out. It's not right, otherwise. But, listen, if we both get up on to land, then I promise you've got a deal. My chief'll be happy for it. You'd like him – he's just your sort of person. We're like you, kind of, my family. We're all making our own way in the world, too. Get us both back, and you've got yourself a deal.'

Wys remained expressionless for a moment, wholly

impossible to read, but then she smiled unexpectedly. 'You're a tricky little pismire, you are,' she told him. 'Well, I reckon it's the Stations then, and there we'll see what we can't do for your friend.'

Travelling with Lyess was strangely like riding in the cabin of an airship. Despite the labouring bell of the creature above them, it was impossible to tell whether they were making headway or just being coasted along by the current flowing outside. For all the creature's size, they were like a speck of nothing amid the vastness of the ocean. By Stenwold's reckoning, most of the time they might as well be stalled in place and going nowhere.

To relieve the sameness of their voyaging, he tried meditating on Art, something he had not done in a decade. He was unsure what malformed Art might come to a man, locked down here in the depths, but the gentle rhythm of the huge jellyfish was conducive to letting his mind wander, and at least it passed the time. Sometimes, when he came to himself, though, he found Lyess sitting right next to him, a fraction of an inch from touching – and watching him, always watching.

*She is lonely*, he understood sadly. *She had not realized how lonely she was until I gave her something to contrast it with.*

When the sea did give his eyes something to feast on, the meals it provided sat ill with him. On one occasion they saw a battle, or at least something like a battle. A Benthic train straggled out in a long dark line against the grey mud of the sea bottom, comprising a chain of armoured beasts and the occasional equally armoured machine. Against them had come a tide of orange and red, and at first Stenwold could not discern what he was looking at. It seemed to be a sea of spines and spikes, a crawling carpet of points and jagged edges. Then his eyes began to single out movement, and he saw that the attackers were great thorny starfish – many-fingered, creeping monsters – along with some that resembled simply impossible balls of lance-like skewers, advancing like tight-knit units of pikemen. In amongst these thronging creatures were men, lithe men with orange skins that seemed likewise rough and spined. Wearing piecemeal armour of bronze, wielding spears and forward-curving swords, they threw themselves at the Benthists in a berserk fury, their animals surging on every side.

The Benthists were swarming to the defence: armoured Onychoi lumbering forth with mauls and swords and the reinforced claws of their Art, while their own creatures snapped and clipped at the enemy with their great claws. They snipped off the spikes of their attackers and pincered through their questing limbs, but Stenwold saw several of the ponderous crustaceans overwhelmed by the crawling onslaught, enwrapped by razor-coated arms and then somehow simply taken apart, pieces of leg and shell drifting off between the assailants in a pale cloud.

The human protagonists were no less savage. Here an Onychoi took his enemy's arm between claw and dagger, and severed it neatly at the shoulder. There one of the attackers brought the honed tip of his blade to bear in cracking through a defender's breastplate. The worst thing was the pace of conflict, for it was all so slow, so weighted down by the water, as though they were enacting some leisurely and complex dance, fighting and dying at such a leaden pace that every victim must have had ample time to contemplate his unavoidable fate.

'What are they?' Stenwold asked, indicating the aggressors.

'Echinoi,' Lyess told him. 'Sometimes they attack the colonies, and they say that's the only reason the Builders tolerate anyone else within their homes. The Echinoi are everyone's enemies. They were first in the sea, the memories say. We other kinden drove them into the deeper places, and they have never forgotten. Some say they possess colonies in the great uncharted wastes, but I have heard of nobody who has seen such things for themselves.'

They drifted on over the sluggish melee, and soon the carnage was left behind in the gloom, only the train's winking lights remaining as distant star-like testimony. Stenwold continued watching for a long time, and saw several of them wink out. Not for the first time did he consider what a terrible thing it would be, to die out here.

Then there were the fish, or at least they looked like fish to Stenwold. He became aware of them only when the progress of Lyess's companion changed, becoming more laboured, and his own stomach told him they were descending fast. He looked about, to find Lyess seeming in a panic, staring about her. There was a dawning light above, like the first silver echo of sunlight, but it was fading, even as he noticed it.

'What's going on?' he asked, but then he spotted them: sleek grey darts swooping about them, lunging in towards the bell above, and then twitching away. There were a half dozen of them attacking from all sides, one after another, and always from above, so that Stenwold thought it would make more sense to get to the surface to protect her companion's top, but instead they continued dropping through the water as swiftly as they could.

The fish were never still, but kept ducking beneath the jellyfish's rippling mantle, each in turn virtually putting a narrow eye up against its transparent flanks. Stenwold's own gaze met theirs, and he experienced a distinct shock of contact, like meeting the stare of some intelligent but utterly inhuman entity. Worse was the expression about the intruders' mouths.

'Cursed fish was *smiling* at me,' he said, shaken.

'They are Menfish,' Lyess spat angrily, and her companion shuddered under a renewed assault. 'They are a bane on the Pelagists. They attack us whenever they can.

They think like humans, even though they are nothing but fish, and they hate us.'

'Can they harm us?' Stenwold asked her. The incessant lunging attack of the Menfish was becoming swifter and more violent.

'They could damage my companion so that we cannot go further, and then they will cut through to us. We must go deep, as they are creatures of the surface.'

Then the Menfish suddenly scattered, all three vanishing into the dark water. It gave Stenwold no relief, since it was all too clearly a flight from some worse monster.

For a moment the travellers held their place in the water, the ragged-edged dome above them expanding and contracting silently. Then a shadow coursed past them, a great armoured form of which Stenwold caught only glimpses: a segmented carapace, paddle-like limbs and tail, folded pincers like the largest of all scorpions. It utterly dwarfed them, and it seemed to Stenwold that it would have dwarfed almost anything.

Lyess was on her knees, staring at the thing as it passed. She was saying something over and over, almost under her breath. Stenwold bent close to hear her, and caught the words, 'Gods of the sea.'

'Gods?' he repeated numbly. The monster of monsters was coming back, making another inquisitive pass. He saw compound eyes, larger than he himself was, glitter in the jellyfish's light, as something behind that broad grid of facets considered him and weighed him, and determined his fate.

'We call them so.' Lyess was almost breathless. 'We meet them seldom. Sometimes they kill us, us Pelagists, but more often they let us live. They are the real powers of the deeps.' Her previous reserve had been stripped from her. Fear and exhilaration raced each other across her face, where Stenwold saw colours – grey and red and deep blue – surface and fade within her skin.

'Do they have' – he hardly dared ask – 'a kinden?'

'Nemoctes believes they do,' she whispered. 'He says that a Pelagist he knew once travelled to the deep places, to some tiny colony where only we and fugitives go. He told how an Onychoi came in like none he'd ever seen before, half again as tall as a normal man, and clawed, no kinden that he'd seen before or since. He swore that it was Seagod-kinden.'

The plated shadow was now receding away on its own inscrutable errands, and in its absence Stenwold could not help thinking, *Sailors' tales, as above, so below?* But he could not deny the fact of the Sea-god, and if it was not actually a god, then perhaps he had no wish to meet anything yet more godlike. *Let us be thankful that the sea keeps its greatest mysteries hidden.*

It was not long after that she woke him, hovering over and almost touching his face, until the sense of her presence broke him from his slumber.

'The Hot Stations,' she announced. 'We have arrived.'

He sat up to see the striking, turbulent vista beyond the clouded walls of Lyess's companion, and the word that sprang unstoppably from his lips was, 'Helleron.'

# Twenty-Seven

'I see you no longer trust me,' Claeon snapped.

Rosander, Nauarch of the Thousand Spines Train, had arrived in full armour, its stony plates grating constantly against one another. The Onychoi gave such an impression of concentrated weight that Teornis was surprised he didn't fall straight through the floor. Tiny traces of powder sparkled in the air where newer pieces of his mail were still establishing their fit against their neighbours. Beside him the Spider-kinden and Claeon and another Kerebroi man all looked like so many children.

'Claeon,' Rosander murmured, 'if the sea were filled with trust, from the depths up to the sunlight, there would not be sufficient trust for me to trust you.' His hard, narrow face broke into an equally hard smile. 'Besides, I must get used to carrying the weight in the air. When my campaign starts, there will be little chance to let the water bear it. So, tell me, when will that be?'

'It would be sooner had your fools not let the land-kinden escape,' Claeon accused, but Rosander was having none of it.

'My bannermen did what they could,' the big Onychoi replied, implacable. 'Your beast let one go and your Dart-kinden the other. I see you have somehow managed to retain the third.' He glanced briefly at Teornis, without much apparent interest. 'Or were you about to hand him over to someone else? Me, perhaps.'

'This man is not for you to torture.' Claeon paced the chamber, which was part of his own suite of rooms. The curved walls were ornamented in golden arabesques that Teornis found beautiful in their execution, but gauche in their effect.

'You think of torture,' Rosander murmured. 'Don't colour me with your pastimes. I might be able to hold him more securely than you, however.'

Claeon rounded on him furiously, storming up to the man's immense bulk as though about to break his hand on that stone carapace. 'Do not be impudent! I am Edmir here! You are strong, Rosander, but do not think, here in the heart of my palace, that you can mock me.'

Rosander looked down at a man who was a fraction of his size, and he sighed slowly. 'The Shell Hunters Train has been trading at Hermatyre during these last few days. Yesterday, twenty of my bannermen asked my permission to take their retinues and depart with the Hunters when they leave.'

Claeon narrowed his eyes. 'And you refused?'

'And I gave them my blessing, for they would go whatever I said, and I would rather they came back to me, when next we meet, than cut all their ties to the Thousand Spines. My people are *bored*, Claeon. They want to move on. *I* want to move on. Give me my war. Give me this landsman, to start with.'

Claeon held up a hand to silence him. 'This one is special. This one will be more use to you alive and happy than would any number of corpses or prisoners. You know Pellectes, of course?'

This was the fourth man, another Kerebroi. The stranger was taller than Claeon, leaner save for having something of a belly. His long hair and beard were lustrous with a shiny greenish hue that Teornis hoped was merely cosmetic.

It was not clear from Rosander's blank expression whether he knew Pellectes or not, so Claeon went on: 'He is the leader of the Littoralists, and his people are already up above, learning about our enemy.' He turned to address Pellectes. 'Rosander will be the agent of our return to the land.'

'So it is foretold,' Pellectes breathed.

Teornis found his eyes meeting Rosander's in a shared look of exasperation. The Onychoi shifted stance in a further chafing of armour, his pose subtly suggesting that his patience was waning fast. 'Tell me then,' he said, 'what's so special about this land-kinden.'

'He claims that the land-kinden that we have been spying on are at war with another tribe of landsmen, and that he himself is a member of this other tribe,' Claeon declared, dismissing with a wave of his hand any number of centuries of landbound politics.

'And it is true,' Pellectes assured them eagerly. 'My own agent within their colony has confirmed it.'

Rosander took two clumping steps forward to stand before Teornis. 'What can you do for us, then?'

The Spider looked the huge man directly in the eye. 'I have agents in Collegium, their colony. I can compromise their defences, guide your soldiers, identify their leaders. It would appear we have a common enemy.'

Rosander's gaze weighed him up, the resulting assessment uncertain. He looked sidelong at the green-bearded Littoralist. 'So where does your orthodoxy feature, in all this?' he grunted. 'First time I've heard your lot ever talk of *friendly* land-kinden.'

'But it is so,' announced Pellectes. 'For just look at him! He is almost kin to us Kerebroi. It is clear that these are our cousins, who somehow avoided the great purge and fled to the further reaches of the land, to find safety. Now we can strike together against our persecutors.'

The Onychoi made a disparaging noise. 'Sounds convenient,' he remarked.

'It is not *convenient*,' Pellectes snapped back at him. 'We have a duty to our ancestors to avenge the wrong done to us. Those that forced us from our homes must now be punished and destroyed. We will reclaim our birthright.'

The dry stare of Rosander swung back to Teornis. 'Anything up there look like *my* brother, landsman?'

'Not that I ever saw,' Teornis told him easily.

'Good. I'd hate to have to kill any bastard as tough as I am.' Rosander looked back to find Pellectes shaking with fury, right before him.

'You dare not mock!' the man shouted in his face.

'I dare,' Rosander growled.

Pellectes's nostrils flared. 'Your ancestors were driven, too. You too have lost a homeland. It is your duty, carried down from parent to child across all the centuries, to reclaim it. It is your destiny to be the agent of our return. How dare you jest at such? What would you say to your ancestors, when you mock their spilt blood?'

'I'd tell them they were weak fools to be pushed around, and that I like the sea just fine. Don't try to infect me with your cant. My bannermen and I, we want conquest and plunder. Keep your ideology to yourself.'

'You must not sully the cause—!' Pellectes started ranting, and then stopped. Teornis had watched Rosander draw a knife, a remarkably understated move for so huge a man. His arm, encumbered by all that weight of stone, had struck swiftly nonetheless. He had the curved blade pressed against one side of the Kerebroi's throat, the curved claw of his gauntlet alongside the other. Two tiny trickles of blood patterned Pellectes's neck. The Littoralist had gone very still, eyes almost out of his head with compounded rage and fear.

'Good. Now keep silent,' Rosander addressed him, and

turned his wrist to take the knife away. The Littoralist stepped back shakily, hands going to the two shallow, bleeding nicks.

'Have this one make arrangements then,' the Onychoi instructed Claeon, jabbing at Teornis with the blood-tipped spike. 'Make it soon, though. Any longer and my train will be on their way. They're not meant for this colony life, and neither am I.'

He turned and lumbered away, trailing faint motes of stone dust.

Pellectes bared his teeth after him. 'The barbarian!' he spat. 'Edmir, there must be some other way to further our cause. Must we rely on such ignorant beasts?'

Claeon folded his hands before him. 'But I *do* rely on him, Pellectes. I need him, alas.' His eyes narrowed. 'Moreover I only need *you* because you're of some use to *him*, and so if he decides to separate your babbling head from your shoulders, I shall cheer him to the echo. You listen to me, now. It was I who made your worthless Littoralists something more than a laughing stock in Hermatyre, and I can undo that just as easily, if you cease to be of use. Do what I say and don't cross me, or I'll have Arkeuthys eat the lot of you – and a sour stomach that would give him, no doubt.'

Pellectes kept his peace stiffly, mortally offended but not deigning to make a reply. Claeon shook his head dolefully. 'Honestly, Pellectes, do you really *believe* all that business? About the land being a place of plenty? I'm reliably informed it's horrible up there.'

'When we retake our ancestral home, it will become paradise again,' Pellectes replied, with absolute conviction.

'Whatever you say. I'll have a message for your spy soon enough. Now get out of the palace and go back to your wretched followers.' He waited until the Littoralist had stalked off, and then turned to Teornis. 'You see what I must deal with? Having brutes and madmen as my allies.'

*Neither of whom you make much effort to keep as allies,* Teornis considered, but he nodded sympathetically. 'You'll want a message from me,' he noted.

'As soon as we can find some way that you can write it.' Claeon shook his head, for it had proved an unexpected barrier. The Kerebroi wrote in some incomprehensible fashion that involved setting patterns down somehow on the thick paper they processed from pressed seaweed. Furthermore, the characters they used were wholly unfamiliar to Teornis, which had quite thrown him. He had never even considered there being a different manner of writing, but the squiggles and half-pictures of the sea-kinden held no meaning for him whatsoever.

That had its advantages, of course. His own script would baffle them equally, so he need have no fear of Claeon or Pellectes deciphering his codes. His messages would reach his own people pristine, and full of hidden meaning.

'And the other matter . . .' Claeon said, with uncharacteristic delicacy. 'Aside from Rosander's war, what about the . . . lost boy?'

'Well, I'm not sure what resources my people will have to hand, without my guidance, but I will have them start the search,' Teornis assured him. *And they will find nothing save tantalizing hints that require a greater knowledge to pursue.*

*And then I shall be out of this foul, damp, barbarous place, and I shall find this prince of theirs if he is to be found, and we shall then see if I cannot make sure Claeon will live in fear for the rest of his days.*

*Helleron.* In this alien place, the familiar name sounded strange inside his head. *It's Helleron-under-Sea, it really is.*

The chimneys were the most obvious parallel. They were twisted columns of stone, impossibly taller than any real factory stacks could be, and what they were gouting could not, of course, be black smoke, but it looked like it, and the shimmer in the water around them was like the heat haze from a foundry or a forge. Other columns around them also mirrored the chimneys, save that they sprouted broad fans or beating arms at irregular intervals. It was a Helleron dreamscape, a nightmare reflection.

At the foot of the chimneys lay the town, and it was a *town*. Stenwold would accept no substitute, certainly not the sea-kinden word 'colony'. This community was not grown by Archetoi, nor was it made from the scooped-out armour of sea-things. Men and women had built this. They were building it still. Even if the pieces that they were assembling it from were of shell and accreated strangeness, even if the crafts they were using would have mystified an honest Collegium carpenter, still they were assembling a kind of shanty town of interconnected hovels, and it would have sat nicely at the rear of a factory in the Helleron slums. *Scuto could have lived here*, he thought, but the idea of thorny Scuto struggling with a caul was too much.

The Hot Stations were lit like a town, too. The globes and baubles of soft light were everywhere, but not as though they had grown there. They were tacked on unevenly, or bobbed at the end of lines like luminous balloons, but the intent was plain to Stenwold: street lighting just like the gaslamps of home. The seabed all around was brightly lit, and there were other little clusters of lamps visible in the darkness beyond, perhaps mining or salvage operations, weed farms or Benthist outposts, who knew? In the ambient light, Stenwold saw other chimneys, as tall and crooked as these smokers but quite dead: hollow spires of marbled stone rising above a bare skeleton of the township, which was even now being removed piecemeal to its new location. Stenwold thought he could discern more exhausted chimneys beyond that. The Hot Stations was a movable feast, it appeared.

There was a remarkable bustle out here. Construction gangs surged between the current township and its deceased echo, bringing over everything that was worth rescuing and finding somewhere new to secure it. The workers were mostly either the diminutive Onychoi or some other kinden, big and grey and heavy-footed, who seemed to be doing most of the nailing down. The simple sight of people doing something as mundane as putting up buildings almost brought a tear to Stenwold's eye. The waters above were not empty either, for there were plenty of swimmers, squid-riders, a half-dozen submersibles carved out of straight or spiral shells, and a broad scattering of domesticated sea life. Nothing ventured too close to the black-belching chimneys, where the water shimmered and twisted like the air above a fire. The 'hot' of the Hot Stations was obviously not to be taken lightly.

There were no others like Lyess and her companion, he saw, and he sensed that she was not happy to be here. He turned and found her staring at him again. There was something desperate about her, but she did not know what she wanted, only that her way of life up till now had been punctuated, mangled by the imposition of a surly, brooding land-kinden.

'I'm sorry,' he said to her, although he was not entirely sure what for. She said nothing in return, did not stir. He sensed that she was searching for words and finding none. *That she will miss me? That she is now well rid of me? That she wishes Arkeuthys had simply eaten me, and spared her this disruption to her life?*

'I am here,' she said at last, to his puzzlement, until a faint hollow voice answered her.

'I shall come to you.' Stenwold recognized Nemoctes's vicarious tones. 'You have done well.'

Lyess's face developed a new expression and, as it did Stenwold realized that she had never truly shown anything of herself in her features before now. It was not pride at having served Nemoctes well, but abject misery, unfiltered and unadulterated. It washed over her and was gone in moments, leaving her face a calm mask with those intent, all-encompassing eyes, but that racked expression would stay in Stenwold's mind for a long time.

*Oh, they have made many sacrifices,* he thought in sudden understanding, *to come to an agreement with the sea monsters they live with. They can survive out in the furthest reaches of the sea, travel the darkest pits of the abyss, but they are human still, even she, and they were never meant for such privation.*

*Did they take this burden on willingly? Or did we drive them to it? Is it true, this story that they tell?*

'Lyess,' he said. She simply eyed him, saying nothing, so he pressed on. 'You spoke about memory, that your beast here has no mind, but only a kind of, what, collective memory?'

She nodded cautiously, as though regretting having mentioned it.

'How far back does it go?' he pressed her.

'Far,' she said, which was all he should have anticipated.

'They tell it, in Hermatyre, that the reason you sea-kinden are down here at all is because you were thrown off the land. By my people, I suppose – my dim and distant predecessors. Does this memory reach that far back?'

'Perhaps,' she said.

'Would you see . . . ? I have to know. If it can be known at all, I must know whether it's true.' *Surely it can't be guilt I feel over this? Or is it indignation at being falsely accused? Is it because I was once a historian that I can't just dismiss it just as 'all a very long time ago'?*

'I can listen to the echo,' she said. 'I may hear what you wish to know. There are no guarantees but, if we meet again, then perhaps I shall tell you.'

He nodded, dissatisfied but sensing he would get nothing more. Apparently ransacking the memories of the jellyfish nation would take some time.

By then they had a companion in the waters, some kind of squid-headed snail, and a man in armour came swimming towards them effortlessly. As a hole began to form in the floor of their chamber, Lyess knelt down calmly and waited, as though Stenwold had simply ceased to be present.

The water beyond Lyess's sanctum was so clenchingly heavy that Stenwold could barely draw breath. Against that, it was warm, and grew warmer as they neared the Hot Stations. Nemoctes had to drag him through two inundated chambers before they found what was obviously a make-shift hatch, comprising just a hinged round plug set off-centre in an uneven wall. When it was levered outwards and open by someone within, a great deal of water cascaded through, carrying Stenwold along with it. He ended up on the floor with water draining away on all sides, at the feet of a broad Onychoi who was wrestling the hatch into a position where the sheer pressure of water would keep it secure.

It was baking hot, Stenwold noticed, and the Onychoi wore nothing but a loincloth. He wondered how Nemoctes could stand there dressed in his armour and not sweat himself to death. *Except, of course, it's not metal armour; it's some weird thing they extrude, or whatever the term is.* Wearily he clambered to his feet, tugging at the neck of his tunic. There were a good dozen people in immediate view, mostly attending to leaks, and they were all dressed in just enough clothing to cover their modesty, but even so Stenwold felt self-conscious. Going without shoes was bad enough. Going bare-chested would seem positively barbaric.

Nemoctes was watching him closely. *And is that all these Pelagics do?* Little had been said before – Lyess's obstinate silence having made things awkward – but Stenwold sighed wearily and asked, 'What now?'

'Come with me,' Nemoctes instructed him.

'Will that markedly improve my situation?' Stenwold asked him acidly.

'Will it see you home, you mean? I hope so, but I make no promises,' the Pelagist replied. 'However, I can swear it will do you another form of good.' He turned and headed past the toiling construction workers, whereupon Stenwold, as so often recently, had little enough choice but to follow him.

The chamber beyond was broad and long, though with a perilously low ceiling propped up by a dozen slanting pillars. It all looked rather slipshod and hastily built, and that very departure from the organically smooth perfection of sea-kinden design might have been welcome, save for the weight of water beyond. 'I suppose you can't persuade your Builder-kinden to come out this far,' Stenwold observed.

'One cannot get the Arketoi to go anywhere.' Nemoctes tossed the words back over his shoulder. 'They build where they will, and others are drawn there to live as their guests. There have always been little hand-made outposts in the depths, places at which my people gather, where the Benthists stop off to trade, where loners go who want nothing to do with any other folk. The Hot Stations are something different. New.'

Stenwold had more questions, but they had now come out into a much grander chamber, which seemed a slum and a ghetto and a market all in one. People of many kinden had gathered here, dumped a sack of goods and a tattered bundle of possessions down, and made it their home. The place boasted a mad assortment of hastily-tacked up screens of the brightly coloured cloth the sea-kinden produced, choked with the sounds and smells of what must have been two hundred people all busy at something. There was food being prepared, mostly in the nature of raw and salted fish, and people haggling over it, and over tools and clothes, leathery paper, elaborate jewelry. A thin Kerebroi woman was tattooing the expansive back of an Onychoi man with an abstract pattern of vibrant colours, using nothing but her bare hands. Another Ony-choi, one of the small ones, sat cross-legged under a ragged awning with a pair of full bowls placed beside him. A faint tracery was taking shape within them as he practised his Art.

Then someone was rushing at Stenwold, pushing through the crowd at waist level, and for a moment he was instinctively reaching for the sword he had not worn in many days.

'Mar'Maker!'

The Fly-kinden was grinning at him like fury, standing before Stenwold with his hands on his hips, as proud as if he was the new master of all they surveyed.

The Beetle smiled down at him wanly. 'I hope you've had a smoother journey than I did, Laszlo.'

'Oh, more than that, far more than that,' the Fly promised him, and then cast a look up at Nemoctes. 'You go in front, shelly. Master Maker and I need to catch up.'

Nemoctes merely looked amused at this, and obligingly led the way, several steps in advance. Stenwold leant down to catch Laszlo's following words.

'You see,' the little man was saying. 'You recall Wys, right? Her that sprung us from Hermatyre?'

'The mercenary,' Stenwold confirmed.

'Very mercenary,' agreed Laszlo. 'And she's got her eyes open, that one. She's not scared of the land, and she doesn't want to make war on it neither. Trade, Mar'Maker, that's what she's after, and she says she'll pitch us up overwater just as soon as she can. Whatever happens, whatever this fellow and that slimer Heiracles and the rest settle on, you do your best to get yourself out of here on Wys's barque.'

'But will Wys go against her employers?' Stenwold pressed, deciding this all sounded much too convenient.

'Heiracles, she doesn't like. Nemoctes she likes, a bit – and so do I, I think – but he's not paying. She knows that if we get something going, her lot and my lot, then everyone will become very rich, and maybe she can set up some place just like this. They say the Man, the one who runs the Stations, he was just a freelance like her once.'

They had caught up with Wys, by then, and Nemoctes was greeting her gravely. The twin shadows of Fel and Phylles were at their accustomed places, one behind either shoulder of their diminutive captain. Stenwold offered the woman a nod, and she grinned at him from a face filled with avarice. Laszlo's words seemed to be written there in a clear script, and Stenwold felt his heart pick up, at a ray of sunny hope that had somehow found its way down here to the depths.

*But play it calmly*, he told himself, and he hoped Laszlo would do the same. If the other sea-kinden became suspicious, then not even Wys would be able to make a clean break from them.

'I've been going mad waiting for you to get here,' Laszlo said. 'We've been here, what . . . four days, I reckon, maybe more.'

'There was some trouble.' Stenwold's tone did not invite question. In his mind he saw again, briefly, the blood-clouded waters where Gribbern had met his end.

'Well, keep our wits about us, and trouble might be a thing of the past, or at least this kind of . . .' Laszlo trailed off. 'Ah, curse it.'

It took Stenwold a moment to see what had gone wrong. Wys had drawn a blade, her face suddenly wiped clear of humour. Fel and Phylles were already stepping forwards, forming up in front of her. Nemoctes's expression, as he turned back towards the landsmen, was startled.

A hand came down on Stenwold's shoulder, and drove him to his knees with the armoured weight of it. Abruptly, monolithic mailed Onychoi were shouldering aside the crowd, approaching from all quarters. Laszlo darted straight upwards, taking them by surprise. He had a knife out, but no way of putting it to much use. Stenwold tried to twist out from under the leaden grip but it closed hard on his shoulder, grating the bones, and hauled him upright again. He struck out at where his attacker's head must be, best guess, and the impact on his elbow numbed his whole arm, the sand-coloured armour feeling hard as bronze.

Nemoctes was striding forward. He held a twisted pick-like weapon in his hand, and demanded, 'What is this? Release that man!' At his raised voice, other people took notice, and Stenwold saw several people slip from the crowd to stand near him. They were Kerebroi, mostly, although one was a dark-skinned woman with a white-speckled scalp, who might easily have been Gribbern's cousin.

'Easy, now, easy.' The speaker slipped out from between two of the Onychoi, pausing before Stenwold to look up at him admiringly. 'No need to get the axe out, Nemoctes. You know all's fair in business.'

Nemoctes looked at the newcomer coldly: a little Onychoi man as bald as the rest of them, save for bushy eyebrows as extravagant as a moth's antennae. He was loaded with gold, about his neck, about his hands, with a veritable belt of interwoven chains and bracers so finely shaped into minutely detailed seascapes that each one of them would probably have persuaded a Helleron magnate to part with his most profitable factory. A swatch of purple cloth, worn over one high shoulder like a half-cloak, completed the overall impression of an extremely successful self-made man.

'Since when do you stand in the way of the Pelagists, Mandir?' Nemoctes asked him quietly. 'Are you so sick of receiving our custom?'

'Don't be angry, old wanderer.' Mandir waved his hands dismissively. 'You've not outstayed your welcome, so come and go as you please. Your prisoners, though . . . well, consider them now freed for the greater good.'

Fel and Phylles stood either side of Nemoctes now, both

obviously looking for an opening, but there were a good eight or nine of the giant Onychoi and they were all armoured head to foot, their gauntlets vicious with spikes.

'You see,' said the extravagantly dressed little man, 'we like Pelagists here, and Pelagists like us. You got any idea how many of your Deepclaw lot have traded in their old beasts for crawlers manufactured right here? The Hot Stations are the next great wave, old wanderer. There's nothing like us anywhere. And so long as I'm the Man of the Stations, the Stations will run according to my rules.'

'And what rule is it that has resulted in this?' Nemoctes demanded.

Mandir pointed a lazy finger up to where Laszlo still hovered. 'Land-kinden are considered the property of the Man, old wayfarer.'

'I never heard that rule before.'

'You never brought me any land-kinden before. The little one with the disregard for where the floor should be has been here a few days, now, long enough for my people to spot he was something special. Now this other fellow turns up, and I'm taking them off your hands, old wanderer. You don't need to worry about them any more.'

'I had not thought,' Nemoctes said, his voice sick with anger, 'that Claeon's reach extended so far.'

'Claeon?' Mandir squawked. 'Oh, piss on Claeon. If it's Hermatyre you're worried about then, trust me, I'll keep them well out of Claeon's grasp. They won't be safer anywhere in all the oceans than with me. Now, how about you and Wys and the rest run along, and everybody can stay friends.'

'This isn't over,' Nemoctes promised darkly.

'Nothing ever is,' Mandir told him cheerfully. 'That's what life's about, isn't it?' As the Onychoi closed ranks about Stenwold, Mandir glanced up again. 'Now you, the amazing, impossible Smallclaw, you feel like coming down?'

'Feel like coming up here to get me?' Laszlo taunted

him, although Stenwold could see that he felt the strain of hanging in the air like that.

Mandir signalled, and one of his Onychoi raised some device. It was a tube of steel – or something very like steel – with two broad grips, and Stenwold understood it immediately, even though he could not have guessed at the principles on which it worked. The simple way it was held told him all he needed. It was the first ranged weapon he had yet seen in sea-kinden hands. The aperture, at the end directed towards Laszlo, was big enough to put a fist into.

'I don't want to hurt anyone,' the Man of the Stations continued reasonably, 'but I can't have you rushing about the place doing impossible things, and making it look untidy. So come down and join your friend before this becomes a regrettable incident.'

Stenwold thought that Laszlo might make a go of it then, just dart off across the wide chamber, moving faster than the cumbersome weapon could follow, but instead he dropped to the ground meekly and walked into the grasp of one of the Onychoi. He managed a covert glance up towards Stenwold, though, and winked at him.

*My man on the inside, is it?* Stenwold reflected, without much hope. *Shame we're now both in the same inside. Betrayed and captured when I'm scarcely inside the door. I was right, this place is* just *like Helleron. . . .*

# Twenty-Eight

It was not true that Caractes was known as the most unsociable man in the sea, but that was only because he stayed out of the way of so many that few even knew of him at all. He was an ancient Polypoi, his skin turned from purple-red almost to grey-blue with age, his hair not cropped in the fashion of his kind but grown out into a long white mane and beard that twitched and curled against the current. He lived at the foot of the cliffs they called the Edge, in the shadow of a great crab shell, that was the relic of a battle of his middle-age, which he had stubbornly dragged there after a moon's worth of travel. His only companion was his beast, which made its home atop the shell, and there sieved the current with its waving, stinging tentacles.

Few of the sea-kinden lived so close to the Edge. It was considered a place of ill-fortune by most of them. A freak current or grand tide could wash away anyone venturing too close to the surface, perhaps casting them onto the deathly shoreline, there to die of thirst or heat, or be taken and eaten by the savage land-kinden. So the stories went, and since the beginning of recorded time the Edge had marked the limit of the sea-kinden world for all but the mad, the overly adventurous, the Littoralists, and a few select families of hunters and gatherers.

Some of these last still remained, although their trade

had declined from generation to generation, so that those who still tried their luck in the shallow waters above were few indeed. Yet, those that held to their old ways found occasional cause to visit Caractes, as did a few of the Pelagists whose yearnings for travel took them not down to the depths but up to skirt the very periphery of the land.

He had a visitor now, and in truth he had wanted one – had impatiently waited for one, for the first time in years. A lean, long-legged Dart-kinden woman had come to his home, leaving her squid mount to hover and seek prey well out of reach of the giant anemone atop Caractes's crabshell house.

The house had no walls, just that hollowed-out carapace propped up with stones, and their speech was conducted by signs: the second language that most sea-kinden learned from infancy, knowing how to perform their first hand gestures before even uttering their first words.

*Caractes.* She assembled the name from its separate syllables. *How do you fare?*

*Lerean,* he greeted her. *Troubled.*

*Old?* with a little mockery in her hands.

He glowered at her, his corona of hair lashing about his face. She was just a third of his age, which made her past her prime for a Dart-kinden, but they tended to age late, and all at once, and she was still swift and strong. *You sit with me and wait, and we'll see.*

*What?* She eyed him suspiciously. They had only met three times before, over five years, and he was a mad old hermit, after all. Caractes pulled himself back under the cover of the shell, where his hands located a wrapped package of pressed fish, and then mutely offered her a piece. She took it and chewed, reclining down beside him in a single elegant motion.

*This had better not be some late tide of romance,* her hands warned him drily.

He sourly raised one shaggy eyebrow. *I have daughters*

*twice your age,* he told her. *There is something new under the sea.*

She took a moment to consider that, still chewing at the fish. Outside, her mount jetted nervously back and forth, and she sent out an Art-thought to calm it.

*Your meaning?*

*Meaning? I mean just what I say. Something new.* His signing was unmistakable, emphatic. *Tell me, you keep the old bargains?*

She stiffened when she saw the hand-signs. The old bargains: it was not a subject her people, the particular families of her people, spoke of, but it was little surprise that Caractes knew of them. The old man was aware of a great deal he had no business knowing. His gaze was fixed on her, now, eyes nested within creases, but sharp as spearpoints for all that.

*We try,* was all she responded, at last.

*You fail,* he jabbed back at her.

She kicked off from her place beside him, abruptly angry. *You know not what you speak of.*

A single slash of his hand cut her off. *You fail, or they fail,* he elaborated, exaggerating his gesture for the 'they'. *Either in their tribute, or your harvest.*

*It is not as it once was. For generations now it has not been so. Contact has been less and less. It is their failure, not ours.*

*Perhaps they do not see it so,* was his return comment on that, and then he was standing, staring upwards as though he could see through the dead old shell above him.

*Each day it comes,* his hands said, as he continued looking up. With a scrabble and a kick, he hauled himself out from under the dead crab's shadow, leaving her no option but to follow.

He pointed, and at first she saw just two lights – two limn-lamps she supposed – being dragged through the water above them. Then her vision compensated for distance and the dark, and she realized they were eyes.

Her mount was beside her immediately, and she put a hand out to comfort it, still staring. *There is something new under the sea*, the old man had said, and here it was – like nothing she had seen. It came sculling through the water on jointed legs, but like no swimming crab or shrimp she had ever seen, lazily coasting along with steady strokes of its six paddle-ended limbs.

*From over the Edge?* she signed, and Caractes nodded grimly. Then he added, to her surprise, *You speak to any Pelagists recently?*

*A few.*

*Go find them again. Tell them to pass this on. I hear from them about land-kinden. I don't know why they talk to me about land-kinden. I never wanted to know. I hear, though, and now I see.*

*That is not land-kinden*, her hands insisted. *It is some Onychoi beast, some new kind, strayed from some other sea, perhaps.*

He made a derisive gesture. *Look, only look*, he insisted. *See what is there, not what you want. Take your steed and go closer, if you dare.*

That last remark stung her, so she took to the saddle and sent her mount speeding backwards in a wide, rising circle, keeping her eyes on the gently rowing creature above. It was large, she saw, but not so very large as all that. She had a backswept holster of spears beside her, and she fingered one speculatively. *A great sea-beast with glowing eyes*, she thought. *That would fetch a great deal at Hermatyre, dead or alive.*

She readied a spear and peered into the nearest burning eye, and saw the faces, and understood what Caractes had meant.

A moment later she was lancing off through the sea, as fast as her beast would take her. Caractes was right. She could not go to Hermatyre with this news, not given the Edmir's nature and history. She must go to those who had the knowledge and impartiality to deal with this. She must find a Pelagist and pass on the word.

'Now, you must be wondering just what's going on, land-kinden,' Mandir addressed them, marching proudly in front of his mob of guards as though he was the tallest denizen of the Hot Stations.

'Not really,' Stenwold said tiredly. 'It's becoming depressingly familiar.'

'Nobody understands the value of you people,' Mandir threw over his shoulder.

Stenwold tried to stop walking, after that one remark, but one of the Onychoi just shoved him onwards. The heat, which had been merely oppressive, was becoming unbearable. Stenwold's ears were expecting the ring of hammer on anvil any moment, but of course they had nothing so wholesomely familiar down here. 'What do you mean?' he demanded. 'Since when were you familiar with people like us?'

Mandir chuckled indulgently. 'You think you're the first land-kinden we've had down here? Think again. It's been a good two dozen we've seen, over the years.'

'You've got two dozen land-kinden here?' Stenwold asked, aghast.

'Well, no, not at the moment. Most of your kind don't take to life down here.' Mandir gave them an awkward smile over his shoulder. 'The food, sometimes, or maybe being cooped up. Some of them turned out to be of no use at all, so it's a gamble, you see, whether you two can do what I need or not. Or some of them tried to escape, which never goes down well, but a few managed to live here a while before they . . . failed to thrive. I hope you'll be more of those. I hope you'll be happy here, for that matter. You do right by me, and you'll get anything you ask for – except out.'

Stenwold exchanged grim looks with Laszlo. 'So I'm to be your slave, am I?'

Mandir turned aside abruptly. Apparently they were nearly at their destination. 'Now, I know that word,' he said. 'Another of your kind threw it at me. She wasn't happy here, I'm sad to say, but if it makes the place feel more like home, then consider yourselves now my slaves.' He was grinning broadly and Stenwold honestly could not say whether he expected them to thank him, or whether he was just being sly.

'I don't understand,' the Beetle said flatly. 'As far as I know, we're the first of our kind to have been subjected to this place. Or have you been kidnapping people from our ships as well?'

'You wound me,' Mandir said, walking up to him cockily. He was half Stenwold's size, and only the clustering armoured hulks all around saved him from a broken neck. 'Rescued, landsman, *rescued*. You people build your little floating barques, but they don't all stay afloat. I have my own people waiting up there beyond the Edge, my scavenging parties, and when the waves are high they keep an eye out. Sometimes they're lucky and they find some of your people about to meet the sea the hard way. So we rescue them. For a while, anyway – if they're useful. I *do* hope you're going to be useful. We have it hard here at the Stations. Everybody works. A lot of your people died from not being able to work.'

Stenwold shook his head. 'And what possible work could you need us for?'

'I'll let our resident expert explain,' Mandir replied. 'Now you're here, you can be his slave. You'll find he's a tough one. A couple of years we've had him now. Of course, he's one of the useful ones, best we've ever had. You listen to him and show yourself a little willing, and maybe life with us won't be so bad.' His expansive gesture narrowed unexpectedly into a simple pointing finger. 'Through here now.'

Stenwold and Laszlo were bustled into an irregular-shaped chamber, its walls and lumpy ceiling cobbled together from disparate pieces, just like the rest of the Hot Stations. What struck Stenwold first was the furniture. It was the sort you'd get if you had described a workbench and a table and some chairs to a blind man, and had him construct them out of organic detritus, but the concept behind them was clear enough. Paper, or the stuff that passed for sea-kinden paper, was heaped in thick stacks everywhere, some of it blank and some of it densely scribbled over with designs.

There was a man present, staring at them. For a moment Stenwold just looked bleakly back, unable to quite understand what he was seeing. The stranger's bluish-white skin was wrinkled and creased, his bare chest showed every rib, the stomach below it withered like a paunchy man gone thin. His hair was long and dirty-white, falling past his shoulders, and he sported a short and ragged beard that showed the scars of sporadic attempts to prune it. He was an Ant-kinden, a Tseni Ant-kinden – there was no mistaking it.

'War Master Maker?' the old Ant croaked. A bulky stylus had dropped from his hand on seeing the new arrivals.

It was the voice that confirmed it. Before hearing him speak, Stenwould would never have placed him.

'Master Tseitus?' he breathed, still not quite believing it.

'I knew,' the Ant breathed. 'I knew you'd come for me, after all this time. I knew you'd come to rescue me.'

He said this despite the wall of mailed Onychoi that stood at Stenwold's back, despite Mandir's grin. His face was childlike in that moment, desperate to make his words become true against all odds. It should have been true, Stenwold thought. There should have been a Collegium army at his back. They should have Mandir in irons, his guards scattered across the waters. It should have been that way, and not this shabby slavery.

'We thought you were dead,' Stenwold told the man softly. 'We all assumed, when you never returned . . .'

'Learned a lot from this one even before we got him home,' Mandir explained, perpetually jolly. 'His barque, well . . . took us half a year to understand it, but we knew just from that that he was special. Not disappointed since, either. Our man here's a genius. You should learn something from him.'

'Tseitus,' said Stenwold, 'just what is it they make you do?'

One bluish hand waved vaguely at the heaped papers. 'Designs. Sketches. They want machines, submersibles, automotives. It's new to them, you see, and they weren't very good at it. They were still . . . oh, you know, they hadn't refined their equations, regarding all the old principles of mechanics, but they're a bright lot and they're learning. So I draw for them, and some of them have even learned our writing.'

'You help these people?' Stenwold wanted to know. 'Willingly?'

'And so will you,' Mandir told him, 'and your little friend.' He prodded Stenwold in the waist. 'Everyone works. No work, no food. You'd be surprised how quickly you see just how reasonable I'm being. Your friend here, as I now see he is, would be dead without us, just like all you land-kinden who end up down here.'

'Not me,' Stenwold snapped at him. 'Not Laszlo, either. We were dragged down here against our will.'

To his surprise, this made a difference to Mandir. He saw the man at least weighing the information up, revealing the first spark of decency he had observed in the Stations' master. Ultimately, though, Mandir's decision was, 'Then you're unlucky, and I'm sorry, but you're much too valuable to us. We need people like you and I can't pass that up.' He nodded, as though convincing himself. 'I'll leave you here to renew your acquaintance. Tseitus will show you what we need.'

'This complete separation of land and sea is a fiction,' Tseitus was explaining the next day. The subject had arisen after several pointed remarks about there being no intended rescue. Stenwold, in short temper, had declared that nobody had even known that there was a *here* down below that he could be rescued from, but Tseitus was not going to relinquish his grievance that easily. He was the first land-kinden, other than Laszlo, that Stenwold had seen for a tenday, but any joy in that encounter was being eroded by the same ascerbic, self-involved attitude Stenwold recalled from the war.

*The war where he did us such good service*, he reminded himself, trying to pay more attention. It was difficult, though.

'Your servant's a mariner, so ask him about sea-kinden,' Tseitus threw at him.

Laszlo had been lounging at the entrance to their work-room, chatting to a couple of Onychoi around the same size as himself. He glanced back and shrugged. 'Stories, Mar'Maker, nothing but. You hear some fellow talk, who spotted people in the waves during a storm, or heard some woman singing, out where there wasn't anyone. Beautiful maids with hind ends of lobsters or cuttlefish or whatnot. Me, I never believed it.'

'That's because you're Apt,' Tseitus told him, having divined this from Laszlo's interest in his sketches. 'If you had Inapt crew with you, they'd be more credulous. Normally that's a poor quality, and why I never really took to the Inapt, but in this case they'd be right.' He jabbed Stenwold in the chest with a thin blue finger. 'Your old

430

masters, the Moths, I'll wager they had links with the sea peoples. Just a shame they never told you about it. In Tsen we always knew better.'

'You're probably right,' Stenwold mumbled. He had pointedly refused to participate in Tseitus's work yesterday, and had just as pointedly not been fed. Hunger had then given him strange dreams.

'They say here that the land means death, but it's a nonsense. Aside from Mandir's mercy missions, I hear of certain cults and societies that hold links with the land, and therefore certain of your Lowlanders that keep faith with the sea. It wouldn't surprise me.'

'Well it surprised me,' Stenwold declared, trying to put a note of finality into his voice, but Tseitus was not accepting it.

'You've never been to the Atoll Coast, have you?' the Ant asked.

'To Tsen? No, my interests always lay eastwards,' Stenwold admitted. There was a dream that kept recurring to him, tearing rents in his sleep and troubling his peace of mind, and he was not quite sure what to make of it. It had been intense, all the more so for a man who seldom recalled such nightly servings of his imagination. A passionate dream, it had been, but it had not involved Arianna, there in his mind. It had not even been like the shameful and lurid thoughts his mind had imposed on Atryssa, Tisamon's beloved, when they had all still been young. Instead, the slender figure that had recently walked through his mind had been that of Lyess of the Medusoi, with her skin so pale as to be near-translucent, her white eyes so wide. It seemed perverse of his mind to conjure such a scene, after the days the pair of them had spent in sullen silence within the chambers of her companion, but in the dream he recalled that almost-embrace, at his lowest ebb, when he had been dragged half-drowned aboard her. In the dream, though, she had broken her awkward reserve and her touch had been cool and yielding, while her arms, her lips, the coils of her hair . . .

Tseitus snorted. 'The east,' he said derisively, as though the whole business of the Wasp Empire would have looked after itself had Stenwold only put his priorities straight. 'You Lowlanders live such soft lives,' he accused. 'Collegium is all luxury: a port city so surrounded by green farmland that your kinden even turn your nose up at fish. Ridiculous! The Atoll Coast is harsh and Tsen, Seym, Cerrih, all of them have to look to the sea. We *know* the sea-kinden.'

Stenwold stared at him. Seeing his expression, Tseitus snorted with satisfied disdain. 'You know, of course, where the name "the Atoll Coast" derives, Maker?' Tseitus was clearly the sort of lecturer that College students loathed. 'Why, because there are islands all along the sea's edge, hundreds of them, and mostly windswept rocks. But yet – they are not rocks: they are coral. There are reefs and reefs, Maker, so that navigators and ships' pilots find themselves in a sought-after and well-rewarded profession. Those reefs are not mere stone, you understand.'

'Arketoi . . .' Stenwold murmured.

'The colony of Grande Atoll is some leagues outside of Seym Harbour,' Tseitus told him. 'They are not so shy, there. Not so very long ago, we learned that land- and sea-kinden meeting means only trouble: a war between worlds that washed earth and water both with blood. After that, over these last centuries, there has been some small contact. I will not say that land and sea go hand in hand, but we have diplomats, even a little carefully controlled trade. We have little they want, though. This' – he waved his hand to indicate what Stenwold assumed was the Hot Stations in its entirety – 'is different. This Aptitude, this lust for artifice, Grande Atoll would not understand. They are all Inapt there, I think, or else just ignorant.' As he spoke, he continued sketching deftly with the strangely shaped reservoir pen the sea-kinden had made for him. 'You don't realize, Maker . . . you don't realize at all.'

*Blank white eyes, and a touch like silk . . .*

Stenwold blinked at the old Ant. 'What don't I realize?'

From the doorway there came a sudden bellow of laughter. Laszlo had enlisted one of the broad-shouldered guards into whatever conversation he was having there. Stenwold saw him gesturing some point and then Tseitus made a loud click of annoyance with his tongue. A moment later the little party, Laszlo included, had stepped outside, smirking.

'You don't realize how lucky we land-kinden were to have got there first. Oh, perhaps there's something about the land that inspires progress, I won't deny. Certainly I understand that the people of Grande Atoll consider the land a very hostile place: too hot, too cold, too barren. The sea provides them with everything they need, whereas we must struggle. But had it been any other way round . . .'

'What?' Stenwold demanded, feeling abruptly combative. 'I've seen sea-kinden engineering. It's nothing special, apprentices are set harder tasks – and that's with you and your predecessors filling in the gaps for them, no less.'

'You miss the point,' argued Tseitus with scholarly derision. 'I would guess that Aptitude here has been widespread for less than a century, or at least they made no use of it before then. They are behind, Maker. They are centuries behind us. No wonder their work looks clumsy. Consider their natural advantages, though, and you will see that if it were we who happened to be behind, the gap would now be that much the greater. Consider their methods of manufacture.'

'This accreation business?' Stenwold said.

'You've seen their ornament – how very fine and delicate the work is?' Tseitus pressed. 'Now imagine machine parts made that way, with infinite precision and detail. All it takes is a craftsman who can envisage what he needs with enough clarity – and they already have them, only a few yet, but there will be more.'

Stenwold's rejoinder died on his lips. 'I see,' he said thoughtfully.

'And their materials, too.'

'I've seen mostly bronze – that and various kinds of shell and cloth, and this paper.'

Tseitus shook his head swiftly, very much the debating academic. 'No no, the clothes and the paper they make from seaweed, or some such. They weave and spin and pulp and stitch just as we do. The rigid materials, though, are accreated, and whilst the wider undersea may consider bronze the cutting edge of progress, here in the Stations it is different. Why do you think they go to the trouble of living here, without the Builders to shelter them? The heat: the heat and the minerals in the water allow them to accreate stronger stuffs. Their metal, Maker, they call it Benthic spring steel. I swear to you it's a finer temper than any you've ever seen above water. So strong, so flexible . . . if we can somehow find out how to make it by conventional means, we could revolutionize half a dozen fields of mechanics!'

'And this is what you're after, is it?' Stenwold asked him. 'This is why you aid them, because, on the side, you're trying to unravel this new metal of theirs?'

'I am a scholar and an artificer, of course,' Tseitus said, as though astonished that the question should even be posed.

Stenwold put his head in his hands. 'Were you aware that they intend to invade Collegium?' he asked wearily. 'Hermatyre has an army of restless Onychoi waiting, even now, for the word.' He looked up at Tseitus, saw the old man caught by a sudden uncertainty.

'I . . .' the Ant muttered, 'I would have died, in my

submersible . . . or they would have starved me, killed me . . . I had no choice.'

'No doubt,' said Stenwold sadly, wondering if he himself would have one either.

Mandir's audience chamber was as makeshift and uneven as the rest of his domain, but the Man of the Hot Stations had taken pains to impress each visitor with his importance.

He had a throne, for one thing, or at least it was a kind of high chair built of pieces of coral and stone and metal, in a blocky, mismatched mosaic. It placed him so that any visitor would have to look up at him, and on either side of it, as evidence of his martial prowess, was displayed a fan of spears, curved swords and other oddly shaped weapons. The pair of Onychoi warriors that flanked his seat added further to such implied potency, but Stenwold's favourite touch, viewing the man enthroned in state, was the cloak. Mandir wore a cloak that fell all the way to the floor, a garment cut long enough to fit a gangling giant, dyed in deeply vibrant purple and edged with shimmering, overlapping discs that Stenwold eventually recognized as polished fish-scales.

'You're looking peaky, landsman,' Mandir addressed him. 'Are you eating properly?'

It had been two days since Stenwold had eaten. He had needed the time to work out what his moral stance was: what he was willing to compromise. In the end, he suspected, hunger had begun to wear down his finer objections. It had been a long while since he had truly been obliged to fast.

'Mandir,' Stenwold named him, wondering if there was some proper form of address. He could hardly call him just 'Man'. The little despot looked satisfied, though, and gestured for him to speak.

'I'll work for you,' Stenwold continued tiredly. 'I will

provide you with designs, and improve the designs your people have already.'

'It's all I ask,' Mandir replied reasonably. 'I'll have my people fix you a solid meal. You look like you could use it.'

'Wait,' Stenwold told him, one hand up. The gesture caused the guards to stir, their armour scraping. 'I have conditions,' he said.

Mandir's forehead wrinkled. 'He has conditions,' he told the air. 'The lord of the land is grown grand again, is he?'

'You want my help,' Stenwold pointed out.

'I do, I do want it. You, on the other hand, *need* to eat. Be thankful we're giving you fresh water on credit.'

'It's not a very great condition, Man of the Stations,' Stenwold said, seeing the formality of address have a placating effect. Mandir made another laconic gesture, and Stenwold went on, 'It concerns my companion, Laszlo.'

Mandir grinned at that. 'I'm hearing a lot about him. He's turning out to be quite a favourite. Shaved his head, hasn't he? Wants to look civilized.'

'So I understand,' Stenwold nodded. In truth, with his stubble cropped, and with the way he held his shoulders now, Laszlo looked uncannily like the small Onychoi found among Mandir's own people. He had taken on the mantle of surrogate sea-kinden with an ease that suggested an interesting past, and Stenwold recalled how Laszlo had served the *Tidenfree* as its factor, the one they sent out to make deals.

'I hear he's quite today's flavour.' Mandir warmed to his subject. 'Does jigs and dances with his Art and all that. I was going to have him to dance for me some time.'

Dancing was perhaps not one of Laszlo's strong points, but since he was the only person in the whole of the depths who could fly, there would be little skill needed to amaze an audience. Mandir's people had been turning up at all hours wanting to see this prodigy from the land.

'He's no artificer, Mandir,' Stenwold explained. 'He's

restless and unhappy. He wants to see more of your realm here. If you let him roam a little, I'll stand surety.'

'Will you so?' Mandir peered down at him as if suddenly regretting the distance. 'Why?'

'Because he's not used to being imprisoned,' Stenwold said. 'Because you've told me how we land-kinden don't thrive down here, and maybe that's because we're always being penned in, never free. Think how you yourself might like it, to be barred up in some strange place, and cut off from everything you know. If he has a chance to get to know people, make some new life for himself here, well . . .'

'And what of you? I'm not letting you go trawling off on your own,' Mandir warned him.

'I will at least have the satisfaction of whatever news he brings back with him and, as long as I am in your hands, you can be sure that he always *will* come back.'

'He'll spy for you,' Mandir accused.

'If that's how you wish to phrase it. But if I can have eyes and ears outside, it will help me adapt, too. I admit, it seems that I'm here for the long haul, so at least give me something more than just the work.' He was not sure how convincing he was being, but then Mandir was no expert in Beetle-kinden expressions, any more than Stenwold could reliably read the Man himself.

'Well,' the little tyrant said at last, 'perhaps . . . Perhaps, but I have conditions too.'

*Oh, yes?* 'What conditions might those be, O Man of the Stations?'

And Mandir reached under the folds of his over-long cloak and produced an object that was small even in his hands, which sent a jolt of recognition through Stenwold.

'Where . . . ?'

'Oh please, landsman, you can answer that one for yourself. From Claeon's people, who took it from you, of course. They had no idea what it was, but my agents in Hermatyre bought it from them because it looked like something I might be interested in.' Mandir's eyes gleamed. 'I *am* interested, too, landsman. I have studied this thing, and I don't understand quite how it does what it does, but I can see its purpose, and it is *beautiful.*' The emphasis, the sudden passion, was surprising, and Stenwold was forced to recast the little man as something more than merely a jumped-up merchant lord. *An artificer, at heart,* he thought: *an artificer now holding a cut-down snapbow.* In Mandir's hands, the two-barrelled weapon that Totho had made for Stenwold shone malevolently in the limn-lights.

'You work on this device, landsman. You plan me a simple version of this thing, that my craftsmen can copy. I'll give your friend the freedom of the Stations in the meantime, so long as he realizes he'll always be watched. But I want one of these. I want the Stations to have these. These,' he announced, with a steely grin, 'are *nice.*'

# Twenty-Nine

The previous lord of the Hot Stations had not kept an audience chamber, had not used a throne, had dressed plainly and been little more than a tavern-keeper to the Benthic trains passing through. The previous lord had not received emissaries from Deep Seep and Hermatyre, bringing him word from their Edmirs as if he was an equal – at least as long as those Edmirs wanted something from him. Mandir contemplated this satisfactory state of affairs as he lounged on his high seat. Claeon had many faults, but the speed of his spies was not one of them, so his representative newly here in the Stations was very obviously sniffing after a certain pair of disappeared captives.

By his order, she came in unarmed and unescorted. They had met before, just the once, a few years ago, but she had not been in this position of responsibility then, merely a pretty adornment belonging to the retinue of Claeon's then-majordomo. Mandir looted his memory and reckoned recalling that the man she then followed had eventually been torn apart by crabs . . . or had he been the one dropped into the stinging coils of a sea-anenome? Mandir had no wish to visit Hermatyre, but it did sound as though the entertainment there was second to none. Claeon was mad, but his madness gave him a distinct sense of style.

'Haelyn, I believe,' he named her, leaning down from his

439

seat. She was as he remembered her, and he remembered her quite clearly. Sepia-kinden were one of the Kerebroi family's minor branches, but so very comely. She now stood in the centre of his audience chamber, hands folded demurely before her, and clad in a long drape of white that had been arranged to hide and suggest in carefully calculated proportions. Her skin fluttered blue and gold and red, as though she was nervous, but her eyes remained steady.

'Mandir, master of the Hot Stations,' she began, 'I bring you greetings from your fellow sea-lord, the Edmir Claeon of Hermatyre.'

'How's the old fellow doing?' Mandir leered. 'Fatter in body and looser in mind? Don't answer that. Perhaps he's doing better after all. His choice of majordomo has certainly improved. How long now since you took that office, Haelyn?'

'Long enough.'

'And what can our poor Hot Stations do for your majestic master?'

She squared her shoulders, tilted her head back. 'He is glad to note that you have recaptured certain renegades, and looks forward to their return to him, to face justice.'

'Renegades from Hermatyre?' Mandir put on a great show of surprise. 'Whatever next? Why would anyone wish to flee a colony governed by a man as fair-minded as Claeon?'

She did not rise to that. 'Certain unusual renegades . . . you know full well I am talking of the land-kinden, Mandir.'

'Land-kinden? Are there such things as land-kinden? Aren't they all ten feet tall and able to kill with a single look?'

Haelyn sighed, folding her arms. 'Shall we dispense now with the formal denials?'

'Consider them spoken. I'm keeping the landsmen, however. Your master can holler and huff as much as he wants.

He forgets that *we* are the coming power now, here in this stretch of the waters.'

'Hermatyre custom feeds your industry here. You are wholly dependent on the trade of others,' she pointed out.

'Hermatyre custom won't stop because Claeon passes an edict. That'll just bring him one step closer to being pulled from his throne and torn apart by his own subjects – may the day be soon,' Mandir replied flatly. 'I never liked him, even before the old Edmir's death. We'd all be better had the boy lived. I say this even though Hermatyre exiles currently throng my streets and do my bidding. Claeon's about mad enough to do something very foolish, so don't think I can't turn away Rosander's Thousand Spines if they end up marching in my direction. You can tell him that as well.'

She bit her lip. 'You're not leaving me much to say to him, that will not have me executed.'

'So don't go back, then,' Mandir suggested. 'We don't get so many Sepia-kinden here. Take on with me. I liked you when I met you that time before. I like you more, seeing you again. Do you dance?'

'Dance?' she spat.

'Sepia-kinden dance? Skin-dancing? Been years since I saw that. Like I say, we don't get many of your kinden, and they don't last here long.'

'Because you kill them?' she suggested bitterly.

He looked at her stonily, letting seconds of silence pass. 'Because life is hard here, and your people are not suited for the heat and the graft. I'm not Claeon. I'm trying to keep a very artificial little world together here, and be as tough as I must, confiscating landsmen included, but I'm not Claeon. I know well what his pastimes are, his hooks and lashes. I like women and good drink, and fine things, but stripping the skin off my subjects has never appealed to me, nor would they stand for it.'

She still glared at him, stubbornly. 'And yet my kinden

do not *last* here, and still you ask me to stay. What sense is there in that?'

'You'll live longer here than at Claeon's side, nevertheless. That's all the sense you need.'

'I don't dance.'

'Shame. The offer's still open.'

'You're serious?' Haelyn frowned at him, incredulous. 'Mandir, you say *Claeon*'s mad? Where would you be, to steal his emissaries? What do you think he might do to retaliate, if he is so very rash?'

Mandir sat back in his seat, plucked at a fold of his long cloak and examined it minutely. 'I don't fear him, for if he sent a pack of Kerebroi here, he'd find half of them would switch sides as soon as they arrived, glad to be out of his shadow. As for Rosander, well, Rosander knows well what toys we have here. He has a few of them himself, and he knows we have many more. If Claeon were to send him here, I'd wager that would be the end of their friendship – which friendship I hear is tottering anyway. So, I keep the landsmen and, if you'll agree to it, I'll keep you too, and keep you well.'

'And would taking to your bed be a condition of that offer?' she sneered. 'I regret that Smallclaw Onychoi have never been to my taste.'

Mandir cocked his head to one side. 'You should review your fancies, Haelyn. When I was a boy, we Smallclaw were always last to the table, even here. The Kerebroi ruled, the Greatclaw were strong and led the trains, the Pelagists had no time for us. We just tagged along with whoever would have us, and made things and fastened armour and tried not to get anyone angry at us. But this is now, and I rule here, and my kinden are coming into their own. We run the Hot Stations, and we're the leading edge of all that's new under the sea. Being half the size of you doesn't mean we have to look up to you any more.' He gestured expansively around at the audience chamber, the guards, the displays of arms. 'But, no, it's no condition. Come to us here and you'll be safe from Claeon, no questions asked. Because I like you. And because I'm not Claeon. The landsmen, you know, they keep what they call slaves in their homes: people who are property, who work until they die, and who live and die according to some *owner's* word, without even a chance to complain.' He paused to watch her reaction. 'That's the land, Haelyn, not death glaring in every eye, but not a paradise either, and more fool the Littoralists for preaching otherwise. But, you know what, Claeon would fit right in. Claeon would make a good landsman, whereas I'm proud to say I wouldn't. Now, you'd better go and work out what you can say to your lord and master that will keep your skin intact, or else work out that you're better off staying here with us. Take your time, either way.'

She nodded, retreated a few steps, and said, 'Thank you,' and then she left.

Within the regularly reconstructed confines of the Hot Stations, the inhabitants occupied space where they found it, and then used it for their own purposes until someone – formerly someone stronger, but these days more likely someone carrying Mandir's writ – took it from them. This chamber, for example, a space like a crumpled dome, contained mostly ranks of sleeping spaces for those who had no special trade, no gift, no contribution to earn them more from their hosts. Here slept the drifters and the refugees, the itinerant Pelagists, the fugitives hopeful of a better life beyond the reach of Edmir or Nauarch. Each life was delineated by a little pile of possessions and a sleeping mat on the uneven floor.

Towards one end of the chamber, the end that linked most conveniently with the main business of the Stations, some larger patches of ground had been claimed. There was a tented space that had a ragbag of used goods for sale or barter, and there was an eating house which served the host of luckless residents with broth, and would buy from them anything they had hunted or gathered. Moreover, the owner was a decent enough brewer, and his personal brand of accreated rotgut had done its share in ensuring that many of the downtrodden rose no higher.

It was also a good place for people to meet unobserved, as it was packed with jostling strangers who asked no questions. There were three conspirators meeting here even now, sitting on a tattered blanket in one corner.

Nemoctes looked the most out of place here for, even without his armour, the Kerebroi Pelagist was a big man, and the shabby cloak did little to disguise him. Still, such was the bustle of the hungry and the inebriated, plenty of them also tall and broad Onychoi, that the crowd had swallowed him up without a trace. Cloaks were common here. since most of the temporary residents might be venturing into colder waters soon enough, and many had good reason to keep their identities hidden. Any spies of Mandir, or anyone else, would have their work cut out for them.

Wys sat beside him, just one Smallclaw amongst many. She was less sure about the company's third, a slender Kerebroi man: all the cowl and cloak in the world could not quite hide how well-groomed and ornamented he was.

'His name is Diamedes,' Nemoctes explained in a low voice. 'He's Heiracles's man here. I have met him before.'

'If he's Heiracles's man, where's his master?' Wys asked.

'The Stations have grown an uncertain place to walk,' Diamedes explained. 'Mandir's seizing of the landsmen has made a lot of people anxious. The little shrimp has not been so bold before, for all his boasting.' Wys bristled at the insult to her kinden, but Diamedes went blithely on, 'Whatever the Man's shortfalls, this is his place. If he should choose to imprison my master and sell him to Claeon, what would stop him?'

Wys continued to look disgruntled. 'Doesn't look like we're going to get far today, then.'

'Wait,' Nemoctes advised her. 'Diamedes informs me that there is one more expected, who will certainly make this meeting worthwhile.'

'Well' – Wys's sour expression whipped away, revealing her grin underneath – 'I'll see your one more, and put in one of my own that will knock him out of the water. You think you're very clever, don't you, you Kerebroi? Well we "little shrimps" can get things done too, and with half the fuss.'

'No doubt,' said Nemoctes drily.

She glowered at him. 'Don't ever get angry, do you?'

'Try living as a Pelagist for a year and a day, Wys. It's calming,' he told her, with a faint smile.

'Boring, more like.' Wys broke off as Fel pushed through the crowd towards them, a small, cloaked figure following in his wake. With a nod he pushed his charge down beside his employer and then stepped back, heading for the door.

'How did it go?' Wys asked the newcomer, leaning close.

'I reckon your Phylles is still leading them all over,' came the reply, 'with that Smallclaw she hired.'

'Cast off your hood, you're among friends,' Wys chuckled. 'Diamedes, I present to you Laszlo Landsman.'

Seeing the bald, stooping figure that the cast-back hood revealed, the other two frowned, looking for the catch. At last Nemoctes raised his eyebrows, impressed. 'It is, isn't it?' he admitted. 'Quite a transformation.'

'And don't I wish I didn't have to go through it,' Laszlo grunted. 'You try shaving your head twice a day – it's no fun, believe me. How are we doing? You worked out how you're going to get us out, yet?'

'How did *that* thing get out?' Diamedes demanded. He was staring at Laszlo with undisguised horror. 'It truly is a landsman?'

445

'Voice down,' Wys advised. 'And, yes, he is. He got out because his chief has talked the Man into it – and he got here because he's a tricky lad with some very unusual Art, and he's good at dodging his minders. Right now, my people are leading Mandir's lot on a grand old chase, so we're short on time. Where's your fifth, Dio?'

Diamedes stood up in a smooth motion, to scan the crowd. A moment later he nodded down at them. 'She's here. She's coming to us.'

'Seriously, though, plans,' put in Laszlo. 'Master Maker's under a lot of pressure right now.'

A woman embraced Diamedes, and they held each other close for a moment before dropping down to rejoin the group. The display of affection lasted no longer than it took for them to sit: a moment's misdirection to confuse any watchers.

'Who's this now?' Wys demanded. 'I don't know her.'

Diamedes named the conspirators for his newly arrived colleague, and added blithely, 'Each one for a different reason, but you can trust them.'

'As much as I can trust *you*?' the acid comment emerged from within the woman's hood.

'I know your secrets already,' Diamedes told her archly, 'so if I wanted to betray you, you'd be dead.'

'Such is the basis of Hermatyre trust: those who have not betrayed you *yet*,' she said, as if it was a proverb. She tugged a little at her cowl, revealing a face that was pleasant at first, and then briefly radiant with shadows of colour. Her eyes remained hard and suspicious. 'Haelyn,' she said. 'My name.'

'Wait, wait . . . wait one breath here,' Wys was saying quickly. 'Now I heard a Sepia of that name was—'

'The Edmir's majordomo?' Haelyn asked her. 'You heard correctly.'

'You're the Edmir's?' Laszlo asked her, wide-eyed.

She looked to Diamedes to explain, and the Kerebroi

man remarked, 'She was always my master's agent within Claeon's household. For years she managed to dance from post to post, to stay useful without incurring Claeon's wrath, which is no small feat. Unfortunately she has now mis-stepped, or perhaps simply time has caught up with her. Claeon has named her majordomo, a position with a lifespan recently measured in moons.'

'It happened one day that I found myself become the most senior of Claeon's domestic staff – the only one of them not fled or dead or far too inexperienced,' Haelyn said bitterly.

'Claeon has sent you here after the land-kinden?' Nemoctes guessed.

'None other,' she agreed. 'I've had an audience with Mandir. He was . . . well, pleasant, actually, but unhelpful, and of course Claeon didn't expect him to just hand the landsmen over. Claeon now wants them dead. His plans have progressed, so I'm not here alone.'

The others exchanged glances. 'Claeon's sent killers, now,' Wys considered, very low. 'I guess we could have expected that.'

'Two Krakind men, both keen to advance themselves in Claeon's service, for reasons that from my point of view are incomprehensible,' Haelyn told them. 'Menes and Theomen, their names. If you have someone follow me, I'll take you to them, so you can mark their faces.'

'Are they good?' Wys asked her.

'They've been cutting throats in Hermatyre for years, I understand. They've silenced a few mouths for Claeon before, but the Edmir mistrusts supremely skilled assassins. They tend to lead shorter lives than a competent majordomo. So these two are passable.'

'We could leak word to Mandir,' Nemoctes suggested thoughtfully.

'And get me killed as well, most likely,' Haelyn argued. 'I'm telling you this so you take action for *yourselves*, not get the Man involved.' She shook her head. 'Why did it even get this complicated? What does Mandir really want with you, little man?'

Laszlo folded his arms. 'Looks like little men like me run this place, lady,' he told her boldly. 'And your man Mandir knows which way the wind's blowing, anyway.' He realized that the expression had left them all quite blank. 'He knows the value of a good land artificer, so he's been kidnapping people from wrecks and ships and the like, putting them to work. You see, I know you lot think we're all savage nasties who eat babies, but your Man here, he knows that we're actually very good at, say, putting a gear train together, or drawing up a set of plans. *You* know.' He pointed to Wys. 'You heard Master Maker talking to Spillage. We know engines, and Mandir knows that we know.'

Nemoctes was looking grave. 'I . . . had not known. Mandir's kept this secret a long time. I'd not have brought you here if—'

'Oh, sure, sure,' Laszlo waved a hand to absolve him. 'Not saying you meant this to happen, old man, but look: Master Maker's being forced to work on something he really doesn't want to, just so's I can get out here to speak to you. So you lot better know how to spring him. So what's the plan?' They exchanged looks again, and Laszlo scowled. 'No plan? Seriously?'

'Mandir controls this place. He builds it as he wants. If they weren't actually *letting* you walk out, you'd still be in,' Diamedes told him sharply. 'Mandir's Onychoi are armed with . . . new weapons. They are very dangerous and I have seen them used. We have no forces to call on, and the last thing any sane man would do is to storm the Hot Stations.'

'So we are waiting,' Nemoctes put in forcefully, over-riding the other man's gloom. 'Well-armed they may be, but they are no army. Mandir has limited warriors to call on, and life in the Hot Stations has always been tenuous. We await a moment when their attention is elsewhere. My

Pelagists have told me there may be an opportunity soon.' This was obviously news to all the rest of them, but he just shook his head. 'I'll say no more now. I do not know how you'd take it, if you knew, but meanwhile we wait. And we watch Claeon's killers, too. It would be best if they do not even trouble Mandir's guards with their intentions. We don't want Mandir any warier than he already is.'

'Leave that to me,' Wys announced. 'I'll put Fel and Phylles on to them. Any trouble and they'll end up in the broth.'

'What a pleasant thought,' Diamedes said. The local broth was a Stations speciality, made with the bitter, boiling water issuing from the vents the place was built around. It was clearly not to the Kerebroi's taste.

'Our time is up,' Nemoctes decided. 'I will have one of my people pass word, if our distraction is to happen. For now, Haelyn, return to your people, and Wys, follow her up. And landsman, back to your minders before they lock you up again.'

When Laszlo returned, Stenwold was bending morosely over some half-sketched plans, whilst Tseitus had a clock-work unravelled on the table and was moving the cogs about like game pieces. The two artificers looked up to see the small man ushered in by Mandir's guards. It had become clear by halfway through their first meeting that there was no actual love lost between the Beetle and the Ant. Despite all logic, Tseitus still resented being left to rot beneath the sea, and he had further made no secret of his contempt for Stenwold's admittedly rusty mechanical skills. On the other hand, Tseitus had never even heard of a snapbow, which invention had reached Collegium after his entombment beneath the waters.

Still, the two of them had one shared interest, which was escaping, and it appeared that the Fly-kinden would be the key to that if anyone would. They waited until the Onychoi had retreated, allowing Laszlo time to uncloak and scratch miserably at his stubbling head, but they were both anxious to hear any news he had to offer.

'I hope you appreciate what I'm doing for you,' was all he said at first. 'This itches like a bastard.'

'A small sacrifice,' snapped Tseitus. 'What is their plan?'

Laszlo shot him a level glance and addressed himself to Stenwold. 'Well, we had a talk – Wys and Nemoctes and Heiracles's people and I – and the most of them couldn't find their arse with both hands if there was a crab hanging off it, to be honest, Mar'Maker. Heiracles and his lot, I wouldn't trust 'em with a bent pin. Nemoctes has something up his sleeve that he thinks we won't like, which in itself's something I don't like. He seems honest enough, but his people have no clout here, and so he's waiting for something to happen. I think he expects that Mandir's people will all go peer out of the windows at the same time long enough for us to simply walk out. I've seen the Man's operation from inside, and it isn't tight, but it's definitely tighter than that. But he obviously believes something's coming. So Wys and I have made our own plans, and sod the rest of them.'

'Plans,' Stenwold said, hoping that the Fly knew what he was talking about. 'What plans?'

'It's all about the Gastroi. You know them?'

'Peasants,' said Tseitus contemptuously.

Stenwold frowned. He had seen them; big, lumbering men and women, heavy-footed, grey-skinned, doing menial work and heavy labour that the Onychoi obviously wouldn't touch. They seemed unlikely rescuers.

'The Ant's half right,' Laszlo said. 'Peasants – farmers, a lot of them, or herders and gatherers. From Hermatyre, too, a fair few. Loads of them live on all those little farms and stations scattered near the colony, Wys tells me. Only Claeon has 'em strung up regularly for a pastime. Just peasants, like our man says, and that's certainly what

Claeon thinks. A lot of them have been turned off their farms or just run away – run here. And they don't like Claeon one bit, but they're loyal to Hermatyre otherwise. They want to see Hermatyre in good hands again.'

'And . . . ?' Stenwold watched him narrowly, seeing Laszlo squirm a little. *Here it comes.*

'Wys and I, we kind of said that if we could get free, we'd be off to find this Aradocles.'

'Who everyone thinks is dead,' Stenwold pointed out. 'Who may well *be* dead, for that matter.'

'But we are off to do that, aren't we? I mean, that was your plan, wasn't it?' Laszlo pressed.

'That was my excuse for talking them into putting us ashore,' Stenwold allowed. 'But as for actually finding him . . .'

'Oh, well, I told them that, anyway, and so did Wys,' Laszlo said, a little awkwardly. 'They're . . . loyal, you see. They hate Claeon because he's a nasty-minded critter, but they want the boy back, and *they* don't believe he's dead.'

'Where is this getting us?' Tseitus demanded. 'So you've swayed the rabble? Does that mean they fight? Will they cast down Mandir? No.'

'No,' Laszlo agreed, 'but they've got all kinds of Art, these Gastroi. I've watched them work. They've got this thing they do with their hands, so that they can just carve into stone or metal, or what have you, and cut it like it's clay. All these pieces that the Hot Stations are made of, they're Gastroi-cut. And that means that when Wys tips them the word, when Nemoctes's moment comes, we're not waiting around for the rescue party. We're going out the back way, and stuff the lot of them. Then Wys will get us out, and we're not *anyone*'s prisoners any more.'

'And you trust Wys, do you?' Stenwold asked. 'Only, our record with these sea-kinden is poor, to say the least.'

'Oh, she's *my* kind of sea-kinden,' Laszlo assured him.

Tseitus snorted and ostentatiously went back to playing

with his cogs. Stenwold sighed and put his head in his hands.

'Hold together, Mar'Maker,' Laszlo told him. 'I've got myself out of worse than this.'

That made the Beetle lift his head. 'Really?'

'No, but I'm always after improving my record. It'll happen.'

'Let's hope so. I won't be able to stall Mandir for long. He's an artificer himself. Whatever I give him must be fit for the purpose, or he'll know.'

'You look like you're losing sleep over it, if I can say so, Mar'Maker.'

Stenwold smiled without humour. 'Oh, sleep I have. Dreams, I have. I think the dreams wear me down more than the waking.' He shook his head. 'I think she *did* something to me,' he added, almost in a whisper.

When Laszlo frowned at him, though, he just waved the thought away.

# Thirty

Claeon burst in, with two guards at his back. It was hard to tell, in that first glimpse, whether he was angry over something in particular, or whether it was merely his sporadic ill temper being given its head. Teornis continued reclining, watching carefully, for to leap to his feet, he decided, would suggest guilt. He had nothing to be guilty about, and no advantage to be gained from feigning it. He donned an enquiring smile.

Claeon jerked his head towards the Spider, and his guards, a pair of sinuous Kerebroi with curved knives, went over and hauled the prisoner to his feet, twisting his arms painfully back. Teornis remained calm, trusting to his assessment of his captor. He had met with Claeon enough times to read the sea-change of the man's moods. This was not the end, just the Edmir throwing some childish tantrum. He told himself that, if his death was due, here, he would see it in Claeon's eyes.

'You can find the brat Aradocles, is that what you're telling me?' the Edmir spat at him, hands clenching over and over. In fact it had been days ago that they had last spoken the missing heir's name, but Teornis had left the dart there, in Claeon's mind, securing it with a little Art to make sure it would fester, and now at last the suppurating fruit had come to light.

'If he still lives, if the dry land has not finished him, I

pride myself that I will find him for you,' Teornis said. He had devised a particular way, by now, of speaking to Claeon: it mingled respect and self-confidence, none of the insolence that would start the man off, but none of the habitual cringing of the sea-kinden staff around him. So far, it had seemed to work.

'You'll succeed, where Pellectes's people have failed – have failed over moons and moons of searching.' Claeon pushed the Spider in the chest, hard enough to wrench his pinioned shoulders.

'But you must have guessed what I have guessed, where Pellectes is concerned,' Teornis said smoothly, hoping that nobody present was a Littoralist.

Claeon's eyes narrowed, and for a moment his arm twitched with the desire to hit somebody, with the Spider as the most obvious target, but a little rare self-control stayed his hand. 'So tell me what you *guess*, land-kinden.'

'Pellectes is mad, to start with,' said Teornis, thinking privately that he had yet to meet any sane sea-kinden. 'But mad in a strange way. Let us be frank, Edmir, you do not believe this business about ancient persecutions from the land or, if you believe, you do not much care. Why should you? The land is a harsh mistress. Why make war and shed blood just to scratch out a living there? But to Pellectes this is the All – the great All transcending logic or reason. All his power and influence, his hold over his followers, comes from this great plan for revenge, and he believes in it, he really does. I'd have thought he was just using the lie for his own purposes but, having met him, he's quite mad and believes every word he says.'

'And yet he has had agents on the land, and your people never suspected.'

'No more we did, but I didn't say he was incapable, just mad as a clam.' A brief moment of wondering over whether clam-kinden actually existed passed him by. 'He doesn't

454

follow you merely because you're the rightful Edmir of Hermatyre,' the foreign words came quite naturally to him now, 'but because you can give him what his madness wants: the land. You, for your part, couldn't care less about the Littoralist dream, but the land's a good playground for your allies, and your woman, whatever her name was, she sent the boy there. To die, perhaps, but, without a corpse, who knows?' Claeon was getting impatient again, so Teornis hurried his speech. 'Why would Pellectes tell his agents to hunt the boy down? Or to tell you about it, if by chance they found him? He worries that, with Aradocles put in the ground – fed to the fish, whatever – you'll not need him any longer, you'll not further his goals. I'll wager his agents have not so much as looked. They're all preparing for their glorious invasion.'

There was a moment of utmost balance, as Claeon's bleak temper teetered between a surge that would earth itself only through Teornis and a rage aimed securely at the Littoralists. Spider eyes watched the thoughts fall into place, the balance tilt, the anger slide inexorably away from him in other directions. With a brutal jab of his chin, Claeon signalled for Teornis's release.

'How can I trust you?' he growled.

'One service Pellectes's people have done you, at least, is they have confirmed my credentials. Those people up there are my enemies, too. Moreover, you'll surely be sending me under an escort. I'd expect nothing less. I will prove myself to you, Edmir, by divining the fate of your missing nephew. If you want, I will then ensure that he stays missing until the end of time. After that, let us talk about Rosander's campaign there for, with my help, he'll grab enough of the land to keep even Pellectes satisfied. Everyone wins except our enemies, and is that not the best way, always?'

He expected Claeon to go off and think it all over again,

as he had so many times before, but unwished-for developments had obviously arisen, and Teornis guessed that Stenwold was still free, still flouting Hermatyre's reach.

'What will you need?' Claeon growled.

'The name of Pellectes's agent, and how to make contact, together with whatever escort you choose to send with me. Your Kerebroi – your Krakind here – can pass for my people, and whilst that won't make them locally popular, they'll at least be taken as land-kinden. I can advise on suitable cloaks and clothes and the like. No Onychoi, though. Just between you and me, to a landsman's eye they look freakish.'

Claeon actually chuckled at that. 'Oh, to me also, much of the time. No, we'll keep them out of it. Even my own Onychoi would rather be with Rosander, I sometimes feel. I can't trust them. I can't trust any of them.'

Looking into the man's small eyes, seeing them stare out of Claeon's heavy face like desperate prisoners, Teornis knew how those Onychoi felt. On land they always said, 'Never trust a Spider', and yet people always did, because his kinden were so good at gaining trust. Still, amongst the Spiders themselves, the value of trust was well known. A Spider-kinden Aristos chose servants and slaves well, and treated them in a way that invited loyalty, respect, even love. Claeon's tyranny would have seemed risible if he hadn't held Teornis's life in his grasping, whip-loving hands.

'I can wait no longer,' the Edmir whispered, and Teornis wondered if he even realized he was speaking aloud. 'The boy, the cursed boy, he haunts my dreams. Even the chance, the *chance* that he might live . . . and return . . .' Those eyes, that had retreated a little into themselves, suddenly blazed out again with renewed fervour. 'And if it becomes known that he died on the land, where that traitress Paladrya sent him, that he was torn apart and eaten by the land-kinden – well, then perhaps Rosander shall have plenty of volunteers for his stupid war. We'll have the whole sea under arms before we're done!' He was smiling joyously now, and Teornis joined him with a strained rictus of a grin, because his complicity was obviously expected.

And then came the fateful words. 'You shall go with the tide, over the Edge and on to the land,' Claeon promised him. 'You shall go tonight.'

Teornis had not been clear on how his re-entry into polite society was likely to be accomplished, conjuring images of riding into Collegium harbour on the back of a giant squid or some such, like an allegorical figure from one of the Spiderlands' more outré operas. The messenger sent to fetch him, however, was not from the ranks of Claeon's regulars, but one of the stunted little Onychoi people. He had taken little note of them, seeing that Claeon's people found them a nuisance underfoot and deemed them a class of menials mostly to be kept outside the palace. His ear for voices was good, though, and when she addressed him he recalled her.

'Chief Landsman,' she said, 'your barque awaits.'

*She was the pilot of the machine that brought us here*, he remembered. *She's one of Rosander's people. Am I being kidnapped again?*

At his doubtless dubious expression she sneered. 'We're doing a little shallow-water testing, Chief Landsman. Claeon's got a mob waiting to go up with us, and you, too, they say.'

'And Claeon's not here to tell me that himself?' Teornis enquired cautiously.

Her mouth twisted sardonically. 'You want to go poke him, see what he says? Or you want out of here?'

She was hard to read, barriers of class, kinden and culture all intervening, and it was a difficult decision for him to say, 'Well lead on then, Chenni.' She looked surprised that he had picked up her name, but just beckoned him to follow.

There was no hulking escort of Onychoi warriors waiting outside, though they had not been shy of forcing their way into Claeon's halls before. For Teornis, the lack of *options* was the frustrating thing. If things took a turn for the worse, he had so little to fall back on. He could not even run for it, for where could he go? The killing sea bounded everything here, so he was made a prisoner by the mere fact of his land-bound ancestry.

'You're quite the favourite of the Nauarch Rosander, I understand,' he said to her, for there might be some small advantage in starting up a rapport. He employed his Art then, casting it over her, tweaking her perceptions of him to make her friendlier, him more trustable. It was something as natural to him as breathing by now, and he hardly knew he was doing it.

'I give him what he wants,' she shot back over her high shoulder, and then, perhaps sensing how this could be misconstrued, 'I make things, build things. I'm chief of his mechanics.'

The word meant nothing to Teornis, of course, save that it smacked of artificing. Another barrier between them, but this time one of aptitude. *I wonder if Claeon has any idea what is brewing amongst these ugly people? No doubt the Moth-kinden remained similarly clueless.* Of all the old overlords, only Teornis's kinden had retained their mastery over the Apt unscathed, and only because they had such a keen understanding of a basic human nature that remained unchanged by machines or magic.

'We'll be swimming back to shore in one of your devices, then?'

'Part-swim and part-crawl. I need to test something,' she replied with more enthusiasm. 'My people have spent what seems like a whole moon in recalibrating the gear weightings to work out of water, but we've sorted it now, looks like. Everything meshes neatly and nothing's going to snap.'

'That sounds good,' said Teornis, letting such talk wash over him. The essence of artifice, as far as he was concerned, was to have someone *else* understand it.

Sooner than he had thought, they were out of the palace, and true enough there was a mob of Kerebroi waiting there, eight of them: six men and two women. They were loaded with gold, their skin tattooed, hair in loose curls, and the men with elegantly curled beards. *And if there's a sight more likely to stand out in Collegium, it could only be an entire Imperial army,* Teornis decided, but he knew he would be equal to this task. And, besides, he wouldn't need to place much trust in them. He was more worried about their resemblance to him having them seen as a bizarre Spider-kinden fancy-dress attack force. *When I'm back on land, when I'm beneath the blessed sky, in the free air, let me start to worry about that.*

There were more Onychoi to be seen ahead. Chenni's party was approaching some kind of dock, such as the one they had arrived by. Teornis expected to see the same slender underwater boat bobbing in the water, but instead there was something that he at first took to be a crab, and then interpreted as some kind of armoured automotive. Its body was comprised of an enormous rounded shield, the tips of many legs just visible beneath its rim. Behind the shield was some manner of machinery that then trailed off into the balancing spine of a long, stiff tail. Teornis was no assessor of vehicles, but it was all built to the heavy, bulky scale of the Onychoi themselves, and the shield looked thick enough to ward off artillery.

'Your barque, Chief Landsman,' Chenni announced proudly. 'We'll have it towed upwards and over the Edge, and after that it'll walk up to shore, sweet as you like.'

'You can't just take *that* into Collegium harbour,' Teornis told her.

'Oh, no worries there. There's a little cove we know, and we're meeting Claeon's spy there, the Littoralist.' She said the last word with marked disdain. 'Now, you get stowed in. Not much room in there for you and the crew, but you'll bear a little discomfort, I'm sure, to get where you're going.'

'Oh, that I will,' Teornis assured her.

That the sea-kinden had achieved a genuine state of Aptitude was amply proved by the nausea and discomfort that the latter part of the journey caused him. The first leg of it, and by far the swiftest, was smooth but tedious, as the automotive was carried up from the depths by what Teornis assumed was one of the Kerebroi's beasts, or some other swimming thing of great strength, that he never saw. When he commented that this looked like a flaw in their machine's design, the little Onychoi, who were all elbows and knees alongside him in the cramped cabin, explained that the vessel would be quite able to crawl the vertical height of the sea-cliff if needed, but that would add days to their journey. After that they started telling him all manner of complex details of their conveyance, and Teornis nodded along, as though any of it made sense to him. *And yet they have the belief that land-kinden are Apt, evidently,* he decided, after over an hour of this. He insinuated his question into the conversation, singling out Chenni and casting a little more of his Art over her, to draw out the details.

'Oh, we go to the Stations often enough,' she said. 'Been hearing odd snips about land-kinden since long before you turned up.'

*Intriguing, but hardly useful,* Teornis considered. Nonetheless he filed it away for later consideration.

The journey back to land was slower than his original entry into the sea world. The knife-like underwater boat that had nipped them away from the fight on the barge had been a fleet little thing. Whatever submerged convoy they were now travelling in took a good two days at their best speed to clear the Shelf – or the Edge as the sea-kinden called it – and then it was a long, stomach-knotting crawl across the seabed towards where breakers marked the boundaries of the two worlds. Teornis ate with the crew, listened to their chatter, watched their constant mothering of the mechanisms of their automotive as it dragged and lurched over the uneven seafloor. The mood was high, the engineering apparently performing.

'You look pasty, landsman. No hurling up in here,' Chenni warned him.

'It's nothing.' He did not want to admit to his Inaptitude.

'It's the equalization, is what it is,' she told him, surprising him. At his querying look she went on, 'When you got brought down here, Claeon's men used their Art on you. It's as old as breathing, that one – when you go from the shallows to the depths, see, you need equalizing, or you die. Nasty death, too. Now we're headed up again, it'll reverse itself, but you'll feel rough if it's your first time, and maybe travelling this way'll make it worse. Felt a little queasy myself, the first time we took one of these up top.'

'You have many of these devices?' Teornis asked Chenni. Before her words he had assumed this was some singular prodigy.

'Oh, a good dozen already, and more on the way. Our long stop in Hermatyre has been good for the manufactory. Otherwise, doing things on the move is always difficult. Of course, when we come for real, we'll have the beasts with us to break up whatever your land lot have built, and carry it away.'

Teornis reminded her that it was not 'his' land lot after all, but she shrugged expressively.

'Makes little difference to me, honestly,' she told him. 'I just know Rosander wants action. Too long in a colony's making him and his lads go half-crazy. But now we've got this war that Claeon and the Lits have hatched for us.

461

Something different, at least. Raiding the land-kinden's probably more fun than raiding another train. Easier too, I reckon.'

*And yet you haven't asked why Claeon's so happy to leave it to you,* Teornis thought. He pictured an octopus, exploring warily with its tentacles, then a crab just blundering in sideways, pincers raised in belligerent threat. *We become them, after long enough. We become our ideal form. My good luck that Spiders are both patient and cunning. I'll have them all in our web yet, beetles and sea monsters, too.*

It was from the heavier going that Teornis guessed they were close to land, the tilt that showed him the seafloor was now a steepening slope. Then he heard the surface waves battering at the metal of the thing's nose, while the gears began making very different sounds. The half-dozen Onychoi became tense, waiting for something to give, but their forward progress, though slower, never stopped as the monstrous machine dragged itself doggedly on to the beach. Chenni let out a whoop of triumph, and for a moment the little half-naked people were hugging each other in an orgy of congratulation.

'We're ashore?' Teornis pressed, when he could finally get anyone's attention.

'Oh we are that, Chief Landsman,' Chenni told him. 'So time for you to make your exit.'

They had to open the hatch for him, of course, and then it was an undignified crawl underneath the rear rim of the machine's great curved hood, on hands and knees through the wet, weed-slick sand, before he could get clear. He did not care. Beneath a cloud-ragged midnight sky, he stood and stretched, with only the solid ground beneath him, only the air above. *To not be trapped in a bubble at the bottom of the sea: whoever could have thought that this would ever be the limit of my ambition?*

His confederates, Claeon's men, crouched, waiting for him, in the surf as though clinging desperately to the last of their world. Whatever they had been promised, to break such a great taboo, they looked less sure of it now. Still, he would not want to be the one to return instead to Claeon, whose temper was less mythic than the deadly, inhospitable land ahead of them, but made up for that by being far more immediate.

Teornis approached them with a smile. 'Which of you leads, here?' he asked. It took some time for one of the men to come forwards.

'I am senior here,' the Kerebroi announced, already shivering in the cold night air, clad in nothing but his loincloth and ornaments. 'I am Geontes.' He was a man who looked close to Teornis's own age, but broader at the waist, as all his kind seemed to be after reaching a certain point in their lives. His beard dripped miserably.

'Well, Geontes, we will have to make a landsman out of you – out of all of you,' Teornis told him, with a kindly smile. 'You can hardly walk into Collegium dressed like the richest beggar in the Lowlands. Assuming you didn't freeze to death before you got there.'

'Your spy's here,' a sardonic voice observed from by his elbow. Chenni was pointing up the beach to where the cliffs began. Teornis's eyes picked out a couple of figures making their careful way down by some narrow path: a Beetle man and a Spider woman ... No, a Kerebroi woman, although he might have taken her for a Spider at a passing glance, had he not known. Here was Pellectes's agent, the worm in the timbers of Collegium.

As for the man ... Teornis found himself smiling as he placed the face. *Oh, now that's interesting. How many masters may a man actually have?*

He now strode forward, every inch the confident Aristos, showing no hint of being a prisoner, of being kept for tendays away from the light and air.

'Why, Master Broiler, as I live and breathe, how splendid!'

463

Helmess Broiler evidently did not find it so – which argued for wisdom. Matters were out of his hands as of now, though, Teornis decided. He bowed low before the woman. 'Madam, you have had word of me, I hope?'

'Some word,' she agreed, regarding him with narrowed eyes. She was a reasonably comely piece of work, he decided, although close-up she did not compare to one of true Spider blood. Still, a Beetle could do worse, no doubt.

'Lady, I am Teornis of the Aldanrael, former Lord-Martial of the Grand Army of the Spiderlands, and implacable enemy of Collegium. You, I take it, are of Pellectes's party, one of the Littoralists?'

The hastily hidden bafflement on Helmess's face was a joy to see. *So I know more than you already, Master Beetle. Therefore beware.*

'Elytrya,' the woman named herself. 'I was told you would be of use to the cause. Is that so?'

'Why else would I be here?' Teornis assured her. 'I bring some lackeys also, for your use, but we must have them properly disguised. It would not do for them to enter Collegium too openly, either as sea-kinden or Spiders.'

'We have clothes, cloaks,' she told him, still distrusting. 'There is a carriage waiting, but these will not all fit in it.'

'They'll have to jog alongside, like servants,' Teornis decided. 'We'll tell them it's a landsman custom. The exercise will do them good, since I daresay Claeon doesn't exercise them enough.' He was watching carefully, and he noticed the slight crease of humour appear in her face. *Oh Claeon, you are held in such low esteem even by your own allies.* 'Shall we go now?' he offered, and she nodded curtly.

Behind them the Onychoi were fussing over the trial machine, but happily in so far as he could judge. Ahead, just a climb up the cliffs and a carriage-ride away, lay the civilized, land-bound comforts of Collegium. Even Beetle hospitality would serve, after what he had been through.

And there would be eyes watching for his return. Teornis had grown tired of dancing to another's tune. It was time to make the melody himself.

The Collegium watch knew Helmess Broiler, that was clear, and were obviously used to his nocturnal perambulations. Teornis wondered if the man had publicly cultivated a hobby such as star-gazing, or collecting moths, to justify his habits, or whether he simply relied on his status as an Assembler to deflect rumour. Considering what he knew of him, Teornis suspected the former, and also guessed that the Beetle had arranged for this particular watch officer to have this particular shift, with open hand and blind eye to the ready. Helmess, he assessed, was a workmanlike intelligencer, and one who had kept a great secret for some time. *So when did I hear that Broiler had got himself a Spider mistress?* It had not seemed important at the time, and it had been quite the fashion after Maker took in Arianna. Waifs, strays and exiles from all across the Spiderlands had ended up as paramours and escorts to the Beetle-kinden men and women of consequence thanks to Stenwold's proclivities. Teornis had seen no reason to have a spy in Helmess's parlour, since he had always suspected Helmess was the Empire's man, and the Aldanrael maintained a spy at the Imperial embassy. So why waste effort on one more old Beetle?

*Oh, what we might have learned, had I done so. However, no regrets now. Time to weep for the past when my enemies are dead, as the poet said.*

Teornis had made sure that, as Broiler's four-beetle carriage was forced to halt at the gates to the city, he stepped just out to stretch his legs. Claeon's people, looking like shabby peasants of no fixed kinden, clustered together behind the carriage, plainly shocked and horrified by Collegium even at night-time. Teornis had laid a reassuring hand on Geontes's shoulder. *I shall spare you too much further discomfort,* he promised inwardly. He grinned up at the stars out of genuine pleasure at remaking their acquaintance, and because there would be those looking out for his face, should he ever re-enter the city.

Then they were rattling through the sleeping streets, the Kerebroi shambling along behind again, and only Teornis spared a moment to look again towards the skies. *Certainly the sea-kinden would not think to, and Beetles are so earthbound.* His keen eyes caught the shudder of wings up there, and an excitement that had been distant till now began abruptly welling up. *I am back in the Dance.*

They encamped at Broiler's townhouse, the Beetle magnate now looking harried, and with good cause. Claeon's men he had already been expecting, and no doubt he felt confident of handling the bewildered, land-lost Kerebroi, but Teornis provided a rogue factor, an element that his planning had not taken into account. The game had changed.

And yet Teornis made sure to appear meekness personified. Though their conversation had been slight, he had shown himself, on the journey, to be Claeon's man, relieved only to be out of the depths. 'Oh you cannot imagine,' he had whispered to Helmess Broiler, 'the darkness, down there, the sense of weight. It is no place for us landsmen, no place at all.' Even so, the Beetle had not seemed convinced.

Geontes and his fellows ended up squatting about Helmess's parlour, their shabby cloaks over their Hermatyre riches giving them the look of larcenous tramps. Helmess's servants were mostly absent, no doubt promptly sent away to avoid telling tales of these remarkable strangers. There was only one on hand to serve some drinks, a stocky man with a cultured air who Teornis tentatively identified as a halfbreed, albeit a very subtle one. *Spider blood, so worth watching.*

'Sands,' Helmess said when asked about him. 'Forman Sands, my man of all work.' He wore a steely little smile as he said it. Teornis knew the expression from his dealings in Helleron long ago. It was polite Beetle parlance for someone that removed obstacles in business and personal life, by whatever means.

'He seems a handy fellow to have around,' Teornis remarked.

'Oh, he'll do,' Helmess agreed, the implicit threat hovering. The Spider only smiled politely.

While the Kerebroi were being served bowls of wine, most of which ended up slopped on the floor, Teornis went to the window and leant out, taking in a deep breath of cool air. Sensing Helmess at his shoulder, he said, 'I am not quite used yet to having a sky up there,' which was true. He smiled back at his host whilst, at the windowsill, his fingers busily spun glinting strands. 'Tell me, Master Broiler, what do you yourself seek from all of this?'

'Why?' Helmess asked him, eyes narrowed. He was suspicious, yes, but suspicious only of the question. The instructions that Teornis's hands were sketching went unseen, save by the eyes outside the house that they were meant for. It was not just the sea-kinden that possessed a silent finger-language.

'Have they promised you a governorship? What on earth does Rosander intend to do with the place, once he has it?'

'I doubt he's thought it through,' said Helmess, drawn into speaking, despite himself. 'And so he will need someone to think for him. I fancy that Elytrya and I shall be appointed king and consort of the city. Surely, Rosander has no clue how to govern the place, and after sufficient raids from the sea he will wish for something more permanent. I will be waiting, and of proven loyalty.'

*I cannot think of any phrase less fitting for you.* 'As you know, my own people will descend on this place soon enough,' Teornis told him, wondering absently if the ships had even left harbour yet. 'Once the back of the Assembly is broken, by whatever means, the picture you sketch may

467

be attractive. An ostensibly independent Collegium will look better to us, and I am sure you will be happy to let our ships ply the sea trade on your behalf. It was all we ever wanted, after all. Such a great fuss over a few coins here or there in a merchant's purse.' He brushed off his hands, their work done, strands of glittering thread ghosting away into the night air.

He turned away from the window, smiling at Helmess, and placed his back to the wall. The Kerebroi sat sullenly as Elytrya spoke to them about the great things that the Littoralists would accomplish, once their long-lost land had been reclaimed. Helmess drank sparingly and remained suspicious.

His man of all work stayed close to his elbow. It was impossible to tell from his face just how far into this conspiracy Sands was. *Has potential, that one*, Teornis noted. *Just how much potential, we'll see in a moment.*

Perhaps half an hour later his people came bursting through every available window.

They were his Dragonfly-kinden, and so had been able to go to ground in Collegium with ease. To the Beetles, Dragonflies meant the Commonweal, who were enemies of the Wasps and therefore nominal friends of the city. Most Beetles had very little idea what a Commonweal Dragonfly should look like and so these men and women, lean and hard in their armour of chitin and hide and with their personal histories written on their skins with scars and tattoos, easily passed muster. The Commonweal was known to be a strange and backward place, after all.

They fell upon the Kerebroi with a will, without hesitation. Geontes was among the first to die. A few of the others had knives out, but tangled in their unfamiliar clothing, before the Dragonflies butchered them. Other intruders had arrows poised on the string, directed at Sands, at Helmess, at Elytrya. Teornis's instructions had been necessarily crude – *kill all Spider-kinden save the Arista and myself*

468

– because the Art-web language was difficult for non-Spiders to follow, and he had not dared to be more specific. Forman Sands, caught at arrow-point standing creditably in front of his employer, owed his life merely to Teornis's need for a simple message, and it was lucky that Teornis's followers had identified Elytrya as the 'Arista' or she would have died too.

It was over so swiftly, with a minimum of fuss. Of the three Dragonfly principalities in exile within the Spiderlands, the warrior-folk of Solorn were those most divorced from their heritage. They had long turned their back on the peace and philosophy of the Commonweal, scratching out a harsh livelihood on their rocky peninsula, bandits, raiders and mercenaries like their cousins in Princep Exilla. Teornis had employed them in his personal house guard and cadre for years.

'Varante,' he greeted their leader. The tall, cord-muscled man bowed in a quick, jerky movement. He was automatically cleaning the blade of his punch-sword with a torn swatch of cloth taken from the cloak of one of the dead. He had served the Aldanrael for twenty years, had Varante, and grown grey and leathery in their service. But not old, never old.

'Lord-Martial,' the Dragonfly addressed him, 'honoured to serve. The bodies in the bay?'

Teornis gave him a wide and genuine smile. His depth of feeling surprised him: how glad he was to see this familiar face, this old retainer who had now restored him to power. 'Not in the bay, no,' he considered. 'That would send entirely the wrong message. Have them taken out and dumped somewhere inland. The further inland the better. Let them become food for ants and worms, but not for fish.' He turned to Helmess and Elytrya, all smiles now. 'You may be feeling some anxiety as to where this is going,' he told them, as though there were not eight corpses being stripped of their valuables and manhandled out of the window one by one. They stared at him, shocked into paralysis. Only Sands seemed able to react, and he was keeping carefully quiet, understanding that he had just become the most expendable person in the room. *I wonder if he would contemplate a change of employer?*

'You' – Teornis pointed at the Kerebroi woman – 'will achieve your conquest of the land. Bring Rosander and his host to Collegium, and that will serve. All I said before remains just as true. And you,' his finger flicked towards Helmess, 'can be governor or king or grand high sealord of this place after we're done, for all I care. Everything goes ahead just as you want.' Teornis's smile was iron. 'But we do it my way. So now let's talk about Aradocles.'

# Thirty-One

'Do you suppose the Spider fleet has reached Collegium yet?' Stenwold asked. The paper swam before his eyes, covered with a scrawl of lines and angles. He was trying to anatomize the snapbow in such a way as to baffle Mandir's engineers without betraying his word, but he had an uncomfortable feeling that they were better artificers than he gave them credit for. The leathery, unpleasant parchment and the awkward excuse for a reservoir pen that Tseitus had been able to construct did not help matters. Though sleep weighed heavily on him, he was reluctant to give in to it. He had been waking each morning with a pounding head and a sense of loss and despair, as though, wherever his dreams took him, it was a place that would not easily let him go.

'Depends,' Laszlo said philosophically, picking at his nails with the point of a knife that he had somehow got hold of. 'If it's a *fleet*, then yes, but whether it'll do any good's another question. What I heard, though, was "armada", and that means something different, over Spiderlands way. That means more than one of their great houses pitching in, and in my experience that sort of thing can take a long time to get organized. If it's an armada proper, if they're serious about this sea-war business, then it's still in harbour like as not, while four overseers and fifty mercenary skippers are arguing about money.'

'I suppose I should take hope from that,' Stenwold said weakly. He looked up as Laszlo padded over. The Fly's expression showed concern.

'We are getting out, Mar'Maker. No doubts. Soon, too, if Wys and Nemmo can be believed. Any day now, they say. Something's coming. Last I went out, everyone seemed tense, but nobody was talking about it. There's trouble, Mar'Maker, and where there's trouble, there's opportunity.'

'The watchword of the *Tidenfree*, I suppose?' Stenwold mustered a smile.

'And of the Bloodfly before her,' Laszlo agreed. 'And the other half of that is, if you can't find trouble, make it.'

'Does Tseitus know that you have such plans?'

Laszlo screwed his face up. 'Not as such, not quite. Not even sure what way that one will jump. I'll tell him when it happens. He can nail his colours then. Until then, well . . . I don't want our sour-faced Ant deciding he prefers it here.'

'Seems hardly likely.'

Laszlo shrugged. 'Who can know what an Ant's thinking, save for another Ant?' He swiped the sheet of paper that Stenwold was working on and frowned at it.

'You have a criticism of my draughtsmanship?' Stenwold asked him archly.

'Is that what you call it? You'll not show this to Mandir, will you?'

'And why not?'

'He might wonder whether your real talents lie elsewhere.' Laszlo reversed the sheet, showing the fruits of Stenwold's labour back to their creator. The tangle of shakily drawn technical plans had trailed off, and instead the pen lines had taken on a woman's likeness. It was rough work, for Stenwold was no artist, but perhaps he had picked up more from his lost friend Nero than he knew. Certainly Stenwold recognized the woman's face.

'I have no recollection of drawing that,' he said hollowly.

'You know,' Laszlo observed, obviously picking his way

472

around a delicate subject, 'Mandir would get a woman in here for you, if you wanted one. He's the soul of generosity sometimes, I've heard.'

'No!' Stenwold said, after a moment of gaping. 'Absolutely not.' The thought of some fearful Onychoi or Gastroi maid being shoved into his chamber was too much. *Besides, my traitor hand has shown to where my mind drifts, and Mandir cannot bring* her *here – and woe betide him if he tried it.*

Laszlo's next shrug eloquently asserted that there were worse bedfellows than sea-kinden, and Stenwold wondered if it was Wys he had lain with, but guessed not. Whenever Laszlo spoke of the submersible captain, the impression left was that their only partnership involved business.

The Fly shook his head. 'Go and sleep, Mar'Maker. You look like one of those big Onychoi lads punched you in both eyes.'

*To sleep, to dream.* Stenwold shook himself in despair. *I have no rest, not anymore.* Still, he dragged himself off to the pallet the sea-kinden had brought for him, which had the same unpleasant texture as their paper, only hoping that he was tired enough to escape whatever waited for him.

He woke because Laszlo was shaking him. He had no idea how much time had passed, as the Stations experienced neither day or night. His mind was still awhirl with images: coiling hair, luminescent limbs.

'What . . . ?' he got out.

'Up, Mar'Maker, up!' Laszlo urged him. 'It's time!'

'Hm?' Stenwold blinked, and then let out a strangled cry and leapt to his feet. 'Time for . . . ?'

'The Stations are under attack,' the Fly told him gravely.

Stenwold stared. 'Attack by Claeon?'

'Just get yourself dressed and ready to run.'

'Or . . . *Nemoctes* is *attacking?*'

'Oh, it's not him. They'd not be scared of him. But they're scared now, all right. Every able sea-kinden has a weapon to hand and is waiting to beat them off. Just get dressed!'

Then Laszlo was gone, flitting out of the room in a blur of wings. Stenwold stumbled into his clothing, the same torn and grimy canvas and leathers he had met Teornis in, with a cloak and tunic of clammy material drawn over that. *No boots.* He sometimes missed footwear almost as much as sun and air.

Thus ready, he waited, but Laszlo did not wing his way back. There was a great deal of commotion from somewhere, shouting of orders, panic and confusion. *An attack? What has Nemoctes done? Or is it Claeon? Surely not just for me, not all of this.*

He was interrupted by a scratching sound from behind him, coming from the wall itself. Turning, he saw something move there, a dot at first, and then a line began grinding a curved path as though some invisible hand was drawing there. He stared for a long time, unable to understand what he was seeing, until at last the line arced back to meet itself, and a circular section of the wall was simply lifted away.

Beyond, there were three figures crowding close, looming into the sudden gap like bad dreams. Broad, stocky, heavy-set types, two men and a woman, with dull, flat faces and grey skin. It took a moment for Stenwold to place them, to recall where he had heard them mentioned: *the Gastroi, Laszlo told me.*

'Come,' one of them said in a low rumble, 'quickly.'

'But Laszlo, my friend, I need to wait . . .'

'Quickly,' the Gastroi man repeated. The other two glanced about anxiously, whether looking out for Mandir's people or for some sign of the attackers, he could not tell.

Stenwold bared his teeth. Laszlo had made arrangements with Wys, after all. He would be able to make his own way out, with ease. Stenwold darted for the hole, then turned back to grab at the table that he had been working at, feeling the all too familiar contours of the original weapon that he had been slaving to duplicate. Then he was out after the Gastroi, as they lumbered away. *Away where?* he wondered. But for now *away* would have to suffice.

Wherever he had been freed into, it was deserted now. The sound of the fighting was not close, but noticeably closer the longer Stenwold listened. His escorts led him at a shambling pace through a brief passage between two rooms, and then to yet another chamber, this time lined with damp pallets. Another circular hole had been bored in the sheet metal of the wall, its rounded edge so neat it might have been machined. Beyond it was a lot of water.

When the first Gastroi stepped out, Stenwold realized that the murk was only ankle-deep, but the very sight of it transfixed him. *There's been a breach.* A breach soon sealed, obviously, but surely this water came from without. How much of a rupture would the Stations need to suffer before they flooded entirely?

'Cauls!' he shouted at the Gastroi. They turned, the second only partway out, staring at him with those coarse, blank faces.

'I cannot breathe the water,' he told them, as simply as he could. 'I need cauls. As . . . as many as you can. Please, I . . .' *I don't want to drown. Any death but that.* But he held that part in, for fear of their contempt. Their baffled stares persisted for another few seconds before one of them nodded, and the one left inside peered about, as though hoping to see a stack of the filmy hoods just waiting for them.

There was a bellow, and abruptly the leading Gastroi disappeared from the hole's vantage point in a spray of blood. Stenwold fumbled for the snapbow, trying to remember if he had loaded it. The second Gastroi had turned, hands raised, but someone ran her through with a short-spear, ramming it up under her ribs. She gave out a harsh, choking cry and swiped at her unseen attacker, but then a second assailant darted in – a nimble little Onychoi – and gashed the entire length of her side with a hooked knife. She fell back through the gap and two small Onychoi scuttled over her instantly, heading for Stenwold. Behind them, the opening was darkened by a Kerebroi man with a full-length spear in his hands.

*Claeon's killers*, Stenwold had just a moment to think. The little spearman went for him, but the final Gastroi, who had been standing still enough to escape notice, lunged in even as he tried to strike, catching the small man by one bicep. The knifeman darted past, and Stenwold pulled the snapbow's trigger. The explosive sound of the weapon's air battery came as an infinite relief, and the Onychoi was punched right off his feet, dead without ever knowing why.

The third Gastroi's face revealed a bleak desperation and, as Stenwold watched, he turned his art on his enemy, and whatever had scored through the walls clipped the surviving Onychoi's arm off effortlessly. As the maimed and scream-ing creature dropped to the ground, the Kerebroi's spear-head lanced into the big, slow man's neck. Stenwold had raised the cut-down snapbow again, seeing the Kerebroi not even flinch, not even recognizing the piece as a weapon.

Then Tseitus had run him through.

The Ant had appeared through the circular gap, wearing a nightshift that was drenched to the knees, and holding something that was as close to a Lowlander shortsword as he had been able to manufacture down here during his years of captivity. He struck twice more, swift and efficient, reminding Stenwold that, however long this man had worn the gown, he had been the child of a warrior city-state once.

'Your Fly says . . . we must go,' Tseitus managed to gasp, breathing heavily. He had surely not fought, not even a backstabbing blow like that, for many years. Laszlo chose that moment to appear, and viewed the carnage with a grey face.

'It wasn't supposed to be like this,' he said faintly. The Gastroi, of course, had been his own recruits for this busi-ness.

476

'Laszlo, what is going on?' Stenwold demanded. The water level outside was rising, and began slopping over the lower edge of the hole.

'Echinoi, they say,' replied Laszlo casually, the name obviously meaning little to him, but Stenwold saw again that spiny orange tide in his mind's eye: its inexorable advance on the Benthic train.

'We have to get out of here,' he said flatly.

'That's what I've been trying to tell everyone!' Laszlo almost shouted at him. 'Come on, we have to find Wys and her lot!'

He darted off, half running and half flying, leaving Stenwold and Tseitus to follow as best they could.

The Stations had been thrown together by many hands and with only a loose plan, so Laszlo was leading them through gaps between rooms, unfinished spaces where the walls were a patchwork of metal and shell and carefully measured pieces of stone, but every so often they would break out into the Stations proper, the public face of Mandir's realm, there to go skittering across a market-place or a sleeping hall. The normal business of the Hot Stations had been suspended and they saw locals frantically gathering up their possessions, while others were arming themselves, with fear and dread on their faces. Here and there, parties of armoured Greatclaw Onychoi lumbered laboriously through the panicking crowd, blades and mauls to hand, and all heading somewhere with obvious purpose. Laszlo paused to watch one troop go by. He had dropped to the ground as soon as he saw them, but nobody was taking any notice of any of the fugitives.

'Stuff it,' the Fly swore mildly. 'Where's Wys, the wretched woman?'

'Laszlo, where are we going?' Stenwold demanded. 'It's not as if we can just kick a door down and walk out of here.'

'I have cauls for us, but only one each.' Laszlo passed him back one of the translucent hoods, while still scanning the crowd. 'But we need Wys – Nemoctes, if we have to, but Wys is best.'

'This is like a circus,' Tseitus complained, just as the screaming began.

At first Stenwold could not see what was happening, but all of a sudden people were fleeing from the little plaza, and the wash of water struck against his calves, freezing him in place. The local inhabitants were dashing for every available exit, but the three landsmen made no move until the Echinoi arrived.

Stenwold saw the colour first, the violent red-tinged orange of them. For a moment it was nothing but a gaudy blur to him, and he could not put a shape to it, but something came oozing out of a gap in the wall, bristling with spines. Its topside bright-hued, its underside a pallid white that seethed with suckered limbs, it unrolled first one arm out into the marketplace, and then another. A five-limbed lump of a monster, it dragged itself over the ground as if pulled unwillingly on strings, its hide waving with dark-tipped spikes. No head, no front, no back, there was nothing of it that admitted any kinship, or anything at all but an inexorable hunger.

And after it came its kinden.

The Echinoi were coloured just like their beasts, in purples, reds and oranges, and there seemed little of the human about them. Their skin was like notched rind, their faces noseless, with eyes like black buttons and mere slashes for mouths. They wore armour of copper and some kind of pale hide, and although some had long, hooked swords made of bronze, their barbed fists looked savage enough in themselves.

They moved swiftly but awkwardly, and that alone was what saved the landsmen. The first three or four rushed for them, wordless and expressionless, but they seemed almost over-fast, out of their own control. Tseitus smashed one across the face with his makeshift blade, and Stenwold was able to simply sidestep another. He gave the creature a shove and it lost its footing and fell past him, although it was back on its feet almost instantly. As they beat a quick retreat he had the fleeting thought: *they are used to fighting in water only. I have been told how they are the only sea-kinden that have no use for the air.*

Then someone was bellowing at him to get out of the way, and he turned to see Mandir, of all people, and a band of his warriors. To the Man of the Stations' credit, there was no order right then, to recapture the landsmen. The Echinoi were all that Mandir had eyes for. He had a dozen of the big Onychoi, and most of them bore the tube-barrelled weapons that Stenwold had noticed before. The heads of the bolts protruding from them were more like axe-blades than arrows. Other men there, of several kinden, had the curved falx swords and two-pronged spears, and there was even a couple of crabs crouched before the line, their pincers wide in threat.

The Echinoi had got into their stride and rushed the line with their crawling, many-limbed beast coursing through the water behind them. Mandir barked a single word, and his warriors loosed their weapons. The shock of concerted release staggered even the great Onychoi, and the sound of a half-dozen spring-loaded plates being released sounded uncannily like a volley of snapbow shot. *Tseitus said they made good springs*, Stenwold thought numbly, as Laszlo tugged at his sleeve. The broad-headed missiles were a momentary blur in the air, and then most of the Echinoi were down. Stenwold saw limbs cut clean away, enormous gashes ripped through corrugated orange hide. One was beheaded entirely, the truncated body standing with sword upraised before dropping to its knees.

The Onychoi were not done, though. As the bowmen began to crank back their springs once more, the balance of Mandir's forces set upon the stricken Echinoi, hacking them limb from limb. The few that remained standing showed no fear, striking out at their enemies even as they were impaled on barbed spears, pinned to the ground and torn apart. Their flesh seemed impossibly tough, and Stenwold saw bristly severed limbs crawling blindly through the water, some with weapons still clutched in their grip. Their great beast suddenly surged forward, knocking a Kerebroi man to the ground and engulfing him, cutting his scream off halfway. The defenders were soon all about the creature, stabbing and cutting, the crabs worrying away at its legs, snapping spines and tearing at the delicate feet beneath.

Laszlo was shouting at him. Laszlo had been shouting at him for some time. 'We have to go!' the Fly's shrill voice insisted, and Stenwold came to himself and realized the man was right. *We are not meant to be here*, he swore, *in so many ways*.

They ducked through another cramped sequence of crawlspaces, with Laszlo forever having to come back for them, two wheezing academics twice his size. The sound of fighting was all about them, frequently the very walls booming and shaking to melee on the far side. The last narrow space that Laszlo urged them through was awash with water whose level was definitely rising. *Mandir's people must have pumps, must be sealing off breaches, but the Echinoi aren't taking no for an answer*.

He groaned and hauled himself out of the crawlspace with Tseitus almost jabbing at his heels. Laszlo hovered above them and, looking up at him, Stenwold almost missed noticing the shadow of movement.

'Duck!' Stenwold cried out, and Laszlo's Fly-kinden reflexes took it from there, hurling him up so fast that he bounced from the ceiling, as a spear whistled past him. Stenwold was granted a moment's grace to regain his feet as the Fly's aerobatics caught their attackers by surprise. It was another Kerebroi man, surely Claeon's second assassin, and he had done better in terms of hired help. There was a couple of the tall, thin Dart-kinden there, with spears at the ready, and a single hulking Onychoi in full armour, foot-long claws curving from his gauntlets.

Stenwold loosed his little snapbow at the big man immediately. *Let's see how Rosander's kin stand up to Lowlander engineering*, was his only thought.

He detected the impact as a puff of dust rose from the mail, but the man barely staggered. Whatever accreted substance his shell was built from, Lowlander engineering was clearly not equal to it. Stenwold scrambled back fast as the two spearmen rushed him.

Tseitus got one of them: he sprang somewhat arthritically out from their entry hole, but Claeon's people had been warned to expect two landsmen, not three. The Ant's home-made sword pierced the lanky sea-kinden under the ribs, a flare of Ant strength driving it up to the hilt. The Ant's expression was gaunt with disbelief at where his life was taking him.

Stenwold was already rushing in, the second spearman briefly distracted, but Tseitus was abruptly disarmed by his own success as the body of his victim took his sword hilt from his hand. The Kerebroi, Claeon's man, kept shouting furious orders.

Stenwold got in past the spearhead before it could turn on him, and caught hold of the shaft with one hand, guessing that he would be stronger than the slender Dart-kinden. For a moment they fought over it, Stenwold hauling with all his weight and the other man twisting almost bonelessly, prying to loosen his grip. Laszlo darted overhead, but his attention was elsewhere. Stenwold heard the sound of grating armour and a shadow fell over him. In sudden fright he pushed where he had been pulling, releasing the spear and sending the Dart-kinden stumbling away. The Onychoi warrior was right there, gauntlet raised, but it was Tseitus who crouched before him. The Ant had just managed to free his sword, and now he swung it with all his might into the enormous armoured chest.

The force of the impact sent the weapon spinning from Tseitus's hand, leaving the artificer yelling with pain and clutching at his wrist. Even as Stenwold lunged forward, the gauntleted fist descended, punching down between the Ant's neck and shoulder with a snapping of bone, the impact driving Tseitus instantly to the floor. Laszlo buzzed helplessly about the Onychoi's helm, ignored and impotent.

Stenwold yelled something wordless, and the spear-butt struck him across the face and knocked him from his feet. He looked up, head spinning, to see the sharp end levelled down towards him. The lean, hollow-cheeked face of his enemy was without pity.

Laszlo passed by again, and the spear tip flicked up to follow him, nearly catching him despite all his agility. He flitted between the spearman and the Onychoi, weaving midway between claw and lance point. His mouth full of blood, Stenwold was half sitting up, still reeling from the blow.

Someone else was standing over him a moment later, a hand extended towards the spearman for all the world like a Wasp-kinden loosing a sting at point-blank range. Stenwold saw it then, the barb-tipped ribbon that flicked from Phylles's palm to puncture the man's skin. It was a pinprick, merely, but the effect was almost instant – the Dart-kinden began staggering and spasming, spear dropping from his hands virtually into Stenwold's own.

Another figure dashed past: *Fel?* But it was Fel in a kind of half-armour comprised of breast and back, shoulders and bracers, and a swept-back crested helm. He looked as lean as whipcord before the bulk of the Onychoi, but once he took his stance, armed only with a pair of narrow daggers and his Art-toughened fists, the huge warrior stepped back.

The spear felt smooth-hafted and alien in his hands, as Stenwold hunched his way over to Tseitus, dragging the man's body up from the swirling water. There was no hope. That single blow had descended hard enough to smash his whole body out of shape. The bluish-white face was strangely composed, the eyes staring with icy clarity at nothing at all.

There sounded two harsh cracks, and Stenwold looked up to see the Greatclaw Onychoi staggering backwards, first one heavy step and then the next. There were now crazed lines jagging their way across the breadth of his breastplate. Meanwhile, Fel was moving fast, shifting from foot to foot in a random, jerky pattern, swaying back from one swinging blow and ducking close in under another. He struck again, a blur that Stenwold barely saw. The hard shell of Fel's knuckles shattered the huge man's shoulder-guard, and stove in the chest armour entirely. Stenwold saw the folded spines flick forwards, turning the fists from bludgeons into punch-daggers.

Beyond the lurching Onychoi he saw the orchestrator of all this: Claeon's hired killer. The slender Kerebroi bran-dished a curved sword, but was backing away, realizing the cause was lost. Stenwold snarled, feeling an unaccus-tomed rush of rage within him, such as he thought he had left behind in his younger days. A moment later he was charging the man, the unfamiliar spear levelled. He heard the voices of Laszlo and Wys cry out his name, but he was having none of it. *Vengeance*, his blood howled. Vengeance for a distant, hostile academic who had never liked him much even back on land, but Tseitus had been a Master of the College and a hero of the Vekken siege, and that deserved some token act of homage.

Stenwold had never even tried to use a spear before.

He dodged past the Onychoi, narrowly avoiding being brained by one gauntleted fist. Fel did something compli-cated with daggers and his spiked fists, and a spray of fine blood dusted Stenwold as he rushed by. The expression on the Kerebroi's face was loathing, but also fear, for here was the landsman, the venomous outlander, and who knew what he was capable of?

Still, he had wits enough to sidestep the spear, and its narrow head rammed the wall, shattering to pieces, only a needle of sharp bone after all. The Kerebroi brought his sword down, the stroke faltering as though even making contact with this land-kinden would carry some kind of contagious death. Stenwold took it on the spear's shaft, which bowed under the impact but held, and then he just pushed hard, ramming the man backwards, putting all his considerable weight behind a shove that propelled the Kerebroi into the piecemeal wall.

The wall gave way. It was just a partition between one internal space and the next. No doubt its builders had never anticipated it being used as a weapon. The wall gave way, and the Kerebroi fell backwards onto a surging sea of spines.

Stenwold had a moment to witness the man's realization of his fate before a dozen quills had impaled him, some keen enough to come jutting out from his front. Then the push was coming from the other way and Stenwold cast himself aside desperately, as the Echinoi beast lurched through in a rippling tide of spikes waving like pike-heads. It filled the breadth of their narrow room, and there were Echinoi warriors following, lipless mouths snarling to bare needle teeth at them, weapons raised. Stenwold watched Phylles, who must have been almost within reach of him a moment before, scrabble to a halt and draw back swiftly. She was on the far side of the beast. They all were. He saw Laszlo gather himself as if to brave the journey across, but the monster's spines were almost scraping the ceiling, leaving no safe gap even for a Fly-kinden. 'Stay back!' Stenwold shouted to him. 'I'll find a way round.'

Then he ran. The Echinoi had spotted him, and he ran, stepping high through the swelling tide. He had no hope, just then, no hope at all. He wished only that Laszlo might go with Wys, and might find a way back to his family.

The Echinoi feet, behind him, were erratic but swift.

# Thirty-Two

Stenwold turned the next corner and found himself facing a battle. There was at least a score of Mandir's warriors in furious close conflict with a mob of Echinoi, both sides hacking at each other with single-minded loathing. He splashed and stumbled across behind them, utterly unnoticed, but there were more of the invaders hot on his trail. He had a moment to consider who his enemies were: those who would enslave him or those who would probably just kill and eat him. In the end, the closer kinship won out.

'Behind you!' he yelled at them, as his pursuers closed.

Two or three of the Greatclaw had just finished tensioning their bows, and at Stenwold's warning they turned, craning past their shoulder-guards to spot the new enemy. The explosive retort of their weapons could be heard even over the melee, a pair of Echinoi hurled from their feet on the instant, one to lie still with half its head missing, the other to twitch and hiss, while its thorned hands plucked at the bolt sunk squarely in its chest. Of the remainder, all but one turned their attention from Stenwold to face this new challenge, descending on the armoured sea-kinden as savagely as beasts but utterly silent.

That one pursuer would be enough, though. Stenwold gripped the broken spearshaft, torn between fight and flight, as the single Echinoi made a slow approach, heedless of its brethren's success or failure. Eyes that were black and featureless examined Stenwold, and perhaps the creature noted that he was different, not its kind's usual prey. Perhaps not, but its rough-skinned visage held no expressions that Stenwold could put a name to. It hefted its bronze sword, elegantly wrought into a forward curve, and went for him.

Since its failure against the Onychoi armour he had almost forgotten the little snapbow, but Totho had made the weapon with two barrels, and one might still be loaded. He brought it up even as the Echinoi closed and dragged on the trigger.

There was a muted click, no charge in the air-battery, even if a bolt was in place. Then that sinuous blade was descending on him. He caught the blow on his makeshift staff, but its impact splintered the spear-shaft almost in two, In desperation he lashed the crooked rod across the Echinoi's face, snapping the weapon entirely but barely making the sea-kinden flinch. The creature swung at him again, overcompensating still in the thin air, and he saved himself by lurching backwards, tripping in the surging waters and tumbling from his feet. The scythe-like edge of the enemy blade passed inches from him as he toppled back. He still held two feet of haft, and he lunged with it as though it was a good Lowlander shortsword, but the jagged point only skidded off the Echinoi's coppery cuirass, and then just as uselessly from its rugged skin. The sword flashed down again.

Something the colour of bone put itself in the way and the Echinoi's blade skittered from a shield of yellowing shell. An armoured form was stepping over Stenwold in one solid stride, shoving the shield in the Echinoi's face and pushing it back. Nemoctes – it was Nemoctes, come from nowhere. He held a weapon like a hook-billed pick in his hand and, as he fended off the Echinoi's next strike he drove the point into his enemy above the neckline of its armour with a grunt of effort. Keeping its sword away with his shield's edge, Nemoctes changed grip on his weapon's haft, ducked low and then put all his strength into wrenching it upwards. Even over the general row of battle, Stenwold heard the splintering of bone as the deep-buried point dragged its way free through the top of the Echinoi's ribs. Then Nemoctes had cast the injured creature away, taking its last weak swing against his greaves.

'Get up,' he snapped at Stenwold. His dark face was grim, splashed with blood.

'I have to get to Laszlo,' the Beetle told him, clambering to his feet out of the water, for what seemed the hundredth time. 'Laszlo . . . Wys . . .'

'You have to get *out*,' Nemoctes interrupted him. 'Anything else is a luxury.' The armoured sea-kinden strode ahead through the water, away from the melee, not even glancing back to see if Stenwold followed.

He followed. He had no other choice.

*If I could have got out with Laszlo and Wys*, he thought bitterly, *Laszlo said she'd take us straight to the surface, to Collegium. But where will Nemoctes take me?*

Ahead he saw movement, and fumbled to raise his piece of broken spear. There was no enemy, though, but a rolling tide of water, coursing waist-high towards him. Nemoctes just forged on into it, taking the brunt of the water with his shoulder, with Stenwold standing in his shadow, clinging to the man's arm to keep his feet. Everywhere abruptly seemed to be filling up fast, meaning the Echinoi must have cut a fresh gash in the brittle skin of the Hot Stations.

'Nemoctes!' he shouted. 'I'll drown—!'

'Just follow!' the other man snapped back at him, pushing ahead. Stenwold caught fragments of combat as they passed, glimpses snatched between one improvised piece of wall and the next: Onychoi and Echinoi locked together, tearing and clawing and chopping, shelly armour cracking, orange skin torn and hewn, all of them now chest-deep in water that swirled with their blood. There were things in

487

that water, that bumped and jostled Stenwold invisibly and, almost as much as the rising tide, he had a sudden fear of a lopped-off Echinoi hand seizing him, digging its thorns into his skin and climbing up his body towards his face. It became harder and harder to force his way ahead even with Nemoctes, shield now slung across his back, half-dragging the land-kinden in his wake. Stenwold finally let go the useless splinter of spear and fumbled for the caul, though realizing that it was good for mere minutes of breath.

*Please not a drowning death*, he kept telling himself. *The sting of a Wasp, the poison of an assassin, the steel of a treacherous Mantis, a snapbow bolt, anything but this, anything.* He would never touch the sea again, he swore, if only he was allowed back onto land. No boats, no ships, not even any long baths. *If there are any of Achaeos's old powers that can hear me, let me die a dry death!*

Something started grappling at him, and he let out a cry of panic at the thought that it might be those Echinoi hands, the writhing severed limbs come to drag him down. Then he realized that he had been stumbling forward with his eyes closed, consumed by his own fear, and it was only Nemoctes trying to wrestle the caul over his head. The water was now up to his chin.

'We're going under!' the Pelagist warned him sharply. 'Just let yourself go limp. Don't fight me and I will take you out!'

He managed to get the translucent hood over Stenwold's head and then, with one swift motion, jerked him off his feet.

Stenwold initially kicked out, but something came to him, some last kernel of self-possession, so that when Nemoctes towed at him, he folded himself into a ball, arms and legs tucked in as though he was an infant in the womb. He had only the loosest idea of what followed, feeling a sudden rush of current against him, Nemoctes holding him firm despite it. Then there were no walls about them, and the armoured man was swimming upwards with sure, powerful strokes, dragging Stenwold towards his companion, his beast, the living thing that Wys's submersible was just the empty shell of. A round, calm eye with a pinhole of a black pupil watched him pass, holding court amid a riot of pale tentacles, and then they found ingress via a pulsing hole where the thing's body met the edge of its shell, and Stenwold entered Nemoctes's domain.

It was not like the cramped space in which Gribbern had lived out his life, nor the great window on to the world that was Lyess's world. It was a house of many rooms, each one smaller than the last, and all cluttered with the memorabilia of Nemoctes's life. There were shells and skulls on the opal-white walls, and weapons and armour too, undoubtedly relics of past conquests. There were arrangements of gold and precious stones that would have beggared some Collegium magnates. There were statues and figurines, most no more than a hand's breadth high, fashioned in jade and jet, pearl and soapstone, depicting warriors and beautiful women, stern tyrants and rampant beasts. Many of these figures were so stylized that Stenwold could not recognize the kinden represented, or sometimes even the subject matter. Above all, there were racks and racks of the sea-kinden's thick paper, some pages bound into sheaves, some simply lying loosely in stacks. The unfamiliar script on them gave no suggestion as to whether they were fables or histories or collections of trade accounts.

Stenwold slowly uncurled, letting the last dregs of the sea run off him. He removed the caul from his head, knowing that he had escaped the ocean's drowning death once more, but that his luck in that respect could not last for ever.

'I have to get to land,' he got out.

'It seems that way,' came Nemoctes's voice.

Stenwold sat up to see the man untying his armour, plate by plate, setting each piece carefully aside.

'What will you do with me?' Stenwold asked him.

Nemoctes shrugged. 'Matters have become more complicated since last we spoke. The Hermatyre politics, that's one thing, but there have been . . . other developments. There is another conclave of those that bear Claeon no love, but perhaps you will be more than just a commodity.'

'Really?' Stenwold held on to no hope. 'Nemoctes . . .' it was a dangerous question, but the sights he had seen during the attack on the Hot Stations would not leave him alone, 'did you lead the Echinoi there?'

At last the Kerebroi stopped, his breastplate lifted half away. 'The Hot Stations are used to Pelagists warning them of visitors, be they Echinoi raiders or the Benthic Trains. I did not lead them there, nor could I, but I asked my people to remain silent. I am not proud, but Mandir challenged me, and all my kind, when he removed you from my protection. I felt honour bound to secure your escape, and I saw no other means.'

Stenwold nodded bleakly, wondering if he should feel the weight of all those deaths on his conscience too. In truth he had been a prisoner too long – of Claeon, of Mandir, of the sea itself – and now had had precious little sympathy to spare. *Save for Tseitus perhaps, who thought I had come to rescue him. Tseitus who would never see the sun again.* Stenwold shook his head wearily, the brutal violence of the last hour still echoing in the back of his mind. *Tseitus who deserved better.*

'The Echinoi . . .' he said slowly. 'Will they destroy the Stations? Will they *win*?' And when Nemoctes just shook his head, Stenwold pressed on, 'Then I don't understand. What was the point for them, even? They died. I saw them killed, and they didn't even seem to care.'

'You saw precious few die, I'd say,' Nemoctes told him. He had taken up a decanter of silver, wrought into the perfect shape of a conch, and now poured Stenwold a measure into a cup like an eggshell.

Stenwold took the drink gingerly. 'I saw them die, hacked to pieces.' The liquid was fierce and bracing, a like strong fortified wine.

'Hacked and dead are different things.' His armour gone, Nemoctes eased himself down to the floor, his back against the curving wall. He looked a lot older, then, than Stenwold had assumed, for the mail had lent him a tenuous strength. 'They do not feel pain like us. They do not bleed like us.' He gave Stenwold a level glance. 'Like us people of the sea, anyway. I cannot vouch for your kind, but I'd wager you're more like us than like the Echinoi. They have become lost in their Art, grown too much like their creatures. For them, wounds that would kill a man three times over will seal up within their flesh, and they can lose arms, legs, who knows what else, and grow back what was lost. Some even say that their limbs, severed from them, grow entire new bodies. Some say raids like these are how they get more Echinoi, that they have grown so far away from us that they have no children amongst them at all. Certainly they live wholly without air, and there is not a Pelagist, even, who can claim to have seen any but the full-grown monsters you met. They are our plague, and I feel sick that I may have aided them in any way.' He drained his cup, tilted his head up to gaze at the arched ceiling. The sense of movement was distant, and Stenwold had to concentrate hard to feel the beast that carried them coursing smoothly through the waters. They might almost be in some scholar's windowless study, or some magnate's private room.

'You'll be returning to your land soon,' Nemoctes told him, still staring upwards.

Stenwold was suddenly alert, feeling hope clutch at him with thin fingers. 'You know . . . ?'

'Things have changed,' the sea-kinden told him, 'as you'll see. Wys wants you returned, I know, and so do I and mine, and now I think Heiracles will find his wishes of less importance than before. Tell me, would you try to find the heir, if you could?'

It was a subject that Stenwold had given much thought to, as he scribed and sketched for Mandir. If he were free, if that mad dream ever came to pass, would he not rather blot the sea-kinden from his mind, like a nightmare? Surely he would not spend a precious minute beneath the sky in seeking to help them.

'Yes,' he said, without hesitation, drawing Nemoctes's questioning gaze.

'Even if you had escaped with Wys, and been taken straight home without these interruptions?' the sea-kinden probed, his wry smile showing that he knew full well what the plan had been.

'Even then,' Stenwold told him. 'I have my reasons.'

'Of that I have no doubt.' Nemoctes nodded slowly. 'It will be a while of travelling, to reach our outpost – a place at the edge of Hermatyre's domain, where Heiracles has supporters but Claeon, I hope, has none. A place near the cliffs that rise towards your land. You'll need some sleep, between now and then.'

After he had slept, tired enough by then to drown any dreams that hovered, and after the horror of the Echinoi was far enough behind them, Stenwold asked about Lyess.

Nemoctes grunted as soon as the name was uttered. He was sitting cross-legged at the broadest end of his suite of chambers, presumably in communication with the creature that was carrying them. 'I know less than you think,' was all he said.

'Has she . . . there must have been others . . . ?'

'That she has travelled with? Not that I've known, and I've known her for a good many moons. She owes me no great favours. Why she broke her lifelong rule, I cannot say.' Nemoctes sighed. 'She . . .'

'Yes?'

'She asked after you, when you were in the Stations. She has been . . . distracted. Not seeming herself. As if I were any judge of what her "self" should be like.'

A hundred questions warred in Stenwold's mouth, but he let none of them out. Somewhere out there, surely not far in terms of how the Pelagists measured their vastly travelled lives, floated her glowing garden and the impossible glory that was her companion.

Waiting for him? Somehow he was sure of it. The thought set his pulse racing, but mostly in fear of what he did not understand. *Why do I care? I do not care. The lonely, alien woman has a claim on my sympathy, no more. So what is this? What is this . . . ?*

The place Nemoctes ferried him to was like Hermatyre writ small. Somehow some Archetoi builders had picked this barren knoll on the sea floor as their project, and now the twisted spires of a new colony had formed, a solitary hall compared to Hermatyre's sprawling city.

The Archetoi were much in evidence inside, passing on their wordless errands, their eyes not deigning to follow or acknowledge their visitors. They were pallid little men and women, their skins tattooed with intricate, accreated patterns, going about their business in a world that barely admitted the existence of the rest of humanity.

They ran into Wys's crew first, just as recently arrived. She gave Stenwold a slightly exasperated look: here was a man who could have been home by now, had he jumped left instead of right. Laszlo had a grin for him, though, albeit a strained one. He was looking pale as a sea-kinden himself by now, and gaunt with it. Stenwold remembered Mandir saying how landsmen never lasted long in the Stations. *We are not meant to be here, and our bodies know it. The gloom, even the air, it is all a slow poison to us.*

'What's this in aid of?' Wys demanded of Nemoctes,

who was clad in his mail once more. 'More Kerebroi games?' Phylles and Fel squared off behind her, their belligerence dominating her small stature.

'For once the games have grown too large for anybody to control,' Nemoctes told her. 'Not Claeon nor Heiracles nor I.' He led the way through to the vaulted, cavernous, empty heart of the new colony. The ceiling was heavy with projecting stalactites and fins that would in time become the pillars and walls of the structure's internal architecture, but for now all that the Archetoi had constructed was a shell. Beneath that arching space two groups stood with a distinct distance between them. One was a rabble of Kerebroi, Heiracles at their head and Paladyra in their midst like a valuable hostage. And the other . . .

Laszlo, with better eyes, gave out a whoop so fierce that Stenwold at first took it for a war cry. Then the Fly was airborne, taking one great leap before descending upon an equally small figure there, clutching her in his arms and laughing madly. Only after she had fought him off did Stenwold recognize her.

'Hammer and tongs,' he said hoarsely, 'it's Despard.' He stumbled forward a few steps, staring at the engineer of the *Tidenfree* as she tried to extricate herself from Laszlo's embrace. Then Stenwold noticed the other two.

Slouching at the back, looking like a man wholly out of his depth in more ways than one, was a lean Beetle youth that Stenwold identified as Maxel Gainer, Tseitus's former apprentice and the builder of the *Tseitan*, which went at least partway towards explaining how he and Despard happened to be here. Their choice of travelling companion, however, was an unexpected one.

She stood in her scale cuirass, in her gold armlets and silver headband, as arrogantly poised as she had been in the College, as she had been aboard *Isseleema's Floating Game*. It was Kratia of Tsen, whose last encounter with young

Master Gainer had nearly been a murderous one. Stenwold approached her falteringly, frowning.

'I give up,' he said, stopping a few paces away from her. 'I just don't understand. Why are you here?'

'Don't thank *her!*' Despard snapped, at his elbow. 'You want to thank anyone, thank us. When we heard that you'd gone under, someone just happened to remember what you said that time when you were asking about the Tseni and their underwater boats. Only they didn't think to bring one with them, so we had to take your lad there's, instead.' She gave Laszlo a push, sending him tottering away, but there were tears glinting at the corners of her eyes. 'We didn't believe you were dead. Not after what she said. We had to look.'

'"What she said"?' Stenwold repeated. 'What did "she" say, Kratia?' He glanced back at Heiracles. 'How are you even free? I'm not overly impressed by sea-kinden hospitality so far, begging your pardons, Master Nemoctes and Mistress Wys.'

Kratia gave him a level look and took out a damp-looking scroll from her belt. It was a moment before Stenwold realized what was wrong with the sight: it was the pulpy sea-kinden paper in the hands of a landswoman. The script on it, surrounded and framed by many-coloured arabesques, remained illegible to him.

'My people had their war with the sea long ago. We have not forgotten, for all that we might like to. This names me ambassador of Tsen to the peoples of Grande Atoll and the greater seas,' Kratia declared simply.

'Lucky you had it with you,' Stenwold told her hollowly.

'War Master, if you had known what lay beneath, would you have set foot on a ship, any ship, without such credentials?'

He shivered. 'Point taken.' Behind him he heard some of Heiracles's people start to shift, and he turned to them, feeling all the might of the Lowlands and beyond arrayed in just those four figures behind him. He had been a prisoner, a fugitive, a slave for a long time. His entire life as he had known it – as an Assembler, a War Master, a spymaster – had been taken from him like a stolen robe. Now he felt it across his shoulders once again, and he almost wept for it: to have power, even a little power, over his own destiny once more.

'So, what now?' he asked them. 'Heiracles, Nemoctes, what now? We are not so ignorant, it would appear. Or at least there are those on land who are far less ignorant than me. There will be others back on land with an interest, too. Despard and Laszlo have a large family. What now?'

Nemoctes was smiling, but the careful immobility of Heiracles's face showed that he had been outmanoeuvred.

'Have you forgotten Rosander?' he hissed, 'and Claeon's invasion? Do you really think your people are *safe*, now? Claeon will care nothing for that document, or the distant frown of Grande Atoll. That place is no more than a name to us.'

'I have forgotten nothing,' Stenwold replied. 'My people are in more danger than you know. We land-kinden are quite capable of making our own lives difficult enough. But we go home, we go to the land. If my home was in flames and soldiers were waiting to put me on crossed pikes, we would go home nonetheless.' The words caused him a stab of pain, the thought of Lyess never to be seen again, never to be touched. For a moment her presence seemed so strong that the soft light of her companion's silver-clear flesh seemed to shine on them like the moon. *No*, he told himself, clinging to what he knew, what he believed in. 'No, we go home.' He looked up, managing a small smile for Nemoctes's benefit. 'Now let us talk about Aradocles.'

There followed perfect silence. Stenwold looked from face to face, amongst Hieracles's delegation, and for a moment he could not find her, and his heart lurched with sudden fear. Then at last he found her, in the shadow of the others. Her eyes drew him to her. She was the only one of Heiracles's people whose expression had not grown hooded at the name of the heir.

'Mistress Paladrya.' The small, brave smile she managed for him provided a calming reassurance out of all proportion, focusing his mind and banishing distraction. 'You took your boy Aradocles to the land, to be out of Claeon's reach. Having met with the Edmir's assassins in the Hot Stations, I now appreciate your caution. I know what the land means to your various kinden. I know also, from Mandir himself, that there are exceptions. You had reason to believe the boy would stand more chance of survival in the sun and air than anywhere beneath the waves.'

From behind Heiracles's shoulder and penned in by the man's servants, she nodded. Her gaze was fixed on Stenwold with a look of absolute intensity.

Stenwold took a step forward, and he felt and heard the other landsmen shift behind him, moving slightly too, as if backing him. *They are not Tisamon but it is good to have friends.* 'Will you come to the land now, to see if he can be found and returned to his people?' he asked her boldly, as though her captors were not there.

'Yes,' she said, simply.

'This is not acceptable,' Heiracles snapped. 'The people of Hermatyre are . . . changeable. I must have something to win them over with, if we are to oust Claeon. This woman is notorious—'

'As the killer of the young Edmir,' Stenwold finished for him. 'I recall it. However, she did not kill him, and he may not be dead. I have witnessed enough to know that the true heir would rally your people far more effectively than any show trial.' He glanced at Nemoctes, then at Wys and her people. Heiracles had brought eight flunkies with him, armed with the sea-kinden's curved knives, so Stenwold weighed numbers and the will to fight, wondering who could be relied on to take a side. 'If Aradocles himself were here, you would support him, would you not, Heiracles?' he asked, in tones dripping with reason.

He saw the battle on the man's lean face, revealing the bitter ambition that the true heir's long absence had fostered. Clearly he had lived the last five years believing the lad dead, and therefore himself the next in line if only Claeon could be removed. Paladrya and her evidence had clearly been not been welcome. *Just as well he wanted her for the people to tear apart, or she would surely be dead already*, Stenwold considered.

'Heiracles,' came Paladrya's soft voice.

His head jerked towards her, while still keeping the landkinden in view. 'You have no voice in this,' he cautioned her.

'You cannot keep the landsmen here, not now. If you tried to do so by force, not only would you fail, but you would show yourself no better than Claeon.'

A brief fragment of expression appeared on Heiracles's face, before he stifled it, but yet it spoke eloquently. He was a man with few illusions, and a great cynicism about others that he assumed was shared by others about him. The idea that anyone might seriously believe that there was any difference between Heiracles's base nature and that of Claeon was obviously a new concept to him. Seeing that bitterness there, so briefly unveiled, Stenwold understood that such a difference did indeed exist, for all that it was whittled down moment to moment by the promise of power.

Paladrya took a deep breath. 'I believe Aradocles is alive, because I cannot bear to believe anything else,' she continued. 'If so, he will return eventually. His heritage will compel him. Perhaps he will indeed bring a landsman army to retake his birthright. Perhaps he will have grown hard, toughened by the hostile land, so that even Rosander will fear him. Who can say what his exile will have made of him? But he will remember me, Heiracles. If he lives, however far he is grown from the boy I knew, I cannot but think that he will remember me. That being so, would you rather he returned to lead his friends against Claeon, to reclaim his throne and reward those who have been loyal to him, or would you prefer he returned later to confront whoever might have unseated his uncle, and whoever might have had his old tutor executed? What will you say to him then? And do you think you will ever sway the people's love so greatly that you shall be safe from its retribution? You are not Claeon. Do not fashion yourself in his image.'

And Stenwold, the veteran of a hundred speeches, found himself wishing to applaud her. Even surrounded by her jailers, she was one of the most impassioned advocates he had ever heard. *The young prince had a fine tutor*, he thought, *and if Heiracles does not agree, then I will take her from him and free her. I will go so far, before I leave the sea, however much I loathe it.*

He felt something tear asunder within him, at that silent vow, the great weight of the ocean pressing down, eager to keep him to itself, and something else perhaps, some stab of anger and loss that was not in any way his own.

'If the heir returned,' Heiracles pronounced carefully, 'he would know me as his most faithful subject.' Everything had drained from his expression but the pragmatism. Chief adviser to a young ruler was not such a poor position, that look said. The ambitions for kingship had sunk without so much as a ripple, and he had recovered his statesman's poise with an ease that would do justice to either a Collegiate Assembler or a Spiderlands Aristos.

Stenwold's relief at the man's response was disproportionate. 'Then I shall need Paladrya,' he declared.

'Of course.' Heiracles moved aside with grace, and the woman stepped tentatively free, moving with steps as halting as an automaton to Stenwold's side, as though she feared being called back at any moment. He put a hand out towards her as she reached him, and she took it gladly, anchoring herself to his party.

'Nemoctes, for the assistance of your people, I thank you,' Stenwold said formally. As he thought of leaving here, of returning home, he felt not clear joy, but a muddied, unsettled sense of displacement. *But that is what I want. What could hold me here, and yet . . .* 'I intend to return,' was all he said, and the Pelagist nodded, frowning at him.

'I shall see you to your land. Perhaps there shall be others also, who will guard your journey.'

Stenwold felt something kick inside him, some irrational surge of emotion, misplaced and out of character. *Stay.* He fought it down. *I cannot . . . I have work to do.*

'How can we know that you'll find the boy?' Heiracles demanded, seeing Stenwold about to leave with his prized hostage.

'Because your own agents shall come with me, if they're willing,' Stenwold replied.

'What agents?' the Kerebroi demanded. His followers became abruptly restless behind him at the mere thought of a land voyage.

Stenwold glanced towards Laszlo, who nodded back, grinning.

'Mistress Wys,' the Beetle said, 'do you dare come with me – you and your fellows?' He watched the question sink in. Phylles's scowl deepened, Fel was blankly hostile as usual, but Wys's face showed every stage of a progression from surprise to fear, to rising eagerness.

'To the shore, land-kinden?' she said. 'To bring back the true Edmir? Sounds like the sort of job that reputations are built on, does it not?'

'You are mad,' Heiracles told her flatly. 'Mad or a Littoralist,' which latter was clearly worse.

'Neither, in fact, but you'll have heard how we Small-claws are always on the lookout for the next new thing,' she told him levelly. 'Now, you'll retain me as your agent?'

'If you're insane enough to go, woman, then go with my blessing,' Heiracles said acidly.

'So go now,' Nemoctes echoed, his resonant voice breaking in. 'I do not like to think how long Claeon's agents will take to track down this meeting, as they did the last.' His eyes met Stenwold's. 'Good luck, landsman.'

'Your lad can come with us,' Wys suggested.

'This one's going nowhere but in the *Tseitan*,' Despard declared firmly, glaring at the Smallclaw woman and holding fiercely on to Laszlo's arm.

The other Fly was already shaking his head. 'No, you take Master Maker,' he told her. 'I trust Wys, here.' He winked. 'We have *business*.'

Despard stared at him as though he had lost his mind. 'And if I have to tell Tomasso that I lost his nephew to *business*?' she demanded.

'Then he'll understand,' Laszlo pointed out.

'Nemoctes is right,' Stenwold told them all. 'Let's go now while the tide is good.'

# Thirty-Three

The interior of the *Tseitan* had been meant to carry two passengers without luxury. With four inside it was low and cramped and stifling, even though one of them was a Fly-kinden. Still, Stenwold's heart soared as they put out from the little colony's dock. It was not just that they were going home to the light and the sky, but the sculling of the *Tseitan*'s swimming limbs, rowing the machine through the water with swift, sure strokes, produced a rhythm that felt more natural by far than the fluid jettings of Wys's machine or the eerie glide of Nemoctes's beast. This was good Collegium engineering.

*And you can see where you're going, too.* It had been so strange to be conveyed by Gribbern in a windowless space within the flesh of a sea-monster. Even Nemoctes's chambers had been like an ornamented coffin. True, it was dark down here, where the sun could not reach, but the limn-lights of the colony shed a pale-blue radiance on their departure. Stenwold saw Wys's submersible bobbing and wavering in the water before the clockwork and the pumps got under way and it surged off, impossibly buoyant, into the dark.

'How did you even make contact,' Stenwold asked, as the *Tseitan* pursued it, 'let alone find where I would be?' His body felt strange, as though being twisted by degrees in an invisible grip. The sea-kinden had warned him, though: it was their 'equalization' being reversed, some other piece of business that all the land-kinden had apparently had to go through, to reach the sea bed.

'As for finding you, we had to rely on them to bring you to us,' came Kratia's clear tones. 'I had planned to invoke the office of an envoy, but these sea-kinden of yours seem an uncivil band of rogues. The people of Grande Atoll possess some manners, at least. The local politics have played into our hands, though, I see, or we'd never have got you back.'

'In a way,' Stenwold admitted. 'Or perhaps it is better to say that we have caught them at their worst, under the hand of a tyrant. They might have been smoother-mannered under their previous ruler, and I hope they will be so under the next.'

'You intend to restore this heir to them?' she asked him.

'If he still lives to be restored.' The possibility that Aradocles would be years dead, slain by the terrors of the land the moment he parted from Paladrya, had been the universal thought that nobody had voiced. *Still, I will be on land and free, and that is surely the greater reward of any bargain I could strike with them. I owe the people of the sea precious little. I have my own worries, after all. I wonder what has gone awry in Collegium, that needed my hand to steady it.* And on that thought: 'You have kept this from the Vekken, I would guess. They would not understand.'

There was no immediate answer, so he craned round to catch her expression. The interior of the *Tseitan* boasted only one dim lantern, but it was easy to pick out the amusement on her pale face.

'Tell me,' he prompted.

'We come here with the Vekken's blessing,' she told him.

Stenwold spluttered over that, and from beside him, Maxel Gainer piped up, 'It's true, Master Maker. There's been all kinds of deals being made concerning your disappearance. They've set up Master Tseitus as a hero, and your man, Master Drillen, has done up some treaty or other over the *Tseitan*, so we're allowed to build more, and they had her and one of the Vekken ambassadors signing something, and then the two of them came to me, with that Fly girl in tow, and said we had to go hunt for you.'

'"That Fly girl" was the start of all of this,' Despard said acidly. 'Without me you'd none of you be here, and don't you forget it.'

'You see, Master Maker, you made your point effectively, to us, and also to Vek. Collegium is rich in ways that we are not, and anyone who turned down such riches would lose place to those that did not. If either Vek or Tsen turned its back on Collegiate trade, then the other would triumph, sooner or later. It's easy to see how Sarn was won over, those years ago. I think that, could we ensure it, either of us would rather have your city sink beneath the sea for ever, but as the best of Vek has failed to destroy you, and as we have no ready means to do it, the only remaining choice is to accept your crooked bargain. So, Collegium is rich, but it's easy to see that the only way that either of our cities get a fair bargain from your people is through you, Maker. We trust you, whereas your fellows would swindle and cheat us. It was a very strange day when I looked into the face of a man of Vek and needed no Art to know that he and I were thinking the same thoughts.'

Stenwold sat back, unexpectedly sobered by the cold logic of it. 'Perhaps, in time, your people shall see this as less of a poisoned chalice, Mistress Kratia,' he murmured. 'The Sarnesh, at least, have voiced no regrets.'

'Because your people have tamed them like pets,' she replied, contemptuously.

Stenwold shrugged, feeling too weary with the whole business to answer. *At least we have them, for now, and Vek also. Two years' hard diplomacy have borne fruit at long last. Strange how the solution to the Vekken problem turned out to involve more Ants, not fewer.*

'Master Maker,' said Gainer from beside him. 'More friends of yours?'

'Hmm?' Stenwold peered ahead. The darkness of the waters seemed near-total to him, now, and he saw only the lights of Wys's barque ahead.

'Another craft just passed between us and them, or something did,' Gainer informed him.

'Probably Nemoctes,' Stenwold decided. 'He's supposed to be somewhere about . . .'

Even as he said it, a shape flashed across their view, pale against the black. It was slim and streamlined, with streamers of tentacles billowing behind it, and there was a brief glimpse of a slender rider couching a lance, leaning forward right above the beast's huge round eye.

It was gone at once, leaving Stenwold with a moment of confusion: *Heiracles or Claeon?* 'Get closer to Wys,' he ordered. His instincts said trouble, sure enough. He could only hope that Wys knew better what was going on.

The dark water was suddenly full of movement. The Dart-kinden riders came sleeting from the abyss all around them, slicing into momentary sight as the lamplight of the *Tseitan*'s ports caught them, before wheeling and vanishing in close formation. He spotted them again, as shadows against the glare of the other submersible, saw them break aside every which way without striking, flurrying back into the dark. It was an attack, beyond question, but one that some trick contrived by Wys had turned aside.

'They've found us,' Stenwold said, feeling a cold hand clench inside him. *So close, so close. Surely they cannot drag me back now.* He felt bitterly the lack of any way of speaking to Wys. Right now, the Pelagists' Far-speech Art would have been invaluable.

The riders were soon back. One made a run straight towards the *Tseitan*'s nose, but turned aside at the very last minute, close enough, as she hauled her beast off, that they could see her narrow, wide-eyed face clearly. Stenwold guessed that the alien nature of the Collegium submersible must be giving them pause, but such hesitation would last only so long. They were getting close to Wys's barque now, Gainer steering the *Tseitan* until they could even distinguish figures within the ornate window set in the vessel's bows. The small figure of Wys was signalling to them, pointing at something, making urgent, exaggerated gestures.

Something pale and shapeless passed in a flurry beyond the far side of Wys's submersible, lit momentarily by the vessel's limn-lights. Stenwold had a brief glimpse of the bar-shaped pupil of a great mottled eye, an eye he had seen before.

'Arkeuthys,' he murmured. The agent of his capture had returned to prevent his escape.

Then the *Tseitan* jerked and shuddered, resounding under the crack of an impact. 'Are we shot?' Despard demanded, eyes wide.

Gainer was wrestling with the controls, trying to keep the vehicle on a level course. A moment later there was a second knock, throwing them to one side, and Stenwold understood: the Dart-kinden were lancing towards them, making swift dives and then breaking their spears against the *Tseitan*'s shell.

'Gainer, what's the hull made of?' he demanded.

Their pilot bared his teeth. 'Magnaferrite over pumice-steel,' he snarled out, all of which material was after Stenwold's day, as far as artificing went.

'That's strong? They're sticking spears into us.'

'Spears?' Gainer let out a strained laugh. 'Let them jab at the body all they want, just please let them steer clear of the *legs*.'

The thought sent a chill through Stenwold. Damage a few of the *Tseitan*'s six paddles and the ship would become helpless prey for Arkeuthys, or it would drift and sink, becoming nothing but an elaborate tomb.

'Gain height,' he suggested. 'They may not like the sun.'

'It's nighttime,' Despard interrupted, and Stenwold blinked in genuine surprise. It had been a long time since he had needed to know.

Another impact came, sounding from right beside the portholes and sending them lurching downwards for a moment, before Gainer could correct them. 'No worries about the glass,' the artificer said, without having to be asked. 'Thick enough that a snapbow couldn't break it, and I know that 'cos I tested it with one.'

They had a mad, wheeling view of Wys's barque, almost on its side but making steady progress, dancing through the water with its pumps rippling in a blur. The Dart-kinden cavalry were pale streamered arrows dashing past it, always breaking away just before striking, their mounts bucking angrily.

Their world, their view, was suddenly blotted from sight. The coiled ridges of a shell surged in front of them, and Gainer cried out and hauled at the sticks to steer them away. They were nearly upside down as they wheeled past the monster's head, itself almost the size of their vessel, with a squid trapped and thrashing within the beast's net of slender arms. Then the giant creature had coursed away, slipping backwards and downwards through the water, and dragging its prey with it.

'What . . . what was that?' Despard squeaked.

'Nemoctes,' Stenwold told her, 'and be glad he's ours.' *And let's hope he's already put the call out to any other Pelagists in the area, because we need all the help we can get.*

Another dart flashed past their ports, its rider yanking it around even as it passed, too close for a spear charge.

'Pull away!' Stenwold said automatically, but Gainer pulled the wrong way, and something heavy and soft impacted with them: the rider's mount itself.

Abruptly they were diving, dragged initially by the creature's weight, then by its own efforts as it tugged at them. There was a hideous screeching, scratching sound from all about them, like nails on glass, as the creature's tentacles took hold. Two or three unrolled across the viewports, their undersides lined not with suckers but with barbed hooks, like little claws, that scratched white lines down the glass as they writhed for purchase. Somewhere around the middle of the ship, above them, came a hollow boom, and then the sound of something strong and savage scoring and gnawing at the metal.

'What are you waiting for?' Despard yelled at Gainer.

'I'm done! It's ready!' he shouted back. 'Arms in, everyone, arms in!'

'What?' Stenwold goggled at him.

'Don't touch the walls, Master Maker!'

Stenwold pulled his elbows in, still insisting he be told what was going on, and then Gainer hollered, 'Now!' Despard, behind them, slammed down the lever she had been poised beside, and for a second every inch of the *Tseitan*'s interior was lit by an uncompromising white radiance.

Stenwold cried out, sure that something had exploded inside the engine. His eyes momentarily blazed with reversed images, then he saw, through the ports, that the tentacles were gone, A moment later a long, bleached form could be seen drifting away, down and away, its tentacles a peeled-back mess, with a separate, smaller body falling beside it.

'What just happened?' he asked, almost reverently, as Gainer dragged them up out of their dive.

'It's a kind of side effect of the engine, which we discovered when we built her,' the pilot said, almost cheerily. 'The engine has a lot of magnets in her, so if you're not careful, you can build up quite a charge differential between the nose and the tail. One of Master Tseitus's apprentices was almost killed, you know, when we discovered that from the original.'

'Are you telling me that . . . ?'

'For a bit of a second the hull was working like a lightning engine,' Gainer confirmed. 'It's a design flaw, but I reckoned it might come in useful some day.'

'Master Tseitus would be proud of you,' Stenwold said. It probably wasn't true, as Tseitus had reserved his pride for his personal consumption. Still, the lad deserved it, and Tseitus deserved to be remembered fondly. The old man's antisocial and cantankerous side could be lost to history.

'I hope so,' Gainer said, and then exclaimed, 'Hammer and tongs, what's that?'

They were in sight of Wys's ship again, but something was dreadfully wrong. For a moment Stenwold thought it had somehow become malformed, but then he realized the truth, and his heart lurched. Curled about the contours of the submersible were the many arms of Arkeuthys. The great octopus held the ship helpless in its grip, and no doubt that great shearing beak was already trying to crack its way in to reach the morsels inside.

'That's . . .' Stenwold ran out of words.

'That looks mighty like what got you into all this in the first place,' Despard filled in for him. 'I got one quick look at it, up top. Didn't want another, to be honest.'

'Do we need them?' Kratia asked coolly.

'Yes!' Stenwold roared at her, and Despard snapped 'Laszlo's in there!' little fists bunched as though she was going to attack the Ant there and then.

'Ram it,' Stenwold suggested. 'Can we ram it?'

'Be like a flea up against that thing,' Gainer said, but his expression was solid determination. 'But we've been saving a little something, haven't we?' He had already set a course towards the stricken submersible.

'Are you telling me this ship's armed?' Stenwold asked him. 'Did we authorize that, back at the College?'

'Master Maker, you were grabbed by an arse-bastarding *sea monster*,' Despard reminded him. 'You think we'd come out here without *something*?'

Their view of the leviathan and the submersible wheeled and circled as Gainer fought to keep the *Tseitan* on a straight course. 'Just like a snapbow,' the pilot murmured between clenched teeth. 'Like a real *big* snapbow with a point on it that you wouldn't believe.'

'Don't hole their ship, then,' Stenwold cautioned. 'Why are we twisting around so much?'

Gainer was backing the *Tseitan* now, the paddles reversing their sweep, then pushing forward again, jockeying the vessel in the water as more Dart-kinden flashed past. 'To aim the bolt,' the Beetle youth explained, 'have to aim the whole ship.'

The piercing eye of Arkeuthys was staring straight at them, as Gainer tugged and cajoled the *Tseitan* into line. Stenwold gazed at it, seeing, in that orb bigger than his own body, the creature's icy concentration – even as its many arms twined and snaked for better purchase, over the shell of Wys's submersible.

'You're there now,' Despard insisted. 'Right there. Just shoot the cursed thing!'

Gainer made a noncommittal grunt, but he was reaching up for a lever above his head. Stenwold glanced back, seeing the Fly's agony of worry for Laszlo, as against Kratia's bland indifference.

Gainer made a tiny adjustment to their heading with his off hand. Stenwold, peering ahead again, saw the enormous eye narrow, and abruptly Arkeuthys had abandoned its victim, casting the submersible end over end, away from it. Somehow it had guessed what even the human sea-kinden had not: the threat that the land-kinden could muster at range.

Gainer shouted 'No!' and hauled down on the lever. The *Tseitan* bucked with the force as a silvery missile flashed in the dim light, leaping like a living thing towards the retreating octopus.

It struck. It must have struck. Suddenly the sea was

boiling black. *Blood!* Stenwold thought at first, but it was ink, of course. First to emerge from that angry cloud was Wys's ship, canted to one side but with its siphons pulsing constantly, limping through the water but still intact. A stream of gleaming bubbles from its side looked like little enough, and Stenwold knew that Wys would have all hands to the pumps to keep the seawater where it belonged.

Then, behind it, Arkeuthys broke from its own screen of ink like a many-armed and angry god, its flowing form vast and all-encompassing. One tentacle was wrapped about the shaft of Gainer's bolt, which it must have hauled out from its flesh, from wherever it had struck.

'Time for your second shot,' Stenwold said tensely.

'There is no second shot,' Gainer stated.

'I don't suppose that *you* have any suggestions, from your city's long experience?' Stenwold put to Kratia.

'Don't start sea wars with the sea-kinden.' She seemed utterly composed, hands clasped on her knees, resigned to their collective fate.

For a time, an unknown time, they all hung there: the *Tseitan* seemingly motionless despite Maxel Gainer back-paddling as fast as he could, Wys's injured submersible, and the great dark-flushed tangle of Arkeuthys looking like some indecipherable glyph in a lost language.

Then the great octopus was retreating, rippling and rolling backwards, away from them, and there was light, a pale, pure light all around.

*I am here.*

Stenwold jumped and stared at the others, looking for some evidence of those words in their faces. *I cannot have heard that. I cannot . . . there is no way.*

As the first streamers of glittering lace brushed past the carapace of the *Tseitan*, he heard Kratia – Kratia of all of them – utter an oath almost reverently. Then Lyess's lambent, pulsing companion dragged a stinging curtain between them and the roiling form of Arkeuthys.

Stenwold assumed the monster would flee, as it had done after the death of Gribbern, but this time the octopus just hung there in the water, glaring balefully as the last shreds of its ink cleared. Wys's barque remained stationary too, its lamps still blazing brightly, while Stenwold thought he saw a moving shadow at the fading perimeter of the light that was Nemoctes's home turning restlessly in the water.

*If we move from her shadow, we expose ourselves,* Stenwold thought. *Unless* . . . He wondered just how far Arkeuthys's understanding went. How human was its mind, of what breadth of vision?

Then the great sea monster was on the move, surging and rippling its way up through the water. Instantly Lyess's glowing companion began ascending, as slow and graceful as an airship lifting off. Arkeuthys was close, moving faster, hovering immediately above. Stenwold saw Lyess's light flash on something bright.

The octopus struck almost gingerly, extending to the very limit of its reach so as to be sure that none of that stinging veil so much as touched it. The tentacles were no longer simply lashing whips: gripped in one of them was the *Tseitan*'s harpoon, while another held a Dart-kinden lance. Stenwold saw them dig in, carve through the soft flesh of Lyess's companion, hesitant jabs and slices as the octopus manhandled the unfamiliar implements. He remembered the Menfish, how they had struck and struck from above, aiming at the jellyfish's blind spot.

'Gainer, bring us up, point us at the monster,' he ordered. 'Bring us so we're looking to pin it between us and her.'

'Us and . . . ?' Gainer began to ask, but Stenwold snapped at him, 'Just bring us up!' The pilot quickly tugged at the sticks, sending the *Tseitan* climbing up the ladder of lights that formed Lyess's long train.

The jellyfish was already shuddering. Arkeuthys could not risk getting close enough for a decisive strike, but it was gaining in dexterity, carving its way in minute portions towards the woman hiding within. Stenwold gritted his teeth, keeping his eyes fixed on the carnage. *We are ascending too slowly.* He stared into the gleaming flesh of the quivering creature, hoping to catch a glimpse of Lyess.

Then a blunt, heavy shape jetted swiftly across the flailing, translucent bell. There was no art to Nemoctes's attack. His creature was no match for Arkeuthys. Still, it was large, and it was armoured, and he directed it straight at the octopus with all the speed its siphon could give it. Arkeuthys recoiled, attack momentarily forgotten. Arms lashed out, briefly wrapping about the ridged, coiled shell, and then casting Nemoctes aside with a single muscular convulsion, sending the ponderous creature end over end away from them, no doubt making a chaos of all Nemoctes's carefully hoarded history.

Then the octopus returned to its task, but now found the *Tseitan* waiting for it.

'Master Maker, there's nothing!' Gainer was saying. 'No second bolt, and we've not the charge for another magnetic shock.'

'Aim us, level us at it like a crossbow,' Stenwold insisted. 'Just as if we had another harpoon to take it between the eyes. Get us as steady as you can.'

'That makes us an easy target,' Kratia warned.

'Do you think it would have any difficulty snatching us from the water when it decides to?' Stenwold asked her.

'That is true.'

The narrowed eye of Arkeuthys bored into them, its twin scalpels poised at arms' ends. Gainer fidgeted and twitched at the controls, until they were absolutely centred on that alien gaze.

With a spasm of rage that seemed all too human, the octopus was abruptly streaming away in, a flurry of tentacles. Then it was gone, lost to the black abyss.

Stenwold settled back, feeling a great wave of relief wash

over him. He could not tell if it was for himself, his return to the land now secured, or if it was because Lyess and her companion still lived.

'Let's go home,' he said softly. 'Only home.'

And in the depths of his mind he heard her soft voice. *You shall come back to me, come back to me, some day.*

# Part Three

# Footprints in the Sand

# Thirty-Four

Using compass and clock and all the tricks that the *Tidenfree* crew had perfected over the years, Despard guided them home. After they had passed the reach of the Shelf, which the sea-kinden had called the Edge, they led rather than followed, with Gainer steering the *Tseitan* in slow, paddling circles from time to time to check that the bobbing shell of Wys's submersible was still behind them. The journey was long, and they had come to the surface several times to take in fresh air, the *Tseitan* lying like a basking thing in the swelling water, whilst the other vessel listed alarmingly beside it, never intended to be brought up to the air. Still, Wys's crew was able to provide food and freshly accreted water, for the *Tseitan* had little room for provisions, what with Stenwold's bulk added to its complement.

At last, though, they came up in sight not only of land but of the city itself: a flare of white stone against a dusk-darkened coast. Gainer guided them in on the wrong side of the sea-wall, where those intent on underhand business moored under the deflected and well-remunerated eyes of the port authorities. The waves were high, though, so no other ship had dared the mooring that night. There were therefore no witnesses as the *Tseitan* rose to the surface, and none to see the rounded bulk of a much larger vessel break the water beside it.

Despard ascended, clutching a rope ladder, which burden

her wings just sufficed to take to the top of the wall. There she secured it and let it down with a flourish. It had been agreed that Gainer would shortly take the *Tseitan* back to its College docks, but for now, Stenwold did not want every scholar and Master to hear of his return, if for nothing else than to avoid the interminable round of questions that his reappearance would spark off. Gainer would therefore keep quiet while, in the meantime, Stenwold would slip into his own city. That was the plan.

Stenwold ascended the rope ladder with more ease than he had descended it all that time ago, when stepping on to the deck of *Isseleema's Floating Game*. Kratia followed him up, with more ease still. As he hauled himself over the top of the wall he saw that the sky was fast greying into twilight: not a glorious red butcher's sunset, not a fiery evening to send comfort to herdsmen and sailors, not a sunset to put Moths and Mantis-kinden to prophesying death and loss. The dusk was pale, almost colourless, the sun on the very point of shrugging its way behind the horizon, almost nonchalantly and without an ounce of showmanship. Stenwold felt something catch in his throat, and tears sprang to his eyes. He fell to his knees on the wall's hard stonework, for it was the most beautiful sight he had ever seen.

There was a soggy-sounding scuffle and Laszlo landed beside him, streaming wet, but grinning like a madman. Stenwold looked up at him: the one person who had shared his ordeal.

'Mar'Maker,' Laszlo nodded, agreeing.

'You're a credit to your family,' Stenwold told him.

The rope ladder was still jerking and tugging, so Stenwold turned to put an arm down to aid Wys, who was scaling it awkwardly, one rung at a time, her eyes focused fiercely on her hands. She took his help gladly when she was high enough, collapsing beside him with ragged breaths.

'You . . . you are mad people,' she said indistinctly. 'Why's it so pissing *cold?*'

Of course, she was wearing just a shift and, of her crew, only Phylles was remotely respectably dressed. 'Despard,' Stenwold decided, 'we'll need clothes for our guests.' He looked down at his own feet, calloused and bare. 'And try for some sandals at least, or we'll all be lame before we reach my house. And tell Tomasso everything you can. Between you and Laszlo here, I owe your crew more than I can count.'

She nodded, looking suitably pleased, and set off into the air in an instant. Wys watched her go with wide eyes.

'Land,' she said. 'This is land, then.' Her gaze shifted from the seaward horizon, turning inland to the shadowed roofs of Collegium. 'I'm not ready for this.'

'In my own city, we receive ambassadors from Grande Atoll, sometimes,' Kratia observed. 'They do not die, of being on land, though they must make certain adjustments. You will not die of it either.'

Wys sat up, nodding. 'Nobody will believe me, that I have seen this,' she said, with a slight smile.

Fel hauled himself up over the edge and crouched there, the spikes on his hands flexing and twitching. Wys reached out and squeezed his arm. He had come wearing his mail, as he had donned it to fight the Echinoi, and his expression was strangely familiar to Stenwold. Only later that night did the connection come to him, for Fel's face was not so unlike a Mantis-kinden's features, and Stenwold had seen that look before, that war between fear and determination, when Tisamon had faced something he reckoned as magic. It spoke of a superstitious awe and terror.

'I must pass on the news of our success to our coalition,' Kratia announced. For a moment Stenwold was thrown, thinking that surely she could speak such words to her sisters even from here, but then he understood: *Of course, she must tell the Vekken.*

'Tell them I shall recompense them, and yourself, in any way I can, beyond the trade with Collegium. I pay my debts.'

'We know it,' she told him. 'Do not think we shall not call upon you for this marker. There are storms coming, Master Maker, and you are a valuable man to be a creditor of.' She nodded him a curt salute and turned on her heel, striding away down the wall's length, towards the city.

Phylles joined them at last, having scaled the wall with her own Art rather than trust the vagaries of the ladder. She clung to the stones, staring up at the sky's vault, at the slowly darkening west. Her hair twitched and flurried.

'Welcome to my world,' Stenwold told the sea-kinden gently. Beneath them, the domed hump of their submersible was descending, and he guessed that, its last passenger having now disembarked, Lej was following some final instruction from Wys. What could they have told him? How long would he wait?

'You're truly after bringing back the heir?' Wys asked him, seeming to have recovered the bulk of her composure. No doubt the fact of Laszlo staying close by her was some comfort. Fel remained standing spear-shaft straight, tense as a wire, eyeing the great built bulk of Collegium, and Phylles seemed to be waiting for the heavens to fall on them.

'Oh yes,' Stenwold said. 'As you just heard, I'm known for the strength of my word.'

'Only,' she grinned weakly, 'I reckon few would blame you if you decided to shaft us a bit. Not exactly open arms, your welcome down there.'

Stenwold shrugged. 'I'm used to mixed receptions. Before Arkeuthys took me, I had no idea your people even existed. Now I leave two kinds of people down below: enemies, and not-enemies. I would rather know that I had friends.' He knelt to put a hand out to the very last of the sea-kinden, who had been labouring her way up the ladder. Paladrya accepted his grasp thankfully, and he helped her carefully to the wall's summit, where she sagged weakly against him.

They all started as Despard alighted again, preceded by a bulging sack. She quickly distributed tunics and cloaks and sandals at random, leaving it to them to sort out what best fitted who. Paladrya held a cape up, a strange expression on her face.

'I remember wrapping him in a cloak, after we took him from the sea . . . I took what care of him I could, but how could it have been enough? If he is dead . . .'

'We can only search,' Stenwold told her. He had taken to Paladrya since their first meeting, prisoners in Claeon's cells. Perhaps it was because, out of all the sea-kinden, her thoughts seemed also for others, not just for herself.

'Come, I'll take you to my house. We can make our plans there,' he told them, sea-kinden and Fly-kinden both. 'Despard, is Tomasso . . . ?'

'At the *Tidenfree*, in harbour. Send word to him if you need him, he says.' She gave him a wry look. 'He'll want the whole story, so don't call him up before you've at least had a night's sleep.'


'Meeting me at your own home, Master Broiler? Either you grow less cautious or more assured of Imperial triumph,' Honory Bellowern remarked drily. When word had come from the Empire's chief agent in Collegium, Helmess had cordially invited him to call, rather than go through all the cloak-and-dagger of their usual meetings. *Let him interpret that how he will*, Broiler considered.

In truth, upstairs were Teornis and Elytrya and a handful of those murderous Dragonfly-kinden the Spider commanded. For all his protestations that they were on the same side, Teornis had suggested, pleasantly, that Helmess might not want to leave his house alone just yet.

'What do you want, Master Bellowern?' the Collegiate Assembler asked. They had better keep very quiet, up above. The last thing he needed was for the Empire to get involved in that particular piece of business.

521

'Orders from Capitas,' Bellowern replied briskly. 'Your moment of greatness arrives. This business with the Spider-kinden is priceless. As soon as their ships arrive, word will go by the fastest means to order the troops to march on Myna.'

'I don't see how that involves me, unless you've made me your messenger boy now,' Helmess grumbled.

'No, no,' Bellowern told him, all smiles still. 'I wouldn't dream of it, not while you're still useful to us in the Assembly. Lucky you didn't lose out *that* badly in the Lots, hmm?'

Helmess scowled at him, which only seemed to fuel the Imperial Beetle's self-satisfaction. 'Now, you must keep them on track for war. Get yourself on a few of their battle councils, or whatever they have. Chair a few committees. You know the sort of talk: "Bring as many ships as they like, the Spiders won't crack this nut overnight." You have to stop some spineless band of silk merchants from talking this into some humiliating *peace*. We want Spider blood shed for every inch of Collegium ground. We want each street corner piled with satrapy dead. All that ingenuity your lot used against the Vekken, all of it turned now onto those wicked slave-takers and web-spinners, hmm? In fact, make sure that the Sarnesh pitch up with a few thousand soldiers from down the rail line. After all, whatever weakens Sarn . . .'

'In other words, business as usual. I'm not sure I needed the reminder, Bellowern.'

'Ah, but' – Honory Bellowern raised a finger and an eyebrow, burlesquing the conspirator – 'you will also be liaising with my agents.'

'Your agents?' Broiler noted, without inflection, thinking, *Oh, yes, and this is new.*

'Just arrived today. Keen lads, most of them our kinden who can do a creditable Co-*lleg*-ium *ac*-cent – hammer and tongs and all that, hey?' Honory drawled. 'I'll be giving

522

them detailed instructions shortly, and I want them to meet you, so they know you're my informant, but in short, their brief is to knock off Aldanrael officers and leaders – bounties all round for actual family members – and Collegium Assemblers, whoever we feel suitable, and then lay the blame on the other party. We'll just keep fanning the fires, and by the time the black and gold flag gets here, they'll be begging us for a little firm governance. Good times, hmm?'

'And you want me to give them lists of names,' Helmess divined.

'You understand me perfectly,' Bellowern agreed. 'And if you have any particular thorns in your side, well, think of that as a little early reward for your loyalty to the Imperial throne. How about Jodry Drillen found with a Spider knife in his throat one morning? Ah, I see you smiling at last. You see, Master Broiler, things are starting to look good. Let's raise a glass to the downfall of Spiders and the Assembly, and the triumph of hidden enemies.'

Helmess Broiler could not keep the grin away, as he sent for the wine.

They made their way into Collegium, while Stenwold still worked out how he would explain his outlandish followers to any guardsmen who might question him. Some Flies, a Spider, a Mantis, or something like a bald Mantis . . . ? but Phylles had *purple* skin and hair that *moved*, and what sort of half-breed could he possibly pass her off as? Best to hope they were not stopped.

The docks had changed since he had last seen them. There were more ships moored, not fewer, but all of them merchantmen. He saw a fair number of Fly-kinden cogs bobbing about, no doubt taking up the slack now that the Spiderlands trade was down. Ashore, the buildings of the port authority, which he had once defended against the Vekken, had been fortified, and there were leadshotters and ballista mounted on the roofs. *Jodry's been doing well in my absence*, he noted approvingly. *But let's hope it will not come to that.*

In the morning he would send to Jodry and to Tomasso. For tonight, though, he would hear Paladrya's story and then he would sleep, and perhaps his dreams would show him where to find a lost prince nobody had set eyes on in four years and more.

*Dead, dead surely.* But he clung on to the idea that somehow this sea-kinden youth had found himself a foothold on the land, had left tracks in the sand that could be followed. A great deal might depend on it.

They made it into the shadow of the first buildings that rose about the harbour. Stenwold had chosen a route leading alongside the river, for that part of Collegium had always been shabbier and less visited by the watch. Still, he and his fellows were challenged within the space of three houses, a quartet of militia appearing from an alley, gaslight glinting on breastplates and snapbows. Stenwold heard Fel hiss, and the sea-kinden were automatically fanning out behind him, obviously expecting a close-in fight. He held a hand out to them urgently. 'Hold!'

'What's this creeping into our . . .' started one of the watch, and then apparently he ran out of words. Stenwold smiled, feeling a surge of fond emotion. Their breastplates were crossed by red sashes stamped by a gold sword and book, and the words *Through the Gate.*

'Yes,' he told them, 'I am returned.'

'Officer Padstock . . .' one started, but another was speaking over him, 'They said you died on the water . . .'

'I live. Inform Elder Padstock. Ask her to come to my home tomorrow morning. But tell nobody else that I am back – not one of them.' Then the thought of repeating this encounter a dozen times, between here and home, struck him. 'In fact, if you could escort me and my companions to my house, I'd be obliged.'

'For you, Master Maker, anything,' one of them said,

and they took him home the quickest way, waving reassuringly to other patrols they passed them. Stenwold saw all three of the merchant companies out on the streets, comprised of men and women of a half-dozen different kinden, all in uniform, all armed with snapbows, pikes, longbows. His escorts told him this was Jodry's doing, keeping an eye out for Spiderlands agents up to no good. Stenwold suspected it was more about assuaging the fears of Collegium citizens, but nevertheless it was a good sign. *You are proving better at this than I gave you credit for, Jodry,* he thought. *We elected the right Speaker.*

When they reached his street, he sent the watch on its way with his message to Padstock. He would make it home without disturbing his neighbours overmuch.

Or so he had thought. As he approached the house, with his ragtag entourage in tow, he saw that lamps were lit in his windows. Stenwold paused, weighing this up. *Has Jodry sent someone to watch my home?* But then the thought came to him: *Che has come back. Che, or Tynisa even!* He started to run, then, letting his fellows catch him if they could, dashing to the door. Finding it unlocked, he flung it open and rushed through to his sitting room.

He found four men gaping up at him from an abruptly halted hand of cards. Stenwold stared at them blankly. The room stank of smoke and worse. There were empty bottles everywhere, on the floor and littering every possible surface. He had spent time in criminal drinking dens that bore less of the stamp of vice than here in his own house.

'What is this?' he demanded.

One of the men had the presence to stand, swaying, his face gone grey with shock. 'Master . . . Maker . . . ?' he goggled. 'But . . . you're a dead man.'

'I've heard that before, and coming from better than you,' Stenwold snapped – and then frowned. '*Cardless?*' In this unexpected context it had taken him too long to recognize the face. Was *this* his manservant, the impeccably turned-out Cardless? All evidence save that drink-slackened face was to the contrary, but the face cast the final vote.

'Dead!' the servant repeated, sounding so aghast that Stenwold almost looked down to see the still-bleeding wounds he must apparently bear. Cardless's fellows, unshaven, unkempt Beetle louts, stared first at him, then back to Stenwold, bewildered.

All the care exercised in getting this far was abruptly gone, swept aside by Stenwold's fury at this invasion of his home. 'Get out,' he ordered flatly. 'All of you get out, if you value your hides. Cardless, you may consider yourself dismissed without reference, at the very *least*. Now leave my house before I throw you from the windows.'

'Big talk,' one of them slurred, standing with a bottle still in hand. 'I count four of us here, old man, one of you . . .'

His voice choked to a stop as Stenwold's fellows finally caught him up, crowding behind him curiously. Stenwold would wonder, later, what those sots must have made of his comrades: the two Flies, Paladrya, Wys, Fel, glowering Phylles. There was surely murder enough evident in Fel's expression alone to prompt their mad dash for safety, as the four of them, babbling incoherently, fled past the newcomers, falling over each other and out on to the street to the sound of a bottle breaking on the flagstones.

*So much for my quiet return*, Stenwold considered. *I couldn't exactly have locked them in the cellar, though, and theirs was hardly a killing offence.* Despite the wreck of his sitting room, and who could know how much of the rest of the house, now they were gone his anger transformed into a bitter humour.

'Oh, hammer and tongs,' he murmured. 'I dread to think what stories will be flung about the city before noon.'

A brief scouting expedition revealed that his own cellar was almost drained dry, only one bottle of inferior wine unopened, and some beetle jerky yet untapped. Remembering his own experiences with sea-kinden food, he hoped it would be seem enough compared with the lobster meat or whatever else they were used to. When he got back upstairs to them, Despard had already flown off to liaise with the family again, so he was left with the ever-faithful Laszlo and the four sea-kinden.

They weren't exactly making themselves at home. Wys had essayed a chair, and was curled up in it, in a position that seemed painfully awkward to Stenwold but apparently bothered her not at all. Fel still stood, as if waiting for the next fight; Phylles and Paladrya had chosen the floor to slump down on.

'I will do what I can to smooth this crossing for you,' he told them, laying down food and drink. 'But it won't be easy.'

'If *you* can do it, we can,' Wys told him. Of all of them she was taking it best.

Stenwold nodded. 'Of course *you*' – he gestured to Paladrya – 'have at least been on land before.'

'Once. So briefly,' she replied, almost in a whisper.

'So tell me. Tell me everything you can about how and where Aradocles left the sea.'

She nodded wearily, taking a moment to gather her strength, while casting her mind back over the years.

'I was Claeon's lover, as you know,' she started.

'We don't know *why*,' Wys interrupted, almost immediately.

Paladrya looked sad. 'He was . . . different before. While his brother was still well, before Claeon began thinking of the Edmiracy. It was ambition for power that poisoned him. But he always talked with me. With whoever he happens to lie with, I think. When the old Edmir fell ill, I knew – from hearing what he did not say, reading the gaps he left – that he would have Aradocles killed. A few years later and the heir would be of age, and everything would have happened differently . . . the temptation would not have been there. But the boy was still young, and Claeon

saw that he himself might become great. And I saw where
his thoughts were leading. I had taught Aradocles for many
years and I loved him as a son. I knew that I had to save
him.'

'And I've seen for myself that it's hard to escape
Claeon's agents,' Stenwold agreed. 'Even so, to the *land*?
Considering the way your people seem to see us, how did
that idea ever come to you?'

'There were very few I could trust, but Aradocles had
some house guards who were loyal only to him. I consulted
with them. One was a Dart-kinden of strange family – an
old family that had lived up against the Edge for many
generations. They do things differently there, and the writ
of Hermatyre – of anywhere – runs thin. Santiren, she was
called. She told me of the ancient customs, rites and rituals
of her people, which had been dying out for ever but still
clung on. Rites and pacts with the land. It was her words
that made my mind up. Left beneath the sea, Claeon would
see Aradocles dead before he became of age. But Santiren
believed that she could broker some contract with the land,
just to keep him safe.'

'Old ways,' murmured Stenwold thoughtfully. 'We
ourselves are not so long established here, my people –
not under our own governance. We were slaves once, and
our rulers were wise and secretive. Who knows what deals
they may have made, and with what powers? Anything is
possible, back in the Bad Old Days. Perhaps the masters of
Pathis-that-was knew more about your people than they
ever bothered to tell us, their underlings.' Stenwold saw
that they were not following him, save perhaps for Laszlo,
and gestured for Paladrya to continue.

'There is little else to say,' she stated. 'I took with us
two of the house guards, both Dart-kinden, Santiren and
another. We rode on the Darts' beasts, myself seated behind
Santiren, and Aradocles behind . . . Marcantor, his name

was. Santiren led the way, and she took us swift and sure, over the Edge, through the shallows, travelling by night, hiding always from the light. Then it was night again and . . . the waters above us became less and less, until we came up into the air.'

'But where?' Stenwold asked her. Abruptly he stood up, rifling across shelves until he found a curled map of the Lowlands.

'I do not know the name of the place. I don't think Santiren did either. It was a forest, like our weed plantations, but instead of the tall weeds there were . . . only crooked, twisted plants. And it was cold, and there was the sky, the moon . . .' She looked up fearfully, as though that great expanse of the heavens still oppressed her even through the ceiling.

'Trees,' Stenwold noted. 'Many of them?'

'There was nothing else visible of the land except the forest,' she said. 'And I bade Aradocles goodbye and returned, and for two years Claeon could not quite believe I had betrayed him, and he hunted everywhere for the boy. Then his suspicion won over his pride, and I became a prisoner, as you found me.'

*And you do not mention the tortures he must have put you through*, Stenwold thought. Her quiet strength impressed him more, the more she spoke. *If only all your kinden had your selflessness*, he considered. *And what manner of man has Aradocles grown into, if he still lives? In your absence, whose hand may have guided him?*

'Trees,' he muttered again. 'Tell me, there was a beach first, perhaps? You scaled a cliff?'

'No, your "trees" extended into the water, so that there was nowhere one could say, this is the land, or this is now the sea. It was an unnatural place, but Santiren swore she had met someone there that still honoured the old compacts.'

Stenwold looked straight into her face – so like a Spider-kinden's, just as Aradocles must surely have seemed a Spider youth – and his heart sank.

'Only one place, that can be,' he declared. They looked encouraged, but he was already shaking his head.

'The Felyal,' Laszlo supplied.

'The Felyal,' Stenwold echoed. His personal feelings for the Mantis-kinden were decidedly mixed, just now, but their feelings for Spider-kind were quite clear and pointed. *Oh he's dead, he's dead, for sure.*

But Stenwold had unfinished business with the Mantids, those refugees of the Felyal that now called Collegium their home. He might as well drag this, the final fate of Arado-cles, into the bargain. What did he have to lose?

# Thirty-Five

Two streets away from Maker's house, Cardless put his back to a wall and tried to think.

His world was falling away from him, leaving him with no visible means of support. How could this have happened? He'd had his life made out, surely? It couldn't all evaporate, as simply as that?

He could go back to Stenwold tomorrow, make it out as a misunderstanding. He had been misled. He had been held hostage. It wasn't his fault.

But then he remembered the grim look of the people Stenwold had brought home with him, the sort of people Cardless would never have thought an Assembler, a College Master, would even know. Killers, mercenaries and pirates, the lot of them. It brought back to Cardless the odd rumours about Maker, his early career, his precise role in fighting the Vekken and the Empire. *Blood on his hands, they say, and not just from the war.*

He could not go back there. He had made too free with Stenwold's possessions. Yet everyone had known the man was dead. Helmess Broiler had been exultant about it. Spider-kinden assassins or something. Everyone knew it, though no two voices agreed just how. He had died out on the water, doing who could know what? His woman, Arianna, had died with him; some even said they had killed each other. The point was that they were *dead*, and the niece was missing, and the rest of the Maker family were so entrenched in internecine feuds that nobody had come to claim the house, the cellar, the larder, the cashbox. That left only Cardless, alone, in that big house, so who wouldn't have started to see it as his own?

Then a written message had come, just days ago, from Broiler's people: *Look out for Stenwold Maker. He may return any day.* Cardless had burned it and laughed. Maker was dead. The sea had swallowed him. No man came back from that – not even Stenwold Maker.

Yet that same old Beetle had stood in the doorway, his face strangely bloodless and grey like a man long without the sun, wearing clothes ragged and stained, and Cardless had almost expected to see barnacles and shells clinging to his skin, seawater pooling at his feet. Stenwold Maker was back from his watery grave.

And now Cardless was out of a job. No money. No job. No *money*. Up until now he had been taking liberties with Maker's credit, and his gambling friends had been happy to take his marker, once he had exhausted Stenwold's stash of ready coin. Now, he *owed*, and some of the people he owed to would not take kindly to being put off. Not now that Cardless had nothing to fall back on.

His mind, still fuddled from drink, at last lit on the only solution: Helmess Broiler. Helmess had told him to watch out for Maker's return. Well, now he was returned, and Broiler would want to know of it. He would pay for that, surely. Perhaps he could find Cardless a new position. It wouldn't have to be working for an Assembler: any decent household would do. Perhaps Broiler had contacts in Helleron. A span of time out of the city wouldn't go amiss, right now.

*Yes, that's it.* Cardless caught his breath raggedly and nodded to himself. Helmess Broiler would want to know that Maker had returned, and then Helmess Broiler would make everything all right again. He was a proper magnate of Collegium, a good Assembler. He would be duly grateful for Cardless's honest service.

Muttering to himself, the dismissed manservant hurried off through Collegium's dark streets.

Helmess was inconveniently asleep when Cardless came calling. The wait in Broiler's antechamber was sobering, and it gave the manservant a chance to put his thoughts in order, to straighten his stained tunic and run a hand through his dishevelled hair. Nonetheless, when he was finally ushered into Helmess Broiler's presence, he was taken aback by the audience present: not only the Beetle magnate and his sultry Spider mistress, plus the pleasant-spoken servant Forman Sands, whom Cardless hoped he could count upon as a brother-in-craft, but there was another Spider-kinden in attendance as well. He was a dark, lean-faced man, slightly bearded, and in clothes that were surely Helmess's own cast-offs and therefore nothing a Spider would normally be seen in. Not this man especially, for Cardless reckoned he could detect an Aristoi when he saw one . . . in fact, now he thought about it, the newcomer's face was decidedly familiar. Behind him stood a ferocious-looking Dragonfly man, all tattoos and scars and a long-hafted sword slung over one shoulder.

Helmess was making impatient gestures to him, so he turned from eyeing the newcomer and got out his story in reasonable order, leaving out any inconvenient details about the precise circumstances that Maker had discovered on his long-delayed return home. He saw the significant looks pass between Broiler and the Spider-kinden man, and allowed himself an eager little smile. Just as he had hoped, his news was obviously valuable, worthy of reward, not only to Helmess but to . . . Teornis?

Cardless felt a little skip of unease within him. Surely this was Teornis of the Aldanrael, who some said had killed Stenwold, and others claimed had been Maker's last victim.

This was a night for dead men, it seemed. Moreover, there was a fair consensus that Teornis was behind the armada even now expected to sail from Seldis and Everis, to bring another war upon poor, battered Collegium. So what was the man doing *here*?

There were rumours, of course, about Helmess Broiler, but then they circulated about any Beetle who ran for Speaker, mostly spread by his opponents. Still, the rumours about Broiler had suggested he was a deal too close to the Empire . . . and now Cardless found himself wondering whether Broiler wasn't a deal too close to some other enemies of Collegium, for here he was sitting right next to one.

He did his best to keep any of the suspicions off his face. He was supposed to be good at that. He just watched as Broiler leant across to the Spider, speaking in hushed tones.

'Well?' Helmess whispered so that this travesty of a man-servant before them would catch none of it. 'I assume you'll have your assassins deal with this.'

'By no means,' Teornis replied softly. 'I would never dream of doing anything so base. Master Maker continues to win my admiration.'

'We have to put him away, now,' Helmess insisted. 'Surely you can see that?'

'That is not how it is done,' was Teornis's light response. 'Nor would it be so easy.' His thought went unsaid, but distinctly understood, that, if there was a choice, to kill Stenwold or kill Broiler, he would not hesitate to cut his host's throat himself. 'Can we dispense with this creature?' He waved a bored hand at Cardless.

'Ah, yes.' Helmess nodded. Then, in louder tones, he said, 'I suppose we've heard enough.'

'Please, Master Broiler,' Cardless said, half obsequious, half desperate. 'I was hoping that I should have some recompense for bringing you this. And . . . I have nowhere to go. Perhaps you have some position . . . or know of one . . . ?'

'Yes, tiresome that you're no longer in Maker's household,' said Helmess. 'Ah well, so much for that. Sands, would you be so kind as to give our friend Cardless his final payment. Be sure he wants for nothing.'

'I would be delighted, Master Broiler,' replied Sands, giving Cardless his best smile and taking him by the elbow. Cardless's backward glance was only one of thankfulness.

Helmess waited until he was gone before adding, 'That is, assuming you're happy for me to dispose of at least *this* irritation?'

'Oh, kill him,' Teornis said dismissively. 'It would be only a day at most before he thought to sell some piece of information back to Stenwold Maker, therefore he's best in the earth. Maker is back, though, and with sea-kinden dancing attendance, no less. He did better than I, for he got out of the water a free man.'

'Sea-kinden?' Helmess was frowning, perhaps thinking of such specimens as Rosander in full armour. 'You're sure?'

'What does your good lady think?' Teornis prompted.

Elytrya nodded reluctantly. 'Yes, the man Cardless's descriptions were clear, even though he did not really know what he was describing. Some, at least, were of the sea.'

'So how did Stenwold persuade them into facing their greatest fear? Are they also Littoralists, plotting the destruction of all land-people? I think not,' Teornis conjectured, 'but what else could drag some of them all the way to Collegium?'

'The heir,' Elytrya spat out.

Teornis nodded enthusiastically. 'None other,' he agreed. 'And I must restate my utter admiration for the resourcefulness of Stenwold Maker. Indeed, it's high time that we made it work on our behalf.'

Helmess regarded him with hooded eyes for a moment,

then made a dubious sound. 'That calls for a great deal of skill, Teornis. I'd not stake even my man Sands on performing that kind of work.'

'Then be thankful that I include amongst my followers some with sharp ears and silent wings,' Teornis told him. 'Varante, you understand my meaning? Keep watch on Maker's house. Have spies to mark his course. Tell me where he goes. Eavesdrop, if you can. Why should we not let the redoubtable Stenwold Maker himself lead us to this errant boy?'

Waking up in his own bed, Stenwold yawned, stretched, flung out a lazy arm across the sheet to reach for Arianna.

A moment of confusion and chaotic memory later, he was sitting up, sweating and hoarse, reaching for purchase under the avalanche of images that came cascading back into place in his mind. Arkeuthys, Rosander, the coiled shell of Wys's submersible and the Echinoi running riot through the Hot Stations. A thought of Arianna tugged at his mind, struggling against this landslide, but when he mouthed her name it was another face he saw: skin so pale as to seem translucent, framed by floating hair.

For a moment, in the pre-dawn silence of the house, he felt her there: Lyess, impossibly with him, somewhere just out of sight in the room, as though she was hiding there with her Art, subtly faded into transparency. There was a gauzy distance between them which was new, but he knew that must simply be the surface of the water – that she would drag him back through eventually. He could not in any way be free of her.

Stenwold had enough self-knowledge to realize that something was wrong here. *She has put her Art on me*, he thought, but it wasn't only that. There was a scent, an indefinable *feel* to any kind of Art that he always recognized. If she had done something to him, it was not something so readily explicable.

*Drugs? Can you drug someone into remembering you? Is it possible to mix a love potion? A love poison?*

He was remembering, now, something that Salma had said, something Che had reported to him just after the lad had left for Tark. Salma had been enchanted, or so he had claimed. A spell, a magic, had been placed on him by the Butterfly-kinden called Grief in Chains – she had bound him to her by sorcery. Stenwold did not believe in sorcery within the walls of his city when the sun was high, but the dawn was barely feeling out the east, and he felt suddenly helpless in the face of this invasion. *But didn't it end well for Salma? He got the girl, in the end.* He had died, in the end, too, and Grief in Chains – who had renamed herself Prized of Dragons – had retreated to the city they were building in his honour. *Death and mourning hardly counts as things ending well.*

He forced himself out of bed, seeking absolution through action. The sea-kinden were all awake, and looking as though they had barely slept all night. Everything here was uncomfortable to them. They would take a while to adjust, and this was even before the brightness of dawn assailed them.

Stenwold woke Laszlo and sent him for victuals, fish if there was any to be found. He explained to Wys and the others, 'We don't eat fish here, you see, not if there's a choice.' They looked at him as if he was mad, and he went on, 'When my people were slaves, we ate fish, and only our masters ate meat. Now we are free, and only the poorest make do with food from the sea.'

Laszlo did his best, though the palates of the sea-kinden nearly bested him. They found the taste of red meat – horse and goat – abhorrent. Stenwold tried them on milk, the least offensive thing he could think of. The very stench of it turned their stomachs, apparently: the whole city smelled bad to them, but the milk seemed to concentrate and epitomize that sour, rotten odour. Bread they ate, thankfully, so he offered them a little honey to go with it – and watched their eyes go wide at the taste. He remembered, belatedly, how he had tasted nothing at all sweet during his long soujourn beneath the waves, and he retrieved the jar from them before they could take too much of it, for fear that they would make themselves ill, like children.

It was shortly after dawn that he finally met with his allies. The sea-kinden were bustled into another room, with Laszlo to watch over them, as into the house came the swaying bulk of Jodry Drillen. In came bearded Tomasso, too, and the plain, honest face of Elder Padstock.

Jodry shook his head, marvelling. There was a genuine tear in his eye as he exclaimed, 'I thought . . . I thought we'd lost you, Sten.'

Padstock nodded soberly. Tomasso explained how she and her fellows had been removed from the barge by the Spider galley, which was intent on learning the fate of Teornis. The *Tidenfree* had come broadside to it, though, half the size of the other vessel, and threatened them with the balance of the Mantis marines, including Danaen, who had flown back to rally more resistance once the Spiders had come alongside.

Stenwold nodded grimly. *And I have a score to settle there.*

In the end they had settled for repatriating Padstock and her people, and then departing.

'You've done well with the sea defences,' Stenwold told Jodry. 'And you should keep it up – keep drilling the companies.'

'But you have another plan?' Jodry guessed, frowning. 'I have received word. The armada is close on sailing. The Spiders are confident enough that they've let it be known, spread the word so as to demoralize us.'

'I do have another plan,' Stenwold assured him, 'though it may not work. At the moment it's looking very dubious indeed, but if it does . . . I have to follow it up, for many reasons. I merely ask you to trust me.'

'Of course,' Jodry replied without hesitation. 'I'll also trust to the Sarnesh to send us a few detachments, if you don't mind. And even the Vekken are making threats.'

'Threats?'

'To come to our aid, if you'd believe. If we get them *and* the Sarnesh both at once I'm not sure we'll need the Spiders to level the city. All in all, I hope you know what you're doing. We've only just rebuilt most of the docklands after the last time.'

Stenwold sent Jodry and Padstock on their way, with some encouragement to keep up the good work. Tomasso he detained, though, and then called for Laszlo to bring their guests through.

The sea-kinden filed in uneasily, frowning at the black-bearded Fly-kinden. When Tomasso clasped Laszlo to him with a grin, the gesture went a long way towards taking the edge off their nervousness.

'This,' Laszlo proudly announced to Wys, 'is just the very man I was telling you about.'

'Is that right?' Her eyes narrrowed. She and Tomasso squared off against one another, and Stenwold had to smile. It was just as though they were any two merchants trying to take each other's measure.

'What have you brought me, boy?' Tomasso asked, seeing a bald Fly-kinden woman of strange looks, with an unfamiliar accent.

'Uncle Tomasso, meet the sea people,' Laszlo told him.

Tomasso raised an eyebrow. 'That so? You don't just mean from some port I've not heard of, some part of the Spiderlands maybe. You don't mean that at all, do you?' He inclined his head towards the Onychoi woman. 'Lady, I'm Tomasso, master of the *Tidenfree* and uncle to this nuisance here.'

Wys shrugged her high shoulders. 'Wys,' she replied

simply. 'I've got a barque and a crew – most of which you see here. The "nuisance" tells me you're into trading the exotic. Myself likewise.'

'What've you got that's exotic?'

'To you, everything.' She grinned, whereupon Tomasso matched her tooth for tooth.

'Looks like you might have trawled something worthwhile up to the surface,' he admitted to Laszlo, still without taking his eyes off Wys. 'Been using your time well, then?'

Laszlo shrugged, ostentatiously nonchalant. 'I like to keep myself busy, skipper.'

Tomasso's eyes flicked towards Stenwold. 'Master Maker, you look like a man with plans.'

'Oh, plans certainly. You don't seem overly surprised to be face to face with people from under the sea.'

'You hear rumours,' Tomasso said. 'Sail these seas enough, and any number of drunk sailors will tell you about the sea-kinden. Never believed it, but that was only for want of evidence. I've travelled, Maker. I've travelled from Cerrih to Sea-Limnis and from Silk Gate to Port Planten, but I've never seen anything like this mob here. They have to come from *somewhere*, so why not the sea? There must be stranger things.'

Stenwold nodded. Silk Gate, as he knew, was on the Silk Road south of Mavralis. The other places were just names. 'I get the impression that you and Wys would like the chance to get better acquainted,' he said. 'May I borrow Laszlo?'

'Not sure I could prise him away from you, in any case,' Tomasso said wryly. 'Master Maker, you have the look of a man about to do something unwise.'

'Oh, unwise, certainly. There is unrest beneath the sea, Master Tomasso, but somewhere here on land there may be the means to cure it. Unfortunately that means was last seen off Felyal, which means our talking to the Mantis-kinden.'

Tomasso grimaced. 'I can't see that Laszlo's going to be much help there. I could find you some lads . . .'

'If it comes to a shoving match, I've already lost it,' Stenwold told him. 'I know Mantis-kinden, though, as well as any outsider can. I know how they think, how they like to see themselves. I only need Laszlo to tell people how I ended up, if I get it wrong.'

# Thirty-Six

It was the same Mantis dive that he had once gone fishing for pirates in, without success. He could only hope to have more luck this time, since the stakes were a whole lot higher.

He ducked beneath the lintel, into a waft of fire-warmed air, out of the night's cool. He would have preferred to visit here by daylight, but had not managed to track down his target until after dusk. Laszlo had trailed dutifully after him all around the city, as he spoke to his informants or avoided people wanting to question him about his absence. Now he gestured for the Fly to stay back. If things went badly, he needed Laszlo to be able to make an escape and tell the story.

It was just as he remembered inside: a forest of wooden pillars cluttering the harbour-front tavern. The Mantids sat with their backs to the virtual trees, talking in low voices, eyes glittering red in the firelight. Winding pipe music came from somewhere, the voices of two instruments entwined, quavering some strange and sad melody.

Stenwold paused just within the doorway, and felt for his courage. There were a good twenty-five or so Mantis-kinden present, of whom he could name only one – and that one was no friend of his, not any more. He called on his memories of Tisamon, but then Tisamon had never been the most typical of his kind. Stenwold hoped that, in this most important thing, he had judged matters right.

He drew his sword. The whisper of steel on leather was barely audible even to himself, but it silenced them all, even the musicians. He felt their eyes settle on him, not with fear or alarm but with a crawling eagerness. Without any transition, weapons were in every hand: rapiers, long knives, spears. A few were even buckling on clawed gauntlets like the one that Tisamon used to wear.

One stood up, a hard-faced woman with a slender blade held loose in her left hand. 'You have walked through the wrong doorway, Beetle,' she told him. 'Perhaps you should go elsewhere with your little sword.'

Stenwold reminded himself bleakly that offering him this chance to withdraw amounted to their most diplomatic level of politeness.

'I'm afraid I know exactly what I am about. My name is Stenwold Maker.'

'What's that to me?' the Mantis woman demanded. There was no sign of any recognition whatsoever in her face.

'You speak for all here? Do you have no name?' Names were important, Stenwold knew, for the Inapt set great store by them.

'Akkestrae, they call me,' she told him. 'Now take your sword and go, Stenwold Maker the Beetle. You are not welcome.'

'I am here to defend Mantis honour.' Those were words that Tisamon had once used, or so Stenwold hoped, relying on a years-old memory. They had their effect anyway. He saw a reaction – an emotion for which the Beetle-kinden had no name – lash across all their faces. He guessed that their offer to let him duck back out and leave had just been withdrawn.

'Hard words for such a soft, fat man to say,' Akkestrae rebuked him. The angle of her rapier had changed even as he spoke, from idle to ready, just a twitch away from running him through. 'Do you think you are the first of your kind to mock us, in your ignorance? The sea lies at your back, Beetle. It can take a good many more corpses yet before it is full.'

'Do not lecture me on what the sea can hold,' snapped Stenwold, with enough fire that she blinked and frowned at him. 'I am here to defend Mantis honour,' he repeated. 'For it appears nobody else will.'

'And who assaults it?' she asked him contemptuously. 'If you know of what you speak, then you must give us a name.'

'Danaen,' Stenwold replied. 'Come forward, Danaen, and defend yourself if you can.'

There was quite a pause, and a murmur of Mantis voices in hissed outrage, before she stepped forward – Danaen, with her scarred face twisted in a look of arrogant disdain. It came to him, then, that the same expression had always been there whenever he met her, but he had previously chosen to interpret it as simple Mantis reserve.

'I hear you are recently back from the dead, Beetle,' she said in almost a whisper, save that the strange acoustics of the place carried it to all ears. 'You must be eager to return there, that you call me out so.'

'Call you out?' Stenwold reproached her, keeping both hands steady on his courage. 'I am here to right your wrong – and a wrong against all your kinden.'

With a tiny movement, so slight he might almost have missed it, her short, slender blades were both in her hands. 'If your life wearies you so much, then I shall cut it from you,' she snarled, her eyes cold.

'Say what you must, Beetle,' said Akkestrae, now sounding bored. 'Speak and then have the grace to die cleanly – if your kind even know how.'

'I have had Mantis allies before,' Stenwold informed them, 'and when I walked in the shadow of a Mantis, I had no fear of failure or betrayal. I knew that, once his oath was given, even Tisamon's death would hardly prevent him carrying out his word.'

'Tisamon!' someone spat derisively from amongst them, and Akkestrae said, 'That is no name to conjure with here, for we know his failings.'

'As did he,' Stenwold replied sombrely. 'Yet he wore the Weaponsmaster's badge, and he earned it. Who denies it?'

Akkestrae watched him as though he was prey that had just offered a certain extra enjoyment in its hunting, but no voice rose to question Tisamon's standing now. It had been Stenwold's main concern that his dead friend's reputation would prove too corroded to bear the reliance he must place on it.

'Tisamon taught me to put faith in the Mantis-kinden.' He addressed the whole room whilst locking eyes with Danaen. 'In the end, whatever his failings, it was his sword that cut the throat of the Wasp Emperor – his sacrifice that took the Wasp armies from our gates. Who denies it?'

'What of it?' Danaen spat, and several voices joined hers.

'So when I sought help once more against a common foe, it was to the Mantis-kinden I turned – and I was betrayed.'

The silence that followed was the most dangerous yet, but before he could break it, Danaen herself did so.

'You went to *talk* with the Spider-kinden scum!' she yelled at him. 'When you found yourself at war with them, you would not fight. Like any Beetle, you would only *talk*. I knew my duty.'

'Did you so?' Stenwold asked. 'Perhaps you refer to drawing blade against the Spider-kinden during our truce, whilst we talked peace?'

'Who faults me on that?' Danaen demanded, and it was clear that few there would.

'Or perhaps you speak of your greater betrayal?'

Stenwold pressed on, and the silence was back, with re-inforcements. He waited, but Danaen did not interrupt again. Her eyes had abruptly become hooded.

'We met out on the water, aboard a barge towed to a precise point. Who made the arrangements? Whose idea was that? And how was it, then, that the barge was attacked, that I and my follower were dragged into the water by new enemies? A trap. It was a trap I stepped into, but none of the Spiders' doing, for they walked into it as well. It was a trap set by those I relied on. The honour of the Mantis-kinden was turned into a trap to exploit my trust.'

Danaen's hands were now white-knuckled around the hilts of her blades. 'And would your city be better off had you sold them to the Spider with your *words?*' she snapped. 'One Beetle or another, why should I take orders from any? If Maker says one thing and Broiler says another, what of it? Why should I not follow the orders that help kill more Spiders?'

*Broiler?* Stenwold's insides lurched. *Helmess bloody* Broiler? *Was selling us to the Wasps not enough, that he has somehow become Claeon's man now?*

'Broiler, you say?'

She glowered at him, but there was something guarded in her eyes, something defensive all of a sudden, and in his mind he had beaten past her guard, his words gathered for a sudden lunge.

'Do any here know what is said of Helmess Broiler?' Stenwold demanded. To his surprise, there was a look of recognition on a few of their faces, a few dark glances, curt nods. 'They say that Helmess Broiler would have sold this city to the Empire, if he had his way. The same Empire that drove you from your homes in the Felyal! And *that* is who Danaen would serve rather than me?'

'Enough of this,' Danaen snapped. 'It is time for me to shed your blood, fat Beetle.'

Stenwold had not entirely thought this moment through,

546

before, but mention of the name Broiler, the man who had been a thorn in his side for so many years, had fired his blood. 'Come on then,' he challenged her, and levelled his shortsword.

Danaen went for him, in a movement faster than he could follow. His parry came in far too late, of course, but the Mantis had pulled back, jerking away from him. Akkestrae's sword was between them.

'What?' Danaen hissed. 'Will you let him speak so lightly of Mantis honour? You heard his words.'

'I heard many words,' the other woman replied flatly, 'and I heard the name of honour in an unfit mouth – but it was not his. You have condemned yourself.'

Danaen sneered at her, looking about at her fellows. 'This is pitiful,' she told them. 'This is what comes of living in this soft city. It has poisoned you.'

They regarded her solemnly, not one of them standing forward to take her part.

'Against the *Spider-kinden*,' she insisted. 'Which one of you would not have struck a blow against the Spider-kinden?'

'I was made a *slave*,' Stenwold said, softly but with feeling. 'Your allies made a slave of me.' The Mantis-kinden, he knew, had strong feelings about slavers. It was one trade they loathed above all others, one fragile piece of common ground they had with Collegium.

'How can you listen to him?' Danaen shrieked at her kinsfolk, and Akkestrae said simply, 'We need only listen to you.'

Stenwold turned away towards the open doorway, lowering his sword. A moment later he heard a sudden flurry of blows, as swift as the rattling of chains, and then a brief cry of pain. When he turned back, Danaen lay on the ground, her body bloody and pierced in many places. Akkestrae was cleaning the long blade of her rapier in minute detail, without even looking at him.

He gave a long sigh of relief and sheathed his sword,

knowing that, waiting outside, Laszlo would note the signal. Two Mantis men took up Danaen's body and dragged it out to the sea's edge, while Stenwold stepped fully inside and went to sit with his back resting against a pillar, pointedly facing into the room. He had to wait a few minutes, as they tried their best to ignore him, but eventually Akkestrae came over to speak.

'What do you want?' she asked him. 'Do not assume we are your friends here, because of this.'

He faced her levelly. 'Oh, no. Just because I am the War Master of Collegium, and have fought our common enemies, because my city has taken you in when your home was burned, or because I have detected the Spider-kinden engaging in their hidden war on my city, and have myself been betrayed into darkness and slavery by your own people, of course I can have no claim on you.'

Her face twisted, her hand hovering at her rapier's hilt, but he felt on more secure ground now. 'What do you want?' she repeated. 'Do you think we fear that you will expel us?'

He saw, although perhaps she did not quite know it herself, that they did indeed fear it. The Mantis-kinden living beneath borrowed roofs in this city of the Apt, without function and without history, were waiting to outstay their welcome. They were baffled, unsure, belligerent, angry at being so useless. *They see no point in themselves. They cannot understand why we keep them here. Perhaps they expect to go down in some grand final stand when we decide to throw them out.*

He sighed, trying to sympathize with them, knowing how he needed their cooperation. 'I value the Mantis-kinden, for no man had a truer friend than Tisamon. There are dark times coming to Collegium: perhaps the Spiders shall bring them, or else the Empire again. We shall be glad of the Mantids then, I'm sure.'

She seemed reassured, if only slightly. 'And yet you want something of us.'

He nodded heavily. 'I am told that there are some from the Felyal who live close to the sea. I am told of pacts, of rituals, and I must speak with one such. It is very important.'

The surprise was evident in her face that a mere Beetle should know anything of that. 'It is a . . . strange old custom, even to us. Few there are who held to it even before the Empire arrived.'

'Is there anybody . . .' Stenwold started, and she interrupted, 'But there is one.'

'Here?'

'The Sea Watch . . . that kind have always walked their own path,' Akkestrae told him. 'But now . . . There is one in the city. She is bitter, and angry, and she walks that path no more. There is a pier, narrow and in need of repair, lying closest to the easternmost sea wall. Most nights you will find her there. Her name is Cynthaen.'

The pier Akkestrae meant was old, too narrow for merchantmen, too high for smaller boats. Had Collegium's sea trade been of more import, then no doubt it would have been torn down long ago for something better. As it was, the rickety construction had been left to rot.

It was past midnight now, for Stenwold had returned home to collect Paladrya, in the hope that she might help win the confidence of this Cynthaen through recounting what details she knew of Aradocles's advent on to the land. He had collected another fistful of bolts for his cut-down snapbow too, for when he had left the waterfront tavern, Laszlo had cautioned him.

'I've not been alone out here, Mar'Maker,' the Fly had said in a low voice. 'The night air's been busy. Nothing so clumsy that I caught a proper glimpse, but . . . they're out there.'

With that warning, Stenwold had requisitioned Fel as well, and the four of them had travelled the long way back to the quays, and located Akkestrae's pier. Paladrya kept herself shrouded in her cloak, for she had quickly understood that her kinden's resemblance to the Spiders might cause her problems. Fel, on the other hand, went in his mail, his vest and bracers of shell over something that was leathery without being leather, and wore his helm with the swept-back crest, as though he was some exotic Mantis prizefighter. Cloaks, Stenwold soon understood, were tangling and unfamiliar to the Onychoi warrior, and he had developed a strong dislike for them.

It would have to do, though. Stenwold had no time to argue, nor did Fel look amenable to persuasion.

The pier was a long one, extending far out to sea on its uneven stanchions. In the waning moonlight Stenwold tried to see if there was anyone standing out there. 'Perhaps this is one of her nights off?' he suggested.

'Someone is there,' Paladrya declared, and the other two were nodding. Fly-kinden had sharp eyes and, of course, the sea-kinden were used to the gloom that was the best their limn-lights could make of the deep sea's utter darkness.

'Just one person?' Stenwold asked cautiously. He saw Laszlo glance suddenly upwards, abruptly suspicious, but the two sea-kinden were again nodding.

'Unless someone could be hiding behind that little structure there,' Paladrya filled in. There was a boxy little shed towards the very end of the pier: a small storage hut, he guessed.

*Out over the water again.* Stenwold found himself remarkably unwilling to step even on to the boards of the jetty. It was not just that they were worm-eaten, and complained creakily about his weight. It was the sea itself beneath. He felt that it was waiting for him. *I escaped it once, and it wants me back.* And he thought: *Yet do I not wish to go back?* 'Return to me', she had said . . . He shook himself irritably and led the way down the pier's uneven length.

He was more than halfway to the end before his eyes could pick out even the suggestion of shape ahead. If something went wrong out here, he would be at such a disadvantage that he might as well just throw himself into the ocean. Irritably he unlatched a lamp from his belt. He had hoped not to have to use it, as whoever was out here obviously valued their moonlit privacy. He struck the steel within, and a wan gas flame ignited, almost white and turned as low as it would go. Despite his misgivings, he felt a great deal better after it was lit.

He approached with caution, Paladrya and Fel shadowing his footsteps and Laszlo hanging slightly back. The lamp illuminated the pier's end, flaring palely on the rotten boards of the storage shed, before touching on the back of the figure at the very end of the pier. It was indeed a Mantis woman, as far as Stenwold could tell, sitting on a barrel and staring out to sea . . . no, she was fishing. As he drew nearer, he spotted that she held a reel of line that was dangling into the midnight waters.

He heard her sigh, and he stopped a prudent distance away, with the shack right by his elbow.

Her voice drifted across to him, sounding weary: 'I'm selling nothing and I'm buying nothing, and I carry no coin, strangers. You'll get precious little from me.'

'We don't mean to rob you,' Stenwold addressed her, 'only to ask you a question, if we may.'

She had a stick in one hand, he now saw, a thick, four-foot length of wood. Without looking round, she leant on it, pushing herself off the barrel with a curiously lopsided motion, turning as she did so. He realized that she was younger than he had thought, her pale hair cut brutally short. Her face had a lot of lines on it, the evidence of pain and bitter feelings.

'Cynthaen,' he addressed her.

'Most of her.' She stepped forward, not Mantis-graceful but with a rolling lurch, and he saw, belatedly, that one leg was just a wooden stump from the knee down. When he lifted his eyes again, she met his gaze with keen cynicism, looking for the pity.

'The Wasps?' he asked her.

'Gift of the Empire, yes,' she said, 'and of a surgeon of your own kinden. Trimmed me and seared me and told me how lucky I was, to be alive. So what do you want to ask me, Master Beetle? Have you found me a foot that needs a new owner?' There was a humour in her voice, but it was sharp-edged.

'I want to ask you about the sea-kinden,' Stenwold told her. 'Your people sent me to you.'

'They remember me, do they?' She lowered herself back on to the barrel, balancing herself between the stick and her sound leg. 'Sea-kinden? Stories, Master Beetle, just stories.'

Stenwold glanced towards his companions, and Cynthaen followed his gaze. When he turned back to her, her face had become closed, resigned.

'So,' she said.

'Your people, your family, made a pact, I am told,' Stenwold explained. 'And some years ago, that pact was called upon.'

'Was it, now?' she said blandly, hunching forward over her stick.

'There was a boy brought up from the sea,' Stenwold prompted. It was clear she knew exactly what he was talking about, but her face would admit none of it. All she would say was, 'Was there so?'

'He would have seemed like a Spider-kinden to you,' the Beetle went on, a little desperately, as Cynthaen simply arched a sceptical eyebrow.

Stenwold opened his mouth, wondering what he could say next, just as Paladrya pushed past him, stepping far too close to the Mantis-kinden woman: almost within reach of the jagged spines on her forearms.

'Please,' the Kerebroi woman declared, simply, 'we have come to take him home. Are there any of your people who might remember?'

Cynthaen had gone very still, and at first Stenwold thought it was because of finding a Spider-kinden woman before her, and was within an inch of striking out at her, but the expression on the Mantis's face was not one of hatred, as he would have expected. Instead it was puzzlement slowly being replaced by something like recognition.

'You,' the Mantis said, and left the single word unqualified for a moment, before adding, 'Was it you?'

Paladrya was now frowning, as the other three gathered closer, trying to work out what was happening here.

'We were few and far between, those of us who kept the Watch, even before the Wasps came,' murmured Cynthaen, very softly indeed. 'Five, perhaps? Six? Dying traditions, they were: the offerings into the deep, and the harvest of the sea. As for now? I don't know if anyone keeps the Sea Watch now. I am the only blood of my house remaining, what's left of me. I recognize you, though. You're of *his* kind, all right, and no Spider.'

Stenwold heard Paladrya's breath catch. 'You . . . ?'

'Do I remember you?' Cynthaen frowned. 'There in the shallows . . . not the two long bastards who came with him, but there was one other. I was watching from the trees. I remember. It could have been you, at that. It could have been. Nigh on five years ago, but I almost think it was you, after all.'

'Do you know . . .' Paladrya's voice was shaking. 'Do you know . . . whether he lives? My Aradocles, does he live?'

'The Wasps came.' Cynthaen's voice went hard again, and she tapped her stick against her wooden leg. 'They burned us out. Torched every logging camp and trading post along the edge of the Felyal, and then carried on till they hit Collegium's walls.'

'Is he here?' Paladrya asked her. 'Please, you must tell me, I have to know. I sent him on to the land, all those years ago, to keep him safe . . .'

Cynthaen gave a barking, incredulous laugh. 'Safe? You chose the wrong place and time, woman. But your lad did fight, I give him that. Fought at the Felyal, and then with the Prince. Went and joined the Landsarmy, he did. Most of the villagers, the traders and the loggers, they couldn't make it here. They moved too slow, had no boats, and the Wasps were already standing in the way. So they went north instead. Signed on with the Prince of the Wasteland.' She nodded at Stenwold. 'You know who I mean.'

'Oh, yes,' Stenwold breathed. 'Yes I do.'

'Then you'll know where they ended up,' Cynthaen told him. 'In that new place of theirs. You want your lad? If he lives at all, he's there.'

'Princep Salmae,' pronounced Stenwold.

'Mar'Maker!' Laszlo shouted an abrupt warning, and Stenwold whirled round to see a figure kick off suddenly into the air, from the roof of the storage shack. Stenwold's hand came up automatically, tugging the little snapbow out of his coat and loosing both bolts, one after the other. One of them must have struck, through luck more than any skill, for the flying figure faltered in the air and then crashed to the pier, smashing through the old boards and vanishing almost instantly into the dark water below.

Almost immediately two others were upon them: lean, scarred men with long-hafted swords glittering, swooping down to avenge their comrade. One of them went straight for Paladrya, and the other stooped on Stenwold.

Fel got himself in the way of that second one. The sword sparked off his bracer, then he and the attacker were trading blows. Dragonfly-kinden, Stenwold saw – and not just Dragonflies but men of a look he had seen before. The swordsman had reach, and kept himself half airborne, swarming about Fel trying to find an opening. The Onychoi warrior left him no gap, pivoting and spinning to keep his opponent in sight, hands raised in a high guard, with their spikes jutting forward. Those blows he could not dodge, he took on his mail or on his Art-armoured knuckles.

Stenwold drew his own blade, turning to aid Paladrya. A second Dragonfly was already crouching low before her, sword held vertically before him. Cynthaen had come to her rescue, balanced on her good leg, both hands resting on her stick.

The Dragonfly struck a cleaving downward blow that should have lopped the Mantis's weapon in half. Cynthaen twisted it a little as she brought it up, though, pulling it apart to reveal a ribbon of steel between a wooden hilt and scabbard. Then she had the blade fully drawn, keeping the sheath in her offhand to block with. Paladrya cowered behind her.

'Mar'Maker, look!' Laszlo was pointing urgently. Up on the shack's roof there was another man, standing tall with a bow in one hand, an arrow just being put to the nock. Cursing at his own stupidity, Stenwold fumbled for more snapbow bolts.

Cynthaen was keeping up a steady defence, but she could not move fast enough to take the initiative, and slowly the Dragonfly's relentless assault was forcing her back, her wooden foot dragging. Stenwold crouched, reloading frantically, and then, in front of him, Fel's opponent was suddenly doubled over. A murderous barbed fist snapped out faster than Stenwold's eyes could follow, ramming four inches of piercing bone under the man's ribs. The bowstring thrummed and Fel was already turning towards the sound, the arrow striking into his armoured chest with enough force to send him to one knee. The mail had taken the worst of it, though, and he was already lurching back to his feet. Stenwold rushed forward, pointing the snapbow wildly in the archer's direction, and the man lifted off, wings flickering in the lamplight before they carried him back down the length of the pier.

The conflict had stilled behind them, and Stenwold turned to see Cynthaen and Paladrya at the pier's very edge. Their opponent lay at Cynthaen's feet, with two deep wounds driven into his back, while Laszlo was cleaning his dagger with an unaccustomedly grim look on his face.

'We've seen these lads before, Mar'Maker,' he pointed out.

Stenwold nodded, drawn unwillingly back to the fatal fight on the barge. Teornis's men, they had to be, which meant that either some other Aldanrael agent was on his trail, or . . .

Or Teornis had got to shore before him. It would surprise Stenwold not at all if that was true. He was a capable man, Teornis, and he would have found some way to manipulate Claeon into freeing him. Abruptly Stenwold felt certain that the Dragonflies had not been sent as assassins, only as spies – that their true prize, the knowledge of where Aradocles might be found, was even now winging its way back to their Aldanrael liege.

'Fel,' he said. 'You're wounded?'

The sea-kinden was staring down at the arrow, looking slightly perplexed now the fighting was done. He tugged at it experimentally and winced, but Stenwold had the impression that the shell mail had done its job and that the wound must be only shallow.

'Never saw that before,' the Onychoi murmured, baffled, and Stenwold was reminded that the sea-people were not well known for archery.

'We need to get to Princep Salmae as quickly as possible,' Stenwold decided. 'If Aradocles is there, we have to find him before *they* do.'

His last glimpse of Cynthaen was to see her staring down at the dead Dragonfly in a kind of helpless frustration, as though she had been robbed by him, as though she would rather have died as a Mantis-kinden should do, than live on as she was.

Varante finished his report, looking sour and vengeful about the death of his kin. They were a proud lot, the Dragonfly-kinden of Solorn, descendants of the retinue of an exiled prince before they became the subjects of the Spider Aristoi. Teornis was only glad that his vassal had retained the self-possession to deliver his report rather than drawing a blade and wading in himself.

*Ah, well, there's no such thing as a perfect slave, as they say.* 'Do you know,' he remarked to Helmess Broiler, 'I have never yet had cause to visit Princep Salmae. Have they even finished it?'

'That place never much interested me.' The Beetle shrugged. 'Just some band of uprooted peasants and former slaves pitching a few tents in the wilderness. Still, I understand the Sarnesh are busy cultivating them, for whatever reason.'

'Well, now it would seem that I must make the visit. Maker will have agents there, of course.'

'Oh, probably. The fellow it's named after was one of his students, after all.' Helmess smiled unpleasantly. 'You'll have your work cut out for you, my lord Spider. Who would talk to you there, when they'll love and revere Maker as a war hero, a saviour? Won't you be at something of a disadvantage?'

'You forget, I'm also a war hero.' Teornis's teeth flashed in a grin. 'Moreover, a Spider-kinden Aristos is *never* at a disadvantage. Stenwold may simply have countered some of my natural superiority, that's all. Secure me a flying machine – for me and Varante and his people.'

Helmess frowned. 'Just like that?'

'It's what you Beetles are good at, isn't it? Machines, logistics? I'll take your man Sands as well. He's nicely inconspicuous. There may be a few too many Common-wealers about for Varante's people to pass unnoticed. What? Don't look so sour, man. After all, we're on the same side, aren't we? We want the same thing,'

'Oh, yes,' said Helmess heavily. His eyes flicked towards Elytrya, and Teornis smiled.

'While you're making the arrangements, I'll keep your lovely mistress company, shall I, just a little insurance for your good behaviour? After all, we wouldn't want you getting any unprofitable ideas.'

# Thirty-Seven

There were few things that might have roused this middle-aged Beetle willingly from his sleep, past midnight, after a late night spent tinkering with the innards of an airship engine. When the rapping had begun at his window, he had done his best to ignore it. The lodgings by the airfield were cheap, frequented by all manner of tramp aviators, small traders and cack-handed artificers. Drunken guests trying to break into the wrong room were not unknown. Yet the noise had continued, and then he had caught, through the pillow he had hauled over his head, the sound of his own name.

Cursing, he had arisen, draped awkwardly in a blanket. A tightness about his head informed him that he had gone to bed with his goggles still on. He took a heavy wrench in one hand and hauled the window shutters open, glaring balefully at the Fly-kinden youth clinging there.

'I don't know you,' the Beetle said flatly. 'Now you bugger off or I'll brain you.'

'Stenwold Maker needs you,' the Fly told him.

For much of a minute the Beetle just stared at him, as though trying to unhear those words by sheer effort of will, but then he swore and threw the wrench into a corner. 'At his place?'

'He's on his way here now,' the Fly said. 'Ten minutes away, maybe.'

'Fine.' The Beetle sighed deeply, then shook his head. 'I'll meet him out on the field, bastard nuisance that he is.'

The Fly dropped from the window ledge, his wings flurrying him away as though a strong wind had caught him. Feeling sour and tired, the Beetle-kinden man began to dress himself, hauling on the hard-wearing leathers of an artificer.

He stumped downstairs to the door of his lodgings. The woman that ran the place, a boot-faced Ant and Beetle halfbreed, was inexplicably waiting ready for him in the obvious belief that he intended shirking payment of the bill. He had stayed at this place on and off for seven years, and yet she still would not trust him an inch or advance him a clay bit's worth of credit.

'I'll be going for a while,' he told her, after settling up. 'Hold the room for me.'

'Where to this time?' Her tone suggested that only the congenitally mad would contemplate a life of travel for themselves.

'No idea,' he replied, confirming her in her conviction. Then he was out of the door, into the night, stamping across to the airfield.

There was a faint mist that had come in off the sea, and the great lamps delineating the airfield's perimeter turned it into a shimmering, silver-red haze. Within it, the shapes of flying machines loomed like the relics of monsters: orthopters with wings folded upwards or back along their sleek lines; lumpen heliopters with their rotors drooping and still; aggressive-styled flyers with two or even three banks of fixed wings. Over them all loomed the grand hulks of the dirigibles, like a convoy of moons strung over the airfield, and the beached ship-hulls that were gondolas awaiting the inflation of their balloons.

The Beetle first went to the hull of his own airship and, with quiet practice, started the pumps that would see her own gasbag fill up. Then he perched in the vessel's prow and watched, waiting for the inevitable, until he saw the promised Stenwold Maker. The old man had changed little since they had last done business: a bit leaner perhaps, but just as strung out with energy and tension. There were a couple of Fly-kinden and a few others clustered about him, but Maker always had possessed a strange taste in friends.

The Beetle aviator let himself down from his airship to the ground, aware that the time had come to put aside – for the night or for the tenday or who knew how long – his commerce and his freedom, and instead dance to Maker's tune once more. A combination of guilt, remembrance and his personal honour meant that he never even thought of just walking away.

'Master Maker,' he acknowledged gruffly, when the man reached him. The Assembler's straggling entourage, he noted, looked even more miscellaneous than usual.

'Jons Allanbridge,' Stenwold named him, with a slight smile. 'It's been a while since the war.'

'Since the last one,' Allanbridge agreed. 'Not dead after all, then?'

'Not for want of trying.'

The two Beetles clasped hands solemnly. Stenwold looked into the other man's face and read enough to guess at secrets – at recent revisions to the man's life that Allanbridge was none too keen to bring to light.

'Where do you trade these days, Jons?' he asked, watching for a shadow to cross the man's face. He had encountered this situation before: a trusted agent left to go wild, and who could know what you would find, when you went back? And Allanbridge had never been Stenwold's man, precisely, just a patriotic free-trader willing to sail where Stenwold asked in return for a fair price and repairs to his vessel.

Allanbridge shrugged. 'Since we'd visited there, I thought I'd have a crack at the Commonweal. Hard going, but I like a challenge.' Something dark was hiding in his face that he wasn't revealing, but for the moment Stenwold trusted that it was just the usual round of smuggling and contraband.

'This isn't the *Maiden*,' Stenwold noted, looking up at the steadily expanding balloon. He had fond memories of Allanbridge's previous craft.

'With the war and all, I raised credit to trade up. Needed bigger cargo space, mostly,' Allanbridge replied, sounding more enthusiastic. 'She's named the *Windlass*. Nice, eh?'

Stenwold nodded. 'Getting ready to take her out, then?'

'Just like old times, is it?' Allanbridge gave a huge sigh. 'Where to, Master Maker?'

'Princep Salmae.'

The destination was obviously a surprise to the aviator. 'That close? I thought you were going to say Shon Fhor or Capitas or Solarno or somesuch. That's all you want me for? Princep Salmae's a two-day trip at most.'

'The quicker the better, though. She can carry all of us?'

'And twice as many again. Get your people aboard and we'll leave as soon as she's fully up.'

Stenwold turned back to his followers: Laszlo and the sea-kinden. With the exception of the Fly, they were staring up at the growing gasbag with astounded awe. The hull itself was enough like a boat for them to recognize, and Stenwold could see that Allanbridge could make a water landing in the *Windlass* easily if he needed, but the balloon itself was immense, building-sized. They could never have seen anything like it before, he thought, until Paladrya murmured, 'Medusoi of the sky.' He looked again, and saw for a moment, in that burgeoning expanse of silk and heated gas, the bell and tendrils of Lyess's translucent companion.

The sea-kinden's reaction to the flight was surprising. At first the lifting sensation completely bewildered them: they looked ill, swaying and lurching in the *Windlass*'s cargo hold, as Allanbridge sent the airship bobbing over the spires of Collegium. They clutched at every available support, and at each other, and their footing skidded and slipped. They were so obviously unsure of what in the world was going on, that Stenwold led them up on to the deck, and showed them the land in all its midnight glory.

They stayed at the rail for a long time, and though he could not see their faces, Laszlo did, skipping around in the air before them, showing off shamelessly. They had looked threatened at first, he told Stenwold later, as though they could never have guessed that horizons could be so far away. Then dawn came up behind them, a few hours later, a pale radiance that their progress seemed for a while in danger of leaving behind, and then a slowly growing red, and finally the sea-kinden watched the sun come up over a landscape, for the first time.

Fel and Phylles wanted no part of it, after that. This was more than they needed to know, it became clear: the sooner they returned to the waves, the better, as far as they were concerned. They went back below to converse, and to pretend they were just in some submersible somewhere, rather than suspended impossibly over miles and miles of distant patchwork fields, above brown hills and the beige expanses of scrubby grazing land. Wys remained, though. She stood at the stern and faced into the sunrise, regarding the land with a seemingly proprietorial air. Stenwold wondered just what she and Tomasso had cooked up together when out of his surveillance, and whether either land or sea would survive their partnership.

Paladrya stayed close to Stenwold until well past noon, until the sun was beating down on them, when she shrouded herself in a hooded cloak to save her skin from blistering. Even Wys was driven below, by then, and Laszlo had tired of his aerobatics, so it was just the two Beetles and the Kerebroi woman left out in the open air. Only then did she approach the rail, looking down over an increasingly arid landscape. She seemed to have no fear of heights, so much so that Stenwold stayed within arm's reach just in case she leant over too far. He supposed that she was used to depths, instead, where there was no such thing as falling.

He took the rail beside her, resting his elbows on it. She glanced his way, her cowl hiding all expression. 'Tell me of your war,' she said. 'The war that my Aradocles must have been caught up in?'

So it was that Stenwold found himself recounting, in miniature, the story of the Wasp Empire and its invasion of the Lowlands, with particular attention to the history of Prince Minor Salme Dien, who had once been his student and had then become a warlord, a champion of the dispossessed, and had at last become a martyr, in whose name a city was being built.

Later still, after napping fitfully in the hold, he stood beside her to see the sun set over Lake Sideriti, staining its blue-green waters red. The city of Princep Salmae lay at the lake's most northerly point, over to the west of Sarn. As the blood-tinted waters passed beneath them, Paladrya leant into him, not flirting, not even affectionate as such, but something comfortably comradely. He sensed her deep worry, her fear that the trail of Aradocles would dry up; that he would merely turn out to be one of the numberless and nameless who had given their lives to slow the Wasp advance.

*After all, even Salma died, in the end.*

The streets of Princep Salmae were picked out unevenly with braziers of burning coals, and Stenwold received the impression of an ordered pattern of buildings, save that most of the buildings were missing and only the pattern itself remained. He had already heard a little about the place: rather than simply start a camp or a village by the lakeside, Salma's surrogate nation had begun with grand ideas. They had measured and paced out all the districts of their perfect city, conferred and voted on what their eventual home should contain, and how it should function. Even to Stenwold, used to Collegium's brand of participatory government, it seemed impossible that anything functional would emerge from such a system – and yet here was Princep Salmae, in outline. Perhaps a quarter of it was built: simple wooden structures in a melange of styles. Even in the twilight, he recognized Commonweal rooftops, Collegiate Beetle designs, plain Ant-kinden dwellings, and other part-built structures that were either in some style he didn't know or something unique to the architect's imagination. Still, most of the city was nothing more than demarcated plots, with a host of ordered tents showing the greater part of the population still waiting patiently for permanent housing. The lakeshore was littered with dozens of small boats, and towards this sketch-city's eastern edge there was a space set aside for an airfield, dotted with a few flying machines. Jons Allanbridge brought the *Windlass* down there with scrupulous care, as Paladrya went below to rouse the other sea-kinden.

Stenwold was first down the ladder, seeing a pair of women approach with the evident air of officials. They were white-haired, though not old, and for a moment he could not place them. Then he recognized them as Roach-kinden, a wandering breed not so often seen in the Lowlands, though commonly found in points north and east. They obviously recognized his name, when he gave it, and seemed more curious than officious.

'I have an old friend at your palace, I think,' he told them, 'who I'd be glad to speak to on a matter of urgency.' It seemed the simplest way of starting his hunt here. 'Do you know Balkus the Ant-kinden? He led me to believe he was the commander of the palace guard, or some such.'

They knew Balkus, certainly, and he was well liked, Stenwold could see.

'But he is not here,' one of them informed him.

'He's at the palace, then?'

She shook her head. 'He is not in Princep. He has gone to the Folly.'

Stenwold frowned at her, aware of the sea-kinden

crowding behind him now, and suddenly understood. 'Mal-kan's Folly?'

'Even so, Master,' the other Roach-kinden said.

That made matters more difficult. The Folly was a fortress the Sarnesh were building on the site of the battle where General Malkan and the Imperial Seventh Army had been defeated during the war. Stenwold had heard the boasts: it was the most modern and formidable piece of fortification ever seen, designed with every ounce of Sarnesh ingenuity to make it impossible for another Wasp army to march on their city. Stenwold had often planned to go and witness the construction. It was inconvenient that Balkus had meanwhile taken to the same idea.

He asked if they knew when the Ant would be back. They did not, but said the man had only left recently.

Stenwold waited until the two of them had gone, before hissing tiredly between his teeth. 'In the morning we apply to the palace,' he suggested. 'For now, we should sleep on the *Windlass*. I'd rather not wander about a strange city at night looking for lodgings.'

He was about to turn for the rope ladder when one of the other machines on the field caught his notice. He frowned, thinking *Surely not*, and walked slowly towards it, squinting in the dying light. It was a big, boxy vehicle, with three sets of rotors drooping from its top, and it looked remarkably familiar except that it was *here*, in this city that had been born as a result of the Empire's tyrannies.

But it was just what he had thought. Closer, he saw the dark and light stripes that sunlight would reveal as black and gold. It was an Imperial heliopter sitting open and bold on the airfield at Princep Salmae. *What is the Empire doing here? What is going on?*

The mute machine gave him no answers, so eventually Stenwold retreated to the *Windlass*, where he would enjoy precious little sleep from worrying.

*

Teornis had his Fly-kinden pilot take the orthopter once around Princep Salmae's perimeter, his Spider-kinden eyes making out the streets and vacant lots with ease in the moonlight. He wondered if Maker had arrived already. It had taken Helmess Broiler long enough to arrange this flying machine that it was entirely possible.

'What do you make of it?' he asked Forman Sands. The halfbreed killer had been unexpectedly good company on the journey, proving well-read and well-spoken. Teornis had watched with amusement as the man's loyalties smoothly segued from being Helmess's man to being the Spider lord's follower, all without a jot of conscience.

'Fascinating, my lord, to see a city in potential. After they build it, it will be nothing but a slum of shacks, no doubt, but as of now . . .'

Teornis nodded, pleased with the assessment. 'Well, we must enjoy it before they ruin it by making it real.' He had the Fly bring the machine down outside the nominal boundaries that passed for Princep's walls, and then sent the flyer away. Once he had Aradocles in hand, if the heir was even here, then he would find his own way back to Collegium without difficulty.

'How do you plan to find your man, Lord Teornis?' Sands asked him. 'Send your Dragonflies hunting through the streets?'

'Only as a last resort,' Teornis replied. 'My former patron, the Edmir Claeon, has some interesting resources. The customs of his people can result in a curious manner of art. See this?' Teornis reached into his tunic and produced the portrait Claeon had ordered drawn. It was a remarkable sketch in purple ink on their thick, spongy paper, but the artist had known Aradocles by sight and, by his skill at accreation, had been able to render the image accurately from his mind straight into the picture. 'We shall take this likeness,' Teornis explained, 'and we shall make enquiries about a Spider youth. There is bound to be

567

someone in this city whose business is tracking and finding, so we shall put them to work for us. And meanwhile we shall find our Master Maker.'

He took the rest of the night to find a Wayhouse, a rough-hewn timber building, still new and unpainted. A generous donation of Helmess Broiler's money ensured that he and his party would not be disturbed there. The brief walk through Princep Salmae had amused Teornis: even after dark, the place was busy just like a Spider town, and it was – also like certain places in the Spiderlands – filled with such a remarkable variety of the lower elements of society. On the road to the Wayhouse he counted a dozen different kinden, most of them not normal residents of the Lowlands, and Roach-kinden most of all. He knew of Roaches from the Spiderlands, where they were itinerant nuisances, vagabonds and charlatans. They had their uses as procurers, spies and informants perhaps, but here they were bustling about everywhere as though Princep was some kind of home for them, and as though they were fit to be considered responsible citizens. That made Teornis smile, when little else had just recently.

Since Princep didn't stop for dusk, there was no reason that their search should. Teornis, however, felt that he had earned some sleep, He passed the portrait to Forman Sands and Varante, and sent them off to locate anyone whose business was the hunting down of fellow human beings. Forman Sands seemed a good man to be asking questions, Teornis had decided, and Varante was a good man to keep a wary eye on Sands, just in case some residual loyalty to Helmess Broiler remained.

With his agents thus dispatched, Teornis took the straw mattress that was all the Way Brothers could offer him, and slept easy, blessed by pleasant dreams.

In the morning he took breakfast, sending another of his Dragonflies out with money to supplement the meagre fare the Brothers could provide. Sands was already back, but first Teornis heard the report of a couple of his men who he had sent off on another errand before even arriving at the Wayhouse.

'Tell me you've found Maker?' he prompted them.

'He came in a flying machine to the airfield,' one of the pair informed him. 'He has several followers: two Flies, a Mantis, a Spider, and one other. The flying machine left this morning, in the direction of Sarn perhaps. Maker is talking to people.'

'Of course he is,' Teornis said absently, but he was thinking – *just random people, Stenwold? No friends from the past? No special contacts? Have I eroded your advantage already, old man?* 'Keep an eye on him,' he instructed, and the Dragonflies nodded, bowed briefly and left the room.

Sands and Varante came in next. Helmess's halfbreed thug wore an odd expression, one that Teornis could not immediately read.

'You've had an eventful night, I hope?'

'We found a tracker, my lord, after a while.'

'Just one?'

'One's all we needed, my lord.'

Teornis rolled his eyes. 'Suspense is for stage actors, Master Sands. Kindly enlighten me.'

And Forman Sands explained what he had learned, and Teornis's eyes went first wide in surprise, and then narrow in careful consideration.

# Thirty-Eight

The architects of Princep evidently intended raising some great edifices to overlook their airfield, but nothing was in place but their plot boundaries as yet. With dawn these became the site of an impromptu foreigners' market, and Laszlo took Wys and her cohorts out to inspect what wares were on show. The peddlers were mostly Roach- or Fly-kinden, so Stenwold guessed that there would be nothing for sale that would have excited a Collegium merchant, but to Wys it would all be both strange and saleable, no doubt.

While they were thus occupied, he found a little eatery with a scattering of chairs and tables, and bought for himself and Paladrya some concoction of rice and roasted mealworms to breakfast on. It took some persuasion to convince her to taste it, but it turned out to be acceptable to a marine palate.

Jons Allanbridge was already airborne by now, heading in the direction of the Sarnesh fortifications named Mal-kan's Folly, in the hope of intercepting Balkus and wringing some information from him. That seemed the best that Stenwold was likely to achieve, left to his own devices.

He cast his gaze about for Laszlo and the others, saw them some distance away, looking at some poor clothier's homespun and woollens: all wonders, no doubt, for the sea-kinden. When he glanced back, he found Paladrya staring at him, and for a moment he held her gaze.

'I am waiting for the strike,' she told him. At his frown she elaborated. 'Some careful, camouflaged creature, waiting as its prey drifts nearer and nearer, drawn in by some lure. Aradocles is the lure, I am the prey. Where is your trap, Stenwold Maker?'

'I am not the trap-laying kind,' he told her.

'Then why? You were safe back with your people, so why are you now here?'

'You think I mean your boy harm?'

She studied him for some time before she said, 'No, but I still don't know why.'

A new voice broke in, 'You forget Master Maker's essential nobility of character.' Someone sat down briskly at their table, as naturally as if this new arrival were an old friend. Stenwold found himself looking into the face of Teornis of the Aldanrael.

For a moment nothing was said. He had his little snapbow concealed inside his tunic, ready loaded but not primed. His sword was at his belt. There were two of Teornis's Dragonfly-kinden standing a respectful distance away, but their blades were to hand, slanted back over their shoulders, and Stenwold had no illusions about his own speed on the draw compared with theirs in response.

'Teornis,' he said, at last, 'this is a . . . surprise.'

'You might at least say a pleasant one,' the Spider remarked, smiling amicably. He gave a nod to Paladrya. 'My lady, outside the Edmir's grasp you look decidedly more radiant – as do we all, I fancy.'

'I knew you would somehow trick your way out of his clutches,' Stenwold observed.

'You make it sound as if that were unfair,' Teornis said. 'Was I unjust to cheat Claeon of his prize?'

'Yes, if you did so by promising him the head of Aradocles,' Stenwold replied flatly. He sensed Paladrya tensing.

For a moment all humour dropped from Teornis's face.

'Remember your slippery friends freed you before Claeon introduced you to his pleasure chambers, Stenwold. You would have promised him a good deal more, I swear it, to be rid of his company. Ask her: I'll wager she and I have that experience in common.'

'But you *are* here for my Aradocles,' Paladyra said softly. 'I can see that much.'

'Oh, certainly,' and all the good nature was back on display. Teornis smiled at her fondly. 'But I won't harm a hair on the lad's head. He's far too valuable for that.'

'You'll use him to control Claeon,' Stenwold confirmed, 'and bring the sea-kinden down on Collegium, as your armada arrives.'

'Even as you'd use him to oust Claeon and remove a threat to your city,' Teornis agreed. 'Were it not for the paltry matter of a disagreement between our peoples, I'd heartily support you.'

'What do you want, Teornis?' Stenwold asked. 'We are now enemies. Your people have made us that.'

'Oh, I know,' the Spider replied, his expression suggesting genuine regret. 'No idea of mine, but we all have our duty. Still, surely we can sit here and speak awhile, without drawn blades? For who else has seen what we have seen? Who else from the land has been within Hermatyre, has endured that darkness, those depths? You and I and your Fly, wherever he is, but none else that has lived to tell the tale. And yet here we are, and don't you think that unites us more than a traders' squabble? We were friends once, Stenwold. When this is over, we'll be so again. You'll want friends in the east when the Empire returns, as we both know it will.'

Stenwold looked at the man's infinitely trustworthy, yet infinitely deceptive face, and shook his head. 'Why couldn't your family be happy with what it had already?' he said, almost in a whisper. Paladrya glanced between them, sensing the weight of their history but knowing that it excluded her.

'Only the dull and the foolish are ever happy with what they've got. Do you sit there, victorious son of the Apt revolution, and preach stagnation? No, and if we'd not moved to jostle the status quo, then one of your greedier magnates would have done so soon enough. Life is all about striving and change, Stenwold. What a bland creature you yourself would be, had the Empire not reforged you, eh?'

'Happier, I'd say.'

'We are not made for stale happiness,' Teornis told him. 'Look at us now, unthanked champions escaped from an impossible prison, returned from certain death, trekking across the Lowlands to hunt down a scion of a mythical kingdom, and to *find* him, too, and what odds would anyone have placed on that?'

Stenwold felt something twitch, within him, but he held it at arm's length, kept it from his expression. 'Long ones, I'd say,' was all he would commit himself to replying.

Teornis stood up, still smiling. 'There has never been a Beetle-kinden like you. Your people sorely underestimate you, and you're wasted on them. After all this has blown over, after we're friends again, come to Seldis. A man of your skills is wasted in Collegium.'

Teornis bowed to them and strode off, just some Spider-kinden Aristos taking the morning air. A moment later, Wys and the other sea-kinden rejoined them hurriedly, staring after Teornis suspiciously.

'Who was that?' the little Onychoi woman demanded.

'Our enemy, unfortunately,' Stenwold explained sadly. Then he frowned. 'Where's Laszlo?'

'He knew your man there,' Wys gestured. 'He went *up*.' She mouthed the word almost superstitiously. The sea-kinden were still finding the concept of Art-powered flight

573

hard to reconcile. They twitched every time some citizen of Princep coursed overhead.

'Up?' For a moment Stenwold didn't understand, but then he rose quickly, trying to spot Teornis, but the Spider and his men were already out of sight. *Laszlo's gone to spy on Teornis, the fool. Doesn't he realize how sharp-eyed those Dragonflies are?* And yet Fly-kinden were a stealthy lot, renowned for getting wherever they weren't wanted, and getting out again with what wasn't theirs. *And also, if I read Teornis's words right, I am in dire need of learning what his plans are.*

He sighed. It was out of his hands now. *Be safe, Laszlo, and next time try not to be so cursed rash.*

*And succeed. If it's possible, succeed.*

'What now?' Wys asked him flatly. 'We've got to wait for him to come back? Is the heir even *here*?' Her gesture took in the busy chaos of Princep, a skeleton city still under construction.

'My "friend" Teornis overestimates me, just as he says my people underestimate me,' Stenwold murmured, drawing confused looks from all present.

'What do you mean?' Paladrya asked him.

'I mean that his own researches are further ahead than ours, and he has told us something that we weren't sure of until now, although Teornis assumed I'd possess the same knowledge as a matter of course. He *knows* that Aradocles is alive, and not only alive but somewhere in this city.'

Forman Sands was waiting when Teornis returned to the Wayhouse, but the Spider waved him away, retreating into his private room with a bottle of the best wine the Way Brothers could provide him, and brooding there for almost an hour. At last he sent word by Varante that Sands should join him.

'Tell me that you were successful at their palace, Master

Sands,' Teornis directed him. At the halfbreed's expression, his face soured. 'Or not, as the case may be?'

'The man I met said only this: she sees no one.'

'Indeed?' Teornis raised an eyebrow. 'I trust you waxed long to him on how important my business with Princep is. Does the name of the Aldanrael carry no weight, these days?'

Forman Sands spread his hands helplessly. 'No one,' he said. The Monarch of Princep Salmae is in mourning and has been since the war. She makes appearances, sometimes, up on her balcony to wave to her people, but receives no ambassadors, no statesmen, no Assemblers, no Aristoi. She'd turn away the Wasp Emperor himself.'

'Scarcely surprising, given recent history,' Teornis murmured. 'Has Maker got to them already? Are they primed against us?'

'It's not the impression I got,' Sands reported. 'In mourning, they said, and in mourning I believe. It's a weird place, this one; doesn't work in any way I can work out. Not a city, just a load of people in one place with the same idea, it seems to me, except . . . this woman of theirs, this Monarch, I reckon they love her for it, even if all she does is mope.'

Teornis made an exasperated noise. 'Well, someone must make the decisions.'

'I'm not entirely sure about that, Master,' Sands replied humbly in disagreement, 'but she has underlings at the palace, yes, even if they are still building it. A whole grab-bag of them, and the man I spoke to called himself her chancellor. Roach-kinden fellow by the name of Sfayot, or something like that. A lot of them looked to be Roaches, at the palace. I reckon old Sfayot has invited his entire family in.'

'We call them vermin in the Spiderlands,' Teornis said disgustedly. 'While here they call them chancellor. Great ladies preserve us! Well, will this Sfayot of yours at least spare me the time of day?'

'He will meet with you in three days' time,' Sands said unhappily, expecting an outburst of anger.

Instead, Teornis merely stared into the dregs of his wine. 'Too long, that. We cannot know when Maker will make his sortie, and he has more influence here than I. We cannot let him get within the palace before us . . .' He broke off as Varante suddenly dashed across the room to the window, drawing out his sword. A moment later the Dragonfly-kinden had squirmed outside, sliding out through the narrow opening with remarkable ease. They heard him on the roof seconds after, stalking about, but there was nothing more, no sounds of violence. Still, Teornis waited, holding up a hand for silence when Sands began to speak, until Varante reappeared the same way.

'And?' the Spider Aristos demanded.

Varante shook his head, looking surly. 'Nothing, my lord,' was all he said, but his head was cocked on one side, still listening out for whatever had set him off.

Teornis sighed. 'Varante is a warrior,' he explained for Sands's benefit. 'His people are loyal, skilled, reliable, but perhaps a little lacking in patience.'

'You don't need to tell me,' Sands agreed vehemently. 'One of the lads you sent with me to the palace got himself cut up on the way back.' At Teornis's frown he went on, 'Some Commonwealer we ran into, and your man decided to start calling him names. They were out with those big swords before I knew it, and each cutting a chunk out of the other.'

'Varante, explain,' Teornis directed.

The Dragonfly looked sullen. 'It is a matter of honour between our peoples. We are of Solorn, one of the Seven Exiles, and we cannot stand by while those who betrayed our ancestors walk free.'

Teornis put his hands to his forehead. Spider-kinden

servants would not have these issues, but then they would not have been so free to act in Collegium, either, and Collegium saw few visitors from the Commonweal. This patchwork city had been named after a Commonwealer, though, and Teornis had already seen plenty of Varante's northern kin out on the streets, curious visitors drawn by the name and reputation of Princep Salmae. When he had originally sent for Varante so long ago, to counter Maker's Mantis-kinden, he had not expected their seven-centuries-old feuding to suddenly become relevant.

'I should not need,' he said stiffly, 'to stress just how important this errand of ours is. I should not need to, because you are of my cadre, Varante, my servants, and therefore any order of mine is important enough to die for. I have relied on you, and I have placed my faith in your honour. Was I wrong?'

There was a glowering pause before Varante replied, 'No, lord.'

'Then you will ensure your men keep to their place,' Teornis instructed him, without an inch of concession in his voice. 'More, we will move tonight. They can deny their palace and their Monarch to visitors all they like, but until they actually finish building the wretched place, it's academic. We're going in to take custody of the heir before Maker does.'

'And Maker himself?' Sands asked.

'Will be slower, I hope.' Teornis looked up at him. 'Why do you ask, Sands?'

'Let me kill him for you,' Forman Sands offered.

'You are ambitious.'

'Master, I killed Beetle Assemblers for Helmess Broiler. They die just as readily as those that vote them in. It's what I do, after all, so just give me the word and I'll make sure Maker's no longer in your way. You've seen this dive: there's no law here. The folks of Princep will barely notice.'

Teornis stared at him bleakly, 'And, of course, Helmess

Broiler will be delighted, should you then find yourself back in his service.'

Sands shrugged. 'Is it wrong if it serves him too?'

Teornis closed his eyes. In repose, his face looked older and wearier, the face of a man who has slept too little, dared too much. When at last he looked on Sands again there was no pleasure in his expression, only a great measure of regret.

'I will not give you the order,' was all he said in the end, and Sands was left to shrug and back out of his presence.

Down in the Wayhouse's common room, Sands, too, procured a bottle of wine from the brothers and reflected. It was not any residual loyalty to Helmess Broiler that motivated him – or not chiefly. It would be useful to hold open the chance of his old employment – trusting a Spider-kinden was never entirely wise – but Sands now felt that it was a philosophical consideration that swayed him most. He had at first been keen to inveigle his way into Teornis's service, for the prospect of learning the trade of the manip-ulator from one of life's masters had been exciting, and he felt that he was becoming blunt in Helmess's service. Everyone knew that Spiders were charming, erudite, ingenious, infinitely deceptive and utterly merciless. He had expected, even looked forward to, all of that. What he had not expected was sentiment.

*Kill Maker.* It was that simple. Maker was a competitor and obstacle to Teornis's ambitions, and therefore he should be removed. Sands could not understand what was staying the Spider's hand. In Sands's world, that curious world he had brewed for himself from academic philosophy and criminal brutality, there were the superior men, and there was the common swarm. The superior man recog-nized his own superiority, evidenced by his sophistication and his freedom of action – no chains of guilt or conscience, of ignorance or instinct, for him. The superior man was above the law, because the law was made to keep the swarm in place, not to check the aspirations of the few men able to master themselves. Stenwold Maker, in Sands's view, was a man who had once had the potential to cross that barrier, but who had squandered his gifts on trying to improve the lot of his inferiors, which was like pouring water into the sands of the desert.

*Kill Maker.* Sands stood up. Teornis would not give the order? But Teornis had not forbidden it, even so. If Sands came to him with Stenwold's blood on his hands, he could be sure that the Spider would smile at the sight. *And perhaps it's a test, after all, for the superior man knows when to go beyond mere orders. The superior man sees what is necessary.* He went to the door of the Wayhouse, stepped out into the street, hands instinctively checking on the hilts of his knives. He examined his knuckles, let the poisoned needles of his Spider-born art slide in and out. After all, he knew Maker, but Maker would not recognize him. It would be easy, therefore, to find a good moment to send the old man to his final rest, and thus satisfy Teornis and Helmess, and the harsh requirements of philosophy.

When the Way Brothers had come here from Collegium to build their hostel, they had arrived with a Beetle-styled building in mind for themselves, which they would normally have built of stone. Stone was in short supply in Princep Salmae, however, so they had made do with wood, putting the whole thing up with beams and planking as best they could, but in the flat-roofed style of a Collegium inn. To keep the worst of the weather off the interior, they had constructed the Wayhouse with a space between the ceilings of the topmost rooms and the roof itself, an open-sided cavity only a foot in height where the moths roosted and the roaches crawled.

It was a tiny, shadowed flatland of a world, but it was just large enough for an enterprising Fly-kinden to take refuge there and hear a great deal of what was said below him. Laszlo now lay spreadeagled in this confined space, Teornis's last words to Forman Sands still ringing in his ears, ready now to make his way to the front of the building for a quick escape and an airborne return to alert Stenwold Maker. He had heard enough, and he had even been able to peek between the boards of the ceiling below him, to catch fragmented glimpses of Teornis' face, and that of the Beetle-looking man he had called Sands.

Laszlo hunched forward, and forward again, knees and elbows doing most of the work with a little sticking Art to give them purchase. He had almost suffered a heart attack when Teornis's Dragonfly thug had burst out of the window below, surely after hearing an incautious movement of Laszlo's. But the Dragonfly's imagination was not a match for his senses, and he had soared straight up to the flat roof, to stalk about angrily immediately over Laszlo's head, unable to locate his quarry.

Laszlo shuffled to the front edge of the building, peering carefully out of the long, narrow gap between wall and shingles that had given him entrance to this hiding space in the first place. The first thing he saw was Sands himself standing at the front doorway below. The man – some kind of halfbreed, Laszlo guessed, but mostly Beetle in his looks – paused briefly, hands going through a brief ritual as casual as if he was adjusting his clothing. A Fly's sharp eyes, though, saw the hilts of the weapons whose presence Sands found so reassuring. The man then strode off into the streets of Princep Salmae, and Laszlo had an uneasy feeling about his intentions, despite all that Teornis had said. His course could be set for a variety of destinations in the city, it was true, but surely Stenwold was in that quarter too.

Laszlo bunched himself for a swift exit, knowing he would make better time through the air than the man walking the streets below him, and thus be able to warn Stenwold just in case. He reached for his Art, about to have his wings eject him from the dark space like a cork from a bottle, when the Dragonfly was abruptly before him, blotting Laszlo's strip of light for a second before alighting on the roof again. Some movement, some shifting of balance on the Fly's part, had been heard, and this time the man was obviously fighting mad, absolutely convinced that there was an eavesdropper, crossing back and forth about the roof, no doubt sword in hand ready to deal death to the intruder. Most often his pacing brought him to the very lip of the roof immediately above where Laszlo lay concealed.

The Fly all but held his breath, keeping deadly still. Of course, he could simply make a run for it the moment the Dragonfly's back was turned, and under any other circumstances he would have trusted to his race's famed agility and speed in the air to throw off pursuit in double time. With Dragonfly-kinden, though . . . if ever there was a race just as comfortable in the air as Laszlo's own, it was they. When the *Tidenfree* had sailed through Spiderlands waters, they had met plenty of Dragonflies from various of the exile principalities that had budded off from the Commonweal centuries earlier. Those from Castilla were as paranoid as Ants, those from Magnaferra polite and elegant as Spiders themselves, and these clowns from Solorn, that Teornis had recruited, were savage and bloody-handed as Mantids, but they were all bad news to have as enemies, swift and sudden, skilled and agile, and utterly relentless. *Probably I could outfly him*, Laszlo told himself, but 'probably' might not be good enough. Those big swords the Dragonflies favoured could cut a poor Fly-kinden in half, given the chance.

The halfbreed was meanwhile out of sight across the city, and his path had looked very much as though it might intersect Stenwold Maker's whereabouts at the airfield. Laszlo itched to go, but the cursed Dragonfly just continued hunting the barren square of roof above him, and would not give up on the scent.

# Thirty-Nine

'This is a gold Central, from the Helleron mints,' Stenwold explained patiently. 'That's the price of a sword, traditionally. These in silver are Standards, ten to a Central. This,' he held up a disc of clay divided into segments, 'is a wheel of bits. You can break it into pieces, and there are,' he squinted at it, 'fifty bits to a Standard here. They fire these wheels locally. They're no good outside the city they're made in.' He laid the coins down at the outdoor table he and Paladrya had commandeered earlier for their breakfast.

At first he thought that Wys was finding all this difficult to take in. Then he realized she was just having trouble *believing* it.

'This . . . this is money?' she asked him, holding up a Central. 'But it's *gold*!'

'Probably no more than half gold,' Stenwold admitted. 'We don't use paper for money, up here.'

'I'm not surprised, since I've seen your paper. Spit on it and it turns to mush,' she said derisively. She stuck out a thin arm, displaying a bracelet of finely interwoven golden threads. 'This is money, then?'

'It's worth money,' Stenwold agreed. 'I couldn't say how much. There's not much weight of gold to it, but the workmanship is fine.'

'It is? Why, thank you.' She grinned at what had apparently been a compliment. 'Everything's backwards here, but

I think I like it. Despite how pissing hot and cold and fussy your air gets.' Her pale skin was roasted pink in places, and she had secured from some vendor a Spider-style parasol to keep off the sun. Fel and Phylles had been driven into the shade before noon, but Wys could not get enough of the land-kinden and their buying and selling.

'Can I keep these?' she asked, of the coins Stenwold had been making his demonstration with.

'Consider them a downpayment,' he told her, and she fairly scampered off towards the nearest peddlers. Stenwold met Paladrya's eyes and saw her smiling.

'The Smallclaw were always the most enterprising amongst us,' she said. 'Hence the Hot Stations, I suppose. Even Claeon has had to make adjustments for them. They will lead the way to our future. I don't imagine they really care who holds the Edmiracy of Hermatyre, in the long run.'

'But you do,' Stenwold told her, 'and I find I do too.' He was waiting now, either for Laszlo to return with something, or for some news from the local messengers he had sent out. It was frustrating to know that Teornis was ahead of him but, lacking a contact in the city due to Balkus's ill-timed absence, there was little he could do. 'What was your plan?' he asked Paladrya. 'Originally, when Claeon took power, what did you foresee?'

'It would have been a grand thing to have had a plan, back then,' she replied, still smiling at him. 'It was all I could do to make that decision: to betray Claeon, save the boy. I thought Claeon would find me out sooner, and kill me in the heat of his rage. Until I met you, I had considered myself unlucky that I had been able to hide my crime from him for long enough for him to wish to keep me alive in order to punish me, rather than destroy me outright.'

There was just a twitch, at her eyes and the corner of her mouth, to hint at the force of Claeon's displeasure. Stenwold covered her hand with his own, trying to find words of sympathy. A moment later a shadow fell over them, and a stout Beetle stood there: a moustached, balding man some years Stenwold's senior, and wearing the working leathers of an artificer. Without introduction he sat down across from them at the crude table, staring narrowly at Paladrya.

'Can we help you?' Stenwold enquired, one hand finding the butt of the snapbow.

'You're the fellow that's been asking questions?' The accent was pure Collegium.

'Some questions, possibly. Are you the man who has the answers?' Stenwold pressed him.

The other Beetle looked from Stenwold back to the sea-kinden woman, who had withdrawn deeper into her cowl, plainly discomfited by him. 'It's a Spider lad you're looking for. Curly hair, barely more than a child. Came in with the Prince's lot.'

'With Salma's people, yes,' Stenwold confirmed. Seeing the flicker of surprise in the man's eyes, he added, 'I knew Prince Salme Dien at Collegium.' *And let that fact carry some weight here, surely?*

'Is that so?' was all the other man would say, then, 'What might you want this lad for?'

Stenwold frowned, wondering if this character was a slaver, perhaps, hoping to offload some random Spider-kinden criminals or debtors. 'To reunite him with his family, Master ... . ?'

'Penhold, Ordley Penhold,' the Beetle told him, but something had set in his face, at Stenwold's words. 'Well, good luck in your search, friend. I hope you find what you're after.' Ordley Penhold stood up, his expression decidedly unfriendly, and stomped off, leaving Stenwold none the wiser.

There were two other enquiries after that: a starved-looking Fly-kinden who almost certainly *was* a slaver's agent, and a Roach woman who tried to get money out of Stenwold by dropping vague hints about the youth he was looking for. The morning was wearing on, and their chances were looking grim, when the halfbreed turned up.

At first Stenwold assumed he was another Beetle, perhaps an associate of the departed Ordley Penhold, but there was a cast to his features that spoke of some mingling of bloods. In truth, Stenwold had already seen many such in Princep Salmae, and he supposed that this new city's unjudging ideology made the place even more attractive than the somewhat forced tolerance of Collegium.

He was a big man, this halfbreed, and well dressed and, when he spoke, his voice was as cultured as a Collegium scholar's. 'Word has come you're looking for a youth that looks Spider-kinden.'

Stenwold sighed tiredly, working up towards yet another wasted conversation, but Paladrya caught his arm.

'Yes,' she agreed carefully, 'he *looks* Spider-kinden.' She eyed the newcomer levelly. 'You have seen such a youth?' The description she had provided was detailed, especially as very few Spiders possessed the curly hair common amongst the Kerebroi. Stenwold felt a slight lift of excitement within him.

'Then you are not the only people searching for him,' the halfbreed murmured. 'He is . . . anxious.' He cast a hurried look about. 'We should go somewhere more private. You have a room nearby?'

Stenwold shook his head. Last night they had slept within the now departed *Windlass*, and he had given precious little thought to tonight's lodgings.

The newcomer grimaced, stepping back from the table. 'Follow me,' he said softly, beckoning them. Without looking back, he headed into a narrow alley between two of the more finished structures, a pair of tall, windowless warehouses.

Stenwold stepped into the buildings' shadow, following the burly halfbreed away from the haphazard bustle of the airfield. Instinctively, once the walls were around him, he glanced back the way they had come, watching for any who might be watching him. Paladrya was behind him, of course, and he saw a moment's alarm in her widening eyes, her mouth opening to shout a warning.

He turned back to meet the assault, his instincts sending his hand not for the snapbow within his tunic but for the sword at his side, dragging it out of its scabbard, but the halfbreed was swifter than he was, lashing out with both fists. Stenwold felt twin lines of pain rake across his face, not the solid impact of knuckles, but the searing lash of claws. He swung his sword towards the big man's midriff and then tried for a lunge, but his arm was growing leaden, his joints abruptly stiff. The weapon tumbled out of suddenly distant-seeming fingers and, the next thing he knew, he was on his knees.

With an expression on his face of quiet amusement, his attacker dragged a long-bladed knife from his belt, while Stenwold fought desperately to regain control of his body, hurling all his kinden's Art against the poison seeping inside him. With swift professionalism, the halfbreed drew his blade back for the kill.

Paladrya pushed past Stenwold, knocking him sideways, and for a horrified moment he thought she would take the blade in her stomach, but she seized hold of the attacker's knife-wrist with one hand, hurling all her weight against it. He whipped her back and forth, trying to loosen her grip, but she had put her own Art into it, and held his knife back no matter how fiercely he tried to wrench it away from, her. Then he struck her hard, smashing his other palm across her face with all his strength, and finally he was rid of her. The incredulous howl that followed was not hers but his, though, for it was not her Art that had given way. The outline of her grasp was written on him still, in raw, flayed flesh where she had stripped his skin.

With a wordless cry of pain and fury he took the knife

in his other hand and moved to stand over Paladrya where she lay. Stenwold saw her glare up at him and spit defiance to the last. He tried to rush forward to intervene, but could manage just a sluggish shuffle.

A moment later, the halfbreed had been shot, or at least he was off his feet so fast that Stenwold's mind reconstructed it so – the poison addling him to such an extent that he could not piece together what he had seen. Only after the killer was floored did he recognize Laszlo rolling off the big man, one arm clutched to his chest, his face twisted and pale with pain.

Wys and the others arrived shortly after, to discover three invalids and a corpse. Paladrya was the best off, though her pale skin was now bruised all the colours of stormclouds and puffed up enough to half close one eye and slur her words. Stenwold was just starting to regain control of his limbs by then. Having experienced the effects of Spider-kinden poison before, he knew how it was soon overcome by a healthy man, especially one with a robust Beetle constitution.

Laszlo was in the worst shape. Seeing Stenwold and Paladrya at the mercy of a man several times his own size, he had used the only equalizer that a Fly-kinden possessed. He had taken his knife in hand, and driven it straight into the man with all the hurtling speed his wings could give him. The weapon had all but vanished under the halfbreed's ribs, but Laszlo had broken his arm and several fingers. Even so, he grinned at Stenwold while blinking away the pain.

'I wasn't bringing you through all that sea stuff just to end up like that,' he hissed. Wys was fussing over him instantly, cursing that she had no salt water at hand to accreate a cast. By then a couple of Roach-kinden had turned up, attracted by the noise, who seemed to be something like the city guard. They leant on their staves and heard Stenwold and Paladrya talk, and they saw that the dead man looked as though he had been able to defend himself, and they sent for someone to have a look at the body, but otherwise seemed to have no interest in arresting or detaining anyone. Stenwold and his company helped Laszlo in the direction of a doctor that the Roach-kinden recommended, who turned out to be a brisk, businesslike Sarnesh surgeon who splinted Laszlo's arm and gave him a concoction to sip at to deaden the pain. The Fly would drink none, though, until he had spoken to Stenwold, so the doctor left them to it, willing to abandon his treatment room to them in exchange for a delicate gold arm-ring that Wys paid him off with.

'Mar'Maker,' Laszlo insisted, 'I heard them. I know where he is.'

For a moment Stenwold thought he meant Teornis, but Paladrya interrupted with, 'Aradocles?' somewhat indistinctly, and Laszlo nodded eagerly.

'They said the palace,' he got out, hunching forward in his haste to tell them, before collapsing back on to the doctor's couch with a groan. 'The Spider's man, that one that went for you, he tried to get inside, but they said their chief here's seeing nobody, not even Aristoi . . . So they're going to sneak in tonight . . . Aradocles is in Princep's palace somewhere, they're sure of it.'

Stenwold glanced from him to Paladrya, and then towards Wys and her crew. 'Then we have to get into the palace, no two ways about it,' he said flatly. 'And if they won't let us, then we'll have to beat Teornis at the sneaking game and get to the boy first.'

Stenwold tried to do it the official way first. He presented himself at the complex that here in Princep they called the Monarch's Palace. It was half-built, but it was large and much of it was composed of stone, so it was clear that the erratic architects of the new city had been putting a great deal of effort into it nonetheless. The approach of the various carpenters and masons and tilers was piecemeal to say the most. The foundations were all marked out, but walls had gone up here and there without any concerted plan, with some parts roofed over and others open to the sky, so that what was probably intended to be a series of interlocking quadrangles currently looked like a complex maze of cane scaffolding, stone and wood. There were gardens cleared around it too, that had been planted the year before with green and were now flourishing. Walking up to the palace doors Stenwold saw a dozen Bee-kinden gardeners, no doubt fugitives or deserters from the Empire, tending shrubs and bushes and transplanted trees with patient, loving care.

This complex was clearly the heart of Princep Salmae – or would be when there was enough of either city or palace to warrant it. The planners had set aside a lot of space for it and given the layout considerable thought. Paths of woodchips meandered through the green, and Stenwold was reminded of his sole visit to the Commonweal, and the ascetic simplicity that dominated everything they built there.

Also a reminder of the Commonweal were the armed men and women whom he took to be the palace guard: Dragonfly-kinden in leather and chitin armour, leaning on spears or strung longbows. *But of course, Princep's Monarch was born there*, he considered. The presence of such guards suggested that Princep Salmae had not been slow in establishing diplomatic relations with its namesake's homeland.

He spent a vexing half-hour talking to a lean old Roach-kinden man called Sfayot. Polite and white-bearded, the Roach explained to him that the Monarch saw nobody.

'You should tell her,' Stenwold stressed, playing his only good card, 'that I was a friend of Prince Salme Dien. I knew him well.'

'Indeed,' said Sfayot gravely, 'Master Maker, do not think your name is unknown to us.'

That brought Stenwold up short. 'But, then, if you knew . . .'

The Roach set off through the gardens, beckoning him to follow, Sfayot walked with a staff, but he trusted little weight to it, and Stenwold guessed that as the habit of a man who had needed to defend himself in places where he could not openly carry a weapon.

'You are indeed known to her, War Master Stenwold Maker,' the Roach said tiredly. 'She keeps herself aloof from the greater Lowlands, but there are certain names she knows. A few, a very few, she will meet with, should they come to her.' He fixed Stenwold with a sharp, pale gaze. 'There is another list of those that she does *not* wish to meet.'

'I don't understand,' Stenwold said, at a loss. 'I was his friend, the man this city is named after.'

Sfayot walked on in silence for some time, Stenwold dogging his footsteps anxiously, but at last the Roach paused before a flowering bush of some variety Stenwold had never seen before.

'Do your people appreciate flowers, Master Maker? Of Beetle cities I have seen only Helleron, and I saw little sign of them there.'

'We can do,' Stenwold said, mystified. 'As tokens of affection, sometimes, or to ornament a room. Yes, we like flowers, I suppose.'

'And once you have used these flowers that you favour . . . ?' Sfayot said, almost too low to hear.

Stenwold was bewildered and weary, and still feeling odd twinges of pain from the halfbreed's poison, so his voice was testy when he replied, 'They die, I suppose. What of it?'

Sfayot nodded mournfully. 'She will not see you, War Master,' he stated, with finality.

Stenwold glared at him. He was on the point of insisting that *something* must be done, because a Spider Aristos and his Dragonfly-kinden killers were going to mount a kid-napping that very night. It would have been the right thing to do, to give the warning and move on, but Stenwold *needed* Aradocles for himself, not just to keep the boy out of Teornis's hands. Any warning he gave might make his own job that much more difficult.

Instead he simply shrugged, as though he was taking the rejection with good grace and intended thereafter to leave, and would trouble Princep Salmae no more. He walked away, but he was looking about him, seeing where the half-constructed palace might best be entered, wondering where any sentries might be stationed after dark. When he glanced back for Sfayot, he thought he spotted the old Roach at the palace doors again, talking to a Beetle-kinden man. He frowned, for the man in question might have been Ordley Penhold, who had spoken so mysteriously earlier that day, but at this distance it was impossible to be sure.

So he returned to his allies, to await nightfall.

# Forty

Looking out from the Wayhouse window, Teornis could watch the western sky darken. No red sky tonight, only angry clouds. That would serve him well enough, but he could not help thinking of the Spiderlands superstition that held a red sky to be a good omen. *Foolishness, obviously, for everyone is beneath the same sky. Everyone can't be lucky all at the same time, surely?* Except that Stenwold Maker, the Apt, the prosaic, read no omens and observed no superstitions.

*Enough of that*, Teornis told himself. 'Varante,' he said quietly.

'Lord?'

'We move.' Teornis had stripped away his finery. Tonight was not the time for the flashy colours he wore for preference. He had on a hauberk of dark leather, backed with folded silk and lined with rows of metal plates, all of it dark. A cloak went over that, hood hauled up to hide his pale face. His Dragonflies had simple chitin cuirasses on, coated with soot, to hide their gleam.

Seldom, indeed, was an Aristos of the Aldanrael required to undertake such skulduggery in person, but the stakes were high and, for all that he prized Varante's skills, there was a delicacy in this venture that the man was not fit for.

Teornis rested a hand on his rapier-hilt. It was his original weapon, rescued by Varante after the great octopus had snatched Teornis from the barge's deck. Light, balanced and razor-edged, it had no gaudiness or jewels in its hilt. The sheer craft that had gone into its making spoke far more about the wealth and taste of its owner. *And I'd rather not have to use it, if I have any say in the matter.*

They departed the Wayhouse swiftly as soon as the sky was wholly dark, creeping from the window, then climbing or flying to the ground. They passed through the half-made streets of Princep Salmae like shadows, heading directly for the palace. There was a scattering of travellers about after sunset, but none of them saw Teornis or his retinue as they closed on the palace grounds.

'Your men understand their job here?' Teornis whispered, catching Varante's answering nod. Teornis had half a dozen Dragonflies with him, and four would now take him into the palace, to grab this troublesome Kerebroi youth and excise him as surgically as possible. The other two were tasked to give Teornis's band a chance at entering unseen. It was a role that would almost certainly see them dead but, when Varante had briefed them, they had simply nodded and bowed. They knew that their people, their families and clansmen back at Solorn, would reap the rewards of their loyal service. Spider-kinden were renowned for their double-dealing ways, save amongst their cadres, their closest servants. Amongst such as Varante, the Aristoi knew that there was no substitute for unquestioning loyalty, and they dealt with them as honestly and generously as might any Collegium philanthropist.

The Commonweal guardsmen that Teornis had been warned about were making their slow patrols about the palace grounds in pairs, and Varante assured Teornis that there were surely a few up on roofs, or casting themselves overhead on shimmering wings. All told, though, there were no more than a dozen guards, and Teornis had the impression that an actual assault on the palace was unthinkable to most living here at Princep. They seemed to hold this Monarch of theirs in a reverence that bordered on idolatry.

Teornis, Varante and their retinue crouched low and waited. The Dragonflies did not seem unduly wary, but they were a sharp-eyed breed, and enough of them carried bows for Teornis to be cautious of an unexpected arrow between the shoulder blades just as he attempted his entrance. He had expected the garden grounds of the palace to be pitch-dark, a friend to the assassin and the spy, but the walled compound of the palace was ringed with lamps that were covered in glass of rainbow hues. The light they shed gave everything an inappropriately festive air.

Just when Teornis was beginning to think that his two decoys had got into trouble in the wrong place, they appeared, standing in the path of the nearest patrolling guardsmen. The two pairs of Dragonflies regarded each other coldly: the neat-looking Commonwealers, with their pristine armour and crescent-headed spears, confronting Teornis's men from distant Solorn, who looked barbarous and scruffy and were obviously spoiling for a fight.

Teornis couldn't hear all of what was said, only catching varying tones of voice. The palace guard sounded shocked and outraged that these exiles should trespass on the Monarch's grounds. The intruders responded by making some extremely unflattering comments about not only the Monarch of Princep, but also the distant Monarch of the Commonweal itself, whose remote ancestor had thrown their equally remote predecessors out into the wide world. As they jeered and jibed, Teornis's men drew their long-hafted swords, making their intentions unmistakable.

The Commonwealers needed no encouragement, and in the next moment they were striking, wings a-flare and spears levelled. Their antagonists were away in the same instant, buzzing low over the bushes with their swords trailing, shouting and jeering and generally making as much commotion as possible. Teornis heard a few gratifying shouts from elsewhere in the grounds, as still more guards were dragged from their appointed watch by the noise. One of the Commonwealers tore overhead, bow in hand, almost close enough for Teornis to put a sword into him, but the sounds of fighting and shouting arose ever further off. The two men tasked with this distraction were doing their job well.

'Now,' he urged, but he did not even need to say it. Varante and the other three were moving towards the palace already, seeking the easiest way in. They ignored the great gates entirely, for the uncompleted wall itself would have afforded them plenty of chances to enter, even if they had been unable to fly. Finding what shadows they could in the coloured light, they chose their gap.

Without any further difficulty, the Spider and his cadre found themselves within the palace of Princep Salmae: that jumble of the part-built, unbuilt and overbuilt that might one day be a vastly grand statement about how the people of Princep valued their rulers, but was today just a confusing and uneven building site.

Teornis nodded to Varante, and the Dragonflies took wing. They would now skulk and flit about the uneven contours of this place, poking and prying, opening doors and peering behind shutters, until one of them eventually found the Kerebroi heir. Then they would grab the lad and lift him out of the city by air – two or three of them sufficient, Teornis hoped, to hoist a slender youth aloft for the necessary distance. Teornis had come along himself only because he suspected his cadre needed his civilizing guidance. Without his master close at hand, Varante might already have gone down for death or glory in a pointless struggle with the palace guard.

Teornis himself stepped forward, now slipping beneath a half-finished roof, now between the struts and diagonals of scaffolding supports, now creeping out into what would be an open courtyard after the builders got around to delineating it with walls.

And, across that space, he came face to face with Stenwold Maker.

Laszlo had complained vociferously about being left behind. Something as trivial as a broken arm would not slow him, he insisted. The fact that he could barely get up from his bed to make this impassioned speech did not help his case.

'What worries me is what will happen to him while we're away,' Stenwold confided to the others. 'Teornis's people may well come here for us, and he's in no position to defend himself if they do.'

Wys shrugged. 'I've got a lot invested in that lad's family, landsman, so I'm not going to let anything bad happen to him.'

Stenwold saw his own frown mirrored in the faces of Fel and Phylles. 'You're proposing . . . ?'

'I'll stay right here at his sickbed and make sure he wants for nothing, surely,' she confirmed.

'Wys,' Phylles murmured, darting a suspicious look at Stenwold, 'Not just Fel and me. Not without you.'

'You'll go with or without me, as I tell you,' Wys declared primly. 'What, you need me to cheer you on? You need my little knife against their great big swords?'

Phylles's face stated bluntly that she wouldn't trust Stenwold an inch.

Wys folded her arms. 'Do what he says. Do what *she* says too, for that matter,' she added, nodding at Paladrya. 'Honestly, the pair of you haven't the sense you were born with. You've had the chance by now to see land-kinden, eh? We've all sat under the same sun, with our skins drying out and going red, eating their chewy food and looking at their daft money. They're people just like us, even if they have chosen a stupid place to live, and this Stenwold Maker's all right. Call me a liar, either of you?'

Fel shrugged, resigning his fate to Stenwold's care, but Phylles still looked mutinous.

'I don't like it,' she said stubbornly. 'What if this is a trap?'

For a moment Wys looked as though she was about to shout at the woman, but then she was grinning despite herself. 'What, all of it?' she asked softly. 'All of this, that enormous city we turned up in first, the one-legged woman, the going-up-in-the-air, this place, all contrived just to put us off our guard? Just go – go with them. Keep Fel out of trouble and keep the Kerebroi woman alive. We need her. She's the only one the heir knows. I'm counting on you, Phylles. And you, Fel, you understand this?'

Fel let out a long sigh. 'I understand less and less, as this goes on. Count on me, though.' His voice was surprisingly soft.

So, leaving Wys to tend to Laszlo, asking him questions about Tomasso and the family, they set off for the palace.

The plan was both simple and complex, all at once. Stenwold had asked himself the question: how do we find Aradocles if he's in that palace? Its interior layout had looked labyrinthine, even in its unfinished state, and he had no information that would allow a reasonably stealthy gang of rogues to creep into the place, rifle it for the missing heir, and then escape with him. Stenwold himself had grown light-footed for a Beetle-kinden, but that was still a long way from being particularly good at sneaking about, and this whole enterprise was looking increasingly hasty and doomed to failure. Without more luck than he could possibly hope for, there was every chance that they would either be swiftly discovered, or would still be searching the place as the sun came up.

So: turn the problem on its head. He had one key

advantage over the undoubtedly stealthier Teornis, because his motives were at least relatively pure. He wanted to restore the boy to his inheritance, while the Spider just wanted to use Aradocles as leverage against Claeon. So what, in fact, did Stenwold need to achieve?

Not to find the boy, for the boy would find them. All they needed was to get themselves into the palace compound. If they were found in the grounds, then the guards would chase them away, just as Sfayot had turned him away in daylight, but if they were discovered within the palace walls, well, that would be a more serious matter by far. There would be questions and threats, and Stenwold would have the chance to tell all. With any luck, by the time he had finished talking, Aradocles might even be among his audience.

Get into the palace, that was the key. That would turn him from someone who could be brushed off like a beggar on the doorstep into someone who held their undivided attention.

The four of them made a careful, hesitant progress through the palace grounds, stopping frequently, using each tree and bush for cover. The guards did their best, but there were so few of them, and they were clearly not expecting intruders. Stenwold had the sense that this posting was something ceremonial for the Commonwealers, a gift from one Monarch to another. The patrols passed blithely by the crouched intruders without ever suspecting their presence.

Stenwold himself was glad for the lanternlight crowning walls, but he quickly conceded that his sea-kinden companions had far better eyes than he, and soon it was Paladrya taking the lead. Cautiously scouting the way, raising a hand to them whenever she saw more guards on the path, she sought no cover herself, for her Art hid her. As she moved, her skin crawled with patterns of light and shade so that, when she was still, she became as invisible as she had been in the cell in Hermatyre where Stenwold had first met her. Her warning upheld palm, as the patrols approached, flashed palely towards them or they would never have caught her signal. Sometimes the Dragonflies walked within feet of her, as she stood motionlessly out in the open, and then Stenwold's own eyes would slide off her, losing her amongst the nocturnal shapes of the garden, until she moved again.

They reached within a short dash of the wall, finding a convenient gap that still jutted with scaffolding and boards. Just as it seemed they would be able to make an unopposed entry, one of the Dragonfly guardsmen appeared around the corner, and chose that moment, and that spot, to stand contemplating the skies, leaning on his crescent-headed spear. Stenwold cursed inwardly, and began to plan if it would be possible to overpower the man without the alarm being raised. He was brought out of his reverie when Fel tapped his shoulder and pointed upwards, directing his eyes to find another man sitting atop the wall, a crooked staff laid across his knees.

*Not this gap, then*, Stenwold thought. That was always going to be the most difficult part: breaching this final line of defence and breaking into the palace proper. Of course, every gap in the walls might similarly have eyes on it, and he had hoped that inspiration would strike once he got here. There was still a good fifteen feet of empty ground between them and the walls, though, and Stenwold could see no way of getting past the sentries without being seen.

Paladrya and Phylles were busy conferring, hands moving silently in the sea-kinden sign language, and a moment later the Kerebroi woman had started towards the sentry in a progress of stops and starts, from unseen to a ghosting shadow, as her skin blurred to keep up with her surroundings.

Stenwold turned to Phylles to ask her what was going on, but she was already moving off as well, not headed for the guards, but for a section of the wall that looked complete, and unwatched. Once there, she began inching her way along the line of it, moving with a slow, continuous motion that offered nothing to attract the eye. She was slowly edging towards where the wall finished, the gap where the guards were stationed, and she glanced up at the man sitting above.

The compound wall was not so very high, Stenwold considered. Could she jump up and grab his ankle? Was that the plan? He looked over to Fel, but the Onychoi man was watching intently, tense as a wire.

A sudden thought came to Stenwold as he spotted that what he had seen as a crooked staff borne by the man aloft was in fact an unstrung bow. He realized that none of the sea-kinden would know it for what it was. He opened his mouth to utter a warning, but to call out would be just as fatal.

Then there was sudden shouting in the garden behind them, like a harsh exchange of insults. Stenwold froze, losing sight of Paladrya entirely. The archer above stood up and strung his bow, all in the same powerful motion, and then was aloft and scooting overhead, already reaching for the first arrow. The spearman took a few steps forward and, for a hopeful moment Stenwold thought he might follow. He stuck to his post, though, until Phylles moved a little closer and he saw her.

The guard's eyes widened, and he made as if to point the spear at her, but then Paladrya was magically beside him, her hands on the weapon's haft. As he wrenched at it, Phylles struck. The whip-like barb of her Art weapon pierced his neck, and he fell, twitching.

Stenwold hurried closer. 'What have you done?' he hissed. 'What will they think of us now?'

'He will wake eventually.' Phylles scowled. 'A little poison only. He will wake after two days, perhaps. Now, are we going in, or shall we stand here and debate it?'

Stenwold nodded curtly, and they slipped inside the walls of the palace.

'We keep going further in until we're spotted. Check everywhere that looks habitable,' he told them, though it was clear that none of it looked remotely habitable to the sea-kinden. Instead they followed him constantly as he went to the nearest sections that were at least roofed over. A glance behind the curtain veiling an arch showed no sign of occupancy, and so they moved on – skulking from a wall to a pile of bricks, and then to a stack of timbers, peering in each window and doorway they came upon. Stenwold saw sleeping forms in one room – two young Roach-kinden girls by the look of it – but no sign of his quarry. They crept on as quietly as they could, finding only yet more incomplete construction, and occasional sleeping figures huddled in random corners beneath blankets, resembling less the staff of a palace than opportunistic refugees.

And then, emerging into a courtyard, Fel hissed abruptly, his hands coming up with daggers in them. It was a moment later that Stenwold identified the dark figure before them as Teornis.

Fel was already moving before Stenwold could stop him, and Teornis let out a shrill whistle as he drew his own slender blade. With no other option, Stenwold dragged the snapbow out from within his tunic and charged it swiftly. Phylles stepped past him to the other side.

The first arrow flashed from above and slanted off Fel's helm, staggering the Onychoi for a moment before he dropped into a defensive crouch. The second shaft lanced through his thigh, but by then Stenwold had spotted the archer as the man swooped overhead, and the snapbow in his hand cracked twice. For once, both bolts struck home and the Dragonfly lurched in mid-air, wings faltering, and was carried out of sight over the next wall by his dying momentum. A moment later two more of Teornis's followers had dropped down beside Fel, their long-hafted swords to hand. A third landed to Stenwold's left and went for him, just as Stenwold dragged his sword from its scabbard.

'Mine!' snapped Phylles, shouldering him aside. Stenwold looked about wildly for Paladrya, spotting her just as she pointed across the courtyard, crying 'Stenwold!' There, Teornis was backing away, evidently intent on locating Aradocles while the melee distracted his rival. Stenwold swore and pushed himself into a run.

Fel was ably holding the two Dragonflies at bay, blocking their sword strokes with his bracers and the natural armour of his knuckles, and taking every chance to lash back with his daggers or the spikes of his Art. They were wisely keeping their distance, using their longer reach to hold him at bay, while trying to take him from two sides at once. Stenwold, dashing past, managed to cut a gash across the shoulder of one, a minor wound but enough of a distraction. He caught a fleeting glimpse of Fel snapping forward in a full-extension lunge, one fist smashing past a Dragonfly's sword, to crunch into shoulder and collar-bone. Then Stenwold's attention was wholly focused on Teornis.

The Spider had paused in his escape as he saw his enemy running for him. Now he had adopted a relaxed stance in the entrance to the courtyard, his rapier lowered so that its point almost touched the ground. His face, visible in the lanternlight, wore a crooked smile.

'Is it come to this?' he asked softly and, as Stenwold stopped to compose an answer, the rapier leapt and touched his cheek, drawing a mere pinpoint of blood, though Teornis barely seemed to have moved at all.

'A warning,' Teornis told him, whereupon Stenwold cast aside conversation and went for him, his shorter, broader blade thrusting in and very nearly getting past the Spider's guard by pure surprise. Teornis shifted sideways a few rapid steps, sliding Stenwold's sword aside each time the Beetle made a jab for him, keeping to the defensive for a little while, and giving ground along the line of the wall.

There was a mess of bricks and loose stones at his back, where the workmen had left them, and Stenwold tried a sudden rush forward to force his opponent on to them. An instant stab of pain shot through his shoulder, and he stumbled back, seeing his own blood on the last two inches of Teornis's rapier.

Then the Spider stopped playing at being wrongfooted, and instead went on the offensive. His narrow sword flickered and darted in the uncertain light, now at Stenwold's face, now cutting stripes in his artificer's leathers, feinting at his knee, his stomach, his groin, making Stenwold lumber backwards awkwardly, with his own blade deflecting barely half the strokes that Teornis whipped out at him. The expression on Teornis's face changed constantly, as though each attack and defence was a conversational gambit that he hoped Stenwold would respond to.

In the courtyard's centre, Fel turned on the spot as Varante probed at his guard, trying to draw him out. The lunge that had dealt with Varante's lieutenant had made a mess of Fel's arrow-wounded leg, and the Onychoi was now concentrating on fending the blade off, unwilling to expose himself to further injury.

'Hold out!' Phylles called to him. 'I'm coming.' Her opponent would not let her get near him, though, retreating into the air whenever she tried to lash out at him with her stingers. It was clear he had no idea what she was but he wasn't taking any chances. He held her off at the length of his sword. Phylles gritted her teeth, knowing that she was running out of time. Paladrya . . .

*Where was Paladrya?*

The rapier's point left a shallow track down Stenwold's side, another thimble-full of blood soaking his under-tunic. Teornis was taking him apart a morsel at a time. Furiously, Stenwold tried to beat past the other man's defence. He was stronger than the Spider, certainly, and the other man could not have blocked a solid strike by Stenwold's sword, but he never tried to. Every attack was met with a sidestep, a neat deflection, allowing Stenwold's energy to waste itself against thin air. Another flick from his opponent, and Stenwold felt a spike of pain in his right calf.

Then something moved behind Teornis: the glint of a dagger's blade. Stenwold pushed forward, watching the Spider sidestep and sidestep, unknowingly getting closer to that near-invisible presence.

'My lord, behind you!' cried Varante, with the benefit of his kinden's keen eyes. He broke off from Fel abruptly, even as the other Dragonfly also kicked into the air, away from Phylles, to come to his master's aid. Fel bunched himself and leapt up, catching Varante by the ankle and dragging him back down. His opponent's sword chopped down at him, striking his shoulder hard enough to shatter the armour, but Fel's right fist rammed home hard enough to bury his Art-spike entirely beneath Varante's chin.

The other Dragonfly, coming from behind, struck Fel a savage blow between neck and shoulder, putting every ounce of strength behind it, and the Onychoi tumbled forward voicelessly over Varante's body.

Teornis had dodged aside at Varante's warning, so Paladrya's desperate stab at him missed entirely. His rapier lashed out at her, more to give himself room than as a serious attack, forcing her back. Stenwold tried to take advantage of the moment, but Teornis got his weapon back into line just in time to catch the Beetle's sword on the quillons of his own. Then the last Dragonfly had landed between Teornis and Paladrya, with the clear intention of finishing the woman off.

Stenwold's stomach lurched at the thought and, before he could think about how unwise this was, he threw himself forward at a full charge. Teornis was caught by surprise, flinging himself out of the way with ease but catching Stenwold only a glancing blow across the shoulder. Then

Stenwold had cuffed the Spider across the face with one wildly swinging fist, batting him aside, and was lunging past towards the Dragonfly, whose sword was already raised.

He knew he was already too late, that he could not save her.

He saw the Dragonfly twist, heard the man's grunt of pain as Paladrya stabbed him under his guard, ramming her dagger in up to the hilt as she bowled into him, the two of them tumbling over each other. Stenwold saw the man's hands jab in too, wicked Art claws curving from his thumbs. Paladrya screamed.

Stenwold was suddenly on the ground and rolling, and there was a fierce line of pain down the back of one leg to join all the other nagging wounds suffered that night. He lurched to his feet, tripped down on one knee again, then managed to stand up, feeling his mauled leg trembling beneath his weight. Teornis was driving straight for him, the point of his rapier dancing in the air like a gnat.

Wholly off balance, Stenwold tried to get his blade back between him and his opponent. The rapier swept over his parry to whip across his face, opening a cut above one eyebrow. Teornis's face was wiped clean of all mockery now, down to the bare bones of his expression: not the cold distance of a killer, but infinite remorse.

'You had to force me to this,' the Spider hissed and his rapier bound effortlessly past Stenwold's own blade, aimed so as to pierce the Beetle between the ribs with merciless precision.

He held off, in the end. Something changed in his face, some expression of bitter regret, and he hauled the sword aside, so that it only scored Stenwold's flank rather than running him through. Stenwold did not possess the same finesse, however, or perhaps that final reserve of restraint, and his instinctive counter-strike jammed his blade up to the hilt between the plates of Teornis's hauberk.

The Spider gasped, a hollow whooping of air, and then he fell, and Stenwold dropped to his knees beside him, bleeding from a dozen wounds and utterly exhausted.

*Paladrya!* something inside him wailed, and his eyes desperately sought for her body.

*She lives.* She lived, though with both hands to her face to staunch the wound the Dragonfly had given her, whilst Phylles stepped back from her assailant's body, the stingers slowly retracting into her hands. The Polypoi woman looked around, her face bleak, and stomped over to where Fel lay, kneeling gently to put a hand on the dead man's arm, as though sea-kinden Art could somehow repel even death. It was clear, though, that there was nothing that would bring Fel back to take his place among Wys's crew

'Stenwold . . .' came a weak voice from beside him, and he looked down to meet the gaze of Teornis. The white-faced Spider was curled about the fatal blade. 'Stenwold,' he spoke again, 'what have we come to?'

Stenwold looked down at him miserably, unable to condemn the other man, even now.

'I lifted the siege of Collegium,' Teornis managed to get out, face twisting with each word. 'I drove the Vekken back, didn't I?'

'You did, at that,' Stenwold agreed quietly.

'Remember me for that . . . and not for this,' the Spider whispered, and Stenwold felt a tide of loss rise within him. Despite it all, despite every piece of treachery brought down on his city by the Aldanrael, he knew he had lost more than he had gained by the killing of Teornis.

Then Phylles stood up swiftly, and Stenwold looked back over his shoulder to see that they were no longer alone there. The palace had awoken at last, it seemed.

A slender Moth-kinden woman was standing there – or so she seemed to him, with her grey skin and white eyes, her expression one of solemn melancholy. A handful of others had moved in behind her, and Stenwold recognized white-bearded Sfayot at the woman's shoulder. Sfayot, who was chancellor, of course, so the Moth he was now deferring to must be . . .

Must not be a Moth. Staring, Stenwold now noticed that the colours cast on her drab skin by the lanterns were not quite the colours of the lanterns themselves.

'Your Majesty,' he ventured, judging that the best way to address the Monarch of Princep Salmae.

The Butterfly-kinden, who had been known as Grief-in-Chains once, studied him coldly. 'Why have you brought death into my halls, Master Stenwold Maker?' she asked.

'Your Highness,' Stenwold repeated, then he was struck by a sudden thought, 'It is said that your Art can heal even terrible wounds.' He gestured mutely at Teornis. 'Please . . .'

The woman's expression softened slightly, but only to retreat to another, more private sadness. 'No more,' she said. 'My touch can heal no more and, besides, he is past help.'

It was true: Teornis lay still. Spider reserve had somehow sufficed to compose his features in a philosophical, almost amused expression.

'Again I ask why you come here to shed yet more blood, War Master,' the Butterfly demanded, but the voice that answered her was Paladrya's. The Kerebroi woman had been standing nearby, still mopping at her bloody face, but her eyes were now fixed on one of the Monarch's small party: a Spider-kinden youth of no more than twenty years, with dark, curling hair.

Stenwold blinked and stared, too, and looked upon the heir of Hermatyre.

# Forty-One

Helmess had expected to find a gang of cut-throats waiting for him, but the crew gathered in the back room of the Endeavour taverna looked surprisingly respectable. He saw Beetle-kinden in artificers' leathers, complete with tools, plan cases and the like, Fly-kinden attired as moderately prosperous tradesmen, factory workers or peddlers, and the sole Wasp-kinden there wore Ant-made chainmail and gave every impression of being a renegade mercenary.

Honory Bellowern strutted before them like a scholar showing off his students.

'Mark this man,' he instructed his followers. 'This is the Empire's man within the Assembly.'

Helmess was uncomfortably aware that their collective gaze contained a measure of contempt. Nobody liked a traitor, even when the treason was convenient.

'I can get the lads of our kinden in amongst the artillerists, or working repairs on the fortifications,' Honory explained. 'Two of them have been here almost a year, getting known and trusted, and they'll vouch for the others. Our Fly-kinden will drop in on the Aldanraels. They should be able to lose themselves amongst the rabble there. When two or more Spider families get together, nobody can keep track of all their servants and slaves.'

'I wonder that you don't have a Spider or two on the payroll,' Helmess observed.

'Ah, well, current policy is not to use Spider agents on Spider business,' Honory explained. 'Can't be entirely sure who's been bought by who, you see. Besides, most Spider-kinden on the Rekef books want to go anywhere *but* the Spiderlands, and nowhere near the Aristoi. I'd be suspicious of those that acted otherwise, frankly.'

'I see the sense in that, I suppose. And your Wasp, where does he fit in?'

Honory laughed. 'Well, General Brugan does like to think we lesser kinden need mothering.'

The Wasp agent eyed him bleakly, but the truth was clear. He was here purely to make this a true-blooded Imperial venture, while the actual work would be performed by the rest.

'I'm glad to see you're back in the game, Master Broiler. You'd kept to your house so much I was getting worried for your health,' Honory remarked, with perhaps a suggestion of threat.

'It has been so long, and I've steeled myself to take this last step, but I will confess I needed a little while to gather the courage,' Helmess replied, with an apologetic shrug. In reality, of course, he was only free to act now because Teornis and his bloody-handed retinue were safely out of Collegium. *And I can't mention them to Honory, or to anyone else.* There were too many secrets involved, that Teornis had pried open, but were still closed to the Empire.

'Well, so long as you're with us now . . . I understand you're on the war council.'

'Much to Jodry Drillen's bafflement,' Helmess agreed. 'You're right, I think he'll crack – if only because he's pointing in the same direction as myself. When he does, he'll fall. Those same warmongers that cheered Stenwold Maker to the echo will take Drillen apart once he suggests peace talks.'

'Splendid, splendid,' Honory said happily. 'Now, for the next few days, you go draw your lists of those we must remove. Better to be over-diligent. A few extra men dead, who did no wrong, will cause us less difficulty than a few alive who might become a problem. We'll see you back here shortly – I'll send word exactly when. My people have marked you, though, so no turning back now.' He said it in a jovial manner, but Helmess as much as heard the clink of chains behind his words.

The youth stepped forward, his eyes fixed on Paladrya. Stenwold would have assumed him just a young Spider-kinden lad, no more remarkable than any of the waifs and strays of the Spiderlands to be found making a life for themselves across the Lowlands. There was no golden glow of kingship about him, no apparent weight of authority: just another of Princep's many orphans.

'Is it you?' the youth whispered, frowning, as Paladrya faced up to his scrutiny bravely. The Dragonfly's thumb-claw had given her a savage, shallow cut, from her brow halfway to her chin, and she held up a torn piece of her robe to it to help the blood clot.

Her own eyes were steady. 'Aradocles,' she said again, and the youth's face dissolved into lines of bafflement and wonder.

'It is!' he hissed, rushing partway towards her, then stopping abruptly. 'What . . . ? How have you come here? What is all this?' His hands took in the bodies strewn about the courtyard, her wound, this desecration of the Mon-arch's palace.

'I came to find you,' she told him. 'We asked . . . we asked that man,' she pointed at Sfayot, 'but they turned us away. These others meant you harm. This was the only way.'

'What is this?' Aradocles repeated, but this time looking back uncertainly at the Butterfly-kinden.

For a moment she regarded him without expression, and

then her voice emerged, surprisingly small. 'I only wanted to keep you safe.'

Guards turned up then, a half-dozen Commonweal Dragonflies with spears. They stared at the carnage, obviously unsure what to do about it.

'Find somewhere for these people within the palace,' the Butterfly directed them, her hand taking in Stenwold and his fellows.

'Monarch . . .' Aradocles started to say, but an imperious gesture cut him off.

'Later,' she informed him. 'You will have your chance to speak to them in the morning. For now they have caused enough harm.'

The guards escorted them to a part of the palace where three adjoining rooms together had been completed, and installed them in the chamber situated furthest in. Nobody seemed sure whether Stenwold's people were prisoners or guests, and the guards hovered awkwardly outside, plainly ready to prevent an escape but without wanting to seem impolite. Blankets and food and drink were brought, and then different food after the sea-kinden turned their noses up at what was offered. Some salt fish was requisitioned from somewhere for them, but the one commodity that was not in the guards' power to provide was answers.

Phylles sat apart, brooding over her grief and blatantly not inviting conversation. Stenwold was left to tend to Paladrya's wounds, and his own, and to think glumly about Teornis. The victory of actually finding Aradocles tasted like ashes in his mouth.

Before dawn, Sfayot came to visit them, his lean old face looking stern in the shadows. His pointing finger picked out Stenwold only.

'She wants to speak to you,' the Roach said, and Stenwold hauled himself to his feet, with wounds and stiffened joints complaining bitterly, and limped after him.

They took him to a cell within the palace complex, just a simple room, unfurnished save for a pallet bed. Had he still been searching for Aradocles, he would have passed by such a place as unfit for anyone more than a menial, and yet it was here the Monarch of Princep Salmae slept.

She stood waiting for him, slender and solemn, with barely a glimmer of light dancing over her grey skin. Looking at her, Stenwold wondered, *Is this what happens? Was the race of Moths born from Butterfly-kinden who lost their way?* For it was clear to him that she had gone far astray from the woman Salma had spoken of – from that bright-fired dancer, the loving innocent with the miraculous healing touch.

*But of course, Salma is dead and, if I recall, she watched him die.*

'War Master Stenwold Maker,' she acknowledged him coldly.

'And what am I to call you? You were Grief in Chains once, I recall.'

'I am Grief again, and no more than that,' she stated. 'Why have you come here, War Master?'

'Seeking the boy. His people have need of him.'

'Arad,' she murmured softly. 'He has served me as my confidant, my companion, while they built these walls around us. He and Sfayot – I have no others to speak to.'

'Are you so alone?' Stenwold asked. 'There's a whole city of people out there who love you, or so I hear.'

'Only because they do not know what I am. My guards say I should have you killed, since you have defiled the palace of the Monarch.'

Stenwold glanced around, but Sfayot had retreated and the guards she spoke of were not visible. Stenwold was alone with the Butterfly-kinden.

'I'd recommend you finish your walls before you get serious about keeping people out,' he said, trying for humour, but the words sounded leaden even as he spoke them and her expression admitted of no amusement. 'I was Salma's mentor and friend,' he told her, watching her shrink at the name. 'I do not deserve your hatred.'

'Do you not? You who held the knife?' she hurled back at him. 'You who cast him into the fire again and again, until at last he could take it no more? You who killed him?'

'The Wasps killed Salma,' Stenwold responded flatly. 'I cannot claim that I took best care of him, when he was in my charge, nonetheless he was a soldier sent by his people to make war on the Empire. He knew that, and he made his own choices in the end.' He stared at her levelly, seeing at last what was written so plainly on her face. 'We neither of us here are to blame.'

She just stared at him silently without any expression he could interpret, and so he added, 'You grieve too much, and Salma would not have wanted that. He would never have wanted your Art to fail, your colours to grow dim.'

A single shudder racked her, just the one, and then she was still again. 'You do not understand,' she told him. 'I am not changed because of Salma's death, but because of the revenge I took afterwards. I am tainted by my own guilt. My people cannot kill, War Master, without losing the essence of what we are.' A great sigh went through her. 'And now you have come to take my page away from me.'

'You know what he is?'

She nodded.

'Then you must know that he too has subjects that need their true ruler. Believe me, I have seen the man who usurped his place, and a less fit man to rule I cannot imagine. I am sorry if this brings you pain, and I would help you if I could. When this is done, ask anything of me, or of my city, and I will try to perform it. For Salma's memory, if for no other reason.'

For a moment a shimmer of colour traversed across her skin, the faintest guttering of what once had been.

'Well,' she said, 'if he wishes to go with you, then I will not stop him.'

The next morning found Stenwold and the three sea-kinden in what would doubtless, at some point in the future, be the palace's grand audience chamber. Now it consisted of two walls and a tiered dais, and an open view across sun-bright grass, and Stenwold thought that it conferred more majesty on Grief that way than ever it would once completed.

They sat on the steps of the dais, the four visitors, with the Monarch of Princep Salmae a step higher than them, and a few servants or staff – or possibly just voyeurs – within earshot. The only other face there that Stenwold knew, apart from Aradocles himself, was the Beetle-kinden Ordley Penhold, watching with a dour and suspicious expression and folded arms as the heir of Hermatyre told them his story.

'At first, when we came to the land,' the youth explained, 'I relied on my guards – on Santiren and Marcantor – for everything, and I waited daily for the call to return to my city, and to the sea.' There was a faraway look in his eyes. 'After a month had passed, I learned to trust Master Penhold here, who had taken us in, and the Mantis Cynthaen who had led us to him, but no others, and I would not talk as they talked, or do the things they did.'

He looked from face to face: Stenwold to Phylles, Phylles to Penhold, but always flicking back to Paladrya in the end.

'After three months, I was learning the land-kinden writing, and keeping stock for Master Penhold, and soon it seemed strange that I had once been a prince of Hermatyre, and lived beneath the waves. After a year, a year without speaking of it even to my two guards . . . in my dreams I remained a sea-kinden, but no more than that, it seemed. I was just Arad Oakleaves, the foundling Spider boy,

Ordly Penhold's ward.' He spared a fond look at the frowning Beetle. 'And then the Wasps came.'

Stenwold nodded. The Imperial Second Army, known as the Gears, had ground its implacable way through the Felyal, killing all those that defied it, driving out the Mantis-kinden, and all the others who had lived a precarious existence at the forest's edge by trading and logging.

'The Wasps arrived, and we tried to flee for your city, Master Maker,' Aradocles explained, 'but the Imperial forces moved too fast and cut us off. They killed Marcantor as we fled the Felyal. North was the only road open to us: hundreds of refugees of all kinden, with nothing but what they carried. I had been a prince, and then a trader's apprentice, and now I became a beggar.'

Paladrya put her hand to her mouth, and he smiled at her. 'Do not mourn for that. Good came of it, in the end. We were found by outriders of the Landsarmy. Those who could fight went to join Prince Salmae Dien for his war.' He stood straighter, on speaking the name. 'I fought,' he stated simply. 'Santiren wanted to keep me safe, but where was safe? I had to order her, in the end. I had to remind myself who I had been, and what my heritage was. I would not let others risk their lives while I remained behind.'

'You fought alongside Salma?' Stenwold wondered at the thought. *I might even have set eyes on this lad, when I took Salma's counsel. Just one more homeless Spider-kinden, I'd have thought.*

'I rode with him in his charge against Malkan,' Aradocles declared, with fierce pride. 'I rode behind him on a beast with six legs and a pincered tail, and I cast my spear. It was a very different mount from those I had ridden as a boy, but my people are cavalrymen more than most land-kinden. Santiren was killed in that charge, but I broke out of their camp again, and lived.'

Paladrya was shaking her head, dismayed at the risks he had taken. 'But what of your own people?' she asked him.

'I had not forgotten them. Salma reminded me,' he replied. 'He was a prince of his people, as I am of mine, but his people better understand what it is to rule. He was our leader not because he wanted power, but because we needed to be led. He led us to fight against the Wasps not for his own gain, but because they had to be fought. Leadership was a burden that his birthright made him shoulder, not just a privilege to abuse. My own people have not properly understood the true role of kings.' When Paladrya started to object he shook his head. 'It is not just Claeon. My father himself cared nothing for his people. He made sure that the Builders, the Arketoi, remained untroubled, and after that his only thought was to enjoy his authority. Small wonder that a man like my uncle coveted his throne.'

'But, if you think so little of us,' Paladrya sounded shaken, 'then what will you do?'

Stenwold reached out and took her hand, as if to steady her.

'I will do what Salma would do, were he in my place,' Aradocles explained. 'I have a life here. I am happy here and I have friends. Yet I must go to Hermatyre and claim my throne. Because my people need me, not because I have any wish to be Edmir. If I thought Claeon the better ruler, I would abdicate for him without a thought.'

'But you'll come back?' Paladrya pressed.

'In all honour, what else can I do?' he asked her, then smiled. 'My old tutor, have I learned my lessons well?'

Stenwold felt a great tension lift from the Kerebroi woman, and she sagged back against the steps, leaning into him. He had not realized that she had been so scared that the youth might refuse.

The sea-kinden and their new-found leader departed with the Monarch's staff but, as Stenwold moved to follow them, Grief held up one dimly luminous hand to stop him. Only the two of them were now left in the unfinished shell of the audience chamber.

'So, War Master,' she addressed him, still without warmth.

'Please don't call me War Master,' he told her. 'Whatever you may think, war is a business I've never sought. It is just that I prefer war to the enduring slavery and repression that the Empire would bring. I'd have thought you'd understand that. Salma did.'

'And now you go to inflict war on Aradocles's people. And you are just as sure of the righteousness of your cause there?'

'Having been prisoner of the boy's uncle and seen his practices, yes, but I will do what I can to minimize the harm that his return will cause. There's more than one way to stage a revolution.'

She stared at him for a long time, as ghosts of faint colour drifted across her skin. 'Your story makes the plight of Arad's city seem urgent. How will you return him to the sea?'

'I had an aviator . . .' Thinking of it, Stenwold cursed his luck, for it could be days before Jons Allanbridge's return. Meanwhile, Stenwold needed him for more than merely transport back to Collegium. 'I suppose we must wait for him.'

'Perhaps it would be best if you and yours were gone with my Arad Oakleaves, before I change my mind and decide that I wish to save him from your latest war,' Grief suggested darkly. 'Do you think he would go with you if I asked him to stay?'

'That depends on how much he believes what he just said about duty,' Stenwold replied levelly. 'Are you suggesting we walk all the way to Collegium?'

'I am suggesting that I have an object lesson for you, Master Maker, on the relative virtues of war and peace.

I will secure the swiftest transport to your city, fear not, though you may not like the means.'

Stenwold sighed. 'Well, if it speeds our journey, I'll not quibble,' he told her.

She inclined her head, watching him from her seat on the topmost step. 'What is it, then?' she asked him.

'I don't understand. What is what?'

'I can see a question in your face, Master Maker – in your very mind. There is something you have wanted to ask me, but you feared to weaken your position before me. Well, now you have all you want, and more. So ask your question, Master Maker, if you dare.'

Stenwold frowned at her, 'There is nothing . . .' he started to say, but the question rose up within him even as he spoke. 'There *is* something,' he admitted awkwardly. 'It is to do with you . . . and Salma.'

Her expression did not exactly invite such a line of enquiry, but she nodded curtly.

'Salma once told my niece that you had enchanted him.' Stenwold got the words out quickly.

Grief went very still, and the smile she conjured up was unconvincing. 'Surely your enlightened kinden do not believe in such things.'

'I have come to find that all manner of things I would once not have believed turn out to be true, nonetheless,' he replied. 'Salma said that you reached out to him because you were a prisoner, and had nobody else to call upon. You made him love you. You put yourself in his mind, so that he kept thinking of you . . .'

'Is that what he said?'

Stenwold looked evasive. 'It is the sense of it, but is it so?'

For a long while he thought she would just turn around and go, and he could not even guess at the thoughts in her head. At last, though, she said, 'It is true,' in a small voice. 'At first, I confess I used the magic of my people on him.

618

As you say, I was desperate. But by the time he came to find me in Tark, my spell was gone. He loved me. Truly, and with no need of magic, he loved me.' She sounded almost defiant.

'Oh, I believe you,' he said, softly. 'Tell me, though, if there was another under such a spell, could you tell? Could you look on him, and see if he were enchanted in the same way'

Now her expression changed, as mere curiosity shouldered aside all that mystic reserve. 'Do you consider yourself enchanted, Master Maker?' she asked. The trace of amusement in her tone cut him.

*But I must make my confession to her, or she will not help me.* 'Since I left the sea . . . no, before that, since I left the presence of a certain sea-kinden, my mind has been drawn towards her. She has come to me many times in my dreams, in my waking imagination. She seems to fascinate some part of me, and yet . . . I felt none of that, when we travelled together. Only afterwards . . .'

'You Lowlanders,' she whispered, 'you *Apt*, you know so little. And yet, Maker, you see so much further than your kind normally can, to even ask that question. Come here, Beetle-kinden, and kneel before the Monarch of Princep Salmae, if you seek her aid.'

Stenwold bristled at that demand, but he did so, lowering himself to his knees with a groan – feeling all the little wounds Teornis had dealt him twinge. He looked up at Grief, and she put a hand to his forehead. Her skin was remarkably warm and, as she touched him, colours danced and glittered about her fingers and up her arm.

'Hah,' she said, almost at once, 'I feel the shell of an old enchantment here, but it is gone, dried up and dead. It holds you no longer. When did this woman last enter your mind?'

'She . . .' Stenwold frowned. 'Since I came from the sea. In Collegium certainly, but . . .' It was true that he had not thought much of Lyess since then. 'Perhaps sea-kinden workings cannot survive in the dry air?' he suggested, hauling himself to his feet and stepping away from her.

'You are blind, still,' she told him. 'Such enchantments die by one means only – just as the spell I set on Salma died.'

'You said it died because he really did love you, as the real replaced the false,' Stenwold objected. 'You think I *really* love this woman?'

'Not her,' Grief told him, almost pityingly. 'You have feelings for another, Master Maker, and they have defended you against this enchantment. It is the only way.' With that she stood up, and the morning sunlight caught her and made her flash and shimmer for one brief second. When his eyes had recovered from the glare, she was walking away, pale and grey as before.

Paladrya had done her best to bring Aradocles up to date with the current politics of Hermatyre, naming all the current powers of the sea-kinden to him: Heiracles, Rosander, Nemoctes, Mandir of the Hot Stations – and Claeon, of course. She and Phylles had introduced him to Wys, and to the convalescing Laszlo, and the five of them were in deep conference when Stenwold found them.

Looking at Aradocles, Stenwold could help not but think, *He is so young for what they will ask of him.* There was a set, determined look to the Kerebroi youth's face, though and if it reminded Stenwold of anyone, it was surely of Salma.

He sat beside Paladrya, letting her speak, while he himself contributed little to the conversation, glancing sidelong at her occasionally. Grief's words to him still echoed in his memory.

Shortly after he rejoined them, Sfayot tracked them down and informed them that the Monarch wished to see them all at the airfield.

★

A crowd had gathered there, a great motley of all the kinden and half-kinden that made up Princep Salmae. It was rare that their beloved Monarch walked amongst them, and Stenwold and his followers had to push and shove through them to make headway. He expected to find Grief surrounded by a ring of her Dragonfly guardsmen, but she had come with only a pair of adherents: the Beetle Ordly Penhold and the ubiquitous Sfayot. The massed citizens meanwhile maintained a respectful distance.

'Ah, Master Maker,' she addressed him, when he managed to extricate himself from the crowd. 'Come stand with me.'

He did so apprehensively, wondering whether she intended to show some manner of favour by this public display. This seemed unlikely, given her attitude so far, so he made his way with caution across the open space to where she stood, almost in the shadow of the flying machines. Aradocles strode at his side, seemingly entirely at ease, and the rest of the sea-kinden followed, with Laszlo jostled and cursing in their midst.

'I have arranged your conveyance, Master Maker, to take you from my city,' she informed him, 'and your pilot also.' She reached out as if to touch the nearest machine, although her hand stopped a few inches from its metal hull.

Stenwold frowned, recognizing the black and gold of its painting. 'There must be some mistake,' he said slowly.

'Indeed?' she enquired archly. 'Ambassador, will you come forth?'

From around the Imperial heliopter's side stepped a familiar figure. He was not dressed in uniform, but was a Wasp nonetheless, and one that Stenwold was well acquainted with through recent bouts in front of the Assembly.

'Ambassador Aagen,' he identified the man.

'There are some few that I shall always be glad of, Master Maker,' Grief declared. 'Aagen is one.' Her tone made clear that Stenwold himself was not in that number.

'So I see.' Despite himself, Stenwold felt slighted. 'Well, Salma told me of the history between you and Aagen. I suppose freedom is a great gift.'

'Hope is a greater one,' Grief told him. 'He comes of a cruel kinden, and yet he is kind. Consider that.'

Stenwold sighed, sourly. *And so I come from a peaceful one and yet make war, is that it? What does the woman expect me to do? Where does she think we would all be, if we hadn't fought the Empire?*

He looked at Aagen, who nodded to him levelly.

'Aagen has sworn to me that he will take you to Collegium as fast as his machine can carry you,' Grief explained. 'Otherwise, Master Maker, you must rely on your feet.'

Stenwold could feel the sea-kinden growing restless, obviously sensing an insult but not understanding the cause. Only Aradocles held himself apart from it all, and no doubt he was used to the Butterfly woman's ways by now.

'You want to see if I can trust my enemy,' he said tiredly. 'Well, I gladly accept the assistance of Master Aagen. I am no Mantis-kinden, to cut off my own fingers rather than clasp hands with someone opposed to my city. '

It was clear that she considered this some kind of victory, and Stenwold could not help but think, *And when the Empire comes again, where will all this love and tolerance get you?* He derived a certain spiteful pleasure from the thought.

'Master Maker,' Aagen said, without mockery, 'shall we go?'

They made a swift departure, after Stenwold left a message instructing Jons Allanbridge to follow on to Collegium with all speed, and after Ordly Penhold had clasped Aradocles's shoulder and given him some almost fatherly words of advice. The sea-kinden's reaction to being in the belly of the flying machine, with its shuddering and clattering and the roar of its engines, was a sight to behold, and Stenwold spent most of the time with his arm about

Paladrya, listening to Laszlo swearing at every jolt and lurch. Just once he went forward to where Aagen sat alone, the Imperial ambassador out flying without any staff or soldiers. The two of them exchanged a few civilized words on recent developments in artificing, and even on a play they had both watched the month before.

By silent mutual agreement they studiously avoided talking politics of any kind.

# Forty-Two

There was a sound from downstairs, and Helmess Broiler stirred sleepily. It must only be his servants pottering about, rising for the day to come.

Which meant it was later than he inwardly felt it should be. He yawned and stretched. Beside him, Elytrya murmured something, and Helmess again wondered precisely how late or early it was, and whether she could be persuaded into a little exercise.

He opened his eyes, looking for the grey of pre-dawn leaching through the east-facing shutters, but the room was near pitch-dark, and the only radiance that outlined the shutters was the faint rose of the street lighting outside.

*So why are the servants . . . ?* He frowned, and wondered, *Am I being robbed?* Thieves seldom dared to intrude where Collegium's great magnates lived. The city guard was prolific and dedicated in those privileged streets, and the lighting well maintained. He listened again but heard nothing.

*Perhaps I imagined it.* But an uncomfortable feeling was growing on him. Something had certainly awoken him; his imagination was not to blame. Helmess sat up and slid his feet over the side of the bed, hearing Elytrya complain wordlessly as she, in turn, was awoken. He reached for a nightshirt and dragged it on.

*Should I call the servants anyway?* he wondered. *If it's*

*nothing, after all, I'll look a proper fool. But if it's something* ... It could be Teornis and his murderous rabble of Dragonflies, back from Princep. Creeping into the place unannounced would probably seem hilarious to that Spider Aristos. The more Helmess thought about it, the more that seemed likely, rather than mere robbers. It was surely about time for Teornis to blight Helmess's life again, and so Helmess would have to find a way to do away with the Spider and his minions, and secure Aradocles for the sea-kinden. If the heir had been found, of course. If the wretched youth wasn't years dead already. Helmess sighed. His world had become particularly vexing recently.

'What is it?' Elytrya sat up, brushing her curls out of her eyes. 'Helmess . . .?'

'Probably nothing,' Helmess assured her, and then there was a distinct creak outside, a heavy footfall on the stair. He remained motionless, as his speculation suddenly broadened to include all manner of possibilities: *What if the Empire has tired of me, after all, and these are Wasp assassins? What if Teornis has sent that traitor Sands after me? What if . . . ?*

The door opened, and Fly-kinden began filing in, so silently and politely that he wondered if he was dreaming. There were almost a dozen of them, men and women, all of them looking like absolute villains and armed to the teeth. Their leader seemed to be a black-bearded fellow who looked particularly ferocious even though he stood no higher than Helmess's chest. Beside him was a little woman in artificer's leathers, with a businesslike crossbow aimed at Helmess's face.

The Beetle magnate stood up slowly, regarding this silent mass of Flies. Most of them looked straight back at him, save for a couple at the periphery who were obviously admiring a particularly expensive Commonweal statuette on his side table.

'To what,' Helmess asked in a hoarse whisper, 'do I owe

the pleasure of this unexpected visit?' He was aware of Elytrya, sitting up in bed clutching the sheet to herself.

'Oh, that's grand,' mocked the bearded leader. 'That's Collegium style, lads. Listen and learn. Well, Master Broiler, it so happens that a good friend of ours asked us to procure a private and intimate audience with yourself, without the need for your guards and servants and such. On that subject, I'd not go shouting for anyone just yet. Not unless you want to have the trouble of interviewing for some vacant domestic positions in the near future.'

'Who sent you, and how much do you want?' Helmess hissed.

'You might as well talk to the man himself,' said the bearded Fly, stepping to one side as a larger figure stepped into the room.

Helmess Broiler's face twisted with immediate hatred. '*Maker!*' he snapped out.

There was a wary silence after this exclamation, but Helmess Broiler was not a man to house his servants too close to his own chambers.

'Hello, Helmess,' Stenwold began calmly.

'By what right do you invade my house?' Broiler snarled at him. 'This is intolerable. What do you think the Assembly will say when I bring this before them?'

'Oh I've no right to be here,' Stenwold told him lightly. 'No warrant, no writ. I'm here merely because you've crossed a line, Helmess.' He met the poisonous gaze of Elytrya without flinching, and nodded pleasantly.

'I have no idea what you're talking about.'

'You've taken the Empire's coin often enough, Helmess. I know that well.'

Helmess's lip curled contemptuously. 'And of course you have proof.'

'I don't need proof, Helmess, because I'm not here to arrest you. I've known you to be the Empire's man for years now. It was easier to leave you be than to root out the identity of whoever would replace you. But now I find it's not just the Empire you'd betray your city to. The Spider-kinden, for example. The Spider-kinden and *her* people.' He gestured at Helmess's companion.

Elytrya bared her teeth. 'You know nothing of my people!' she spat.

'Oh, I know all too much about your crooked-minded people,' Stenwold replied, still perfectly calm. 'I know now that you must be a Littoralist spy, and you're desperate to help your people "reclaim the land". And you've found a willing accomplice in Helmess here because he's prepared to sell out his own people to any bidder at all, it seems.'

'This is utter fiction,' Helmess protested, with great dignity. 'It's no secret that you dislike me, Maker, since I've always been your political opponent. If you have some concrete accusation to make, rather than all these flights of fancy, then bring it before the Assembly, rather than—'

'Danaen let your name slip, Helmess,' Stenwold interrupted.

The other man's eyes narrowed. 'The word of a Mantis-kinden . . . ?'

'She won't testify against you. She's dead.'

Helmess flinched, ever so slightly. 'Maker, I don't know what you think you're doing, but—'

'No formal charges,' Stenwold informed him. 'No militia. No Assembly hearing. No courts of law. No proper procedure. My Arianna *died* as a result of your treachery.' And, at last, his voice shook a little with the force of the emotion he was holding back, and Helmess shifted uneasily, beginning to comprehend the magnitude of his situation.

Stenwold smiled to see it. 'But I see you have your own companion. Not quite a Spider-kinden, but almost as decorative. Enough to pay the debt you ran up when you caused Arianna's death, perhaps.' Around him the Fly-kinden villains shifted and grinned, their weapons much in evidence.

Helmess's fleshy face went taut and still, and Stenwold smiled. 'Ah, good,' he said, 'so you *do* care about her. That will make this easier.'

'Now, Maker,' said Helmess hurriedly, 'don't do anything you might regret. This is Collegium, after all. You can't just . . .'

Stenwold's smile turned hard. 'How swift you are to cling to Collegium when it suits you. Well, Helmess, I cannot tell you how much I would like to have you pay for your treacheries, and your sea-kinden spy alongside you.' The Fly-kinden moved in on cue, surrounding the bed. The black-bearded man hopped up between Helmess and Elytrya in a flurry of wings, brandishing a blade in either hand.

'On your word, Master Maker,' he said, plainly enjoying himself immensely.

'Maker—!'

'Listen to me,' Stenwold cut him off sharply. 'I will give you and your woman one chance only. If you do what I say, then you live, for now. If something should happen to me, though, or any others that I care about, you will suffer for it, and for once I will be as heedless of civilized propriety as your beloved Wasp-kinden. No law and no procedure, Helmess. If you dare cross me then my people will gut you and leave you to die. Understand?'

The other Beetle-kinden met his gaze bleakly. 'What then, Maker? What is your price?'

Stenwold nodded, and abruptly there was a dagger-blade touching Elytrya's throat. 'Madam,' he said formally, 'you will now tell me everything of your arrangements with Rosander of the Thousand Spines Train: how your messengers reach him, what words they use. I wish to meet with Rosander. You will compose a message for him immediately, and if he has not arranged to meet with me in a few days' time, then I will let my followers do what they will with you.'

'He . . .' She was now staring at him, wide-eyed. 'He will not come to the city, not without his army. He will suspect a trap.'

'I shall have a boat moored out by the Edge, and he may meet me there. He surely cannot refuse such an invitation. We will tell him I wish to renew my acquaintance with him, so as to save my people from his wrath.' Stenwold nodded to one of the Flies, a bald, hunched woman, and Helmess recognized her belatedly as one of the Smallclaw Onychoi. 'Wys here will take the message – once you have briefed her on what to say, and who to say it to. If something happens to her, then something worse will happen to you – for I will keep you close, spy, until Rosander and I have concluded our business.'

'You will regret this, Maker,' Helmess growled softly.

'Oh, I'll regret letting you live, no doubt,' Stenwold snapped, 'but right now the good of my city comes above my own preferences. A novel perspective for you, I'm sure.' He clicked his fingers abruptly, making Helmess start. 'There is just one thing more.'

Helmess glared at him mutinously. 'I sense it would seem rude of me to refuse. What do you want, Maker?'

'Details of how the Empire is going to exploit the situation.'

'I don't know what you're talking about.'

'Wrong!' Abruptly Stenwold had his sword aimed straight at Helmess's sagging chins. 'My crew here have followed you to meetings with Honory Bellowern, and why would you sell us just to two separate factions, when you can throw in the Empire as well? Tell me where they fit into this, or I swear you'll be signing all your contracts with your left hand from now on.'

Walking away from Broiler's place, with a hastily clad Elystrya under guard by the *Tidenfree* crew, Tomasso said, 'I'll have the ship made ready then, Master Maker, for this sea-kinden gambit of yours.'

Stenwold shook his head. 'Not this time,' he told the Fly. 'I have a different vessel in mind.'

The four barques rose smoothly from the lightless depths towards the sun, bullying their way up the gradient of gradually lightening water until they broke through the mirrored glitter of the surface, breaching the waves on all sides of the little ship's dark silhouette.

Three were slender, dart-shaped craft, driven up from the abyss by water forced through their siphons. The last was far broader, a great curved carapace with a dozen busy paddling arms below to flurry it through the water. From this last vessel emerged Rosander.

He had taken the time to dress well for the land-kinden. He wore his armour of pale stone, even down to the helm, so that what now crawled from the barque's interior looked less like a man and more like a huge, jagged statue. Behind him, his select followers climbed up into the light, shading their eyes: little skittering Smallclaws, hulking Greatclaws in armour of accreated shell, lithe Kerebroi with spears and knives. The smaller vessels began disgorging their crews, too, crawling out to crouch on the rolling hulls and look up at the landsmen's ship.

It was a little enough thing, that ship, and Rosander knew that the land-people had far greater vessels they could launch. If they wanted to overwhelm him by main force, this little vessel surely could not hold enough land-kinden to accomplish it. *Why, I alone could probably overcome their crew, surely.* He looked up at the great round sail that bellied up there in the wind, sagging and wrinkled in places. *Perhaps they do want to surrender or talk terms, though I cannot think that they will accept such terms as I'm minded to offer.*

Rosander grinned to himself. 'Chenni,' he said, 'want to see some land-kinden craftsmanship?'

'Surely,' the Smallclaw artificer piped up, and Rosander

reached out for the curving hull, ready to jam his spiked gauntlets into the wood to give him purchase for the climb.

'Wait, wait!' called a voice from above, and a ladder of cloth was unfurled before his face. He regarded it doubtfully, but the voice explained, 'It's silk woven with steel thread. Come on up.'

Rosander heard Chenni make an approving sound. 'I'll get you one, never fear,' he assured her, and then applied himself to ascending the ladder. It was an awkward climb, swaying and creaking, and he took it steadily to avoid looking foolish before his own people. The ladder was as strong as the landsmen claimed, confirming that they were an ingenious lot, which fact would make the impending land campaign all the more profitable. *About time that worm Mandir was knocked off his pedestal*, Rosander reflected. Perhaps the booty from this land venture would be enough to break the Hot Stations' stranglehold.

He hauled himself over the rail which, being less cunningly reinforced than the rope, snapped in three places. Nevertheless, he was left standing on the deck of the land-kinden ship: he, Rosander, Nauarch of the Thousand Spines Train and future conqueror of the land.

'Bring on your warriors,' he instructed, waiting for the lower reaches of the vessel to disgorge further land-kinden. All around the ship his people waited, ready to dig their claws into the hull and haul themselves over the side, to butcher every landsman on board. Rosander glanced around, the narrow eyeslit of his helm sweeping the deck, but no angry hordes of landsmen became apparent. Indeed he saw only two men, dark and stout the pair of them. The nearest, who had let down the ladder, was now edging backwards, staring at Rosander with alarm, while the other . . .

'Hah,' Rosander grunted. 'And it *is* you, at that. I didn't believe it.' He stomped his way forward, hearing the deck beneath him creak, while Chenni pattered along beside him. This particular landsman faced up to his scrutiny without fear, as well he might. 'You escaped,' Rosander rumbled. 'I heard the news. You escaped the Edmir and you escaped the Man of the Stations too, all the way back to your home on the land. You've warned your people, no doubt. They'll give us some sport, then, which is all to the good.' Rosander reached up and tugged his helm off, squinting a little in the bright sun. 'You impress me, landsman.' He grinned abruptly, showing surprisingly delicate teeth in his narrow mouth. 'Kneel, kneel before me now and swear yourself one of the Thousand Spines, and I'll make you my deputy on land when I've conquered it.'

The land-kinden regarded him with a slight smile. 'I fear that's an honour I can't accept, Nauarch Rosander,' he said. 'Even so, I'm glad you remember me. My name is Master Stenwold Maker of Collegium and I am here to speak for my people. Will you hear me out?'

Rosander regarded him almost fondly. 'You were free,' the Nauarch said. 'You had escaped, and now you come back. My warriors surround this ship. Are you so eager to rejoin us down in Hermatyre? Hear you out? Oh I'll hear you out, Master Stenwold Maker, but I make no promises.'

He saw a gratifying twitch in the man's expression when return to Hermatyre was mentioned. Rosander couldn't blame him, for Claeon was never a kind captor. *Well, let us see how my becoming master of the land tilts the balance against Claeon. Perhaps my next campaign will see me take Hermatyre and bring some justice to that wretched place.*

'Perhaps we should go below,' Stenwold suggested, 'out of the sun.'

'Get him to show me the engines of this contraption,' Chenni prompted.

'Do it,' Rosander ordered the landsman, and Stenwold nodded and gestured them to a hatch that led below. Before heading down, he glanced over at the other land-kinden present.

632

'Master Allanbridge?' he said, making the name a question.

'I'll be fine,' the other replied, obviously uneasy all the same.

Stenwold nodded and set off into the ship's interior. 'I had forgotten your companion for a moment,' he confessed as they descended, every step of Rosander's eliciting a groan of tortured wood. 'She piloted the barque that brought me to Hermatyre. She also did her best to keep me out of Claeon's hands. For that she's earned a look at our engines, if nothing else.'

The space below had only two rooms, one of which housed the engine. The other, Rosander saw as they reached the foot of the stairs, had a table set out, and furniture that he identified after a moment as designed for sitting on. Apparently these land-kinden believed that there really was something to talk about. *Surrender terms, perhaps? Or maybe this Stenwold will sell his people yet.*

'Come on, then,' Chenni prompted. 'Let's see what you've got.'

Stenwold paused, then called back up. 'Jons! Are you done there?'

'As much as,' came the reply.

'Would you come down here and show Mistress Chenni how the engines work?'

'With pleasure.' A moment later they heard the man stomping above their heads, and then he was letting himself down the ladder.

'We should talk,' Stenwold told Rosander, gesturing at the table. 'Amongst the land-kinden, one debates with one's enemies around a table, to try and find another solution than war.'

Rosander grunted and went over to one of the chairs, reaching out for it and turning it between armoured finger and thumb. As Stenwold headed about the far side of the table, the giant Onychoi brought his fist down on it, with no great display of force, and instantly reduced it to matchwood.

'Got anything stronger, or should I stand?' he growled.

Stenwold, not the least put out, sat down across from him. 'You are Rosander, Nauarch of the Thousand Spines Train.'

'Well done.' Rosander put his helm down on the table. 'What do you *want*, Stenwold Maker? Amongst the sea-kinden, the Kerebroi may talk and talk, but *we* act. Debate is a coward's excuse for putting off the strike.'

'I'm sorry that you feel that way,' Stenwold replied. 'Nauarch, you are not Claeon.'

Rosander's lips twisted into an unwilling smile. 'Nicest thing anyone's said about me for at least a moon,' he shot back. 'So what?'

'I mean you are not consumed by malice, nor are you terrified of losing your power. You are secure in what you possess, whereas Claeon is not.'

'A fair assessment.'

'Neither, unless I guess wrong, are you one of the Littoralist movement,' Stenwold went on. 'You don't lap up all that business of theirs about the destiny of the sea-kinden to reclaim the land from the hated land-kinden, who drove your ancestors from it a thousand thousand years ago, or whatever.'

'Fools and madmen,' agreed Rosander.

'So, why do you make yourself my people's enemy?' Stenwold asked him.

Rosander shrugged, stone pauldrons moving massively. 'I bear your kinden no ill will. Surrender to me and you'll not be ill-treated, though we'll be disappointed if we don't get our fight. As you say, I'm no tyrant, but I am an adventurer, Maker. And now I know the land is there for the taking, that is the new adventure I choose. To be the man that conquers the land! To be remembered for ever as he who took that great step.' Rosander was grinning even at the thought. 'And my Train would follow me even beyond the sea, despite all the tales they have been told at their mother's tit. I would reward them for that loyalty, because I would make them all princes of the land, with landsmen to wait on their every need. And I would do this, Maker, because I can.'

There was now an odd vibration running through the wood of the vessel, which he assumed to be the engine working. 'If your servant has any ideas about taking us elsewhere, be assured my people have orders to hole this barque and take it to the bottom, if necessary,' he warned Stenwold. Listening out, he could hear voices over the rumble of the engine: Maker's man explaining something to Chenni. 'I thought it was the sails that made these things go, anyway. Obviously I was misinformed.'

The hull lurched slightly beneath him, not enough to make him shift his balance, but a new movement he did not entirely like. 'Maker,' he cautioned softly, 'do you think I cannot kill you if you've planned some treachery?'

'With ease,' Stenwold Maker agreed, although there was a tension to him that Rosander could clearly read. 'Perhaps . . . some fresh air, maybe?'

The hull shuddered and swung again and Rosander nodded. 'You go in front of me, Maker, and gather your servant up too. I suddenly suspect that you are trying to be clever, and that may in turn mean that you're being unwise.'

'Jons!' Stenwold called out. 'Bring Mistress Chenni above decks, if you would.'

'That time already, is it?' the other landsman replied. 'Well then, little miss, if you'd come with me.'

Rosander waited at the foot of the steps for his aide, who came pattering around from behind the landsmen, looking enthusiastic.

'It's a fine piece,' she said. 'Not clockworks at all, but burning some kind of oily stuff to make it go. Knocks Mandir's tricks into a barrel. We should certainly get one.'

'Yes, but what is it *doing*?' Rosander stressed.

She goggled up at him. 'Why, it's . . . working.' She frowned.

'Go on up, Nauarch. You shall see all,' Stenwold Maker said softly.

Rosander glared at him and stomped up the steps, heedless of the tortured sounds they made as his weight bent and bowed them.

'If you think . . .' he started, but it was never clear what he imagined Stenwold might think, because his voice trailed off.

The slack, bellying fabric he had taken for sails had grown taut now, forming a great rounded bulk above them. And the sea . . .

The sea was gone. There was no horizon. Rosander stormed towards the rail, furious . . . and stopped dead.

There was the sea, still, but it was a dark canvas far below them, glittering with pinpoints of reflected sunlight. He could see no sign of his people, or even their vessels. Instead the water was fast giving way to something lighter: green and grey and dusty tan. The *land*.

'We are not just land-kinden, you see,' Stenwold remarked quietly, beside him. 'We are air-kinden also.'

Rosander's gauntleted hand lashed out and grabbed him by the arm, painfully tight. 'Take us back,' he hissed. 'Take us back down, *now*.'

'Oh, we will. This is no kidnapping. You can see for yourself we are in no position to overpower you,' Stenwold assured him, his voice catching slightly with the pressure of that grip. 'But look, there is your new kingdom. There is the land.'

Despite himself, Rosander found his eyes drawn to the great expanse that now filled the whole of their view, stretching as far as his eyes could squint in the bright, dry light.

'There is my city,' Stenwold, pointed. 'There is white

Collegium, your intended victim. But inland of Collegium lies the city of Sarn, where the soldiers of the Ant-kinden march, and they would march to our defence, as would other allies. The Vekken from down the coast, for example, and the Tseni by sea. Who knows who else?'

Rosander made a growling sound in his throat, where-upon Stenwold spoke swiftly on, 'But the warriors of the Thousand Spines are fierce and brave, so perhaps you would best all who came against you, and then capture my city. But my city is not the land, Rosander, for beyond Sarn there is the city of Helleron, many tens of miles further inland, where they mine and smelt and craft – our own version of the Hot Stations. That marks the edge of the Lowlands, which is the region I call home.' The land-scape was still passing swiftly beneath them, with no sign that it would come to an end any time soon. 'But perhaps, eventually, you would prevail, Rosander. Perhaps. So I must tell you that, beyond Helleron, there is the Empire of the Wasps, a warlike nation that in size is greater than all the Lowlands. Then there is the Three-City Alliance and the Disputed Principalities, and of course, if you go north past the great ridge, the Commonweal, vast and ancient, greater than all the rest. All this might you conquer – in twenty years or fifty years of never seeing the sea.'

Rosander's grip on his arm was looser now, the Nauarch staring out at the dust-hazy horizon.

'And even then,' said Stenwold, 'you would not have conquered the *land*. To the east of the Empire, to the north of the Commonweal, to the south of the Spiderlands, the land goes on, with more and more peoples to resist you, and still no end in sight. My people have charted their own courses for five hundred years, and our maps do not define how far the land goes, any more than yours can delimit the sea. What would you conquer, Nauarch? All your warriors, all the warriors of a hundred such trains, would be lost for ever in just a fraction of all that land.'

'I could take just your city,' argued Rosander, almost desperately.

'And we will fight you,' Stenwold said. 'And who can say how that fight would go? You would make many early gains, no doubt, by striking from the waters where we could not reach you, but we have submersibles now, and eventually you would find that we would carry the war down to you. But what of it? Win or lose, what would you achieve in conquering a mere fistful of earth, against all this?'

For a long while Rosander stared out over the rail of the *Windlass* at the wider world beyond, and Stenwold stepped back, out of the clutch of his now-loose fingers, and let him look. After a moment, the diminutive form of Chenni went to her leader, putting a small hand up to reassure him.

Jons Allanbridge shook his head as Stenwold came over, leaving the giant sea-kinden at the rail.

'I thought he was going to throw you over the side,' he said.

Stenwold shrugged. 'It was always a risk.'

'So why did you not have some lads with snapbows and nailbows to do the bastard over once we got aloft?'

'Because that might precipitate the very war that I'm trying to prevent. By my assessment he's not a tyrant, nor even a conqueror like the Wasps are – or as the Vekken were! – and, if I can shake hands with the Vekken, then I owe it to Rosander, if nothing else, to offer him my hand now.'

The great form at the rail turned to him and said, 'And what exactly do you offer?'

'Help us take Hermatyre,' Stenwold said instantly. 'Depose Claeon with your own hands. Can you really say that wouldn't give you pleasure?'

Rosander stared at him levelly. 'Invade the sea on behalf of the land-kinden? I think not.'

'Not a land-kinden will be present, save perhaps for

myself,' Stenwold assured him. 'Retake Hermatyre for its true heir.'

The Nauarch snorted incredulously, then he frowned. 'You mean it, don't you? You've *found* him? I always thought Claeon'd had him killed years back.' For a moment he seemed to be weighing up the very thought of it, but: 'No, not for Aradocles, and not for you.' He held up a hand, forestalling Stenwold's objections. 'If I'd wanted Hermatyre, I'd have taken it by now, and Claeon couldn't have stopped me. There are those amongst the Thousand Spines that have been pressing me to do just that – to sack the greatest city of the sea. My people resent being made to wait on Claeon's pleasure every bit as much as I do. Claeon promised—'

'You have seen the truth of what he promised,' Stenwold interrupted.

'I have.' Rosander looked down at Chenni, or maybe at his own feet. 'I have stayed my hand from Hermatyre, simply because what my warriors would leave of it would not be Hermatyre any more. I have a fondness for the place, despite its poor taste in rulers.'

'So what will you do?' Stenwold asked him.

'I will take my warriors back to the depths, where we belong. We will tread the deep paths again, and fight the Echinoi, and terrorize the small colonies, and be as we were meant to be. But maybe we will return to Hermatyre soon, to buy and sell, and I would not be heartbroken if we found some other Edmir on the throne.'

639

# Forty-Three

Daven tugged his hood a little higher, for all he and his fellows were in a private room in the Fair Licence, a respectable merchant's taverna within sight of the College. It was not that it was so very difficult, to be a Wasp in Collegium. He had been given only a couple of months to establish his cover here, masquerading as a mercenary factoring for a Helleron trade cartel, and he had expected to live every hour under the hostile glares of the locals, but the Collegiate merchants were paragons of venal acceptance just now. One would never think that an Imperial army had been at their gates recently enough to have left scars on the stonework.

His life here had been quiet enough at first, waiting on orders from home, liaising covertly with the diplomat Bellowern. In the midst of profit and loss, the flow of trade, socializing with his false peers, the myriad of entertainments that Collegium had to offer, he had found it difficult to remember that he was a spy.

Then the orders had finally come, following hard on the heels of reports about the new war with the Spiderlands. Then had arrived his reinforcements.

There were eight of them seated about this table in the Fair Licence, all dressed in canvas workshop leathers and over-robes, like any Collegium artisan just in from the road. If they seemed a little uniform, perhaps it was simply

Daven's military eye picking up on it. They were all Beetle-kinden men, and none of them looked like more than journeymen artificers or travelling merchant's clerks. They were Rekef Outlander, every one of them, however, and here to play their parts in bringing down Collegium.

'Stenwold Maker,' suggested one of them – Daven had not quite got their names straight yet. He sat back, sipping at the wine he had grown rather too fond of over the last few months, and let them get on with it. They had been briefed exhaustively, and they were brimming over with enthusiasm for the task and, although he was supposed to be their commanding officer, he felt surplus to requirements.

'There seems to be some doubt over whether he's still with us,' another noted.

'No, he's definitely been seen recently. He's still on the list. In the midst of the fighting, one of us will have to arrange something for him.'

'The file on him doesn't suggest he's a man too careful of his own wellbeing,' another added, almost approvingly, as though commending the absent Master Maker for such consideration.

'The Speaker, Drillen?' another noted.

'Put him on the list,' said the man who was so keen on lists. 'And some random Assemblers, whoever we get a crack at?'

'No, nothing that might make them throw the fight. If their leaders start fearing for their own lives, they'll sue for peace in an instant,' broke in one who had not spoken before. 'Special targets only, amongst the Assembly. Other than that, our targets must be those whose deaths will cause outrage, and those buildings whose destruction will fan the flames of Collegiate passion.'

Daven found that rather too flowery for spy talk, but said nothing. Really, watching these men was like seeing some horrible machine set in motion, one that nothing could stop.

'The College workshops,' one of them said, while another named a handful of public monuments. A third put in for a rather good theatre that Daven had visited a couple of times. Still he contributed nothing.

'Come now,' said one of the eldest. 'What are you thinking of? The College library must burn, surely, or what will we be doing with ourselves?'

'That's going beyond our brief, surely?' Daven was surprised at the words, more so because they were his own. Eight dark Beetle faces stared at him.

'How it will inflame them, though,' said the poet drily. 'No, you're right, the library must go. That will commit the Collegiates to the fight like nothing else.'

'Do we have enough incendiaries to accomplish it?' asked a more practical voice.

'If we cannot secure the makings for incendiaries here in Collegium then we're altogether in the wrong business,' said the list-maker expansively, refilling his wine bowl. 'Burn the library, yes. That'll teach those bloody pompous academics to look down on the rest of us, eh? Now, where's this cursed traitor of ours, Captain?'

Daven took the slightest second to connect the title to his own rank, in that other life he had lived in the Empire, not so very long ago. He opened his mouth to reply and the door was kicked in violently.

The Rekef men leapt to their feet, daggers and swords clearing scabbards, and at least two small crossbows being dragged from packs or from under the table, already cocked. Daven himself had his hand out immediately, palm open towards the doorway. By that time there were four armoured Beetles crowding into the room with snap-bows trained, and more of them behind. They wore the bar-visored helms and engraved breastplates of the new merchant companies.

One of the crossbows let loose, its bolt just slanting off the lead intruder's breastplate. A snapbow bolt then took the Rekef man responsible through the eye, sending him backwards over his chair. A second Collegium shot killed another of the Rekef men down the table, by a reflexive, accidental release. By that time there were at least eight of the weapons directed at them from the open doorway.

'I am Chief Officer Padstock of the Maker's Own Company, and you are all under arrest,' came the clipped tones of the woman that led them. 'Drop your weapons and surrender to the authority of Collegium.'

Her eyes sought out Daven's, facing down his open palm without fear. He could kill her, he knew, but that would get him and all his men slaughtered in instant retaliation. For a moment the temptation to do so was almost overwhelming, which he realized was due to the prospect of getting this pack of venomous infiltrators butchered along with him.

Taking a deep breath he lowered his hand and stepped back, feeling at most ambivalent about the whole situation.

It had taken a moment for Stenwold to gather his courage, before he could step back down into the coiled interior of Wys's submersible. For a moment he had wavered on the brink, sensing the great lightless abyss beneath him, limitless and monster-haunted, as alien and unconquerable to him as the land had seemed to Rosander.

'You don't have to go,' Paladrya had told him, resting her hand on his arm. 'I know your people have their own fight.'

'I will see this out,' he announced, more for his own sake than for hers, and in he had gone.

When Wys had come back from passing word to Rosander, she had brought some new passengers. Word of the new-found heir had been passed to the Pelagist network while she was hunting down the Nauarch of the Thousand Spines. From there it had reached Hermatyre's exiles.

By the time Stenwold struggled through the hatch, the

battle lines had clearly been drawn. Aradocles stood firm, a slight young challenger, while across the main chamber from him waited the tall figure of Heiracles. The elder Kerebroi had brought two servants or guards with him, and they had knives, as all sea-kinden seemed to have knives. At the same time, the stance of Paladrya, Phylles and the big engineer Lej made it clear that they would be weighing in on the heir's side should the newcomers try anything disagreeable.

Despite everything that separated Stenwold from these sea people, he found he could read Heiracles quite clearly by now. It was plain the man had never expected Aradocles to be still living. It was also plain that he had coveted the throne for himself, and had planned to appropriate the heir's name and cause to that end. Seeing Aradocles there brought a sudden end to all that, unless some swift treachery could be accomplished. Stenwold observed all that behind the man's eyes, the last flowering of ambition that had clung on even after the hunt of the heir had set off, and watched Heiracles make a coldly rational decision and let it all go. Chancellor of Hermatyre was better than king of nothing, his expression said, although Stenwold resolved to warn the young prince to surround himself with trusted and capable bodyguards, should he at last reclaim his kingdom.

Then Heiracles knelt and bowed his head – less to a man than to the inevitable. 'Welcome back, Your Eminence, my Edmir,' he declared.

With a studied disregard for the knives, Aradocles went to assist Heiracles to his feet. In that moment, the way the youth moved reminded Stenwold very much of Salma. The heir nodded. 'Use that title only once I have earned it,' he reproached the older man. 'I'm not in Hermatyre yet. Tell me, how do we stand there?'

'The word has gone out to our . . . your supporters,' Heiracles informed him. 'Those of the Pelagists who have taken sides are gathering. A host is ready to march on Hermatyre.'

'And their numbers?' Aradocles queried.

'Still mustering as yet. I hear from Wys that the Thousand Spines . . .' He glanced at Stenwold for more.

'I hope that they shall not be a problem,' was all Stenwold would commit to. *Or have I misjudged Rosander and his priorities?* he considered.

'Then the numbers should be close to even and, once word reaches Hermatyre that you are with us, we expect the colony's defenders to undergo a change of heart. Claeon can command obedience, but no love.'

The submersible had begun to descend. Stenwold watched the water outside darken and darken, until there was nothing but black. He could not suppress a shudder.

'I do not want to come to the throne wading waist-deep in the blood of my own subjects,' Aradocles said, frowning.

'If they cling to your false uncle, what can they expect?' Heiracles asked dismissively.

'And how are they to know that I am truly with you, that my name is not merely an empty boast? Claeon will tell them that I am slain, that it is merely a trick to unseat the colony's true ruler.'

It was clear from the way that Heiracles paused before answering that he was well aware of this. 'I am assured that the people of Hermatyre are eager for your return, Edmir.'

Aradocles shook his head. 'Not enough, Heiracles. I will not have my people slaying one another, each believing that they fight for the true ruler. If I were to show myself to them . . .'

'There'd be enough there who'd gut you, because they're Claeon's parasites,' Wys put in immediately. 'And with you dead, boy, where's that leave everyone? All it'd take is one lancer, or one of those new Stations weapons that can lob a spear ten yards. Getting close enough to see who you are is getting close enough to kill you.'

The heir to Hermatyre frowned, looking down at his hands, and, with a shock of familiarity, Stenwold recognized a mannerism of his own, doubtless transmitted to the youth via Salma.

A lengthy journey through darkness took them to where the loyalists were gathering. During the long hours, Stenwold sat alongside Paladrya and tried not to think about the Spider-kinden fleet and the progress it must be making down the coast, or about the Wasp armies massing to take advantage of Collegium's downfall.

At last there was light: the limn-lamps of a small colony transforming the deep sea in shades of pale blue and gold. Stenwold joined the others in looking out across a crawling seabed. There were crabs and lobsters and similar beasts there, jostling for leg-room, harnessed and saddled, and the swift darting of squid-borne cavalry passed overhead. Spiral shells bobbed and danced around one another, hanging in the water like airships, and some trailed living tentacles while others were propelled by mechanical siphons. Around it all there were the sea-people, a military mob of them, without order and without distinction, and belonging to all kinden.

They docked, and for Stenwold there was the usual awkwardness of them dragging him, cauled again, over to the encrusted mound that was the colony. It had been a long enough absence that the pressure, the cold and the claustrophobia were not the least dulled by his past familiarity. Still, he had been given his chance to avoid this reacquaintance up at the Collegium docks, and he had only himself to blame for being a prisoner of the sea once again.

They held a council of war, whereupon a handful of Krakind nobles and Pelagist leaders got to see Aradocles, so that they could vouch to their followers that this was the true heir after all. Some attempt at a plan was made, but Stenwold soon gained the uneasy feeling that these sea-kinden were simply not used to war. Their idea of such a fight, even with the numbers they had amassed, was to hurl their people at the enemy, as swiftly and fiercely as possible, and hope to let sheer individual skill and inspiration carry the day. Of all the sea-kinden he had met, Stenwold wondered if the only one who might understand how to conduct a war was Rosander.

The Krakind let their discussions run on, till most of the Pelagists gave up on the whole business and went off to tend to their machines or their animals. Stenwold now looked up as he heard one approaching him.

'Nemoctes,' he named the arrival.

'Stenwold Maker.' Nemoctes was wearing his shell mail, the same shield slung across his back. 'I have a message for you.'

Something twisted inside Stenwold. 'From . . . ?'

'Her, yes. Lyess.' Nemoctes looked troubled. 'She told me that you'd put a question to her, before you left, and that her companion has the answer now. She told me also that you were coming back to us. She seemed very sure of that.'

Stenwold nodded tiredly. 'Take me to her.'

'You need not, if you do not wish it,' Nemoctes cautioned. 'She is . . . behaving strangely. I have never before known her like this. Something has changed with her.'

'Take me to her,' Stenwold repeated, and levered himself to his feet. Nemoctes's expression darkened but he nodded, gesturing for Stenwold to follow him.

On the way to the hatch, Paladrya approached him, her expression suddenly one of alarm, and he wondered what she had guessed at, and by what means. She reached out a hand to him and he touched fingers briefly, feeling like a man going to his own execution.

He found that his memories had strayed, during that period when Lyess and her domain had been so much on his mind. In his thoughts, during his incarceration at the Hot Stations, during the flight in the submersible, he had recalled pure light, as though he had travelled with Lyess in a room full of windows: as though the clean sunlight had shone in from every point.

Now, standing before her again after so long, he discovered that his mind had glossed over the shapes in the translucent material of the creature around them: the coils and sacs and organs casting their shadows through the ambient glow. His mind had rewritten the place, gilded and edited it until he found he recalled something like a domed hall of lucent marble, when all along he had been dwelling within the guts of a monster.

Lyess, though, his memories had not needed to alter: beautiful as a statue and just as cold; blank-eyed as a Moth-kinden, or as the Monarch of Princep Salmae. He could feel the shreds of old glamour stir at the sight of her, her skin paler than alabaster, her form so perfect in its curves and in its grace that she seemed more the work of some arch-genius artificer than a product of nature. About her shoulders her hair stirred and waved under unfelt currents.

'You came back,' she said. He could not read her face because, like an Ant-kinden, she had lived all her life in a communion that had never needed facial expressions. Unlike the Ants, though, that communion had denied any human contact, until now.

'Nemoctes said you had an answer for me,' he said slowly, thinking carefully on his words lest he commit to something without realizing.

'You asked me to seek out the memories of our ancestors,' she told him. 'You wished to know if the Littoralists were right and if your forebears drove ours from the land.'

Stenwold nodded, not trusting himself to speak. *It means nothing*, the better part of his mind insisted. *At this remove, what difference can it make?* But he was a scholar – a tactician, a spymaster and a statesman yes, but a scholar first. He wanted to know what guilt and what blood stained the hands of all those on the land.

'Kneel,' she instructed him and, when he raised his eyebrows at that, she cocked her head to one side and smiled, though it was an awkward attempt at the expression. 'Or you will fall,' she explained, 'when my companion touches your mind.'

Suddenly he was less keen to know. The pulsating, curving walls around them seemed to loom always on the point of closing in. 'My *mind*? Can you not simply tell . . . ?'

'You have called on the memories of ancient days, Stenwold Maker. Do you not wish to share them, now that they are laid before you?' That smile was still there, and as false as ever, but there were real feelings behind it, though terrible feelings. To kneel before her would be to open himself to more than old memories, he realized. There was a need in her, that was desperate, yearning and predatory. She had put her barbs in him before, to lure him back to her, yet he felt bleakly that it was nothing of Stenwold Maker that she sought. It was merely that he was the first, the only, human being that she had shared her domain with, and after he had gone, she had been lonely.

*But I do want to know!* And would it be such a crime to toy with her affections, to profess things he did not feel, in order to discover what no man of Collegium had ever known before?

'Come, Stenwold.' She held out a hand to him, the skin so delicate that he could almost see her bones through it. He remembered now what it had been to touch her, and how he had felt as her power, her enchantment, had encroached on him.

*A lifetime of that? A forever of being slave to her magic, a slave to the sea?*

'Can you not . . . just tell me?' he asked plaintively, staring at the proffered hand.

'Words are but sounds,' she told him simply. 'In the

deep, words are nothing. Sight is nothing. There is only feeling and knowledge. Would you turn away the gift of pure knowledge?' And, as he hesitated still, two words forced themselves out from her resolve: 'Please, Stenwold.'

He knew then how it would be a crime, a terrible crime, to buy her knowledge with false coin – and a crime that would come with its own form of punishment. If he knelt before her, if he even took her hand, it would be as if he had signed a contract, made a vow. From that point on, the very creature that contained them would enforce her right, more terribly than any bride's father in dragging him to his nuptials.

'I can't.' He heard his words and watched her face, half expecting that it would remain calm as ever even so.

'You must!' she insisted. 'You are mine! I marked you as my own. You have thought of me, only of me!' Her features twitched and quivered, without ever forming a coherent expression.

'No longer,' he explained. 'Perhaps the land air has washed all the sea from me.' *Or perhaps the Monarch was right, and I have been saved by my admiration for another.* But he said none of that.

'But you want to know,' she insisted, and her hand, still offered to him, kept clenching and unclenching.

'I do, but I cannot meet your price, Lyess.'

For a second she stared at him, and some emotion flowered at last in her face. It was rage, pure rage, as callow and raw as a youth's, flooding through her and contorting her features until her perfect teeth were bared, her eyes turning into daggers.

'No!' she shrieked, and lunged towards him faster than he had expected. The hand that had been offered to him was at his throat in an instant, still feeling cool and slick. He stumbled back, and she went with him, until she had him pressed against the yielding flesh of the wall. He had a hand on her wrist by that point, and her grip was not strong, but then something writhed against his neck, something in her palm, and he went very still.

*Phylles's Art*, he thought, having seen the lashing barbs of Wys's crew-woman kill their share of victims, and now it seemed that Lyess's kinden possessed a similar weapon. Thinking of the curtain of stinging tendrils her companion trailed behind it, he realized that he should have guessed at that before.

'You are mine,' Lyess insisted. Against her so-pale face, in the grey-white light, it was hard to tell if she was weeping or not, but her voice suggested it. 'I was led to you! You were given to me!'

'By who?' got out Stenwold. 'Nemoctes?'

'Nemoctes?' she spat. 'What would he know? He is so concerned with Edmirs and heirs and doing right. Do you think I was close by to save you, by chance? It was destiny! It was pure *destiny!*' She pushed him back against the wall again, but there was very little strength to her, even in her rage. Only the poisoned sting in her palm held him captive.

'What destiny?' he asked, in his most calming voice.

'The Seagod said,' she told him. 'The Seagod promised. It sent me to rescue you.'

Stenwold recalled that vast segmented shadow, that clawed silhouette. Even as a landsman, even as an Apt landsman, he had felt a power off the Seagod, radiating an all-encompassing awareness that no mere beast could own. 'It saved us from the Menfish,' he said softly.

'It told me of you when I travelled in the deep places,' Lyess whispered reverently. 'It spoke of the landsman, and told me where I must be – and when. I hated it then, for we Pelagists must be free above all, but then we took you within ourselves, and I . . . I have never . . . never known . . .'

*Never known being close to another human being*, Stenwold

finished inwardly, but the scholar in him enquired, 'What could this Seagod want with me? It makes no sense? Why would it care?'

Abruptly she was holding his face between both her hands, drawing him close to her, almost close enough to kiss. 'It told me of you,' she whispered. 'There is blood coming from the land: a great outpouring of blood that shall wash over everything until it comes to where the land meets the sea. The sea is great, but that blood is the blood of ages past, and if it is not stopped on land, there will be no end to it. In the end, the sea itself shall be red with it, and all that we are shall be destroyed, even to the furthest Pelagists, even to the Seagod itself. If it can be stopped at all, then you are the man who might do so. So, I must save you from Arkeuthys, and take you with me, admit you to where no trespasser has ever been suffered, where only the distant voices of my fellow Pelagists have ever spoken. Thus you were given into my care. So you are *mine*.'

Stenwold was frowning at her. *And where have I heard prophecy like that before, talk of blood on blood?* 'I cannot be yours, Lyess,' he said, as gently as he could. He felt her Art writhe and twitch against his face.

'I will kill you,' she breathed. 'Do you think I cannot?'

'And what will become of this prophecy then? And your Seagod, too?'

'Must I care?' she hissed. 'Must I believe in prophecy? I *want*! I have never *wanted* before. If you cannot be mine, then I shall kill you.' But, even as she said it, the wrath began ebbing from her, like a high tide that time could not sustain. Her shoulders shook, and she collapsed against him.

'It's not fair,' he heard her say. 'I asked for none of this. For all my life I needed no one. Now how shall I live, knowing that there is more?'

He wanted to tell her that there would be others, that he was Stenwold Maker of Collegium, who believed in neither prophecy nor destiny, and was not worth such despair or longing. He said nothing, though, but let her sag into his arms, the porcelain-delicate translucence of her, and held her close until the distant, transmitted tones of Nemoctes's voice came, querulous and faint, to announce that Aradocles's army was preparing to march.

# Forty-Four

Haelyn had not wanted to bring Claeon the news. It had seemed a good moment, after the report came to her, for her to abandon her post and seek anonymity within the twisted chambers of Hermatyre. Being Claeon's major-domo was a career that promised no longevity, but she had already lasted longer than most. Telling a paranoid tyrant that his enemies really *were* moving against him seemed like suicide to her.

*Yet here I am*, and she knew it was through pure self-interest. When this was over, she wanted to be alive, yes, but she also wanted the gratitude of the winner. If she abandoned Claeon now, and he triumphed, then she would undoubtedly regret it. There would be resentful hands enough to drag her from whatever hiding place and cast her in front of his throne. Worse, if she stepped into the crowds now, and the insurrectionists won, then Heiracles, of notoriously short memory, would have forgotten her assistance long before she was able to make a claim on his generosity. She must stay the course, and hope that Hermatyre fell to the attackers before Claeon's madness killed her.

But first she would have to survive this moment. 'Your Eminence, great Edmir,' she began.

Claeon sat hunched on his throne. His mood had been foul of late. He had known that Heiracles and the other malcontents were mustering, and although he had sent his soldiers out to break heads and shed blood, the insurrectionists had evaded them easily. Worse, a number of his own people had not come back at all, and Haelyn strongly suspected that they had cast their lot with the other side.

He was glowering silently at her now, waiting for her to speak on. There were two Dart-kinden guardsmen at the door, and at a word they would have her on the floor, their spears crossed over her neck. Then Claeon would climb down from his throne, knife in hand and full of bravery against a helpless victim.

'They're coming, aren't they?' he asked, his voice very soft, and to her surprise she thought she heard fear in it. *What has he heard?* The rumour was rampant throughout the colony that Aradocles had returned, but nobody knew for sure if it was true, not even she.

'Our scouts confirm it, Edmir,' she reported, bracing herself, but the explosion of anger never came. Instead he crouched motionless upon his throne, one hand gripping the coral of it painfully hard.

'Guards,' he said, no shout but just a flat command. Even as Haelyn flinched, he instructed them, 'Have all my warriors prepare for war. Spread the word through the colony, that all those who can fight must now show their loyalty to the true bloodline. Have them arm themselves, have them rouse their beasts. Our colony is under threat from greedy, violent men who seek to depose the rightful Edmir, men who seek to sully this throne with their ignoble, unworthy heritage.' He stood up, and for a moment he seemed cloaked with an authority that Haelyn had never witnessed before. 'Tell them that Hermatyre will stand or fall through their resolve. Have them make ready, therefore. And send for Rosander and Pellectes. I will have orders for them, too. We will crush this rabble, this pack of upstarts with their pretender heir.'

The guards marched out swiftly to bear their leader's

words to his people. Claeon took a few steps away from the throne, suddenly a smaller man, divested of majesty. 'Mine,' he whispered. 'Mine. What I have taken must not be taken from me.' His narrowed eyes found Haelyn again. 'What do the Arketoi?'

'The Arketoi?' she asked, baffled. 'Nothing. No more than they ever do. They build. They repair.'

'Good.' He seemed more comforted by this news than she had expected, and strode past her, his progress jerkily swift, out of the throne room and into the antechamber with its great window. 'Where are you?' he demanded of the view outside – and almost at once it was occluded by a coiling bulk that half crawled, half slid from somewhere above. A vast, penetrating eye pressed itself to the clear membrane.

'Arkeuthys,' Claeon addressed it, 'rally your people. All that we rule is under threat. Draw them from every crevice, every crack. Bring all of your kin, arm them and direct them. To war, Arkeuthys, to war!'

What words the great octopus might have then sent back, through Claeon's Art-forged link, Haelyn could not guess, but a moment later the beast had thrust itself away from the colony's uneven stone and was jetting off into the black void.

There was a light cough from the doorway, and Haelyn saw Pellectes there. The green-bearded Littoralist leader looked awkward and out of place, giving Haelyn the distinct impression that he had been interrupted in the middle of preparing his own exit.

'Your Eminence?' the man enquired.

'Come here,' Claeon bid him curtly, and Pellectes crossed the throne room to the window with obvious un-willingness.

'You must rally your people,' Claeon continued, with false heartiness. 'Have you not heard that all our freedoms are under threat? Call on your Littoralists. They shall be chief amongst my armies.'

'Your Eminence,' Pellectes demurred, 'we are visionaries, idealists, but we are no warriors.'

Claeon had seized the Littoralist's arm in an instant, and Haelyn saw the flesh go white under the Edmir's grip. 'Oh, but you have spoken so boldly of invading the land, of thus taking what is ours by right! You talk such a fight as all the world has never seen, Pellectes!' Claeon's tight smile was painful to behold. 'Have I not supported your cause? Have I not even enlisted Nauarch Rosander and primed him to carry the Littoralist banner on to the shores of the land?' He yanked the taller Kerebroi close, the smile becoming a snarl almost without transition. 'And do you believe, if the boy should triumph, he will have any time for your nonsense? Do you not think, instead, that there are plenty of tattle-tales in this colony who would be only too happy to point out to him those who once had my ear, and shared my confidences? You have more enemies than you know, Pellectes, and if I am undone, you yourself shall never step safely in Hermatyre again. Now, go arm your people, every one of them, for you have as much to lose as I do!'

He hurled the man from him, sending the Littoralist sprawling on the floor, and Haelyn watched Pellectes stumble back to his feet, already running for the door.

Even at that moment one of his guards returned and the Edmir bellowed furiously at him, 'Where is Rosander?'

'Edmir, he musters his Thousand Spines already,' the guard promised him, and at that, Claeon smiled.


'Do your people believe in destiny and prophecy and that kind of thing?' Stenwold asked, trying his best to sound casual. He was back in Wys's submersible again, which he trusted in a battle more than Nemoctes's living vessel.

Wys made a face at that question. 'Destiny? Not likely.

Destiny's what you make for yourself. Ain't that right, Spillage?'

'Sounds right to me,' came the voice of the Greatclaw engineer from above.

Phylles was looking less certain, though, so Wys prodded her. 'Don't tell me you're still hung up on all of that stuff?'

The Polypoi woman looked stubborn, so Wys explained. 'Her folk are all about omens and telling the future, sitting and seeing what the currents send past them, cryptic messages from the dead, all that rot. But we civilized her – or at least I thought we'd civilized her.'

All around them the dark sea seemed studded with stars: the limn-lights suspended from the larger craft and creatures in Aradocles's fleet.

Paladrya laid a hand on Stenwold's shoulder, and he smiled.

'Say what you like,' she addressed them all, 'we all have destinies, and those destinies can be uncovered. I have seen it done.'

'Reckon the lad's destiny is to win this battle, then?' Wys asked her. ''Cos if we could know that beforehand, I'd feel a lot easier.'

'What about prophecies delivered by a Seagod?' Stenwold chanced. That drew a long silence from all of them.

'Right,' said Wys at last. 'Seagods? Prophecies? You've been drinking with Pelagists too much, is what that is.'

Stenwold looked to Paladrya, but she shook her head. 'Stories only,' she told him. 'Such prophecies have led to the founding of colonies – or their destruction. I've never met anyone who's even seen a Seagod. And Wys is right – Pelagists delight in telling tall stories to us Obligists from the colonies.'

'I saw a Seagod once,' came Lej's voice from above, but Wys gave a rude snort and told him that he certainly hadn't.

*

It was not long after that before pale light began to leach into the darkness outside, outlining what Stenwold might have thought of as a horizon, under more civilized conditions. Before that, all had been as dark as midnight, with only the limn-lights of their fellow travellers to provide a shifting constellation around and below them. Now there was a growing radiance ahead, and Stenwold realized it must be Hermatyre.

'I hope the boy knows what he's doing,' Wys muttered, uncharacteristically fretful. Stenwold expected Paladrya to leap to her protégé's defence, but she was merely biting at her lip, looking worried.

'He's shifting,' Wys noted a moment later. 'Make sure you stay with him.'

It had been Aradocles's contribution to ocean skirmish to use the Pelagists and their far-speaking Art. Stenwold knew that Salma had done the same with Ant-kinden, using their mindlink to coordinate the various wings of his army. Here, in the crushing, soundless depths, there was no tradition of military coordination. Each warrior fought alone and fell alone, guided only by his personal tactical sense. Aradocles had split up his force into detachments, each with a Pelagist at its heart. He himself rode with Nemoctes, hidden within the living shell. Wys's barque, the dead exterior of a similar creature with a clockwork engine installed, tacked and bobbed to keep up as Nemoctes adjusted his course towards the colony. All around them the army shifted and swirled, following the glowing bells of jellyfish, the mud-crawlers, the nautili, as they followed their leader's orders and came about.

Hermatyre was soon the brightest thing in the sea, shedding varicoloured radiance into the inky water. That radiance showed how the water before the colony was busy, seething with mustering bodies. The pale pens of squid darted or hovered in glimmering schools, each with its lance-wielding rider. Untidy ranks of Kerebroi spearmen, nimble and lightly armoured, clustered and straggled across the seabed between the city and its enemies. The armoured forms of crabs and lobsters squatted, claws drawn in like shields, the long spiny whips of their antennae twitching at the drifting of the currents.

And then there were the octopuses, Arkeuthys's people. Scores of them clustered across the face of the colony. None was as large as their master, but one in three was a match in size for Wys's submersible. Squinting into the underwater radiance, Stenwold saw metal and pale shell glinting: spikes and blades crudely made, tentacles coiling about makeshift hilts. He remembered the *Tseitan*'s battle with Arkeuthys, and the great sea-monster taking their harpoon and using it as a spear. *Did we teach them that?*

Stenwold had only the loosest notion of how many dissidents Heiracles had managed to muster. 'How do the numbers look?' he asked, for it seemed to him that there were a great many who had rallied to Hermatyre's defence.

'We're short of theirs,' Wys replied bluntly, her small hands clenched into fists, and Stenwold could see her now wondering whether she had made the right decision.

'But we fight on the side of the true heir,' Paladrya insisted loyally, although her face seemed bloodless. 'Who would fight so hard on behalf of Claeon?'

'Well, let's hope *they* know we've got the true heir with us, because I don't see them trailing banners with his face on,' Wys told her. 'Oh, I'm getting less fond of this . . . and there are Rosander's lot, of course.' Something went out of her expression. 'Piss on it,' she said, almost sadly.

A column of armoured crustaceans was emerging around the Hermatyre's lumpy, coral-encrusted curve. They trudged out before the defenders, ten abreast at least, and around them marched Rosander's warriors of the Thousand Spine Train. Almost all of them were Onychoi of one sort or another, many armoured in colossal plate, proceeding with a strangely ponderous dignity. There were other kinden among their number, too: squid-riders, Kerebroi, even a few Pelagists and some of Phylles's kin. Their passage stirred up the mud beneath, as though the seabed smoked beneath their feet.

And they kept coming, this column emerging inexorably into view, tens and tens and then hundreds of men and women and beasts, until Stenwold felt weak just to watch them. 'So many,' he whispered, and Wys gave him a wry look.

'What, you thought there was only a *thousand* of the bastards? Just a name, landsman, just a name.'

'Look.' Paladrya was pointing, but it was not clear at what. Then Wys had seen it, too, rushing over to the panes of her viewport to get a better look. Stenwold remained baffled, unable to see anything in this advancing horde beyond the doom of their plans.

'It is *all* the Thousand Spines,' Phylles explained to him quietly. Her eyes were still intent on the scene outside.

'Well, yes, that's the problem, isn't it?' Stenwold suggested.

'No, land-kinden, *all* of them. All their goods, their wagons, their crèches, their infirmaries, everything that they need to live, out in the depths.'

Stenwold frowned, trying to understand it. True, a great many of the crawling beasts were heavily laden, but he had assumed that was the norm for this place and these people. 'Then . . . ?'

But by then it was clear. The direction that Rosander's Benthists was taking would neither draw them up before the city nor crash into the advancing dissidents. Instead they were simply going away, heading off across the seabed towards the depths, resuming the Benthist life after living so long on Claeon's promises.

'Save me from sea-kinden with a sense of drama,' Stenwold murmured, but then Paladrya was hugging him, hard enough to drive half the breath from his body.

'You did it!' she shouted. 'You drove away Rosander!'

He put an arm about her, finding that the gesture could be both affectionate and comradely, without any awkwardness. 'Just talk, that's all it was. The sort of talk my people are good at, though.'

She kissed him, without warning or apparent premeditation, and their eyes locked, Paladrya seeming more startled by it than Stenwold himself.

'I don't want to piss on your party, or anything, but there's still more of Claeon's lot than of us,' Wys pointed out sourly.

Stenwold eyed the defenders, seeing them eddy and mill aimlessly now that the Thousand Spines were abandoning them. More of them than the attackers, yes, but not so very many more that victory would be swift for them. In fact, this looked like a recipe for a bloody and mutually destructive contest. He shivered at the thought.

The attackers' advance became swifter now, and he could see the defenders forming into a rabble of a line, ready to receive them. Then something detached itself from the pitted surface of Hermatyre, and rippled towards them in a flurry of tentacles. Stenwold found that he recognized it: not only because it was far larger than any other of its kind there, but from its very attitude, the pale and rubbery hide laced with scars, those great flat-pupilled, white eyes.

*Arkeuthys.*

The sea-monster that had dragged him down into this nightmare world the first time. All across the surface of Hermatyre, the smaller octopuses were now squirming into the water, fanning out across the defenders, coming to rest on the seabed or simply undulating back and forth. Arkeuthys just hung there before the attackers, though, like a vast tentacled skull, as the attackers' advance began to slow to a crawl. The reputation alone, the very name of the great monster, seeped into each mind like a curse.

*

Aboard Nemoctes's companion, Aradocles lifted his head.

'It's the big beast, Arkeuthys,' Nemoctes suppied, watching through the eyes of the creature that carried them. The Pelagist was fully geared for war, shell armour and shield and hook-headed axe.

'Oh, I know that,' said the heir of Hermatyre softly. It had been a long time since he had used the Art of Speech, years indeed since he had been close enough to one of Arkeuthys's brood. Now he felt the mind of the creature just like a sun, burning away in the water with the malevolent fire of its long years. The octopuses, the Krakind's namesake beasts, were more than mere animals. They were guardians and patrons to the humans who claimed kinship with them, and in return the beasts lived longer and longer, lifespans stretching from the brief span allotted to their lesser cousins until they could count their years as men did, or longer. As they aged, they grew wiser, too, more cunning in the ways of the world, and of humanity. They had always been a force here, in Hermatyre, a silent but influential counsel in the affairs of the Edmirs.

*Arkeuthys*, sent out Aradocles, into the watery void. *Hear me.*

He was not sure that he had properly recaptured the Art of it, until that slow voice came back, sounding like stone grating on stone. *So, you have returned after all.*

*Did you ever doubt it?*

*It would not be the first time*, Arkeuthys replied, *that rumours of you have stirred up fools. I have personally defended your honour by putting down such lies. Has the idiot Heiracles not told you of his previous attempts at unseating your rightful blood? Or would he perhaps clothe himself in virtue now, as though it could be accreated, like metal or shell?*

*I have no illusions about Heiracles*, Aradocles replied. The presence of Arkeuthys in his mind was vast and heavy, and it made his knees want to buckle, his bowels to loosen.

But he stood all the straighter, under the force of that vast scrutiny. *Heiracles knows his place, now.*

*And do you?* There was bleak amusement in the great monster's thoughts. *Your rabble cringes from me even now. What did you expect, Aradocles?*

*From them? That they would follow me this far – and further, as they must.* Aradocles took a deep breath, sensing the abyss beneath him that he must plumb. *And from you? Obedience, as due to your rightful Edmir.*

There was a very long pause indeed, and the eventual response was not words at all, but a feeling that indicated amusement – only amusement.

*Hear me, Arkeuthys,* Aradocles persisted. *You served my father well, and you are a great ruler of your own people. After I was lost to Hermatyre, when I was believed dead, you then served my uncle. Why should you not? He was thought by all to be the rightful Edmir of Hermatyre, so it was not your place to question him. Now you know the truth of my return, why should you not serve your rightful lord, and turn from the false one?*

He sensed the quality of the silence change at the far end of his link with Arkeuthys. At last the great beast murmured, *Claeon has valued my support, and given me much freedom. He has made me a very Edmir of my people, as he is Edmir of yours.*

*As he was,* corrected Aradocles sharply. *Arkeuthys, you are your people's ruler. It has never been the place of the Kerebroi to interfere in such matters. Do you think I would try to unseat you because you have served others in my family? Only continue to serve my family still, and why should I bear you any grudge?*

And the baffled reply followed fast on the heels of his words. *But your people will remember only too well what I have done in Claeon's name, little one.*

*They will remember that it was done in Claeon's name,*

*that is all. And if they should ever complain, well, if they would have me as their Edmir, then they will live by my decision.*

The attacking force's advance had stopped entirely now. All eyes, on both sides, were fixed on the giant octopus, as it undulated slightly between both lines, its eyes narrowed to the merest of slits.

*Claeon would not make such a generous offer, nor would your father, if they found themselves in your place. You must be aware of the reality of what I have done, of the weapon I have made myself in Claeon's hands against those who resisted his rule.*

*I have spent time amongst strange people,* Aradocles replied simply. *I have learned new arts. Their word for this is amnesty, and that is what I offer. Do you see its meaning, here in my mind?*

*I do . . .*

*Then speak to the Krakind Kerebroi gathered amongst the defenders. Tell them one thing only. Tell them I have returned, the true heir, to claim my throne. Do this, and you shall remain to me as much as you ever were to Claeon – and with one advantage more.*

*And what is that?* pried the thoughts of Arkeuthys.

*Why, that I am* not *Claeon,* Aradocles told the creature drily. *Surely you cannot claim that you actually liked my uncle?*

Arkeuthys began abruptly jetting backwards in the water, as Nemoctes reported, coiling and pulsing until he hung over the defenders. In Aradocles's mind, though, echoed the faint suggestion of laughter.

It was only when Aradocles's troops entered Hermatyre that Stenwold realized just how messy things could have become. The city possessed dozens of the double-doored hatches, but each outer one could have been held with ease by just a few spearmen, and then again at the inner door.

There were no defenders in evidence, though. Stenwold himself had watched as Arkeuthys had drifted over Claeon's marshalled forces, expecting a sudden charge, the first blood of the war. There had been a change plain to see in the enemy army, though, a ripple of shock passing through them. As the attackers had drawn closer Stenwold had witnessed a great deal of the sea-kinden's busy underwater hand-speech as Krakind Kerebroi – the kin of Aradocles and Claeon – passed on news to their allies of other kinden.

And the defending force had soon begun to break up. Individuals had sidled off, and then whole troops of them, the majority of the defenders simply giving up and going home. Some even left their weapons behind: spears driven point-first into the seabed or the falx swords abandoned. The octopuses – all of Arkeuthys's crawling, lurking kindred – had simply slithered away across the great gnarled dome of the colony, leaving the way clear.

Some of the defenders had not disbanded, though. A number had come to join the attackers, gladly switching sides for no reason that Stenwold could understand just then. Others, however, had remained under arms, and they hurried back into Hermatyre, desperate to get inside its coral walls before the heir's forces reached them. There were not enough that they could have held the city, however, even if they could have been sure of support from the rest of the populace.

Aradocles's forces began the slow process of filing into the colony, streaming in through every entrance and forming up in their separate detachments, braced for Claeon's counterattack. For Stenwold, this was the longest part of the assault, watching the foot-soldiers of the assault force queue and mill until their own turn came. Hermatyre had not been built with such a grand number of visitors in mind.

'I suppose, if we'd needed, we could have used the

Gastroi to cut our way in,' he suggested. The looks he received from the others revealed nothing but horror.

'You cannot *cut*,' Paladrya told him, as if even the mention of the word was sacrilege. 'The Builders, the Arketoi, would be angered.'

Stenwold remembered those pale little tattooed men, the mysterious kinden who had constructed Hermatyre and all the other colonies across the seabed. 'I didn't see any of them in the battle line,' he said. 'I didn't think they really, well, noticed this kind of thing.'

'Battles? Politics?' Paladrya replied. 'Oh, sometimes they do, and woe betide anyone who attracts their attention. Break any of the substance of Hermatyre, though, and you'd never be able to go near a colony ever again. The entire kinden, they'd *know*.'

At last it was Stenwold's turn, and he took up his caul and let Paladrya pull him over to the city's stone outer skin and help guide him inside. He had come this far, and he wanted to see this finished.

The army had divided into different cohorts, and now the Pelagists' far-speech would not help them for, of Nemoctes's people, only the man himself was entering the colony. Meanwhile each cohort, entering by a different gate, would start moving through the twisting paths of Hermatyre, seeking out resistance wherever it was to be found.

Stenwold himself followed close behind Aradocles, with Paladrya to one side of him and Phylles to the other. He had never gained much of a sense of Hermatyre's layout before, while being bundled through the streets by Claeon's men or Rosander's, but now he had a chance to appreciate the colony's bizarre architecture, its curious beauty and its utterly alien design. A living city, surely, or one that had been grown and then died, as more city was grown on top of it, over and over. Within that stratified crust, the colony was expressed in diverse hollows: chambers as small as a cramped room or as great as a city square; the walls patterned, segmented, moulded into symmetrical designs of unknown import in the secret architectural language of the Builders. The tunnels interlinking the chambers led up and down seemingly at random: ribbed passageways of stone winding and twisting like worms through the city's heart. Everywhere there was limn-light, those coloured globes of radiance that the sea-kinden crafted for lamps, casting dim-coloured veils across the pale stone, and across the grim faces of the invaders.

They had expected Claeon's people to fight them from room to room, but there was barely any resistance, just a few straggling defenders caught up by the attackers' tide. The residents of Hermatyre watched Aradocles and his people pass, making no move to stop them, but nor did they cheer. Instead they waited, untrusting and unsure, to see the outcome. Stenwold was reminded that Aradocles had been absent for years, and their memory of him was of a mere youth, and not a king. Rightful heir he might be, but these people had been living under Claeon's capricious and heavy-handed rule, and they had no guarantee that the Edmir's nephew would prove any better.

And then they came out upon a vista that Stenwold did recognize, at last. Here he had returned, by all the strange roads that fate had led him along, to the Cathedra Edmir, the heart of Hermatyre, the great plaza that gave onto the gates of the Edmir's palace complex. This was the place that he had first been dragged to, feeling bewildered and battered, for his first introduction to the sea-kinden. This was where Paladrya had been imprisoned since Claeon's suspicion fell upon her, until Wys's people had broken them both out.

And this was where the Edmir's loyalists had chosen to make their stand, and there were many. All Claeon's remaining supporters were assembled here, every villain

668

and sycophant who had prospered so much under his reign that their lives would be forfeit if he fell. All the cruelty, the greed, the petty tyranny and casual brutality that had grown fat under Claeon's rule had now gathered to defend him, knowing that they were dead men otherwise.

Some remained within the palace, others were lined up outside it: Dart-kinden and Krakind Kerebroi, Onychoi large and small, a few that were kin to Phylles even. They stood in clumps, forming an uneven battle line: some with mauls or falxes, others with hooked knives, but most of them with spears. Some had weapons that Stenwold took for lances at first, but then he noticed that, instead of a head of metal or bone, they had something else twined around the shaft like a living thing.

'Well,' he murmured to Paladrya, 'I think this is as far as words and peace take us,' to which she nodded soberly.

# Forty-Five

'What are they waiting for?' Pellectes demanded. The Littoralist leader clutched a spear in both hands, peering out over the heads of the warriors lined up in front of the palace. 'He has more men than we do, doesn't he? Or does he?' He craned left and right, trying to see clearer without exposing himself to the eyes of the enemy.

'This is but part of the boy's force,' growled Claeon sourly. Since the bulk of Hermatyre's defenders had betrayed him – since *Arkeuthys* had betrayed him! – he was running out of options. 'The other packs of vagabonds are combing the streets even now.'

'Then what are *we* waiting for?' Pellectes demanded, almost jostling Claeon as the two of them stood at the back of their forces, in the gaping entryway of the palace itself. 'Why not attack now? We have more warriors than he does, I think. Yes, I'm sure of it.'

'And we'd be shorn of our walls, open to attack on all sides. No, all they have to do is wait.' Claeon had come to the fight prepared, clad head to foot in armour of bone-coloured shell that had been minutely accreated to fit every line of his body. The bronze-beaked gold head of his maul rested on the ground before him.

His fingers itched to stick hot knives into Aradocles, his wretched nephew. To have had so much, and then so great a fall, all because of one sickly boy. If only it had been his own agents who had first located the heir, out there on the hostile land. *How could it all go so wrong?*

'Something's happening,' Pellectes said suddenly, and Claeon leant forward to see a figure stand forward from the throng of insurgents.

'Is that him?' the tall Littoralist asked, frowning.

Claeon stared at the Krakind youth's face for a long time before nodding. Yes, that was the visage, that was the look of his nephew, for all that exile on the land had toughened and leathered him.

*A sudden strike now?* he considered. With Aradocles dead, numbers would barely matter. What would the invaders be fighting for? The true bloodline would rest only in Claeon.

'Where is Claeon?' the boy out in front demanded. He wore no armour, and carried merely a short-bladed sword of unfamiliar design. 'Claeon, my uncle, come forth!'

A lot of Claeon's men were now looking back at him, but the Edmir made no move to present himself, scowling silently within his helm as Aradocles called him out.

'Come to me, uncle! Let us not waste the lives of our people. Will you not fight me? Will you not decide this by single combat?'

No armour, and just that brief sword, but the boy was young and strong, and Claeon was no great warrior. *And, besides, one look at me and they'd rush at me, tear me to pieces. Why should I trust this boy's honour? Or even his control of his own forces?* Claeon leant forward until he could murmur to the nearest of his men.

'I promise great riches to any man who can send a spear into that strutting youth,' he spat. 'Shed his blood for me, and I shall reward it.'

Throwing spears was an uncommon art amongst the sea-kinden, as it was near-useless in the water, but there were a few who had made a practice of it to better surprise unwary opponents. Of these, one man at least was bold enough, or desperate enough, to listen to the Edmir's promises. A lean, sinewy Dart-kinden, clad in a breastplate of overlapping scallop-shells, shouldered his way forward between his fellows.

'Claeon!' Aradocles called out again. 'Do you fear me so much, uncle?'

Claeon ground his teeth angrily.

It was over in a moment. The spearman had reached the fore, and now had the spear cocked back for casting in one smooth motion.

There was a sharp snapping noise, and the Dart-kinden dropped, stone dead with a hole punched through his armour.

Utter silence descended, the sea-kinden on both sides staring. Claeon saw, though. He saw, in the front rank of the insurgents, there was a broad, dark, balding man of foreign features, a man who had once been confined in Claeon's clutches, inside his very oubliette. Now the man had one hand directed forward, with some small rod in its grip, too tiny to be any serious weapon save that he had simply pointed it at the spearman, and the spearman had died.

'The land-kinden,' Pellectes moaned, and Claeon saw at last how the man really did believe his own fictions. In the mind of Pellectes, the land-kinden were the great monsters, the eternal enemy, the things that would *get you* if you erred. A sheen of sweat had broken out on the man's high forehead, and he kept pointing with a shaking hand. 'The land-kinden!' he gasped again, as though the arrival of just one was enough to stave in the walls of Hermatyre.

'Kill him!' Pellectes shrieked, pointing a quivering hand that encompassed both the landsman and Aradocles, and a dozen people around them. 'Kill him now! Or we're all doomed!' He shoved at shoulders, kicked and pushed and yelled, and then some of the defenders were surging forward, and then more and more who were out of earshot of

Pellectes but saw the advance and assumed an order had been given, and then the entire mass of defenders was moving forth to do battle away from the protection of the palace.

'Claeon, we must destroy the land-kinden!' Pellectes cried out, and turned to see the Edmir backing away. The head of the maul dragged along the palace floor, and the plates of Claeon's beautifully crafted armour scraped and slid, but Claeon's face was ashen, and he backed and backed, and then he turned and ran into the palace.

Stenwold expected commands to be shouted, for the front rank of the insurgents to raise a fence of spear-points against the enemy, but it seemed to him that the entire force suddenly went to pieces, shouting challenges and war cries, half of them rushing forward, half of them standing still to receive the charge.

'Get behind me, land-kinden!' Aradocles snapped at him, readying his sword. For a horrible moment Stenwold thought the youth, carrying all that priceless royal blood, was about to rush headlong into the fray, but, even if he had intended to, his own followers got in his way, meeting the onrushing loyalists and clashing fiercely with them. Stenwold had seen the sea-kinden of the Hot Stations in their bloody hacking at the Echinoi, and he had seen their swift cavalry actions in the open sea, but here he saw the Kerebroi fighting their with own kind, and it was savage.

They were swift and lithe, these sea-kinden, and they were not soldiers such as the Ants or the Wasps might field. Instead they reminded Stenwold only of the old Inapt of the land, of the Mantids and the Moths. They descended on one another as individuals, fought a hundred separate duels and shifting skirmishes. Here Dart-kinden spearmen leapt at one another, spinning and turning, clashing shafts against one each other, sweeping their weapons' butts around and lancing with the bone needles of their heads.

Greatclaw Onychoi, hulking in their grand suits of armour, laid about with mauls and their terrible curved swords, the falxes that could shatter mail or bones with a single ponderous stroke. Others carried deadlier weapons: staves about which were twisted stinging cells that lashed and stabbed at their foes across a man's length of space, killing with agonizing venom the moment they struck. They were good only for a single death, though, and soon abandoned, their wielders reversing the same weapons to present spearheads to the enemy. Around them a great number of the sea-kinden had resorted to daggers. Krakind ripped and tore at one another with their hooked blades, and sometimes just with the tearing Art of their bare hands. Swiftclaw Onychoi, Mantis-lean creatures that were kin to Fel, hammered and punched with their spines or with narrow-bladed stilettos. Those few of Phylles's kinden walked through the fighting like bleak death, the stingers of their hands shooting left and right, and held off only by the greater reach of spearmen. Phylles herself was gone, lost sight of in the fury of the fighting, but Stenwold had no doubt that she was doing more than her fair share of the killing.

It was just what Aradocles had wanted to avoid. It was what might have happened on so much grander a scale outside the colony, if the great army of the defenders had not disbanded.

The heir himself waited. He had his Helleron-made shortsword in his hand, watching the ebb and flow of the convoluted melee. Stenwold had by now lost track of who was on whose side, but all the locals seemed to know.

A spearman leapt at the heir from the press, screaming a battle cry. Stenwold's hand moved and the man was thrown back, the retort of the little snapbow lost amid the shouting. His hands reloaded mechanically. Aradocles glanced back at him, expressionless, and then nodded.

'Land-kinden, follow me,' he instructed. 'We go to find Claeon.'

Stenwold had been in more than a few fights in his life, from seedy knifings in the back streets of Helleron, through skirmishes with enemy agents in a dozen cities, all the way to the hammer of war brought by the Wasps against Myna or the Vekken against Collegium. Never a fight like this, though. For him the melee had become something surreal and dreamlike. He was surrounded by sea-kinden: he and Paladrya ringed by Aradocles's most fervent followers. The prince, the young Edmir himself, simply forged ahead, leading with his blade, but never needing to bloody it. On either side, the spearmen of his vanguard pressed forth, desperate to keep pace with their leader. They could not protect him, though, constantly moving as he was, and yet he was not touched, nor did he strike a single blow.

Stenwold, having long lost track of who was insurgent and who were those still clinging to Claeon, simply judged everyone by watching Aradocles. Those that raised a weapon against him, those that he levelled his sword at, they died, the snapbow punching them from their feet without their ever understanding what it was that killed them. Aradocles surged forward, dragging his warriors with him, and Stenwold shot and reloaded, shot and shot and reloaded, over and over. The range of his weapon was a little less than twenty feet at most, as he leant round Aradocles to take aim. His victims were busy concentrating on the young heir, barely understanding at first that the stubby twin-barrelled piece in Stenwold's hand was a weapon at all. Here in Hermatyre they had nothing like it.

He had brought a sufficiency of snapbow bolts.

*Ah, but this would be different in the Hot Stations*, Stenwold admitted to himself, finding plenty of time for reflection in that almost casually bloody advance. *A few of those spring-bows, those harpoon-launchers of Mandir's, would lay us low in short order. We catch the sea-kinden here at the very turning point of Aptitude.* But clearly the Man of the Hot Stations was jealous with his inventions, and none had made it as far as Hermatyre, and so the little device that Totho had crafted for his old mentor, that little trinket of murder, brought death like a plague upon Aradocles's enemies.

Had there been more Greatclaw Onychoi there with their heavy mail, then Stenwold might not have had such an easy time, but the Kerebroi relied on speed and close-in fighting, and none of them was faster than a snapbow bolt.

At one point the defenders, almost in the entryway of the palace itself, had formed up a respectable row of spears, the Dart-kinden standing side by side with a discipline the rest of the field had not witnessed. Aradocles paused, glancing back at Stenwold, who merely nodded.

The young Edmir pointed his blade like a wizard from the Bad Old Days, some Moth Skryre bringing down a curse on his enemies. He pointed his blade, and a man in the centre of the line pitched backwards. He pointed again, and the next man's helm cracked, a small hole drilled neatly into the skull beneath, which became a gap the size of a fist in the back of the luckless man's head. The fatal sword selected a third target. By now Stenwold found he could load his snapbow without even looking at his hands, but then it had always been the genius of Totho's weapon that any fool could become proficient with it after only a little practice.

A Kerebroi man, a lean figure with a greenish beard, was now trying to hold the defending spearmen together. Aradocles singled him out emotionlessly. In the last moment before Stenwold followed suit, the enemy leader met the landsman's gaze, his face twisting into a mask of fear and loathing. Then Stenwold's shot took him in the temple, snapping his head back, his body vanishing behind the rank of his followers.

The spear line broke apart, the lean and swift Dart-kinden falling into a chaos of struggling warriors trying to get out of the path of that deadly blade – and Aradocles advanced up the steps of the palace.

A shock went through the enemy. Stenwold saw it in their movements, as though a school of fish suddenly changed direction, all at the same time. Looking across the battle from the elevation of the steps, he realized that another contingent of Aradocles's followers had finally arrived from the left, Nemoctes, in his mail and shield, driving a wedge through the weakened defenders. The battle had come to a close then and there, with his flanking assault, and Claeon's wretches were being killed if they tried to resist, disarmed if they surrendered. Many who surrendered were still killed, Stenwold noticed, a hundred grievances and revenges being written out in blood. There was nothing he could do about it, and this was hardly a vice found only beneath the waters.

'Claeon!' Aradocles called out again, and entered into the palace – making it his own even as he did so.

Claeon descended hurriedly, wondering just how long Pellectes's incompetent defence would hold the bastards back. Time enough for an escape, perhaps, if an escape was possible. *Out into the open sea, head off into the depths. Someone will take me in. Some Benthist train, some minor colony out there. Then I'll raise a warband and I'll come back here. I'll have that boy's head on a spear, I swear it!*

The door ahead of him swung open at a touch, a little water gushing past his feet. The next door would take him into the ocean.

And yet he paused. There could be insurgents waiting just beyond, hanging in the water, staking out his private dock. After all, they knew about it – when Paladrya and that cursed land-kinden had been taken from his oubliette, it had been this way they had come to escape. This, his private egress into the sea, and it had been sullied by base freebooters and fleeing prisoners.

He paused then because, of course, this hatch only opened outwards and, in all the excitement about the prisoners' exit, he had never considered how their rescuers had got *in*.

He reached his hands towards the hatch once more, but hesitated. What if there was somebody out there?

And in the trembling fastness of his mind he heard the mocking words: *Oh, there's nobody out here, Claeon. Nobody at all.*

'Arkeuthys?' He spoke the name out loud, unable to stop himself.

*Indeed.* That familiar pressure, the great mind of the sea monster.

*You betrayed me!* Claeon sent back to it, agonized. *Why?*

*The boy is persuasive,* the giant octopus replied idly. *Come out, Claeon. Come into my arms and let me finish this. Your head would make a valuable gift.*

*If you truly wanted to kill me, then you'd not have warned me,* Claeon divined.

*Perhaps that is the extent of my sentiment,* came the murmured reply, like distant rocks falling. *Ah, Claeon, we have had such times together, have we not? We have been partners in each other's misdeeds.*

*But you betrayed me!* Claeon insisted. *You were always my other half. You took joy in the work I set you! Why throw that away now?*

Arkeuthys chuckled, unrepentant. *Well, I always thought that I had matched you in wickedness for wickedness, Claeon, but then the boy explained to me that I had just been loyal to the man everyone thought was the true Edmir, so I decided that I would rather be the other half of someone less demanding. It's over, Claeon. Give up now. Perhaps the boy will just hang you in a cage as a warning, rather than peeling your skin off.*

Claeon whimpered and backed away, clutching the heavy maul closer to him, and then he was bolting back up into the main body of the palace, clumsy in his armour, rebounding from the walls and staggering. He could hear the sounds of the fighting getting closer every moment, it seemed, and he had only one place to go.

The throne room, his sanctum, provided no shelter now, but where else was there for an Edmir to meet his end?

He stumbled through the passageways of his palace, all abandoned now – as he had been abandoned, save by those fools currently being butchered under the incompetent command of Pellectes. *Littoralists! I should never have reached out my hand to them. This is all Pellectes's fault! If he hadn't had me kidnap the landsman ... but then how would I have enticed Rosander to keep the peace for me, save by dangling the land before him like a dead fish?*

And he burst into the throne room, seeing the seat of all his power and command, yet taking no joy from it.

His throne room had a door, though it was very rarely closed. Now he got his hands about the rim and hauled at it until the valve-like disc closed shut behind him.

But there was no way to seal it. This was no pressure door, such as led into the ocean. Aradocles could pry it open with ease. Claeon had always relied on guards to keep out his enemies. Now he had no guard but himself.

He thought he could hear shouting beyond the closed portal. Were the cursed boy and his landsmen even now approaching, calling out his name? Claeon whimpered with dread and hate, raising up his maul. *Can it be done? Then I shall do it.* With a great cry, he launched the weapon's beaked head at the door's hinge, striking away jagged fragments of stony stuff, compacting the hollow chambers of the coral. Shouting incoherently, he struck four, five times, smashing the substance of the frame, pressing it in on itself. Either the door would fall completely away, leaving him not greatly worse off than he was before, or ...

Panting heavily he stepped back and looked at his handiwork. He had exposed the tombs of a thousand tiny creatures: the barren little cells that their brethren had sealed them up inside, when they were built over, when Hermatyre was being laid down. The door still held its place, though and, when he tugged at it, it was wedged solid. He had now sealed himself within his throne room.

'What have you done?' a woman's voice demanded, and he whirled about with his maul raised. Stepping from behind the throne came Haelyn, his majordomo. The Sepia-kinden woman looked aghast.

'*My* throne,' Claeon snarled. '*I* am the Edmir, no other. He shall not have it. This is *mine*.'

'And what will you do now?' Haelyn asked incredulously. 'Do you think they won't find a way in? And if they don't, will you starve? Or what?'

'I will defy them to my last breath. If I die, I shall be the last Edmir of Hermatyre to sit here and rule.'

'Claeon, listen to me,' she insisted, 'there is another way. For all that has gone wrong between you, Aradocles is your nephew still. If you beg it of him, he will be merciful.'

'Why?' The Edmir scowled at her. 'Why mercy, when he has me by the throat? Mercy is not for Edmirs. Mercy is only for the weak.'

'What other chance have you?' she yelled at him, stepping down from the dais. 'Listen to yourself, Claeon!'

His eyes narrowed abruptly, and she stopped. 'Who let them in, Haelyn?'

'Who let who in?'

'When they stole those land-kinden from my oubliette, when they took my dear Paladrya from me, who let them in? Who was it who betrayed me? I am betrayed, and who better for that than one who held my utmost confidence?'

Until then, he had only the faintest suspicion, his paranoia seeking any target, but now he saw the faintest flush of colours swirling over her skin. A flinch, a twitch of guilt, revealed even under the shadows of her Art, and he knew.

'Traitor!' he shrieked, and in the next moment he was

running at her, maul upraised. She retreated upwards beside the throne, shouting his name, but he was done with that – done with her. His majordomos always failed him, sooner or later. Well, this last one would not survive him. He would regret only that he could not finish her off properly, and at his leisure, but perhaps it was fitting that his last act as Edmir should be a brutal one.

She dodged behind the throne, and his next swing smashed the back of it in a cloud of fragments, obliterating its beauty in a single moment. He would indeed be the last Edmir to govern Hermatyre from that seat. Haelyn retreated and retreated, but Claeon was mad with fury now, whirling the maul about him, cracking dents in the floor, in the walls, until at last she tripped and fell.

She screamed, and he savoured it, standing over her with the comforting weight of the maul in his hands. It was grimed now with pulverized coral, but he'd wash that off soon enough. He raised it high.

Her eyes had slipped away from the weapon, from his own gaze. She was staring now at something beyond him. He was a fool for doing so, but he could not stop himself craning around to look.

The Arketoi stood there, some half-dozen of them: pallid little hairless men and women, tattooed and almost naked, as like unto each other as siblings. They stared at him wordlessly, for they never spoke. Even as he watched, a few more of them trickled into the throne room, twisting their way through the walls, walking somehow in between the infinitesimal spaces between the dead coral. Some had gone over to the door, and were examining its smashed hinge.

'Do not touch that! Do not heal it!' Claeon protested. The majority of the Arketoi just stared at him reproachfully. 'What do you want?' he demanded.

'You hurt the colony,' Haelyn whispered. 'You hurt *them*.'

681

Claeon snarled. 'It's *my* colony! I'm the Edmir!' But he saw Haelyn's face and her immediate reaction. *It's their colony. It always has been. We are but guests.*

The Arketoi began shuffling towards him, and he threatened them with his maul. One by one, they raised their hands towards him, as if in salute.

'Get back!' Claeon howled. He struck one a blow with the maul – not solidly, but the little man was such a frail piece of work that he crumpled immediately. The others simply came on at him, reaching out with their pale fingers. More and more of them crept into the room from every crack and corner, from nowhere at all. There were twenty – no thirty, at least – all focusing only on Claeon.

He swung the maul to all sides of him, catching another pair, but then they reached him, and Haelyn screamed again, not from fear for herself but for what they then did.

When Aradocles, Stenwold and Paladrya finally entered the throne room, through a perfectly functional door, they discovered Haelyn pressed against one wall, hands covering her mouth, and, in the centre of the room, nothing but the rough shape of a man – as though a statue had been abandoned to the ocean many decades past, and become thoroughly encrusted over by barnacles and coral.

# Forty-Six

'You know what you're doing, of course,' remarked Tomasso philosophically.

Stenwold just shrugged, his eyes fixed on the sea. Overhead the *Tidenfree*'s sails bellied and flapped, lowered halfway and turned from the wind so that the crew could let down the ship's boat in safety.

'Still in sight of Collegium harbour, as well,' said the Fly captain, approvingly. 'A right piece of theatre. I'll wager they're cramming the sea wall with telescopes in their hands. You're a man with a knack for building your own legend.'

'I never wanted a legend,' Stenwold said softly. 'If I could have lived my whole life merely as a tinker and a scholar, that would have suited me.'

Tomasso made a rude noise, and then said, more solicitously, 'You don't want anyone along with you? You're sure, now? I've got good hands here, who'd gladly do it. Stab me, but Laszlo would come, if only he had four whole limbs. I'd not be able to keep him back. Prefers you to me, these days.'

'We went through a lot together,' said Stenwold fondly. 'No – no others. Anyone with me is a hostage being handed to the enemy.'

'Well, then,' said Tomasso. 'Ready the boat. Master Maker's fixing to leave us.'

Parting had been hard, after all that dagger work had been done. Aradocles had wanted him to stay just a little longer. There was to be a procession, a ceremony, where the boy would make pledges to the people of Hermatyre such as an Edmir had never offered before. He was going to make Salma proud of him, Stenwold knew. He would rule the colony as a true Commonweal prince, whose first concern must always – or should always – be for the well-being of his subjects.

But Stenwold could hear a clock ticking in the back of his mind. *How long for them to raise their grand armada, and sail on Collegium? How long for the Black and Gold to take note and start their next grand war?* He had made his apologies, after begging one simple audience with the new Edmir. After that, he had headed for the water, where Wys's submersible was waiting to carry him, as swiftly as possible, back to his home.

The ratcheting of the hoist brought him back to the here and now. Despard the artificer was supervising the little tub's swinging, positioning it over the water beyond the rail's edge. This was a tiny little boat for a big Beetle man, but it was not as though he would need to do much rowing in it. His destination was coming to him.

He cast another look at the sea, and then back to Tomasso. 'You're sure you can get under way in time?'

'We'll go wide, let the engine take us into the wind,' the Fly explained. 'We're faster than any of theirs, towards that point of the compass. Don't you worry about us, Master Maker.'

'Stenwold. Call me Stenwold, Tomasso. If anyone's earned that, you and your people certainly have.'

Tomasso had been there, of course, at the urgent and secret meeting Stenwold had called as soon as he struck land. It had been a matter of putting his affairs in order, of making sure that everything was set and in place, in case . . . well, just in case.

Tomasso and Wys, and an increasingly incredulous Jodry Drillen, these had been his co-conspirators. A precious two hours of his life had been spent explaining to the Speaker for the Assembly just who Wys was, and where she came from. At the end of that, Jodry had been sitting back in his seat, mouth hanging open, the frontiers of his world now pushed beyond the horizon in an unexpected direction.

'Just what am I expected to do with all of this?' he had demanded of Stenwold. And then Stenwold had told him, laid it out for him: the secret deal that he had told nobody of until then. Tomasso and Wys had been given their first hearing of it then, as well, and Stenwold had been desperately trusting to his assessment of them – that what he was offering would be appealing enough, and that they were honest enough, to make it work. Honest enough in their own way, of course, for a pirate and a mercenary. Stenwold had always found himself mixing with people like that, whose lives were bought and sold. He knew two types: those that wanted enough, and those that wanted it all. He could only hope he was right in assuming that Tomasso and Wys were amongst the first and not the second.

'You're happy with the arrangements?' he asked, stepping out into the *Tidenfree*'s little boat. He knew that it was too late now, if Tomasso decided to change the deal, but he felt driven to ask, even so.

'Oh, you're right there, Stenwold,' the black-bearded Fly agreed with a grin. 'You came through for us, all right – and then some.' There had been all the respectability that a Fly-kinden family could dream of, as part of that deal. Tomasso would have Jodry's seal of approval, a mercantile contact of the first water, and never a whiff of piracy. There would be a College scholarship waiting for whoever Tomasso chose to send, and citizenship for the entire crew. Stenwold reckoned that, amongst those flying through the rigging or hauling on the ropes, there was probably at least one new Assembler here, give it a few years. But there was more to it than that, for Tomasso would have more than just empty promises backing his new position in the city.

He had laid it out piece by piece, at that secret and hasty meeting. It was an arrangement he had been given plenty of time to construct, as he was passed from one set of sea-kinden hands to another. This had to work for *everyone*.

'First,' he had told Jodry, 'forget about everything you just heard. Nobody must know.' He looked from surprised face to surprised face and smiled sadly. 'We are not yet ready for the sea-kinden, and they are not ready for us. There's a thousand years and more of prejudice on their side: they think we're monsters; some of them think we're their ancient enemies – and perhaps we are. But it's more than that. It's economics, merchant business. All of us here know how the business of merchants is the real crank handle of the world, without which nothing turns.'

The little boat rocked as they lowered it, the ropes straining under the load. Stenwold tried to compose himself, aware that, even if matters went well for Collegium here, he could still find himself in a bad way soon enough.

'What do we have that the sea-kinden might want?' Stenwold had asked them, rhetorically. 'We have artifice. They've made great strides in the last few years, but that's mostly after they found Tseitus's original submersible.' He had managed to speak to the Tseni ambassadors, very quickly, to ask how they dealt with their own seagoing neighbours. They did not trade, they explained. In fact trade was strictly prohibited by both sides, punishable by death. Their history, the near-disaster that their city had staved off, had taught them that, and it bolstered Stenwold's determination to get this business *right*.

'Artifice, some centuries of learning, which could revolutionize the sea-kinden way of life,' he explained. 'And what do they have, in order to buy this from us?' He smiled sadly, thinking of the injustices of history. 'They have limitless supplies of gold, a metal that they account merely decorative, without intrinsic worth.'

He had been studying Jodry's face, when he had said that, and what he had seen there was only reassuring. Not goggling greed but a sober thoughtful look: Jodry had understood immediately.

'An influx of our newest and most complex inventions would turn Hermatyre inside out. Nobody could then say what might happen. The Edmiracy might be overthrown entirely. Anarchy could ensue . . . And then there are the Inapt of the sea-kinden, who would soon be driven to the wall. So far, the sea has managed a very polite version of the Apt Revolution. I would not want to undo all that by an over-generous hand. If we tried to turn them into us, we would destroy them.' He had given the matter plenty of thought. 'And in recompense, as they connived at their own destruction, they would destroy us in turn. Our currency would become worthless. We would destroy the Helleron mint, which smelts coin for the Lowlands and half the Empire and the Spiderlands, now. Nobody would profit from such a liberalization of trade.'

He unhitched the boat from the hoist and felt the sea take it, rolling and pitching it as he fumbled for the oars. The muted growl of the *Tidenfree*'s engine sounded up, and the wooden wall of her hull began to pull away from him, turning his little rowboat in lazy circles along with the swell. He thought he heard a high voice shout his name, and guessed that it was Laszlo wishing him luck, having finally fought his way abovedecks.

He had not explained the other reason why there must be no open trade, nor even open knowledge regarding the sea-kinden. Jodry, however, had seen at once what would happen if certain of the merchant class heard that there was gold to be had in the sea. Who would be the first of them, Stenwold wondered, to start construction of a fleet of submersibles? Who would mount a mad invasion of the depths, just as Rosander had planned his war on the land? Gold would spur them on, and their machines would grow more and more sophisticated, and the land-kinden would become the enemy that the superstitious sea-kinden believed them to be.

Stenwold had never rowed before, but Tomasso had carefully explained to him the principles. He paddled about, trying to wheel the boat, turning and turning until it was pointed in the wrong direction and he, by contrast, was facing in the right one. It was, he had to admit, a remarkable view.

He had told them, then, that he was not willing to sever all contact, that land and sea might yet have a use for one another. He had then put the deal to them: Tomasso and Wys, and their crews, would be the new Sea Watch, a link between their worlds. There would be a carefully measured flow of artifice to Hermatyre, and a return of gold and accreated goods into Collegium. Tomasso would take his cut, and Jodry would arrange the disposal of the rest. Aradocles would have a source of wealth that would allow him to keep his colony strong and free. Even Mandir and the Hot Stations would not be left behind, because they would retain their monopoly on the heat-forged metals only they could create.

There was an old, abandoned Wayhouse, up on the cliffs, that would become a lighthouse as soon as it had been refurbished. Tomasso would lease it from the Assembly and make it the heart of his new merchant empire, and everyone would no doubt wonder where the money came from, and would assume some source of trade overseas that the Fly-kinden were guarding closely. It was near enough the truth, save that over should read under.

Stenwold had stayed for the marriage, but only because the *Tidenfree* would not have sailed until it was done. It had been a strange ceremony, held below decks aboard the ship.

Tomasso looked magnificent in silks of many colours, with beads threaded into his beard, and Wys, bald and slightly hunchbacked, had decked herself out in enough gold and pearls to buy a townhouse in sight of the College. Tomasso's second had been Laszlo, his arm still in a sling, while Wys's had been the hulking figure of Lej, who they'd been forced to lower in through the cargo hatch.

With that done, they had set sail – and not a moment too soon. The defenders of Collegium had been mobilizing even as the *Tidenfree* set out, and everyone had thought her just a merchantman escaping the brawl, until Jodry put out word that War Master Stenwold Maker himself was on board.

It had been hard, tuning their deal to the minutest detail so that, like a well-made machine, it would work without needing him to hand, for, after today, he might well be in no position to intervene and make adjustments. It had been hard to get all those people into that room, and to convince Jodry. Harder still to entrust so much to a pair of thieves and a statesman.

But hardest of all, for him, had been the parting, in Hermatyre.

Not Aradocles, not Nemoctes, not the coral halls lit in strange colours. Most certainly not Arkeuthys or all of the monster-haunted, crushing, drowning sea. Stenwold would miss none of it.

She had come to him as he prepared to embark. As she reached for his arm, he had turned to see her: Paladrya, his fellow prisoner, his fellow questor after the lost heir. They had been through a lot together, in a strange way, and been through more while apart. They had suffered and lost, both of them, moulded into soldiers from unlikely clay.

She had looked into his eyes, and her lips parted, but the words had failed her. She had it all now: most trusted adviser of the young Edmir, her wisdom balancing out Heiracles's ambition. Her student, her surrogate child, had come home in glory at last. Stenwold knew all that, but he would have guessed none of it from her expression.

And at last he had given in, felt the walls within him crack at last, letting past the intolerable admission: *That witch in Princep Salmae was right, curse her!*

It was not the fierce passion he had known for Arianna, born from an old man's glee at his young and clever lover, that had fired him, and near-destroyed him when it all went wrong. He felt that such love had been burned from him now. But here was a woman that he could have lived with, and grown old with, and respected. Here she was, kind and loyal and quick, a woman to aid him in his wars, and not tire of him come peacetime.

And she was of the sea.

'Will you . . . come back?' Paladrya had asked, and he saw from her face that she knew the answer.

'Would you come with me?' was his reply. In his mind had been the brooding oppression of a life there without the sun, a life where he would be a cripple, the only adult capable of drowning in a world saturated with water. In her mind, he was sure, was the parching dryness of the air, the scorching sun, the sheer horror of that vast and empty sky.

'If I live,' he had said, 'I shall send word by Wys. I'm sure she'll not object to carrying . . .' And he had stopped there, because he knew that she could not read his script, nor he hers.

And there had been no tears – at least not there and then. She and he were alike in that, too. She had just nodded sagely, fencing away that part of her mind that cared for him, because she could not have him, and there was other work still to do. Seeing that, her workaday bravery and sacrifice, he came closer than he could imagine to swearing that he would return.

Now he rested his oars, looking eastwards into the morning sky, where the horizon was lost beneath a vast spread of canvas. The painted sails of Seldis and Siennis and a dozen satrapy ports had arrived, a force four times as great as the one which Teornis had led to lift the Vekken siege. The Spider-kinden were taking no chances. Their armada had come to Collegium at last.

Alone in his little boat, Stenwold waited for them, rowing only enough to keep him directly in their path.

*Here goes nothing*, he thought, as their shadows fell across him.

The first hull, a one-masted vessel of the *Tidenfree*'s size, knifed through the water and past him. *What if they don't stop?* he wondered, imagining himself bobbing along in his little boat, left behind in the armada's wake, abandoned and irrelevant. Then another vessel, a larger one, was heeling around, Spider-kinden sailors appearing at the rail.

'Hoi, Beetle, who are you?' one of them demanded, as the ship turned and slowed ponderously.

'I'm the Collegiate navy!' he shouted back. Not long after, they threw him a line and, when he had clambered up, he found himself at sword's point. They took him that seriously.

They searched him, but found not even so much as a knife. Then they gave him over to a copper-skinned Ant-kinden, who searched him again, looking for devices or explosives that the Spiders might have missed. Stenwold was impressed by the thoroughness of it all.

'I am a representative of Collegium,' he informed them, frequently. 'I would speak with your leader.'

They kept him below decks for some time, and he felt the ship shudder and creak all around him as its crew put it through its paces. He had some sense of these things, now, and he knew when the vessel was turning, and when it was taking on more sail to regain its place in the armada's progress. Later, he would know when it was slowing, the sail being reefed in. He made his calculations and, when they led him abovedecks again, he found he had it almost exactly right. The armada had taken anchor within clear

691

sight of the Collegium sea wall, well out of range of any artillery. On every ship there were men preparing, and Stenwold had a good view of them all: mercenaries or conscripts from a dozen satrapies, together with hundreds of the Spider-kinden themselves. He saw flying machines being assembled on the decks of some ships, ballistae and leadshotters on others. The pace was leisurely, though. It was past noon already, so it was plain that the Spiders were intending to commence festivities on the morrow.

'You're on your way to her ladyship,' said a Spider woman, who was presumably master of the vessel that had taken him on. She was a lean, sun-weathered woman with a scarred chin, and she grinned at him. 'Collegiate navy, I like that. You speak nice to Herself, and you'll come away with an intact hide, you hear?'

Stenwold thanked her courteously, and they put him in a boat that was somewhat bigger than the last one, so that four Spider marines could row him over to a nearby ship of the armada. It was a large, strongly made vessel, but by no means the grandest or the largest, and he was glad that his recollections about Spider-kinden shipping had proved accurate. Things might have become difficult otherwise.

So it was that, by passing through a succession of firm hands, Stenwold found himself before the admiral of the armada.

She was a woman of perhaps his own years, with the usual caveat that Spiders aged gracefully, and hid their age more gracefully still. Her hair was silver, but intentionally so, and there were perhaps a few lines on her face that no amount of craft could hide. In the privacy of her cabin, she was dressed in a simple white gown, without decoration or ornament. She wore it like a queen, and Stenwold had no doubt of her authority from the moment he saw her. She was a woman for whom the world turned, such was her invulnerable self-assurance. Beside that, the fact that she kept the marines at hand became a mere detail. There was no suggestion in her behaviour that they might be *necessary*.

More than this, though, he recognized a resemblance in her face, and he felt his heart sink slightly.

'Good afternoon, Sieur Beetle,' she addressed him, and a Fly-kinden servant that Stenwold had not even noticed was already at his elbow, pouring him some wine into one of the tall, narrow goblets that the Spider-kinden preferred.

'They tell me that you are the Collegiate ambassador,' the woman continued, taking up her goblet as soon as it was filled.

Stenwold lifted his own, letting the two silvered vessels clink together. 'That may as well be true, for I have come to speak for my city.'

'I had hoped someone would,' she acknowledged. 'I am the Lady-Martial Mycella of the Aldanrael. Whom do I have the pleasure of addressing?'

'My name is Stenwold Maker.'

'Good.' She nodded politely. 'A serious envoy, then, for serious times. My son writes approvingly of your acumen, Sieur Maker.'

*No more, he does.* Something obviously showed in Stenwold's face, because abruptly she was very still.

'Your son is Teornis,' he said heavily.

'One of them.' She saved him further confession, already reading it from his face. 'Then he is dead.' At Stenwold's nod, she asked simply, 'And did you slay him?'

'I did.' For she would have seen it in him, deny it as he might.

Had there not been a heartbeat's pause then, when she remained utterly without expression, he would never have known. That was all she let him see of her loss.

'You have not improved your bargaining position,' was all she said, and when he made to tell her that he had not meant to, not wanted to, she waved him away, killing the words with a slight gesture. 'Tell me that Collegium sues for peace,' she instructed.

'It does not. It stands ready to defend itself at all costs,' he told her formally.

'Then there seems little point in your coming here and putting yourself in my power, Sieur Maker. Under the circumstances, one might imagine that matters will go poorly for you.'

'I bring a warning, my lady,' Stenwold replied gravely. 'I would ask you to take your ships back to their home ports.'

'No doubt, but I am not in the vein to grant petitions at this moment, unless they include a prayer for leniency, coupled with a surrender.'

'May we go above?' he said suddenly.

She frowned suspiciously. 'You wish to signal to your compatriots? I think that would be unwise. I have no wish to announce to Collegium which is my flagship.'

'A fair point,' he conceded. His heart was beating very fast now, as though he was waiting for a bomb to go off. 'In that case, could I recommend that you have the ships' boats standing ready to be launched, as many as you can.'

Lady-Martial Mycella stared at him, trying to pry some meaning from his face. He felt her Art plucking at the edges of his mind. *Tell me, tell me.*

A rap at the door frame announced the arrival of a Spider-kinden man dressed in armour of chitin and boiled leather.

Mycella frowned at him. 'Speak.'

'My lady, it is the *Glorious Phaedris,*' the man got out. 'He is in . . . difficulty.'

'What sort of difficulty?' Mycella snapped, and when the man gaped at her, she set her mouth in a hard line and marched past him. 'Hold the Beetle until I return,' she shot over her shoulder, as she left.

Stenwold drained the goblet, trying to calm himself,

wondering just how advanced the *Glorious Phaedris*'s difficulties would be by the time Mycella reached the deck.

Scant minutes later she sent for him, and the baffled marines hauled him up into the sunlight.

It was easy enough to spot the *Glorious Phaedris*. He – as the Spiders would say – was a colossal vessel, fore and aft decks bristling with leadshotters, whose three masts would have hoisted a spread of canvas to put any other ship in the armada to shame. His hull was painted in a pattern of red and gold that glittered in the bright sunlight, making it seem as though fire scorched his flanks.

That fire was now being doused. The great ship tilted at an alarming angle, stern proud of the water, and very clearly sinking. His nearest companions in the fleet were hurriedly readying their boats, getting them into the water as swiftly as possible, to take on the ailing giant's crew.

Mycella stood at the rail, observing this scene with every appearance of detachment. 'Clever,' she remarked, as though they were watching some piece of theatre.

'It had to be the largest ship in the fleet,' Stenwold confirmed. 'It was a reasonable calculation that I'd not be aboard it, when I was brought before you.' When she rounded on him, he added, still sounding eminently reasonable though his heart thundered, 'After that, of course, all bets are off. It could be this one next, as easily as any other.'

'Sabotage,' she stated flatly. 'Some spy of yours is amongst us. Well, scuttling a single of my ships shall not save your city, Sieur Maker.'

'Shall we wait to see which vessel is next?' he asked her. 'I predicted that you might need convincing. We won't wait long now, so I advise you to have all boats ready.'

He had explained everything to Aradocles in great detail. It would have been easy for the new Edmir to forget any debt owed to the land, but whether it was through his service to Salma, or his own good character, Stenwold had never doubted the boy for a moment.

'My lady,' said one of Mycella's crew hoarsely. 'The *Costevan*.' His shaking finger picked out a long-hulled armourclad, an Ant-crewed vessel clad all in metal. What sails could not have shifted had been brought here by engines, showing that the Spiderlands had more at their disposal than mere galleons. Being so armoured, it was sinking far swifter than the *Glorious Phaedris*, rolling uncontrollably to port as its crew clambered about it, struggling for higher ground. Stenwold grimaced, knowing that the rescue boats would come far too late for most of the armoured soldiers. Then he saw the water ripple at the edge of the sinking boat, and a twisting grey tentacle squirmed its way up the canted deck and whipped about the ankle of one of the floundering Ant-kinden, pulling taut in an instant and yanking the man into the sea. Stenwold felt his stomach lurch with horrible memory.

*Arkeuthys.*

'I beg you,' he said, 'mobilize your fleet. Take your ships away from my city. Unless you go, they shall all be destroyed before you even touch land. It is set in motion now, and I cannot stop it.'

They had seen Arkeuthys's contribution to the sinking. What they had not seen was the Gastroi – the tireless, hard-working Gastroi – swimming up to the underside of the hulls, using their Art to cut through wood or metal as easily as they could grind their way into stone. The results of that labour were already plain to see, though: two ships sinking, indeed one very nearly sunk, and every other ship's captain thinking, *And who's next?*

He saw Mycella consider coldly what would happen if she now ordered full sail against Collegium, saw her evaluate the sea wall defences, the time it would take for beach landings where the coast allowed it, both east and west of the city. There were not so many suitable anchorages, only a few rocky coves and the one broad beach that the Vekken had used when they had tried to take the city by land and sea. How long, to disembark all her soldiers, all the machinery of war, the supplies and the ammunition, while all the time her ships were being taken, one by one? How many would be left of her army, to menace the walls of Collegium? Even as she considered it, the cry went out that yet another ship was failing. The sea-kinden were gaining confidence.

'Up sail, all ships. Send the order through the fleet,' Mycella said, her tone clipped. 'Have all boats ready, as well.' She rounded on Stenwold. 'And as for you, no doubt this . . . *thing* will plague me all the way to Seldis, unless I put you back in the water.'

Stenwold nodded. In truth he suspected the ships would soon enough outpace the sea-kinden, whether he was alive or dead.

'Put him in one of the boats,' Mycella instructed. 'Have him rowed into harbour under a peace flag. Let the legend of Stenwold Maker acquire one more chapter.' As her sailors scrambled to obey her, she said, 'My son was right to admire you, Sieur Maker. I do not know how you have accomplished this, what underwater engines your people have constructed, but it is duly noted. Today is yours.' Only when he was already in the boat, and the sailors were beginning to lower it hand over hand into the water, did she call back to him.

'There will come a tomorrow, Sieur Maker, when we shall speak again. Remember that.' And the sheer depth of her pain and anger, shorn for a moment of all her veils, chilled him to the bone.

# Glossary

## *Characters*

**Aagen** – Wasp-kinden ambassador to Collegium

**Accius** – Vekken Ant-kinden ambassador to Collegium

**Achaeos** – Moth-kinden lover of Cheerwell Maker, died in the war

**Akkestrae** – Mantis-kinden in Collegium

**Albinus** – Ant-kinden intelligencer in Kanateris

**Aldanrael** – a Spider-kinden Aristoi family

**Amnon** – Khanaphir Beetle-kinden expatriate

**Ancient League** – the Moths and Mantids of Dorax, Etheryon and Nethyon, allies of Collegium in the war

**Aradocles** – Krakind heir to Hermatyre

**Arianna** – Spider-kinden lover of Stenwold Maker

**Arkeuthys** – giant octopus

**Arvi** – Fly-kinden secretary to Jodry Drillen

**Balkus** – renegade Sarnesh Ant-kinden

**Berjek Gripshod** – Beetle-kinden academic

**Bloodfly** – notorious Fly-kinden pirate from a generation ago

**Caractes** – Polypoi hermit

**Cardless** – Beetle-kinden servant to Stenwold Maker

**Cheerwell Maker ('Che')** – Beetle-kinden, niece of Stenwold Maker

**Chenni** – Smallclaw Onychoi, Rosander's artificer

**Claeon** – Krakind Kerebroi, Edmir of Hermatyre

**Cynthaen** – Mantis-kinden fisherwoman

**Danaen** – Mantis-kinden raider

**Daven** – Wasp-kinden Rekef agent

**Despard** – Fly-kinden artificer of the *Tidenfree* crew

**Diamedes** – Krakind Kerebroi, agent of Hieracles

**Ebris of the Ganbrodiel** – Spider-kinden pirate

**Elder Padstock** – Beetle-kinden, Chief Officer of the
  Maker's Own Company

**Elleria of the Aldanrael** – Teornis's cousin

**Elytrya** – Krakind Kerebroi Littoralist agent

**Epiphona** – Greatclaw Onychoi, Nauarch of the Three
  Red Fish Train

**Fel** – Swiftclaw Onychoi, of Wys's crew

**Fernaea ('Fern')** – Fly-kinden seer, of the *Tidenfree* crew

**Filipo** – Fly-kinden rogue in the employ of Forman Sands

**Forman Sands** – Halfbreed assassin in the employ of
  Helmess Broiler

**Geontes** – Krakind Kerebroi, agent of Claeon

**Grampos** – Tarantula-kinden in Kanateris

**Greenwise Artector** – Beetle-kinden magnate in Helleron

**Gribbern** – Deepclaw Onychoi Pelagist

**Grief** – Butterfly-kinden, Monarch of Princep Salmae

**Gude** – Fly-kinden helmswoman of the *Tidenfree* crew

**Haelyn** – Sepia-kinden Kerebroi, majordomo to Claeon

**Heiracles** – Krakind Kerebroi, insurgent leader

**Helmess Broiler** – Beetle-kinden Assembler

**Honory Bellowern** – Beetle-kinden, Imperial diplomat

**Isseleema** – Spider-kinden ship-owner

**Jaclen Courser** – Beetle-kinden ship's master

**Janos Outwright** – Beetle-kinden, Chief Officer of the
  Merchant Companies

**Jodry Drillen** – Beetle-kinden Assembler

**Jons Allanbridge** – Beetle-kinden aviator

**Kratia** – Tseni Ant-kinden ambassador

**Laszlo** – Fly-kinden factor of the *Tidenfree* crew

**Lej ('Spillage')** – Greatclaw Onychoi engineer, of Wys's crew

**Lerean** – Dart-kinden Kerebroi wanderer

**Lineo Thadspar** – Beetle-kinden, former speaker for the Assembly – died during the war

**Lyess** – Medusoi Pelagist

**Malius** – Vekken Ant-kinden ambassador

**Mandir** – Smallclaw Onychoi, the Man of the Hot Stations

**Marcantor** – Dart-kinden Kerebroi in Aradocles' service

**Marteus** – Ant-kinden chief officer of the Coldstone Company

**Maxel Gainer** – Beetle-kinden artificer, Tseitus's apprentice

**Menes** – Krakind Kerebroi assassin in Claeon's service

**Nemoctes** – Wayfarer-kinden Kerebroi, leader of the Pelagists

**Ordly Penhold** – Beetle-kinden merchant

**Paladrya** – Krakind Kerebroi tutor to Aradocles

**Partreyn** – Beetle-kinden deputy speaker of the Assembly

**Pellectes** – Krakind Kerebroi, leader of the Littoralists

**Phylles** – Polypoi member of Wys's crew

**Piera** – Fly-kinden of the *Tidenfree* crew

**Plius** – Tseni Ant-kinden agent, died during the war

**Praeda Rakespear** – Beetle-kinden academic

**Pserry** – Gribbern's beast

**Rones Failwright** – Beetle-kinden Assembler, shipping magnate

**Rosander** – Greatclaw Onychoi, Nauarch of the Thousand Spines train

**Salme Dien ('Salma')** – Dragonfly-kinden noble, died during the war

**Santiren** – Dart-kinden Kerebroi in the service of Aradocles

**Sfayot** – Roach-kinden chancellor of Princep Salmae

**Stenwold Maker** – Beetle-kinden spymaster and statesman

**Teornis of the Aldanrael** – Spider-kinden Aristoi

**Termes** – Vekken Ant-kinden ambassador

**Thalric** – Wasp-kinden former Rekef agent and Regent

**Theomen** – Krakind Kerebroi assassin in Claeon's service

**Three-City Alliance** – Myna, Szar and Maynes; cities formerly under the control of the Empire

**Tisamon** – Mantis-kinden Weaponsmaster, died during the war

**Tolly Aimark** – Beetle-kinden ship's master

**Tomasso** – Fly-kinden master of the *Tidenfree*

**Tseitus** – Tseni Ant-kinden artificer

**Tynisa** – halfbreed Weaponsmaster, daughter of Tisamon

**Tyresia** – Spider-kinden information broker

**Varante** – Dragonfly-kinden leader of Teornis's cadre

**Wys** – Smallclaw Onychoi mercenary

## Places

**Arvandine** – trading post at the edge of the Felyal

**Capitas** – capital of the Empire

**Collegium** – Beetle city, heart of the Lowlands

**Deep Seep** – sea-kinden colony

**Everis** – Spider-kinden island city

**Felyal** – Mantis-kinden forest, now mostly burned

**Grand Atoll** – sea-kinden colony off Tsen

**Helleron** – Beetle-kinden industrial city

**Hermatyre** – sea-kinden colony

**The Hot Stations** – sea-kinden industrial colony

**Kanateris** – Spider-kinden pirate town

**Khanaphes** – ancient Beetle-kinden city

**Merro** – Fly-kinden town

**Princep Salmae** – city newly founded by war refugees

**Sarn** – Ant-kinden city allied with Collegium
**Seldis** – Spider-kinden city
**Siennis** – Spider-kinden city
**Sonn** – Beetle-kinden city in the Empire
**Tark** – Ant-kinden city, devastated during the war
**Tsen** – Ant-kinden city on the far west coast of the
    Lowlands
**Vek** – Ant-kinden city recently at war with Collegium


## *Organizations and things*

**Amphiophos** – the seat of Collegiate government
**Assembly** – the governing body of Collegium, elected by
    Lots
**Benthist** – a member of a nomadic sea-kinden group
**Coldstone Company** – a Collegium merchant company
**Edmir** – the governor of a sea-kinden colony
*Isseleema's Floating Game* – a floating gaming house
**Lots** – the election of Collegiate Assemblers
**Maker's Own** – a Collegium merchant company
*Migrating Home* – Jaclen Courser's merchant ship
**Nauarch** – the leader of a Benthist train
**Obligist** – a sea-kinden living in a colony
**Outwright's Pike and Shot** – a Collegium merchant
    company
**Pelagist** – a sea-kinden that leads a solitary, travelling life
*Pelter* – Tolly Aimark's ship
**Rekef** – the Imperial secret service
**Speaker** – the leader of the Collegiate Assembly
*Storm Locust* – Ebris of the Ganbrodiel's ship
**Thousand Spines Train** – Rosander's followers
*Tidenfree* – Tomasso's ship
*Tseitan* – Maxel Gainer's submersible
*Very Blade* – pirate vessel
*Windlass* – Jons Allanbridge's airship